THE GEORGE FELSE OMNIBUS

Also by Ellis Peters:

Inspector Felse mysteries
A NICE DERANGEMENT OF EPITAPHS
BLACK IS THE COLOUR OF MY TRUE LOVE'S HEART
THE KNOCKER ON DEATH'S DOOR
RAINBOW'S END
FALLEN INTO THE PIT
DEATH AND THE JOYFUL WOMAN
THE GRASS WIDOW'S TALE
THE HOUSE OF GREEN TURF

Brother Cadfael mysteries
A MORBID TASTE FOR BONES
ONE CORPSE TOO MANY
MONK'S-HOOD
ST PETER'S FAIR
THE LEPER OF SAINT GILES
THE VIRGIN IN THE ICE
THE SANCTUARY SPARROW
THE DEVIL'S NOVICE
DEAD MAN'S RANSOM
THE PILGRIM OF HATE
AN EXCELLENT MYSTERY
THE RAVEN IN THE FOREGATE
THE ROSE RENT
THE HERMIT OF EYTON FOREST
THE CONFESSION OF BROTHER HALUIN
THE HERETIC'S APPRENTICE
THE POTTER'S FIELD
THE SUMMER OF THE DANES
THE HOLY THIEF

THE FIRST CADFAEL OMNIBUS
THE SECOND CADFAEL OMNIBUS
THE THIRD CADFAEL OMNIBUS
THE FOURTH CADFAEL OMNIBUS

Ellis Peters writing as Edith Pargeter
The Heaven Tree trilogy
THE HEAVEN TREE
THE GREEN BRANCH
THE SCARLET SEED

THE HEAVEN TREE TRILOGY (ONE VOLUME)

THE MARRIAGE OF MEGGOTTA

MOST LOVING MERE FOLLY

THE GEORGE FELSE OMNIBUS

Ellis Peters

Fallen into the Pit
Death and the Joyful Woman
A Nice Derangement of Epitaphs

WARNER FUTURA

A *Warner Futura* Book
First published in this omnibus edition in 1994 by
Warner Futura

This omnibus edition copyright © Edith Pargeter 1994

FALLEN INTO THE PIT
first published by Heinemann in 1951
Published by Futura in 1991
Copyright © Edith Pargeter 1951

DEATH AND THE JOYFUL WOMAN
first published by Collins in 1961
Published by Futura in 1991
Copyright © Edith Pargeter in 1961

A NICE DERANGEMENT OF EPITAPHS
first published by Collins in 1965
Published by Futura in 1988
Reprinted 1988 (twice), 1989, 1990
Copyright © Edith Pargeter in 1965

The moral right of the author has been asserted

*All characters in this publication are fictitious and
any resemblance to real persons, living or dead, is purely
coincidental*

All rights reserved
No part of this publication may be reproduced,
stored in a retrieval system, or transmitted, in
any form or by any means without the prior permission
in writing of the publisher, nor be otherwise circulated
in any form or cover other than that in which
it is published and without a similar condition including
this condition being imposed on the subsequent purchaser

A CIP catalogue for this book
is available from the British Library

ISBN 0 7515 1031 9

Phototypeset by Intype, London
Printed and bound in Great Britain by
Clays Ltd, St Ives, PLC

Warner Futura
A Division of
Little, Brown and Company (UK)
Brettenham House
Lancaster Place
London WC2E 7EN

Contents

Fallen into
the Pit

To JIM,
and the survival
of
his memory and ideas
through his friends

Contents

Chapter 1

The Time –

I

The war ended, and the young men came home, and tried indignantly to fit themselves into old clothes and old habits which proved, on examination, to be both a little threadbare, and on trial to be both cripplingly small for bodies and minds mysteriously grown in absence. Things changed overnight changed again next day. Nobody knew where he stood. Even the language was different. At the 'Shock of Hay' you could hear goodnights flying at closing-time in two or three tongues besides English. Blank-eyed, blond youths with shut faces worked side by side with the hard old men in the beet fields, and the sons of the old men, coming home laboriously with the distorted selves they had salved from the blond youths' embraces all over the world, wondered where they had been, and to what country they had returned. But they had known for some time, the most acute of them, that if England meant the country they had left, and Comerford the village, this would be neither Comerford nor England. Fortunately the names meant much more than their own phases, and the lie of the land, obscured behind many changes, remained constant even at this pass.

Those who came back first had the easiest time. Those who had still to linger a year or more of their time away in the tedium of suddenly purposeless armies, or adjust themselves to the fluid situation of other people's crumbling countries, limped home with more bitter difficulty, to find the fields full of displaced persons, and the shops of a new lingua franca evolved for their benefit, the encrustations of pits suddenly congealed into the nationalised mining industry, whole hills and valleys turn out by the roots under the gigantic caresses of surface mining machinery, and in the upper air of the mind every boundary shifted and every alignment altered. It was all a bewildered young man could do to find his way around this almost unrecognisable land. The old did not try; they sat in the middle of it in contemplation, waiting for the eyes to adjust their vision, and the legs to acquire the mastery of this new kind of drunkenness. Only the young had so short a time before them that they could not afford to wait.

They tried, however, to cram themselves back into the old round holes, and mutilated their unaccountably squared personalities in the process. Time eased the fit for some; for some, who had sent their minds home ahead of their bodies, the adjustment was neither long nor unwelcome, though it could not be without pain; to some the whole of Comerford seemed now only a green round hole, not big enough to hold them. They despised it both for what had changed in it and for what had remained the same, because they had lived too long enclosed in the changes and monotonies of their own natures, and could no longer distinguish great from small.

If day-to-day life could halt at such a time, and give all the lost people time to get their bearings, things would be easier; but it went on steadily, or rather unsteadily, all the time, full of all the old snags and spiteful with new ones. Colliers' sons went back to the pits, and found themselves working side by side with Ukrainians, Poles, Czechs, Lithuanians, Letts, whose wartime alliance was just falling apart into a hundred minor incompatibilities; and soon came even the few screened Germans out of their captivity to fester among their ex-enemies without being able to reunite them. Nice-looking, stolid young men, hard workers, a good type; but they did not always remember to keep the old 'Heil Hitler!' off their tongues; and the left-ward-inclined youngster with Welsh blood in his veins and a brother dead in some stalag or other was liable to notice these things. Maybe he picked a fight, maybe some older and cooler minds broke it up, maybe he just got his room at the hostel rifled and his books shredded, or maybe some evening in the dark, pepper found its way into his eyes. No one knew how. No connection with the war, of course; the war was over.

Meantime the topsoil of two small fields and an undulation of rough pasture and furze was scoured off and piled aside in new mountain ridges, and the grabs lifted out the stony innards of Comerford earth to lay bare the hundred and eighty thousand or so tons of shallow coal which the experts said was to be found underneath. As if the earth cried, instant outcry broke out over the issue, one faction crying havoc for the two fields, a smaller and less vociferous group welcoming the levelling of the furze mounds, and tidying of the ground long ago mauled by shallow dog-hole mining. But the small army of weathered men swarming over the site, performing prodigious surgical operations with uncouth red and yellow instruments, took no notice of either party in the controversy. They assembled about them every conceivable variety of weatherproof and wear-proof ex-Army clothing, making their largeness larger still under leather jerkins and duffle coats, and so armoured, they busied themselves in making hills and valleys change places, the straight crooked and the plain places rough. But when they moved on they left a level dark plain, and though inimical voices clamoured prophetically of soil made barren for a lifetime, and drainage difficulties had to be stabbed at twice after an initial failure, in one year grass was growing delicately over the whole great scar. Poor grass beside that which formerly grew on the two small fields, but beautiful, improbable grass over what used to be furze, bramble and naked clay.

9

And from the returned young men themselves, wise and foolish, willing and unwilling soldiers in their time, proceeded outward through their families and their friends shuddering cycles of unrest, like the tremors before earthquake. They came trailing clouds of tattered and tired glory which they could neither repair nor shake off. The unimaginative were the luckiest, or those whose supposedly adventurous Army career had been spent largely among mud and boredom and potatoes; but some came haunted by the things their own hands had done and their own bodies endured, growths from which no manner of amputation could divide them, ghosts for which Comerford had no room. They had been where even those nearest to them could not follow, and daily they withdrew there again from the compression and safety of lathe and field and farm, until the adjustment to sanity took place painfully at last, and the compression ceased to bound them, and was felt to be wider than the mad waste in the memory. Then they had arrived. But the journey was a long one, and others besides themselves might die on the way.

There was, for instance, Charles Blunden, up at the Harrow. His was a mild case, but even he had fought his way in a tidy, orthodox fashion twice across North Africa and all the way north through Sicily and Italy to his demob. in 1946, and had then to become, all in a moment, an upland farmer. Or Jim Tugg, who came home three times decorated, trailing prodigious exploits as a paratrooper before and after Arnhem, and shrank suddenly to the quiet dark shape of a shepherd on Chris Hollins's farm. Who believed in it? When he went by, double his pre-war size, light as a cat, close-mouthed and gaunt-eyed as a fate, the ground under his noiseless tread quaked a little, and small boys expected lightnings to come out of the ends of his fingers and dart into the earth.

Or, of course, Chad Wedderburn, whose legends came home before him, the extremest case of all. Captured in Italy, bitterly ill-used by both Italians and Germans after three attempts to

10

escape, at the fourth attempt he had succeeded, if that could be called escape which smuggled him across the Adriatic from one mortal danger to another. For the rest of the war he became a guerrilla at large all over the Balkans, living from minute to minute, tasting all the splendours and miseries of the mountain life among the Yugoslav patriots, sharing their marathon marches, their hunger, their cold, their sickness and wounds, for which there was seldom medical attention and almost never drugs or anæsthetics. He knew, because he had had to use daily during that last year, all the ways of killing a man quietly before he can kill you; and because he had been an apt pupil he was still alive. It was as if an explosion had taken place in Comerford the day he was born, to fling fragments of violence half across the world.

When he came back in 1949, after a year of hospital treatments in many places, and another year of study to return to his profession, it was an anticlimax, almost a rebuff. He looked much thinner and darker and harder than pre-war, but otherwise scarcely different; he was even quieter than he had ever been before, and of his many scars only one was visible, and that was a disappointment, just a brownish mark running down the left side of his jaw from ear to chin. The village tried to bring him out of his shell by drawing him into British Legion activities, and he astonished and offended them by replying decisively that personally he had been a conscript, and he thought the sooner people forgot whether they had worn a uniform or not, the better, in a war which had involved everybody alike, and in which few people had had any choice about the manner of their service.

But this fair warning meant little to the boys at the grammar school, when he returned there at length as classics master. They had caught a reputed tiger, and a tiger they confidently expected. They conferred together over him with excited warnings, and prepared to jump at the lift of his eyebrow, and adore him for it. But the tiger, though its voice was incisive and its manner by no means timorous, continued to behave like a singularly patient sheep-dog. They could not understand it. They began to test the length of that patience by tentative provocation, and found it elastic enough to leave them still unscathed. His way with them was not so unreasonably mild as to let these experiments proceed too far, but he let them go beyond the point where a real tiger might have been expected to pounce. On a natural human reaction to this disappointment they began to fear, prematurely and unjustifiably, that what they had acquired was merely the usual tame, doctored, domestic cat, after all. But the legend, though invisible, like the potential genie in the bottle, still awed them and stayed their courage short of positive danger. With tigers, with cats for that matter, you never know.

II

The Fourth Form, who had tamed more masters than they could remember, discussed the phenomenon in perhaps the most unwise spot they could have found for the conference, only ten yards from the form-room window, in the first ten minutes of break, while the latest manifestation of Chad Wedderburn's mildness was fresh in their minds. They had sweated Latin and English under him for the whole of the summer term, which was just drawing to its buoyant close, and got away with everything except murder. That he managed none the less to get the work out of them, and to keep a reasonable and easy order, without resorting to sarcasm or the cane, had escaped their young notice, for work was something on which their minds took care not to dwell out of the classroom. The fact remained that he was not the man they had thought him.

'If you'd planted a booby trap like that for old Stinky,' said the largest thirteen-year-old, levelling a forefinger almost into Dominic Felse's eye, 'he'd have skinned you alive.'

'It wasn't for old Wedderburn, either,' said Dominic darkly, 'it was for you. If he didn't come in so beastly *prompt* to his classes he wouldn't walk into things like that. Old Stinky was always ten minutes late. You can't *rely* on these early people.' He chewed his knuckles, and frowned at the memory of flying books and inkwell, thanking heaven that by some uncanny chance the lid of the well had jammed shut, and only a few minute drops had oozed out of its hinges to spatter the floor. He cocked a bright hazel eye at the large youth, whose name was Warren, and hence inescapably 'Rabbit' Warren. 'Anyhow, you try it some time. It felt like being skinned alive to me.'

'Sensitive plant!' said Rabbit scornfully, for he had not been on the receiving end of the drastically quiet storm, and had in any case little respect for the power of words, least of all when delivered below a shout.

Dominic let it pass. He felt peaceful, for people like Rabbit seldom interested him enough to rouse him to combat. All beef and bone! He looked small enough when he was turned loose with Virgil, Book X!

'But when you think what he's supposed to have *done*,' said Morgan helplessly, 'what can you make of it? I mean, stealing about in the mountains knocking off sentries, and slipping a knife in people's ribs, and marching hundreds of miles with next to nothing to eat, and rounding up thousands of Germans – '

'And now he's too soft even to lick a chap for cheek – '

'Never once – not all the term he's been here!'

'Of course, we could be rather small fry, after all that,' said Dominic, arrested by the thought.

'Oh, rot, he just hasn't got the guts!'

'Oh, rot, yourself! Of course he has! He *did* all that, didn't he?'

'I tell you what,' said Rabbit, in very firm tones, 'I don't believe he did!'

The circle closed in a little, tension plucking at them strongly. Dominic unwound his long, slim legs from the boundary railing

13

and hopped down into the argument with a suddenly flushed face.

'Oh, get off! You know jolly well –'

'We don't know jolly well one single thing, we only know what they all say, and how do they know it's true? They weren't there, were they? I bet you it's all a pack of fairy-tales! Well, look at him! Does he look like a bloke that went around knocking off sentries and rounding up Germans? I don't believe a word of it!'

'You can't tell by looking at people what they are, anyhow. That's just idiotic –'

'Oh, is it? And who're you calling an idiot?'

'You, if you think you can just wipe out old Wedderburn's record by saying you don't believe it.'

'Well, I don't see! I don't believe he ever killed all those Jerries they say he did. I think it's a pack of lies! I don't believe he ever saw Markos, I don't believe he ever was knocked about in a prison camp, see? I don't believe he's got it in him to stick a knife in anyone's ribs. I bet you he never killed *anybody!*'

'I bet you he did, then! Who do you think you are, calling him a liar? He's worth ten of you.'

'Oh, yes, you would stick up for him! He let you off lightly, didn't he?'

'That's got nothing to do with it,' said Dominic, meditating how little he had ever liked Rabbit's face, and how pleasant it would be to do his best to change it.

'Well, all right, then, I still say it's a big lie about his adventures – all of it! Now! Want to make something of it?'

'It wouldn't settle anything if I did fight you,' said Dominic, tempted, 'but I'm considering it.'

'You don't have to, anyhow, do you? Not you!' And he raised his voice suddenly into the taunting chant from which Dominic had suffered through most of his school years: 'Yah, can't touch me! My dad's a p'liceman!'

Dominic had finished considering it, and come to a pleasing

decision. His small but solid fist hit Rabbit's left cheek hard on the bone, and distorted the last word into a yell of quite unexpected delightfulness. Rabbit swung back on his heels, and with the recovering swing forward launched himself head-down at his opponent with both arms flailing; but before they could do each other any damage a window flew up in the classroom, and the voice of Chad Wedderburn himself demanded information as to what the devil was going on out there. Everybody ducked, as though to be shortened by a head was to be invisible, and the latecomers on the outside of the circle faded away round the corner with the aplomb of pantomime fairies or stage ghosts; but enough were left to present a comical array of apprehensive faces as supporting chorus to the two red-handed criminals pulled up in mid-career. They all gaped up at the window, made themselves as small as possible, and volunteered not a word.

'Felse and Warren,' said the unwontedly awful voice, crisply underlined by the crook of the selective forefinger, 'up here, and at the double! The rest of you, beat it! And if I catch any of you fighting again, take warning, I'll have the hide off both parties. Get me?'

They said, in one concerted sigh, that they had indeed got him.

'Good! Now scram!'

It was popular, not classic, language, and it was certainly understanded of the people. They departed thankfully, while with mutual recriminations Dominic and Rabbit scrambled up the stairs and arrived panting before the desk at which Chad sat writing. He looked them over with a severe eye, and then said quietly: 'What you fellows argue about is your business strictly. Only what you fight about is mine. Understand me once for all, fighting is something not to be considered short of a life-and-death matter, and something I will not have about me on any less pretext than that. It proves nothing, it settles nothing, it solves nothing, except the problem of who has the most brawn and the least of any other qualities. There could be times when

15

nothing else would serve, but they're not likely to occur in the school yard – and they *always* indicate a failure by *both* sides, wherever they occur.'

A rum couple, he thought, comparing them. On such an occasion the face is, of course, worn correctly closed and expressionless, but the eyes become correspondingly alive and responsive; and while the eyes of Warren were respectful and solemn and impervious, the light, bright, gold-flecked eyes of Felse were extremely busy weighing up his judge. A little puzzled about him the child seemed, but getting somewhere, and probably not, to judge by the reserve of those eyes, exactly where he would have liked the young mind to arrive. Be careful, Chad! In this small package is unsuspected dynamite.

'Understand me?'

'Yes, sir!' If he said it, he meant it; but the reserve was still there. He understood, bless him, but he did not altogether agree.

'Well, then, let's put it this way. You two have still got a score not settled. Give me your word you won't try that way again, and we'll say no more about this time. Is it a deal?'

Rabbit said: 'Oh, yes, sir!' promptly and easily. The other one looked worried, and a little annoyed, even, as if something had been sprung on him before he was ready, and from an unfair angle. He said, hesitating, standing on one leg the better to think, a method by which he often wrestled the sense out of a more than usually tough line of Virgil: 'But, sir, could I – ?' He wanted Rabbit to go, so that he could argue properly.

'All right, Warren, remember I've got your word for it. Now get out!'

Dominic still stood considering, even after his enemy was gone in a clatter of grateful haste down the staircase. Chad let him alone, and thoughtfully finished the sentence of his letter which their entry had interrupted, before he looked up again and said with a slight smile: 'Well?'

'You see, sir, it isn't that I don't think you're right about

16

fighting being the wrong way to do things, and all that. But, sir, you *did* fight.'

'Yes,' said Chad, 'I did fight.' He did not sound displeased; Dominic raised the fierce glance of his eyes from the floor, and looked at him, and he did not look displeased, either. 'Not, however, at the drop of a hat. And not because some lunatic threw at me: 'My dad's a policeman!', either.' He smiled; so did Dominic.

'No, sir! But that wasn't why I hit him. I'd just made up my mind I would, and that didn't make any difference.'

'All right, that's understood, if you tell me so. But I'm still sure that what you hit him for was something a thousand miles from being worth it. And what I said still goes. All the more because you were certainly the aggressor. Either you give me your word not to go and re-open that fight in a safer place, and not to start any more so lightly, either, or else we'll settle our account here and now.'

Dominic followed the turn of his head towards the cupboard, with hurt and incredulous eyes. 'But, sir, you can't! I mean – you *don't!*'

'On the contrary,' said Chad remorselessly, 'on this occasion I can and do.'

Dominic's mind calculated values frantically. He said in a small, alert voice: 'Sir, if a fellow *made* another fellow fight him, you wouldn't blame the other fellow, would you? Even if he'd promised never to fight, would you?'

'In that case I'd hold the attacker responsible for both of them. He'd have quite a charge-sheet to answer, wouldn't he? Come along, now, no side-tracking. I want an answer.'

Dominic thought, and squirmed, and would not give in. He said almost apologetically: 'You see, sir, it's like this. Didn't you decide for yourself what was worth fighting about? I mean, wouldn't you insist – Well, it isn't even a thing you can put on to conscription, is it? Because lots of fellows, if they felt like

17

that, refused to fight. I mean, it's just *oneself* who must decide, in the end, isn't it?'

He looked a little harassed, and Chad felt sufficiently appreciative to help him out. 'You're doing fine. Don't mind me! What's the conclusion?'

'I think, sir, that I ought to decide for myself, too.'

'Ah!' said Chad. 'Then if you've gone as far towards maturity as that, you have to take the next step forward, whether you like it or not, and realise that in any society you have to be prepared to pay for that privilege.'

'Yes, sir!' sighed Dominic, resigned eyes again straying. 'I *have* realised it.'

Chad was sorry that he had got himself into this situation, and even sorrier that he had dragged this new kind of schoolroom lawyer into it with him. But there was no way out of it now. To let him off would be to insult him; even to let him down lightly would be to make light of his conclusions. Chad dealt with him faithfully, therefore, and left, in the process, no doubt of his own ability. But the persistent child, even when dismissed after the humane minute or two allowed for recovery, did not go. He lingered, breathing hard, with his burning palms clenched uneasily in his pockets, but his eyes once again speculative upon the future.

'Sir, could I ask you – you go home by the road, usually, don't you? I mean – not over the fields – '

'Sometimes,' said Chad, examining him with respect. 'I have been known to walk through the fields.' The eyes clouded over ever so slightly, but he saw the cloud, and understood it. 'But this afternoon I shall be going home as you supposed – by the road.' The cloud dispersed, the eyes gleamed. Chad knew himself transparent as his adversary, and the knowledge dismayed him considerably. If they were all like this one, he thought, I'd have to get out of this business; and that would be the devil, because if they were all like this one it would be well worth staying in it.

'Yes, sir! Thank you, sir!'

'You won't, however,' said Chad delicately, 'be in very good condition to give of your best. Why not change your mind? No discredit to you if you did, I assure you – quite the reverse.'

The child, still tenderly massaging his hands in the deeps of his pockets, said hesitantly: 'Sir, I hope you won't think it awful cheek, but – well, it wasn't a question of odds with you, always, was it?'

The water was getting too deep for him, he made haste out of it, slipping away out of the room before Chad knew how to reply. It was reassuring to find that he supposed any situation to be beyond him.

On the way home by the fields, that afternoon, Dominic finished what he had begun, and conclusively knocked the stuffing out of Rabbit. He was a little handicapped by the puffiness of his hands, but he managed, and the fact that it hurt him somehow added to the satisfaction he got out of it. He marched home flushed and whistling, one cheek a little bruised and the eye discolouring, his hands now hurting at the back as well as the palm, because he had skinned the knuckles, but his crest well up and his self-esteem buoyantly high. One couldn't, of course, even by a roundabout method, tell the person most concerned how the affair had been concluded, but it was really a pity that he couldn't simply know.

The oblique illogic of proceedings which seemed to him directly logical did not worry Dominic at all. If you fight for somebody who doesn't believe in fighting, and has choked you off for it in advance, that's still your own affair. Especially when you have already paid for the privilege and, like the village blacksmith, owe not any man.

III

Dominic came in to tea scrupulously washed and tidied, because
Aunt Nora was there, and six-year-old Cousin John; but in spite
of all his precautions he did not escape from the table again
before his mother had observed and interpreted more or less
correctly the various small changes in his appearance. It might
not have happened but for the brat John, for he was taking care
to keep his knuckles as far out of sight as possible. John had so
far resisted all attempts to teach him to recognise letters, and
was not interested in figures for their own sake, but he could
count éclairs on a plate and people round a table as fast as
anyone, and make them come out right, too. Having observed
by this means that the éclairs out-numbered the people by one,
and that he himself was the youngest and most indulged person
present, he had assumed that the extra one would be his as of
right; and it was a serious shock to him when Dominic's acquisi-
tive hand shot out and abstracted it from under his nose. He
let out a wail of indignation, and seized the offending hand by
the wrist as it flicked back again with the prize, and both
mothers, naturally, leaned forward to quell the argument before
it could become a scrimmage. Maybe Aunt Nora did miss the
significance of the skinned knuckles and tender palm, but Bunty
Felse didn't. Her eyes sought her son's, she frowned a little,
and then laughed, whereupon he scowled blackly, relinquished
the éclair, and hurriedly put his hands out of sight under the
table. But she didn't say anything. She wouldn't, until the others
had gone, and by then, with luck, Dominic himself could be
out of the way for an hour or two. Maybe she'd forget, maybe
father wouldn't notice. Inside an hour he could finish his homework and be off to the kitchen-yard of the 'Shock of Hay' to
collect Pussy.

Unhappily in his haste to get rid of his homework he forgot
to conceal his hands, and the jut of scored knuckles from a
chewed pen was too obvious to escape Sergeant Felse's notice

when he sat back from his late tea. George wasn't yet so far from his own schooldays that he couldn't interpret the signs. But George had an inconvenient conscience which moved him occasionally to demand more from his son than he had ever provided for his father. He reached over Dominic's shoulder, took the inky hand and turned it about in his own palm, and held on to it firmly when Dominic attempted to slide it away again. Dominic, sighing, thought and almost said: 'Here it comes!'

'Hm!' said George. 'Interesting! Who licked you?'

Dominic fidgeted, and frowned, and said: 'Old Wedderburn.'

'Oh. I thought he didn't go in for violence?'

'This time he did,' snapped Dominic. 'Look out, the pen's going to drip. Mind my algebra!' He wriggled, and was released; he grumbled just above his breath, like a half-grown pup growling, and mopped the small blot in the margin with unnecessary energy, to divert attention from his injuries. But he heard George chuckle.

'What was it all about? Fighting? Oh, don't trouble to duck, I've already seen your eye.'

'Does it show much?' asked Dominic, fingering it rather anxiously.

'Going to be a beauty. Somebody else licked you, evidently, besides old Wedderburn.'

'He didn't!' said Dominic indignantly. 'You just ought to see him, that's all. I bet he'll have more than just a black eye to show by tomorrow.' The gleam came back to his eyes readily, brightening them to the colour of home-made marmalade. He pushed his chair back from the table to balance it on its two back legs, and wound his own long, flannelled shanks bewilderingly about the front ones, braced on his taut brown arms, suddenly grinning, suddenly gloating, the little devil, about as subdued as a cock robin in the nesting season. Four feet seven of indiarubber and whalebone, with a shock head of dark chestnut hair growing in all directions, and a freckled nose, and an

21

obstinate mouth; a good deal like his mother, only Bunty's hair was frankly red, and her skin fair and clear of freckles. George's resolution to be properly paternal, and read the appropriate lecture, went by the board, as it usually did. After all, he spent all his days being serious, even portentous, about minor crimes, he couldn't quite keep it up after hours with his own boy; and he was well aware in his own heart, though he never admitted it, that while he was more ready to threaten, it was usually Bunty who performed. She had a way of advancing with perfect calm and patience to the limit of what she would stand, and then, only occasionally and with devastating effect, falling on her startled son like a thunderstorm. And George's conscience, aware of shortcomings, impelled him sometimes to express concern ahead of her, so that he might at least appear to be the seat of authority in the house. She never snubbed him, she only smiled, and said with suspicious sweetness: 'Yes, darling, you're perfectly right!'

Tonight, when he followed her into the scullery and took the teacloth out of her hand, she turned and gave him the too demure smile which made him feel about Dominic's age; and with a very natural reaction he resolved to be his full thirty-nine years, and be damned to her.

'Our Dom's been in trouble at school,' he said with gravity.

'So was his father before him,' said Bunty, 'many a time. It didn't make the slightest impression on him, either. Dom's all right, don't you worry.' Aunt Nora and John were already down the road and waiting for the bus back to Comerbourne Bridge, and Bunty could laugh at both George and Dominic if she pleased, without hurting either of them. She patted his cheek disconcertingly with her wet hand, and snatched a cup from him just in time to prevent him from dropping it. 'You're so like him, it just isn't true.'

George took exception to this. 'He's the spitting image of you, and you know it. Try and make him go the way he doesn't want, and see how far you get with it. But he *is* a little devil!'

He recaptured the paternal frown with some difficulty, for heavier things than Dominic had been on his mind all day, and this was by way of self-indulgence at the end of the common task. Sometimes he thought: 'Why did I ever go into this police business, anyway?'

'What was it this time?' asked Bunty serenely.

'He fell foul of Chad Wedderburn over scrapping with some other kid. Seems there are some things that get Chad's goat, after all. They had to hunt for a long time before they found one of 'em – it took Dom to do it! – but he's managed it this time. A queer lad,' said George thoughtfully. 'Chad, I mean. Would you suppose that his particular red rag would be fighting?'

'I can conceive it,' said Bunty, rinsing the sink. 'Hasn't he had about enough of it to last him a lifetime?'

'That isn't really any reason, though, why he should grudge our Dom his bash.'

'It's on the right side, anyhow,' she said comfortably. 'Not that Dom usually goes hunting for that particular kind of trouble, to do the little tyke justice. You didn't ask him anything about it, did you?' A hazel eye very like Dominic's regarded him sidelong for a flash, and appeared satisfied with his indignant stare; off duty she found little difference between her husband and her son. 'Sorry, darling! Of course you didn't. Neither did I. He looked so on his dignity, I didn't dare. But he won,' she said positively, 'it was sticking out all over him.'

'I wish some of his elders had learned enough sense to quit scrapping,' said George. 'Win or lose, it's a mug's game, but there are always more mugs than plenty.' He hung up the towel neatly and rolled his shirt-sleeves down. 'Dealing with kids must be money for jam compared with our job.'

'The child,' murmured Bunty, 'is father to the man. I don't suppose there's much to choose. Had a bad sort of day then?'

'Not exactly – just ominous.' He liked to talk to her about his job, at night, when he could kick it out of his mind for a short time if he wished, and therefore with human perversity ceased to wish it. Closer than his skin was Bunty, the partner of partners, and often she could help him to see a little more daylight through the opaque human creatures who vexed and made interesting his days. 'I wouldn't care to say that our D.P.s are any less honest by nature than we are, but their dependent circumstances, or all they've been through, or something, has certainly given some of 'em the idea that they're entitled to be carried for the rest of their days. *And* that all we've got is theirs for the taking. Rum, you know, old girl – I could have swallowed that, but they pinch from *one another*. That I just don't get. Nobody dare leave anything lying around in the camp these days. And how the farm workers do love 'em, to be sure!'

'Cheer up,' said Bunty helpfully, 'the knives haven't been out for three nights, not even at turning-out time.'

'Knock on wood when you say things like that, just to please me. Still, the land's awake, all right, maybe we've got to thank the visitors for that. And I suppose they have had the rough end of it for some years, poor devils – but what we'll stand from somebody who couldn't get on with his own country – or hasn't risked trying it – is nobody's business. Mind you,' said George scrupulously, 'there are some fine chaps among 'em, too. They're the ones I'm sorry for. There may be some place in the world where they belong, but it certainly isn't among their fellow-exiles here in Comerford.'

'A man without any national roots,' said Bunty gravely, 'is the last person to make a good adopted child in another country.'

'That's the hell of it. The last person to make any kind of internationalist, either. But we've got 'em, and we've got to try and digest 'em.'

It was almost invariably at this hour in the evening, when slippers, and pipe, and a drowsy evening with the wireless floated comfortably in George's mind's eye, that the office telephone rang. It did so now, and Dominic, already on the doorstep with trunks and towel rolled under his arm, shrieked back unnecessarily to inform them of the call, and ask if he should answer it. Either way he was content; he wanted to go and fetch Pussy out from her tiresome music lesson and go swimming in the pool of the Comer, but it would also be gratifying to listen in to the beginning, at least, of some interesting incident. However, he departed blithely when George came out to the office himself, for trouble would keep, and the golden July evening would not.

'Hell!' said George, reaching for the receiver. 'This is what comes of drawing fate's attention to – Hullo, yes! Felse here!' Bunty saw the official tension settle upon his face, and heaved a resigned sigh. When he hung up she had his cap already in her hands, and was holding it out to him with a comical resignation.

'Who mentioned knives?' said George accusingly, ducking his head into it wrathfully, ducking a little lower still to kiss her as he hooked open the door. 'From now on, woman, keep off that line of talk, you've got me a real casualty this time.'

'Where?' cried Bunty. 'Not the camp?'

'The Lodge – young miner at the hostel copped it from a P.O.W.'

'He's not badly hurt?' she shrieked after him, leaning forward in the doorway as he flung a leg across his bike and pushed off hard along the empty evening road.

'Be O.K., I think – I hope!' He was gone, and the rest of the story with him. Bunty went back dispiritedly into the kitchen and turned up the radio, but it was not much company. One might almost as well not have a husband; D.P.s, labour rows, neighbours swopping punches over a shared front path or a drying-ground, Road Safety Committee meetings, lectures, drunks, accidents, there was no end to it. And now some poor kid in trouble – maybe two poor kids, since most of the ex-P.O.W. recruits at the miners' hostel were no more. Say good-bye to that cosy evening with George, he won't be back until all hours.

'Maybe I should get me a dog,' said Bunty grimly, 'or take up fancy-work.'

IV

The Lodge had cost the Coal Board more than it was worth, and more than they need have paid for it if they had had the courage of their convictions; but it was house-room for thirty men. The warden was a decent, orthodox, middle-aged man who expected his troublous family of Welshmen, local boys, Poles, Germans and Czechs to behave in as orderly a manner as children in a preparatory school, and was out of his depth when they did not. The whole set-up was too new for him; he preferred an arrangement tried and hardened by use, where the right procedure for every eventuality was already safely laid down in black and white for a simple man to follow. Improvisation was not in his nature. He opened the studded imitation Tudor door to George, and perceptibly heaved all his responsibilities into those welcome navy-blue arms at sight. His wife would be less than useless; she had political convictions but no human ones. If the boy was really hurt they'd better get him out of there, thought George, before she gave him a chill.

'Doctor here?' he asked, half-way up the stairs with the warden babbling in his ear.

'Just ten minutes ahead of you, Sergeant. He's with the lad now.' There is a certain type of man who persists in using the word lad though it does not come naturally to him; the thing has a semi-clerical ring about it, a certain condescension. You get the feeling that a young male creature of one's own class would have been a boy, while this person is subtly different.

'Good! No verdict from him yet?'

'There's scarcely been time, Sergeant. This has been a terrible business, it might so easily have ended in a tragedy. This collier's

26

lad – ' A shade more of definition, and one step down; we're getting on, thought George.

'Which?' You didn't say who the victim was. Local boy?'

'Young Fleetwood. He's been here only a month, and really – '

'I know him,' said George. 'What about the other party?'

'A young man named Schauffler, Helmut Schauffler. I must say he's never given me any trouble before. A good type, I would have said. And, to be quite fair, I can't say he has been altogether to blame – certainly not the only one to blame – '

'Where is he now?'

'Down in my office. My assistant is there with him.'

'You weren't there when the thing happened? – wherever it did happen? Was anyone?'

'It was in the day-room. Three other men were present. They were playing darts. I don't know if you – '

'That's all right,' said George, marching across the landing, which betrayed its period by being lit with a large stained-glass window in improbable armorial bearings, notably of a violent blue. 'Let's see what the damage is, first. Which room?' But the murmur of voices had drawn him before the warden could reply, and he walked in upon the end of the doctor's ministrations without waiting to be led. There were more people round the bed. The warden's wife, holding with an expression of reserve and distaste an enamel bowl of water stained darkly red. A scared-looking eighteen-year-old backed up against his bed in the far corner; the rest of him trying to be invisible, but his ears sticking out on stalks. And somebody long and lean, or appearing long by reason of his leanness, standing with his back to the door and talking down to the boy on the bed across the doctor's bowed shoulder. A quiet, reasonable voice cheerfully advising the kid not to be an ass, because everything would be taken care of, including letting his mother know. The speaker looked round at the small sound the door made in opening, and showed the unexpected face of Chad Wedderburn, the slanting light magnifying his scar. Tonight he had another mark, too, a

27

small punctured bruise upon the same cheek, of which at the moment he seemed completely unaware.

The doctor was a little, grimly gay, middle-aged man with brilliant eyes, and false teeth which slipped at the most awkward moments, and which he plugged testily back into position with a sudden thumb whenever they tripped him. He looked over his shoulder at George, and with a welcoming grin, as who should say: 'Ah, trouble!' pulled him directly into consultation. Trouble was the breath of life to him, not because he enjoyed seeing people tormented, but because his energy was tumultuous, and demanded an exhausting variety of interests to employ it through the day.

'There you are, Sergeant!' he said, as if George had been there from the beginning. 'What did I tell you? Only a perfectly clean wound, touched a rib, no damage, not the ghost of a complication of any kind. Thinks he's going to die because he bleeds freely. Thinks I'm going to forbid you to badger him, I dare say. Your mistake, my boy! Put you through it as much as he likes, I've no objection. Eat you if he likes! He'd find you tough enough if he tried it!' He was all this time busily finishing a bandage, and buttoning a stained shirt over it again with fingers which flew as fast as his tongue, but more steadily. The boy on the bed looked a little bewildered at the spate of words, but a little reassured, too, and stirred docilely from side to side as the hands directed him. 'Good boy! You're all right, I promise you. Nothing in the world to worry about, so take that scared look off your face, and relax. All you've got to do is exactly as you're told for a few days. Something new for you, eh? Eh?'

Apprehensive but faintly soothed grey eyes flickered from the doctor's face to George's, and back again. Young Fleetwood was seventeen, sturdy but small for his age; on his own here now, George remembered, the family had moved south. Clever, idealistic kid, out to save the country and the world, so he by-passed the chance of teaching, and set out to cure what was wrong with the mines. Probably end up as a mining engineer, and

28

maybe that would reconcile his old man, who had been a collier himself and learned to look upon it as something not good enough for his sons. All the more important because there was only this one son now; the elder was dead in the last push into Germany, in 1945.

'I'm taking him into hospital for a few days,' said the doctor briskly. 'No great need, but I'd like him under my eye.'

'Best thing for him, I'd say. How bad was it?'

'Quite a gash – sliced wound, but the rib stopped the knife, or it might have been a bad job. The ambulance will be here for him in about ten minutes, but if you need longer – ? Let him down easy, he's had a fright.'

'That's all right, he wouldn't know how to start being scared of me,' said George cheerfully. 'Known me all his life.' He sat on the edge of the bed, and smiled at the boy until he got a wan smile in return. 'Can we have the room to ourselves until the ambulance comes? Let me know when you're ready for him, doctor.'

Jim Fleetwood let the room empty of everyone else, but turned his head unhappily after Chad Wedderburn, and reached a hand to keep him, but drew it back with a slight flush, ashamed of hanging on to comfort. Chad said quietly: 'It's all right, Jim, I'll come back.'

'Stay, by all means,' said George, 'if he wants you. That's all right with me. I know the feeling.' The door closed after the others, and it was quiet in the room. 'That's better! How did you get here? Just visiting?'

'Jim asked for me, and his room-mate called me on the phone. I was ahead of the doctor. His family are a long way off, you see; I suppose I seemed about as solid a prop as he could think of off-hand.' He looked, at that, as if he might be. The broken bruise on his cheek burned darkly; he saw George's eyes linger on it, and said evenly: 'Yes, I walked into it, too. This was a present from the same bloke. The row was barely over when I got here, everybody was arguing, down in the day-room, what

29

happened and what didn't happen. Schauffler happens to be a kind I know already. He didn't much like being known. But he'd given up the knife by then, luckily for me. I was turning away from him at the time,' he explained gently, but with a certain tension in his voice which hinted at stresses underneath. 'I had Jim in my arms. The Schauffler kind chooses its time.'

'I wish you'd lit into him then,' said Jim, feebly blazing. 'I wish you'd killed him.'

'You're a fine pal, to want me hanged for a Helmut Schauffler!'

The boy paled at the thought, and lost his voice for fear of saying something of equally awful implications with the next breath.

'There isn't going to be any trouble, is there? I don't want my people to get it wrong.' He began to flush and shake a little, and George put a hand on his shoulder to quiet him.

'The only trouble you've got is a few days in hospital, and the job of getting on your feet again. Just tell us all about it, and then quit worrying about anything except getting well. We'll see that your parents don't get it wrong. You can trust us. If I don't make a good job of it, Wedderburn will. Now, how did this business start?'

'It's been going on a week or more, ever since I was coming from the showers one day, and saw him just leaving some more German chaps outside. They saluted each other the Nazi way, and said: 'Heil, Hitler!' – just as if there hadn't been any war, and our Ted and all the other chaps gone west for nothing. I dare say I oughtn't to have cut loose, but what can you expect a chap to do? I couldn't stand it. I suppose I raved a bit – honestly, I can't remember a damned word I said, but I suppose it was all wrong and idiotic. I should have hit him, only Tom Stephens and some more fellows came, and lugged me away. I didn't put any complaint in – I couldn't, because I was ashamed I'd made such a muck of it, and anyhow he hadn't done anything to me, only stand there and grin. But ever since then he's picking on me here – nothing you could get hold of, because there never was anyone else around to see and hear – but he'd slip remarks in my ear as he went by – he got to find out about Ted, somehow. I think he's been prying here in my room. But I can't *prove* any of it. I'm telling you, but it's only my word for it. Only, honestly, I haven't made it up, and I'm not imagining it, either.'

'I wish you'd had the sense to come to me days ago,' said Chad Wedderburn.

'Well, but I didn't want to make trouble for you, and it was all so slippery. You can see it's no good now. I only made you take the same sort of nastiness I've had.'

'What about tonight?' prompted George.

'He was down in the day-room, playing darts with three of the fellows. They didn't often invite him in, but I suppose he was there, and they took him on. I didn't even know. I went down there to borrow a fine screw-driver, because I'd broken the strut of Ted's photo, and I was putting a new one on it. When I went in he was sitting by the table, and he had a clasp-knife, and was trimming the end of a dart that wouldn't fly true. I never took any notice of him. I just put the photo on the table – as far from him as it would go, but it's only a small table – and asked Tom Stephens for his pocket gadget, and he gave it to me, and went on with the game. And I went back to pick up my picture.' He stirred painfully on his pillow, and shut his teeth together hard to stop a rising gulp. 'It's Ted in his uniform – I went and left it down there – '

'Don't worry, we'll take care of that. Go on!'

'He sat there whittling away with the knife, and he looked at me over it, and then he spat – making believe he was spitting on the blade, and then stooping down to sharpen it on the sole of his shoe – but he knew what he was about, all right! He spat on Ted's photo – spattered it all over the face – He spat on my brother, and grinned at me! A dirty little Nazi like that!'

'So you went for him,' said George equably.

'Of course I did! What would you expect me to do? I dropped the screw-driver – anyhow it was a little pocket thing, all closed up, like a lipstick – and went for him, and hit him in the face, and he started to get up and lunge at me, all in one movement. The knife went into me, and I fell on the top of him, and then the other three came and pulled us apart, and I was bleeding like a pig – and – and I was scared like a kid, and started to yell for Mr. Wedderburn, and Tom went and got him – and that's all.'

Not all, perhaps, that could be told, but all that Jim was capable of telling just then, and it was as full of holes as any sieve. He looked speculatively at Chad's darkening cheek, and asked: 'What about your little incident? If you had the kid in your arms at the time, *you* can hardly have started the rough stuff.'

Chad smiled sourly. 'I didn't even call him rude names. It was all strictly schoolmaster stuff. He was sitting like a damp sack until I turned to go out of the day-room, and then he shot up like a rocket, and took a hack at me. I – hadn't been complimentary, of course. His poor English might have led him to find words there which I never used.'

'Don't put words in *my* mouth,' said George hastily.

'Just the words you'll probably find in his. He has them all, there's been time to find the right ones. But it would hold up an assault charge,' he said simply, 'if you're hard up. Every little helps!'

George thought it might, but discreetly said nothing. He patted Jim with an absent-minded cheerfulness, as he might have done a Dominic smitten with stomach-ache, bade him do as he was told, like a good chap, and not worry about anything; and with the exchange of a glance committed him again to the surprising care of Chad Wedderburn, who was inexpertly putting together the small necessities of a stay in hospital from the chest-of-drawers. 'See him off, and keep him happy. Come along to the station on your way back, will you? I'll take care of brother Ted, you can be easy, you shall have him back safely.'

He went down, not very well satisfied, to collect three vague and confused statements from the dart-players. An incident only three seconds long is not seen clearly by men whose minds are concentrated on a dart-board placed on the other side of the room. Tom Stephens, who was the most anxious to back up his room-mate, said he had seen the blow struck, and didn't think it was any accident. He had also seen the insult to Ted's photograph, which still lay on the table with half-dried stains of spittle undoubtedly marking the glass, and his firm impression was that that had been no error of judgment, either, but a deliberate provocation. But the other two were less ready to swear to it. The German had started up to defend himself, and the open knife was already in his hand; what could you expect in the circumstances? Jim had hit him first, and quite possibly on mistaken grounds. They wouldn't like to say he had meant any harm.

As for the warden, he wanted everything smoothed down into a chapter of accidents, the eruption of contrary temperaments intent on thinking the worst of each other. Schauffler had always been a good, quiet fellow, a little sullen and defensive in this place where he felt himself unwanted, but anxious to avoid trouble rather than to court it. The position of an anti-Nazi German soldier allowed into industry here was certainly a difficult one, and it was the warden's opinion that hot-headed young people like Jim Fleetwood did nothing to make it easier. All this he poured into George's ear as they went along the corridor to his office to have a look at this vexed case in the flesh.

The warden's assistant was sitting at a desk near the top-heavy Victorian fireplace, and opposite him in a straight-backed chair, perfectly still and inert, sat Helmut Schauffler. He was perhaps twenty-three or four, blond as a chorus-girl, with a smooth face weathered to dark ivory, and light-blue eyes a little moist and swollen, as if he had been crying, and could cry again at will. But the rest of his face, smooth across broad, hard bones, was too motionless to suggest that any sort of grief was involved in the phenomenon. He should, thought George, be a pretty impressive specimen when on his feet, broad-shouldered and narrow-flanked, with large, easy movements; but just now he didn't look capable of movement at all, he sat, as Chad had said, like a damp sack, helpless and hopeless, with his flaccid hands dangling between his knees. They didn't look as if they had bones enough in them to hold a knife, much less steer it into another man's ribs. When George entered, the blue eyes lifted to his face apprehensively, like the eyes of an animal in a trap, but the rest of his face never moved a muscle.

His voice was deep but vague in pitch, fitting the sullen indefiniteness of his person; his English was interestingly broken. He burst easily into a long and pathetic explanation of the whole incident, the burden of his song being that here he was an outcast, misinterpreted, misunderstood, that his most harmless gestures were held to be threats, and the most innocent lapses of his tongue, astray among the complexities of the English language, taken as deliberate affronts. Once animated by his own woes, his body exhibited some of the tensions which had been missing, drew itself into the compact and muscular mass it was meant to be, with double the adolescent strength of Jim Fleetwood in it. It appeared, in fact, to enjoy its own animal competence. The hands, flattened along his thighs, no longer looked incapable of killing.

'I never wish to hurt this boy, I never wish to insult his brother, never. That one was a soldier; I too, I respect him. It is by a bad chance it happens like that. But the young brother is so hot, all at once he runs at me, strikes me in the face – I do not even know what it is he thinks I have done! When I am struck so, I jump up to fend him off – who not? The knife I forget, all is so suddenly happening, I am so confused. It is only he, running at me, he runs on the knife in my hand – What am I to say? If I am not German, this does not happen. If I am

34

not German, he does not so quickly think the worst in all I do. What is it, to be here in this country a German?'

George reminded him delicately of the Nazi salute which had not passed unnoticed at the colliery. He admitted it, tears of despair starting in his blue eyes.

'Thus we are taught so long, thus it must be done years of our lives, can we so soon lose it? It comes to my hand, so, my will does not know what I do. Never have I been a Nazi, only one must conform, or for parents, family, all, is very bad life. I am young, I do as I am taught. And now it makes me to seem an enemy here, where I would be only a quiet citizen.'

His depression deepened when the unwarrantable blow at Chad Wedderburn was recalled to his memory. Five people had seen that, and to deny it was purposeless; even excuses might carry less weight here, but he could try. He enjoyed trying, George could see that. As the tragedy and doom of his eyes deepened, the exultation and sleekness of his body became more clear and insolent, like the arrogant stretchings of a cat before a fire.

'That was a bad thing, I own it, I regret it. But even that I do not mean. I am confused, angry, I am in trouble and afraid, no one helps me, no one explains or wishes to make things easier. This man, it is well understood he is very angry for the boy Jim. But he rages at me – half he says I do not understand, and so perhaps I think it worse than it is. I lose my head, and strike him because I am in despair. But when I have done it I am sorry, I no longer wish to hurt him. I am very sorry and ashamed.'

He wept a subtle tear or two; George was impressed in spite of himself. He went away to phone Weaver, and get a car from Comerbourne. This hostel was no place for Helmut Schauffler now, from any point of view; even the warden would be glad to get rid of him, though one felt that he would be equally glad to get rid of Jim. And in view of the fact that somebody, somewhere, was due to have considerable trouble with Helmut in the future, maybe a few days in custody wouldn't do any harm; especially as the tears and broken words were due to flow for the magistrates' benefit even more readily than they had done for George's, and he doubted if a charge of unlawful wounding or causing bodily harm was going to stand up successfully under their weight.

He didn't forget to collect Ted's photograph, clean it gravely of the traces of Helmut's attentions, and commit it to the care of Tom Stephens until Jim came home. It was the usual conventional photograph of a simple young man in uniform: candid-eyed, vulnerable, not too intelligent, very much Jim's brother; easy meat, the pair of them, for a Helmut Schauffler. George felt depressed, and not altogether because of the immediate upsets of Comerford. Something was going wrong here which had also larger implications; it wasn't in a few months' time that the world was due to hear about it, but in twenty years or so, after a few people had shouted their hearts out about it and been shrugged aside as mental for their pains.

George went home at last, late and slowly, and found Chad Wedderburn talking to Bunty in the kitchen. The cut on his cheek was discolouring badly, and by tomorrow would be a focus of extreme interest for the Fourth, George said, remembering the beginning of his evening as if it drifted back to him from a thousand miles away: 'I hope Dom hasn't seen that. If he has, you're liable to be sued for breach of contract, or obtaining money on false pretences, or something.'

When Chad laughed, the stiffening cut quivered and laughed with him. 'I'm afraid he has. He was a little late getting home, and we met on the doorstep. His eyes popped out of his head, almost. He's probably hanging over the banisters now, all ears.'

'I hope,' said Bunty, 'he's asleep by this time, or there'll be not getting him up in the morning. What would you like him to be told, if he assumes I've got the whole story out of you?' And though she said 'if ', it was immediately clear to George

36

that indeed she had. She wore a satisfied look, as if she had not been altogether left out of events.

'I leave it to your husband,' said Chad, grinning at George. 'Or haven't you got a clue, either?'

'I could tell him the truth, I suppose, but he'd be pretty disgusted with you.'

'Oh, I don't know!' said Chad, smiling down a little sombrely at the curling smoke of his cigarette. 'He'd see the arguments for non-violence – in the circumstances. Still, I do admit – '

'You'd have liked to pulverise him, wouldn't you?'

'It would have been a pleasure,' said Chad, in voice and word still understating.

'Why didn't you? Oh, I know, you were thinking about Jim, you wanted him safe out of the rotten business without any more harm – and all that. Still – why didn't you?'

The hard, lean fingers closed gently together on the end of the cigarette and crushed it out. 'I was afraid,' said Chad, very simply, 'that if I started I should probably kill him.'

V

Helmut Schauffler was discharged on the bodily harm charge, though with a warning that it was dismissed only by reason of an element of doubt as to his motives, and the extent to which sheer accidental circumstances had framed him. On the assault charge he was fined £2, which within the allotted time he contrived to pay. The magistrates gave full weight to his passionate plea that everybody was against him, and the worst construction automatically put on everything he did; so anxious were they to be excluded from the everybody thus censured that they leaned over backwards to be generous to him, and expressed the hope that he would yet find his niche in England, and settle down happily among his neighbours. The local colliery administration had already decided by then that they would be

courting trouble by taking him back, and in their turn hoped
that something else might be found for him, something more
retired from the frictions of hostel life. Say some job on a farm.
He was able-bodied, and a hard worker by inclination; if he had
to deal only with a very small group of individuals who were
prepared to take a little trouble with him, the results might still
be admirable. The magistrates called this case to the attention
of any local farmers who might be in need of a hand, and hoped
one of them would feel able to make the experiment.

Gerd Hollins read the local weekly religiously from front
page to back every Saturday evening. She put it down and
looked at her husband over the carefully folded sheets at last,
and was quiet for a long time. Whenever she fixed her eyes on
him thus, Chris Hollins felt their plucking as the strings of a
harp feel the fingers that wrest music out of them, and had to
look up and meet her dark glance before he could have any rest.

They had been married now for ten years; she had been in
England for twelve, and her speech was flawlessly English, per-
fected even with the leisurely country softness of Comerford,
where she had learned most of it. But she kept still some little
opulent gestures and elaborations of manner which set her apart
as clearly as an accent would have done. She had been assimilated without being changed; sometimes it was merely plain that
she was not English, sometimes one could safely judge her
country to be Germany. Always, though her quietness withdrew
it into the background of her personality, the discerning eye
could be sure that she was a Jewess. Her father had been a
teacher in Dessau; there had been three brothers, and one more
sister. Now there was only Gerd. She had escaped in the autumn
of 1937, and by interminable ways round Europe arrived in
England, where she had found domestic work, and begun to
scrape together all the money she could, in readiness for the
day when some other member of the family should follow her.
But nobody ever came. It was only by the most elaborately
capricious of chances that she herself had ever arrived. Long

after she had married Christopher Hollins she had gone on hoping and believing that the others would turn up, after the war; and after the war she had traced at least her youngest brother, but to a cardboard box of ashes on a shelf in a room of the crematorium of Osviecim. And that was all.

Gerd was in the middle thirties, and already less handsome than she had been; but Chris was fifty, and found her very beautiful. Even if her figure had rounded and spread far more disastrously, and the understandable grey in her smooth, rather coarse black hair been more obtrusive, he would still have thought her a beauty, for he was still in love with her, and probably always would be. He had lived all his life in the constant round of his little lands, a hill-farm just above the village, mostly sheep-pasture; but she had brought here in her person all the romance and all the tragedy of Europe, and in spirit he understood it better, and burned with it more deeply, than many who had wandered through it in uniform and seen it for themselves, but without an interpreter. Most people found him narrow and dull and virtuously uninteresting, but inside the placid shell she had found house-room for all the havoc of humanity's hopes; and living alone with him was not boring to her.

She folded the paper more firmly, the dry half-column of 'Magistrates' Courts' framed between her hands. 'Chris, have you seen this?' She gave it to him. He read it silently, and looked at her again, and gravely.

'Perhaps you'll think it a counsel of desperation,' she said, 'but I want you to take in this man.'

'But all these years,' he said, astonished, 'you've avoided having any contact with Germans. Why should you suddenly want to have one here? I'm dead sure it would be a mistake. Better not to think of them, even, not to remember they exist.'

'I know! I've been wrong to avoid the issue. If by trying one could really forget they exist, that might be well. But I have tried – as you say, I've tried for years – and without success. How long can one go on running away from a fact, I wonder?

39

Chris, I haven't done you or myself any good. You can't pretend things haven't happened. I'm tired of trying. If I could make this effort, it would be better for us both.'

'It's too big a risk,' he said. 'We should be fools to go looking for trouble. He'll only remind you all over again, every time you look at him. That's no way to get rid of memories.'

'I've tried smothering them,' she said, 'for years. It's no good that way, Chris. I can't forget things that way. There's only one thing for it, and that's to admit everything and accept everything, and find some way of living that doesn't mean always sitting on top of a chest of grudges, trying to keep the lid from opening. If I could get used to the idea that Germans are much the same as other flesh and blood – if there could be some ordinary boy, stupid perhaps, difficult perhaps, I don't care – only someone who could have something in him worth forgiving – '

'You seem to have picked a difficult case if you want this one,' he said bitterly.

'There are no easy ones. Anyhow, what would be the good of an easy one? It would mean nothing. But he's young – and if it succeeded, I should be a lot happier. Chris, I want to try. Let me try!'

'I don't know!' he said. 'I'll have to think about it. Give me a little time to consider. I'm involved in this, too.'

'Yes,' she agreed, 'because you, too, would be happier if we could get rid of this past that follows us about.'

It is not easy to shake off memory by any method; and gentle and still as she was, and spotlessly innocent of any act which should haunt her afterwards, and unfair though it is that the acts of other persons should haunt us, Hollins had felt her always being followed by the hate and horror which even she could not escape. He did not reflect that her nature was soft, and should have been unretentive. He was not given to thinking except by such processes as lift the shoot to the light. But he could perceive, and he perceived that she made the best of things, and even enjoyed some happiness, always with the footsteps treading on her heels. Ten years had not achieved a cure by leaving well alone; it might be worth even the risk of meddling.

So he thought about it, and sought another opinion because thought was such unfamiliar country to him. He talked it over with Jim Tugg, in the late afternoon when he came back tired from the last of the dipping. Jim listened, and his black brows drew together over the gaunt deeps of his eyes.

'Your wife's a saint,' he said, wasting no words, 'but she's a fool, too. If you do a daft thing like that, you'll be buying trouble for everybody.'

'That's what I'm afraid of,' admitted Hollins; 'but she's set her mind on it.'

'More fool her, to think it could do any good. And more fool you, if you let her have her way. Forgive! You might as well forgive an adder for being an adder, and pick it up in your hand, and expect it not to bite you.'

He was no comfort. He said the same things to Gerd, and in much the same words. She heard him attentively, fixing her great, black, young, sad eyes on him trustfully, for he was friend as well as shepherd. When he had done, she said: 'You may be right. Yet if it could be only one accidentally decent boy, he would do. If I could *like* one of them, and be able to bear it that I came from the same race, it would be enough. And there must be some who are good – you know it is impossible there should be none at all.'

'Some there may be,' he said, 'but don't look for them here. The best go back, they want to do something for their own country. What do you expect to find here? There's so little in any of them except what someone with more will has planted – they've got no bones of their own to stand up by.'

'I cannot go on all my life hating,' said Gerd. 'I wasn't made for it.'

Jim turned his dark, massive face towards her, and said:

41

'While there's hateful things gong on every day side by side with us, what's wrong with hating?'

'It's painful. It deforms one. Perhaps it even kills.'

'Not a chance!' he said with a fiery smile, sultry and sudden like the red of a bonfire breaking through the damp smouldering blanket of sods. 'It keeps alive, sometimes. With no other solitary thing to live for, hate can keep you alive.'

'It is not a way in which I can maintain life,' she said, looking at him plaintively; but she was never angry, never condemned his angers, never said things heatedly without considering first if she truly meant them. And therefore, for one who loved her, it was necessary always to listen to her earnestly, and try to make the adjustments which alone could help you to understand her.

'No,' he said, staring at her steadily, 'no, I don't suppose you could.' She did not know, because she thought so little of herself she did not guess, even when he looked at her like that, that he adored her. Why should she suspect it? She was a few years older than he, and looked older still; she was greying, her figure was growing soft and shapeless and middle-aged, and her face had never been striking, even in first youth. 'Try, then!' he said, and abruptly turned away. 'Have it your own way! If it doesn't come off – if he's all I think he might be – there's always me around to deal with him. But if he turns out to be the usual kind,' said Jim Tugg, 'I'll kill him.'

She did not think anything of that, not because he was given to saying such things, but because everyone says them sooner or later. Her mind had gone too far with the idea to turn back; if she had retreated from her purpose now it would only have been one more ghost on her heels, like the spectral bastard of the older memories.

So Helmut came. He came lumpishly, defensively, with closed face and warding-off eyes, as if he feared everyone he met might hit him. They received him without fuss or too much favour, like any other hand, lodging him in the attic room over the house end of the stables, and feeding him at their own table. But getting his head out from between his shoulders was a labour for Hercules during the first few days, and tools were needed to prise out a few whispered words. He worked willingly, even anxiously, and looked years younger than his age because he seemed so lost and timorous; but it was true that the actual lines of his face, in their solidity and stillness, did not quite bear out the unformed, grieved questing of his eyes. He seemed so young that Gerd was moved, and the warmth of it came into her heart gratefully, and she believed she had succeeded.

She was not even very unwise. She called him Helmut, because Jim was always Jim, but used it very seldom because it came stiffly to her tongue. Only if she had to use a name for him, that was the name. And on his part there were few words except: 'Yes, Mrs. Hollins!' and 'No, Mrs. Hollins!' like a dutiful boy new from school. Jim behaved to him with careful but competent coolness, as to an awkward gate-post freshly painted. And in a few days Helmut began to expand to his full size, instead of going about shrunk defensively into himself; and in a few days more, when he had his true height, only an inch below Jim's, and his great, loose young breadth of shoulder spread for all to see, his gait and all his movements, down to the extending of a hand to accept a plate, acquired a glossy, exultant smoothness, his step an effortless spring, his voice a resonance hitherto unsuspected.

'He comes to himself,' said Gerd, and was pleased, as if the triumph had been hers.

He did come to himself, and with a vengeance. He was late in to his dinner one day, having stayed to finish a repair job on one of the distant fences; and by the time he arrived Hollins was away again, and Jim just leaving. She served Helmut alone. He watched her as she came and went, and his light blue eyes had stopped being young and pathetic, and were bright, opaque and interested. They travelled all over her, and enjoyed their sapience. Suddenly in the very same tone in which he had just

43

thanked her for his pudding he said in German: 'You like it better here than at home, do you? The English are more long-suffering?'

Her step faltered for only the fraction of a second. She put a cup of coffee at his elbow, and said quite calmly and levelly: 'Do not speak German to me. I prefer not to use it.'

'You want to forget it?' he suggested sympathetically, and flashing up at her a quick, cold grimace which was not quite a smile.

'I prefer not to use it. If you speak in it I shall not answer you.'

'In English then,' he said, and laughed so briefly that the sound was gone almost as soon as recognised. He stretched himself, leaning back in his chair to have her the more securely in view. 'Do you think even the English do not tire at last? There are some who are tired already of harbouring you. They make little noise yet, but the time will come when you will hear it, even in this very nice comfortable place.'

No protests came to her lips, because there was no use in them. She turned her back and went away from him, carrying dirty dishes into the scullery, as if he did not exist, or only as precisely the same rather lumpish and harmless young man he had been five minutes before. Behind her he said, a little more sharply for her apparent calm, but still with a shy, subtle quietness: 'You hear already, but a Jew crawls away only when he must. Even when you kick him out at the door he creeps in by the window again.'

She closed the door between them, and began to fill the sink, as if nothing in the world had happened; her heart in her breast was like a white-hot stone, heavy, dragging her body down into a dark place she did not know, but she began to whisk soap powder into the water, to slide the knives into it, and clatter them out again on to the draining-board.

Presently he brought his dishes in to her there, the door opening almost apologetically as on his first day, and his big, fair body coming in sidelong. She felt him there, though she did not turn her head, and all she saw was his hands as he put down the plate and cup on the table at her right hand. Then, as he was going, he touched her; his fingertips, first so softly that the contact was hardly perceptible, then with a sly, savouring firmness, in the soft flesh of her back, drawing lines, drawing a subtle shape there on her body.

'Even in this nice country,' he whispered, with a stupid little giggling breath of excitement and pleasure in her ear, 'you will wear here, some day, a yellow star.'

He was gone, even a little hastily in the end, shutting the door loudly over her motionless silence. She stood there at the sink staring at her raised hands with a slight, concentrating frown, while the lather dried on them in little iridescent bubbles with the smallest of moist, bright sounds. She seemed to be contemplating some domestic complication such as the next week's grocery order. What she was actually seeing was a long, dark earth corridor, and six people walking down it, father, mother, Walter, Hans, Frieda, Josef; and at the end of it a crematorium trolley, into which, one by one, they quietly climbed and vanished.

Chapter 2

The Place —

I

The farms at Comerford, cheek by jowl with the collieries, lay round the rim of a misshapen bowl which circled a bend of the River Comer. Over all the high ground sheep-pasture jostled with the waste tips and shafts of the mines, and the relics of old forest filled every cranny of the hills still left to them. But the greatest acreage on these levels belonged to new and fantastic forest, which had eaten at the pastures until almost sixty per cent was absorbed. The pits had begun to dump here a hundred and fifty years ago from great numbers of sudden, shallow shafts; and having created about itself queer mud-pie shapes of clay, each shaft finally failed and was abandoned, the area being thereupon left for the wind to plant again, and the seasons to reclaim. On the better places a wild, deep, elastic grass grew, then heather, then the unconquerable silver birches which came from nowhere, by fragile-seeming colonies, to seed and flourish upon starvation. The casing of the shafts fell in, their perfunctory wooden surrounds disintegrated or were impounded in bad winters for firewood, and there remained, quite simply, a series of highly dangerous holes in the ground, which were nobody's business. Presently about these death-traps the high woodlands thickened with bramble and heather and bilberries, and made

46

soil enough for other trees to feed there; and a few more
enterprising landowners, like Selwyn Blunden of the Harrow,
covered the barren places with young plantations, and turned
parts of them into preserves, since they would raise no other
crop. So from forest Comerford circled round again to forest,
but these woods had the bizarre outlines of the high places
of Assyria, instead of the suave folded lines of the primeval
England.

Slithering inward from the cooler winds, the village coiled
itself inside the bowl, three convoluted streets, so involved that
one could nowhere see more than fifty yards ahead, and a maze
of footpaths kept clear by the obstinacy of the inhabitants, who
used them on principle even when they proved to be the longest
way home. And downward still from the village went the rich,
sheltered fields of the lower farms, greening, greening into the
black prolific water-meadows, and the serpentine curves and
bright calm pool of the Comer.

The main road, winding up the valley, made the passage of
the village perforce, for as yet there was no by-pass to spare
motorists the convolutions of the Comerford street. The railway
was just over the coal-rim and out of sight, with the local station
nestling a lane's length from the last wood of the Harrow
preserves.

On the rim the opencast unit camped like a giant circus,
leisurely stripping up the more naked of the clay hills, under
which the coal seams ran obliquely towards the Harrow; and on
this sacred land, too, the Coal Board had designs, so that the
contractor and his men sat and looked with shining eyes at
the fat wooded lands, and the heathery open levels extending
from the edge of their present site round to the skyline above
the river. Old Blunden had shrugged his shoulders over the
hectic changes in the landscape, in the social pattern of England
and Comerford, even in the day-to-day business of farming, and
had seemed to accept the necessity of adjusting himself to all
these things; but he was human, and when the encroaching

finger of change tried to creep over his own boundaries he stopped being quite so philosophical about it. The odds were that if the fight went against him he would pay up and look big, for he had always been a sporting old chap; but he would see to it that there was a fight first. His appeal was a massive responsibility, for he was one of the powers in the district still, for all his virtual retirement. The farm might be nominally his son's responsibility now, even his son's property, but their voices in this matter were one voice, and that was the old man's.

Meantime, the large, leather-coated, weather-beaten gypsies and their monstrous machines went on methodically building new mountains and gouging out new valleys, and the dark top-soil, neatly isolated, began to grow a fresh young grass even in the autumn, in the first decline of the beautiful year. And for the time being this edge of Comerford looked like a stretch of the baked clay deserts of Sinkiang. People who had never-turned a hair about the open shafts in the woods were never tired of lamenting this temporary devastation. Even the more thoughtful residents looked forward to the day when the lie of coal would be exhausted, and the site would be folded level and bare again to heal slowly in the soothing flow of seasons. Only the little boys, exulting in strange friendly men and the pleasures of change, collected new grotesque tractors and grabs and loaders as they had formerly collected cigarette packets and stamps, and gravitated to the site on their way home from school as dogs to a bone. Just as the twentieth-century nomads, the new navigators, gravitated inevitably to the pubs of Comerford in the darkening evenings, and boiled among the regulars like an incompatible ingredient in some chemical mixture, with larger bodies, louder voices and different accents, a race of good-humoured giants left over from the primitive world.

The 'Shock of Hay' was the largest pub in the village, snug under the shadow of the church tower, with the trim oval green drawn around it like a nicely arranged skirt about a demure woman posing for her portrait. It had a creaking picture-sign so faded that it might have been anything, and a large stable-yard from the heyday of horses, and an erroneous reputation of being a coaching inn, though the truth was that no coach in the history of transport ever ran so crazy a route as to pass through Comerford. The house was warm and red and squat, with ceilings rather low for Georgian, but rooms of the commendable spaciousness which gives a large man license to stretch his legs as he sits, without tangling them in the iron stand of the next table, or tripping up his neighbour in the gangway. The sunshine miners liked it because they could sprawl; but they liked it also, as everybody did, because it possessed the inestimable asset of the person of Io Hart.

Joe Hart owned and ran it. He had been born there, and his father before him, and though he had had a few vicissitudes in his young days, sown a few unexpected crops here and there, been a boxer and a fireman and a lumberjack for brief periods, it had always been taken for granted that when the old man died he should come here and take over the business. And so he had, as to the manner born.

Mrs. Hart had been dead for four years now, but Io, the elder daughter, who was twenty-two, had everything at her finger-ends, could manage the whole diverse flow of customers year in and year out without disarranging a curl of her warm brown hair, and make her father, into the bargain, do whatever she wanted. When she knew what she wanted, which wasn't always. Folks were beginning to say that she didn't know which of two young men she wanted, and that was shaping into quite a serious matter, especially when they would come and do their quarrelling in the snug, and over any mortal thing under the sun except Io. Luckily, the only other girl was thirteen, a safe age yet. Her name was Catherine, but it had been shortened to Cat early in her schooldays, and from that had swivelled round into Pussy, by which unexpected and in many ways unsuitable name everyone in Comerford knew her. She was an extremely self-possessed young woman, shaped like a boy rather than a girl, though not so

lumpy at the joints; she could outrun most boys of her age, skim
stones over the Comer with a flick of the wrist like a whip-lash
while the shots of her rivals sank despondently in mid-stream,
climb like any monkey, throw from the shoulder, keep up her
end one-handed in school or out of it, and had generally, as
her father proudly said (though not in her hearing), all her
buttons on. She would never be the beauty Io was, but in another
way she might be pretty disturbing in a few years, with her
direct green eyes and her snub nose, and all that light-brown
hair now impatiently confined in two long plaits, one over either
shoulder. But the only kind of cat she recalled was some rangy
tigerish tom, treading sleekly across the gardens in long strides
with his soft, disdainful feet; not the kind of cat one would call
Pussy. Because of its inappropriateness the name stuck; people
are like that.

Io was darker of eyes and hair, though fairer of face. She had
a pink-and-white skin which glowed softly, and when she smiled,
which was often, the glow seemed to brighten and deepen,
warming her whole face. She was one of those fortunate people
who are dainty by nature, invariably dainty without any effort
on their part, whose clothes always fit, whose hair always curls,
and to whom dust never adheres, while mud-splashes in the
street deflect themselves from touching even their shoes. Her
very gestures had a finished delicacy, and no spot ever spilled
overboard from a glass while she carried it. She was plump,
frankly plump, with some shape about it, the new feminine turn
of fashion might have been designed expressly for her soft, firm
figure. Her arms even had dimples in them near the elbows,
dairy-maid fashion, and even those village connoisseurs who
theoretically were devotees of the attenuated celluloid lovelies of
Hollywood found this generosity of Io's person singularly agree-
able to behold. In fact, the chief drawback of the 'Shock of Hay'
was that sometimes even its ample spaces became uncomfortably
full.

The two who were seriously upsetting the peace of the place

on Io's account were Charles Blunden and Chad Wedderburn. Not that they ever came into the open about it; they just sat there in their particular corner of the snug, perhaps one or two nights a week for an hour or less, and bristled at each other like fighting terriers. But it was quite obvious what goaded them, by the jealous way they sharpened their words and threw them like darts whenever she came near them. They were always arguing about something, and the something was never Io; it might be politics, it might be books, or music, or even football; but most often it was something abtruse and high-flown, amply provided with long words and formidable terms, so that their neighbours admired the more as they understood the less. They had always been friends, and for that matter had always argued, in a casual way, so that the effect was not of a change, but only of a sudden and devastating acceleration in the inflammable progress of their relationship. But it left people with an uneasy feeling that some day it might get really out of hand, and refuse to stop.

Now wouldn't you think, said Comerford to itself, that two young men who had been half across the world during the war, and lived through two or three lifetimes of adventure and discomfort and danger, could be trusted to behave with some restraint and calm over the simple matter of a girl they both admired? Yet that was the one thing that set them both off like the fuse to explosives; after all they'd been through! True, there were lulls of common sense between, chiefly when Io, who had a temper of her own if it came to that, had visibly been pushed to consider knocking their heads together. Then the odds were that one or other of them would laugh, though rather discomfort-edly, and they would come to their senses and go off together apparently friends, and both out of spirits.

Charles, of course, would have been quite a catch for any girl, with all the Harrow land in his hands; but the other one had still the rags of that glamorous reputation of his, for all his attempts to claw himself naked of them. Most people when they

51

thought about the issue at all, thought Io would be a fool if she didn't take Charles; and most of the observers who had watched the rivalry, in its comedy setting, most closely, gave it as their opinion that in the end that was what she would do. They claimed to see the signs of preference already; but the only person who really saw them, with cruel clearness, was Chad himself. He saw them all the time whether they existed or not. And to tell the truth, his temper was not improved by the fact that as often as not he was ashamed of his subjection, and knew himself every kind of fool. Diagnosis, however, is not cure, and a fool he continued, kicking himself for it all the way.

II

An hour before closing time, on this particular evening towards the end of the August holidays, they were arguing about the Blunden appeal, which hung in suspense somewhere in the legal wilds, as yet unheard. It had come up because the sunshine miners were making vast, unpleasing harmonies in the bar, and their presence had reminded Charles how the grabs were steadily scooping their way nearer to his boundary fence.

'They say there's nearly two hundred thousand tons of the stuff under the heath and the top pastures,' he said gloomily. 'As if that's worth tearing the guts out of those fields for! At the price it costs 'em to get it, too!'

'Only about twenty acres of the ground they want from you is pasture,' said Chad unpleasantly and promptly, 'and you know it, so don't go around pretending they're proposing to take good agricultural land in this case. *I* can't see why you're kicking.'

'They very often have taken good agricultural land, and you know that. Years and years to get it back into shape!'

'I've seen that view questioned by better-informed people than you. It doesn't take half so long to put it back in condition as you people make out. Read some of the books about soil, and see if they don't bear me out.'

'I'm a farmer myself, and I know – '

'But farmers disagree about it themselves. And in any case, this time it's just twenty acres of not so brilliant high pasture, and no more. The rest's all waste land, being used for precisely nothing, not even building. Fit for nothing! If it was levelled at least it could be built on.' He had begun simply by taking the opposite side because he must, but by this time he was serious, dead serious, on one of his queer hobby-horses, almost all of which consisted in finding the good to be said for anything which was being denounced publicly and loudly, and in some cases with suspicious facility, by the majority of other people. He leaned across the table and spread his lean, nervous hand under Charles's eyes. 'Look! I know it looks like hell, I know it makes a positive wilderness while it lasts, I know it's the fashion, almost the rule, to damn it out of hand. I know it *does* put land back from its full usefulness for some time – we needn't argue how long, the experts are busy doing that – and I even know some bad mistakes have been made in judging the priorities in some cases, and good land *has* been taken. But for heaven's sake, do consider this particular case on its own merits, and don't just hand me out the arguments that might be justifiable if you were growing wheat on every acre they want to take up.'

'Twenty acres is twenty acres,' said Charles obstinately. 'And they want the whole of the preserve, as well.'

'Oh, don't let's pretend that's of any great value! You and your old man like to play with a little shooting there yourselves, but that's all there is to it. The woods there are pretty enough to look at, but it isn't a case of valuable timber or loss of soil. I bet you that land could be pasture at the most three seasons after it was relaid – I could show you land that was bearing a pretty good grass the second year after – and that's what it's never done in my lifetime or yours.'

'I very much doubt it. And anyhow, it's an asset as it is – it's woodland.'

'Private woodland, about half of it, with your fence round it, and not so hot at that. Come off it, Charles!'

'As much an asset, at any rate, as two hundred thousand tons of rubbish at an uneconomic price.'

'But the plant's here, the labour's here, it's a continuation of the very job they're doing, and if you let them carry on you'll be bringing the price down, and handsomely. That's the point!'

'Never within miles of the cost by the old way,' said Charles positively and truthfully; for his grandfather had been in the dog-hole colliery business in the later stages of Comerford's shallow-mining past.

'Are you seriously holding up the old way as a present-day possibility? As an alternative to surface-mining?' Chad really looked startled, as if his friend had proposed a return to the stage-coach; so much startled that Charles coloured a little, his broad, florid face burning brick-red under the dark, pained stare. But he felt the weight of listening opinion in the snug to be on his side, and answered sturdily:

'Why not? It got the coal out, didn't it? Not that we need, in my opinion, to get such poor stuff as this out at all!'

'But it's there, and the odds are it will be wanted out at some time. And it may as well be while the site here is open – clear the whole lot, and let's have the ground back in service – whether in two years or ten, at least once for all. If you win your appeal, and they re-lay this site and go away, sooner or later that shallow coal left under your ground *is* going to be wanted. Supplies aren't so inexhaustible that we can suppose any deposit of two hundred thousand tons can be ignored for ever. Then how do you propose to get it out? Shallow shafts? – like last century?'

'Why not?' said Charles defiantly. 'It was effective, wasn't it?'

Words failed Chad for a moment to express the deadly effectiveness of uncontrolled shallow mining in Comerford. He

54

leaned back with a gusty sigh, and reached for his beer. Io, watching them from the doorway as she went out with a tray, thought them unusually placid tonight, but did not suspect that for the moment she was forgotten. Her reactions if she had suspected it, however, would have been simple relief, only very faintly tinged with pique.

'Shallow mining,' said Chad, carefully quiet as always when he wanted his own prejudices to stop overweighting his case and erecting Charles's defences against him, 'has done more damage to this district than any other kind of exploitation. Just at the back of the Harrow – off your land – there's a perfect example, that little triangular field where all those experimental shafts were sunk when we were kids. You know it. Could you even put sheep on that field?'

'No,' admitted Charles, after a moment of grudged but honest consideration. 'I suppose you couldn't. Anyhow, *I* wouldn't care to risk it.'

'No, and if you did you'd lose half of them. It's pitted all over. They've had to wire off the path and take it round the two hedges instead of straight across, for fear of losing somebody down one of the holes; and even under the hedge the path's cracking and sliding away. Until that ground's finished subsiding it's done being used for anything. And that may be for good, it's certainly several lifetimes. You can't even hurry the process. If you put heavy machinery on that ground to try to iron it out, you'd simply lose your machines. But it could be stripped and opencast, and at least you'd have some sort of useable land again.'

'But that's a very extreme case,' objected Charles. 'It's hardly fair to judge by one small field that's been ruined. The rest of the shafts round the district are fairly scattered.'

'Pretty thickly! Do you know there are at least fifty on your own land?'

They were warming again to enmity, perhaps because Io's blue dress filled the corners of their eyes, and Io's small, rounded and pleasing voice was saying something gay and unintelligible to a group of colliers just within earshot.

'Candidly, I don't believe it,' said Charles, jutting his square brown jaw belligerently.

'You mean to say you don't know?'

'I'm as likely to know as you, but no, I don't know the exact figure. And neither do you! But I don't believe there are anything like fifty!'

'All right, let's prove it! One way or the other! Come round with me on Saturday afternoon, and I'll show you shafts you didn't know were there.'

'It's likely, isn't it? said Charles, jeering. 'I've been going around with my eyes closed all this time, I suppose?'

'I suppose so, too.'

'My God, I never saw such infernal assurance!' spluttered Charles.

'Well, come and see! What have you got to lose?'

'Damn it, man, it's *my land!*'

'All right, then, *you* take *me* all round it, and show me how little damage your precious shallow-mining did to it.'

They would go, too, wrangling all the way in precisely the same manner, with the same more peaceful intervals, in which they would discuss the problem earnestly and even amicably, but disagreeing still. They were temperamentally incapable of agreeing upon any subject, and the more serious they were, and the less obsessed by their differences, the more sharply defined did those differences become. The inhabitants of the snug listened tolerantly and with interest, grinning over their beer; and the vigorous singing of the sunshine miners in the bar subsided gently into the tinkling of the piano, and reluctantly ceased. It was at this moment of calm that the lower pane of the window suddenly exploded inward with a shattering noise, and slivers of glass shot in through the curtains and rang like ice upon the table.

A single voice, indistinguishably venomous and frightened,

began bellowing outside in the lane, and there was a sound of heaving and grunting struggle under the window, but no second voice. The snug rose as one man, emptying glasses on the instant of flight, to pour out by the side door into the lane and see who was scragging whom. They were not greatly surprised, for fights, though comparatively few, were potentially many these days; and the usual speculations came out in staccato phrases as they left their seats, answering one another equably.

'That Union Movement chap again with his ruddy literature, maybe – said he was asking for trouble, coming here!'

'D.P.s, I bet!'

'More likely sunshine miners and colliers arguing the toss.'

They tumbled out by the side door to see for themselves, all but Chad Wedderburn, who sat regarding his linked hands on the table with a slight frown of distaste and weariness. Even when Charles got up with somewhat strained casualness and said he might as well see the fun, too, Chad did not move. The sounds of battle had no charm for him. Io came in resignedly from the bar, and found him still sitting there, finishing a cigarette. He looked round at her, and even for her did not smile.

'What, one superior being?' said Io, none too kindly. 'Are you made of different clay, or something?' She sounded hard-boiled, and a little ill-tempered; but she looked upset, and more than a little scared. It was all very well pretending, but she didn't like it much, either. She went to the window, and began to brush tinkling splinters of glass out of the curtains and down from the sill; but at every louder shout from outside she started just perceptibly. A dozen people were talking at once, now, and the heaving and crashing had almost ceased, there was just a breathless trampling, a babel of argument and expostulation, and the virtuous youthful tones of Police-Constable Weaver, pitched high, to assert who was master here.

'Now, then, what's going on? What's going on here?'

He was very young, he liked to say the correct thing, and

Chad was tempted to suppose he even practised the tone in which it should be delivered.

'All over!' said Chad, smiling at Io. 'The law's arrived. No need to worry about possible bloodshed any more.'

'I wasn't worrying,' said Io smartly, kneeling over the dustpan. 'I couldn't care less! Men! They're no better than dead-end kids, got to be either hitting someone else, or watching two other men hit each other. Even a football match is no good unless it ends in a free fight!' She marched away furiously by one door as the dispersing spectators came in by the other in a haze of satisfied excitement, with fat voices and shining, pleased eyes, doing their best to justify her strictures, and settled down contentedly to their drinks again with a topic of conversation which would last them all the rest of the evening.

Charles, tweedy and broad-set, the perfect picture of the young yeoman farmer, came back to his chair rather self-consciously, trying to look as if the spectacle of two men trying to take each other apart had really rather bored him. In fact the mind of Charles moved with a methodical probing caution which ruled out boredom. He said with a shrug and a smile:

'Another case for the old man's bench next week! Disturbing the peace, or assault – if they can sort out who hit whom first – or whatever is the correct charge these days.' But he couldn't disguise the excitement which flushed his fine, candid face, ruddy and solid and simple with all the graces Chad's black-visaged person lacked. He leaned over the table as if he had a secret, though a dozen full-voiced conversations about him were tossing the same theme. 'It could have been a bad business. Didn't you see them? My God, Jim meant making a job of it this time! I knew there'd been some bad blood up there, and I believe they've already been pulled apart a couple of times, but this looked like being the real thing.'

'Jim? Jim who?'

'Tugg. Good Lord, didn't you really look? Lord knows it

does seem asking for trouble to take in a German labourer on the same farm – '

'A German?' said Chad, his lean brows drawing together. 'Schauffler?'

'Whatever his name is! The fellow they've got up there. Big, fair-haired chap nearly Tugg's own size. I heard Hollins had had a bit of trouble with them already. Seems it's Jim who usually starts it – '

'Yes,' agreed Chad thoughtfully, remembering another, safer, easier Jim who was just out of hospital and back at the hostel, with only a long scar on his ribs to show for it, 'yes, it would be.'

'Oh, I don't know!' protested Charles, failing to understand. 'He's usually a reasonable enough chap, I should have said. There must be something behind it. Tugg doesn't just fly off the handle. But a German, of course – it was a fool trick to have him there, if you ask me.'

So everyone would be saying, of course, and so perhaps it was; but where, thought Chad, as he finished his drink and quietly took his leave, where *is* the right place for the Helmut Schaufflers? What's to be done with them? No keeping Helmut on the Hollins' farm, after this, however big a something there is behind it; and no other farmer will touch him with a barge-pole, with the certainty of upsetting all his other labour. And yet we can't get rid of him. If he does something too blatantly his own fault and no one else's, we can deport him, he's still German; but he won't ever be left visibly the *only* guilty party in any clash; it will always be the other fellow who begins it.

He was depressed. He went out, and began the green walk home by the field path, up towards the rim of the bowl; and before long, as he walked slowly, someone overtook him, and he found himself walking side by side with Jim Tugg. Jim was quite untouched, that was easily seen in the early dusk; he was neat and light and long in his walking, quiet of face, content but dark, gratified but not satisfied. He greeted Chad from the outer edges only of a great preoccupation, but in a friendly tone, and accepted a cigarette. He didn't have to act as if nothing had happened, because everyone knew by now that it had. No need even to wonder if it had reached this particular person; it had reached everybody.

'That'll mean a summons for assault, I suppose,' said Chad.

'Be well worth it,' said Jims serenely, narrowing his far-gazing eyes against the blown smoke of the cigarette.

'What did he say to you?'

'Who? Weaver?'

'Helmut. What was it he said, to make you hit him?'

Jim turned his big, gaunt face and looked at him narrowly. 'What makes you think he didn't hit me first?'

'The Helmuts don't – not unless you're small, peaceful, and at a disadvantage – and they have no other immediate way of getting at you.'

The dark look lingered on him a long minute, and then was withdrawn, and Jim gazed up the rise of the fields again, and walked intact and immured in his own sufficiency.

'Didn't say nothing to me. I got tired of waiting.'

'He knows how to angle for sympathy,' warned Chad.

'He can have all of that.'

'Well, you know your own business best. But you could find yourself in gaol unless you're more forthcoming in court. If you don't put him in the wrong, he'll take jolly good care he doesn't put himself there.'

'Thanks for the goodwill, anyhow!' said Jim, and smiled suddenly, and went on up the rising path with a lengthened stride, to disappear in the twilight.

III

The chairman of the magistrates was Selwyn Blunden, the old man himself, Charles's father. He behaved admirably, eliciting, as on the bench he frequently did, some less obvious aspects of what on the face of it was a simple case. As a result of which astute activities, the bench discharged Jim Tugg on payment of costs, and with a warning against taking the law into his own hands. His previous unspotted record of civic usefulness, especially his war reputation, stood firmly by him; his plea of guilty, which spared everybody the trouble of lengthy evidence, did him no harm. Even Helmut's able display of hunted and frustrated good intentions, his portrait of a misunderstood young stranger in a very strange land, did not appear completely to convince Blunden. He delivered a short but pointed lecture on the responsibilities of an ex-P.O.W. to a country which had made repeated efforts to find a niche for him. It had been a generous gesture on the part of Hollins, said the chairman, to take him in after a previous conviction, and it could not be accepted that the failure of the experiment was due only to Tugg; it would appear that something in the nature of a special effort was now required from Helmut himself, if he was to remain *persona grata* in this country.

Afterwards he admitted to George that he had some qualms about Helmut. Maybe the difficulties of his position had not been sufficiently appreciated. Maybe England still owed him one more chance; but how was it to be arranged, in order to protect both parties? People must be a little tired of taking risks on Helmut.

'To tell the truth,' said the old man candidly, 'I have a horror of doing the young wretch less than justice. Maybe I'm leaning over backwards to avoid it – I don't know – if he were anything but German it would be easier to discount the feeling. But at any rate, I would like to see him have one more shot before we decide he's quite irreconcilable.'

'The difficulty,' said George, 'is what to do with him. He might have ideas himself, but I very much doubt it. I think he intends to be carried. He'll work – oh, yes, everyone admits that! – but he won't take one crumb of responsibility for himself if he can leave the load on us.'

Selwyn Blunden pondered, and stroked his broad brick-red forehead, from which the crisp grey hair had receded into a thick, ebbing wave. He was very like his son Charles; the authentic yeoman flavour, indefinably not quite county, glossed him over healthily and brightly, like a coat of tan. He was between sixty-five and seventy, but he still looked somewhere in the fifties, walking as straight as his son, carrying himself, thought George, rather like a retired general, if generals ever retired in such good condition. He had a beautiful big white moustache, behind which he was accustomed to retire when deep in thought, caressing it meanwhile with a large and well-shaped hand to enlarge the screened area.

'I could say a few words for him in quite a few directions,' he said thoughtfully, uttering no more than the truth, since he probably carried more influence than any other man in the district, 'but I want to see him somewhere where he can't do any more mischief – and not on false pretences, either – must let 'em know what they're biting off, whoever's bold enough to take him on. Wouldn't bother about him, as a matter of fact, only the fellow's so young, after all.' He fingered the moustache's gleaming curves, emerging from its shelter reluctantly. 'Tell you what, I think the best bet might be the opencast contractors. Tough company there, all right, tough enough to hold him down, I should think. They're still taking on men when they can get 'em, I'm told, and everybody admits the boy does at least work.'

'Seems to be his one virtue,' said George.

'Well, no harm in trying, at least. I'll have a word with the contractor's man, give him the facts straight, and we'll see how he feels about it.' He frowned for a moment, and George guessed that he was thinking about the delicate matter of the appeal, still pending, still threatening the effectiveness of the unit's operations in Comerford. 'Hm! Equivocal position, very!' he said cryptically, but shook the embarrassment away from him with a twitch of his big shoulders and a flash of his old, bold blue eyes. Better-looking than Charles, on the whole; sharper-boned, more acid in him. 'I'll have a word with the young fellow, too,' he decided. 'Might do more good in private. I don't know – never been a P.O.W. myself – I dare say it does seem as if we're all incurably against him.' He shook his head doubtfully, sadly but firmly, and marched away. It was curious that the back view of him undid some of the effect of talking to him face to face. His gait, after all, wasn't so young; he bowed his shoulders a little, he leaned forward heavily. One was reminded that he was getting old, that he had had his reverses in his time. From behind it was possible to be sorry for the old man; from in front one wouldn't dare.

When Bunty heard the story, her eyes opened wide, and she laughed, and said: 'The cunning old devil!' almost in her son's tone. 'What effrontery!' she said, but with admiration rather than indignation. 'He pretends it's an embarrassing position for him, to have to approach those people when he's doing his best to keep them off his own ground; but he knows jolly well they'll jump to do as he asks them all the more eagerly, because they'll think, if we oblige the old boy over this he can't very well go on being awkward about the appeal. Maybe that would be their reaction, but it won't be his. No amount of favours done for him could restrain him from being awkward where his own privilege is concerned, and they ought to have sense enough to know it by now. They'll find out later!'

'He says he's abiding by the result, bad or good,' said George, 'and I believe he means it. The old chap's getting a streak of fatalism in his latter years, and honestly, I don't think he minds as much as he would have done ten years ago. The world's changing, as he's never tired of reminding us.'

'He's fondest of reminding other people of that, though,' said Bunty, grinning. 'He might not be so keen on having it pointed out to him.' She added, thoughtfully tossing the probabilities in her mind: 'Bet you five bob, evens, Helmut gets taken on!'

George looked scandalised, pulled her hair, and told her she would get him into trouble yet. The truth was, as Bunty maintained, that he was afraid of losing his money. By and large, Blunden was the next thing to God around here.

However, he was absolutely frank with the agent in the little concrete hut office above the gouged-out valleys of the coal-site. The name of Gerd Hollins had not even been mentioned in court, but for all that, the old man had not missed her significance; and the story he told was the full story.

'I'm no racialist myself, thank God! But that boy's had the principles drummed into him ever since he began school, I suppose, and we can hardly be surprised if he retains 'em still. Telling's not much use to that kind of fellow. Now if you could surround him with Jews doing the same work, doing it better than he does, and well able to knock him down if he reverts to type – well, to my way of thinking it might be more effective. But that poor, well-meaning lady at the farm has had more trouble, I fancy, than she's let anyone else know. Tugg has eyes, and a brain. I may be wrong! I may be quite wrong! But I fancy that's very much what happened. A Jewess is still a Jewess to Helmut, and a Jewess going out of her way to be kind to him was asking to be trampled on.'

'That at least couldn't happen here,' agreed the agent, watching him respectfully. He was a young, hard, experienced man, but he was not past being flattered; and besides, if the old boy could bring himself to ask favours, even in this fashion, he could be handled, he could be sweetened. Up to this they had had no direct contact, and men can keep up an enmity on paper which won't survive the personal touch. 'If he steps out of line here he's liable to get hurt; and being that kind of chap, he'll have gumption enough to size up the odds, and stay in line.'

'I can't guarantee it, but I think he will. And the one good thing about him, as everyone agrees, is that he will work. Strong as a horse, willing, handy, even, in that way, entirely trustworthy. It's an odd thing, that, but at any rate it gives one some hope of him. I tell you frankly, he'll need keeping in his place; but duly kept there, he could be a useful man.'

He could, if he only managed to place the old fellow under a very small, but strongly binding, obligation. Costs on this site had been, to tell the truth, alarmingly high, and though the extended range was a desirable way of bringing them down, if the Blundens were going to put all their weight into the appeal and fight every inch of the way, frankly it wasn't going to be worth while pushing the matter. But if this tiny seed of love was going to stay the defending hand, ever so lightly, and let the thing go through in comparative peace, then it was going to be very well worth it. One hypothetically troublesome hand, thought the agent contentedly, was a very small price to pay for that consummation.

'All right!' he said, making his decision. 'He can start, if the employment people O.K. it. We'll make the experiment, at any rate. I take it he'll want help with getting somewhere to lodge? There might be a vacancy where some of the men are staying. Anyhow, we can see to all that for him.'

He thought: This really ought to be worth a little goodwill. Hope the old boy appreciates it! And it appeared to him by small but gratifying signs – for of course one must not expect too much too soon – that the old boy did.

Helmut came, and it appeared that he did too, for a more anxiously accommodating, earnest, subdued young man had never been seen on the site. He had shrunk a little from his full size again, his face was tight shut and grey with reserve, he applied himself grimly to the safe outlet of work, picked up things very quickly, and heaved his weight into the job as if his life depended on it. Perhaps the old man, briefing him for this

third onslaught on reconciliation, had succeeded in impressing
on him the fact that, indeed, his life did depend on it.

IV

Charles and Chad came down through the silvery woods,
between the quivering birches, the intervals of naked whitish
clay crunching and powdering softly under their feet after the
hot, dry summer. They were still arguing, in much the same
terms as they had argued three weeks ago, when this expedition
had first been suggested.

'I still don't see that such poor-quality coal is worth getting
at all, at a time when there's no shortage of deep-mined stuff.
The question of *how* to get it ought not to arise.'

'But it would arise some time – or there's a long chance it
would.'

'Not in my time, or yours,' scoffed Charles, as if that clinched it.

'And that's all you damn well think about! My God, you
sound like something from the nineteenth century! "It'll last
our time!" Is that all that matters?'

The suggestion that anything else ought to matter certainly
jolted Charles, but some sensitivity in him recognised at once,
against the whole armoury of his training, that he ought to
resent the implication of his short-sightedness.

'I dare say I do as much thinking a generation ahead as you
do, for that matter – '

'So you never put a plough into the ground, or plant a tree,
until you've calculated whether it's going to be you or your
grandchildren who's going to get the benefit of it! Leaving clean
out of the question anybody else's grandchildren!'

'You're a damned sanctimonious prig!' said Charles, and
unexpectedly scored a hit. Chad was sometimes horribly afraid
that he was. His dark cheeks flushed. But even if it was true, it

couldn't be helped; and what he had said of Charles was certainly no less true.

'Sorry! It's something you've got to decide yourself, I suppose. Do it how you like!' He kicked at the thick blond tussocks of grass, and the trailers of bramble in his path, and moved a little aside from Charles to skirt a place where the rains of many years had made a deep channel, too permanent for even this dry season to obliterate. Aside among the scattered trees and clearings of new saplings, funnel-shaped pits, a dozen yards across and often as deep, punctured the level crest of the mounds. These were so frequent, and so taken for granted, that the infants of Comerford, though reared only a mile from genuine and normal hills, thought it more fitting to have them of waste clay, and pitted with holes.

Charles, strolling moodily with his hands in his pockets, thought; I suppose we do rather tend to talk about uneconomic propositions where we can't look forward to covering costs inside a very few years. Maybe it is a mistake, at that! Only it seems crazy to have to look thirty years ahead for a thing to pay for itself – even if it saves no end from then on. And even the entertainment of the doubt was new to him, and made him feel like looking guiltily over his shoulder.

'Anyhow,' he said generously, 'you were right about the numbers. I didn't think there were so many shafts – never bothered actually to count 'em.'

'And about the mess they made?' asked Chad, with a fleeting grin.

'Oh, well, I knew they didn't exactly improve the place. Being brought up in the middle of it, one forgets about it, rather, but the facts were always there to be seen. It didn't need you to point 'em out.'

'Some of the ground could be put back into use, I'm sure of it. Oh, I know it sounds odd to be recommending surface-mining as a method of reclaiming land, but it does happen. There was a piece of the old canal-bed running round one side of a field at Harsham, and they had it all up, and put it back level. Farmer's got a field double the size now. If it does nothing else, it certainly can iron out the creases, and you must admit you've got more than your share of the creases up here.'

'Oh, in that way there isn't all that much to lose, I suppose. Except that even a rather seedy wood with some sort of growth on it is better than a bare patch. After all, hasn't this generation got its rights, too, as well as the next? They've had their fair share of ugliness, I should have said. Is it so selfish to leave a bit for the future?'

Chad said nothing. They came to the hedge, and the gate in it, and leaned looking down on the undulating slope, and over into the crater where the scored underworld of red and yellow machines lay, with its knife-edged deep where the water drained down into a dwindling mud-circled pool. Deep as a quarry in places, with lorry tracks running up the beaten clay mountains, and the larger, crueller marks of tractors patterning the whole surface. A growth of huts lay on the distant rim from them, with the canyon in between made deeper by the blue evening shadows.

'I'm not really so sure,' said Charles, gazing into the depths, 'that they're as keen on going here as they were. They haven't had much luck lately, and they say the cost per ton is getting rather alarming – I mean alarming even to the people who believe in the method. Naturally the contractor isn't going to carry the can back if he can help it. Did you know they lost a digger over the edge there the other day? Lord knows how! Sort of accident you get sometimes in stone quarries – probably the driver's miscalculation, but there's no knowing. The kid driving was pretty lucky to come out of it alive, but the digger's a dead loss. Crazy expensive business! The boy's in hospital, but they say he'll be all right.'

'I heard about it,' said Chad. 'They've had quite a run of accidents lately. Must have some pretty deadly mechanics, to

judge by the number of tractors they've had to send away for
major repairs.'

'You hear all about 'em, evidently,' said Charles.

'What my boys don't know about every piece of machinery
down there isn't worth knowing. We have no train-spotters any
more, only tractor-spotters. On the whole I think it's a safer
amusement.'

They moved on, detaching themselves with a countryman's
reluctance from the top bar of the gate. The undulating ground,
dryly prolific with brambles and bilberry wires, descended with
them on its many and complicated levels, here and there cracking and falling away into new funnels about the bricked-over
shafts, more often falling clear into holes, only half-boarded up,
and already rotting away within.

'The old man had a lot of these filled,' said Charles, 'in 1941,
after he lost a calf down one of 'em at the back of the long
field. It wasn't a very good job, because labour was busy on
other things, and all they could find time to do was rush round
about twice with a tractor, and shove as much clay and stuff
down 'em as the machines could move. But they didn't do the
lot, and even those they did do are falling in again. Some of
'em have sagged yards in these few years, and I wouldn't care
to trust any stock around them now. I hand you that much, if
it's any use to you.'

'You don't need me,' said Chad, surveying the wreckage of
land still beautiful. 'It speaks for itself. What made your old
man suddenly decide to fill the things, just when labour and
machinery were non-existent? Not,' he added frankly, 'that that
isn't typical!'

'Oh, I suppose the calf touched it off, turned it into that
particular channel; but the fact is he was trying to work himself
to death at that time, any way that offered, to take his mind
off his troubles. Don't you remember the business about my
stepmother? But I suppose you were walled up somewhere in
Europe at the time, it wouldn't reach as far as that – not even

my dad's troubles carried that far in 1940. She left him, you know – went off with some fellow he didn't even know existed, and left him a characteristic note saying it had all been a failure and a mistake, and he wasn't to try and find her, because she could never be happy with him. I dare say you heard bits of it afterwards. They still talk about it round the village, when there's no more recent stink to fill their nostrils.'

'Oh, yes, I did hear something about it, of course. Not very much. But I remember seeing her around, just pre-war – she was rather pretty, wasn't she, and quite young?'

'Not so frightfully, but too young for him. Old man's folly, and all that. *I* wasn't surprised,' said Charles, 'when it went smash. Tell you the truth, I never could stand her myself. Stupid, fluffy-brained, self-centred woman – I never could see why it cut him up so. But you know, it wasn't so much being deserted, it was the way she did it. It was 1940, and the scare was on, and lots of people, especially comfortably-off old-style lads like my father, were talking about getting the women and children out of the country and clearing the decks for action – expecting invasion any minute, and all that. She had quite a lot of property in jewels, and securities and so on – not terribly rich, but it was a good little nest-egg, all told. She went about quietly realising the lot, turned everything into cash, explaining in confidence to every dealer that the old boy was sending her to the U.S.A. to be safe and off his mind. Her nerves! She was one of those women who have nerves! Well, you can see it made sense, he was just the chap who might do exactly that. Then she disappeared. Just left him this note, saying she was off with her lover – Well, he's a stiff-necked old devil, and he didn't try to find her, he let her go, since that was what she wanted. But it knocked him, all the same, especially as the rotten story leaked out gradually, as they always do. That was the first he'd heard of this tale she'd put up. Poor, silly old devil, he was the only one who knew nothing whatever about it! People didn't talk about it in front of him once they had the rights of it – but how would you feel, having been made to look that kind of a doting fool?'

'Not so good,' admitted Chad. 'So he went about working off his losses anyway he could! Ramming up these holes in the ground for one thing – well, he might have done worse!'

'Oh, it's an ill wind! And mind you, I believe he does realise by now that she was no great loss, but I'm dead sure he'd never admit it. Funny thing!' said Charles pensively, 'everything he touched after that seemed to turn up trumps. He prospered every way except the way he wanted. That's the way things often work out in this world.'

'Surely your old man never had much to complain about in the quality of his luck,' said Chad, with recollections of a childhood in which Selwyn Blunden had loomed large and fixed as any eighteenth-century squire.

'Oh, I don't know! It hasn't been all one way with him. Just before the war he had a bad patch – not that he ever confided in me, I was still looked upon as a bit of a kid. But I knew he'd had a disastrous spell of trying to run a racing stable. It wasn't his line of country, and he should have had sense enough to leave it alone. He did, luckily, have sense enough to get out of it in time.' Charles laughed, but affectionately. 'A great responsibility, parents! It was after that woman left him, though, that he first began to seem almost old. When I came home he was glad to turn over the farm to me, I think, and sit back and feel tired.'

'Not too tired to continue calling the tune,' said Chad provocatively.

'It would be diplomatic to let him think he called it, in any case. Besides, his tune usually suits me very well.'

'This appeal, for instance?'

'This appeal, for instance! You haven't made me change my mind, don't think it.'

They went on amicably enough down the rutted track through

the blond grass, towards the spinney gate and the dust-white ribbon of the lane.

'If you did change your mind,' said Chad to himself, 'I wonder, I really wonder, which way the tune would be whistled then?'

Chapter 3

– And the Loved One

I

Gerd Hollins went down to the end of the garden in the late
September evening, past the small green door in the high wall,
which Jim Tugg had painted afresh that afternoon. The screen
of the orchard trees separated her from the house and from her
husband's uneasy, questioning eyes, and now there was no living
creature within sight or sound of her but the silly, self-important
hens, scratching and pecking desultorily in their long runs.
They came screeching to meet her when she went in and filled
their troughs. She filled her basket with eggs, going from shed
to shed, stooping her head under every lintel with the same
patient, humble movement, rearing it again as she emerged with
the same self-contained and self-dependent pride. But as she
was dropping the peg into the last latch, her back turned to the
narrow path by which she had come, she stiffened and stood
quite still, her fingers frozen in the act, her breath halting for
a moment. She heard and knew the step, though he walked on
the grass verge to soften it. She had asked Jim to lock the door
in the wall when he finished the job, but he must have forgotten.
She could scarcely blame him, when the door had never been
locked before in his experience.

'You didn't expect me?' said Helmut, in the soft, pleased

voice every inflection of which she knew and hated. 'You are not glad to see me? It is ungrateful, when I go to so much trouble to pay you these visits. How would you remember your own language, if it were not for me?'

Gerd let the peg fall into place, and picked up the basket. When she turned to face him, she saw him astride the path, where it closed in hedge to hedge, so that she could not pass him unless he chose to let her. Everything about him was now hideously familiar to her: the heavy spread of his shoulders, the forward jut of his head upon the thick young neck, the blond, waving hair, and the coarser, duller fairness of the face, now fallen a little slack with enjoyment. He had scarcely to speak at all, only to appear, and drink and eat the quiet despair and loathing of her looks; he did not need to have any power to touch or harm her, because he was a reminder of all the harm she had already suffered, all the rough hands which had ever been laid on her.

'I like to spend a few minutes with you,' he said softly. 'It is like home again for you, isn't it? Like home, to see someone look at you again not like these stupid sentimental people – someone who doesn't weep silly tears over you as a refugee, but sees only a greasy, fat, ageing Jewess, a creature to spit on – ' He spat at her feet, leisurely, and smiled at her with his blue, pleased eyes. 'You Jews, you like to have a grievance, it is bad for you when you cannot whine how you are persecuted. I am something you need – why are you not grateful to me?'

'Why do you come here?' she said, in a very calm and level and unreal voice. 'You have been beaten already, more than once. Do you want to be killed for this amusement? Is it worth that much?'

She had never spoken to him like that before; in the whole incredible relationship she had spoken as little as she could, in his enforced presence remaining still and withdrawn, shutting him out from her spirit as well as she might. Now she came suddenly out of her closed space to meet him, and he was stimulated by the new note in her voice, and came closer to her, giggling softly to himself with pleasure. He put out his big right hand, and felt at her arm, digging his fingers into it curiously, probingly, as into a beast.

'You Jews, you think to grow soft and fat on this country now as you did on us. You are like slugs, without bones. You will not take much crushing, when the English learn sense.'

'You had better go,' she said, 'if you wish to be safe. You've had your fun; be warned, it can't last for ever.'

'Safe? Oh, I know already where your men are, both of them. I am quite safe. Presently I will go – when it pleases me – when the smell of Jew is too strong for me.'

'Why do you come here?' she said. 'What do you hope to gain? You can't harm me. We are in England now, not Germany. I am protected from you here.'

'You are not protected,' he said triumphantly, 'because you will not claim protection. Why don't you tell your fool of a husband how I come to torment you? Because you want a quiet life, and still you hope to find one. You don't want to tell him, or the other one, either, because they will want to kill me if they know, and it will be nothing but trouble for you all, whether they succeed to kill me or fail, only trouble. And then to help them you would have to stand up in court and tell all this for the papers to take down, and they would make a good story with all your sad past in Germany, for people to buy for a penny and read, people who don't know you, don't care more for you than I do. You will die before you do that – you have only one kind of courage. So you hope if you keep very quiet and pretend not to hear, not to see me, this bad time will pass, and no trouble for these men of yours, and even for you only a short trouble. No, you don't go to the law! Not to the law, nor to your husband! It is just a nice secret between you and me, this meeting. I am quite safe from everyone but you. And you are too soft to do anything – too soft even to be angry.'

She looked at him without any expression, and said in the same level tone: 'It might be a mistake to rely too much on that.'

Helmut laughed, but looked over his shoulder all the same, and took his hand from her arm, which had all this time refrained from noticing his touch sufficiently to wish to shake it off. He was, for him, very careful now; he appeared only when he was sure of finding her alone. There was no hurry; if he went softly he had a whole lifetime in which to drive her mad.

'Bah, you would even lie to him, to keep him from knowing. I have the best ally in you. But it is an offensive smell, the smell of Jew, and even for the fun of seeing you hate me I cannot bear it long. So I am going, don't be afraid. It isn't time for you to be afraid yet – not quite time. You have not to go back to the ghetto and the camp – yet!' He laughed again, and touched her cheek with his hard finger-tips, and shook and wiped them as if her pale, chill flesh had soiled them. Then he turned carelessly on his heel, and went away from her in a quick, light walk, and slid through the green door in the wall, closing it gently after him.

Gerd stood for a long time staring about her, while the empty twilight deepened perceptibly about her, and grew green with the green of the trees. She ought to have become used to it by now, and yet the shock never grew less, was always like the opening of a black pit under her feet. She had almost forgotten, until he came, that it was possible to hate anyone like that. He was all the shadowy horror of her life rolled into one person, and he came and went protected and secure and insolent about her, reminding her softly that he had been the means of destroying her family, and would yet be the means of destroying her; for in spite of the war and the peace and all the good resolutions, it appeared that governments were still on his side, not on hers.

She went on into the house, bracing herself to meet her husband's eyes and tell him nothing. She had brought him sorrow and trouble enough. But Hollins was not in the house. She supposed that he had merely gone out into the yard upon some late job or other, or up the fields on his usual evening round; but she sat with her sewing for a long time, and he did not come in.

She sat and thought of Helmut. And continually out of nowhere the thought of Christopher's old service revolver came to her mind. She looked at it calmly, and did not either embrace or put away the suggestion, but only let it lie there in her mind, like a seed patiently waiting to grow.

Helmut went up through the woods towards the rim of the bowl, his hands deep in his pockets, his feet muttering in the scuffle of pine needles and drifted twigs under the trees, and silent in the deep grass of the open places. He whistled as he went, for he was very pleased with events. He liked his job, he liked being in a private lodging, he liked the money he jingled in his fingers as he walked, he liked the evening, and his errand, and the feeling of well-being which his methodical visits to Gerd gave him. He liked his own cleverness and everyone else's stupidity, which fed it without effort on his part. He liked the large black eyes of the Jewish woman, defying him but believing him when he told her that he was only the vanguard, that racial hate was not far from her heels, even here, and would bring her down at last.

Behind him in the shadow of the trees, out of hearing and screened from sight, someone walked with him, step for step.

II

Pussy and Dominic came down the wilderness of hills on an evening in the second week of the autumn term, crossed a discouraged little field full of nibbling sheep-tracks now thick with white dust, and came to the squat brick hut of Webster's well. It lay in an arm of hedge at the rim of the next woodland, the ground falling away behind it in a staircase of sheep-paths, with only fringes of tired grass between them, to the channel of the brook and the shadows of the trees which overhung it; while on the other side, the homing side, the path wound uphill among clumps of silver birch saplings for a time, and then descended along the rim of the Harrow preserves until it reached the lane, and the road into the village.

The brook passed along the side of the field, gathered in the powerful overflow from the pipe in the back of the well and spread itself wallowing over the whole basin of low ground behind the brick hut, carrying so strong a flow of water that in winter it was a small lake lying there, and even now after the dry summer there were two or three considerable channels threading the churned-up bowl of clay mud, trodden into great, white, deep holes by the drinking cattle. Only the supply of water in the well never seemed to decline, for it enclosed two vigorous springs, and the overflow sprang out from its pipe with force enough to strike your hand away if you held it against it. Dominic and Pussy knew all the interesting things which can be done with a strong jet of water, provided you do not mind getting a little draggled in the process. They had outgrown most of them, but tonight they had lingered longer than usual in the Comer pool, and emerged already far too late to get back to Comerford in time for the Road Safety Committee's lectures to senior school-children, to which an hour and a half of their evening should have been dedicated; they felt, accordingly, guilty and abandoned enough to enjoy playing babyish games with water for a further twenty minutes or so, while the sun went down.

'They'll be halfway through by now,' said Pussy cheerfully, wringing out water from the ends of her pigtails, when they were tired of making fountains.

'Not worrying about it are you? It was an honest mistake, anyhow. I really didn't notice the time.'

'You're the one who has to worry,' said Pussy heartlessly. 'Io

78

might nag a little, but Dad hardly dare pretend to be concerned about road safety, I should think – not until his own driving improves a bit. You're the one who's going to catch it! Penalty of being the police-sergeant's son!'

'Most of the time,' said Dominic peacefully, 'I can manage him pretty well. But he does get parentish sometimes – I guess he has to, really, in his position. And I suppose it was rather letting him down, to stay away when he's got to give the lecture. But I didn't do it purposely.' This fact alone was enough to make him feel as virtuous as if he had not done it at all. He sat teasing burrs out of his wet hair with his fingers, and making faces over the snarls he found in it. 'Got a comb, Puss? I seem to have been rolling in a patch of burdocks.'

Pussy had reached the stage of carrying a comb constantly upon her person. She fished it out of the top of her stocking, since the pocket of her skirt had somehow contrived to slit itself wide open in a thorn-bush on the way up the slope from the river; and having detached it from the folds of her handkerchief, she flicked it across to him, and went on wringing drops from the ends of her hair.

'What time is it?' asked Pussy then, flinging the plaits over her shoulders as a mettlesome horse tosses its mane and starts at the touch of it. She scrambled up from the grass and went to the well, to cup her hands in it and drink the icy water.

'Nearly half-past eight. They'll be at it for another half-hour yet. Bit of a nerve, when you come to think of it,' said Dominic, stiffening into belated indignation as he squinted out from behind his tangled chestnut forelock with horrible grimaces, 'to expect us to go to a lecture, *and* do our homework, and then go straight to bed, I suppose, without any fun at all. I didn't forget the time on purpose, but I'm rather glad, all the same. And I don't care if they do check up on us, either, it was worth it.'

The inconsiderate female administered comfort as cold as the water she was drinking: 'Your father would be sure to look for you, anyhow. Almost anybody else could be missing without being noticed, but *you* can't expect to.' She added, as a casual blow over the heart: '*Our* homework was excused!'

Dominic emerged to gape at her in incredulous envy. 'Ours wasn't! And I've only done part of it yet, too. My goodness, you girls get away with everything.' He thrust the dark red mass of his hair back from his forehead, gave it a last smooth with his hand, and waved the comb at her disgustedly. 'Here, catch!'

The throw was strong and astray, perhaps with the injured weight of his unfinished homework behind it, and Pussy's hands were wet. It sailed through her grabbing fingers, and flew over the top of the well, to vanish soundlessly down the dimpled slope below.

'In the brook, probably,' she said, giving him a hard, considering look. 'Now you can jolly well go and find it – or buy me another, which you like.'

'If you weren't such a muff – ' he grumbled, nevertheless climbing docilely to his feet.

'If you could throw straight, you mean!'

Dominic went over the crest, and began to trot down the slope from path to path towards the watery hollow, looking about him on the ground. When Pussy looked over the roof of the well again he was down among the tree shadows, looking before him into the water, and paying no attention to her. She called impatiently: 'It can't have gone as far as that!'

Dominic turned his head and looked back with a start. His eyes seemed very big in the shadows, his face suddenly and rather unwillingly serious. 'No, it's all right, I've got it. It's only – wait a minute!'

He went nearer to the stormy clay sea, with the two or three murmuring tides still flowing through it in deep channels, green with the reflected green of the overhanging trees. She saw him leaning forward, peering; then, as she began to follow him down the slope, he turned and came back at a stumbling run to meet her, crying as he came, in a peremptory tone which made her

80

hackles rise at once: 'Don't come! I'm coming now! I've got it!' As if she cared about the comb, when her thumbs had pricked at the wide light gleam of his eyes, and his face so white that the freckles looked almost vermilion by contrast. But when he reached her he caught her by the wrist, and turned her about quite roughly, and hustled her back up the slope with him, tugging and furious.

'What is it? What on earth do you think you're doing, Dom Felse? Let me go! Do you want a clip in the ear?'

But she was only angry as he was masterful, by reversion from some other emotion not at all understood. She wrenched at her wrist, and at his fingers which held it, and panted: 'What did you see down there? Loose my arm! I'm going to look what it was.'

'No!' said Dominic, with quite unexpected violence. 'You're not to! I'll hit you if you try it!' But before he had dragged her a dozen yards past the well on the homeward path his pallor became suddenly green, his knees quaked, and he leaned helplessly into the long grass and lost all interest in Pussy. She did not wait to hold his forehead, but with a ruthless singleness of mind flew back to bound down the hill like a chamois, and probe the depths where he had seen whatever it was he had seen. Between sympathy and curiosity Pussy plumped for curiosity, though she would not be the first cat it had killed. Dominic, for the moment, was too busy being sick to observe that she had deserted and disobeyed him, and in the circumstances he would not, in any event, have expected anything else. Only in extremity would he have thought of giving orders to Pussy.

By the time he had recovered sufficiently to see and hear again, she was just coming back, at a rather automatic walk, and half her face was a green, scared shining of eyes.

'You would go!' said Dominic with pallid satisfaction.

'Anyhow,' said Pussy, equally malevolent and equally shaken, 'I wasn't sick!'

81

'I'm sick easily. It's a ph–physical reaction.'

Pussy sat down in the grass beside him, because her own knees were none too steady. She sat hugging her hands together in her lap, while they looked at each other forlornly, but with the dawning of a steadying excitement deep in their eyes. When you have something to do in an emergency, you are not sick, and you forget to be frightened.

'He's dead, isn't he?' said Pussy.

'Yes.' Saying it made it at once more normal; after all, it is normal, there are funerals every week in almost every village, and you hear your parents talking about this one and that one who have died. Not always old, either, and not always naturally. And then, books and films have made the thing a commonplace, even if parents do frown upon that kind of film and that kind of novel. It only takes a bit of getting used to when you suddenly fall over the thing itself in a corner of your own home woods. 'Did you see who it was?'

She shook her head, ashamed to admit that she had not waited to look closely, but on recognition of a man's body in the nearer channel of the brook had turned and run for her life.

'It's that German fellow – Helmut Schauffler.' His voice quavered hollowly upon the words, for giving the body a name somehow brought the issues of life and death right to his own doorstep.

'He must have fallen in,' said Pussy strenuously, 'or fainted, or something.'

'No, he – no, I'm sure he didn't. What would he be doing down there, leaning over the water, if he felt faint? And besides – ' But his voice faded quite away before the details could come tumbling out.

'What have we got to do?' asked Pussy, for once glad to lean on him for guidance; and she drew a little nearer in the grass, to feel the warmth of his shoulder near her, in the sudden chill which was not altogether the fruit of the falling evening. She began to shiver, and to be aware that she was wet and cold.

'We've got to get my father here at once. One of us ought to stay here, I think – I'm almost sure – to make sure nothing's disturbed until he comes.'

'But there's no one to disturb anything,' protested Pussy, thinking of the long run home alone, or, far worse, the long, chilly wait here in this suddenly unpleasing place.

'No, but there might be before he came. Anyhow, I shall stay here. You go and get Dad – please, Puss, don't argue this time, do go! You can run, it's all downhill, nearly, and you'll get warm if you run. Will you?'

And she did not argue, nor complain, nor tell him frankly that he was no boss of hers, nor do any of the things which might have been expected of her, but with exemplary sweetness suddenly smiled at him, and jumped to her feet.

'He'll still be lecturing, but you'll have to interrupt. He won't care, when he knows why. But don't let anybody shush you and make you wait, promise!'

She could give him that assurance with goodwill; and indeed, the curative effect of having something definite and essential to do in the matter had brought back the colour to her cheeks and the flash to her green eyes. Even the prospect of insinuating herself with shocking news into the middle of the Road Safety Committee's lecture began to tickle her resilient fancy with suggestions of enviable notoriety. She actually made a spring upon her way, and then looked back and suddenly peeled off her blazer.

'Here, you have this, if you're staying here in the cold. I shall be warm enough, running. You *would* come out without a coat of any sort, wouldn't you?'

'Well, it was quite warm enough then,' said Dominic, startled and recoiling.

'Well, it isn't now. Don't be silly, put it on. You look pretty green still.' She thrust it into his arms, and ran, and her white blouse and flying plaits signalled back to him from the rising

83

path until she crossed the crest, and disappeared from view without a glance behind.

Dominic sat where she had left him, hugging the blazer and staring after her. He felt hollow, and queasy and limp, and if he did not actually feel cold, he was nevertheless shivering; and besides, he had given himself inevitably the inactive part which left him nothing to do but think; and thought, at this moment, was no very pleasant employment. He had lived no nearer to this sort of thing than Pussy had, but he knew instinctively rather more of its implications. The first, the worst, shock was that it could happen here; not in someone else's village, in some other county, but here, less than a hundred yards from where he sat huddled in the grass like a rather draggled bird. Once that had been assimilated, the rest was not so bad. And most potent of all, he had his share of curiosity, too, and curiosity can cure as well as kill.

Something else was in his heart, too, something presumptuous, perhaps, but none the less authentic and strong and full of anxiety. Dominic felt himself to be a piece of his father, accidentally present here ahead of the rest. Every crisis is also an opportunity. And he wanted George to do everything surely and perfectly; he was very fond of George, though he had never bothered to be aware of it. That was the chief reason why he pulled himself up out of the crushed grass, and went back to the hollow of clay behind the well, dragging Pussy's blazer about his shoulders as he went. And with every step his brand new, burning zeal to be helpful flamed up a little higher. He needed its warmth badly to take him down the darkening slope, for he felt very empty within, and the air was growing acidly cold, and the silence and loneliness which he had not noticed before hung rather heavily upon his senses now that he had such quiet and yet such unforgettable company.

The light was failing, but it was still sufficient to show him most of what he had seen before. He stepped down to the trodden edges of the water, where the tufts of long grass were powdered with clinging white dust; and climbing out upon the corrugations which the cows had trampled up to bake in the sun, above the small pits of dark, oily, ochreous water, he looked closely and long at the body of Helmut, face downward, composed and straight under the trembling flow of the water.

Pale things at this hour had a lambent light of their own, and the back of the blond head, breaking the surface with a wave of thick fair hair, was the first alien thing he had seen, and fascinated him still. The face he could not see, but the head was just as unmistakable from the back; and the clothes, too, the old Army tunic faded and stripped of its buttons and tabs, the worn grey cord trousers, the soft woollen scarf round his neck, these were familiar enough to identify him. He lay there half-obscured by the cloudy, ochreous quality of the water, which reddened him all over, all but the patch of fair hair. And to Dominic, staring intently with eyes growing bigger and bigger, it seemed, as it had seemed at first, that the arch of skull under the hair was not quite the right shape.

III

Pussy sneaked into the chapel schoolroom by the side door, and found the room full of people, and all dauntingly attentive to George, who was in full flood, and doing rather well. Interrupting him was not, after all, quite the picnic she had foreseen, the respectful hush of concentration, real or simulated, shut her firmly into the obscure area off-stage for several minutes before she recovered breath and confidence and a due sense of her own importance. The vicar, as chairman, was firmly ensconced between her and her quarry, and hedged about with cardboard models and miniature working traffic lights, George looked as inaccessible as any lighthouseman from the mainland. But he also looked large, decisive and safe, and she wanted this most desirable of reinforcements to reach Dominic with all speed.

She edged forward among the cardboard buses, and became for the first time visible to the audience as she plucked the vicar by the sleeve. The audience stirred and buzzed, deflecting its keenest attention with suspicious readiness; the vicar frowned, and leaned down to her to say: 'Hush, little girl! You can ask your questions later.'

Pussy recoiled into a cold self-confidence which had needed some such spur as that. She said very firmly: 'I must speak to Sergeant Felse at once – it's urgent!'

'You can't interrupt now,' said the vicar with equal but more indulgent firmness. 'Wait ten minutes more, and the sergeant will be closing his little talk.'

This conversation was conducted in stage whispers, more disturbing by far than fire-crackers; and its quality, but not its import, had reached George's ready ear. He looked round at them, and paused in mid-sentence to ask directly if anything was wrong. The vicar opened his lips to assure him confidently that nothing was, but Pussy craned to show herself beyond his stooping shoulder, and said indignantly: 'Yes, Sergeant Felse! Please, you're wanted at once, it's very serious. *Please* come!'

And George came. He handed back the meeting to the vicar with the aplomb and assurance of one presenting him with an extra large Easter offering, slithered between the cardboard showpieces, and in a few minutes was down with Pussy in the wings of the tiny stage, and heading for the quiet outside the door, steering her before him with a hand upon her shoulder until they were out of earshot of the audience.

'Now, then! What's the matter? Where've you left Dom?' For it went without saying that Dom was in the affair somewhere. 'He isn't in trouble, is he?' But the excitement he saw in Pussy was not quite of the kind he would have looked for had any accident happened to Dominic.

'No, Dom's all right. At least – he was sick, and I nearly was, too, only don't tell him – and besides, he really looked, and I only half-looked – ' She threw off these preliminaries, which

were supposed to be perfectly clear to Dominic's father, in one
hopping breath, and then took a few seconds to orientate herself
among events, and become coherent. 'He's at the brook, just
behind Webster's well. He said when one found something like
that one ought to keep an eye on it until the police came, so he
stayed, and I came to get you. We found a man in the water
there,' she said explicitly at last. 'He's dead.'

'*What?*' said George, jolted far past the limit of his expectations.

'It's that German who had the fight with Jim Tugg – Helmut
something-or-other. But he's quite dead,' said Pussy, large-eyed.
'He doesn't move at all, and he's right under the water.'

'Sure of all that?' demanded George. 'Not just something
that might be a man who might be that particular man?'

'I didn't look *who* it was, but it was a man, all right. And
Dom said it was *him*.'

'Did you come straight down? Any idea what time it was?
Did you hang around up there – before or after finding him?'

'I came straight down, as soon as – as we thought what we
ought to do. Only a few minutes before we saw him I asked
Dom the time, and he said nearly half-past eight.'

'Good girl! Now listen, Puss, you go home, drink something
hot, and talk Io and your father silly with all the details, if you
want to – get 'em off your mind. Don't bother about anything
else tonight, and I'll see you again tomorrow. Got it?'

'Oh, but I'm coming back with you!' she said, dismayed.

'Oh, no, you're not, you're going straight home. Don't be
afraid you're missing anything, Dom will be coming home, too,
just as soon as I get to him. I'll see you in the morning. O.K.?'

Pussy was at once displeased and relieved, but he was the
boss, and as one accidentally drafted into service she was particularly bound to respect his orders. So she said: 'O.K.!' though
without any great enthusiasm.

'And go to bed in good time, when you've spun your yarn.
No wonder you're shivering, running around without a coat.'

He turned her towards the 'Shock of Hay', and set a rapid course for the bright red telephone box nestling in a corner of its garden wall.

'I had a blazer,' said Pussy, liking the feel of the official hand upon her shoulder, 'but I left it with Dom. He hadn't got a coat at all.'

'He wouldn't have! Lucky one of you had some sense. He shall bring it over when he comes home. All right, now you cut off home, and forget it.'

She wouldn't, of course, it wasn't to be expected; but she went home like a lamb. He thought Io would get the story in full before another half-hour had passed, but with Pussy one could never be quite sure. Io might not be considered sufficiently adult and tough to be entrusted with such grisly secrets.

George called Bunty, and asked her to send Cooke up to Webster's well after him as soon as he came in, which he was due to do in about a quarter of an hour. Then he called Comerbourne, and passed on the warning to the station sergeant there, so that ambulance, surgeon and photographer could be on tap if required; and these preliminaries arranged, he plucked out his bike from the back yard of the chapel school-room, from which the vicar had not yet released his audience, and rode off madly by the up-hill lane out of the village towards the woods.

Dominic was down in the hollow still, prowling up and down the tussocks of grass and ridges of clay carefully with his light weight, as if he might obliterate the prints of tell-tale shoes at every step; though in fact every inch of ground above the water was baked hard as sandstone, and armies could have tramped over it without doing more than flatten the more thin and brittle ridges. He had searched right from the edge of the field to a hundred yards or so downstream from the body, as closely as he could by the fading light, and had found absolutely nothing except adamant clay, rough strong grass insensitive to any but the heaviest tread, and the old stipplings made by the cows coming to water; and all these were now frozen fast into position, and had been unchanged for weeks. He didn't know quite what he was seeking, but he did know that it wasn't there to be found, and that was something to have discovered. No one ever picnicked here; there wasn't even a toffee-paper, or a sandwich bag. There was only the man in the water, lying along the stream's channel and almost filling it, so that the water made rather louder ripples round him, and a faster flow downstream from him.

Nobody falls into a stream as neatly as that; it fitted him like his clothes. Nobody deliberately lies in a stream in such a cold-blooded, difficult fashion, no matter how fiercely determined he may be upon suicide. Not with the whole of the Comer just over the heath and down the hill! And nobody climbs painfully across twelve yards of crippling lumpy clay in order to faint in one yard of water, either. So there was only one possibility left.

It seemed to him that George took an unconscionable time to get there, and it grew colder and colder, or at any rate Dominic did, perhaps because of the emptiness within rather than the chill without. When he looked at his watch he was staggered to see how short a time he had really been waiting. He knew he mustn't touch the body, even if he had wanted to; but he went and sat on his heels precariously balanced among the clay ridges, to examine it at least more closely. The light was going, it was no use. And now that he looked up, the light was really going, in dead earnest, and to tell the truth he didn't like the effect very much.

George appeared rather suddenly on the iris-coloured skyline by the well, and Dominic started at the sight of him with a first impulse of fright; for after all, it wasn't as if Helmut had died a natural death. But the same instant he knew it was only his father coming loping down towards him, and the leap of grati-tude which his heart made to meet him frightened him almost as much as the momentary terror had done, because it betrayed the state of his nerves so plainly.

To George, springing down the slope with a reassuring hail,

his son's freckled face looked very small and pinched and pale, even by that considerately blind light. He kept his torch trained on the ground, away from the shivering boy who clearly didn't want to be examined too narrowly just now.

'I thought you were never coming,' said Dominic querulously. 'Did Pussy tell you everything?'

'Only the fact,' said George, and balanced forward to pass the light of the torch slowly and closely along the length of Helmut's body, strangely clothed now in the surface gleam of the water, quivering over him like silver, and stirring the intrusive pallor of his hair like weed in its ripples. 'Well, that's Helmut, all right! No doubt about it.'

'I thought one of us ought to stay here,' said Dominic, at his shoulder as he stooped, and clinging rather close to its comfortable known bulk. 'So I told Pussy to come and butt into your meeting, and I've kept an eye on things here. That was right, wasn't it?'

'Absolutely right!' said George, still surveying the busy, untroubled flow of water round the blond, distorted head; but he reached for Dominic with his spare hand, and felt a trembling shoulder relax gratefully under his touch.

'Where is she? Didn't she come back with you?'

'She wanted to come back, but I sent her home to bed. And that's where you're going, my lad, just as soon as you can get there.'

'I'm all right,' said Dominic, promptly stiffening. 'I want to stay and help.'

'You can help better by not staying. Comerbourne are hanging around for my next call, and you can go down and tell your mother to ring them. I'll give you a note for her.'

'But –'

'No buts!' said George placidly. 'You can stay until Cooke come up, and fill in the time by telling me exactly how you dropped on this affair, and what you've been doing while you waited for me.'

Dominic told him, fairly lucidly, even to his own inadequacy. George sat on his heels the while, and passed his fingers thoughtfully through the obtrusive clump of fair hair which now held all the remaining light seemingly gathered into its whiteness. Everything was evening itself out from a chaos into a methodical channel of thought, and the steady flow of probability was certainly carrying both their minds in the same direction.

'He couldn't have fallen in,' said Dominic. 'If you even tried to fall into the bed of the stream just like that, I don't believe you could do it. And if you did, unless you were stunned you'd get up again. There aren't any stones just there to stun him. And – and he's sort of really wedged into position, isn't he? Like a cork into a bottle!'

George turned his head, and gave him a long, considering and rather anxious look, switching the torch off. 'I see you've been doing some thinking while you waited. Well, then, go on with it! Get it off your chest.'

'There wasn't much to do except think,' said Dominic. 'I went right back to the hedge there, and all down the stream to the bend, looking for just any kind of mark there might be; but you wouldn't know there'd been anything here but cows for months. The only bits that could hold tracks now are deep inside these clay holes, where the water's still lying, and they're shut in so hard you couldn't get to them. You might as well look for prints in solid concrete. But the light got so dazzly I couldn't see any more, so I stopped. Only I didn't find even the least little thing. Maybe – on *him* – you know, there might be something, when you get him out. But even then, that flow of water's been running over him for – Do you think he's been there long?'

'Do you?' asked George, neither encouraging nor discouraging him, only watching him steadily and keeping a reassuring hold of him.

'Well, I think it must have happened last night. I mean, this way isn't used very much, but in the daytime there might always be one or two odd people passing. It was broad daylight still when Pussy and I got here tonight. So I think last night, in the dark – wouldn't you?'

'It might have been more than one evening ago, mightn't it?' said George.

'Yes, I suppose so, only then he might have been found earlier. And – they begin to look – different, don't they?'

The more he talked, and the more staggering things he said, the more evenly the blood flowed back into his pinched, large-eyed face, and the more matter-of-fact and normal became his voice. Thinking about it openly, instead of deep inside his own closed mind, did him good. A rather tired sparkle, even, came back into his eye. Helmut dead became, when discussed, a practical problem, and nothing more; certainly not a tragedy.

'Even if a man wanted to drown himself,' said Dominic, knitting his brows painfully, 'he wouldn't choose here, would he? And even if he did, and lay down here himself, he wouldn't lie like that – look, with his arms down by his sides – When people lie down on their faces they let themselves down by their arms, and lie with them folded under their chests or their foreheads – don't they? I do, if I sleep on my front.'

George said nothing, though the grotesque helplessness of the backward-stretched arms, with hands half-open knotting the little currents of water, had not escaped him. He didn't want to snub Dominic, but he didn't want to egg him on, either. Just let what was in his mind flow headlong out of it, and after a long sleep he would have given up his proprietary rights in the death of Helmut, and turned his energies to something more suitable.

'Besides,' said Dominic, in a small but steady voice, 'he was hit on the head first, wasn't he? I haven't touched him – and of course you can't really see, and there wouldn't be any blood, after the water had kept flowing over him – but his head doesn't look right. I think somebody bashed his head in, and then put him here in the water, to make sure.'

He couldn't tell what George was thinking, and his eyes ached with trying to see clearly in a light meant only for seeing earth and sky, comparative shapes of light and darkness. He gave a shivering little yawn, and George tightened his embracing arm in a rallying shake, and laughed gently, but not because there was anything funny to be found in the situation.

'All right, you've used your wits enough for one night. Time you went home. I can hear Cooke coming down the path, I think. Want him to come back with you?'

'No, honestly, I'm all right, I can go by myself. Does Mummy know why I'm so late? And I didn't finish my homework – do you think they might excuse it this once? It wasn't my fault I went and found a dead body – '

'She knows it's all on the level. And if you like, you can tell her all about it. Forget about the homework, we'll see about that. Just go straight to bed. Here, hold the torch a moment, and I'll give you a note for Bunty.' He scribbled rapidly the message which would launch upon him all the paraphernalia of a murder investigation. Why not call the thing by what was, after all, its proper name? Even if it seemed to fit rather badly here! A lamp flashed from the crest of the ridge, and the incurably cheerful voice of Police-Constable Cooke hallooed down the slope. 'Hullo, come on down!' cried George, folding his note; and putting it into Dominic's hand, he turned him about, and started him up the slope with a gentle push and a slap behind. 'All right, now git! Make haste home, and get something warm inside you. And don't forget to return Pussy's blazer as you go through the village. Sure you don't want company? I wouldn't blame you!'

'No, thanks awfully! I'm O.K.!'

He departed sturdily, swopping greetings with Cooke as they met in the middle of the slope, quite in his everyday manner. George watched him over the brow and out of sight, frowning against the chance which had brought him this particular way on this particular evening. If Comerford had to have a murder case, he would much have preferred that Dominic should be well out of it; but there he was, promptly and firmly in it, with his quick eyes, and his acute wits, and his young human curiosity already deeply engaged; and who was to get him out again, and by what means? George feared it was going to prove a job far beyond his capacity.

Cooke came bounding down the last level to the mud-side, and strode out across the dried flats, to gaze at Helmut Schauffler and whistle long and softly over him. Whereupon he said with no diminution of his customary gaiety: 'Well, they say the only good one's a dead one! Looks like we've got one good one, anyhow!' And when he had further examined the motionless figure under its quivering cloudy veil of ochre water: 'I wouldn't say the thing had a natural look, would you?'

'I would not,' said George heavily.

'And I doubt very much if he was the kind to see himself off – whereas he was precisely the kind to persuade somebody else to do the job for him.'

George agreed grimly: 'It certainly looks as if Helmut got himself misunderstood once too often.'

'Once too often for him. What d'you suppose happened? Coshed, or drowned, or what?'

'Both, but it'll need a post-mortem to find out which really killed him.'

'This means the whole works, I suppose!' said Cooke, with a slow, delighted smile. He saw parking offences and minor accidents and stray dogs suddenly exchanged for a murder case, the first in his experience – for that matter, the first in George's, either – and the prospect did not displease him. 'Makes a nice change!' he said brightly. 'Sounds the wrong thing to say, but if he had to turn up in a brook, it might as well be ours. Not that I expect anything very sensational, of course! He certainly went around asking for it.'

Fallen into the Pit

George stood looking moodily at Helmut, a trouble-centre dead as alive. He saw what Cooke meant. In the books murders are elaborate affairs carefully planned beforehand, and approached by a prepared path, but in real life they are more often sudden, human, impulsive affairs of a simple squabble and a too hearty blow, or a word too many and a spasm of jealousy to which a knife or a stone lends itself too aptly; tragedies which might never have happened at all if the wind had set even half a point to east or west. And the curious result seemed to be that while they were less expert and less interesting than the fictional crimes, they were also more often successful. Since no path led up to them, there were not likely to be any footprints on it.

Consider, for instance, this present set-up. Ground baked clear of any identity, no blood, no weapon, no convenient lines to lead back to whoever had met Helmut, perhaps exchanged words with him, and found him, it might be, no nastier than Fleetwood, and Jim Tugg, and Chad Wedderburn, and a dozen more had found him on previous occasions – only by spite or design hit him rather harder. There, but for the grace of God, went half of Comerford! And short of an actual witness, which was very improbable indeed, George couldn't see why anyone should ever find out who had finished the job.

But unnatural death sets in motion the machine, and it has to run. Even if everyone concerned, except perhaps the dead man, wherever he is, would really rather it refused to start at all.

'I tell you what!' said Cooke. 'This is one time when the coroner's jury ought to bring in the Ingoldsby verdict on the nagging wife – remember? "We find: Sarve 'un right!" But I suppose that would be opening the door to pretty well anything!'

'I suppose so. Among other things, to a final verdict of: Sarve 'un right! on us. Tell me,' said George, 'half a dozen people who would have been quite pleased to knock Helmut on the head!'

Cooke told him seven, blithely, without pausing for breath.

'And all my six would have been different,' sighed George. 'Yet, believe me, we're expected to show concern, disapproval, and even some degree of surprise.' All the same he knew as soon as he had said it that the concern and disapproval were certainly present in his mind, even if the surprise was not. For murder is not merely an affair of one man killed and one man guilty; it affects the whole community of innocent people, sending shattering currents along the suddenly exposed nerves of a village; and the only cure for this nervous disorder is knowledge. Censure, when you come to think of it, habits in quite another part of the forest.

Chapter 4

First Thoughts

I

The word murder once uttered in Comerford, everyone began to look at his neighbour, and to wonder; not with condemnation, not with fear, only with concern and disquiet. For the crack in Helmut's head was also a crack in society, through which impulses from the outer darkness might come crowding in; and of disintegration all human creatures are mortally afraid.

When George saw Helmut in the mortuary for the last time, still and indifferent, stonily unaware of the flood he had loosed, he felt even less sympathy for him than on the occasion of their first meeting. Then at least he had been a young, live creature in whom there might yet be discovered, if one dug long enough and deep enough, some grains of usefulness and decency; now he had not even a potential value, he was past the possibility of change. Nasty, devious and unwholesome, he had run true to type right to the end, and dead as alive had turned in the hands of chance, and put his enemy in the wrong; and in his death, as in his life, George suspected that his enemy had been something at least finer and more honest than the victim.

George, in fact, would have been disposed almost to regret that justice must be done, but for the fact that he had realised to whom justice was due in this case; and it was not out of any

97

zeal for Helmut's cause that he fixed his eyes obstinately on the end and went shouldering towards it by the best ways he could find. It was not even simply because it was his job, though his conscience could have driven him along the same ways with only slightly less impetus. It was the thought of every man turning suddenly to look at his neighbour and wonder; for the sake of everyone who hadn't bashed in Helmut's head, for the sake ultimately even of the one who had, George wanted to travel fast and arrive without mishap.

Others were travelling by the same road, and it was by no means certain that they would always be in step. Inspector Logan, for instance, whom Cooke deplored and Weaver resented, and of whose heavy but occasional presence George was glad. He was a decent old stick in an orthodox sort of way, and capable of giving a subordinate his head and a free run over minor matters, but a murder was something with which he couldn't quite trust even George. And at the other end of the scale of significance there was Dominic. He was very quiet, very quiet indeed, but he was still there, saying nothing, trying to make himself as small as possible, but keeping his eyes and ears wide open. He had been warned, he had been reasoned with, he had been urged to forget about the whole affair and attend to his own business; and when that failed to remove him from the scene of operations, he had been threatened, and even, on one occasion, bundled out of the office by the scruff of the neck, though without any ill-will. The trouble about telling Dominic to get out and stay out was that he couldn't do it even if he wanted to; he was in the affair by accident, but climbing out of a bog was easy by comparison with extracting his tenacious mind from this mud of Helmut's making. And George didn't like it, he didn't like it at all. That was one more reason for making haste.

The evidence of the body was slim enough. The doctors testified that his fractured skull had been caused by three determined blows with some blunt instrument, but probably something thin and heavy, like a reversed walking-stick or the head of a well-weighted crop, or even an iron bar, rather than a stone or a thick club. What mattered more exactly and immediately was that the injuries could not have been self-inflicted, and could scarcely have been incurred by accident. They were precise, neat and of murderous intention; and the coroner's jury had no choice but to bring in a verdict of murder against some person or persons unknown. In a sense Helmut had been twice murdered, for though the doctors expressed certainty that he had died from his head injuries, he had done so only just in time to avoid death from drowning. He had breathed after he was put into the water, for a negligible amount of it was in his lungs. And though everyone agreed that he had asked a dozen times over for all he finally got, there was still something terrifying about the ferocity with which he had been answered.

On Thursday evening the children had found him; according to the doctors, he had died on Wednesday evening, at some time between nine and eleven. As for the exact spot where he had been attacked, no one could even be sure of that; George and the inspector and all of them had been over the ground practically inch by inch, and found nothing. What could be expected, after such a dry season, and on such adamant soil? There was no sign of a struggle, and it seemed probable to George that there had been none. The blows which had smashed Helmut's skull had been delivered from behind, and there had been no great or instant flow of blood, according to the medical evidence. Somebody's clothes, somewhere in Comerford, might bear marks, but probably even those would be slight. And no time had been wasted in carrying or dragging the body at least across the trodden level of clay, and possibly down the slope. By his size and weight, Helmut had not been moved very far to reach the water, and even over a short distance considerable strength must have been needed to carry him. Could one rule out the possibility of a woman? George was very wary of drawing conclusions from insufficient premises. There is very little, when it comes to the point of desperation, that a woman cannot do. A body can be rolled down a steep slope if it cannot be carried. Grass will bend under its passing and return, dust will be disturbed and resettle; and when the body has been in the brook under a strong flow of water for twenty-four hours it will tell you nothing about these things.

So that was all they got out of Helmut or the field or the basin of clay. No weapon, no blood, nothing. His pockets had kept their contents relatively unimpaired, but even these had little to say. His papers, surprisingly well and carefully kept in a leather wallet rubbed dark at the edges with much carrying, but nothing there except the essentials, no letters, no photographs; a disintegrating ten of cigarettes and a paper of matches; a small key, a handkerchief, a fountain pen, the same clasp-knife which had marked Jim Fleetwood; another wallet, with a pulpy mass of notes in it; and a miscellaneous handful of small change. Rather a lot of money for an ex-P.O.W. to be carrying around with him; twelve pound notes, old and dirty notes of widely divided numbers, which pulled apart in rotten folds when separated. And finally, a strong electric torch, heavy enough to drag one coat pocket out of line. There was one more interesting thing; the lining of his tunic on the left side was slit across at the breast, making an extra large pocket within it, but the interior yielded nothing but the usual accumulation of dust, sodden now into mud, and some less usual fluff of feathers, over which the experts made faces because there was not enough of it to be very much use to them.

His lodgings, a single furnished room in the same house with a husky from the coal-site, confirmed the interesting supposition that Helmut's life had been run on a pattern of Prussian neatness. He had not many possessions, but every one of them had a place, and was severely in it. His actions and thoughts appeared to have been the only things absolved from this discipline. Perhaps he had learned it in the Army, perhaps even earlier – in the Hitler Youth, which he had at one time decorated with his presence and enlivened with his enthusiasm, to judge by the few photographs he had left behind in one drawer of his table. The key they had found in his breast pocket opened this particular drawer, and all his more personal papers were in it, including a diary which disappointed by recording only the dispatch and receipt of letters, and an account of such daily trivia as his laundry, his wages and expenditure, reminders of things he must buy, and small jobs of mending he must do. Of what went on inside his head nothing was set down, of his prim housewifely domestic existence no detail was omitted.

The most interesting thing was that in the table drawer they found another bundle of notes, rolled in an elastic band. Counted, these produced no less than thirty-seven pounds, in notes old and much-travelled, a jumble of any old numbers, like those which had been found on his body. The daily record of income and expenditure in the diary made no attempt to account for any such sum; here were only the few pounds he earned weekly, and the slender housekeeping he conducted with them. Nor, to judge by his records, could he possibly have saved up so much gradually from his pay.

'It looks,' said George, fingering through the creased green edges of the notes, 'as if Helmut had got himself a nice little racket on the side. Ever hear of him in any of the regular lines?'

'No,' said Cooke thoughtfully, 'but now that I come to think of it, the lads on the site seemed to think he was uncommonly flush with money. None of 'em had anything much to do with him off the job, except maybe the bloke who lodges here with him, and he professes to know nothing.'

'So does the landlady. He was just a fellow who paid for his room, as far as she was concerned.' The house was one of a row built on the outskirts of the first colliery district just outside the village, a bit of industrial England suddenly sprawled into the fields; and the landlady lived on her pension and what she could get for her two small, cluttered rooms, which was every reason why she should accept a good payer thankfully, and ask no further questions about him. 'She's obviously honest. And besides, he'd been here only just over a month, even if she'd been a busybody she hadn't had time to find out very much about him. And anyhow, how much identity have any of these exiles got? Scarcely anything they have about them goes back to any time before captivity, or any place outside this country. We know no more about them than if they'd fallen from Mars. No more about their origins, their minds – or their deaths, either, as far as I can see yet.'

'He had plenty of enemies,' said Cooke, summing up with extreme but acute simplicity, 'and more money than according to all the known facts he should have had. About some people who get themselves murdered we don't even know as much as that – native English, too.'

But this point, from which they started, seemed always to be the same point where they also finished.

All of this came out at the inquest, and after that airing of their very little knowledge the atmosphere was not quite so oppressive; but the intervening days were bad, because everybody had the word murder in his mind, but was studiously keeping it off his tongue until authority had spoken it. It is not, after all, a word to be bandied about lightly. Conversation until then was a matter of eyes saying one thing and lips another. Suspicion seemed the wrong term for that emotion with which they eyed one another; it was rather an insatiable curiosity, sympathy and regret. The state of mind which had led to the act, the states of mind to which the act had led, these were the wrong and terrible things; the act itself was nothing. By whatever agency, however, the crack in the known world was there, was growing, was letting in the slow, patient, feeling fingers of chaos.

Take just one household, involved in only the safest and most candid way. Dominic hovered on the edge of his parents' troubled conferences, all eyes and ears, and inadvertently let slip the extent of his knowledge one evening. Pussy was there, or perhaps he would not have been so anxious to cut a figure, and would have had more sense than to interrupt.

'Dad, do you think he could have been making his extra money on the black market? You know some chickens were missed a few weeks ago at the poultry farm down at Redlands.'

'Extra money?' said George, frowning on him abruptly out of the deeps of a preoccupation which had blotted out his existence for the last half-hour. 'What do you know about his money?'

'Well, but I heard you say to Mummy that – '

'How many times have I got to tell you to mind your own business? Have you been creeping about the house listening to other people's conversations?' George was tired, and irritated at the reminder of his worst personal anxiety, or he would not have sounded so exasperated.

'I didn't listen!' flared Dominic, for whom the verb in this sense involved hiding behind doors or applying his ear to key-holes. Dominic didn't do these things; he just came quietly in and sat, and said nothing, and missed nothing. 'I only heard you say it, I wasn't spying on you.'

'Well, once for all, forget about the whole business. Keep your nose out of it, and keep from under my feet. This is absolutely nothing to do with you.'

So Dominic cheeked George, and George boxed Dominic's ears, a thing which hadn't happened for over three years now. Dominic wouldn't have minded so much if it had not been done in front of Pussy, but as it had, his feelings were badly hurt, and he sulked all the evening, very pointedly in George's direction, and was sweet and gentle and obedient with Bunty to mark the difference. Pussy, not caring one way or the other about the actual clout, was enchanted to discover that it gave her such an unexpected hold on him, and preened herself in his tantrums, experimentally teasing him back into resentment whenever his naturally resilient heart threatened to bound back into good-humour. By the end of the evening George's hands were itching

103

to repeat the treatment upon Dominic, and Bunty's to duplicate it upon Pussy. It was wonderful what Helmut could do in the way of putting cats among pigeons, even when he was dead.

These stresses seemed slight, and were slight; they seemed to pass, and they did pass; but they also recurred. And what might be the atmosphere up at the Hollins's farm, for instance, if it was like this even here, in this scarcely affected family?

Bunty did a little scolding and persuading in two directions, and received a double stream of indignant confidences, all of which she kept faithfully, without even wanting to reconcile them. She said what she thought, and listened to what you thought, and that was the beautiful thing about her.

'I only wanted to help him,' said Dominic. 'You'd have thought I was trying to muck things up for him, instead of that. And I *haven't* listened when I wasn't meant to – if he didn't want me to be here when he was talking about it he could have told me to go right away, couldn't he? He could *see* I was here! I can't *not* hear, can I, when I'm in the same room? And I can't help *thinking* about it. Surely it isn't forbidden to *think!*'

'Now, you understand him a great deal better than that, if you'd be perfectly honest with yourself,' said Bunty serenely. 'He's worried that you should be spending your time thinking about this particular subject, and whether you like it or not, you know quite well it's on your account he's worrying. He'd be a great deal happier if you didn't have to think about it at all – and frankly, so would I.'

'I don't have to,' said Dominic. 'I want to.'

'Why? Is it a nice thing to think about?'

He considered this with some surprise, and admitted: 'No, not nice, I suppose. But it's there, and how can you *not* think about it? I suppose it might be rather good not to know anything about it; but it's interesting, all the same. And *how* can you not know anything about a thing, when you've *seen* it?'

'It can't be done,' she agreed, smiling.

'Well, but he won't see that. You can see it, why can't he?'

'He can,' said Bunty. 'He does. That's what worries him. He wouldn't be so unreasonable about it if he wasn't fighting a losing battle.'

'Well, if I'm not allowed to talk about it,' said Dominic, between a prophecy and a threat, 'I shall think about it all the more. And anyhow, he shouldn't have hit me.'

'And you shouldn't have given him that final piece of lip. And the one wasn't particularly like your father, and the other wasn't particularly like you – was it?'

Dominic, aware that he was being turned from his course, but unable to detect the exact mechanism by which she steered him, gave her a long, wary look, and suddenly coloured a little, and again as suddenly grinned. 'Oh, Mummy, you are a devil!'

'And you,' said Bunty, relieved, 'are a dope.'

George wasn't quite so easy, because George was seriously worried. Maybe he would eventually get used to the idea that his son had senses and faculties and wits meant to be exercised, sooner or later, beyond the range of his protective supervision; but at the moment he was still contesting the suggestion that the time for such a development had arrived.

'It's sheer inquisitiveness,' he said stubbornly, 'and unhealthy inquisitiveness, at that. You don't want him to grow into a morbid Yank-type adolescent, do you? – lapping up sensation like ice-cream?'

'Not the least fear of that,' said Bunty, with equal firmness. 'Dom got pulled into this, whether he liked it or not. Do you think you could just forget about it, if you were in his shoes?'

'Maybe not forget about it, but I could keep my fingers out of it when I was told, and he'd better, or else – '

'I doubt very much if you could have done anything of the kind,' said Bunty severely. 'The same conscience which makes you try to head him off now would have kept you in it up to the neck then. So for goodness' sake, even if you feel you must slap him down, at least don't misrepresent him.'

George, as a matter of fact, and as she very well knew, already regretted his momentary loss of temper; but he had not changed his mind.

II

The local inhabitants were left to George because he knew them every one, and they all knew him. Such a degree of familiarity raises as many new difficulties as it eliminates old ones, but at least both sides know where they stand.

He went up to see Hollins on the day after the inquest. Mrs. Hollins met him in the yard, and brought him into the kitchen, and sat down with him there with the simplicity of every day, as if she did not even know that a man she had hated was dead; and yet she had had dealings with the police before, and could certainly recognise the occasion. George began the interview wondering about her calm, and ended understanding it. She had been through such extravagances of persecution, suspicion and compression already that nothing in this line was any longer a novelty to her, and therefore there was nothing to get excited about. It was as simple as that. Her linked hands, rather plump and dark upon the edge of the table, had unusual tensions, but it did not seem to him that they had much to do with his visit; her eyes were certainly wide, luminous and haunted, but he thought by older things than the death of Helmut Schauffler. On the whole it seemed to him that she was not steeling herself up towards a crisis, but relaxing from one.

'You'll want to see Chris, I dare say,' she said. 'He'll be in pretty soon now, all being well. Let me make the tea a little early for once. You'd like some, wouldn't you?'

He didn't object. The easier the atmosphere remained, the better pleased he would be; and she had a kind of graciousness which he wished to assist and preserve for her sake and his own, instead of putting clumsy official fingers through it. They sat in the hearth of the big, dark farmhouse kitchen, under the warped black beams stuck with iron hooks; there were seats set into the ingle on either side of the fire, and only the firelight, no daylight, lit their faces here. It was a room looking forward to winter before summer was over the hill; and she was a tired, autumnal woman, content with a retired quietness and a private warmth for the rest of her life. She had seen too much and travelled too far already to have any palate left for wilder pleasures. However, they drank tea together, and blinked at the fire, which she kept rather high for so bright an autumn day.

'I came to ask you about Helmut Schauffler,' said George. 'Your husband, too, of course.'

'But it's a month now since he left us. I'm afraid there's nothing we can tell you about him since then.' She looked up and met his eyes without a smile, but tranquilly. 'You know already all about that affair. It was an experiment that failed, that's all.'

'I wouldn't care to say I know all about it,' said George. 'I always wondered what made you take him on.'

'Considerations which ought to have kept him out, I suppose. It was my suggestion.' She gave him a long, clear look, as if she wondered how much she could express and he understand. 'I am legally an Englishwoman, perhaps, but I am still German. You can't get rid of your blood. I lived for years by ignoring mine, but you can't even do that for ever. I hoped to be able to reconcile myself with my race through just one man who should prove to be – at any rate, not altogether vile. It sounds romantic, but it was in reality very practical. I was asking for very little, you see, even an occasional impulse of decency would have done – even the most grudging effort to live at honest peace with me. It would have been like recovering a whole country.'

'But it didn't work out,' said George. 'I see!'

'He was what he was. He was satisfied with what he was. You must know it as well as I do by this time.'

'I doubt if anyone knows it as well as you do,' said George, watching her squarely. 'Better tell me exactly what did happen to the experiment. It wasn't so simple, for instance, was it, as if you had been merely an Englishwoman who took a similar chance on him? – or even any other German woman!'

'No,' said Gerd, after a long minute of silence, during which her eyes seemed to him to grow larger, darker and deeper in her still face. 'My case was that of a German Jewess, exactly as it would have been in 1933. I think, Sergeant Felse, you have wasted your war!'

'Tell me!' said George. And she told him; from the humble entry of Helmut to the shock of his first expansion, through dozens of similar moments, nightmare moments when she had been left alone with him only by the normal routine of the day, only for seconds at a time, but long enough to look down the dark shaft of his mind into the abyss out of which she had climbed once at terrible cost. 'And you think you have changed something, with your war! You think you have drained that pool! It's only frozen over very thinly. Wait for the first, the very first thaw, and the ice will give like tissue-paper, and you will be swimming for your lives again. And so shall we!' she said, with piercing quietness.

'You didn't tell your husband anything about this persecution. Why not?'

She told him that, too. He believed her. She was accustomed to containing her own troubles rather than make them greater by spreading them further, like ink through blotting paper.

'But Jim Tugg found out? Or at any rate, suspected!'

'I never told him anything, either, but he is better acquainted than my husband with people like that boy. He often pestered me with questions, and I tried to put him off. But yes, he knew. Knew, or guessed. There was some trouble between them once or twice, and Jim began to try to stay in between us. It was – sometimes – successful. Not always!'

'And the night when he attacked Schauffler in the village? He told us as little as possible to account for it, but it was a determined attack, and my impression is that he'd followed him that evening with a very definite purpose. He meant driving him off this farm at least, if not off the face of the earth.' George watched her eyes, but they met his gaze emptily, looking through him and beyond, with a daunting, dark patience. 'What happened to bring that on? Something even worse than usual?'

'Only the last of many scenes like those I've described already. But I was tired, and Jim came at the wrong moment, and I said more than I meant. It was a weakness and I was sorry for it. But it was too late then. He went away to find him, and there was nothing I could do to stop him.'

'Did you want to stop him?' asked George simply.

Her look remained fixed, and a little strained. 'I would sometimes have been very glad to see Helmut Schauffler dead. Why not admit it? I had every reason to dislike him. But I have never quite reached the point of wanting someone to kill him. There has been more than enough killing. Yes, I would have stopped Jim if I could. But if you know him you certainly know he is not an easy man to stop.'

'And so you got rid of Helmut,' said George, 'without much cost to Jim, as it turned out. But your husband must have had more than an inkling of what was going on, by then? He could hardly miss it, after that, could he?'

'There was no longer any need to make a secret of it, when the boy was gone. I told Chris all he needed to know – there was no need to dwell upon details. It was over.'

'Was it?'

She looked at him with the first disquiet she had shown, and raised her head a little warily. 'What do you mean?'

'He was still in the village. Didn't he come near you again? It could happen.'

'After Jim had beaten him like that? Helmut was brave only when he *knew* the odds were on his side.'

'But very painstaking and persistent in seeking situations where they *were* on his side. Remember,' he said, 'I've seen him in action before, on a boy who was probably much less capable of dealing with him than you were, but in similar circumstances. I know how patient and devious he could be in pursuit of amusement.'

'He didn't trouble me again,' she said firmly.

'He never came here – when you were on your own, for instance?'

'No, I had no more trouble.'

'Then you can't give me any more information about his movements the day he was killed? He was at work as usual during the day, came back to his lodgings at the usual time, about half-past five. In the evening he went out again, the landlady saw him leave the house about a quarter to seven. A boy tinkering with his motorbike by the side of the road at Markyeat Cross says he saw him pass soon after seven, and climb the stile into the field. Since then no one seems to have seen him until he turned up the following night in the brook. That field–path leads up this way. I just wondered if he'd been here again.'

'I haven't seen him since he was in court,' she said.

'And Jim? He hasn't run into him, either?'

'Jim hasn't seen him,' she said. 'Why should he? Jim knows nothing at all about him since they fought, and you know that part already. That's finished with.'

'I hope so,' said George equably, and watched her for a moment with curious, placid eyes. 'But you never know, do you, what's finished with and what isn't? How well do you remember that evening? Can you tell me what you were doing here while Helmut was coming up the field-path?'

'Wednesday!' she said, recollecting. 'Yes – I was ironing most of the evening. I fed the hens, as usual, about eight o'clock, and collected the eggs, and then finished the ironing. And then I went on making a dress, and listened to the wireless. That's all!'

'You didn't go out at all that night?'

She smiled, and said: 'No.'

'Nor your husband, either?'

'Oh, yes, Chris went out half-way through the evening, to see Mr. Blunden at the Harrow. They were planning to transport some stock together to some show in the south. But he can tell you all about that, better than I can.'

'What time did he get back?'

'Oh, I suppose about half-past ten – I can't be sure to a quarter of an hour or so. He's a little late, but when he comes he can tell you more exactly, I expect.'

And when Chris Hollins came, clumping in a few minutes later from the yard, he did fill in the picture with a few dredged-up details; the time of his call at Blunden's, about nine o'clock, as he remembered, for the wireless was on with the news; the route of his long and leisurely walk home; his arrival somewhat before half-past ten. He had taken his time coming home, certainly; it was a lovely night, and he'd felt like a walk. But as he had chosen the more obscure heath pathways, and the woodland tracks, he had met hardly a soul after leaving the lane by the Harrow, until he had stopped for a moment to talk to Bill Hayley the carrier almost at the foot of his own drive.

He was not, naturally enough, so accomplished at this kind of thing as his wife, and he exhibited all the signs of guilt which the innocent show when questioned by the police. George in his unregenerate 'teens, coming away from the orchard-wall of this very farm with two or three purloined apples in his pocket, had felt himself going this same dark brick-red colour even upon passing close to a policeman. Besides, there are so many laws that there exists always the possibility that one or two of them *may* have been unwittingly broken. Hollins's lowered brow, board and belligerent as the curly forehead of his own bull, did not quicken George's pulse by a single beat. Yet he was deeply interested. Chiefly in the way they looked at each other, the stocky, straight, blustering, uneasy, kind husband and the dark, quiet, relaxed wife. After every answer, his eyes stole away to hers, seemed to circle her, looking for a way into that calm, to bruise their simple blueness against it and withdraw to stare again. And she met them with her dark, self-contained gentleness, closed and inviolable, and did not let him in. However often he scratched at the door, she did not let him in. Like a fireguard, fending him off, she spread the grieving glance of her black eyes all around her to keep his hands out of the fire. But deep within her head those eyes were watching him, too, more inwardly, with less of composure and quiet than she had in keeping her own counsel.

George did not know nor try to guess what was going on between them in this absence of communication; but at least he knew that something was going on, and something in which they both went blindfolded as surely as he did.

'You didn't see anything of Schauffler, then, on the day he was murdered?' said George, choosing his words with deliberation. He added, snapping away the pencil with which he had noted down the scanty details of Hollins's walk home: 'Either of you?'

She didn't turn a hair. She had lived with the reality of murder, why should she start at the word? But her husband drew in his head as if the wall had leaned at him.

'No, we didn't. Why should you think we had, any more than anybody else around the village? He'd left here a month before. He hasn't been up here since. Why should he?'

'Why, indeed?' said George, and went away very thoughtfully from between the two fencing glances, to let them close at last.

But for some reason he did not go down the drive. He turned aside when he left the yard, and went along the field-path by the remembered orchard-wall. There was a narrow door in it, almost at the end, he recalled. It had just been painted, bright, deep green paint, maybe a few days old.

III

Jim Tugg was quite another pair of shoes, a pair that didn't pinch at all. He looked at George across the bare scrubbed table in his single downstairs room, as spare and clean and indifferent as a monk's cell, and stubbed down tobacco hard into the bowl of a short clay pipe which ought to have roasted his nose when it was going well, and made a face as dark as thunder in contempt of all subtlety.

'Turn it up!' he said, bitterly grinning. 'I know what you're after as well as what you do! I'm one of the possibles – maybe the most possible of the lot. God knows I wouldn't blame you, at that. Too bad for you it just didn't happen that way!'

'You didn't have much use for Germans in the lump, did you?' said George thoughtfully, watching the big teak-coloured forefinger pack the pipe too full for most lungs to draw it.

'I'm calculable, but I'm not that calculable. Men don't come to me in the lump, they come singly, with two feet each, and a voice apiece all round. Germans – maybe they rate more rejects than most other kinds, but even they, when they go out go out one at a time. If you mean I hadn't any use at all for Helmut Schauffler, say it, and I'll tell you the answer.'

George gave him a light, and said: 'I'm listening.'

'I hated his guts! Who didn't, that ever had anything to do with him at close quarters? I could have killed him and liked it, I dare say. I did bash him, more than once, and I liked that, too, I liked it a lot. I should have liked to bash him again on the twenty-sixth of September, and I wouldn't have minded even if it had turned out one bash too many, either. Nothing more probable ever happened. Only this didn't happen. I never saw him that day, or it likely would have done – but I didn't see him, and it didn't happen.'

'What had he done to you?' asked George with deceptive mildness.

'Nothing. He was like a leech creeping round me feet, he

113

loved me the way a leech loves you. Until I hit him the first time. Then he kept out of my way all he could, unless there was half a dozen other fellows close at hand.'

'Then what did you have against him so badly?'

'You know already,' said Jim, looking up under his black brows from cavernous dark eyes. 'You've been to the house, I saw you come round the orchard to my gate. You know what I had against him.'

'Only the persecution of Mrs. Hollins?'

'Only?' said Jim, and small, rose-coloured flames spurted up inside the dark pupils of his eyes, burning out the angry centre of his being into a hollow, sultry fire.

'Don't mistake me! Nothing on your own account?'

The flames subsided. He sat leaning forward easily with his elbows on his knees, and his hard, sinewy forearms tapering down strangely into the lean, grave hands which held the pipe between them, ritually still. He thought about it, and thought with him was leisurely on the rare occasions when he let it come of itself, instead of igniting it like explosive gas while it was still half-formed. He narrowed his eyes against the spiral of smoke, and said: 'Yes, maybe there was something on my own account, too, growing out of all the rest. Sergeant, we only just finished a war. I don't kid myself I won it single-handed, but I had my hand in it all right, and what's more, I knew what it was in there for. I wanted my war used properly. God damn it, didn't I have a right to expect it? And every time I looked at that deadly, dirty, arrogant, cringing little spew of a Nazi, and knew him for what he was, I knew we'd won and thrown the whole stakes away again, poured it down the drain. Look, Sergeant, I don't know what other fellows feel, but me, I didn't much like Arnhem, I didn't much like any damn part of the whole dirty business. It's no fun to me, in the ordinary way, to get another chap's throat between my hands and squeeze – and the hell of a lot of fun it was picking up the pieces of other chaps I knew who didn't squeeze hard enough. Well, it made some sense while we thought it was *for* something. But if the Schaufflers can come squirming out of their holes only a few years later, and spit on Jewish women, and tell 'em they're marked already for the camps and the furnaces – here in our own country, my God, in the country that's supposed to have licked 'em – will you tell me, Sergeant Felse, what the hell we tore our guts out for?'

George looked sombrely between his boot-heels on the bare wooden floor, and said: 'Seems to me someone else, though, was due to collect that particular bash on the head – if everybody had his rights.'

Jim grinned. It was like looking down the shaft of a pit, such improbable dark depths opened in his eyes.

'Ah!' he said, 'if we only knew where to deliver it! But Schauffler was here under my feet, something I *could* get at. I could land off at him with some prospect of connecting. Only I didn't. Don't ask me why. I let him alone so long as he let her alone; and if he didn't, I thrashed him – when I was let, but there were too many of your lads about, half the time. He got a bit more careful after the first mistake, but he only went farther round to work, and kept a bit sharper an eye on me. He couldn't leave her alone, not even to save his life – after all, torturing people was what he lived on.'

'But after all,' said George, arguing with himself as well as with the shepherd, 'he couldn't actually harm or kill her here.'

'No, he couldn't kill her, he could only sicken her with living. She had a war, too, and it looked as if all her efforts were gone to hell, same as mine. You ought to try it some time,' said Jim acidly, 'it's a great feeling.'

After these daunting exchanges it was none too easy to get back to straight question and answer, to the small beer of where were you on the evening of Wednesday, September 26th. But he was forthcoming enough.

'I was down at my sister's place, in the village, until about eight o'clock that evening. Mrs. Jack Harness – you know her.

115

Then I went to the "Shock of Hay", and I was in the snug there a goodish time. I don't remember what time I left, except it was well before closing-time. Maybe about half-past nine, maybe not quite that. I dare say Io might have noticed, or Wedderburn, or some of the fellows who were there.' He mentioned several names, indifferently, drawing heavily on the packed clay pipe. 'I came home up the back way, over the fields. It's quicker. Didn't meet a soul, though; you won't get no confirmation of my movements once I slipped up the lane by the pub.' He looked once around the clean, hard little room, monastically arid in the slanting light of the evening. 'Nor you won't get no confiding woman here to tell you what time I got in that night. I could tell you, roughly – soon after ten. But I can't prove it. There's nobody here but me and the dogs, and they won't tell much.'

Hearing himself mentioned, the collie thumped the floor with his tail for a moment, and lifted his head to look at his master. He was a one-man dog, nobody existed but Jim. He would gladly have deposed for him if he could.

'Then that's all you can tell me about this business?' said George.

'That's all I can tell you, and that's no better than nothing. I never touched him that night. If I had, I'd tell you – but if I had, he wouldn't have been stuck in the brook to finish him off. My way'd be no better, maybe – but that ain't my way.'

George looked at him with blankly thoughtful eyes, and asked: 'Would you say it was more a woman's way?'

Jim straightened from his leaning attitude, not suddenly, not slowly, and came to his feet. The scrubbed deal table in between them, blanched and furry with cleanness, jarred out of line as his hip struck against it; and the startled collie rose, too, and growled from between his knees. He stood staring down at George, and his face had not taken fire, but only glowed darker and more savagely self-contained in shadow, averted from the window.

'What do you mean by that? What woman's way?'

'Any,' said George. 'Do you think they haven't got the same capabilities as you? But they might not have the same strength, or the same knowledge of how to do that kind of thing. And that's where the water would come in very handy. Wouldn't it?' He looked up at the gaunt, weathered face looming over him, and smiled, a little wearily. 'Sit down, can't you! Do you think I found Helmut any more pleasing than you did?'

Said Jim, not moving: 'You're on the wrong tack. She wouldn't hurt a fly.' And it was somehow immediately apparent that he had in no sense been tricked into assuming a particular she. He knew which woman George had in mind, and he saw no point in dissembling his knowledge. All his cards went on the table. Or had he perhaps still one he wasn't showing, one he was never likely to show?

'Why should she?' said George. 'No fly's been hurting her.'

'I never knew her even feel like being violent to anyone or anything. She wouldn't know how. I tell you, Gerd Hollins is an angel.'

'For all I know,' said George, 'I may be looking for an angel.'

'Then why don't you stop looking?' asked the dark mouth very softly.

IV

George went into the yard of the 'Shock of Hay' by the private way, and tapped at the scullery door; and there was Io filling a kettle at the tap, and putting it on the gas-ring for the late cocoa on which they usually went to bed. It was getting round to closing-time, and warm, merry murmurs came in from the bar along the passage, the mellowest noise George had heard in Comerford all that day. It took a solid evening of drinking, leisurely but devoted drinking, to get rid of the hag on

Comerford's back these days. There were no individual voices in this noise, it was as communal as the buzzing of a hive of bees, and as contented. He liked to hear it; it soothed his over-active mind, even welcomed him with an unsuspecting smile. Pussy, of course, was in bed already, though it was questionable whether she was sleeping. No one who wanted information would have dreamed of going to the 'Shock of Hay' until after Pussy's bedtime.

'Come on in!' said Io resignedly. 'We're nearly through, and you don't have to be official tonight – Dad's going to be only too glad to get 'em out on time, believe me. Go into the kitchen, will you, Sergeant, and I'll be with you in a minute. And keep your voice down, or the quiz-kid will be out of bed and stretching her ears.'

'Anybody'd think you were expecting me,' said George, duck-ing his head under the low scullery doorway, where even Joe Hart, who was about five feet seven inches square, had to stoop.

'You'd have hard work to find one person among that gang out there,' she said, nodding briskly in the direction of the murmurous bar, 'who isn't expecting you – any minute. You're the most expected man in Comerford, bar none.' But he could tell from the serenity of her voice and the undisturbed tiredness of her eyes that the true meaning of what she said had not yet penetrated into her own mind. She looked at him, and he was still human, he had not become a symbol. She smiled at him nicely, following him into the kitchen and patting the back of a chair at him invitingly. 'Sit down until I can get Dad for you. I'll take him off in the bar until ten, it won't be long.'

'No, stay!' said George. 'I'd like to talk to you. In fact, I probably need to talk to you more than to your father – if you were looking after the snug last Wednesday, that is.'

Io had already turned cheerfully away to relieve her father of his duties in the bar, but she swung round in the doorway and looked back at him with eyes suddenly widening and darkening, in a sharpened awareness. She came back slowly into the room, and closed the door behind her, one hand smoothing uncertainly at the skirt of her pink cotton frock.

'Me? The night before Pussy came in and – the night before they found him?'

'The night he was murdered,' said George.

'Yes, I see! You know,' she said slowly, 'that's funny! I knew what you'd come about, of course. What else could it be? I guessed that much. And I knew everybody was somehow mixed up in it – I mean, from the impartial view. But the only person I didn't think of as being involved was me. Do you suppose that's the same with all those fellows out there? Everybody's talking about the murder, there isn't anything else worth talking about in Comerford just now. But how funny if every one of them sees all the rest as actors and himself as the audience!'

'Until I come along,' said George wryly, seeing the first veil of removal drawn between his eyes and hers. He felt himself being geometricised into a totem as she looked at him. The law! An idol which does condescend to wield a certain benevolent guardianship over us; but beware of it, all the same, it exacts human sacrifice.

'Poor George!' said Io, breaking all the rules deliciously. 'It isn't very nice, is it? But you can't help it. Go on, then, ask me anything you like. I don't quite see how I can be any good, I didn't know anything about it until you sent Pussy home, and even then she wouldn't let on what had happened, the monkey! She had an awful nightmare in the night, and then I found out. By next day it was a great adventure, and she was Sexton Blake and Tinker and Pedro all in one, but it didn't look quite such a picnic at one o'clock in the morning. I was in the snug as usual that evening – I mean the Wednesday evening. So go ahead, and ask me things. But I can't imagine I'll be much help.' She sat down opposite him, and folded her hands submissively in her lap, and looked at him gravely with her large brown eyes.

'Can you remember who was in, that night? All the regulars? Wedderburn and Charles Blunden? Jim Tugg?'

119

Io shut her eyes and recited a list of names, fishing them up out of her memory one by one, the first few readily, including the quarrelsome friends of whose presence she could never go unaware for long, then single names coming out of forgetfulness with distinct pops of achievement, like champagne corks. 'And Tugg – yes, he was in some time that evening, I'm sure. I remember his dog having a bit of an argument with Baxter's terrier. You know what terriers are. Yes, he was here.' She added disconcertingly, suddenly opening her eyes upon doubt and wonder, upon the crack in the wall of Comerford's peace: 'Why did you ask me specially about him? You don't think that *he* –?'

'I just collect facts,' said George. 'If witnesses can account for every minute of a man's time between nine and eleven on that evening, so much the better for him. Every one cancelled out is one with a quiet mind – at least on his own account. So let's not look any further for my motives. What time did Jim come in?'

'Oh! Oh, dear, that's something quite different. I served him, of course, and I know he was there, because of the dogs – but what time he came in, that's another thing. The news was on when the terrier came in and started the row, I remember that. But honestly, I can't remember how long he'd been there then.'

'Never mind! You could hardly be expected to keep the lot of 'em in mind.' The news had been on, and Jim Tugg noticeably there at the 'Shock of Hay'. The news had been on, and Chris Hollins talking cattle-transport with Blunden at the Harrow. 'What time did he leave? Any clue?'

She shook her head helplessly. 'I didn't notice him go. You know, he isn't a man who makes a noise about what he does. I think – I'm pretty sure he wasn't there at ten, when everybody was saying good-night. But he seldom stayed until ten, so perhaps I'm not really honestly remembering that, only taking it for granted. Doesn't he remember himself?'

'Not exactly. He thinks he left about half-past nine, maybe a little earlier.'

'One of the others might remember properly,' she said, with a sudden warming smile. 'Baxter might, after having his dog nipped for its cheek. Only I'm not sure he wasn't away first himself. I never thought it would be so difficult to answer these questions, but it *is*. I didn't have any special reason to take note, you see.'

'Of course not! Don't strain your memory, or you'll begin to imagine things and mix up days altogether. If anything flashes back of itself, well and good, but don't chivvy it. One of the others may have had things fixed in his mind by some little incident.' He met her eyes squarely, and asked without warning: 'What about Wedderburn and Blunden? Any clear recollection of their comings and goings?'

As if he needed to ask! Everyone knew that she had no peace from them, that she was forced to take notice of them because they took fierce notice of her, of every word she shed in their direction, and every glance, skirmishing over them like rival centre-forwards in a hockey bully. Her pink-and-white face flamed, but she smiled, not too grudgingly, sensing first only his delicate little poke at her own self-esteem. Only then did the second stab reach her. Chad and Charles, they came into it, too. He saw her smile ebb, and her breath halt for an instant as it went home. Nobody is safe! Take care how you speak of one friend to another friend from now on. Take care particularly of every word you say to George Felse. After all, he is the police. And virtually, you've got everybody's life in your hands. Charles's life among the rest! Or was it Chad's she thought of first? Comerford would have said Charles's, but there was no way of being sure until she was sure herself.

George felt her withdraw herself, not stealthily, only delicately, in a shocked quietness, as decisively as if she had walked backwards from him out of the room, to hold him in her eye every step of the way. Her look, which had been as limpid as crystal, grew opaque and shadowy as a thicket of bracken in its covert brownness. Her voice quietened by a distinct degree, answering discreetly: 'Well, they were both here, but I didn't notice exactly when they came in, I was rather busy. Only when they began to fight, as usual, I couldn't very well help noticing, could I?'

'Literally fight?' asked George, with a smile he was far from feeling.

'No, of course not, it was only the same as it always is.' Her brow darkened, clouding over at their idiocies. 'But they were far too busy with each other to be wasting any time thinking of knocking anyone else on the head,' she added firmly.

'They were there when the dogs began to scrap?' asked George again, doggedly ignoring his dismissal from individual personality.

'Yes, I'm sure of that. Charles was nearest, and he caught hold of the collie by the tail to make him break. They were both here before nine.'

'And did they leave together?'

She said rather grudgingly: 'No. They – behaved a little worse than most nights – at least, Chad did. Good Lord, wouldn't you think after all he's been through he'd have some sense of proportion? Wouldn't you, honestly? And yet, just because Charles asked me to go to the carnival dance at Comerbourne with him, and I said I would – Why shouldn't I go to a dance, if I'm asked?' she demanded of George, forgetting for the moment how much of a policeman he had become, and how little of a friend and neighbour. 'Oh, not a word about the actual issue, of course, he just quarrelled with Charles and with me and with the whole snug about everything else you can think of. Half of it was in Latin, or something; anyhow, I didn't even know what he was calling us. He got rather tight, and went off in the sulks, before ten o'clock. I can't be exact about the time, I didn't look at the clock, but it seems it must have been nearly half an hour before closing-time when he went.'

'They don't give you much peace between them, do they?' said George, greatly daring.

Io looked at him for a struggling moment between indignation and laughter, and then collapsed without warning into an amused despair somewhere between the two. 'Sometimes I'd like to knock their two silly heads together, and see if I could knock any sense into either of 'em. *I* don't want to be bothered with them, I've something better to do with my time; but I'd *like* them both, if only they'd let me. When they act like squabbling children, it isn't so easy.'

Even in her confidences, now, there was a note of constraint, as if she watched him covertly to see how he took every word. Not only the wicked, apparently, flee when no man pursueth, for reach as he would, he could lay no hand on Io.

'Was he very drunk when he went off? That's most unusual for him, isn't it?'

'Well, it's hard to describe. He was more drunk that I've ever seen him, and he'd been drinking in a more business-like way than usual, but he was perfectly capable. Walked straight as an arrow. It seemed to make him more and more of a schoolmaster, if you know what I mean. By the time he went I couldn't understand a word he was saying, it was so high-flown.'

'I take it he was heading straight for home?'

'Oh, you must ask him that, *I* don't know.' She brightened at having reached something she honestly did not know, and stretched her small, shapely feet out before her with satisfaction. The murmurs from the bar, coming in only very softly, sounded like bees in lime flowers, drowsy and eased at the end of the day.

'I will. And what about Charles? He stayed till ten?' Why shouldn't he, reflected George, when he had got rid of his rival for once, and scored a minor triumph with the girl? He wouldn't go home until closing time that night, of all nights.

'Oh, he was the last out of the snug. He wanted to hang around and talk, even at that hour, but I was tired, and fed up with the pair of them.' She made a wry face which somehow only accentuated the softness and sweetness of her mouth, the brown, harassed gentleness of her eyes. 'I didn't behave so well myself. And he went home. But he was quite pleased with himself, was Charles. And Chad – well, I don't honestly think either of them had any time to think about anyone but himself that night.'

'Probably not,' agreed George, cocking an ear towards the bar, where the clock was just striking, a few minutes ahead of its time. 'Is Chad there tonight? I need to talk to him; perhaps I could catch him now.'

Io let him go, watched him go with a grieved, withdrawn face. Chad was certainly there among the regulars stirring in the snug, they had both heard his voice lifted in good-nights just after the clock struck; and certainly he would go home to his rather rigidly retired cottage up the hill, where his mother kept house for him in a chilly, indifferent gentility, by the lane and the fields, on which quiet road one could talk to him very earnestly, and not be observed or interrupted. And of course she was sure that Chad could fill in the details of his better-forgotten evening minute by minute, like a school exercise. In any case, what was Chad to her but an ill-tempered nuisance? Still she watched George's purposeful exit to the yard and the lane with reluctance and regret, and would have liked to put a few miles between them until someone, someone who knew how to be more wary for Chad than he was likely to be for himself, had pointed out to him how times and people were changed in the village of Comerford.

A hand reached down through the banisters, and tweaked at the topmost of Io's brown curls. Green eyes shone upon her quietly from the stairs.

'What did I tell you?' said Pussy, dangling her plaits as deliberately as if they had been baited. 'He thinks it's old Wedderburn! Now what are you going to do about it?'

V

When they fell into step on the way up the fields, neither of them was in the least surprised. This was the way home for only a handful of people, and Sergeant Felse was not among them, but Chad Wedderburn merely looked at him along his wide, knife-sharp shoulder, and smiled rather wearily, and left it at that. He said: 'Hullo! On business?' Over the hill and beyond the ridge of trees was the small, genteelly kept house which had caused him such a panic of claustrophobia when he first came back to it, and the acidulated gentlewoman whom he had found it so hard to recognise as his mother. The likeness had come back into her unchanging face for him after a while, and they had fitted together the creaking parts of their joint life, and found it not so bad a machine, after all; but there were still times when he suddenly felt his heart fail in him, wondering what she had to do with him. She was so well-bred that she could not embarrass him by any parade of pride in him, nor shatter him by too unveiled a love, and altogether he was grateful to her and fond of her. But it could not be called an ecstatic relationship. She provided the background she thought most appropriate; he appreciated and conformed to it as his part of the adjustment. Only now and again did it pinch him badly, after a whole year of practice, and usually he could put up with these times and make no fuss. More than once in Croatia he had tasted surgery without anæsthetics, it was a pity if he couldn't keep silence now when he got the anæsthetic without the surgery.

The brown scar was like a pencil mark down his neck from the ear, a very small earnest of what he bore on his body. It drew his mouth and cheek a little awry, George noticed, a thing which was hardly observable by daylight; but now the twilight of a clouded three-quarter moon plucked his face into a deformed smile even when he was not smiling.

'On business, of course!' he said, answering himself equably. 'Don't bother to be subtle about it, just say it. By now we all know that we're in it up to the neck – some of us rather above the neck, in fact. I know no reason why you shouldn't look in my direction rather pointedly. I know no reason why I should go out of my way to deny that I killed this particular man. I can hardly be indignant at the suggestion, can I, considering my history?'

His dark cheek, hollow and frail in the half-darkness, twitched suddenly. He looked as if a little sudden light would have shown dully clean through him; too brittle and thin to be able to beat in a man's head. And yet he spread his own hand in front of him, and looked at it, and flexed it, as if he stood off to regard its secret accomplishments, with awe that they should repose in such an unlikely instrument. The Fourth Form in their innocence had not wondered more at that than he had in his experience. He shivered in a quiet, inescapable disgust, remembering what was supposed to have been the achievement of his manhood. 'It's almost a pity,' he said, 'that I can't make it easy for you, but I don't know the answer myself.'

'I'm just beginning to find out,' said George, rather ruefully, 'what's meant by routine investigations. They don't follow any known routine for more than one yard before running off the rails. But if you want to ask the questions and answer them, too, go ahead, don't mind me.'

'There was the Fleetwood affair,' said Chad, mentally leaning back to get it in focus, 'and I'm not going to try and make that any less than it was. Only an incident, maybe, but it was a symptom, too. And I seem to remember saying something rather rash about not wanting to start anything in case I killed him. Has been heard to threaten the life of the deceased man! And there was even the Jim Tugg affair, too; I was a witness to that if I needed any reminders.'

'I didn't attach too literal a meaning,' said George, 'to what you said about killing him, if that's any comfort to you.'

'Your mistake, I meant it literally. But you may also have observed that, because I was afraid of how it might end, I took

126

good care, even under considerable provocation, not to let it begin.'

'Granted!' said George. 'Why go out of your way to make a case for and against, when nobody's accused you? I should sit back and wait events, if I were you, and not worry about it.'

'I think you wouldn't. Haven't you noticed that that's the one thing none of us can do? Comerford's too small, and murder, even so piteous a specimen of the art, is too big. Besides, I find your presence conducive to talk, and I'm interested to see how good a case can be made – for and against.' He was indeed talking to the night, which was no more impersonal than Sergeant Felse to him. 'I find the motive angle a little under-supplied, don't you? The Fleetwood affair passed over safely, one doesn't kill this week for what one felt last week. A little roundabout, too. People do terrible things on behalf of other people, but things even more desperate for themselves. And what had Helmut ever done to me?'

This was more interesting than what George had foreseen, and he fell in with it adaptably enough, moving unhurried and unstampeded up the leisurely swell of the darkened field, with the vague black ghosts of the straggling hedge trees marching alongside on his right hand. Not too much attention need be paid, perhaps, to the matter, but the manner had peculiarities. Maybe Chad had drunk a little more than usual even tonight, in pursuit of some quiet place he couldn't find within his mind when sober. Or maybe he was instinctively putting up a barricade of eccentricity about his too questionable, too potential loneliness, to persuade the paths of all official feet to go round him reverently, as for a madman where madmen are holy. Or maybe he was just fed up, too fed up to be careful, and had set out to heave all the probabilities in the teeth of authority, and dare them to sort everything out and make sense of it.

'Jim Tugg suggested a very apposite motive, I thought,' said George mildly. 'It would apply to you just as well. He said he had it against Helmut Schauffler that he was the living, walking, detestable proof of a war won at considerable personal cost by one set of men, and wantonly thrown away by others. If the Helmuts, he said, can sidle about the conquering country, only a few years later, hiding their most extreme nastiness behind the skirts of the law, what on earth did we tear our guts out for? I'm bound to say I find it a better motive than a great many which might seem more plausible on the surface.'

'A motive for anger,' said Chad, his voice slow and thoughtful in the dark, 'but not for killing – not unless you could be sure that removing one man would make some difference. And of course it wouldn't.'

'An angry man doesn't necessarily stop to work out the effects of what he does.'

'Some do. I do. That's why I didn't do it. I had some training in calculating results, and doing it quickly, too. It comes almost naturally to me now.'

'Moreover,' went on George placidly, 'the removal of Helmut might have been expected to have a very good effect indeed. He was like a pen-knife, chipping away industriously at the mortar between the stones of a perfectly good, serviceable wall – picking away at it and prising it apart bit by bit, for no positive purpose in the world, only for the love of destroying things. Nobody likes to feel the roof being brought down over his head, in my experience.'

Chad turned his head suddenly, and looked along his thin shoulder with a small movement of such desperation and pain that even George was startled. 'If you mean this damned inadequate society that's supposed to keep the rain off us, what makes you think I'd be sorry to see it go? What gives you the idea I've found it weatherproof, these last few years? Wouldn't I be more likely to forgive him the rest, if only he could bring this down on the top of us, and force us to put up something better in its place?' He drew a breath that hit George's consciousness like a blow, and caused him to flinch. No doubt of the hurt here, no doubt of the bitterness. He tried to close the

128

door on it again, but his voice was laboured. 'Never in my life,' he said deliberately, 'did I strike a solitary blow for English society, and make no mistake, I'm never likely to start now.'

'Perhaps not,' said George, clairvoyant, 'but for something bigger you might, or for something smaller. For the idea of human decency and dignity, for instance – '

'By reducing something human to an indecent and undignified mess in a ditch?'

'Something which had already offended so far that it had become a sort of renegade from its own kind. Perhaps! More is required to make up humanity than two arms, two legs, and all the rest of the physical catalogue. But far more likely, for the peace of mind of a very small unit of society – about as large as Comerford. I'm not so sure that the disintegration of this one little community would leave you so completely cold.'

'I'm not so sure,' said Chad, 'that it would. But haven't you seen already, and don't you suppose I could have seen in advance, that Helmut dead is a more effective agent of disintegration than he was alive? My God, do you suppose you're still the same person you were ten days ago? Do you suppose I am? They talk, oh, yes, they shout over the garden fences just as usual, and talk their little heads off, and even enjoy it in a way. But they can all feel the ground quaking under them, just the same, and they can all see, now, that the bloke next door is just about as near to them as somebody from the moon. It's beginning to crumble apart, faster than one rather nasty young man could have prised it while he was alive. And the only way of stopping it is by catching and hanging some poor devil who probably meant well by all of us. Nobody could possibly deserve to die merely because he smashed Helmut's head in, but I'm not at all sure that he doesn't deserve it for his damned stupidity, for what he's done to Comerford. While he was alive, Helmut was never quite real, but, by God, he's real enough now he's dead!'

'You have,' allowed George ruefully, 'very definitely got something there.'

'I thought by the sound of you that you had it, too. Not a nice job, yours,' he said more quietly, and even smiled in a wry, grudging way. But he had said too much already for his own peace of mind, and the less he added now, the better. He lifted his head with a gesture of putting something from his back, not without effort. 'This is all a little in the air. Shall we touch down again? I loathed Helmut Schauffler, but I didn't kill him. I object to killing, for one thing, and for another, in this case it would have been the worst possible policy, and I think there never has been a moment in my dealings with him when I failed to remember that. But you don't, of course, have to believe me. Go ahead and ask me things, what you like!'

The voice in which he answered questions, George noticed, was not quite the same voice, but carefully flattened into a level of indifference, a witness-box voice. He had nerves which needed to be steadied by these little extra attentions; one does not drag one's life suddenly through half a dozen phases of chaos and emerge impervious, it seems one may even come out of it with sensitivities more acutely tuned than before to the vibrations of danger and exasperation.

'You were at the "Shock of Hay" last Wednesday evening about the usual time for a call. When the nine o'clock news was on you were there. Any idea what time you left?'

'Not exactly. I wasn't noticing time very much. Well before closing time, though, it was just getting really full – and a bit noisy. I'd say about twenty to ten, but somebody else might know more about it than I do. Charles might – I'd just called him something not very complimentary – and not particularly usual. In certain circumstances I tend to become polysyllabic – especially on brandy.'

'So I've heard,' said George. 'What time did you get home?'

'You could, of course, get that from my mother. She always knows the time when everything happens, especially if the routine goes wrong.'

'I'm trying,' said George gently, 'to get it from you.'

130

'Clever of you,' said Chad, 'to be so sure I should know. She called my attention to it directly I came in. Oh, not in any very censorious manner, merely as you point out a slight error in the pence column to a junior clerk toward whom you are, on the whole, well-disposed. It's a habit, actually. I suspect she tells the cat when he's ten minutes late. One isn't, of course, expected or required to take very much notice of the small reproof. It was twenty-five minutes to twelve.'

'And what happened to the two hours in between?'

'I spent them sobering up, and walking off a pretty evil temper. I bring enough moods home as it is – this one I preferred to leave somewhere in the Comer.'

'You didn't go swimming?'

'I did. Half-tight – rather more than half – but I could still swim. It wasn't a cold night, and the pool's safe as houses if you know it well. I'm not saying I'd have done it if I hadn't been rather beyond myself, as a matter of fact – but something had to be done! I didn't go straight there, just walked; keeping off the roads. Over the mounts, through the larch plantation, down the woods the other side. Went a long way towards the bridge along the water-meadows, then changed my mind and came back to the pool, and bathed. After that I didn't linger, I was too damned cold, I came back into Comerford the same way, only dropped down from the mounts by the steep path through the quarry. Home – exactly twenty-five to twelve.'

'Meet anybody anywhere along this route?'

'At that hour, along this route, I wouldn't expect to. And beyond that, I took good care not to meet anyone, that was the last thing I wanted. Nobody who isn't drunk or in love walks by the river at eleven o'clock at night, and the lovers choose the less exposed bits, even when there are no other people there. I did pass one boy pushing a bike when I crossed the lane on top there – we swopped good-nights, but I didn't know him, and I don't suppose he knew me from Adam. After that it was fine, I never saw a soul.'

131

'Might be finer for both of us now if you had,' said George. 'Why did you have to choose that night to be difficult? And come to think of it, when you crossed the mounts towards the larches you must have been fairly near to the basin by Webster's well. That would be about – let's see! – ten o'clock or soon after, wouldn't it?'

'About that, I suppose.'

'You didn't see anyone hanging around there? There's a place where the ground dips from the high paths, and you can see down into the basin behind the well. Nothing out of the way to be seen there then?'

'Not that I remember. I can't say I do remember even glancing towards the well, really. But in the wooded part, just past the dip, there was somebody moving around. Nothing for you, though, I'm afraid. The preserve fence begins about there, and not being a gamekeeper I find it etiquette not to look in the direction of poachers when I hear 'em at work. I took it for granted that was what he was up to, but he was rather a noise of footsteps than anything I saw. Just somebody running lightly in the underbrush, away from me to get deeper in shadow. It was pretty dark; he didn't have to go far to be lost. But it was a man, all right. Just a blur with a face and hands, and then gone, but a man. It's happened before on occasions; and as I say, I was tactful, and went right ahead without another look.'

'That's helpful!' said George glumly. 'Nothing else to report at all?'

'No, I think not. Sorry about that, but I couldn't know it was going to be important. And as a matter of fact, I still think pheasants were all he was after. I know the kind of running, and the place and time were right for it. Still, it's your man-hunt.'

There was no more to be had from him, either directly or by observation. They parted at the junction of the field-paths, and in a few minutes a high hedge hid them from each other. George went very thoughtfully back into Comerford's deserted green, let himself into the station, and telephoned Inspector Logan at

Comerbourne. There was something about Helmut's tunic that he wanted to confirm; and he thought, after all, he would go over and make certain now, and not risk leaving it until the morning.

Chapter 5

Second Thoughts

I

'Well,' said Selwyn Blunden, settling his considerable bulk well back in the big chair, 'that was an experiment that didn't last long. Poor young devil! – but he was a devil! Pity, it seemed to be beginning rather well, so I heard from the manager fellow down on the site there.' He nodded towards the window which lay nearest to the ravaged valleys of the coalsite, still out of sight and sound, still held at bay from the Blunden fences, but creeping steadily nearer. 'Said he was an excellent worker, excellent! Well, nobody's going to get any more work out of him now – or have any trouble with him, either.'

'Except us,' said George. 'My troubles with him seem to be only beginning.'

'Yes, in that way I suppose you're right. Bad business altogether, bad for the village, unsettles everybody – bad for the boy himself, who after all might have made a decent fellow in the end – bad for your lad, and that young thing with the plaits, too, by God! How did your young man take it?'

'Oh, Dom's all right. Stood up to it like a professional, but it's had its effect, all the same, I wish it hadn't. He's taking far too proprietary an interest in the case for my liking.'

The big old man looked up under his bushy eyebrows and

smiled through the thin clouds of smoke from his cigar. 'What, enjoying the sensation, is he? You never can tell with children. These things simply don't frighten them until some fool of a grown-up goes to the trouble to explain to them that they ought to be frightened.'

'Oh, not that, exactly. Dom's rather past the stage of having to have these things explained to him. Consequently he's quite capable of frightening himself, without any help from anyone. No, I wouldn't say he's enjoying it. But it happened to him, and he doesn't want to let go of it until it's all cleared up. Feels committed to it. Neither soft words nor fleas in his ear discourage him.'

'I see! Bound to admire his spirit, I must say, but damned inconvenient for you, I quite see that. One likes to have one's family kept rather separate from things like murder.' He sighed deeply, and exhaled smoke like some wholesome old dragon in an unorthodox fairy-tale. 'Difficult times all round, Sergeant. I do appreciate your troubles. Got some of my own, but nothing to speak of by comparison. Result of that appeal should be through almost any day, and between you and me, win or lose, I'll be glad to see it. Can't carry this sort of war of attrition as well as I used to.'

'How do you think it's going to turn out?' asked George with interest.

'Oh, it's anybody's guess – but I think the appeal will be allowed. Yes, I really expect it to go through. Site's almost an uneconomic proposition as it is, after the run of bad luck they've had down there. Well, back luck! – more likely over-confidence and over-haste, I'd hazard, if the truth be told. Put any amount of machinery out of action in a very short time, crashed one grab clean over and damned nearly killed the lad driving it – too much of it to be simply bad luck. It's my opinion they were trying to rush this last stretch to make a good case for moving into my ground before the winter closed in, and were in such a hurry they took too many chances, and made a botch of it.

But *I* don't know! Their business, not mine. I'll abide by the decision, this time, bad or good, but I admit I hope for success. Can't expect me to enjoy the prospect of having the place torn up by the roots, can you, after all?'

George allowed that it would be rather a lot to expect. He suppressed a grin which would have done no discredit to Dominic, and asked demurely: 'How's the shooting this year? Client of mine tells me the pheasants have done rather well.'

The white moustache bristled for a moment, the bold blue eyes flashed, but he relaxed into laughter before their blueness had quite grown spearlike. 'Ah, well, haven't had too many taken yet, all things considered. And your job's a bit like the confessional, isn't it? So I won't ask you for his name. Yes, they've done quite well. With only half a keeper, so to speak, one couldn't ask more. Briggs is a complete anarchist, of course, won't be ruled by owner, expert or predecessor, but he does rear the birds, heaven knows how. I've stopped interfering.'

'I heard the guns out for the first time yesterday evening. Sounded like autumn!'

'Oh, that would be Charles and a couple of friends he had down. I haven't been out myself yet, haven't had time. Perhaps this week-end we may get out together for a few hours – can't let a whole week of October slip away without a single bird. But there won't be any big parties this year. I can't do with the social life, Sergeant Felse, it takes too much out of a man, and I'm not so young as I once was. And then, it needs a woman to take charge of the house, or there's no heart in it –'

For a fleeting moment his blue eyes glanced upward at the wide, creamy expanse of wall opposite, where the best light in the room gathered and seemed to cluster upon a large, framed photograph. A woman, young but not very young, pretty but not very pretty, somehow too undecided to be *very* anything; and yet she had a soft, vague charm about her, too. A lot of fluffy light-brown hair, a formless yet pleasing face which looked as if it might yet amount to something if every line in it could be tightened up, a soft, petulant mouth, a string of carved imitation stones round her plump neck. Why should so vigorous, hard and arrogant an old man have lost any sleep over the flight of such a wife?

The sight of the picture never failed to astonish George with the same query. But human affections are something over which even the most practical people cannot be logical. Nobody likes to be left naked to laughter, either, even if leaves have fallen and cold winds come, especially if he happens to be the local panjandrum. And since the quick glance was never more than a momentary slipping of his guard, George was no wiser after it than he had been before. Maybe it was love, maybe only outraged dignity, that dug knives into the old man. Or maybe both had worn off long ago.

But to think of a woman with a face like that having the brains and patience to go quietly about from dealer to dealer, selling her jewellery, getting rid of her securities, telling them all – and all in confidence, of course! – that he was sending her to safety in America. If two of them had ever compared notes they would have known that she was collecting together more money than she could possibly be allowed to take out of the country; but of course every deal was private and confidential, and they never did compare notes. In a way, thought George irreverently, the old man ought to have been rather proud of her, she made a thumping good job of it. And he appreciates tactics, as a rule! Maybe, at that, it was from him she learned all she knew.

But this was not what he had come for. He pulled his mind sharply back from this most fascinating side-track, and asked: 'You're exhibiting at the Sutton Show, I suppose?'

'Yes, hoping to. Sending some stuff down by road, with Hollins. Pretty good prospects, I think.' He began to talk stock, his eyes kindling, and George let him run for a while, though most of it went past him and left no mark.

'Hollins came to see you about the arrangements, I

understand, last Wednesday night. He says he was here about nine. Do you remember it?'

'Yes, of course. Came just after I turned the news on, I remember. Stayed maybe a quarter of an hour or twenty minutes. He was away before half-past nine, at any rate. Rather a dull stick, young Chris,' said the old man, looking up suddenly under his thick eyebrows with a perfectly intelligent appreciation of the meaning of these questions, 'though a good sheep–farmer. Not at all a likely suspect for murder, one would think.'

'None of 'em are,' agreed George. 'All next-door-neighbours, everybody knowing everybody, murder's an impossibility, that's all about it. Only alternative to thinking nobody could have done it is thinking anybody could have done it – and that's a thing one hopes not to have to face.'

'It's a thing nine out of ten of us couldn't possibly face. We know enough to shut our eyes tight when it comes along, and keep 'em shut until it's gone by. It's that or lose hold of every mortal thing. But still – I'd put Hollins well down the list of possibilities, myself.'

'No one will be more pleased than I shall,' agreed George, 'if I can account for every minute of his evening, and put him clean out of it. You've accounted for twenty minutes or so, and that's something. What sort of frame of mind did he seem to be in? Just as usual? Not agitated at all? Not even more with-drawn than usual?'

'Didn't notice anything out of the way. He talked business in the fewest words that would cover it, as always. He never talked much. Came, and said what he had to say, and went, and that was that. No, there wasn't anything odd about him. Maybe a bit brisker than usual, if anything. He was a fellow who liked to sit and light a pipe as a sort of formal preliminary to conference, and come to the point briefly, but at his leisure. This time he got off the mark without smoking. That's positively all there is to be said about the interview, as far as I remember.'

138

'He didn't say anything about where he was going when he left you? Nothing about any calls intended on the way home?'

'No, nothing that I remember.'

'Oh, well – thanks for your help, sir.' George rose, and old Blunden's heavy bulk heaved itself out of the arm–chair to accompany him to the door. Again he noticed the ageing thrust of the big shoulders, the slight stoop, for all the glint of his eye which had still more devilry in it than Charles could compass in the whole range of his moods.

'I won't ask you anything,' said Blunden, leading the way through the sudden dimness of a hall which faced away from the morning sun. 'But I don't mind telling you, Sergeant Felse, that I feel very concerned for that poor woman Hollins married. Not much of the truth ever came out, but I gathered what sort of a life young Schauffler had been leading her, all the same. Wish you luck all the more when I think about her. I do indeed! The sooner this case is closed, once and for all, the better I'll be pleased.'

'So will I,' said George with even more fervour; and went away very thoughtfully to find Jim Tugg, who was leaning on one of his hurdles at the lambing-fold down in the bowl of the fields beyond the farm, chewing a grass and contemplating a number of well-grown and skittish Kerry Hill lambs. He appeared to be doing nothing beyond this, but in fact he was calculating the season's chances, and putting them pretty high, if nothing went wrong with the weather. He was dead sure he'd got the best tup he'd seen for years, and was looking forward to an average higher than last year. He was not thinking of the police at all, and even when he looked up from the black knees and black noses of the fat young ewes to the incongruous navy-blue figure of George, the contemplative expression of his eyes changed only very slowly and reluctantly.

George was nonetheless familiar by now with this change. In most people it happened instantaneously, the brief flare of intensified awareness, and then the quick but stealthy closing of the door upon him, with an almost panicky quietness, so that he should not hear it shut to. In Jim the pace was slower, and only the eyes changed, the rest of the dark face never tightening by one muscular contraction; and in Jim the closing of the door had a deliberation which did not care so much about being observed. The collie stopped bossing the sheep about, and came and stood at his knee, as if he had called it.

'Well, Sergeant?' said Jim. 'Thought of some more questions?'

'Just one,' said George, and found himself a leaning-place on the hurdles before he launched it. He wanted more than an answer to it; he wanted to understand the expression that went with the answer, but in the end all he could make of Jim's face was a mild surprise when he asked at length:

'That green door in the orchard-wall up at the house – Which day did you paint it?'

II

Gerd Hollins put down the large hen-saucepan she had been about to lift to the stove, put it down carefully with a slow relaxing of the muscles of her olive forearms, and straightened up wiping her palms on the hips of her apron, where they left long damp marks in a deeper blue. She stood for a long minute looking at George without saying a word or moving a finger, quite still and aware, with her big eyes, strangely afraid but more strangely not afraid of him, fixed steadily on his face.

'How did you know?' she said. 'Was there someone who saw us? Who was it who told you?' And suddenly the tensions went out of her, ebbing very quietly, and she sat down limply in the nearest chair, and leaned her linked hands heavily into her thighs, as if the weight of them was too much to hold up any longer. But it was odd that she should first ask that. Why should she want to know if someone had told him? Because in that case the same person might have told someone else?

There was only one someone who could count for her in such an affair or at such a moment. Or perhaps two? The second of whom had just manifested nothing but rather scornful surprise at being asked about the newly-painted door. But in any case her husband was in all probability the only creature about whom she really cared. Was it safe to conclude, then, that, as far as she knew, her husband was unaware of Helmut's last visit, and that the fear she felt was of the possibility that, after all, there might have been someone willing and able to enlighten him?

When she let herself sag like that she was middle-aged, even though her face continued dark, self-contained and handsome. She looked at him, and waited to be answered.

'On Helmut's tunic-sleeve,' he said, 'there were very faint traces of green paint, not much more than a coating on the hairy outside of the pile. The kind of just noticeable mark you get from a quick-drying paint when it's tacky. It tallies with the new paint on the door in your orchard-wall. Jim painted the door, he says, last Wednesday afternoon.'

She passed her hand across her forehead, smoothing aside a strayed end of her black hair. 'Yes,' she said, 'he did. He left it unlocked afterwards. Yes – I see! So no one actually told you?'

'No one. I've come so that you can do that.'

She looked up suddenly, and said: 'Jim –?'

'Jim is still wondering what the devil I meant by the question. He doesn't know it could have anything to do with Helmut. This is just between me and you.'

She gave a long sigh, and said: 'I'll tell you exactly what happened. It affects no one but me. Chris didn't know. Jim didn't know – at least – no, I'm sure he didn't know about that night, at any rate. He was down in the village before Helmut came near me.'

Yes, she could care about more than one man at a time, it seemed, even if not in quite the same way. A stubborn, deliberate loyalty to Jim Tugg crossed at right-angles the protective love she felt for her husband. Might there not even be some real conflict here in this house, where the two of them went about her constantly, either loving her in his fashion? George caught himself back aghast from this complication of human feeling. Good God! he thought, I'm beginning to see chasms all round me, complexes in the kitchen, rivalries in the rickyard. Why, I've known these people for years! But he was not quite reassured. How many of the people you have known for years do you really know?

'It was the fifth time he'd been up here,' said Gerd, in a level voice, 'since he left us. He didn't come too often, partly because it was a risk – and you know he always liked to have the odds on his side – but also, I think, because he wanted me never to get used to it, always to be able to think and hope I'd seen the last of him, so that he could come back every time quite fresh and unexpected. Twice he came over the fence and through the garden, when both Chris and Jim were off the place. He must have stayed somewhere watching until they went. The third time he found the little door in the wall. That was perfect, because in the evening I have to go there to feed the fowl and shut the pens, and there it's quite private, right out of sight of the house or the yard. And narrow! I could never pass until he chose to let me. The fourth time was the same. There'd been eight days between, and I almost thought he'd tired of it. Then I had a lock put on the door, and kept it locked until the Wednesday. Jim forgot to lock it again after he finished. It never used to be locked, you see, it was no wonder it slipped his mind.'

She paused, rather as if to assemble her thoughts than in expectation of any comment from George, but he asked her, because it had been mystifying him all along: 'But what could he *do* here? What satisfaction did he get, to make the game so fascinating to him? I mean, you'd expect even a Helmut to tire of simply tormenting someone – especially, if I may say so, when the victim was quite beyond being frightened.'

She weighed it and him in the deeps of her appallingly patient eyes, and explained quietly: 'Fright is not everything. There may even be a new pleasure to be got out of someone who is not – frightened, exactly. I think Helmut must have got rather bored with people who were just frightened of him, during the war. They seem to have stopped being amusing to him. He liked better someone who was desperate, but couldn't do anything about it. I was desperate, but there was nothing I could do. Maybe it wouldn't be easy to make you understand what Helmut was like, those times when he came here after me. Since I'm telling everything, I'll try to tell you that, too. He very seldom touched me, usually just stood between me and where I was going. Towards the end he began to finger me. Even then it was in his own way. My flesh was only attractive to him because it was in a way repellent, too. He just kept me with him while he talked. He talked about all those places in Germany where my kind of people were herded, and used, and killed. He told me how it must have been for my family. Especially how it must have ended. He told me that all in good time it would be like that for me, that I was not to believe I had finished with these things. He said England would learn, was learning fast, what to do with Jews, niggers, Asiatics, all the inferior breeds. Do not be obvious, and tell me that I am in England, and protected. He was real, was he not? He was there, and he was protected. Oh, I never believed literally in what he said. But I believed in *him*, because every word he said and every thought he had in his mind proved that he was still very much a reality. Things have been so badly mishandled that, after all we've done to get rid of him, he's still one of the greatest realities in the world. In some countries almost the only reality – except poverty. And not quite a rumour in other countries – even here!'

She had regained, as she spoke, the power and composure of her body, and looked at him with straight, challenging eyes, but palely unsmiling.

'I wasn't afraid of him,' she said steadily, 'but I was afraid of

143

the effect he had on me. I'd forgotten it was possible to hate and loathe anyone in that way.'

'I can understand it,' said George sombrely. 'But did he really get so much satisfaction out of these visits that he went on taking such risks for it?'

'He got the only bits of his present life that made him feel like a Nazi and a demi-god again. What more do you suppose he wanted? And he took very little risk. Almost none at all. He was always careful, he had time to be careful.'

'He could watch his step, yes, but at any moment you chose you could have told your husband the whole story. Why didn't you? I can understand your keeping quiet at first, but after Jim's flare-up with Helmut the story was out. Why didn't you keep it that way? Why go to so much trouble to pretend the persecution had ended? If you didn't lie to your husband, you must have come pretty near it. You certainly lied to me. Why?'

She did not answer for a moment, and somehow in her silence he had a vivid recollection of Helmut's body lying in the brook, with ripples tugging and twisting at his blond hair. Perhaps, after all, it was a silly question to ask her. With that ending somewhere shadowy at the back of her mind, she had gone to some trouble to ensure that for the one person who mattered there should be no motive. And Hollins was a man for whom she could do such a service successfully, a limited man, a gullible man, a fond man, not so hard to blindfold. A woman like Gerd, experienced in every kind of evil fortune, might easily take it upon herself to shut up his mind from anger, his heart from grief, and his hands from violence. What was another load more or less to her, if he was back in the sun and serenity of his fields, innocent of any anxiety?

'Did you have any suspicion,' said George suddenly, 'that this would happen?'

'This?'

'Schauffler's murder.' He used the word deliberately, but there was no spark.

144

'Like it did happen – no, I never thought of that. I thought of anger, and fights, and magistrates' courts, and newspapers, and all the stupidity of these things. I didn't often think of him dead, and when I did, it was openly, in a fight – some blow that was a little too hard. But that would have been enough, you see.'

Yes, he saw. So perhaps the motive she was so resolute not to let slip into her husband's hands had only lain waiting and growing and hardening in her own.

'It seems, you understand,' he said carefully, 'that, but for whoever killed him, you must have been the last person to see Helmut alive. The last word we had on him was from the boy who saw him leave the lane for the field-path at Markyeat Cross, soon after seven. It was after that, obviously, that he came here, since he seems to have been heading straight for you then. Tell me about that visit. What time did he come in by the green door? How long did he stay?'

She told him as exactly as she could, dragging up details from her memory with a distasteful carefulness. It must have been nearly eight o'clock when she had gone out to the poultry-houses, therefore according to the time when he had passed Markyeat Cross he must have waited for her coming at least twenty minutes, but his savouring patience had not given out. He had left her, she thought, rather before a quarter-past eight. Where he had gone on closing the green door between them she did not know. By eleven o'clock, according to the doctors, he had been dead and in his brook, snugly tucked into the basin of clay under the edge of the Harrow woods and the waste lands. And between the last touch of his pleased and revolted fingers on her bare arm, and the blow that killed him, who had seen him?

'I wish to heaven,' said George suddenly, 'that you'd told me the truth long ago!'

'When you questioned me about these things there was

already a body to be accounted for. In such a case one lies –
rather too easily.'

'I meant long before that, before it ever came to that. If you
wanted your husband protected, as I'm sure you did, at least
why didn't you come to *me*?'

She gave him a long look which made him feel small, young
and nakedly useless, and said without any irony or unkindness:
'Sergeant Felse, you over-estimate yourself and your office. To
the police people simply do not go. Nor to the Church, either.
It seems there are no short cuts left to God.'

It was horribly true, he felt as if she had thrown acid in his
face. All the good intentions, all the good agencies, seem to have
grown crooked, grown in upon themselves like ingrowing toe-
nails, and set up poisoned irritations from which people wince
away. In real trouble, unless he is lucky enough to possess that
rare creature, a genuine friend, every man retires into himself,
the one fortress on which he can place at any rate some reliance.
As Gerd had withdrawn into herself and taken all her problems
with her, that no one else might stumble over them and come
to grief.

The only people who still ask the police for protection,
thought George bitterly, are the Fascists. What sort of use are
we?

'It sounds impossible,' he said, 'that a woman can be persecuted in her own house, like that, and have no remedy she
can feel justified in taking. Tell me honestly, had you yourself
ever thought of a way out?'

She looked at him impenetrably, and said: 'No. Except to go
on bearing it, and take what precautions I could to avoid him.'

'Did your husband ever say anything to make you think he
had his suspicions. I mean, that Helmut was still haunting you?'

'No, never.'

'Nor Jim, either?'

'No, nor Jim.'

She heard, just as she said it, Christopher's feet at the scraper

outside the scullery door, methodically scraping off his boots
the traces of one of the few damp places left in the hollows of
his fields, the shrunken marsh pool in the bottom meadows.
George heard it, too, a slow, dogged noise like the man who
made it. He saw the slight but sudden rearing of Gerd's head,
the deep, perceptible brightening of her eyes, the quickening of
all the tensions which held her secret. But not a gleam
of welcome for him now, no gladness. Not for the first time,
Chris had done the wrong thing. She got up with a quite
daunting gesture of dismissal, picked up the hen-saucepan, and
put it on the large gas-ring, and resolutely lit the gas under it.
But George did not move. Just as the porch door opened he
said clearly:

'In that case I hope you realise, Mrs. Hollins, that you seem
to be the only person in Comerford who had an excellent motive
for wanting him dead, and who knew his movements that night
well enough to have followed him and killed him.'

III

Chris Hollins heaved himself into the doorway and stood there
looking up under his lowered brows, like a bull meditating a
charge. Gerd, turning with the matches in her hand, gave him
a look so forbidding that at any other time he would have retired
into a dazed silence, following her leads, saying what he believed
she wanted of him; but now he stood and lowered his head at
her, too, in his male indignation, and demanded menacingly:

'What's this you're saying to my wife, Sergeant?'

George repeated it. Not because he was proud of it; indeed,
the second time it sounded even cheaper. But it had certainly
made Hollins rise, and that was almost more than he had
expected. He said it again, almost word for word, with the calm
of distaste, but to the other man's ears it sounded more like the
calm of rock-like confidence.

147

'And what grounds have you got,' he said thickly, 'for saying any such thing to her? How do you know a dozen more people didn't know of his movements, and hadn't better reason to want him dead than ever she had?'

'There may have been a hundred,' agreed George, 'but there's curiously little sign of even one. You find me the evidence, and I'll be more than interested.'

Gerd said: 'In any case, it's no desperate matter, so don't let's get melodramatic about it. Sergeant Felse has his job to do. I haven't been accused of killing him, so far, and there's no need to act as if I have.' Her eyes were large and urgent on her husband now, with no time for George; and for that reason he was able to make more sense of their questioning than ever he had made before. She wanted the subject dropped. She wanted either an end of the interview, or Chris miles away; for it was plain, for one dazzling moment, that she simply did not know what he might be about to say, and feared it as she had never feared Helmut Schauffler. 'I've told all I know,' she said. 'I don't think he can have anything more to ask you.'

'I might,' said George, 'ask him why it doesn't surprise him to hear that you knew all about Helmut's movements the night he was killed. After all, yesterday you both denied you'd seen hide or hair of him since he was in court. He seems to take it all as a matter of course that we should have come to a different conclusion today.'

The exchange of glances was fluid and turbulent, like the currents of a river. One minute he thought he had the hang of it, the next it seemed to mean something quite different. They were at cross-purposes, each in fear of what the other might give away, each probing after the other's secrets. Certainly it seemed that Helmut's last visit to the farm had been no secret from Hollins, however securely Gerd had tried to hide it. Now she was at a loss how to say least, how to keep him most silent, agonised with trying to understand at every stage before George could understand, and so steer the revelations into the most harmless channel. But Hollins was past giving her any co-operation in the endeavour. Concealment was alien to his nature, and he had had enough of it, if it could end in his wife's being singled out as a likely suspect of murder. He swung his heavy head from one to the other of them, darkly staring, and said bluntly:

'Well I knew he'd been here, and talked to her, and carried on his old games at her, like before! And well I knew she told you lies when she said the opposite yesterday. Do you wonder she kept as much as she could to herself? If it was a mistake, it was a mistake ninety-nine out of a hundred would have made.'

She stood there staring at him with blank, shocked eyes. When she could speak she said: 'Why didn't you tell me? I thought you at least knew nothing about it – I wanted you not to know! But when you found it out, you might have told me!'

'Trying to shut up trouble doesn't work so well,' he said grimly. 'But I thought it was my job to think of something, and not to put the weight of it any harder on you. Not that it came to anything – not even murder. I might as well say, why didn't you tell me, and not leave me to find out for myself what was going on. But I don't ask you any such thing.'

'Well, having gone so far,' said George, 'you may as well tell me all you know. Look, I don't pretend to be the children's friend to any very wonderful extent, but wouldn't it have been better to trust me a little further in the first place?'

'Maybe it would, but try being in our shoes, and see what you'd do. Not that we'd anything guilty to hide,' he said with quite unwonted violence, as if he were trying to convince himself, 'but just on the run of events can put you in a bad spot without any help on your part, and it comes natural to play down the awkward bits that don't mean anything, but have a nasty way of looking as if they do.'

George, with his eyes on Gerd, agreed reasonably that this made perfect sense. 'But now let's have all the facts you've got to give, even if they look nothing to you. They help to fill in an evening, and reduce the time about which we know very little. For instance, we know now that Helmut came here, accosted Mrs. Hollins in the orchard at about eight o'clock, made himself as objectionable as usual, and left at about a quarter-past the hour. From then until eleven o'clock, when apparently he must have been dead, we know nothing about him. It seems you knew the persecution was still going on. How long had you known it? Before that night?'

Hollins turned his head from side to side, thrusting at them both as if they might make simultaneous but not concerted attack. After a thick pause he said, quite quietly: 'No.'

'You found it out that night?'

'Yes. She was a long time. I had a devil nagging me that there was still something wrong. I went down the garden and looked through the trees there, and saw them. He had her by the arm – '

Gerd cried out suddenly, in a voice too high-pitched for her: 'He's lying! I do not believe it! He's making up a tale for you, to draw you off from me. Don't listen to him! He knew nothing, he saw nothing, I am absolutely sure he was not there – '

'I did more than see. It was all I could do not to come out at him and wring his neck on the spot, but if you could keep me out of things for my own good, so could I you. I went back to the house,' he said, breathing hard, 'and got my old revolver, and loaded it, and then I went round to the edge of the spinney, where I knew he'd go sneaking away after he left you. Oh, no, Sergeant Felse, my wife wasn't the only one to know all about his movements that evening. I knew them better than she did. I saw him alive long after she did. When he went off up the mounts and into the wood, I went after him.'

Knotting her hands at her waist into a tight contortion of thin, hard fingers in which the knuckles showed white, she said: 'You are a fool! You take the wrong way, the foolish way, to protect me.'

George, looking from one to the other, prompted delicately:

'You said, Mrs. Hollins, that he went out half-way through the evening.'

'I was gone before she got back to the house.'

'It's true, he was gone,' she said, trembling now, 'but I knew he was going to Blunden's, I took it for granted that he should simply leave when he was ready. And he did go to Blunden's – the old man will tell you so.'

'He has told me so already. But it doesn't take three-quarters of an hour and more to go from here to the Harrow.'

'On a fine evening, why should he hurry? There was nothing else to claim him. But this other story he has made up, to help me, to make you think that Helmut lived long after he left me, and there can be no suspicion on me – '

'Look!' said George, suddenly going to her and taking her firmly by the elbow. 'Take it easy, both of you! You sit down, and don't rush things before you come to them.' She looked surprised, even, he suspected, a little amused, as he put her into a chair, but she sat there obediently looking up at him, and her face was eased. 'Look, I know I started this, and in a not particularly fair way, either. But I'm not trying to get more out of you than just the plain, stupid truth. Just because you're anxious to show me that he didn't kill Helmut, there's no need in the world to fall over backwards and tell me that *you did*. It's long odds Helmut *was* seen alive long after he left here, maybe by several people, if only we knew how to find 'em. If your husband can fill in a bit of the missing time, so much the better for both of you in the long run. Only give up the idea that pushing the bits you don't much like under the rug is going to make things better for anybody. It's only going to make me mad, and that does nobody any good.'

She began to smile, and then he felt better, even though the smile was faintly indulgent, as to a crazy juvenile. 'All right, if it's understood that you don't either of you have to talk in a hurry, we can hear the rest.' He looked up at Hollins, but the heavy remoteness of that face had not changed at all. 'You followed him. Go on!'

Hollins shook back his shoulders, and went on: 'I kept behind him all up the woods, out of sight and hearing of him, but close. The revolver was in my pocket. I don't know whether I meant to kill him or not. I know I meant at least to half-kill him, maybe I meant more.'

'But it was after nine when he was killed,' cried Gerd, 'and at nine – '

'At nine, or a couple of minutes later, your husband was at the Harrow,' said George. 'Also, Helmut was not shot. And it does seem a little unlikely that a man with a loaded revolver in his pocket should go to the trouble to use a less certain method for the same job.'

'I didn't use it for any job, in the end. It's still fully loaded, it hasn't even been used to bash somebody over the head. I suppose those fellows of yours who examine these things can tell that by looking at it?'

'They can try, at any rate,' said George. 'Go on, where did you leave Schauffler, and at what time?'

'I kept behind him until he came on to the ridge above the river, and sat down there for a while. He was very pleased with himself, humming and singing to himself in German, and grinning as if he'd pulled off something very clever. He sat there quite a time. I had time to think, and I thought better of it.'

George asked, with genuine and personal curiosity: 'Why?'

'Well, he wasn't such big stuff. I meant getting him, and I watched and waited for him to move on; but he got to looking smaller and smaller as it got dark. And I cooled off this much, that I began to think how much trouble I should be laying up for her, as well as myself, with how little use or satisfaction. I knew about him now, and I could put a stop to him as far as my wife was concerned, without starting something worse for her, like murder in the family. She'd gone to a lot of pains to

152

avoid what it looked like I was bent to bring on her. So I went off and left him there. I went to the Harrow – we weren't two hundred yards from the wicket in the fence – and left him to go to hell for all I cared.'

'Virtually,' said George, 'he did. What time did you quit?'

'I'd say about ten to nine. I went straight to Blunden's, and it wouldn't take above ten minutes to do it from there.'

'And you didn't see anything of him on the return journey?'

'Not a sign. I told you the way I came home, and that was all truth, if the rest wasn't. I took my time over it, to get it all off my mind before I came back where anybody could see me. I needed to walk him out of my system, or *she'd* have known with one look at me. From my point of view, after I turned my back on him up there we were both done with Helmut Schauffler.'

Unfortunately no one was yet done with Helmut Schauffler. That was the devil of it. Not George, not all the spasmodically talkative, suddenly quiet neighbours leaning over Comerford garden fences, not the cheated heroes looking for a world fit for humankind, certainly not these two unquiet lovers. It was plain when their eyes met, drawn together unwillingly, that wells of doubt were opened within them, never to be filled by any amount of protestations or promises. Only certainty was of any use; nothing else held any peace for anyone in this haunted village.

She looks at him, thought George with pity and horror, as if she believes he's lying. And he looks at her as if he *knows* she's told only part of the truth. And yet he could not be sure even of this. 'My lad,' said George to himself, 'you'd better get a move on, for everybody's sake!'

IV

'I never noticed before,' he said to Bunty, in the late evening, when Dominic was safely in bed and his ears no longer innocently stretched after a solution of problems which were his as surely as anyone's, 'I never realised how opaque people's looks can be. We read meanings into them every day, but suddenly when it's a matter of life and death it makes you look again, and start weighing possibilities and separating them from suppositions – and altogether in the end you're terrified to think anything means anything. For a moment I could have sworn that each of those two was seriously afraid the other had done it. And then I couldn't be sure if that was really the meaning of the looks they were giving each other, or if it was something shared, or what it was.'

Bunty looked at him with her practical partisan sympathy, and agreed: 'That's a pity. Because if each of them really believed the other had done it, that would mean neither of them had done it, and then at least somebody would be safely out of it.'

'Not quite, because an expression in the eyes isn't evidence. But at least I could have felt sure of something in my own mind. Now I'm sure of nothing. It's as open as ever it was – in their direction rather wider open. Because there was an intent to murder, I'm sure of that, and while it's credible that it should evaporate as suddenly as that – because he's a sane man with both feet on the ground, and only too deeply aware how much trouble his wife's been dragged through already – still it's also a strong possibility that it *didn't* evaporate.'

Bunty, aware of his hand's vague undirected searching for something in his pockets, got up and brought him the tired man's solace, his tobacco pouch and pipe, and the necessary matches. She put them into his lap, and watched his fingers operate them mechanically. Even over the first deep draws he made a face of disappointment. It was his own growing, and he always forgot to be prepared for the shock; but he was too stubborn to admit that it was unsmokeable. Maybe he hadn't got the knack of curing it properly; anyhow, it was pretty awful. Bunty had never before noticed his distaste quite so clearly, and she made a mental note to buy a tin of his old brand the very next morning, and leave it somewhere for him to find, quite by accident.

'And another eye-opener,' said George fretfully, 'is the ease with which well-known citizens can walk about this darned place for hours at a time, and meet nobody. You wouldn't think it possible.'

'In the dark, in a scattered country district where everybody drops off home by his own particular bee-line across the mounts, well, it isn't really so astonishing as it seems,' said Bunty reasonably.

'Not when you come to weigh up everything, perhaps. But it's confoundedly inconvenient. Here we've got Wedderburn going off in the sulks to walk off a slight load before he goes home to his mother. And Jim Tugg wandering home by devious ways, alone but for his dog – but I grant you, there's nothing new about that, Jim likes his dog's company far better than most men's. And Hollins stalking Helmut, by his own confession, with intent to knock hell out of him at the very least, and then taking his disordered fancy for a walk until the agitation set up by the thought of murder had passed – '

'And Mrs. Hollins,' said Bunty very soberly, 'at home by herself all this time, shut up with the thought of Helmut. Nobody to take her mind off it, nobody to see what she did, nobody even to tell us whether she was really there or not.'

George looked through the detestable smoke of his unthrifty crop at her, and found her looking very solemn and rather pale under the ruffled red hair. Awfully like the shivering but acute waif, so pale, so important, so large and scared of eye, who had met him in the clay-flats by the shrunken brook, standing over the blond head of Helmut.

'You don't really think, do you, that she might have done it?'

'I think *I* might,' said Bunty, 'in her place. Especially if I had reason to think that *you* might be thinking of doing it for me. She had a background of desperation. I don't mean it came naturally to her, but her scope had been rather forcibly widened, you see. And she had, if we come to it in earnest, the finest motive you would wish to see.'

'But the fact that her mind was used to dealing with these awful things would also mean that it was trained and equipped to resist them. I mean, she could not only seriously consider murder, after all she'd experienced – she could effectively reject it, too. I'm not satisfied that it's the strongest motive we have to look for. People of insignificant balance kill for insignificant things – sometimes almost lightly. And we haven't quoted the tenth part of Helmut's enemies. There are dozens of them, more trivial ones but real ones, round this village unaccounted for. There's at least one good union man who began the ideo-logical feud with him long before young Fleetwood ever opened his mouth. And plenty of others, too. And there's something about this whole affair that makes me feel it never was planned. It came out of nowhere, out of some man's mind through his hands so fast he never had time to stop it or even see what it was, until it was done. That's how it feels to me.'

'It could still have been a woman,' said Bunty, 'even that way.'

'It could. Women have murderous impulses, too. But wouldn't a woman have been – more disastrously subtle about it, after-wards? I don't know. This was so short and simple. No messy attempts to cover up, but a clean walk-out.'

'And no weapon,' said Bunty, biting her underlip. 'I suppose the revolver didn't show any sign?'

'Not a mark. Nobody's head was beaten in with the butt of *that* gun, that's certain.'

'If only,' burst out Bunty, speaking for Comerford with authentic passion, 'if only it weren't for all the people whose lives are being bent out of shape now, I'd pray like anything that nobody'd ever solve it. But it's the village that's being murdered, not Helmut. Oh, George, isn't there any way out of it?'

'Only one. Straight ahead and out the other side – one man short or one woman short,' said George, 'whichever it turns out to be. And the sooner the better, for everybody concerned!'

Chapter 6

Feathers in the Wind

I

It was odd how all the games which came into season with the autumn, the ranging games which can extend over a whole square half-mile of country, had gravitated this year towards Webster's well, which sat, as it were, in the midst of a charmed circle of play. The younger boys evacuated their gangs from the village into this particular wilderness out of all the circle of pit-mounds open to them, and files of Indians moved up the shadowed side of the high field hedge there, while the hollows of birch saplings scattered in the clay wastes began to heave with commandos. There had always been cycles of fashion in playgrounds, of course, and usually for the most unsuitable reasons. Once for a whole autumn the favourite place had been the ruined engine-house on the brambly, naked mounds near the station. An elderly man of none too sound mind had been found hanged there, and horrid fascination had drawn all the boys and many of the bolder girls to haunt it for months after, especially at the shadowy hour between evening and night, when it was most terrifying, and lingering there repaid terror well-concealed with the most enviable kudos.

Another year a farmer's horse, grazed in a field with a brook at the bottom, got itself bogged to the neck during the night, and had to be rescued by the inevitable and long-suffering fire-brigade, whose entire working life, in these parts, appeared to be spent in fetching kittens down from telegraph poles, or dogs out of pit-shafts. The rescue lasted all day, and a crowd large enough for a fair-ground had gathered to witness the end of it; after which the marshy corner had become haunted ground for at least a month, and all the mothers of Comerford had more than usually muddy children.

But this year it was Webster's well. Webster's well and the mounts round it had no rival. Even the older children, past the stage of pretend games, took their elaborate versions of hide-and-seek up there to play. Pussy had a splendid variation of her own, which involved dusk, and pocket torches, and therefore could only be played in the end of daylight, which meant at the extremest end of a thirteen-year-old's evening, until summer time ended, later in October. Usually they wound up the fine evenings with a bout of it, before they went home to bed. Pussy was trailing a gang at the time. She had her solitary periods and her periods of communal activity, and Dominic, largely independent of his company though willing to co-operate with any numbers, acquiesced in her moods but retained to himself, formidably and irrevocably, the right to secede. He didn't care how many people she collected about her, if the result continued to entertain him; but if they proved boring, and began to waste too much time in argument and wrangling, he was off. Life, even at thirteen, was too short for inaction.

It was growing dark on this particular October evening, with the silvery darkness of autumnal, clear nights when frosts have not yet begun. The occasional reports of guns in the preserves had already become so snugly familiar that they fell into the silence almost as softly as drops of dew from the trees. They sounded warm when the warmth of the day ended, prolonging activity long into the inactive hours like an echo; and now with dusk they chimed once or twice more, and ceased upon a stillness. The earth sighed, stretched and relaxed, composing itself for sleep.

At this point even the games grew stealthier, brigandage molten into witchcraft. The fat child with the gym tunic, and the sandy-haired boy with glasses, who were hunters for the occasion, sat in the grass close beside Webster's well, counting up to two hundred in leisurely, methodical whispers, no longer shouting out the numbers belligerently as by daylight. The flock scattered into the waste woods voiceless and soft of foot. Pussy and Dominic scrambled across the ridges of clay and went up the terraced slope beyond on hands and knees, for it was steep, and it does not take long to count to two hundred. Through the hedge at the top, by enlarged dog-holes which no one bothered to repair, and headlong into a wilderness of furze and birch saplings, tunnelling like rabbits among the spiny places, slithering like lizards through the silvery, slippery leaves.

'Where shall we go?' asked Pussy in Dominic's ear; and at this eerie hour even Pussy whispered.

It was the tail-end of the evening's play, and they had almost exhausted the charms of every ordinary hiding-place. At this hungry and thirsty and yearning hour, with the uneasiness of the dark and the inevitability of bedtime clutching at them, something more was needed than the spidery tunnels of the furze and broom, and the clay hollows of elders and watery pits of willow, full of lean shadows. Rustlings and whisperings and tremors quivered across the vanishing face of the waste land after the feet of their companions. The pit mounds inhaled with one great sigh, and the children were swallowed up. And Pussy and Dominic, straight as arrows, restless, wanting something more, set their course directly upward from the well across the ribbon of wilderness, and fetched up breathlessly under the pale fence of the Harrow preserve, looking into a sweet, warm, olive-green darkness within.

Dominic panted: 'I never thought it was quite so near.' He shook the pales, and looked along the fence, and saw nothing on his side but the same thickets in which he had already buried himself grubbily half a dozen times this same evening.

'Where shall we go?' repeated Pussy. 'Quick, they'll be coming, if you don't make up your mind.'

But he had made up his mind already. It might not have happened, if the pale had not been broken out of its place, rotted away with its top still dangling in the circle of wire. Only fifty yards along the fence there was a gate, and with no wire atop, either, and a path ran tidily away from it into the dark of the plantation, heading for the Harrow farm; but the gate would not have charmed him, because it was a right of way, whereas this was a way to which he had no right. And all the guns had ceased now, and the darkness had a hush upon it as if the wood held its breath to see if he would really come. He slid one leg through. The pale behind him gave unexpectedly, swinging aside to widen the gap as his negligible hip struck it. He didn't even have to wriggle.

'You'll catch it,' said Pussy practically, 'if anyone comes.'

'Who's going to come, at this time of night? Come on – unless you're scared!'

But though she put the case against it, she was already sliding through the gap after him. Her head butted him in the side smartly. He tugged her through and away into the warm grass-less deeps of the trees. 'Come on! I can hear Sandy moving off. You take an *age!* – and the gap's big enough for a man.'

Pussy said giggling: 'Who d'you suppose made it? I never knew about it before, did you?'

'No, but I'll bet there are dozens like it. Poachers, of course! Who d'you think would make quick ways out, if it wasn't poachers?'

'Dope, I meant which poachers! Because I know several of the special ways that belong to special people, so there!'

'Oh, yes, they'd be sure to tell *you!*' said Dominic, unkindly and unwisely.

'I keep my ears open. You ought to try it some time! I could draw you maps – '

They crashed suddenly a little downhill, slithering in the thin, shiny coating of pine-needles, blind, wrapped in a scented, sudden, womb-like darkness. They were not accustomed yet to the black of it, and Dominic, treading lightly and quick upon the light, quickening heels of his intuition, suddenly checked and felt ahead cautiously with one toe, putting out a hand to hold Pussy back as she made to pass him.

'Look out, there's a hole!'

'I can't see a thing,' she said blithely, leaning forward hard against the pluck of his arm.

'Shine the light! You've got it.'

'But they'll see it. We don't want to show it till we have to.'

'They won't see it from here, if you keep it this way on the ground. Be quick!'

Clawing it indifferently out of the leg of her school knickers, she felt for the button of the pencil-slim torch, the button which always stuck, and had to be humoured. 'Besides, I'm not sure we're not cheating, coming in here. They'll take it for granted it's out of bounds beyond the fence. Nobody ever does come in here.'

'Well, there's never been anything to stop 'em. We never *said* it was out of bounds. And anyhow, when we have to shine the torch they'll know.'

'I don't believe the silly torch intends to be shone. I can't get it on.' She shook it, and it made a ferocious rattling, but no light. 'Maybe the bulb's gone. And if old Blunden comes along and hears us in here there's going to be trouble.'

'Well, why did you come, if you're scared? *I* never made you! And I don't believe old Blunden would be so very fierce, either; he's always quite decent about things, if you ask me.'

'Not people with torches in among his pheasants at night,' said Pussy positively.

'Well, we haven't got what *I'd* call a torch – '

But they had. The button sprang coyly away under her finger at that precious moment, and a wavering wand of light sailed out ahead of them and plucked slender young tree-trunks vibrating out of the dark like harp-strings, with a suddenness which sang. They saw each other's eyes brilliant and large as the eyes of owls in the night, as the eyes of cows encountered unexpectedly nose to nose when short-cutting by gaps in the hedges. Their hearts knocked hard, for no good reason except the reminder of the combat of light and dark, before they even saw the chasm yawning under their toes. Then Pussy squeaked, and scuffled backwards and brought them both down in the pine-needles.

But it wasn't the abyss it had seemed at first glance. Dominic took the torch from her, and crawled forward on his knees to shine it into the hole, and the plunging hell of dark dwindled into a pocketful of dingy, cobwebby shadows. A filled-in pit-shaft, narrow among the trees, but still thrusting them a little aside to make room for it. Grey clay slopes breaking barrenly through poor grass and silt of needles, like a beggar's sides through his tattered shirt; a few bricks from the shaft beaten into the composite of clay and earth, showing fragmentarily red among the grey and green. The place had been levelled, long before the trees were planted, but the earth's hungry empty places underneath had not been nearly satisfied, and now the inevitable shifting fall had made once again a pit, ten or a dozen feet deep, and steadily settling deeper. Grass clawed at the rims of it, trying to hold fast. The slopes of clay which descended into it were furrowed and dried and cracked into lozenges by the dry season, and down in the bottom a small abrupt subsidence within the large and slow one had exposed a curved surface of brickwork pitted with darker holes. Round it the young trees leaned, fearfully and inquisitively peering in, and Dominic with the torch in his hand was only one more strange young staring tree, curious and afraid.

'Just another old shaft!' said Pussy, recovering her aplomb.

'Yes. I didn't know about this one, did you? But there are dozens all over the place.'

"'Tisn't a nice sort of place, is it?" said Pussy, wrinkling her nose with distaste. 'Look at those holes down there! I bet you there are rats!'

'I bet there are! It's all right, though. I thought for a minute it was an open shaft, didn't you?'

They had forgotten Sandy and the fat girl, until a sudden howl and hubbub broke out on the other side of the fence, rustle of stealthy footsteps first, then giggles, then a shriek of triumph and discovery, and crashing of running bodies among the bushes.

'It's Pat and Nancy – I heard you! Come on, Pat, you devil – show!' And a pencilly beam of light, wavering and striped among the branches as the detected pair switched on, and the thunder and protest of pursuit, sibilant slithering of willows, hard obstreperous clawing of gorse, dangerously near.

'Duck!' hissed Dominic, clamping a hand over the torch until she could wrestle the button back. 'Quick, they're coming this way!' She struggled, and the thread of sheathed light dwindled away into the warm dark of his palm. The hunters, returning in triumph, quested along the fence, traced by their steps back and forth, back and forth, whispering.

'Someone else up here! Sure of it! Who? Can't be! Can't hear a thing! But there *was* somebody. Who? Try Dickie! Oi, Dickie! Come on, show a light – Dick-ie!!' No light, no sound. 'Hullo, here's a paling loose. Think anybody'd dare go inside?' 'It's trespassing. And there might be traps!' 'Rot, it's against the law.'

The pale creaked. Danger prickled at Pussy's spine, at Dominic's. Only one way to go for cover. Softly, softly, over the rim of the slope, his hand on her wrist, down the smooth-rough, needle-glazed, heat-ridged sides of the funnel, down into the pit, down among the cobwebs, down where the rats go. They slid down inch by inch on their bellies, feeling the way gingerly with outstretched toes, and holding by the tufts of coarse grass which had such a different texture in the dark. Right down into the uncomfortable oubliette at the bottom, by the invisible shatterings of the arched brickwork and the black holes which Pussy preferred not to remember. The darkness here had a smell, dry, musty, faintly rotten. It made their nostrils curl with repulsion and yet quiver with curiosity – like the vaults of the Castle of Otranto, perhaps, or the family tomb of the Baskervilles. They huddled together in it and froze into stillness, until the stealthy crunching of feet in the pine-silt had withdrawn again, afraid to venture so far beyond the pales.

'How if they fall in?' breathed Pussy in Dominic's ear, tremulous with giggles.

'Can't fall far – and we'll be under. Shut up!'

But the night, settling lower in its pillows, breathing long and gently toward sleep, brought no more echoes of pursuit down to them; and in a few minutes they relaxed, and sorted out their tangled legs from among the dirty trailers of bramble and spears of discouraged grass.

'They've gone!'

'I think! But don't shout too soon. Give them a minute or two more.'

'Be damned!' said Pussy elegantly. 'I want to get out of here.' She fumbled at the torch again, and swore because as usual it refused to light until she had almost broken her nail on it.

'Why, what's the matter with it here? Been in a lot worse places.' Dominic stretched and heaved himself upright by the edges of brickwork, and fragments came away in his fingers and all but tumbled him down again. He groped, and encountered dankness, the caving softness of earth hidden from the sun, cool, dirty, unpleasing opening of one of the holes. Strange how cold! Touch the clay above in the open mounds, and it warmed you even after dusk, but this involuntary contact added to the shock of its recession the shock of its tomb-like, dead chill, striking up his wrist, making the skin of his arm creep like running spiders. He was glad that Pussy was busy stamping on his little vaunt, as usual, so that she failed to hear his minute gasp of disgust.

'Oh, yes! Old Tubby's study this morning, for instance – I heard all about it!'

Half his mind gathered itself to retort, but only half, and that uneasily. How could she have heard all about it? Nobody knew all about it except the headmaster and Dominic himself, and he was jolly sure neither of these two had told her anything. And anyhow, the old boy had been in quite a good mood, and nothing had resulted except a lecture and a few footling lines, which he hadn't yet done. Oh, hell! Silly old-maid things, lines! The hole went back and back; he stretched his arm delicately, and couldn't feel any end to it. Filthy the cold earth felt in there. And there was something, his finger-tips found it, something suddenly soft, with a horrid, doughy solidity inside it, soft, clinging to his fingers, like fur, perhaps, or feathers. He drew his hand back, and the soft bulk followed it a little, shifting uneasily among the loosened soil. Not alive, not a rat. It just rolled after the recoil of his hand because he had disturbed it, but it was small and dead. Rabbit? But not quite that feel. Spines in the softness, longer here. Feathers – a tapering tail.

'Something in here,' he said, drawing his hand out; and his voice had the small awareness which could stop Pussy in mid-scramble, wherever they happened to be at the time, and make her turn the beam of the suddenly compliant torch upon his face. He was a little streaked and dusty, but not so bad, on the whole; it took a second and longer look to discover how far his mind had sprung from hide-and-seek. He sniffed at his own hand, and wrinkled his nose with shock. A clinging odour of rottenness prodded him in the pit of his vulnerable stomach, but his inquisitiveness rose above that. 'Wait a minute! Shine the light this way again. There *is* something there. I believe it's a bird – '

He was groping again, more deliberately this time, with his

166

eyes screwed up, as if that would prevent his nose from working since he had no free hand with which to hold it, and his teeth tight clenched, as if through their grip was produced the power which propelled him.

Pussy said, sitting firmly half-way up the slope, where she had turned to stare at him: 'Don't be so daft! What would a bird be doing down a hole like that?'

'Daft yourself! He's just lying there, dead, because someone put him there, that's what. And why did somebody put him there? Why, because he didn't want to be caught carrying him – Wait a minute, I can't – There are two of 'em! What d'you know? A brace!'

'Pheasants!' said Pussy, leaping to catch up with him, and came slithering to his side again, a minor avalanche of clay dust and pine-rubbish accompanying her.

They were not, when he drew them out into the light of the torch, immediately recognisable as anything except a draggled and odorous mess, fouled with cobwebs and earth. He held them away from him, swivelling on his heels to get to windward, even where there was no apparent wind; and his stomach kicked again, more vigorously, but he would not pay attention to it. A nasty, mangled mess, with broken feathers, and soiled down. Rat-gnawed, too, but the wobbling light failed to show Pussy the traces. Dominic's spine crawled, but the charm was already working, his tightening wits had their noses to the ground. He reared his face, taking a blind line across country, clean over Pussy's stooped, inquisitive head. The fence only a few yards away, the hole in the fence, the tongue of waste land, the clay bowl under the outflow of Webster's well. He himself had said, only ten minutes ago: 'I never thought it was quite so near.' And how long did it take for birds to get – like these were? In a hole in the earth like this, with rats for company, would – he calculated with lips moving rapidly, tantalising Pussy unreasonably – would ten, eleven days produce this stage of unpleasantness? He thought it might. He had shifted the draggled corpses uneasily, shaking his fingers as if he could get the unclean feeling off them that way. Must tell Dad, as soon as possible. It might not be anything, but then it might, and how was he to be sure? And he hadn't even been looking for them, they were honestly accidental. Except that he would certainly be told, for Pete's sake keep away from that place!

'Well, some poacher got disturbed,' said Pussy easily, 'and thought it best not to be caught with the goods on him, so he dumped them in here. That's simple enough. If he used this ground he'd know all about the holes already. Maybe he's hidden things down there before. Anyhow, what's the song and dance about? Ugh! Put them back, and let's get out of here. They're horrid!'

'Well, but,' said Dominic, leaning into the thread of wind which circled the funnel of the pit, and surveying his finds out of the wary corners of large eyes, 'well, but if a poacher just put them there because he thought he was going to meet somebody who could get him into trouble – maybe the owner, or the keeper – well, he put them away pretty carefully so they'd stay hidden until he could come and collect them, didn't he? He wouldn't want to waste his trouble.'

This she allowed to be common sense, jutting her underlip thoughtfully. They had forgotten the very existence of Sandy and his partner by this time.

'Well, then, why didn't he collect them afterwards? Look, you can see for yourself, they've been there days and days. He must have meant to go back for them when the coast was clear. Why hasn't he been?'

'I don't know. There could be any amount of reasons. He may have been ill ever since, or something.'

'Or dead!' said Dominic.

The minute the idea and the word were out of him the darkness seemed a shade darker about them, and the malodorous carrion dangling from his reluctant hand a degree more foul. Dead birds couldn't hurt anyone, but they could suggest other deaths, and bring the night leaning heavily over the pit-shaft in the wood, leaning down upon two suddenly shivering young creatures who observed with quite unusual unanimity the desirability of getting to some cleaner, brighter place with all haste.

'Outside,' said Pussy uneasily, as if they had been shut in, 'we could see them better. It won't be quite dark yet.'

'We don't want the others to know,' said Dominic, suddenly recalling the abandoned game. 'We'll go the other way, down the little quarry. They'll soon give us up and go home. Or you could go and tell them I – tell them my mother wanted me, or something – while I go straight home with these.'

Pussy turned at the rim of the pit to give him a hand, because he had only one free for use. She took him by the upper arm in a grip lean and hard as a boy's, and braced back, hoisted his weight over the edge. Waves of nauseating, faint rottenness came off the drooping bodies. She had no real wish to see them, by this or any light; she reached the open and still kept going, only drawing in a little to be just ahead of Dominic's other shoulder.

'Oh, they'll go home, they'll be all right. I'm coming with you.' As they crawled through the swinging pale she asked: 'Do you really think they were that German's pheasants? Dominic, really do you?'

'Yes, really I do. Well, look down there the way we came, it's only a few minutes to the path by the well, to the – to where he was. And unless it was someone who was dead, wouldn't he go back for his birds? Some time before a whole week there *must* be a chance. After he hid them so carefully, too, because they weren't just dropped in the bushes, he wasn't in as big a hurry as all that. He just wanted them out of his pockets, because there was someone he heard in the woods, and he wanted to be able to pop through the fence and march off down by the well quite jauntily, nothing on him even if it was the keeper, and if he got awkward.'

'But we don't know that Helmut had been poaching,' she objected.

'Well, we know he was as near as that to the preserves. And don't you remember, the lining of his tunic was slit across here, to make an extra-large pocket inside. Why should he want a pocket like that, unless it was to put birds or rabbits in? And where we found him – well, it's so near.'

They skirted the high hedge, and took the right-hand path down into the small overgrown quarry, instead of bearing left towards the all-significant well. What was left of the light seemed warm and kind and even bright upon them, greenish, bluish, with leaves, with sky, and the soft distant glimmering of stars almost invisible in the milky blue. Not even a hint of frost now, only the cool regretful afterbreath of summer, mild and quiet, ominous with foreshadowings, sweet with memories. Clamour of voices from the slackening game they had left came after them with infinite remoteness.

'He put them there until the coast was clear,' said Pussy, hushed of voice, 'and he went slipping back on to the lawful path, bold as brass. What harm am I doing? Because he heard someone coming in the wood, you think? It might have been the keeper? Or it might have been anyone, almost – '

'Yes. But by the well, going along looking all innocent, as you said, he met someone. And that was the person who killed him. So he never had the chance to go back for them.'

Once out of the closed, musty, smothering darkness, where panic lay so near and came so lightly, they could discuss the thing calmly enough, and even step back from it to regard its more inconvenient personal implications. As, for instance, the unfortunate location of the pit where the discovery had been made.

'Of course,' said Pussy, 'the very first thing he'll ask you will be where did you find them? And you'll have to admit we were trespassing.'

'He won't have to ask me,' said Dominic, on his dignity. 'It'll be the very first thing I shall tell him.'

'Well, I suppose that's the only thing to do – but I don't suppose it'll get you off.'

'Can't help that,' said Dominic firmly. 'This is more important than trespassing. And anyhow, everybody trespasses, sooner or later, you can do it even without knowing, sometimes.' But to be honest, of course, he reflected within himself, that was not the way he had done it. However, he was not seriously troubled. What is minor crime, when every official mind is on a murder case?

They hurried down through the narrow, birch-silvered path which threaded the quarry, and into the edges of the village where the first street-lights were already shining. Horrid whiffs of decay tossed behind them on the small breezes of coolness which had sprung up with the night. They let themselves in unobtrusively by the scullery door of the police-station, and sidled into the office to see if George was there. But the office was empty. George had to be fetched away from his book and his pipe in front of the kitchen fire, and brought in by an incoherent Pussy, almost forcibly by the hand, to view the bodies, which by this time were reposing on an old newspaper upon his desk, under the merciless light of a hundred-watt bulb. The effect was displeasing in the extreme, and Dominic's self-willed inside began to kick again, even before he saw his father's face of blank consternation halted on the threshold.

'What in the name of creation,' said George, 'do you two imagine you've got there?'

II

Half-way through the explanation, which was a joint affair, and therefore took rather longer than it need have done, Bunty began to be suspicious that she was missing something, and as the parties involved were merely Dominic and Pussy, she had no scruples about coming into to demand her share in their

171

revelations. Besides, there was a chance that someone would be needed to hold the balance between her husband and her son, who on this subject of all subjects still obstinately refused to see eye to eye. The note of appeasement, however, was being sounded with quite unusual discretion as she entered.

'It was an absolute accident,' Dominic said, 'honestly it was. We weren't even thinking about that business, and it was only one chance in a thousand we ever found them. If the pale hadn't been loose we shouldn't ever have gone in, and if Pussy's torch hadn't been phoney I shouldn't have grabbed off in the dark for a hold in the grass, and put my hand down the hole. It was just luck. But we couldn't do anything except bring them to you, once we'd got them, could we?'

'You'd no business there in the first place,' said George, heavily paternal. 'Serve you right if Briggs had caught you and warmed your jacket for you. Next time I hope he does.'

Bunty remembered certain events of George's schooldays; but she did not smile, or only within her own mind. Dominic grinned suddenly, and said: 'Oh, well – occupational risks! But old Briggs isn't so hot on running.'

'I'm surprised at you, Pussy,' pursued George, not strictly truthfully. 'I thought you had more sense, even if he hasn't.'

There was really no need to argue with him, for his mind was all the time on the dingy draggle of nastiness obtruding its presence from the desk. Thirteen days now! It could be. And the minute fluff they had harvested from Helmut's tunic-lining came easily back to mind. On his last evening he had been observed on the edge of the preserves, his body had been found not a hundred yards from the fence, and at about ten o'clock, melting into the shadows with the typical coyness of his kind, Chad Wedderburn had caught a glimpse of what he could only suppose to be a poacher. And among the miscellaneous small belongings found in Helmut's pockets –

'He had a torch, didn't he?' asked Dominic, his eyes fixed

insatiably on his father's face. 'A big, powerful one. I remember – '

Yes, he had had a torch on him, big and powerful, dragging one pocket of his tunic out of line. Trust Dom to remember that! Found practically on the spot, equipped for the job, and dead just about as long as these birds; and as the kids had pointed out, what poacher but a dead poacher would leave his bag cached until it rotted on him? He supposed he had better call at the Harrow, instead of making straight for the pit.

'Can we come back with you?' asked Dominic eagerly. 'We could take you straight to it – and there are several holes down there, you might not know which it was.'

'It's almost bedtime now,' said Bunty, frowning upon the idea. 'And Io will wonder where Pussy is.'

'Oh, Mummy, there's nearly half an hour yet, we came away before any of the others. And we'd come straight back, really, it wouldn't take long.'

'Nobody'll be worried about me,' said Pussy, elaborately casual. 'I'm not expected home till half-past nine.'

'Better have a look on the spot,' said George to Bunty. 'I'll send them straight back as soon as they've told their tale.'

The trouble was, of course, that he would and did do precisely that. As soon as they had collected Charles Blunden from the farmhouse, with brief explanations, and led their little party to the pit in the pinewoods, and indicated the exact repellent hollow from which they had removed the pheasants, the adults, of course, had done with them. Pussy expected it, Dominic knew it. In the pitchy, resiny darkness, even with lights, expressions were too elusive to be read accurately, but dismissal was in the very stance of George, straightening up in the heel of the pit to say briskly:

'All right, you two, better cut home now. Unless,' he added unkindly, putting ideas into Charles's easy-going head, 'Mr Blunden wants to ask any questions about fences before we let you out of it.'

'Eh?' said Charles, with his arm rather gingerly down the
dank hiding-hole, and only a corner of his mind on what had
been said, just enough to prick up to the sound of his own
name.

'Violating your boundaries, you realise – that's how the thing
began. Knock their heads together if you feel like it, I'll look
the other way.'

'It was my fault,' said Dominic, demurely sure of himself.
'We only wanted somewhere new to hide, and we didn't mean
to go far or do any harm. And anyhow, we did come straight
back and own up to it as soon as we found the birds. You're
not mad, are you, Mr. Blunden?' He daren't be, of course, even
if he wanted to; Pussy wasn't Io's young sister for nothing. Io
might call her all the little devils in creation on her own account,
but it wouldn't pay Charles Blunden to start the same tune;
families are like that. So Dominic trailed his coat gracefully
close to impudence, and felt quite safe. They were about to be
thrown out of the conference, in any case, so he had nothing to
lose.

'Oh, that's all right,' said Charles, disappointingly not even
very interested. 'A fence like that asks to be violated. Not that
I'm advising you to try it while Briggs is about, mind you, or
even to let my father spot you at it. But there's no harm done
this time. Just watch your step, and we'll say no more about it.'

'And we did right to go straight back and report, didn't we?'
pursued Dominic, angling for a re-entry into the council
through Charles, since George certainly wouldn't buy it. 'I say,
do you think it was really like we worked it out? Do you think – '

George said: 'Git! We want to talk, and it's high time you
two went home to bed. You're observant, intelligent, helpful
and reliable people, no doubt, in fact almost everything you
think you are; but there isn't a thing more you can do for us
here. Beat it!'

'I suppose it's something to be appreciated,' said Pussy

sarcastically, as they threaded their way out of the wood by the slender gleam of the torch, and went huffily but helplessly home.

III

'Nothing more there, I'm certain,' said Charles, after twenty minutes of combing the pit and its spidery caverns inch by inch with torches. 'Try it again by daylight, of course, but I think there'll be nothing to show for it. It looks as if the kids weren't far out.'

'Oh, that was a deliberate cache, all right,' agreed George, frowning round at the queer gaunt shadows and lights of the young tree-trunks, erect and motionless, circling them like an audience. 'Things don't fall into sidelong holes like that, even if they were dropped over the edge of the pit in a hurry. They were meant to be well out of sight, and I must say only the merest freak seems to have unearthed them again. There's only one thing worries me – '

'About the Helmut theory? I thought it was pretty sharp of your boy to have jumped to it like he did. Why, what's the snag? I can't see any holes in it.'

'I wouldn't go so far as to say it is a hole. People do such queer things, and do the simplest things so queerly. But in my experience poachers *don't* go to such elaborate shifts to hide their birds, even when they have to ditch them for safety. This place is isolated enough to begin with, and here's the pit, ready to hand, what's wrong with just dropping the birds in one of the hollows under the hang of the grass? Ninety-nine fellows in a hundred would.'

'Just wanted to make doubly sure, I suppose.'

'He didn't expect to be leaving 'em a week or more, I take it. It's long odds the things would have been safe as houses like that for the time they'd have had to wait.'

'Still, if he had to scramble down into the pit in any case to find a hiding-place, why not go the whole hog? And anyhow, isn't the very thoroughness of the thing an extra argument for thinking it was Helmut who planted them? He being a poacher rather out of our experience than in it, and given to habits of Prussian thoroughness? Where another bloke might favour rapid improvisation and a bit of risk, I should think he might easily have proceeded with this sort of methodical mak sikker. Makes sense, doesn't it?'

'Maybe, if you put it like that. But it still looks far-fetched to me! Let's get out!' he said, digging a toe into the crumbling clay slope. 'Nothing more we can do here.'

They ploughed their way to the upper air, which was scarcely lighter by reason of the enclosing trees; and on the rim of the pit George turned to look down once again into the deep, dismal scar. 'How far back does this date? It's not one of your father's war-time operations — trees are too well-grown for that by — what, ten years? Must be that at least.'

'Oh, yes, this patch is one of the first, though mind you these beastly conifers do give a false impression, they're such mushrooms. Can't remember the exact year, but late in the 1920s it must have been. He had all this mount levelled and planted. But you can see it wasn't a very good job they did on the pit-shafts.' His own voice, regretful and even a little bitter, sounded to him for a moment like an echo of Chad's. He wasn't succumbing to Chad's persuasions after all, was he? But the old man could have made a job of it, while he was about it. And if he was alert enough in the 1920s to level a mound for his own preserves, why couldn't he see that he owed the village a bit of levelling, too, for all the chaos the get-rich-quick mining grandfather had created? Still, it was easy to be both wise and enlightened twenty years after the event. They were of their kind and generation, no better but anyhow no worse. 'With proper protection on replacing and levelling,' he said, almost apologetically, 'some of these ruined villages could still have been rich. Why don't we think in time?'

'Up to a point,' said George dryly, turning on his heel from the unpleasing prospect, 'they did.'

'Up to the point of private preserves they did, but not an inch beyond.'

'Strictly on that principle,' said George, 'the century proceeded.'

'The old boy's late operations were all out on the heath patches the other side of the house,' said Charles. 'Near the boundary, actually. The open-cast gang will be ripping them all up again, *if* they decide it's worth their while after all these disastrous expenses they've run their noses into recently, and *if* they win the dispute.'

He didn't sound to George as if he cared very much either way about that, or indeed knew very clearly what he did want. They walked singly through the close-set trees, Charles leaning the torch-beam to the ground for George's benefit. 'We didn't even make a good job of the planning,' he said sadly. 'I'm all for mixed woods myself, these quick pay-offs with conifers play hell with the soil.' They came out from the warm, cloying stomach of the wood, where the soft darkness beyond seemed almost light by comparison, a striped light through the pales. 'This time,' said Charles, 'I really think you should leave by the gap in the fence. See for yourself!' He groped along the pales until the loose one swung in his hand. 'Here we are! I must get that seen to right away. No need to encourage 'em!'

George, looking through the film of trees beyond the fence, could trace at a little distance the cleared line of the path by which Chad Wedderburn had plotted his angry course that night of the death. Somewhere about here he had heard and glimpsed, if his tale was true, the figure of a man, presumed to be a poacher, withdrawing himself rapidly and modestly into the shadows. Could it have been Helmut Schauffler himself? Last heard of previously at about ten to nine, about five hundred yards from this same spot, very pleased with himself, singing to himself in German. Sitting, waiting for the spirit to move him to the next mischief. Or perhaps for the night to fall.

If the shy figure seen at somewhat after ten had really been his, the time during which his death might have taken place was narrowed to slightly under one hour; and Chris Hollins, marching home at last about half-past ten, was almost certainly absolved from any shadow of guilt. For though it did not, as George had said, take three-quarters of an hour to reach the Harrow from Hollins's farm, it did take at least twenty-five minutes to do the journey even in the reverse direction, which was mostly downhill. And the time of Hollins's arrival did not rest solely on his wife's evidence, for there was the carrier's cottage at the bottom of his own drive, and the carrier who had leaned over his gate and exchanged good-nights with him. At twenty-past ten, he said, and he was a precise man. If he was right, and if the shadow among the shadows was Helmut, then Chris Hollins could not have killed him.

'Not a very promising line, after all, I suppose,' said Charles, sounding, as everyone did, quite cheerful at this reflection. In a way, no one wanted the wretched case solved; in another way no one would have any peace, and nothing would ever be normal again, until it was solved. 'Still, you never know. Some witness may turn up yet who'll really have something to say. Anyhow, if there's anything I can do when you come up again, you know where to find me.'

George went home to Bunty very thoughtfully. It was all, *if*, whichever way he turned. *If* Chad's elusive figure at ten had been Helmut, Chris Hollins was out of it. *If*, of course, Chad was telling the truth. And that was something about which no one could be sure. His whole attitude was so mad that it was quite conceivable he had not only seen him, but knocked him on the head and rolled him into the brook, too, and come back to tell half of the tale, when he need have mentioned none. It sounded crazy, but Chad was hurling provocations into the teeth of fate in precisely this bitter-crazy manner. Or, of course, he

178

could be telling the whole truth, in which case it became increasingly desirable to identify his poacher. Most probably some canny regular who had nothing to do with the business, but still he might know something. See Chad again, in case he could add anything to his previous statement. See all the poachers he could think of; business is business, but murder is murder.

And did it necessarily follow from the (hypothetical) clearing of Chris Hollins, that Gerd was equally innocent? George looked at it from all directions, and could only conclude that it did not. Chris had been home shortly before half-past ten, just as he said, because Bill Hayley had seen and talked to him. But there was no proof that Gerd had been there to meet him, except her husband's word. And what was that worth where her safety was concerned? What would you expect it to be worth?

Exhausted with speculation, George's mind went back and forth between the Hollins' household, Jim Tugg, Chad Wedderburn, with the uneasy wraiths of Jim Fleetwood and many like him periodically appearing and disappearing between. There was no end to it. And the mere new fact that Helmut had added poaching to his worse offences did not greatly change the picture. All it did was slightly affect his actual movements on the night of his death, and perhaps give an imperfect lead on the time of his exit, since it argued that he had been alive and active after the darkness grew sufficiently positive for his purposes. In George's mind the death drew more surely into the single hour between ten and eleven; but stealthily, and he feared unjustifiably.

Bunty met him in the office, and indicated by a small gesture of her head and a rueful smile that Dominic was just having his supper in the kitchen. She closed the door gently in between, and said with a soft, wry gravity: 'Your son, my dear George, is seriously displeased with you.'

'I know,' said George. 'I don't blame him, poor little beast. He finds 'em, I appropriate 'em. But this time, as a matter of fact, he isn't missing a thing, there's nothing to miss. Only a lot of useless speculations that go round in circles and get nowhere.'

'Then you can afford to talk to him, and at any rate pretend to confide in him a little. Now's the time, when you can do it with a straight face.' She took his cap from him, laid it aside, and reached up suddenly to kiss him. 'I wouldn't trust you to try it when you really had anything on your mind, because he'd see through you like glass. But if there's anything to tell, even you can say so and remain opaque. Let's go and be nice to him, shall we? Or he'll only imagine all sorts of lurid discoveries.'

'That's all I'm doing,' said George bitterly. But he went, and he was nice. Somebody might as well get some satisfaction out of the incident, if it was any way possible; it was precious little George was getting.

IV

It was Constable Cooke who said it, after they had been over and round and through every fact and every supposition they possessed between them. They had it now in positive terms that not only had Helmut's tunic-lining retained rubbings of down from the pheasants' feathers, but the pheasants' feathers had acquired and guarded, through their long repose in the clay of the pit, distinct traces of the fluff from Helmut's tunic-lining. Leaving no doubt whatever that these were the very birds, and very little that they had been planted in precisely the same way, and probably for the same reasons, as their discoverer had supposed. That was something at any rate, though it led them no nearer to a solution. They were left counting over their possibilities again, reducing them to the probabilities, which seemed to be four, and weighing these one against another to find the pennyweight of difference in their motives and opportunities. And Constable Cooke, who was light of heart because he was less surely involved, said what George had refrained from saying.

'Among four who had equal reasons for wanting him dead, and equal opportunities for killing him,' he said brightly, 'personally I'd plump for one of the two who're known to have had enough experience to be good at it. A sweater, after all, is most likely to have been knitted by someone who can knit.'

George sat looking at him for a moment in heavy silence, jabbing holes in the blotting-pad of his desk with a poised and rapier-pointed pencil, until the over-perfected tip inevitably broke off short. He threw it down, and said glumly: 'You may as well elaborate that, now you've said it.'

Cooke sat on the corner of the desk, swinging a plump leg, and looking at his sergeant with the bland, blond cheerfulness which filled George sometimes with a childish desire to shock him; like a particularly smug round vase which no right-minded infant could resist smashing. He would have been quite a nice lad, if only God had given him a little more imagination.

'Well, it's obvious enough, isn't it? There's Mrs. Hollins, admittedly she was being pushed to extremes, and you can never be sure then what a person can and can't do. But I'm not professing to be sure, I'm only talking probabilities. There's a woman who never hurt anybody or anything in her life, as far as we know, and never showed any desire to; and even if she got desperate enough to try, it would be a bit of a fluke if she made such a good job of it, the first time, wouldn't it? And then old Chris, how much more likely is it with him? I bet he never killed anything bigger than a weasel or a rabbit in his life. A more peaceful chap never existed. Not to mention that he had less time for the job than some of the others. But when you come to the other two, my word, that's a different tale!'

'The other two, however,' said George, 'had much less solid motives for murder. I'm not saying they had none, but there wasn't the urgency, or the personal need. And I'm inclined to think, with Wedderburn, that while people will certainly do desperate things for the sake of other people, when it comes to it they'll do far more desperate ones for their own sakes.'

'Well, but according to that, even, they had as much motive as Hollins had. More, because they had more imagination to be aware of it. If Hollins might kill for his wife's sake, so might Tugg, if you ask me, he thinks the world of her. And Wedderburn had a grudge on Jim Fleetwood's account, as well as a general grudge that a German, and a near-Nazi at that, should be able to live here under protection while he stirred up trouble for everybody in the village.'

'Very natural,' said George, 'and common to a great many other people who'd come into contact with Helmut round these parts. You could count me in on that grudge.'

'Well, yes, most of us, I suppose. But in different degrees. And still you're left with this great difference, that Tugg and Wedderburn have both had, as you might say, wide experience in killing. They knew how to set about it, easy as knocking off a chicken. And even more, they'd got used to it. Most people, even if they could bring 'emselves to the actual act, would shrink from the idea. But those two lived with the idea so long that it wouldn't bother them.'

George continued to stare at him glumly, and said nothing. The door of the office, ajar in the draught from the window, creaked a little, naggingly, like a not-quite-aching tooth. It was evening, just after tea, and faintly from the scullery came the chink of crockery, and the vague, soft sounds of Bunty singing to herself.

'Well, it's reasonable, isn't it?' said Cooke.

'Reasonable, but not, therefore, necessarily true. You could argue on the same lines that people in London got used to the blitz, and so they did, but the reaction against it was cumulative, all the same. It was in the later stages they suffered most, not from the first few raids. Long acquaintance can sicken you, as well as getting you accustomed to a thing.'

'Yes, but in a way this death was like a hangover from the

war, almost a part of it. You can easily imagine a soldier feeling no more qualms about rubbing out Helmut than about firing a machine-gun on a battlefield. For years it had been their job, a virtue, if you come to think of it, to kill people like Helmut. And it was a job they were both pretty good at, you know – especially Wedderburn, if all the tales are true.'

George thought what he had been trying not to think for some time, that there was something in it. Not as much as Cooke thought, perhaps, but certainly something. In time of war countries fall over themselves to make commandos and guerrillas of their young men, self-reliant killers who can slit a throat and live off a hostile countryside as simply as they once caught the morning bus to their various blameless jobs. But to reconvert these formidable creations afterwards is quite another matter. Nobody ever gave much thought to that, nobody ever does until their recoil hits the very system which made and made use of them. Men who have learned to kill as a solution for otherwise insoluble problems in wartime may the more readily revert to it as a solution for other problems as desperate in other conditions. And logically, thought George, who has the least right of any man living to judge them for it? Surely the system which taught them the art and ethics of murder to save itself has no right at all. The obvious answer would be: 'Come on in the dock with us!'

And yet he was there to do his best for a community, as well as a system, a community as surely victims as were the unlucky young men. And the best might have to be the destruction of one victim for the sake of the others. But he knew, he was beginning to feel very clearly, where the really guilty men were to be found, if Jim Tugg or Chad Wedderburn had committed murder.

'So your vote goes to the schoolmaster, does it?' he asked, stabbing the broken point of the pencil into the wood until powdered graphite flaked from its sides. The door went on creaking, more protestingly because the outer door had just opened, but he was too engrossed to remark it.

'Well, look at his record! It's about as wild a war story as you could find anywhere, littered with killings.' Cooke, who had not suffered the reality, saw words rather than actualities, and threw the resultant phrases airily, like carnival balloons which could not be expected to do any harm. 'He must be inured to it by now, however much he was forced into it by circumstances to begin with. After all, to a fellow like Wedderburn, who's seen half the continent torn into bloody pieces, what's one murder more or less to make a fuss about?'

Dominic's entering footsteps, brisk in the corridor outside the open door, had crashed into the latter part of this pronouncement too late to interrupt it short of its full meaning. Too late Cooke muttered: 'Look out! The ghost walks!' There he was in the doorway, staring at them with his eyes big and his mouth open, first a little pale, and then deeply flushed. George, heaving himself round in his chair, said resignedly but testily: 'Get out, Dom!' but it was an automatic reaction, not too firmly meant, and Dom did not get out. He came in, indeed, and pushed the door to behind him with a slam, and burst out:

'Don't listen to him, he's crazy, he's got it all wrong! Chad Wedderburn *isn't* like that!'

'Now, nobody's jumping to any conclusions,' said George gently, aware of a vehemence which was not to be dismissed. 'Don't panic because you hear a view you don't like, it's about the five hundredth we've discussed, and we're not guaranteeing any of 'em!'

'Well, but you were listening to him! And it's such a lot of damned rubbish – ' he said furiously. His hazel eyes were light yellow with rage, and his tongue falling over the words in its fiery haste.

'Dominic!' said George warningly.

'Well, so it is damned rubbish! He knows nothing about old Wedderburn, why should he go around saying such idiotic things

184

about him? If that's how the police work, just saying a man was a soldier five years ago, so this year killing somebody comes easy to him – I think it's *awful*! I bet you hang all the wrong people, if you've got many Cookes! I bet – '

'Dominic!' George took him by the shoulders and shook him sharply. 'Now, let's have no more of it!'

'You listened to him,' said Dominic fiercely, 'you ought to listen to me. At least I *do* know Mr. Wedderburn, better than either of you do!'

'Calm down, then, and stop your cheek, and you'll get a better hearing.' He gave him another small, admonishing shake, but his hands were very placid, and his face not deeply disapproving. 'And just leave out the damns,' he said firmly, 'they don't make your arguments any more convincing.'

'Well, all right, but he made me mad.'

'So we gathered,' said Cooke, still complacently swinging his leg from the corner of the desk, and grinning at Dominic with impervious good-humour. 'I never knew you were so fond of your beaks, young Dom.'

'I'm not! He's not *bad*! I don't like him all that much, but he's decent and fair, anyhow. But I don't see why you should just draw far-fetched conclusions about him when you don't even know him beyond just enough to speak to in the street.'

'And you do? Fair enough! Go on, tell us what you think about him.'

'Well, he *isn't* like what you said. It went just the opposite way with him. In the war he got pushed into the position where he had to learn to live like you said, because there wasn't any other way. And he did jolly good at it, I know, but he *hated* it. All the time! He only got so good at it because he had to – to go right through with it to get out, if you know what I mean. But he just *hated* it! I don't believe anything could make him do anything like that again. Not for any reason you could think of, not to save his life. It's because he's learned so much about it, because he knows it inside-out, that he wouldn't ever bring himself to touch it, I'm absolutely sure.'

'He may talk that way,' said Cooke easily, 'but that doesn't necessarily prove anything.'

'He doesn't talk that way. He acts that way. Well, look what happened when he came home! The British Legion wanted him to join, and he wouldn't. He said he was only a soldier because he was conscripted, and it was time we forgot who'd been in uniform and who hadn't, and stopped making differences between them, when they'd most of them had about as much choice as he had. And at school some of the fellows tried to get him to talk about all those things he'd done, and he wouldn't, he only used to tell us there was nothing admirable in being more violent than the other fellow, and nothing grand about armies or uniforms, and the best occupation for anyone who'd had to fight a war was making sure nobody would ever have to fight another. He said fighting *always* represents a failure by *both* sides. He said that to me, the day I started a fight with Rabbit. He was always down on hero-worship, or military things – any fellows who tried to suck up to him because of his record, he was frightfully sarcastic with them at first, and then he got sort of grave and sad instead, because he isn't usually sarky. But he always squashes those fellows if they try it on.'

'Some of those who value their own achievements most,' said George, with serious courtesy, and looking him steadily in the eye, 'also resent being fawned upon publicly.'

'Yes, but I think not when it's that kind of achievement, really, because the kind of man who loves being a hero, and getting decorated, and all that- well, don't you think he has to be a bit *stupid*, too? – kind of blunt in the brain, so he doesn't see through all the bunk? Mostly they *love* being fussed over, so they must be a bit thick. And old Wedderburn isn't stupid, whatever he may be.'

George looked at his son, and felt his own heart enlarged and aching in him, because they grow up, because their intelligences begin to bud and branch, to be separate, to thrust up sturdily to the light on their own, away from the anxious hand that reaches out to prop them. Even before their voices break, the spiritual note has broken, odd little rumblings of maturity quake like thunder under the known and guarded treble. Little vibrations of pride and sadness answer somewhere in the paternal body, under the heart, in the seat of shocks and terrors and delights. My son is growing up! Bud and branch, he is forward, and resolute, and clear. It will be a splendid tree. This is the time for all good parents to try their mettle, because the most difficult thing in life to learn is that you can only retain people by letting them go. George looked at Dominic, and smiled a little, and elicited an anxious but confiding smile in return.

'That's quite a point,' he said. 'No, he isn't stupid, and he doesn't like adulation, I'm sure of that. D'you want to tell us about that row you had over the fight? It might explain more than a lot of argument.'

'I don't mind. It was funny, really,' said Dominic with a sudden glimmering grin, 'because it was about him, only he didn't know it. He turned out such a mild sort of beak, you see, old Rabbit started throwing his weight about and saying he didn't believe he'd done any of the things he was supposed to have done, and it was all a pack of lies about his adventures in the war, and all that. Well, I didn't care whether old Wedderburn wanted to get any credit for all those things or not, but I didn't see why Rabbit should be allowed to go about saying he was a liar. Because Wedderburn isn't sham, anyhow, that's the biggest thing about him. So we argued a bit about it, and then I hit Rabbit, and we didn't have time to get any farther because old Wedderburn opened the window and called us in. He never jaws very much, just says what he means. He said what I told you, that fighting never settles anything, it's only a way of admitting failure to cope with things, and the only thing it proves is who has the most brawn and the least brain. He said was always

wrong short of a life-and-death matter, and anyhow, he just
wouldn't stand for it. And then he said we'd say no more about
it, if we'd both give him our word not to start the fight again.'

'And what did you say?' asked George, respectfully grave.

'Well, Rabbit said O.K. like a shot, of course he *would*! And
I was a bit peeved, really, because you want time to think when
you get something like that shot at you. So he sent Rabbit away;
I thought that was a pretty good show. And I thought pretty
hard, and I said I thought he was right, really, about fighting
being a bad thing, but still he *had* fought. But he wasn't mad,
he just said yes, but not over nothing, like us. And he said I
had to make up my mind, and promise not to start scrapping
over it again, or else! He'd never licked anybody, not since he
came, but he told me straight he would this time, so I had to
think frightfully fast, and maybe it wasn't such a bright effort.
Only I couldn't see why *I* shouldn't be allowed to judge what
was nothing and what wasn't, and I still couldn't see why Rabbit
should call him a liar and a cheat, and get away with it. At
least,' he said honestly, 'I could see that I couldn't exactly be
allowed to judge, but I didn't see why I shouldn't *do* it, all the
same. So I explained to him that I'd rather not make any
promises, because I thought that I ought to decide for myself
what was worth fighting for, and what wasn't.'

'And what did he say to that? Was he angry?'

'No, he – You know,' said Dominic doubtfully, 'I think he
was *pleased*! It sounds awfully daft, but honestly, he looked at
me as if he was. Only I can't think why, I expected him to be
mad as the dickens, because it sounded fearful cheek, only it
really wasn't meant to be. But I honestly *didn't* see how it could
be right just to let somebody else makes the rules for you,
without making up your own mind at all.'

'Did he agree with you?'

'Well, he didn't exactly say. He just said that when you've got
to that stage of maturity, you have to go the next bit, whether
you want to or not, and realise that in any society you have to

be prepared to pay for the privilege of making up your own mind. I can't remember all the right words, but you get what he meant. He didn't seem a bit angry, but I knew he wouldn't let me off, and he was giving me a chance to back out. But I wasn't going to. So I said yes, all right. I *would* pay.'

'And then he licked you,' said George.

'Well, he had to, really, didn't he?' said Dominic reasonably.

'Wasn't that a bit illogical,' suggested Cooke, with his hearty, good-natured, insensitive laugh, 'for a bloke who'd just been preaching non-violence?'

Dominic replied, but punctiliously to his father's look, not to Cooke who was in his black books: 'No, I don't think so, really, because he had to make up his mind, too. If you see what I mean!'

'Yes,' said George, 'I see what you mean.'

'So you see, don't you, that what Cooke was saying about him is just bunk? He didn't get used to it, it *sickened* him, only there just wasn't anything else then for him to do. And honestly, he's the last man in the place who could have done a murder – even that murder. Dad, don't make an awful mistake like that, will you?'

'I'll try not to,' said George, softened and gentle with astonishment at seeing his son's face all earnest anxiety on his account. 'Don't worry, Dom, I'll remember all you've told us. It's perfectly good evidence, and I won't lose sight of it. Satisfied?'

'Mmmm, I suppose so. You know, it's so easy to say things like Cooke was saying, but it isn't true. All kinds of fellows had to fight, thousands and thousands of them, but they were still just as much all kinds in the end, weren't they? I think it may have got easier for some, and harder and harder for others. And anyhow, you can't just lump people all together, like that.' He flushed a little, meeting George's smile. 'Sorry I swore! I was upset.'

'That's all right. Going out again now?'

'Yes, I came to tell Mummy I might be a bit late, but I shall only be at the Hart's. Mr. Hart is picking the late apples, and they want to finish tonight, so a few extra hands – ' For whom, thought George, there would be ample wages in kind at the end of the picking, even if they came only half an hour before the daylight began to fail.

'All right, I'll tell her. You cut along.' And he watched him spring gaily through the door without a glance at Cooke, with whom he was still seriously annoyed.

An odd, loyal, disturbing, reassuring kid, sharp and sensitive to currents of thought and qualities of character. If he didn't like Chad Wedderburn 'all that much', very decidedly he liked him in some degree, and that in itself was an argument. But the weakness of the evidence of a man's own mouth is that it often has two edges. Fighting never settles anything, cannot be right short of life-and-death matter. But a man must and should be his own judge of what is and what is not a matter of life and death, because that is ultimately an issue he cannot delegate to any other creature. And having reached that stage of maturity, he must realise that in any society – because societies, state or school or church, exist to curb all the non-conforming into conformity – he must pay for the privilege. So far, if he had perfectly understood him, Chad Wedderburn.

Even Cooke was thinking along the same lines. He looked after Dominic with an indulgent smile, and said appreciatively: 'Well, I hope the folks who don't like *me* all that much will stick up for me as nobly. Poor kid, he doesn't know what it all adds up to. Call your own tune, pay your own piper! Well, and what if he did just that? He allowed Dom the right to, you can bet he'd insist on the same rights for himself. What did he decide about Helmut, do you suppose? That it would be worth it?'

George said nothing. It could follow, but it need not follow, that was the devil of it. Only something else echoed ominously in his mind, the hot, reiterated note of Chad's revulsion from bloodshed, genuine, yes, too terribly genuine, but was it perhaps pitched in an unnatural key? Did it not sometimes sound like the prayers of a man's mind for deliverance from his own body? Might not a man thus passionately denounce what he feared most of all in himself? A man who was wise enough and deep enough to dread his own facility in destruction, an adept whose skill terrified him. And then the last remote, unexpected case, argued over and over in the mind, where this dreaded efficiency in killing, held so fiercely in restraint, began to look once more legitimate, began to argue its right to a gesture almost of virtue.

'Call your own tune, pay your own piper!' said Constable Cooke, brightly. 'Some merely get hammered, some get hanged. It's a matter for the individual whether he finds it worth-while!'

191

Chapter 7

Treasure in the Mud

I

Pussy and Dominic were in the loft over the stables at the 'Shock of Hay', in the warm, clean, high roof, smelling of straw and fruit; they were polishing and wrapping the biggest, soundest apples for keeping until the spring, and laying them out on wooden trays slatted to let the air through. The picking was already done, and the great unsorted baskets of fruit lay below them in the horseless stables, keeping company with the car, and the lawn-mower, and all the garden tools. From time to time Dominic slid himself and his basket down through the trapdoor by the shaky stairs, and selected the finest to haul back with him into the loft. They were working so hard that they forgot to eat, and neglected to light their lantern until the light was almost gone. It was middle evening, the sky outside suddenly clouded, the air heavy as a sad cake.

The end of the long drought came in a puff of air and a thudding of heavy drops down the roof. When the thunder had spent itself the sweet green night would smell heavenly of fresh foliage; but first the noise and the downpour, the ominous drum-roll of the earliest scud, and then the clouds opening, and the crashing, splattering fall.

Somebody caught in the garden, where the benches circled

the chestnut tree, gave a squeak of protest and ran headlong for the stable door. The two above heard the door crash back to the wall before a precipitate entry, and a gasping laugh, and quick breathing. Sounds came up to them with a strange, dark clarity, cupped and shielded and redoubled in the arch of the roof-beams. They went on peaceably wrapping, intent on finishing their job and earning their wages. Kneeling in the straw by the low shelves, they themselves made no sound.

A second person running, a sudden foot at the brick threshold, and a perceptible check. The rain streamed coolly, wildly, over the tiles of the roof, giving the voice from below a brook's moving but monotonous sound.

'Oh, it's you! I'm sorry – I'll go!' And he actually turned to go, his heel harsh on the gravel. Dominic and Pussy heard, and knew Chad Wedderburn's voice, but it hovered only in the borders of their consciousness, so occupied where they with their apples.

And the other one was Io, and Io instant in exasperation, bursting out after him angrily: 'Come *back!* Good Lord, haven't you got *any* sense? Come out of it, and don't be a fool! I shan't give you the plague.'

The slightest of scuffles indicated that she had proceeded beyond words, and unceremoniously hauled him back into shelter. They stood gasping, and shaking and slapping the rain from their clothes, and he said in a harsh, constrained voice: 'Aren't you afraid you might take it from me?' But he made no second attempt to leave her. She must have looked formidably angry.

'What's the matter with you? Can't you even act naturally for ten minutes, till the rain stops? Am I diseased, or something, that you take one look at me and run for your life? Don't be afraid, I'm going back to the house as soon as I can get there without being drowned on the way. You won't be bothered with me a minute longer than I can help.'

Shrinking away from her in the shadows within the door, he stood drawn into himself hard, and said nothing; and in the

193

moment of silence Dominic and Pussy looked at each other guiltily, stirred back from a world of nothing but apples to a situation they had not foreseen. In the greenish, watery gloom under the skylight, with the refractions of rain flowing across their faces like the deeps of the sea, they stared stilly at each other, and wondered silently that they ought to do. It was now or never. In the first minute you can cough loudly, or drop a tray, or kick over the watering-can, or burst into song, but after that it's too horribly obvious. And if the first minute passes and is away before you can clutch at it, there is absolutely nothing to be done except hold your breath, and pretend you are not there. To be sure, in other circumstances they would have nudged each other, and giggled, and made the most of it, but somehow it was immediately apparent that this was not the occasion for such behaviour. The voices, both of them, had overtones which raised the blood to their cheeks hotly.

'I'm sorry you had to be marooned with such an uncongenial company.' Such a tight, dark voice, a disembodied pain. 'It could just as easily have been someone more pleasing. Charles, for instance!'

'Oh, lord!' groaned Io. 'I expected that! Must you carry on like a bad-tempered child?'

'I hope to God,' he said, 'there are no children in any way resembling me. It would be better to put them away quietly if there are.'

'How can you talk like that! I suppose you're half-tight,' said Io viciously.

'Not even half. What's the use, when it doesn't take?'

And now it was palpably too late to do anything about it. There they were, crouching mouse-still in the loft, holding their breath with shock, and not even looking at each other any more, because it was as disturbing as looking into a mirror. It would be awful if the two below should ever find out that they had been overheard. It was awful having to sit here and listen, but it was far too late to move.

The voice resumed, corrosive and unnatural in the void quiet, under the liquid lash of the rain.

'I can't make you out. *I* call it cowardice, to carry on as if you had nothing to live for, as if you were crippled, or something, just because things don't fall into your hand. For God's sake, what happened to you during the war? You got the reputation of being able to stand up to anything, but it must have been a mistake.'

'It was a mistake,' he said harshly, 'the worst I ever made. The intelligent people lay down, for good.'

'You make me mad!' she said furiously. 'Moping like a sick cow, for want of your own way! And you haven't even the wits to see that if you're not careful, and don't pull yourself together, you could die yet. Do you *want* people to believe you're a murderer? The police think so already.'

'Why not? I am – a hundred times over.'

'Don't go on talking like that! What happened in the war wasn't your fault, and it's over. And anyhow, most people found your part of it rather admirable,' she said indignantly.

'Admirable!' he said, in a soft, indrawn howl. 'My good God almighty!'

'Well, I didn't invent your reputation. I can't help it, if you don't like being a hero!'

'I don't like it!' he shouted hoarsely. 'I loathe it! Don't insult me with it! I never want to hear it from you, whatever the damned herd choose to think. Hero! Oh, yes, it's a fine thing to be a hero! – to have the identity ripped clean out of you – to be violated – in the middle of your being – '

It was awful, frightening; his voice broke in a terrible ugly second, and then there was just an almost-silence, full of a sort of heaving and struggling for breath, like a drowning man fighting to regain his footing. Dominic turned his face right away from Pussy's sight, and leaned hard against the shelves, because he was trembling. His inside felt hollow and molten-hot. His head hurt him. He wanted to think that Chad was really a little

195

drunk, but he didn't believe it. He wasn't very experienced, but he knew a true grief from a drunken one even by its sound. And now somebody was crying. Io was crying, very quietly and laboriously and angrily, muffling it in her hands and the shadows and an inadequate handkerchief. And the painful quaking of the air which emanated from Chad had suddenly stilled into a listening silence.

'Why are you crying? As you said, it's over. And if it wasn't you've no reason to shed any tears over it – you find it admirable.'

'I find you detestable,' cried Io furiously.

'I know! You've made that quite plain.' And after an uneasy moment of the rain's song he said with sour, grudging gentleness: 'Don't cry, Io! It isn't worth it.'

'I'm not crying! Go away! Get to hell out of here, and leave me alone!'

He seemed to hesitate a moment, and then the heel of his shoe rang violently on the threshold, and he ran lurching through the downpour away from her.

Instant upon his going, she began to cry in earnest, candidly and stormily in a long, diminishing outburst, until her tears and the thunder-storm ebbed together. She went out slowly, splashing mournfully across the gravel path starred with sudden pools, and in a few minutes the two in the loft could move and breathe again. They stirred and looked at each other with quick, evasive, scared glances.

'Wasn't it awful? If they'd heard us!'

'Awful!'

They relaxed, and sat trembling, stiff with bracing themselves in one position, all large, wild eyes in the green gloom under the skylight.

'I've been worrying about her,' said Pussy, 'for a long time. You know, it's true what she said – your father thinks it was him who did the murder. Doesn't he?'

'I don't know. I tried to tell him it was crazy, but I'm afraid he does think it. I know he's making an awful mistake.'

'He jolly well mustn't make it, then!' said Pussy with fierce energy. 'I'm not going to have my sister made miserable like that all her life, no fear I'm not. If nobody else will do anything about it, we've got to, Dom, that's all.'

Dominic, a little puzzled and still shaken by the sudden and searing contact of other people's misery, blinked at her for a moment without understanding. 'Well, but I thought your sister – I didn't know that she – everybody always said it was the other one. And she – well, she wasn't being exactly nice to him, was she?'

'Oh, use your loaf!' said Pussy impatiently. 'He wasn't being exactly nice to her, but everybody knows he's stuck on her so bad it's half-killing him. What d'you think she was crying about? Of course he's the one! I've thought so for a long time. They wouldn't bother to fight if they weren't gone on each other, because there'd be nothing to fight about. But, Dom, what on earth are we going to do?'

'If only we could solve it ourselves,' said Dominic wistfully.

'Well, couldn't we at least try? It doesn't seem as if anyone else is doing much about it, and somebody's got to.'

'My father – ' began Dominic, his hackles rising at once.

'Your father's a dear, and I know he's trying all he can, and listen, I'm too upset to argue with you. I'm only asking you, couldn't we try? It's awful when you think about people being so miserable. If only it wasn't for this business hanging over them, maybe they could act a little more sensibly, maybe it would come out right. But as things are, what chance have they got? Dom, let's at least try!'

'I'd like to,' said Dominic, 'I want to. But I'm trying to think. What is there we can do? We haven't got a clue. We don't know where to look for one. There's only the basin by the well, where we found *him*. And the pit where the pheasants were, but there's nothing there, the police have been over it with microscopes, practically. And we don't even know what we're looking for,' he admitted despondently.

'If only we could find the weapon – or even a trace of it – '

'Well, there's only one thing we can do, and that's go over and over the ground inch by inch, for *anything*, anything at all. Anyhow, there's no harm in trying. Are you game?'

'Yes, of course I am. When shall we go? Tomorrow?'

'The sooner the better. I'll meet you there as soon as I've done my homework. I'll bring a really good torch. Anyhow, if there is anything there, this time we won't miss it.' He looked at Pussy crouching on the floor among the straw, and was touched to see the bright scornful eyes blinking back tears. He knew they were only going on a wild-goose chase, he knew they might just as well start going through the Harrow stacks for the proverbial needle, but he wouldn't admit it, if the pretence could comfort Pussy. He clapped her on the shoulders, a hard, comradely clout. 'It'll be all right in the end, old girl, you see if it isn't. We'll try tomorrow, and we'll go on trying till we jolly well get somewhere. We've got to get ourselves and everyone else out of this mess, and we're going to do it, too.'

Pussy said: 'You know, Dom – I know I go on about Io, sometimes, but she's really not bad. I – I *like* her!'

II

It rained heavily most of the night, and the thirsty earth drank madly, but still there was water to spare next day, lying in all the dimples of the road, and making a white slime of all the open clay faces on the mounds. By the time Dominic came home from school the clouds were all past, and the sky from east to west hung pale and faint and exhausted into calm.

Just when he wanted to rush his tea and his homework, and be away on the job in hand – though when it came to expecting any results from it he might have been regarded as a despairing optimist – Cousin John was at the house visiting, and without his mother, so that it inevitably followed that Dominic was expected to help to look after and amuse him. Not that young John was such a bad kid, really, but who could be bothered with him on this particular day? Dominic made an ungracious business of it, so much so that Bunty was a little hurt and put out at his behaviour. He was usually an accommodating child. Still, she admitted his right to his off-days, like the rest of us, and good-humouredly, if a little coolly,· relieved him of his charge as soon as she had washed up. Dominic rushed through his French, made a hideous mess of his algebra, and scuttled out at the back door in a terrible hurry, with George's best torch in his pocket. It wasn't that he expected to find anything, really, but there was somehow a satisfaction in furious activity, and, after all, if one raked around persistently enough, something might turn up. At least he had keyed himself to the attempt, and he meant to leave no blade of grass undisturbed between Webster's well and the Harrow fences.

This was the day on which the news went round Comerford that the Harrow appeal had been allowed. In view of the objections raised by the owner, the Ministry had decided not to proceed with the extension of the open-cast site, but to cut their losses and end their operations in Comerford at the Harrow borders. Nobody was much surprised. The Blundens almost always got their own way, and it wasn't to be expected, in view of what Comerford had yet seen of nationalised industries, that the new set-up was going to alter the rule very much. It took more than a change of name to upset the equilibrium of Selwyn Blunden when it was a case of manipulating authorities.

Dominic had heard, distractedly from behind a French prose extract, the discussion round the tea-table. He wasn't surprised, either; everyone had been saying for weeks that it would go that way, but somehow long delay raises disconcerting doubts far back in the mind, behind the façade of certainty. Every speculation always ended with: 'But after all, you never know!' Well, now they did know, and that was done with. Now there was only one topic of conversation left in Comerford.

At the last moment, just as he was sidling out at the gate, Bunty called him back, and asked him to see John safely on to the bus for Comerbourne Bridge; which meant that he had to go all the way round by the green, and stand chafing for five minutes until the wretched bus arrived, instead of taking all the most convenient short cuts to his objective. But as soon as John was bundled aboard, off went Dominic by the fields and the lane and the quarry, heading by the longer but now more direct route for Webster's well.

He came to the stile in the rough ground outside the Harrow preserves, where the silvery green of birches fluttered against the background black of the conifers; and there was Charles Blunden sitting on the stile, with a shot-gun on his arm and a brown-and-white spaniel between his feet. He was looking straight before him with mild, contemplative eyes, and he looked vaguely pleased with the contents of his own mind, and rather a long way off. But he smiled at Dominic when he came up, and said: 'Oh, hullo, Dom! Made any more interesting discoveries yet?'

Dominic had walked off the remnants of his impatience and ill-temper, and grinned back quite cheerfully at him. 'No, nothing new! Did you get any birds tonight?' He peered through the stile, and saw a brace dropped in the grass by the side of the path. The spaniel, sad-eyed, poked a moist nose into his palm; its brow was covered with raffish brown curls, and its front legs were splayed out drunkenly, spreading enormous feathered paws in the wet grass. It had a pedigree rather longer than its master's, and shelves of prizes, and rumour had it that he had refused fabulous sums for its purchase; but it was not in the least stuck-up. Dominic doubled its ears and massaged them gently in his fingers, and the curly head heeled over into his thigh heavy and lopsided with bliss.

'I heard,' said Dominic, looking up into Charles's face, 'about the result of the appeal. I bet you're glad it's settled, aren't you?'

'Settled? Ah!' said Charles absently. He grew a little less remote, his wandering glance settling upon Dominic thoughtfully. 'Tell me, Dom, as an intelligent and unprejudiced person, what do you think of that business? What were the rights and wrongs of it? Don't mind me, tell me your opinion if it kills me.'

'I hadn't exactly thought,' said Dominic, taken aback.

'Neither had I, until the thing was almost settled. D'you know how it is, Dom, when you want a thing against pressure, and want it like the dickens – and then the pressure's withdrawn, and you find you don't really want it, after all?'

'Oh, yes,' said Dominic readily, 'of course! But I don't –'

'Well, after all, we seem to have made all this fuss about twenty acres of second-rate pasture. It got to looking like the fattest agricultural land in the county to me, while the fight was on. What do you think we ought to have done? I'll bet you had an opinion one way or the other. If you didn't, you're the only person over the age of five in Comerford who didn't.'

'Well, I don't know much about it,' said Dominic doubtfully. 'It does look an awful mess when the land's being worked, but the old colliers say the shallow pits made a worse mess in the end. And it's all shallow coal, isn't it? So if it's ever going to be got at all, it's got to be one way or the other, hasn't it? It seems almost better to have the mess now, and get it over. It doesn't last so long as when the ground caves in, like under those cottages out on the Comerbourne road – all pegged together with iron bars. And even then the walls are cracking. I know a boy who lives in one. The bedroom floors are like this,' said Dominic, tilting his hand at an extravagant angle.

Charles looked at him, and the odd, finished peacefulness of his face broke into a slow, broad smile. 'Out of the mouths –' he said. 'Well, so you think we raised a song and dance for next to nothing, and on the wrong side?'

'Oh, I don't know about that. I only said – And I told you, I don't really know much about it.' Dominic was uncomfortable, and found it unfair that he should be pinned into a corner like this. He scrubbed at the bunched curls of the spaniel's forehead, and said placatingly: 'But anyhow, in the end it seems the Coal Board didn't want it as much as they thought they did, either. Especially after they started to have such rotten luck. If it was luck! You remember that grab that went over the edge? I was talking to one of the men off the site once, and he told me *he* thought somebody'd been mucking about with the engine.. He said he thought a lot of those repairs they had were really sabotage, only he couldn't say so openly because he couldn't find any proof. I don't suppose there's anything in it, really,' owned Dominic regretfully, 'because I've often talked to the same man, and he likes a good story, and anyhow if there wasn't the least bit of evidence there may not have been any sabotage, either. But still, it was funny that they had so much trouble so quickly, wasn't it?'

'I never heard that story,' said Charles.

'Oh, he wouldn't dare tell it to anyone responsible, he's known for an awful old liar. Anyhow, the whole unit will soon be packing up now, I suppose, so there isn't any point in guessing.'

Charles looked at him, and smiled, and said: 'Maybe they won't after all. It rests with them entirely.'

'But – they've nearly finished the rest of the site, and now that they've allowed the appeal – '

'Oh, I took it to a further appeal, Dom. I told you, I stopped being indignant as soon as I got my own way. I've been walking round having another look at all my grandfather's wreckage this evening, since we heard the result. I'm going to withdraw my objections, and waive the result of the appeal. Tomorrow, while I know my own mind. They can carry right on, and be damned to grandfather and his methods.'

Dominic, staring with open mouth, perceived that Charles meant what he was saying. This was no joke. The tired, satisfied, almost self-satisfied glow which Charles had about him this evening emanated from this decision, and he wanted someone to share it so that it would be irrevocable, underlined, signed and sealed, with no room anywhere for another change of heart. For which rôle of witness even Dominic had sufficed.

He asked, swallowing hard: 'Does Mr. Blunden know?'

'Not yet!' Charles laughed, a large, ruddy, bright sound in the evening, breaking the sequence of gunshots, far and near, which were now the commonplace of the season, and almost inaudible unless one consciously thought about them. 'Expecting me to get a thick ear? Don't you worry, if I know him he's lost all interest since he heard he's carried his point. That's what mattered with the old man, to have his own way. I suppose it's in the family. Besides, it'll please his cussed nature, making 'em sweat blood losing the ground to him, and then chucking it to 'em when he's won. Take his side of any argument, and he's sure to hop over to yours. No, this is really hot news, young Dom. You're positively the only one who knows it yet.'

As a consequence of which accident, he was now unusually pleased with Dominic, and suddenly fishing out a half-crown from his pocket, flipped it over into his startled hand. 'Here, celebrate the occasion, while I go and break the news.' He swung his legs over the stile, hoisting the shot-gun clear of the gate-posts, and gathered up his birds from the grass. Dominic was stammering delighted but rather dazed thanks, for he was not used to having half-crowns thrown at him without warning, or, indeed, at all. The cost of living, so his mother said, was turning her into a muttering miser, and causing her to cast longing eyes even on her son's weekly one and sixpence, and occasional bonuses.

'That's all right!' said Charles, laughing back from the shadow of the trees. 'Buy your girl a choc-ice!' And he whistled the spaniel to heel, and marched away into his dark woodlands with his half of the momentous secret.

III

Pussy and Dominic hunted all the evening, inexhaustible, obstinate, refusing to be discouraged even by the fact that they were hunting what appeared to be a different country. After a night of thunder and heavy rain, the bowl behind the well, the frozen sea of clay, had thawed most alarmingly. It was now a glistening expanse of yellow ochreous slime, indescribably glutinous and slippery, with swollen, devious streams threading it muddily; and the overflow from the back of the well was a tight, bright thrust of water as thick as an arm, jetting out forcibly with a mule's kick. It was always strong of course, but this was storm pressure, and would soon diminish. In the meantime, they had chosen the worst possible conditions for their search, as they found after the first skid and fall on the treacherous greasy slopes going down into the bowl. Pussy got half-way down, and then her feet went from under her, and down she slid, to rise with the seat of her gym knickers one glazed grey patch of wet clay. Dominic, trying to enjoy the spectacle and pass her at speed at the same time, made a terrifying spin and left long ski-tracks behind him, but merely came down on one hand and arm to the elbow, much to the detriment of his jacket. He had also to work his way sidelong a dozen yards by the current sheep-track to find a tuft of grass big enough and dry enough to wipe his hands fairly clean.

As for their shoes, in a few minutes they were past praying for, clay to the ankles; but at the time they brushed these small catastrophes aside as of no importance. In any case, after the first fall there was not much point in being careful, and they began to stride recklessly about, skidding and recovering, slithering on to their behinds and climbing precariously up again, with their tenacious minds fixed on their objective, and fast shut to all regard of consequences to their clothing or skins. They'd come to look over the ground yet once more, and look it over they would, even if the rain had transformed it overnight and a fortnight of time made the quest practically hopeless in the first place.

The dusk came, and they did not even notice it until they were straining their eyes upon the ground. Then the torches came out, and the dark came, and as their eyes were bent assiduously upon the circles of light upon the trampled ground, it quite startled them to look up suddenly and see that the sky had stars already, and was deeply blue between the clusters of them, fully dark. The gradual brightening of the discs of gold, the gradual darkening of the walls of dark, had passed unnoticed.

'It must be getting late,' said Pussy dubiously.

'Oh, rot, can't be!' He had not his watch on him, but he was quite confident, because it seemed to him that he had been there no time at all. 'It gets dark very quickly, once it starts. But it can't be past nine o'clock yet.'

'Seems as if it's hopeless, though,' said Pussy, staring at the well. They were dishevelled, tired and unbelievably dirty. Clay even in Dom's hair, where he had come down full-length once, and slid downhill on his back. Smears of ochre down his face. She had an uneasy feeling that she did not look very much better herself. Now that she came to look at him, the effect was awe-inspiring. She said: 'Wait till your mother sees you! My word, isn't there going to be a row!'

'My mother will listen to me,' said Dominic firmly, 'she always lets people explain. If you're scared, go on home, or anyhow, go on up to the level and wait for me. I'm not afraid of my mother.'

'Well, anyhow, we've looked everywhere, and it seems a dead end.'

'I know,' he said, dismally smearing a clay-stiffened cheek. He had not expected much, but he did not admit that, there was no point in making Pussy feel worse than she did already. 'And yet if we quit now, there won't be any chance of finding anything after. We've trampled the whole place up, and after a few more rain-storms it'll be hopeless. But I suppose it was a thin chance – after so long. If we couldn't find a weapon or any sign of one that first time, we couldn't very well expect to find it now.' He stared at the back of the well, where the fierce, quiet jet of the outfall poured into a little pebbly hollow, and ran away downhill through boulders and small stones to join the stream. 'You know, I always thought – '

'Thought what?' asked Pussy, following his stare and the strong beam of the torch.

'Well, if *I*'d hit somebody over the head with a club, or whatever it was, close here by the well, I shouldn't throw it away and leave it to be found. And of course he didn't, either, or we should have found it. But if – if there was any blood, or anything, I shouldn't want to carry it away like that, either. They said it was something thin, like a walking-stick or a crop, so if it was you could easily walk away carrying it, even if you met a dozen people on your way home, if it was just clean and normal. But you have to be careful about getting even the smallest drop of blood on your clothes, because they can tell even months after what group it is, and everything.'

'Plenty of water down there,' said Pussy, shivering, 'where he put the body. He could wash it.'

'Yes, but that's the stream, and it's ochre water; I should think if there were any grooves, or if there was a plaited thong, like in some crops, or anywhere that dirt could lodge, that fearful yellow stuff might get left behind. Enough to be traced, they don't need much. But here,' he said, jerking his solemn head at the muscular arm of the outflow, and gnawing at his knuckles forgetful of their coating of clay, 'here's clean water, and with a kick on it that ought to wash anything off anything if you just stood it in it firmly for a few minutes. Very nearly wash the paint off, too. Only, of course, it wasn't quite so strong as this then. But it was pretty hefty, all the same. Remember, we were mucking about with it that next night, throwing jets around, and it was all you could do to keep your hand still in it.'

Pussy drew a little nearer to him at the stirring of that

memory, steadying herself by his arm. 'Yes, that's right! I remember, just before you found him – '

'If I'd to get a stick cleaned up after a job like that,' said Dominic, 'I should have wedged it in among the stones there so that it stood in the outflow. I should think if you left it there just while you dragged the body down and put it in the stream, and then came back for it and walked right on into the village, or wherever you were going, there wouldn't be even a hair or a speck left on it to show. Anyhow, that's what *I* should have done. Like anybody who had a drop of blood on his hands here would just run there and wash them. It stands to sense.'

She agreed, with a shiver, that it seemed reasonable. Dominic climbed up the slope and pulled a stick out of the lush foot of the hedge, and scrambled with it up into the stony fringes of the outflow. 'Like that!' He planted it upright, digging the point deep between the stones and into the soft underneath of the bed, and it stood held and balanced in the direct jet of the water, which gripped it solidly as in ice. 'You see? It couldn't be simpler.'

The spray from the tiny basin spattered him, and, shifting a precarious foothold, he stepped backward to one unluckily more precarious still. A rounded, reddish stone rocked under his foot, and slid from its place, bringing down in one wet vociferous fall Dominic and a large section of the stony bank together. He yelled, clawing at the boulders, and tumbled heavily on one hip and shoulder into the descending stream below the outfall. His hands felt for a firm hold among the stones under the water, to brace himself clear of it and get to his feet again; and sharp under his right palm, deep between the disturbed pebbles, something stung him with a sharp, metallic impact, denting but not breaking the skin.

Pussy, slithering along to help him out, sensed his instant excitement in his sudden quietness. She had reached for his arm, but he was grubbing instead in the bed of the brook, and bringing up some small muddy thing which was certainly not the weapon with which anyone had been killed; and until he had it washed clean of encrustations of silt he was not even interested in getting out of the water. He scrambled backwards to his feet, and dipped the thing, and rubbed it on his handkerchief, which in any case was already soaking wet and smeared with clay.

'What have you got?' asked Pussy, craning to peer over his shoulder with the torch.

'I don't know. We'll have a look at it in a minute, when you can see it for muck – but it's something queer to find in a brook. Look, it's beginning to shine. I believe it's silver.'

'Tin, more likely,' said Pussy scornfully.

'No, tin would have rusted away in no time, but this was so covered in mud it must have been there some time, and you can see it's only sort of dulled. If one edge hadn't stuck in me I wouldn't have known there was anything there at all.'

He climbed out of his stony bath, shivering a little in the chill night air, but too intent on his find to pay much attention to his own state. It was Pussy who observed the shiver.

'Dom, you're terribly wet. You'll catch cold if we don't get home double-quick.'

'Yes, all right, we'll go in a minute. But look – now look!'

In the light of the torch they examined, large-eyed, a small irregular oval of silver, mottled and discoloured now, but showing gleams of clean metal; a little shield for engraving, but never engraved, dinted a little, very thin apparently from long use and sheer old age, for all the lines of its pattern were worn smooth and shallow. Round the outline of the shield curved decorative leaves, the flourish of the upper edge buckled and bent a little. It bore five tiny holes for fastening it to a surface, and by the strong round curve of its shape they could guess what kind of a surface.

'It's like on that walking-stick we gave to old Wilman when he left school two years ago,' said Dominic in a hushed voice, 'only a different pattern, you know. And a bit smaller, not so showy. But you can see it *is* off a stick. I can't think of anything else that would make it curve like that.'

'Or an umbrella,' said Pussy. 'It could be.'

'Yes, only people don't often give umbrellas for that sort of present, and put names on them, and all that. They're such stupid things it would look too silly. But lots of walking-sticks have these things on. And – we were looking for something that might belong to a walking-stick.' He looked up at her across the tarnished glimmer of his treasure, and his eyes were enormous with gravity. She stared back, and asked in an almost inaudible whisper:

'But how did it get *there?*'

'I think it was like I said. He *did* shove the weapon in there to wash off the traces. And this plate had worn very thin, and the top edge was bent up, like you see, so the water had something to press against there, and it tore it right off and washed it down among the stones there, and it lodged tight. And when he grabbed the stick again to make his get-away – because he wouldn't want to hang around, when for all very few people do come here, somebody easily *might* – he was in too much of a hurry to notice that the shield was gone. Or if he did notice it, he didn't think it safe to stay too long looking for it, and so there it stayed. Well, it's reasonable, isn't it? How else should a silver plate off a stick get in a place like that?'

How else indeed? Pussy said with awe: 'Then we *have* found it! After all, we didn't come out for nothing. And now if we can find the stick this shield came off – ' She shivered in her turn, remembering the strange pale island of Helmut's hair in the centre of the brook's channel; and suddenly she didn't at all like this place by night, and wanted to be anywhere out of it. She clutched urgently at Dominic's arm with a thin, strong, dirty hand, and besought him in a low voice: 'Let's go, Dom! We've found it, now let's get home. You ought to get it to your father, quickly – and anyhow, it's awfully late, I'm sure it is.'

He could not tear himself away too easily, now that he had

something to show for it, something to advance as sure proof that he had real ideas about the case which they wouldn't allow to be his, that he wasn't just being inquisitive in a totally aimless way. He was torn two ways, for he had an uneasy feeling that he had let time slip by more rapidly than he had realised, and it would be well for him to make all haste to placate his parents. But also he wanted to pursue success while he had hold of her skirt. What more he could expect was not certain. He knew only that he was on an advancing wave, and to turn back seemed an act of folly.

'And you're terribly wet,' said Pussy. 'You will catch cold if we don't run for it.'

So they ran, taking hands over the rough places, he with the little shield clutched fiercely in his left palm in his damp trouser-pocket, she with the beam of the torch trained unsteadily on the path ahead of them. Half-way down the mounds, Dominic remembered the other item of information he had to pass on to his father, the odd decision of Charles Blunden to reverse his policy toward the Coal Board. Not, of course, that that had anything to do with the Helmut affair, or could compete in importance with the silver plate; but still it was, in its way, interesting.

IV

Dominic arrived blown and incoherent at the back door just as the church clock chimed the half-hour, and wondered, as he let himself in with unavailing caution, whether it was half-past nine or half-past ten. It couldn't really be only half-past nine, though the thought of the later hour made his heart thump unhappily. What on earth had made him forget to put on his watch? But he had a talisman in his pocket, and a tongue in his head; and anyhow, they were always willing to listen to reason.

He had not time to steel himself, for the kitchen door opened to greet him, though he had made no noise at all; and there was George bolt upright in front of the fire looking distinctly a heavy father, with one arm still in the sleeve of a coat which he had just been in the act of putting on, and was now in the act of taking off again, with some relief; and there was Bunty at the door, with a set, savage face like angry ice, and eyes that made him wriggle in his wet clothes, saying as he halted reluctantly: 'So you decided to come home, after all! Come in here, and be quick about it!'

Quite ordinary words, but a truly awful voice, such as he had never heard from Bunty in the whole of his life before. Dominic's heart sank. Suddenly he was fully aware of every smear of grime on his face, of his encrustations of clay, of his appalling lateness, of the fact that George had been about to come out and look for him, and, into the bargain, of every undiscovered crime he had committed within the year. The scrap of silver clutched in his hand no longer seemed very much to bring home in justification of all these enormities.

He stole in unwillingly, and stood avoiding Bunty's fixed and formidable eye. In a small, wan voice he said: 'I say, I'm frightfully sorry I'm late!'

'Where,' said Bunty, levelly and coldly, 'where have you been till this hour? Do you see that clock?'

Now that she pointed him to it so relentlessly, he certainly did, and he gaped at it in consternation. But it couldn't be true! Half-past ten he could have believed, though even that seemed impossible, but half-past eleven! He said desperately: 'Oh, but it can't be right! It was only seven when I went out, it just *can't* have been as long as all that – '

'And what *have* you been doing? Just *look* at you! Come here, and show yourself!' And when he hesitated discreetly among the shadows in the doorway, his heart now somewhere in his filthy shoes, she took two angry steps forward and hauled him into the light by the collar of his jacket, and like any other

211

mother gasped and moaned at the horrid sight. 'George!' she said faintly. 'Did you *ever* – *?*'

George said blankly: 'My God, what an object! How in the world did you get into that state?'

'I'm awfully sorry,' said Dominic miserably, 'I'm afraid I *am* a bit dirty – '

'A bit!' Bunty turned him about in her hands, and stared incredulously, despairingly, from his ruined grey flannels to her own soiled fingers. 'Your *clothes!* They'll never clean again, never! Why, it's all over you. It's even in your hair! How on earth did you get like this? And where? Nearly midnight, and you come strolling in as if tomorrow would do. And filthy! I never saw anything like you in my life. And you're wet!' She felt at him with sudden exasperated palms, and her ice was melting, but into a rage which would need some manipulating. 'You're wet through, child! Heavens!' she moaned, 'you're supposed to be thirteen, not three!'

She usually listened, and tonight she wouldn't listen. She was always just, yet tonight she didn't give him a chance to explain, she just flamed at him as soon as he opened his mouth. It was a shock to his understanding, and he simply could not accept or believe in it.

'But, Mummy, I – yes, I know, I fell in the brook, but it was because – '

'I don't want to hear a word about it. Upstairs!' said Bunty, and pointed a daunting finger.

'Yes, I'll go, really, only please, I want to explain about – '

'It's too late for explanations. Do as you're told, this minute.'

George, an almost placating echo in the background, said dryly: 'Better go to bed, quick, my lad, before something worse happens to you.'

'But, Dad, this is important! I've got to talk to you about – '

'You've got to get out of those wet things, and go to bed,' said George inflexibly, 'and if I were you I'd do it without any arguing.'

212

'No, honestly, I'm not trying to make any excuses, it's – '

Bunty said, in the awfully quiet voice which indicated that the end of her patience was in sight: 'Upstairs, and into the bathroom, without one more word, do you hear?'

It wasn't fair, and it wasn't like her, and Dominic simply couldn't believe it. A flash of anger lit for a moment in the middle of his confusion and bewilderment. He burst out almost with a stamp of his clay-heavy foot: 'Mummy, you've *got* to listen to me! Don't be so *unreasonable!*'

Bunty moved with a suddenness which was not natural to her, but an efficiency which was characteristic, boxed both his ears briskly, took him by the scruff of his neck and ran him stumbling and shrilling out of the room, up the stairs, and into the bathroom, quite breathless with indignation. She sat him down upon the cork-topped stool, and swooped down upon the taps of the bath as if she would box their ears, too, but only turned them on with a crisp savagery which made him draw his toes respectfully out of her way as she swept past him.

'Get out of those clothes, and be quick about it.'

She stooped to feel the temperature of the water, and alter the flow, and when she turned on him again he had got no farther than dropping his jacket sulkily on the floor, and very slowly unfastening his collar and tie. She made a vexed noise of exasperation, slapped his hands aside quite sharply, and began to unbutton his shirt with a hard-fingered, severe speed which stung him to offended resistance. He jerked himself back a little from her hands, and pushed her away, childishly hugging his damp clothes to him.

'*Mummy!* Don't treat me like a baby! I can do it myself.'

'I shall treat you like a baby just as long as you insist on behaving like one. Do it yourself, then, and look sharp about it, or I shall do it for you.'

She went away, and he heard her moving about for a moment in his bedroom, and then she came back with his pyjamas, and his hair-brush, and gave an ominous look in his direction

213

because he was still not in the bath. The look made him move a little faster, though he did it with an expression of positive mutiny. She was in a mood he didn't know at all, and therefore anything could happen, especially anything bad; and the bath seemed to him the safest place, as well as the place where she desired him to go. He wanted to assert himself, of course, he wanted to vindicate his male dignity, his poor, tender male dignity which had had its ears soundly boxed, exactly as if it had still been a mere sprig of self-conceit; but she looked at him with a pointed female look, and reversed the hair-brush suggestively in her hand, and Dominic took refuge in the bath very quickly, with only a half-swallowed sob of rage.

The silver shield, which he had fished carefully out of the pocket of his flannels and secreted in his tooth-mug while she was out of the room, must on no account be risked. If it came within her sight she might very likely, in her present mood, swept in into the waste-bin. But he was in agony about it all the time that she was bathing him. For she wouldn't trust him to get rid of the clay unaided, even though he protested furiously that he was perfectly competent, and flushed and flamed at her miserably: 'Mummy, you're *indecent!*' She merely extinguished the end of his protest with a well-loaded sponge, and unfairly, when he was blind and dumb, and could not argue, told him roundly that she intended to get him clean, and to see to it herself, and further added with genuine despondency that she didn't see how it was ever to be done.

The battle was a painful one. Having no other means of expressing his resentment of such treatment, Dominic developed more, and more, obstructive knees and elbows than any boy ever had before. Bunty, retaliating, adjusted his suddenly unpliable body to the positions she required by a series of wet and stinging slaps. The tangled head which would not bend to the pressure of her fingers was tugged over by a lock of its own wet hair, instead. Dominic fought his losing fight in silence, except when her vigorous onslaught on the folds of his ears dragged a squeal of protest from him:

'Mummy, you're *hurting!*'

'Serve you right!' she said smartly. 'How do you suppose I'm ever going to get you clean without hurting? You need scrubbing all over.' But for all that, she went more gently, even though the glimpses he got of her face in the pauses of the battle, between soapings and towellings and the rasp of the loofah, did not indicate any softening in her anger and disapproval. Still, in spite of her prompt: 'Serve you right!' so determinedly repeated, she wiped his eyes for him quite nicely when he complained that the soap was in them; and suddenly, when her fingers were so soft and slow with the warm towel on his sore, sulky face, he wanted to give in, and say he was sorry, and it was all his fault, even the bathroom war. But when he got one eye open and glimpsed her face, it still looked dauntingly severe, and the words retreated hurriedly, and left an unsatisfied coldness in his mouth. And then he was angrier than ever, so angry that he determined to make one more attempt to assert himself. The thought of his hard-working evening, the feel of the little shield stealthily retrieved and secretly cradled in his hand as he pulled on his pyjamas, stung him back to outer realities.

He waited until he was padding after her into his bedroom, his hair smugly brushed, his tired mind stumbling with sleep but goaded with hurt self-importance. Bunty laid the brush on his tall-boy, turned down the bed, and motioned him in. He felt the sharp edges of his discovery denting his palm, but she didn't look any more approachable than before, and there was still no safe ground for him to cross to reach her.

'I'll bring you you some hot milk,' she said, 'when you're in bed. Though you don't deserve it.'

But for that fatal afterthought he would have got across to her safely, but as it was he turned back in a passion of spleen, and said ungraciously: 'I don't want any, thank you!' He wasn't going to want anything she said he didn't deserve.

He hesitated at the foot of the bed, gazing at her with direct, resentful eyes, his newly-washed chestnut hair standing up in wild, fluffy curls all over his head. 'Mummy, there's something I want to talk to Dad about, seriously. I've got to tell him – '

It was no use, she rode over him. 'You're not going to talk to anyone about anything tonight. We've both had enough of you. Get into bed!'

'But it's awfully important – '

'Get into bed!'

'But, *Mummy* – '

Bunty reached for the hair-brush. Dominic gave it up. He made a small noise of despair, not unlike a sob, and leaped into the bed and swept the clothes high over him in one wild movement, leaving to view only the funny fuzz of his hair, soft and delicate as a baby's. Under the clothes he smelled his own unimaginable cleanness, revoltingly scented. 'The wrong soap,' he muttered crossly and inaudibly. 'Beastly sandalwood! You did it on purpose!'

Bunty stooped over him, and noticed the same error in the same moment. He hated a girl's soap. She wished she had noticed in time. She kissed the very small lunette of scented forehead which was visible under the hair, and it and all the rest of Dominic's person promptly recoiled in childish dudgeon six inches lower into the bed, and vanished utterly from view in one violent gesture of repudiation. Unmoved, or at any rate contriving to appear unmoved, Bunty put out the light.

'Don't let me hear one word more from you tonight, or I'll send your father in to you,' she warned.

'I wish you would!' muttered Dominic, safely under the clothes. 'At least he'd listen to reason.'

When she was gone, he lay clutching his treasure for a few minutes, and then, mindful of the danger of bending its thinness if he fell asleep and lay on it, and so losing perhaps the most vital aspect of his clue, he sat up and slipped it into the near corner of the little drawer in his bedside table. Then he subsided again. He was still very angry. He lay tingling all over with hot water and scrubbing, and slaps, his mind tingling, too, with offended pride and slighted masculinity. He was too upset to sleep. He wouldn't sleep all night, he would lie fretting, unable to forgive her, unable to settle his mind and rest. He would get up pale and quiet and ill-used, and she would be sorry –

Dominic fell off the rim of a great sea of sleep, and drowned deliciously in its most serene and dreamless deeps.

V

When he awoke it was to the pleasant sensation of someone rocking him gently by the toes, and the gleam of full day-light, with a watery sun just breaking into the room. He opened one eye into the rays, and closed it again dazzled and drowsy, but not before he had glimpsed George sitting on the foot of his bed. He lay thinking about it for a moment, trying to orientate himself. Around his snug and blissful sense of immediate well-being there was certainly a hovering awareness of last night's upsets, but it took him an interval of thought to remember properly. He opened his eyes, narrowly against the glare, and yawned, and stared at George.

'Come on, get out of it,' said George, smiling at him without reserve, but he thought without very much gaiety, either. 'I've given you a shake three times already. You'll be late for school.'

'I didn't hear you,' murmured Dominic, with eyelids gently closing again, and nose half-buried in the pillow.

'You wouldn't have heard the crack of doom if it had gone off this morning. That's what you get for staying out till half-past eleven. Remember?'

He did remember, and became instantly a shade more awake; because a lot of uncomfortable trailing ends from yesterday suddenly tripped his comfortably wandering mind, and brought him up sharp on his nose. He sat up, fixing George with a sudden reproachful grin.

'You're a nice one! Why didn't you help me out last night?'

'More than my own life was worth,' said George. 'I'd have been the next to get my ears clouted if I'd interfered. You be thankful you got off so lightly.' He gave his waking son a nice smile, full of teasing and reassurance in equal measure, the intimate exchange between equals which had always been an all-clear after Dominic's storms. 'Now, come on, get up and get washed.'

'Don't need washing,' said Dominic, reminded of his many injuries, and looking for a moment quite seriously annoyed again; but the morning was too fine, and his natural optimism too irrepressible to leave him under the cloud any longer. He slid out of bed, and stuck his toes into his slippers. A slightly awed, pink grin beamed sideways at George. He giggled: 'If you'd seen what she did to me last night, you'd think I could skip washing for a month. Anyhow, I haven't got a skin to wash, she jolly well scrubbed it all off.'

'She had to relieve her feelings somehow. If she hadn't skinned you with washing, I dare say she'd have had to do it some other way. You be thankful she only used a loofah!'

'She didn't,' said Dominic feelingly, 'she used a hair-brush, too. *My* hair-brush, of all the cheek! At least, she threatened me with it. She wouldn't listen to a word. And I really did have something important to say, because I didn't go off and stay out all that time and get into all that mess for nothing. *Do* I do things as stupid as that, now, honestly?'

George, thus appealed to, allowed that he did not, that there was, somewhere in that disconcerting head, the germ of a sense of responsibility. Dominic, vindicated, completed the interrupted shedding of his pyjamas, and turned to reach for his clothes in the usual place. A clean shirt, his other flannels, the old blazer; Bunty had laid them there with a severe precision which indicated that some last light barrier of estrangement still existed between them, and it would behove him to set about the process of sweetening her with discretion rather than with audacity. There is a time for cheek and a time for amendment; Dominic judged from the alignment of his clothes upon their chair that this was the time for amendment. He sighed, a little damped. 'Is she still mad at me?'

'No madder than you were at her last night,' George assured him comfortably. 'Just watch your step for a few days, and be a bit extra nice to her, and it'll all blow over. Now hurry up! Go and wash the sleep out of your eyes, at least, and brush your teeth. Your breakfast's waiting.'

'But I want to talk to you. I still haven't told you about it.'

'You can talk through the door, I'll stay here.'

Dominic talked, and rapidly, between the sketch of a wash and the motions of cleaning his teeth, and padded back into the bedroom still talking. 'It was only a thin chance, but that was the only place we could think of to start. And I know you told me to keep out of it, over and over, but honestly I couldn't.' He paused in the middle of slithering into his flannels. '*You*'re not mad at me now, are you?'

'What's the use?' said George. 'That wouldn't stop you. So that's why you went to such a daft place on a night when it was sure to be sodden with rain!'

'Yes, and honestly, I hadn't the remotest notion how late it was, it didn't seem to have been any time at all. I suppose we were just busy, and didn't notice, but really, I had a shock when I saw the clock. Well, then we were in a bit of a mess already, and I thought of the outflow, and climbed up on the stones. And one of the silly things rolled away and let me down in the water, and that's when I put my hand on this thing I told you about, right down between the pebbles in the bed of the stream. And that's what I wanted to tell you about last night, only I couldn't get a word in for Mummy. Look, it's here!' He loped across to the drawer, and fished out the shield, and laid it triumphantly in George's palm. His light, bright hazel eyes searched the judging face anxiously. 'You do see what it is, don't you? It's off a walking-stick – or anyhow, off something thin and round like a walking stick. And tapered, too, because look, the curve at the bottom of the shield is a little bit closer than at the top. I was awfully careful not to bend it out of shape at all. And you see, it fitted in with what I'd been thinking so exactly. So I brought it for you. Because how else would a silver plate from a stick get in there under the outflow, except the way I said?'

'How, indeed?' said George absently, staring at the small thing he turned about in his fingers. 'Can you show me exactly where this was? The very spot? Oh, I'll guarantee you absolution this time, even if you fall in the brook again.'

'Yes, of course I can!' He began to glow, because George was taking him seriously, because George wasn't warning him off. 'I made a note – there's a special dark-coloured stone with veins in it. I could put this right back where it was wedged. You *do* think it's important, don't you?'

'I think it is, I'm sure it may be. But we shall see if they can find anything interesting in these grooves of the pattern. Can't expect much of a reaction after a fortnight in the brook, I'm afraid, but with a crumpled edge like this top one, you never know.'

'And it was partly silted over,' said Dominic eagerly. 'That would protect it, wouldn't it? And if we could find the stick it came from, there ought to be marks, oughtn't there? Even if he tried to hide them. The shape of the shield might show, and anyhow, the tiny holes where it was fastened. Dad, before you take it away, d'you mind if I make a tracing of it? In case, I mean, I might see a stick that might be the one.'

George gave him a distracted smile, and said: 'Yes, you can do that. But make haste and brush your hair – straighten it, anyhow. Detective or no detective, you've got to go to school, and you'd better be in good time. Don't worry, I won't shut you out of your own evidence. You shall know if it helps us. Fair's fair! Now get on!'

'But my copy,' said Dominic agitatedly, through the sound of the brush tugging at the ridiculous fluff of his hair. 'I shan't have time to make it now, and you'll take it away before I come home.'

'I'll do it for you. Mind you, Dom, I should like it much better if you'd do as I asked, and stay out of it. It's not the sort of business for you, and I wish you'd never been brought into it in the first place.' Dominic was very silent indeed, for fear of being thought to have made some response to this invitation. George sighed. 'Well, it wasn't your fault, I suppose. Anyhow, you shall have your copy.'

'If only Mummy had let me speak, I could have told you all about it last night.' The point was still sore, because it was so unlike Bunty to close her ears; and Dominic kept returning to rub incredulously at the smart. 'It wasn't a bit like her, you know. I mean, she's always so *fair*. That's what I couldn't understand. What got into her, to make her like that? I know it was awful to be so late, and all that, but still she always listens to what I've got to say, but last night she wouldn't let me say a word.'

'It's quite understandable, in the circumstances,' said George. 'If I could have been at home with her it wouldn't have been so bad. But I came home only about ten minutes before you did, and found her frantic, still waiting for you. She'd been along finally to the 'Shock of Hay', and found that Pussy was missing, too, but nobody'd got a clue where either of you had gone. She'd just finished telling me all about it, and I was putting my coat on again to come out and look for you, when you sneaked in. No wonder you caught it hot, my lad!'

'Well, no, but still – Mummy isn't like all the others, who fly off the handle for nothing. I mean, she doesn't *panic* about lateness, and jump to the conclusion that people have been run

221

over, or murdered, or something, just because they don't come in when they ought to. Not usually, she doesn't.'

'Not unless there's a reason,' said George, 'but last night was a bit different. She was scared stiff about you, and that's why you got rather a rough time of it when you did turn up. I may as well tell you,' he said soberly. 'You'd hear all about it at school, anyhow, and I'd rather you heard it from me.' Dominic had stopped brushing, with the length of his disorderly hair smoothed down over his forehead, partly obscuring one eye, and in this odd condition was staring open-mouthed at his father. Something made him move close to him, the brush still forgotten in his hand. George took him by the arms and held him gently, for pleasure and need of touching him.

'You see, Dom, last night there was another death. Briggs, the gamekeeper up at the Harrow, rang up soon after eight o'clock from the top call-box, and told me he'd just found Charles Blunden in the woods there, with his own shot-gun lying by him, and both barrels in him. He hadn't dared tell the old man, I had to do that when I got up there. It may have been suicide. It could just, only just, have been an accident. Only people here don't believe in accidents any more. It went round the village like wildfire. That's why,' he said, soothing Dominic's blank white stare with a rather laborious smile, 'a late son last night was a son who – might come home, or might not. Like the old man's son! So don't hold it against Bunty if she took it out of you for all the hours she'd been waiting. If I'd known you weren't home I'd have been pretty edgy myself.'

Dominic's sudden small hand clutched hard at his arm. 'Did you say Charles Blunden?' His voice was a queer small croak in moment of stress, already beginning to hint at breaking. 'But – when did he find him? And where?'

'He rang up soon after eight. The doctor said Charles hadn't been dead any time, probably not more than half an hour. It's by sheer luck he was found so soon, because nobody would have paid the least attention to the shots. There were several guns out all round the village, one report more or less just vanished among the rest. He was up in the top wood, apparently heading towards the house.'

Dominic, with fixed eyes and working lips, made frantic calculations. 'I went out a bit before seven, didn't I? The bus from the green is at five minutes to. Yes, I must have gone out more like a quarter to, because John dawdles so, it would take nearly ten minutes down to the green. And where was it they ·found him? In the top wood?'

'Yes, lying by the path about two hundred yards in from the stile on to the mounds. You'll be late, Dom. Go and eat, and we'll talk about it this evening. After all, the poor devil's dead, we can't do anything for him.' George put a rallying arm round his son's shoulders, and gave him a shake to stir him out of what appeared to be a trance; but Dominic seized him by the lapels, and hung on to him with frantic weight.

'No, no, *please!* This is frightfully urgent, don't make me go until I've told you. You see, I *saw* him! Last night, at the stile! He gave me a half-crown – it's in my pocket, Mummy must have found it.' Odd, excited tears, such as he had not experienced by Helmut's body, came glittering uncertainly into his eyes now, and his voice wouldn't keep steady. Disgusted and distressed, he clung to George, who was solid and large, and held him firmly. 'It's awful isn't it? It didn't seem to matter so much when it was somebody I didn't know much, and nobody liked. But Mr. Blunden – I was talking to him last night. I think I must have been the last person who talked to him, except – you know – if somebody killed him, the somebody. He gave me half a crown,' said Dominic, with trembling lips. 'He was *pleased* with himself, and everything. I'm sure he didn't do it to himself, not on purpose. Oh, I don't want his half-crown now, I wish he hadn't given it to me – '

George drew him round to sit on the bed beside him, and shut him in with a large, possessive arm, and didn't try to hurry him, or even to keep him to the point. School could wait.

Indeed, if this meant what it appeared to mean, Dominic would be occupied with other matters than school for most of the morning, and if he seemed in a fit state to benefit by a return to normality he could easily go in the afternoon. Meantime, he leaned thankfully into George's side, and shook at little intervals, but with diminishing violence.

'Why shouldn't he give it to you?' said George reasonably. 'And why shouldn't you spend it? He wanted you to have it, didn't he? He'd be a bit hurt, wouldn't he, if he knew you'd let it be spoiled for you. What did he say when he gave it to you?'

'He said: "Go and celebrate for me." And when I thanked him, he said: "That's all right. Buy your girl a choc-ice." '

'Then that's what you do, and don't disappoint him. You don't have to tell Puss where the money came from, that's just between you and him, and none of her business.'

'I suppose not.' His voice sounded a little soothed. 'I'd better tell you about it, hadn't I? I wish I'd had my watch, because I can't be quite sure about all the times. Only I know I started from the green as soon as the bus had gone, and it was on time, and that's five minutes to seven.'

'Well, that's a good start. You went up the lane to the quarry, didn't you? That's the nearest way.'

'Yes. And when I got up to the stile, Charles was sitting on it. How long do you think that would be after I started? I should think it would take me about twenty minutes from the green, because I went as quickly as I could, to have some of the daylight left. But I could walk it again and time it, if you liked. I think it must have been about a quarter-past seven when I got there. He'd been shooting. Did they find any pheasants with him?'

'Yes, Briggs found a brace. Charles spoke to you first, did he? And then you stayed there for a few minutes, talking to him?'

'Yes, I told him I'd heard about the appeal being granted, and then he asked me what I thought about it. I didn't know what to say, really, because I'd never thought much about it, but

I said maybe surface-mining was better than shallow mining, anyhow. And then he said that although the appeal had been upheld, it was up to the Coal Board whether the contractors went on working on the site, because he was going to tell them tomorrow – that's today – that they could have the land, after all.'

'What?' George held him off incredulously to stare at him, but the intelligent, slightly stunned hazel eyes stared back firmly, and with an admirably recovered calm. 'But they'd been fighting like tigers to keep it, why should he change his mind now? Are you sure you didn't misunderstand him? That couldn't have been what he said.'

'Oh, yes, really it was. He said he'd been walking round having another look at the mess his grandfather left behind, the old way. He said you want something like the devil when someone tries to get it from you, but if they give up trying you can see it's only twenty acres of not very good pasture that'll have to come up sooner or later, one way or the other, if there's really that much coal there. So he'd made up his mind to tell them he'd give up his objections, and they could go ahead. I think he wanted to tell somebody quickly, so he wouldn't get uncertain again, and it was just that nobody happened to come along except me.'

'You mean he hadn't told anyone else at all?'

'No, he hadn't. Because I thought there might be a row about it, and like a crumb I said, did his father know? And he laughed, and said no, he didn't yet, but it was all right, he wouldn't care, what mattered to him was getting his own way, and after all, he *had* got that.'

This had a credible sound to George's ears. And wasn't it possible that the long arguments with Chad Wedderburn, which had made life wearisome for so long in the snug of the 'Shock of Hay', had had some odd, cumulative effect in the end? When, as Dominic had said, the pressure was removed, and Charles could afford to think, instead of merely feeling, in the contra-suggestible way of all his family? The whole thing began to make a circumstantial tale, and the stimulation of telling it had pulled Dominic together valiantly after the shattering shock of learning its ending. He had drawn a little away, leaning easily into the circle of George's arm, facing him with colour in his cheeks again, and animated eyes.

'And then he said this was really hot news, and I was the first to hear it. And he threw me the half-crown, and told me to go and celebrate, and said he was going home to break the news. Then he got over the stile, and picked up his birds and went off along the path towards the Harrow, and I went on to the well to meet Pussy. I don't think I can have been there at the stile with him more than ten minutes, but that would make it about twenty-five past seven, wouldn't it? And he only got such a little way along the path. You know,' said Dominic, his eyes getting bigger and bigger, 'you go over a ridge there to the well, although it's not far, and I don't think the sound would carry so sharply. Especially when there were quite a number of guns going at the time, you know, all round the valley. But I think it must have happened awfully soon after I left him, don't you?'

'It looks like it. You didn't see anyone else up there? While you were talking or after you left him?'

'No, not a soul. I didn't see anyone else until Pussy came up from the village.

'There's nothing else strikes you about it?'

'No,' said Dominic, after a minute or two of furrowing his brow over this. 'Should it?'

'Oh, I'm not being clever and seeing anything you didn't see. Just collecting any ideas you may have. Usually they seem to me worth examining,' said George, and smiled at him.

Unexpectedly Dominic blushed deeply at this, and as suddenly paled under the weight of being appreciated and praised thus in intoxicating intimacy. Something inside him was growing so fast, these days, that he could feel it expanding, and sometimes it made him dizzy, and sometimes it frightened him.

It was deeply involved, whatever it was, with George, and George's affairs, and when George trusted him and paid him a compliment it quickened exultingly, and opened recklessly like a deep, sweet flower feeling the sun. He said hesitantly: 'There is one thing. Only it isn't evidence, really; it's only what I think myself.'

'I should still like to hear it.'

'Well – it's only that I'm sure he didn't do it himself. At least, not on purpose. When I talked to him, he was in an awfully good mood. Something special, I mean. He wasn't thinking at all about ending things, more of starting them. He'd sort of gone off the deep end by telling me, and he was *glad*. It's like this!' pursued Dominic, frowning down at a slim finger which was plotting the obscure courses of his mind on George's coat-sleeve. 'He's been in the Army, and all his life apart from that he's worked the farm for his father, and – well,' he said, suddenly raising bright, resolved eyes to George's face, 'he seemed to me as if it was the first real decision he'd ever made for himself in his life, and – and that's what he wanted me to celebrate.'

Chapter 8

The Pursuit of Walking-Sticks

I

At the opening of the inquest on Charles Blunden, only evidence of identification was taken.

The church room was packed on the occasion, and the air within heavy with an uneasiness which took effect like heat, though from ill-fitting windows an elaborate network of draughts searched out every corner. It was the first really cold day. Outside, the air pinched. Inside, the entire population of Comerford, or all those who could squeeze in, stared and sweated and whispered. Comerford was full of whispers, sibilant over fences, floating down lanes, confided over counters, drawn out across pints of bitter in the bar of the 'Shock of Hay', where Io Hart seldom showed herself now, and always with pale face and heavy eyes. From grief for Charles, people said to one another wisely. But Io withdrew herself, and said nothing at all. She did not come to the inquest, though the cord of tension which was tugging the whole village into one congestion of feeling had drawn to the hall even the most unexpected and retiring of people. It was not quite curiosity. In this case the community was a party involved, deeply, perhaps fatally, and it behoved them to sit watchfully over their interests so long as there was anxiety, so long as there was hope.

Fallen into the Pit

The old man came. Everyone had been sure that he would not appear, but he did, suddenly lumbering through the narrow gangway with a heavier lurch than usual, and a more ungainly stoop, as if his big, gallant body had slipped one or two of its connections, and was shaking unco-ordinated parts along with it in a losing struggle to reassemble them. His wholesome ruddiness had become a stricken mottle of purple and white, with sagging cheeks and puzzled old puffy eyelids, though the bright blueness of his eyes continued sudden as speedwell, alive and alert in the demoralisation of his face. Charles had been his only child. There was not much point in the Harrow for him now, and none in his old amusement of making money, of which he had more than enough already for a dwindling middle age without an heir. People pitied him. If he knew it, he gave no sign, though it must have galled him. He had been so long kowtowed to and envied. People held their breath, pitying him. He lumbered to his place, and sat as if he believed himself to be sitting alone. And when the time came, he identified his son in a harsh, shocked, but defiant voice, daring fate to down him, even with weapons like these. But George observed that the tell-tale back view, which had always betrayed him, was now that of an old man indeed, sunken together, top-heavy, disintegrating. The old, however, sometimes have astonishing recuperative powers, because with one's own death at least fully in sight, few things are any longer worth making a lengthy fuss about, even the deaths of the young.

Three days adjournment, at the request of the police, who were not yet ready to present their expert evidence; and therefore the tension remained and tightened, wound up with whispers, frayed with fears. Few people hesitated to use the word murder this time, though there was no verdict yet to support it. Few people waited for the evidence, to conclude that though the connection was not immediately apparent, this murder was fellow to the first. Murder begets murder, and the first step is the hardest. There even began to be a name in the middle of the whispers, blackening under them as under a swarm of bees settling. Who else had any motive for killing Charles Blunden, except his inseparable quarrelling partner, his rival in love, his opponent in ideas, Chad Wedderburn? Who was already held to be the most probable suspect in the first crime, and showed now as almost the only one in this, unless Chad? The first death an impulse of understandable indignation, they said, from a man of his record and reputation; and the second one the fruit of the first success, adapted now, too easily, to his own inclinations and desires. Out at large, somewhere without witnesses, on the first occasion, and this time, by his own account, peacefully at home marking test papers in Latin, but alone, for his mother had been away for some days in Bristol, visiting a sister of hers who had arthritis. Again no witnesses to his movements all the evening. And when all was said, who else was in it?

Of course there was no evidence – yet – that he had gone out to meet Charles in the woods, and turned his own gun against him, and emptied both barrels into his chest. But there was no positive evidence that he had not, and by this time that was almost enough for Comerford.

Bunty came home shocked and distressed from her morning's shopping, having been offered this solution confidently with the fish. She had stamped on the theory very firmly, but she knew that she had not scotched it. As well join Canute in trying to turn back the tide. The strain on Comerford had to find outlet somewhere, it was only to be expected. And after all, who could say with certainty that they were wrong? The most one could say was that they were premature.

She argued with herself that the two young men had always been friends, in spite of their endless wranglings, for what else could have held them together? But some insecurity within her mind answered dubiously that human creatures cling together for other reasons besides love, that there are the irresistible attractions of enmity as well. And further, that friendship has often reversed its hand when some unlucky girl got in the way. She had no peace; no one had any peace, and no one would have now until the thing was finished. Meantime, there was Charles's funeral to focus public feeling, and she had ordered flowers, as much for Dominic's sake as anyone's. To lay the ghost of the flung half-crown, and the easy, gay voice which had bidden him buy his girl an ice to celebrate a gesture of self-assertion, the first and the last, made only just in time.

Pussy and Dominic compared notes in the loft, over the last apple-wrapping, and the note of desperation had somehow stolen into their councils unawares.

'She won't go out, or do anything, or take any interest in anything,' said Pussy. 'She just does her work, as usual, and says nothing all the day long. And he doesn't come in any more. He did come in once, and then it was so awful he went away very soon. I think that's when he realised how it was. And that's why he won't come near her now.'

'She doesn't think he did it, though, does she?'

'No, of course not. But all the others do, and he won't even bring that feeling near her. If he's going to bring bad luck he's determined he won't bring it here. You know, everybody's saying it now, everybody.'

'Well, everybody's wrong,' said Dominic, cussed to the last.

'Well, I think so, too, but how to prove it? Was he at school today?'

'Yes, we had him first period this morning.'

'It must be pretty awful for him,' she said.

'He looked kind of sick, but he acted just the same as ever. But – ' Dominic scowled down at the apple he was wrapping, and said no more.

'What are we gong to do?' asked Pussy grimly.

'The same we've been doing, only twice as hard. Just go on watching out for walking-sticks – anywhere, doesn't matter where, doesn't matter how you do it, only get a close look at all you can, until we find the right one.'

'I *have* been doing. And it isn't so easy, because I'm not allowed in the bar and the snug, but I've done it. I bet I haven't missed many this week, and I'll bet almost every stick in the place has been in by now, but I haven't seen anything like we're looking for. And it's all very well for you, but I've nearly been caught two or three times creeping about with my little bit of paper, and you can't always think of something credible to say.'

'All very well for me? I like that! You've got it easy, you just sit around and wait for people to bring the sticks to you, but I have to go out and look for them. I'm fagged out running errands, just to get into people's halls and see if there are any sticks. All this week I've run about for Mummy like a blinking spaniel,' said Dominic indignantly, but miserably, too.

'I bet she thinks you're sickening for something,' said Pussy cynically.

'Oh, well, she thinks I'm trying to get round her by being extra good because of the row we had when we came home late that night.' He looked a little guilty at this, however convenient he had found it to be; for he had inherited something of Bunty's sense of justice, and was uncomfortable in even the shabbiest of haloes when he had not earned it. 'But that's not all. Even from school I've collected notes to deliver, and all sorts of beastly errands, just to get into more places, and I can tell you it isn't such fun getting yourself a reputation like I'm getting with the other fellows. But I wouldn't care, if only we could *get* something from it.'

'Is it any use going on?' asked Pussy despondently.

'What else can we do? And I'm absolutely sure that if we can only find that stick, Pussy, we've done it, we're through.'

'Well, of course, it would be a big thing,' she owned dubiously, 'but I don't know that everything would be settled. This other business – it seems to make the stick a bit of a back-number now.'

'It doesn't, I'm sure it doesn't. I've got a hunch. The two things are connected somehow, I'm certain. And the only clue we've got in either case is this.' He fished the little paper shield out of his pocket, and smoothed it ruefully on his thigh, fingering the faint convolutions of the leaves. 'So you can please yourself, but I'm jolly well going on plugging and plugging at this until I *do* find the stick it came from. Or until I can think of something better to do.'

'O.K.!' said Pussy, sighing, 'I'm with you. Only I can't say I'm expecting very much.'

Dominic could not honestly have said that he was expecting very much himself, but he would not be discouraged. He had a hunch, and not being in a position of exact responsibility, as his father was, he could afford to play his hunches. That seemed to him the chief difference between them; he was a piece of George, bound by no rules and regulations except the normal ones of human decency, and he could do, and he would do, the things from which George was barred, like following will-o'-the-wisps of intuition, and butting his head obstinately against the weight of the evidence – such as it was – and taking subtle, implied risks which he himself could not define. And what he found he would give to George, and where he failed no one was involved but himself. But he must not fail. There was only one channel to follow, and therefore he could give every thought of his mind, every particle of his energy, to the pursuit of the walking-stick.

Sitting back on his heels among the straw, he argued the possibilities over again, and could get nothing new out of them. It is possible to burn a stick, or drop it down a pit; but would the murderer think it necessary, just because a tiny plate without a name had been lost from it? Because there was always a risk of things thrown away turning up again in inconvenient circumstances, and even things committed to the fire had been known to leave identifiable traces behind. Much simpler to keep the thing, and see if the plate came into the evidence at the inquest. And of course it had not, and even now no one knew anything about its discovery except Pussy, Dominic and the police; ergo, in all probability the owner would congratulate himself on the way things had worked out, and behave as normally as usual, destroying nothing where there was no need, not even hiding the stick, because no one was looking for it. He might use it less than usual for a time, but he wouldn't discard it, unless he'd been in the habit of ringing the changes on several, because its disappearance might be noticed and commented on by someone who knew him. Every man, even a murderer, must have some intimates.

Conclusion number one, therefore, and almost the only one: it was worth looking in the normal places, hallstands, and the lobbies of offices, and the umbrella-stands in cafés, or in the church porch on Sundays, where one could examine everything at leisure. And the obsession had so got hold of him that he had even crept into the private staff hall at school, and hurriedly examined the single ebony cane and two umbrellas discarded there. And almost got caught by old Broome as he was sneaking out again, only luckily Broome jumped easily to the conclusion that his business had been with the headmaster, and of a nature all too usual with Dominic Felse; and he couldn't resist making a rather feeble joke about it, whereupon Dominic took the hint, and got by with a drooping crest and a muttered reply, and took to his heels thankfully as soon as he was round the corner.

Sometimes even he became despondent. There were so many walking-sticks. Among the young they were not so frequent, perhaps, but lots of older men never went anywhere without them, and the old grandees like Blunden, and Starkie from the Grange, and Britten, the ex-coal-owner practically collected the things. Dominic had never realised before how many were still in constant use. Ordinarily they constituted one of the many things about the equipment of his elders to which his selective eyes were quite blind, they came into sight only when they threatened him; and the days of his more irresponsible scrapes, in which he had occasionally been involved with indignant old men thus armed, were some years behind him now, so that he had forgotten much of what he had learned.

Fortunately he had a strain of persistence which had some-times been a nuisance, and could now for once be an asset. A single objective suited him very well; he fixed his eyes on it, and followed stubbornly.

George played fair with him. The silver plate was Dominic's piece of evidence, honestly come by, and he was entitled to know what they could discover of its significance. George would much have preferred to edge him out of the affair, even now, but if he insisted on his rights he should have them. Therefore the results of the tests on the shield were faithfully, if briefly, reported as soon as completed. Dominic expected it; almost the first thing he did when he came home from school each day was to put his head in at the office door to see if George was there, and if he was, to fix his brightly enquiring eyes on him and wait for confidences without asking, with a touching faith.

On the evening after the inquest opened, George was late, and Dominic met him as he came in. Inky from his homework, the brat couldn't wait.

So George told him; it was like cutting out one of his own nerves to hold out any part of the complications of living and dying to Dominic, thus prematurely as he felt it to be; but he owed it to him. Yes, there were positive reactions. The crumpled upper edge of the shield had retained, soon covered by sand and silt as it had been, the faintest possible traces, in its threads of tarnish and dirt, of something else which was undoubtedly skin tissue and blood.

Dominic's eyes grew immense, remembering how the whole accumulation of matter in those furrows had been no thicker than a rather coarse hair, and marvelling how many tests could extract from them exact information about particles he could not even see.

'Could it be his? Can they tell that, too?'

'They can tell that it could be, but not that it is. Yes, it may be Helmut's.'

'Well – ' said Dominic on a long, deep breath, 'being found right there, and if it *could* be – there isn't much doubt, is there?'

George owned soberly that the odds in favour were certainly heavy.

'Then we've only got to find the stick!'

George merely smiled at him rather wryly, clapped an arm round his shoulders, and drew him in to supper. It sounded so very simple, the way Dominic said it.

II

The wreath for the funeral was delivered late in the evening. Dominic went into the scullery, where it reposed upon the table, and stood looking at it for a minute as if he hoped it had something to tell him, with his face solemn and thoughtful, and his lip caught doubtfully between his teeth. Then he said to Bunty, somewhat gruffly: 'I'll take it up to the farm tomorrow as I go to school.'

'It would mean getting up awfully early,' said Bunty comfortably. 'Don't you bother about it, I'll take it up later, or George will.' Penitence was nice, but she didn't want him too good.

'No, I can easily get up in plenty of time. I'll take it.'

For a moment she was at a loss what to say, and looked at him narrowly, hoping he wasn't genuinely moping about Charles and the unhappy meeting with him at the tail-end of his life, and hoping still more sternly that he wasn't doing a little artificial moping, dramatising the encounter into something it had certainly not been in reality and his past interest in Charles into a warm relationship which in fact had never existed. She felt vaguely ashamed of supposing it possible, in this most healthy and normal of children, but round about thirteen queer things begin to happen even to the extroverts, and it pays to knock the

first little emotional self-indulgence on the head, before it begins
to be a necessity of life. But Dominic chewed his lip, and said
joltingly: 'You know, it wouldn't seem so bad if I'd even *liked*
him. But I didn't much, and it's awful hum-bug trying to
pretend you did because a fellow's dead, isn't it?' He misinterpreted Bunty's relieved silence, and looked at her a little
deprecatingly. 'It sounds a bit beastly, maybe I shouldn't have
said that. I do think he was quite a good sort of chap – only
sort of secondhand. You know – there wasn't anything about
him you couldn't have found first somewhere else. And – and
there ought to have been,' said Dominic firmly, 'he had plenty
of chance.'

'You didn't know him so very well,' said Bunty. 'I dare say
there was more to him than you found out.'

'Well, maybe. Only I don't want to go putting on any act. It
doesn't seem decent sucking up to a fellow just because he's
dead, and you were somehow sort of dragged into it at the end.
It's awfully difficult, isn't it,' said Dominic, turning on her a
perplexed and appealing face, 'knowing how you ought to behave
to people, not to be dishonest, and not to be just beastly, either?
I get all mixed up when I start thinking about it.'

'Then don't think about it too hard,' advised Bunty. 'It only
gets you a bit hypnotised, like staring at one thing till you begin
seeing spots before your eyes. Mostly the spots aren't really
there.'

'Well, but does it go *on* being as complicated as this?' he
asked rather pathetically.

'Much the same, Dom, but you get used to picking your way.
Don't you worry about it, I'll back your instincts to be pretty
near the right balance most of the time.'

Dominic frowned thoughtfully at the brilliant bronze and
gold chrysanthemums of the wreath, and said definitely: 'Well,
I've got an instinct I owe him something.'

The half-crown? thought Bunty for a moment; for even that
was a legitimate point, to a punctilious young thing who had

lost the chance of returning satisfaction for a gift. But no, it wasn't that. What stuck in his conscience and made him feel bound to Charles was the confidence which had suddenly passed between them. It had hardly mattered to Charles, at the time, who first received his news in trust; but it mattered to Dominic.

So she made no demur, even in the way of kindness; and Dominic, rising half an hour earlier than usual, and without being called more than twice, at that, set off through the fields and the plantation for the Harrow farm.

It was a meek sort of morning, grey, amorphous, not even cold, the tufts of grass showery about his ankles, the heather festooned with wet cobwebs in a shadowy, silvery net, and the subdued, moist conversations of birds uneasy in the trees. Dominic hoisted the heavy wreath from one hand to the other for ease, and found it awkward however he carried it. His mind behind the musing face was furiously busy, but he was not sure that it was getting anywhere. Point by point he went over all he had told George, and wondered if he had left anything out. It isn't always easy remembering every detail of an encounter which you had no reason to believe, at the time, would turn out to be evidence in a murder case. They hadn't yet said it was murder, of course, officially, but all the village was saying it, and Dominic couldn't help imbibing some of that premature certainty. Charles, who had taken him into his confidence, and had thereupon astonishingly died, nagged at him now to make use of what he knew. He owed him that much, at any rate.

And seriously, who could have wanted Charles dead? It wasn't as if he had been positive enough and individual enough to have any real enemies. You don't kill people you can't dislike, people who haven't got it in them to rouse you at all. As for old Wedderburn, that was bunk. Maybe Charles Blunden had been in his way where Io Hart was concerned, but then Io had never shown any obvious inclination to single out either or them. Maybe, thought Dominic doubtfully, fellows who've got it bad for girls imagine these things; but it seemed to him Chad

regarded his chances with Io as marred at least as surely by his
own past as by the existence of Charles. As though he'd lost a
leg, or something, so that he could never think of marrying,
and yet couldn't stop thinking of it, either. Was it really possible
to feel yourself maimed for life, merely because you had been
pushed into killing other people in a war in order to stay
alive yourself? In a war, when most people thought themselves
absolved for everything? But the fellow who goes the opposite
way from everyone else isn't necessarily wrong.

So apart from his instinctive certainty that Chad was not the
murderer, Dominic was not even impressed with the arguments
of those who thought he was. People don't remove their rivals
unless it's going to make enough difference to justify the effort,
let alone the risk. And it didn't look as if Chad thought the
removal of half her male acquaintance could ensure him a peaceful passage with Io.

And if Chad didn't seem a likely murderer, no more did
anyone else of whom Dominic could think at the moment. What
earthly reason could they have? Maybe, after all, it had been
the result of an accident. Powder-marks on his jacket, but no
particular scufflings underfoot or round about to indicate that
there had been any struggle for the shot-gun. Accident, they
said, was a bare possibility. Suicide, thought Dominic definitely,
wasn't even that.

He came through the broad rickyard, past the long barns and
the byres, and into the kitchen-yard. He hadn't liked to go to the
front door, where he might encounter the old man; and at this
hour the cook-housekeeper and the maid, both of whom slept
at home in the village and went in daily, would be in and out
of the kitchen door, and see him coming in, so he would be
giving the least possible trouble. Also, though he did not admit
that this weighed with him, if he ran errands to the Harrow at
this time of year, and took care to discharge them into Mrs.
Pritchard's hands, there were usually late pears to be harvested,
and yellow, mellow, large pears are very welcome at break.

In the yard, backed against the wall of the house, was a kennel, and lying before it, chin on outstretched paws, a brown-and-white field spaniel, staring indifferently at the day through half-closed eyes. When he opened his eyes fully at Dominic's approach, their blank sadness seemed preternatural even for a spaniel. He did not move until Dominic stooped to scrub civilly at the curls of his forehead, then his tail waved vaguely, and he leaned his head heavily to the caressing hand, but made no warmer response. He was chained to his kennel. Dominic never remembered having seen Charles's dog chained up before.

Of course, that was one thing he'd forgotten to mention to George: the dog. Not that it made much difference. Only, now that he came to think of it, George hadn't mentioned him, either, when he told who Briggs had run up to break the news. Dogs were taken for granted in Briggs's life, of course, maybe he wouldn't think to say there was a dog there. Only someone must have taken him home, for it didn't seem to Dominic that he would leave his master's body of his own will.

The dog was moping; that was natural. He liked being saluted by his friends, but even this pleasure he accepted now abstractedly, and soon let his broad head sink to his paws again, staring slit-eyed at the day. And Dominic went to meet Mrs. Pritchard in the kitchen doorway.

She took the wreath, and being touched by his somewhat misunderstood solemnity, desired to cheer him with pears. He went back to the dog while he waited for her, for the dog worried him. Such a fine creature, in such resplendent condition, and lying here so listlessly at the end of a chain. He set himself to woo him, and did not do so badly, for the tail began to wave again, and with more warmth; and presently the great, sad head lifted, and the soft jowl explored his lowered face, blowing experimentally with strong, gusty breaths. So far they had progressed when a footstep sounded at the door, and the dog stiffened, peered, and then withdrew into the dark inside of the kennel, belly to the ground, and lay there. The feathery front

paws disappeared under the spotted chin. Only a bight of chain
coiling out from the kennel and in again, and the round luminous whites of two staring eyes, betrayed that there was any dog
within. He made a small whining sound, and then was quiet,
and would not come out again in spite of Dominic's wheedling
fingers and winning voice.

Dominic gave up the attempt. He got up from his knees,
dusting them busily, and looked up full into old Blunden's face.
He had expected Mrs. Pritchard returning, and was speechless
with surprise and shyness for a moment; but the old man smiled
at him, and seemed quite himself, in spite of his ravaged face
and forward-blundering shoulders. The loss was not by him,
but the shock was, and his toughness had not let him down.
The bold blue eyes had still a rather blank, dazed look, but the
old spark of intelligence burned deep underneath the surface as
bright as ever, lustrously intent upon Dominic.

'I shouldn't bother with him,' he said quietly. 'Poor brute's
been temperamental since Charles went, you know. Pining here,
I'm afraid. His dog, you see – with him when it happened –
whatever did happen.' He seemed to be talking as much to
himself as to Dominic, and yet a sense of sudden isolation, of
terrifying intimacy, made Dominic hold his breath. 'You're
Felse's boy, aren't you?' said the old man, smiling at him quite
nicely but rather rigidly, so that his senses went numb, and his
mouth dry. Very seldom in his life had Dominic been as tongue-
tied as this.

'Yes, sir!' he whispered, like any second-former new at school.

'Wanting me? Or is Mrs. Pritchard seeing after something
for you?'

'Yes, sir, thank you, she – she said she'd get me some pears.'

'Ah good! Plenty of 'em, goodness knows, plenty! No boys to
make inroads in 'em here. May as well fill your pockets, take 'em
where they'll be welcome, eh?' His eyes went back regretfully to
the round, unwavering, white stare in the shadows at the back
of the kennel. 'Yes, poor brute, pining here! Might do well yet

at some other place. Fresh start good for dogs, as well as for humans, eh, my boy? With him when it happened, you know. Came home alone!'

Dominic stood looking at him with awed eyes and wary face, wishing himself away, and yet painfully alive to every accent, every turn of voice or tension of body. And presently, as if soothed with staring, he did not wish himself away any more. He had an idea; at least, it felt like an idea, though it seemed to come out of his bowels rather than his brain, making him ask things before he knew he was going to ask them.

'Do you have to tie him up? He isn't used to it, is he?'

'Roams off, poor beast, if you loose him. Back to where it happened, mostly. Get over it in time, no doubt, but once off the chain now, and he's away.'

'Isn't it odd,' said Dominic, automatic as a sleepwalker, 'that he should come home that night, and now he goes back there as often as he can.'

'Don't know, my boy! I didn't think much about it at the time. Enough on all our minds, no time for the dog. But they're queer cattle, too, you know – individual as humans, every one, and almost as capricious. Suffer from shock, too, like humans. Poor brute came home and crept into the stables, and hid in a corner. Heard him whining when I came through the yard. Had to hunt for him, wouldn't come out. Found him only just before Briggs turned up with your father. Had to chain him, no doing anything with him since then. But he'll get over it if he goes to a new home, with decent people – fresh surroundings, and all that – no reminders.' He looked through Dominic with a fixed face, the smile dead on it, and repeated absently: 'No reminders!'

Dominic ventured: 'We're all most awfully sorry, sir.'

'Yes, son, I know, I know! Your father's been very good – very good!' He patted Dominic's slight shoulder, and sighed. 'Here comes Mrs. Pritchard with your pears now.'

Dominic accepted a bag almost as heavy as his school satchel, and distributed thanks between them, as both appeared to be involved in the gift. To tell the truth, he had little energy or attention left over from coping with the idea, which was occupying his body with the intensity of a stomach-ache, making him feel light and sick with excitement. When Mrs. Pritchard had gone away again into the house, and left them moving slowly towards the rickyard together, he struggled to grasp the moment and turn it to use, and for a minute or two was literally without words. Unexpectedly the old man helped him.

'You've been taking a real interest, so your father tells me, in this bad business that's got hold of Comerford.' He sounded, in his preoccupied way, as indulgent about it as all the rest, as if it were something quite unreal and childish, a kind of morbid game. But he was old, and one had to make all kinds of allowances.

'Well, I don't know!' Dominic said uncomfortably. 'It was just an accident that it happened to be Pussy and me who found him. And you can't just forget about a thing like that. But there hasn't been anything we could do.'

'Very few leads of any kind, more's the pity,' agreed the old man. 'For you, or your father, eh? – see, now, what's your name? Dominic, isn't it?'

Never particularly pleased with this admission, the owner of the name sighed that indeed it was.

'Still, you're an intelligent boy. I hear you've been trying, anyhow – doing your best. That night you saw the last of my lad – ' The hand on Dominic's shoulder tightened, just perceptibly, but the pressure sent a quaking shock through him; needlessly, for the old man's voice was level, spiritless and resigned, and Charles relinquished already, because there was no help for it. Only the old or the cold can resist trying to help what cannot be helped. 'That was the occasion of some amateur sleuthing, wasn't it? Eh, Dominic? And got you into some trouble on the rebound, too, didn't it? No more late nights for a while, eh?'

To be teased with laughter so mournfully soft was dreadful.

Dominic felt himself crimsoning to his hair, and vowed to reproach his mother bitterly for talking to outsiders about what should have remained a private matter between them. It wasn't like her, either; but that had been a night of near-panic among the households of Comerford, and no doubt all the women had compared notes in the greengrocer's and the butcher's afterwards. Maybe she hadn't really told very much, only that he was out late poking his nose into his father's business – she wouldn't have to tell them how angry she had been, that would be clearly visible without any words. Still, he would make his protest. It would be foolish to let one's parents get out of hand.

'It wasn't a great success,' he said rather glumly.

'No, there's been no luck for the police from the beginning. No luck for the village, one could say.' They had reached the gate of the rickyard, and here the hand left his shoulder, and the heavy feet pacing beside him halted. 'So you didn't find anything of interest. Pity, after such a gallant try!' The old, indulgent, sad smile dwelt thoughtfully upon Dominic's face. He felt the fluttering excitement inside him mounting to speech, possessing his lips. And just for a moment of panic he had not the least idea exactly what he was going to say. Frightened of his instincts, trying with a too belated effort to control them into thoughts, and shape what was already shaped, he heard himself saying in a tight, small voice:

'I *have* got something now, though. I didn't give it to my father, because – well, it may be nothing at all to do with it, and they've had so many false starts, and – well, he doesn't like me butting in. So I thought, if I could find out first whether it really means anything, then he'd be pleased – and if it's no good, well, I shan't have caused him any trouble, or – or – '

'Or got into any yourself,' said Blunden, the smile deepening almost affectionately in his blue, bright eyes. 'Well, maybe you're wise. They've certainly got more than enough irrelevant nonsense to sort out, without our adding to it. You do that, Dom, my boy! You make sure of your evidence first!'

Fallen into the Pit

Dominic closed the gate between them, and hoisted the bag of pears into the hollow of his left arm. 'Yes, sir, I think I will. Only I shall need *somebody*'s help. You see, it's something I can't understand myself, it's – ' He hesitated, flushed and smiled, resettling his satchel on his shoulders. 'I say, sir, I'm awfully sorry! I didn't mean to start worrying you with my affairs – and I expect it's all tripe, really. I'd better get on now. Thanks awfully for the pears!'

'That's all right, my boy! If there's anything *I* can do – '

'Oh, I didn't mean – I say, I *am* ashamed, bothering you, when – ' He made to say more, then resolutely turned himself to the drive. 'Thanks, sir, all the same! Good-bye!'

'Oh well, it's your pidgin! Good-bye, Dominic!'

Dominic went ten yards down the drive, gnawing his knuckles in extreme indecision and then turned, and called after him: 'I say, sir!'

The old man was only a few yards from the gate, moving heavily, and at the call he turned at once and came back. The boy was coming back, too, dragging his feet a little, still uncertain. Big hazel eyes, dark with solemnity, stared over the bitten fingers. 'I say, sir, do you really think I might – If you honestly don't mind – '

'Come on, now, better share it!' said Blunden kindly. 'What is it that's on your mind?'

'I haven't got it here, but I could bring it to you. You see – can you read German, sir?'

They stared at each other over the gate with wide, conspiratorial eyes, half-hypnotising each other. Then the old man said, not without some degree of natural bewilderment: 'As a matter of fact, laddie, I can. But what's that got to do with it?'

Dominic drew a deep breath, and came back through the gate.

245

III

It was not a nice day for a boy with his mind anywhere but on his work. To begin with, he was late, which made a bad start; and a part of himself, the part with the brains, had been left behind somewhere on the way, to haggle out a worse problem then ever cropped up in algebra. It was a pity that the headmaster now took Fourth-Form maths. He wasn't a bad sort, and he wasn't even in a bad temper that day, but he was a man who liked a little application even where there was no natural aptitude, and above all he couldn't forgive lack of application where the natural aptitude did exist. Dominic suffered from the reputation of having a fairly liberal share of brains; it was usually what went on out of the classroom, rather than what happened in it, that got him into hot water. But today he couldn't do anything right. He was inattentive, absent-minded, dreaming in a distant and rather harassed world where a and b, x and y indicated people, not abstract quantities. In the middle of theorems, Dominic floated. Challenged, he gave frantic answers at random, dragging himself back in a panic from some mysterious place to which he had retired to think. The Head was not convinced that what occupied him there was thought. Chewed to fragments, Dominic did not really seem to mind as much as he should have done, but only to wriggle and circle uneasily, like a dog anxious to get back to a bone from which it has been chivvied wantonly by spiteful children. If the tongue-lash left him unstung for two minutes, he was off again, blank-eyed, into the depths of himself.

It went on like that all day, and by last period in the afternoon, which was Latin, he had even begun to look a little ill with the indigestible weight of his thoughts. Virgil could hold him no better than x and y, though he had normally a taste for the full, rolling hexameters which were round in the mouth as a sun-warmed apple in the palm, tactile satisfaction somehow molten into the ear's delight. He made a stumbling mess of passages which would ordinarily have made his eyes lighten into gold; and Chad, after a succession of rather surprised promptings and patient elucidations, gave him a more searching look, and on the strength of it let him out gently with a few lines before he had intended to do so. Dominic retired ungratefully, with bewildering promptness and a single-mindedness Chad could not help admiring, and sank his teeth once again into the throat of his own peculiar problem. Which by then he had almost settled, in so far as it could be settled short of the assay.

Chad set some written work, and perceiving, as he expected, that one pen was loitering after only a few tentative words, called Dominic to him. 'The rest of you,' he said almost automatically, as the few inevitably inquisitive heads were raised to follow Dominic's resigned progress, 'get on with your work. We're no better worth prolonged examination than we were five minutes ago.' The 'we', Dominic thought, was rather decent of him.

The Fourth Form, as always, looked mortally offended at being told to mind their own business, and elevated their eyebrows and looks down their noses in their best style to indicate their total lack of interest in anything so insignificant as Dominic Felse and Chad Wedderburn. And if here and there an ear was flapping a little in their direction, it flapped in vain. Chad had a quiet voice, and leaned forward over his desk to reduce the distance between them so that it might be even quieter and still adequate. He looked, now that Dominic examined him closely, distinctly worn and haggard, and his scar stood out more lividly than usual, though his manner was exactly as they had known it ever since his return, unhurried, calm, past surprise but wryly alert to impressions, and sensitive in response to them. If sleep had largely left him, if he knew as well as they did that the whole village was settling his guilt and seething with speculations as to his future, he gave no outward sign of it, made no concessions. And he could still see sufficiently clearly to observe that one of his boys had something on his mind. The only mistake he had made was in thinking that it might be something which could be got rid of by sharing it.

'Come on, now,' he said quietly, 'what's the matter?'

'Nothing, sir,' said Dominic, but in a discouraged tone which did not expect to convince.

'Don't tell me that! Your mind hasn't been on what we're doing here for one minute this afternoon. I know your work well enough to know that. What's wrong? Are you feeling off-colour?'

'Oh, no, sir, really I'm all right.'

'Then there's something worrying you sick. Isn't there? Don't you dare hand me: "Oh, no, sir!" again,' he said smartly, warding off another disclaimer, 'or I'll take you at your word, and make you pay through the nose for what you just did to the shield of Æneas. How would you like it if I kept you here for an hour after school, and let you make me a decent translation of the whole passage?'

Dominic's face woke into sudden alarm and reproach, because his inner world was touched. He breathed: 'Oh, but, sir, *please* – You don't really mean it, do you? Please not today! I've got such a lot to do this evening, honestly.'

'I'm sure you have,' said Chad, watching every change of the vulnerable face, and at a loss as yet to account for the success of his pinprick. 'Suppose you tell me the truth, then, and talk yourself out of it. Or, of course, you could regard it as merely getting a load off your chest, in strict confidence. Wouldn't you like to unload?'

Dominic would, as a matter of fact, have liked to very much; but if he couldn't entirely trust George with it, how could he give it to anyone else? No, as soon as it was shared it was rendered ineffective. He had to carry it through alone, or some ham-handed well-intentioned adult would throw sand in the works. He had it ready now, exactly planned out in his own mind, and no one knew anything about it except himself, and no one was to know except Pussy, who had only a minor part and could in any event be trusted to the death. So nobody could ruin it. And that was the best, the only way.

'It's only something I have to do,' he said carefully, 'and I would like to tell you, but I mustn't – not yet.'

'Something as anxious as you've been looking? Couldn't you use some help, then? It might not look so bad if you compared notes with somebody else over it.'

'Oh, it isn't *bad*,' said Dominic, opening his eyes wide. 'It's a bit difficult, but really, it'll be all right. Only it's important that I should have this evening free; truly it is. I'm sorry I mucked up the construe, I didn't have my mind on it.'

Chad looked at him silently and thoughtfully for what seemed a long time; and by the pricking of his thumbs he was warned that the child was most certainly up to something. No light employment, no mischief, no slender personal affair to be squared up in half an hour of getting round someone; but a serious undertaking. Nothing less could account for the odd, withdrawn look of the hazel eyes, which regarded him from beyond an impassable barrier of responsibility. A look at once calm and desperate, resolved and appealing. 'I'd like awfully to tell you,' said the eyes, 'but I can't, so don't ask me. I've got to do this myself.' And deep within all the other expressions they held was a bright, still excitement which made him very uneasy.

'You'd rather I didn't pursue the subject. Well, I can't press you to tell me, if you don't want to. But at least remember, Dom,' he said, suddenly flicking a petal of colour into Dominic's cheeks with the unexpected use of his name, 'that there's no need for you to look far for help, if you do want it. If it's something you don't want to take home – well, even beaks are capable of listening to something more important than Virgil, on occasion. I hope you'd feel you could come to me, if ever you did need a second judgment.'

Dominic, pink to the temples, but remarkably composed, said, 'Thanks awfully sir! Only I can't – not yet.'

'All right, leave it at that. You can go back to your desk.'

Somehow the probing of that level, illusionless voice, and its unexpected kindness, had shaken Dominic's peace of mind, making him turn and look more closely at what he was doing; and he was a little frightened at what he saw, but it was fright without the possibility of retreat. He had started the thing already, and it would have to run.

When he was released from school he ran nearly all the way back into the village, and caught Pussy just biking into the yard of the 'Shock of Hay', wobbling across the dipping threshold with her eyes alert along the road for him. They retired to the loft, which was their usual conference hall when the cooler weather came; and before he was well out of the trap-door and into the straw beside her, Dominic had her by the arm in a hard, sudden grip which made her stare at him in astonishment. Pussy saw the excitement, too, and glimpsed, but did not recognise, the desperation. She asked promptly: 'What on earth's the matter? What's going on?'

'Listen! I've got to go, awfully quickly, so listen seriously and don't make any mistakes. There's something you've got to do for me, do you understand? *Got* to! If you muff it, goodness knows what will happen.'

'I'm no more likely to muff things than you are,' she said, the hackles of her pride rising instantly. 'Have I ever let you down? Have I?'

'No, you never have. You've always been fine. And listen, this is the most vital thing you ever did for me, and there's nobody in it but just us two. So you can see how I'm trusting you.'

'Well, and you know you can. Is it something about the case, Dom? Have you found out something?'

'I don't know – I think so, but I don't know. It may turn out wrong, that's what we have to test. I'm taking a chance on something, and you've got to work this end of it, and you've got to work it right, or I shall be in a spot. And not only me, because everything may come unstuck, and then we'll be back where we started, or even worse off. So make absolutely sure for me, Pussy, *please*!'

'You don't have to go on about it,' she said with spirit. 'Just tell me what I've got to do, I won't make a mess of it.'

Bright and feverish, his eyes gleamed yellowly in the shadows, burning on her with a frightening light. His hand kept its slightly convulsive hold of her arm. She had never seen him like this before, not even when they found Helmut in the brook.

'You know where the top lane from the station comes up to the gate into the Harrow grounds? The one among the plantations? You've got to get hold of my father, tonight, and make him go there with you. Cooke or Weaver, too, if you can get them, but there must be my father, and some other witness, too. You've got to get them into hiding in the wood there, near the gate, where they can hear and follow if anyone comes along the path, and you must have them there before nine o'clock. That's vital. I shall come along there just after nine. I want my father to hear and see everything that goes on, and keep pretty close to me. Is that quite clear?'

'Clear enough! But is that all? What happens then?'

'Nobody knows that yet, idiot!' Dominic's nerves were a little ragged, and his manners frayed with them; but for once Pussy did not combat the issue. 'That's what we've got to find out. That's what my father's got to be absolutely sure to see. You've got to keep him quiet until something does happen, and you've absolutely got to keep him within earshot of us, or I'm wasting my time.'

'But how am I going to do it? What am I to say to him, to make him take me seriously? He may be busy. He may not listen to me.'

'Tell him I'm on to something important. Tell him I'm in a jam – I probably shall be by then,' said Dominic. 'If he doesn't believe I've got anything for him, maybe he'll believe I've got myself into a mess, anyhow, trying. But it's your job. I don't care what you tell him, provided you get him there. Now I've got to go,' he said, wriggling through the straw with a dry rustling, 'but Pussy, please, for Pete's sake don't let me down. I'm relying on you.' He slid his long legs through the trap, and his foot ground on the rungs of the ladder.

Pussy clawed at his sleeve. 'No, wait, Dom! It's something dangerous you're doing – isn't it?'

'I don't know – I keep telling you, I just don't know what will happen. It may be!'

'Why not tell him about it, instead of just dragging him about by guesswork in the dark? Wouldn't it be better ? Tell him, and let him help properly, instead of being blindfolded. Think how much better and safer it would be!'

'Oh, don't be a fool!' said Dominic ill-temperedly. 'If I told him, there wouldn't *be* any experiment. He'd never let me try it. All I'd get would be a flea in my ear, and we'd be no farther forward. And this is something I've started already – if he made me give it up we'd be wasting everything we've done. That's why I've got to go off tonight and give the thing a push without Dad knowing anything about it. And that's why you've got to look after his end of it, after I'm gone. Do talk sense! This is something the police couldn't do, it wouldn't be right for them. But *I* can! And then they've *got* to help me finish it, because it's the only way of getting me out of the mess.' He ended a little breathlessly, and the sick shining of his eyes scared her.

'But can't you tell *me*? I could be more use if I knew what you were doing. If anything goes wrong, I shan't know what to do, because I don't know what you want. I shan't even know, perhaps, if something does go wrong. And suppose your father wants you at home tonight? How can you make a good enough reason for not doing what he wants? It's all so sloppy!' said Pussy helplessly. 'A lot of dangling strings!'

'No, it isn't. I'm going to gobble my tea and be out before my father comes home. I'm not staying to ask any questions, or to answer any. Before nine o'clock I've got things to do. And if I'm right,' he said, shivering a little in excitement, so that the ladder creaked as he stepped lower, 'you'll all know what to do. And if I'm wrong, it won't matter, I'll have made such a mess of everything, nothing can make it any worse.'

Watching him sink slowly through the floor, like a demon in a pantomime, resolutely drawing away from her and leaving her with all the weight of his project in her hands and none of the fun, she began to protest further, and then stopped, because there was nothing more to say. She would do as he asked, no matter how it enraged her to be treated in this fashion, because heaven knew what mess he would get himself into if she did not. And there would be time afterwards to take it out of him for hogging his secret.

'I can't stay any longer,' he said vanishing, 'or I'd tell you everything, honestly. You'll know by tonight. Don't be late!'

'We'll be there,' said Pussy, flatly and finally, and slithered after him down the ladder.

Dominic hurried home, by the same road which Charles Blunden's funeral had taken that morning, on its way to the church. It had been a long funeral, the biggest Comerford had seen for years. The coffin had been hidden under the mass of the old man's white and gold and purple flowers.

Chapter 9

Babes in the Wood

I

Chad Wedderburn hesitated until nearly eight o'clock, but he went in the end.

The remembrance of Dominic's overburdened eyes had haunted him all through the marking of two batches of homework, and made a small counter-circling pool of uneasiness on the borders of his own taut and isolated disquiet. He knew he was letting things go, lying down and letting events run over him, because he was sick of himself and his unsloughable memories; and because where one hope – but had it ever reached the stage of real hope? – had blotted out all lesser and more accessible consolations, and remained itself forever out of reach, there was no longer any inducement to stand upright, or any point in fighting back. He resented his own bitter acquiescence, but it was logical, and he could not stir himself out of it. He had suffered, whether by his own fault or the mismanagement of others, injuries to his nature which unfitted him for loving or being loved by an innocent like Io; and only the artificial stimulus of rivalry with Charles had ever made him quicken to the possibility of so happy and normal a relationship, exult in what seemed to be hopes, and sulk over what seemed to be reverses. Only seemed to be. With the stimulus withdraw, the thing was seen to be still a simple and irrevocable impossibility. But surely poor Charles didn't have to get killed to show him that.

He knew, none better, that they were already saying he had killed Charles. With all the acquired stoicism of six years of warfare, he found himself still capable of unpractised emotions not so easy to contain as pain, exhaustion and fear had proved; and he supposed there was little Comerford did not know about his feelings for Io Hart. Busily misinterpreting what they knew, they had made him a murderer, because he was a dog with a renowned name, which the spiral courses of history were about to use to hang him. He had, had he not, been a great killer in his day?

So he let fall out of his hands every intention of defending himself. For what? There remained a certain interest in watching the events which moved in on him, but no point whatever in caring about the issue.

Yet other people went on existing, side by side with him in the world, with a certain intermittent warmth and poignancy which still troubled him. Especially when they looked at him with harried, adventurous young eyes like Dominic's, and reluctantly declined to confide in him. Another human being taking large and probably disastrous decisions, too early and too anxiously, perhaps mutilating himself before he was even whole. And because one had resigned all responsibility for one's own fate, did it follow that one could not care for his?

He hesitated a long time, but he went in the end. Down to the village, among the covert, regretful, fascinated eyes, and knocked at the door of the police-station, and asked for George. He wondered if the three youths passing with their girls believed that he was in the act of giving himself up. More than likely they did.

Bunty was surprised to see him. She stood the door wide, and asked him into the office, to close the door on the chill of the evening. He thought how very like her son was to her, even to the tilt of the head and the disconcertingly straight eyes.

'I'm sorry, but George is out at the moment. He's been gone ever since mid-afternoon, and told me he might be late getting home.' She smiled at him, rather wryly. 'I don't even know where he is. I haven't seen much of him myself, lately. Is it something urgent?'

'Well, I hardly know. It isn't business exactly, I only wanted to talk to him about Dominic. But since he's already out of reach, I dare say tomorrow will do as well.'

Bunty, looking intensely serious in a moment, asked: 'Dom isn't in any trouble, is he? He hasn't been getting himself into any bad scrape?'

'Not any scrape at all that I know of. Don't worry, it's nothing like that. Just that I think it might be useful if your husband and I compared notes about him. He's a nice kid, and got more gumption than most of his age. But perhaps he's reached a difficult stage of development rather early.'

It sounded portentous, but Bunty seemed to understand better than the turn of phrase had deserved. Her eyes lit much as Dominic's did when his partisan interest was kindled. 'Yes, hasn't he?' she said, and bit her lips upon a slightly guilty smile, remembering how little respect she had paid to his budding manhood when her dander was up, and with how little subtlety she had approached his new complexities. Good old Dom, the first really adult quality he had acquired had been an ability to humour his elders and make allowances for them. 'Have you been having trouble with him? He likes you, you know, and that's the first essential for being able to manage him.'

A slow, dark flush mounted Chad's lean cheeks as he looked at her. She found it astonishing and touching that the mention of a child's liking for him could make him colour so painfully. He must be awfully short of compensations to make so much of so small a one.

'I'm glad! I like him, too, and by and large, the sort of

trouble he gives me is the most encouraging kind. No, I'm only concerned, probably quite unnecessarily, with Dom's own state of mind. Isn't there something weighing a bit heavily on him, just lately?'

Bunty hesitated, for they were approaching a subject which had thorns wherever one touched it. 'Well, of course, he's been thinking far too much about this Schauffler case, but that was hardly avoidable, since he found the body. But naturally we've been keeping an eye on him, and I can't say I've thought there was much wrong with his reactions. One can't just forget a thing like that, but there's nothing morbid about Dom.'

'Good God, no! I never meant to suggest it. No, he hasn't an ounce of humbug in him, I'm sure of that. I was thinking of something much more positive and active. Are you sure he's not up to something on his own? By the way, where is he now?'

'He went out, immediately after tea.' Her eyes widened in suspicion and apprehension. 'He was very quick and very quiet, but so he often is. He didn't stop to do his homework first, as he usually does, but that happens, too, when he has something on. And I've never asked questions, it's never been necessary, and I'm not going to start now. You don't think he's up to anything really hare-brained?'

'Never quite that,' said Chad, and smiled, and was glad to see her smile in response.

'That's awfully nice of you. He *is* a capable boy, I know that. But we might not think exactly alike about what's crazy and what isn't. You see, trusting him and leaving him his privacy has been easy while he stayed transparent and calculable – maybe not so much of a gesture, after all, because we often didn't need to ask, we could see for ourselves. But now he isn't quite transparent, even though I think he's as honest as ever he was. And he isn't, he certainly isn't, quite calculable. That's when the pinch comes.'

'I may be thinking more of it than it really is,' said Chad, 'and troubling you with what amounts to nothing. It's only today he's been in this peculiar state, so one can hardly blame Schauffler for it. It may even be some odd score he's got to settle with some other boy, only he seemed to be taking it very seriously. All today he's been miles from school, working out something which did seem rather to be giving him trouble. I wondered if between us we couldn't find out a little more about it, without treading too heavily on his toes.'

'There was the bad business of Charles Blunden,' said Bunty carefully. 'That was rather on his mind, because – ' She remembered in time that the adjourned inquest had so far produced only evidence of identification, that Dominic's last meeting with Charles, and the queer confidence it had produced, were known to no one except herself, the police, and the boy. Maybe Dom had stretched his promise of secrecy so far as to admit Pussy, who was half himself, but she was sure he had extended it to no one else; and it was not for her to publish it to Chad Wedderburn, whatever she believed of him. 'But I'd swear he was all right,' she said, 'when he went off this morning. I wish I'd paid more attention to him at tea, but there was nothing particularly odd about him being silent and a little abstracted.'

'Of course not! I had different opportunities. In the middle of the Æneid, Book Eight,' he said with a fleeting smile, 'one is apt to notice complete absence of mind. Especially in the intelligent. The middle of tea is rather another matter.'

Bunty, looking uneasily at the clock, said: 'With all his home-work still to do, he ought to be thinking of coming back by now. Usually he does it first.'

'You don't know where he's gone?'

'No, I rather took it for granted it was down to the 'Shock of Hay' to pick up Pussy for some project or other. I thought maybe they needed what was left of the daylight, hence the hurry. Now I don't know what to think.'

'Go on thinking the same,' said Chad, 'and I'll go and see if he's down there. But I think I ought to apologise in advance for scaring you for nothing. We're all a shade jumpy, maybe it's affected my judgment.'

She was nevertheless deeply aware that it had taken some very strong uneasiness to send him down here tonight on this or any other errand. It might prove baseless, but it had been profoundly felt, and since it was on Dominic's account she warmed to him for it. 'Hadn't I better come down with you, and make sure?'

'Had you better? If he's harmlessly fooling around there with Pussy and their gang, it might be a little galling – '

Bunty thought deeply, and smiled, and said: 'You're very right. He'll hardly suspect you of coming along simply to reassure yourself he isn't in mischief, but I couldn't get by so easily. All right, I'll wait. No doubt he'll come blithely in when it suits him, or when he's hungry. No, I couldn't make a fool of him in front of Pussy, of course.'

'I'll come back this way, and let you know. But I'm sure it will be all right.'

That, he thought and she thought, as the door closed between them, is precisely what one says when one is by no means sure of any such matter. The street-lamp just outside the police-station shone on him briefly through the near-darkness, which in unlit places would still be scarcely more than dusk. A small, slender figure, coming at a run, butted head-down into his middle, and being steadied from the impact, gave a gasp of relief, and called him Sergeant Felse. He held her off, and recognised Pussy. She had a certain fixed and resolute look about her which fingered the same sore place Dominic's eyes had left in his consciousness. He said: 'Hullo, where are you off to in such a hurry? What's the matter?'

'Oh, it's you, Mr. Wedderburn,' said Pussy, damped but well-disposed. 'I thought you were Dom's father. I've got to see him.'

'Bad luck! I came on the same errand. He's out, and he won't be back till late.'

Pussy, with her hand already reaching out for the latch of the gate, stopped dead, and stared up at him with large green eyes of horror. 'He's out?' she echoed in a shrill whisper. 'Where? Where could I find him?'

'I doubt very much if you can. Mrs. Felse doesn't know where he is, only that he's been gone since this afternoon, and told her not to expect him back until late tonight. Why, what's the matter?'

'But what am I going to do?' she demanded in dismay. 'I've got to find him.' She pushed headlong at the gate, for a moment intent on bursting in to pour out the story to Bunty, since George was missing, and somebody had to take action. Then she closed it again, and stood chewing her underlip and thinking more deeply. No, it wouldn't do. She couldn't frighten his mother until she knew there was reason. The last time had been bad enough. 'Is Weaver in there? Or even Cooke, but Weaver would be better.'

'No, there's no one but Mrs. Felse.'

'Oh, hell!' said Pussy roundly. 'And they might be just anywhere!'

'No doubt they could be found, if it's as bad as that. And why won't Mrs. Felse do?'

'She – well, she's a woman,' said Pussy in sufficient explanation. 'I can't go scaring her, and anyhow there's nothing she could do. I need *men*. And I haven't got time to look for them.' Her voice grew deeper and gruffer in desperation, instead of shrilling. 'I need them now, at once. I was relying on Sergeant Felse. I left it as late as I dared, so he wouldn't have too much time to think. I was dead sure of finding him at home. He ought to have been home long before now. What on earth am I going to do?'

For answer, Chad took her by the arm, and turned her firmly about, and began to march her towards the distant lights of the 'Shock of Hay'. 'Come on, if it's as bad as that, you can walk

260

and talk at the same time. You're going home, and on the way you're going to tell me what this is all about.'

Not unwillingly trotting alongside, she uttered breathlessly: 'But I can't – it isn't my secret, I can't just tell anyone.'

'Don't be finicky! You want men, and I'm the nearest. In the bar no doubt we can find more, if you can convince me by then that you seriously need them. So go ahead, and tell me the whole story. Where's Dominic?'

She began to tell him, half-walking and half-running at his side in the dark, gratefully anchored by his large, firm hand. She had disliked the whole business from the beginning, as she disliked and distrusted any plan of which she possessed only half the essential outline; and now that it came to the point, she was glad to pour it out to him, glad of his unexclaiming quietness and terse questions, glad of the speed he was making with her, though it left her gasping; and more glad than ever of his procedure on arrival. For he released her arm at the main door, shepherded her by one shoulder straight through the bar, where she was not allowed to go, walked up to Io without hesitation, and said:

'Come through into the kitchen, please, Io. There's something bad afoot, we need five minutes' thinking.'

Io pushed a draught Bass across the bar, scooped in a half-crown, and automatically dispensed change, without any alteration of her expression. She raised her eyes to his face suddenly, their rich brown a little stunned and misty with bewilderment, but large and calm, and ready to light up with pleasure. He had just shouldered his way clean through something which had hung between them for so long that she had almost forgotten how he looked when he was not obscured by it. She did not feel the eyes of every soul in the bar converging upon them, with a weight of speculation which would have hurt her only ten minutes ago. She was not aware of the sudden silence, and the equally sudden discretion of voices veiling it, rather too quickly, rather too obviously. She did not stop to argue, but did

261

exactly as he asked her; she had been ready to do exactly as he asked her for quite a long time, and the real trouble had been that he had never asked her. She turned, and flashed through the rear door, holding it open for him to follow; and the surprising creature, turning to run a critical eye over the whole company assembled in the bar, singled out Jim Tugg as the most potentially useful and the most proof against astonishment, and jerked an abrupt head at him to join the conference in the kitchen.

'Lend us a hand on a job, Jim?'

Jim left off leaning on the corner of the bar, and hitched his muscular length deliberately after them, the collie padding at his heel soundlessly. The men of Comerford, glasses suspended in forgetful hands, watched his dark, shut face pass by them, going where Chad Wedderburn called him, uncommitted, apparently incurious, certainly unsurprised. They fell silent again, their eyes following him until the door closed between. Joe, rolling back from the snug with an empty tray, looked them all over and asked blankly: 'Who's been through? The Pied Piper?'

When they told him, he shrugged his wide shoulders, and went on drawing beer. He was at sea already with Io; better to keep his fingers crossed and leave her alone.

In the kitchen Io turned on Chad and Pussy wide-eyed. 'What is it? What's the matter? Where did you find her, Chad, and what's wrong with her?'

Chad looked at the clock; it was twenty-five minutes to nine. He looked down at Pussy, whose green eyes were blazing again hopefully, almost gleefully. 'Now, then! Get your breath back, and tell all that tale again in less than five minutes. No interruptions, there isn't time. If you or he are pulling our legs, look out afterwards, that's all. But now, we're listening!'

Pussy recounted in rather less than three minutes the instructions she had received from Dominic, and the way he had looked and acted at that interview. Io and Jim kept their eyes on her throughout the recital, but Chad's were on Io, and when Pussy's breath and facts gave out together Io seemed to feel the compulsion of his glance, for she looked directly up at him, and both of them smiled. A rather anxious, grave, and yet very peaceful smile, confirming, where there was no time for more, that while what was about to happen was extremely uncertain, what had just happened was the most certain thing in the world, and neither accident nor mistake.

'Well, what's the verdict?' asked Chad.

'We must go, of course,' said Io. 'I don't say he's really on to anything important, but almost certainly he's going to be in some sort of trouble if we don't fish him out of it. Either way, he needs rescuing.'

Jim said: 'What is there to lose? If the kid's father isn't here to lug him out of mischief, somebody else better take over. All the more if there's more to it than mischief.'

'There is,' said Pussy earnestly. 'I tell you, he's dead serious. I think he was a bit scared, really, but he's got some clue, I'm sure he has. Let's go, quickly! There's only just time.'

They slid out from the scullery door to the yard, Io clawing a coat from the hooks in the passage as she went. It was the mackintosh she wore when feeding the hens, but she didn't care. And suddenly in the half-lit scullery Chad turned and caught her hand restrainingly as she struggled into it.

'No need for you to come, Io. Stay here! We shall come back.'

'What do you take me for?' she demanded indignantly, and remained at his shoulder as they scurried across the yard. 'This may be something real – have you thought of that? You know Dom. He isn't a fool. He doesn't go off at half-cock.'

'Yes, I've thought of it. So go back and help your old man, and take Pussy with you. Who's going to look after the bar if you quit?'

'Damn the bar!' said Io. 'If Pussy and I stay behind, who's going to look after you?'

263

II

Dominic went up the last fifty yards of dark birch-coppice with his heart bumping so heavily that it seemed to him its impact against his ribs must be clearly audible a long way ahead, like a clock with an enormous tick. If it went on like this, it would be difficult to talk. He tried to restrain its leaping, breathing deeply and slowly, clenching his hands and bracing his muscles to struggle with the pulse that shook him. It was ten minutes to nine. He had just seen the smoke of the train, a pallid streak along the line with a minute rosy glow at its forward end, proceeding steadily in the direction of Fressington. It would take the old man the full ten minutes to walk up the lanes from the station and reach his forest gate. So Dominic had time to think, and time to breathe slowly.

He came to the gate and waited there. Behind him the absolute dark of the first belt of conifers, beyond which the older mixed woods began; but in both, darkness enough, only the wide drive making a perceptible band of pallor until it lost itself among the trees. Very close to the pathway the bushes and trees leaned. He thought of them, and felt comforted. Before him, across the green track, the clumsy, crumpled mounds, half-clothed in furze and broom and heather, blundering away into a muddle of birch trees once more. On his left, the winding lane dipping down into the meadows and coiling to the station; and on this side it seemed almost light by comparison with the blackness of the firs within the Harrow fence. On his right, grass-tracks meandering to the bowl of the well, autumnally filled now with coppery ochre-slime and stained, iridescent water.

Dominic's feet were caked to the ankle, and felt too heavy to lift. He groped along the dark ground for a broken end of stick, and began to clean the worst accumulations from under the waists of his shoes. The little notebook he was clutching, still damp to the touch, and soil-coloured almost to invisibility in the last remains of the light, could hardly suffer by such smears as found their way to its covers. It was already a disintegrating mess. But he had better keep his face and hand fairly presentable. The former he scrubbed energetically with his handkerchief, the latter he rubbed even more vigorously on the seat of his flannels. The moist October night settled deeper about him, an almost tangible silence draping his mind like cobweb, when his wits had to be so piercingly clear. He pulled the little torch out of his pocket, and tried the beam of it. Not too big a light, not so bright that it made vision easy even when held to the page. The faint, faded ink-marks in the book, widened and paled by soaking in water, sunk into the swollen texture of the pulpy leaves, winked and seemed to change and shift under the light, sometimes to vanish altogether with his intent staring. But here and there a word could be read, and here and there a column of figures, conveying its general significance but not its details.

Down the lane from the station there began the sound of footsteps, heavy but fairly swift, though the old man was climbing a decided slope. Presently there was a bulky, in-crescent shape vaguely discernible against the sky, gradually lengthening to a man's full height; and Selwyn Blunden, puffing grampus-like, and leaning heavily on his stick, came labouring to the gate.

'Hullo, young man! So there you are! Afraid I'm late. Confounded train behind time, as usual. I hope you haven't been waiting long?'

'Oh, no, only a few minutes. I saw the train pulling out.'

'Well, shall we go on up to the house? We can't do anything here in the dark. You've brought this little book that's been worrying you so much, have you?' He put a hand to the latch of the gate, and his walking-stick knocked woodenly against the bars as he led the way through. Dominic followed, but rather slowly, with some appearance of reluctance, and closed the gate after him with a flat clapper-note of the latch which echoed through the bushes. Straining his ears, he thought how deathly silent it was after the sound, and his heart made a sick fluttering in him. 'What's the matter?' said Blunden, wheeling to look at him with close, stooping head, in the darkness where the small shape was only another movement of shadow. 'You have brought it, haven't you?'

'Oh, yes, look, here it is. But – couldn't you look at it here? I was only a bit worried – I don't want to be too late getting home, and if we go right up to the house won't it take us rather a long time? My mother – '

A large hand behind his shoulders propelled him gently but firmly forward. 'That's all right, we won't give your mother any reason to complain this time. I'll take you home in the car afterwards. Mustn't get you into trouble for trying to be helpful, must we? But I'm not a cat, laddie, and I can't see in the dark. Come on up to the house like a good lad, and let's have a real good look at your find.'

Dominic went where he was led, but walked no faster than he had to. He kept silence for a minute as they walked, and the black, coniferous darkness closed behind them like another gate. He listened, stretching his senses until he could imagine all manner of sounds without hearing one; and then he thought there was the lightest and softest of rustling steps, somewhere alongside them in the bushes, and then an owl called, some- where apparently in the distance, with a wonderfully detached, undisturbing note. But he was aware by a sudden quivering of the nerves that it was not distant, and not an owl. He held his breath in apprehension that what was perceptible to him should also be obvious to the old man; but the heavy tread never halted.

Dominic drew a deep breath and felt better. Someone, at any rate, had kept the tryst. He ought to have known; he ought to have trusted Pussy, she never let him down, never once. He clutched the little book, braced his shoulders, and said firmly: 'I'd better tell you about it, sir.' His voice sounded clearly in the arching of the trees, a light thread through the darkness.

'Look, you can see from the look of it why it took me a long time to make anything of it.' The beam of the torch, shaken by his walking, wobbled tantalisingly upon the sodden greyish covers with their stains of ochre. 'It was the day before yesterday, when we were coming up from the Comer and crossing by Webster's well there, and you know it's an awful mess now, after the rain. We were fooling around, ever so many of us, and I found this right in one of the holes in the clay by the brook there. It must have been there some time, and I should have thrown it away again, only, you know, for the murder. But we all used to hope we'd find something that would be a clue.'

'Every boy his own Dick Barton,' said Blunden, with a laugh that boomed among the trees; and he patted Dominic with a pleased hand. 'Very natural, especially in the police-sergeant's son, eh? Well, so you showed it around, I suppose, among you?'

'No, I kept it just to myself,' said Dominic. 'I don't know exactly why. I just did.'

'Why didn't you give it to your father, right away?'

Dominic wriggled and admitted reluctantly: 'Well, I should have, only – the last time I tried to help, there was an awful row. My father was awfully mad at me, and told me not to interfere again. He didn't like me being in it at all. And I didn't want to get into more trouble, so I tried to make it out by myself, this time, at least until I could be sure I'd really got something. And I just couldn't, though I'd cleaned it up all I could. But honestly, I didn't like to risk showing him until I was sure. Most of the time I didn't think it was anything, really,' he confessed, 'only it just *could* be, you see. So then when you were so decent this morning, I thought perhaps if you could read German – and you could!'

'Could and can, old man, so we'll soon settle it one way or the other. How much did you find out on your own? This is very interesting – and damned enterprising, I must say!'

'Well,' said Dominic, slowly and clearly, 'it's got a lot of dates in it, and some columns of figures, though you can't make out just what they are, at least not often. It looks like somebody's accounts, and a sort of diary, and it *is* German, honestly it is. Look, you can see here!' He stopped, the better to steady the light upon the warped and faded page, and the old man bent his head into the glow beside his, to peer closely, and shut one hand on the nearer side of the book; but somehow Dominic's hand was interposed, and kept its closer hold.

'Look, that's a German word, you can read that – it's the German word for machine. That's funny isn't it? And look here, again – ' he pulled himself up suddenly from a skid into enthusiasm, moving on again slowly from under the massive bulk of the old man.

Softly in the dark Blunden said, behind him, over him: 'But, my dear boy, you're perfectly right, it *is* German. No doubt about it. Now what do you make of that?'

'Well, you see, it's just that it was found *there* – where we found him. And *he* was German. I know it seems far-fetched, but I do sort of wonder if it can have fallen out of his pocket somehow. And at the inquest it came out how very careful he was, and kept records of everything he did, almost, even his washing and mending. Only there was quite a lot of money without any records. And in here, look, there's what seems to be something about money. Columns of figures, and everything. Could it be, do you think, that he was just as careful about that extra money he had, only it was a bit shady where he got it, and so he kept it in a separate book? You do see, don't you, how it would sort of make sense?'

'Oh, yes, I quite see that!' said the old voice softly, humouring him. A sudden hand reached out again for the book. 'Let me see it closer! Of course, I don't want you to be disappointed, after so much ingenuity, but much better settle it quickly.'

Dominic held on to it, bending the torch upon its pages industriously, and frowning over the unfamiliar syllables. When the hand would have touched, he stopped abruptly, the better to study the inside cover. 'Just a minute, sir! It's funny – a trick of the light, I suppose – there's something here I've tried and tried to make out, even in a good light, and now, all of a sudden – '

'Let me see! Perhaps I can tell you.' He came nearer. Dominic hesitated, and backed a step, looking up at him oddly. 'Well, come on, child! You brought it for me to see, didn't you?'

The torch went out, and left them a moment in the dark, the velvet-black night between the trees extinguishing faces and voices. The wind sighed a little in the bushes, and somewhere on the left a twig cracked, but softly, moistly in the damp undergrowth. When the tiny beam erupted again, glow-worm-like, they were three yards apart, and the small, upturned face, lit from under the chin and very faintly, was an awestruck mask with hollow, staring eyes.

'I think, sir,' he said in a pinched voice, 'I ought to go straight home now. If you don't awfully mind.'

'Go home? After coming all up here for a special purpose, go home with nothing done? Nonsense, child! There's no hurry, you'll be home just as quickly in the car.' And the big body, powerful and silent, leaned nearer, seemed to Dominic's fascinated eyes simply to be nearer, without a sound or a movement. He backed away by inches, trying to keep the distance between them intact. The hands of the bushes, sudden and frightening, clawed at his back; he did not know quite how he had been deflected into them, but they were there, nudging him. He felt sick, but he was used to that, it happened in every crisis, and he was growing out of it gradually and learning to control it.

'Yes, sir, but – It's very good of you, but I ought to go straight back to my father. I ought not to wait. And there isn't any need for me to bother you now, I've just found what we needed. It's quite all right now, thank you. So if you really don't mind – '

The darkness round his little glow-worm of light confused him. He was trying to stay steadily between Blunden and the gate, now perhaps a hundred yards behind them; but somehow in his anxiety to keep his face to the old man he had allowed himself to be edged round into the rim of the drive, into the undergrowth; and now he had no sense of direction at all, he was just marooned on a floating island of inadequate light in a sea of dark. He knew he would see better if he switched the torch off, but he knew he must not do it. Other people, mere whispers in the bushes – and how if they were only owls and badgers, after all? – they had to see, too; they had to see everything.

'And what,' said the old man softly, 'what have you found? What is this magic word that settles everything? Show me!' And the ambling, massy darkness of him below the shoulders shifted suddenly, and he was nearer, was within touch. Something else moved, too, from, left hand to right; the walking-stick on which he had leaned so heavily, so ageingly, since Charles was killed. He was not leaning on it now, his back was not sagging, the stoop of his head was a panther's stoop from muscular, resilient shoulders. Dominic felt behind him, and was lacerated with holly spines.

'It's his name,' he said in a little, quaking voice which longed rather to shriek for George than to pursue this any farther. 'I tried and tried, and couldn't read it before, but it *is* his name, Helmut Schauffler – So it's all right, isn't it? I must go quickly, and give it to my father. It was very kind of you to help me, but I've got to go and find him at once – '

'Pretty superhuman of you,' said the old man's voice heartily, 'not to have shown it to someone long before this. Didn't you? Not even to some of the other boys?'

'No, honestly I didn't.'

'Not to anyone at all?' The hand that held the stick tightened its fingers; he saw the long line of descending darkness in the darkness lift and quiver, and that was all the warning he had.

'No, nobody but you!'

Then he gathered himself, as if the words had been the release of a spring, and leaped a yard to his right, stooping his head low, the light of the torch plunging madly as he jumped. He saw only a confusion of looming, heavy face, immense bristling moustache, exaggerated cheeks, set teeth and braced muscles steadying the blow, and two bright, firm, matter-of-fact blue eyes that terrified him more than all the rest, because they were not angry, but only practically intent on seeing him efficiently silenced. He saw a dark, hissing flash which must have been the stick descending, and felt it fall heavily but harmlessly on his left arm below the shoulder, at an angle which slid it down his sleeve almost unchecked, to crash through the holly branches and thud into the ground. Then his nerve gave way, and he clawed his way round into the line of the drive, and ran, and ran, dangling his numbed left arm, with the heavy feet pounding fast behind him. He threw the little book away, and the torch after it, and plunging aside into the bushes, tore a way through them into somebody's arms.

He didn't know what was happening, and was too stunned to attempt to follow the sounds he heard, though he knew that someone had screamed, and was dimly and rather pleasurably aware that it had not been with his voice. Confused impressions of a great many people erupting darkly from both sides of the drive cleared slowly into a sharper awareness. Voices regained their individuality. Pussy had screamed, and he thought he had heard his father's tones in a sudden sharp shout, and then after the crashing of branches and thudding of feet and gasping and grunting of struggle, a heavy fall. He didn't care much. He was satisfied to be alive, and held with a sort of relentless gentleness hard against a big, hard body, into whose shoulder he ground his face, sobbing dryly, and past caring who heard him.

'All right, all right, son!' Jim Tugg was saying in his ear. 'We was by you all the time. If you'd held still I had me hands on you, all ready to lug you backwards out of harm's way. Never mind, fine you did it your own way. All over now bar the shouting!'

There wasn't much shouting. It had gone very quiet. Dominic drew calming breaths that seemed to be dragged right down to his toes. 'Did they get him? Is it all right?' he managed between gulps.

'We've got him all right. Don't you worry!'

So presently he took his face out of Jim's shoulder, and looked. Several torches had appeared in a random ring of light about the torn holly-bushes and the scuffled patch of gravel in the drive. Chad Wedderburn and Constable Weaver were holding Selwyn Blunden by the arms, but though all his muscles heaved a little in bewilderment against the restraint, he was not struggling. His big head had settled like a sleeping owl's, deep into the hunched shoulders, and his face had sagged into a dead, doughy stillness; but the blue, icy eyes which stared hard at Dominic out of this flabby mask were very much alive. They had not hated him before, because he had been only a slight bump in the roadway, but they hated him now because he was the barrier into which a whole life had crashed and shattered. He stared back, and suddenly, though he couldn't be ashamed, he couldn't be proud either. He blinked at the rest of them, at Io just starting towards him a step or two in impulsive tenderness, with Pussy in her arms; at his father just picking up the fallen walking-stick in his handkerchief, hurriedly and without due reverence because his mind was on something else, and thrusting that, too, into Io's hands. It wasn't all over bar the shouting, at all; it had only just begun, and it was he who had begun it. He'd had to, hadn't he? There wasn't anything else to be done. But he turned his face into Jim Tugg's patient sleeve, and said:

'I want my father! I want to go home!'

George was by him already, lifting him out of Jim's arms as by right, hugging him, feeling him all over for breaks and bruises, and finding nothing gravely wrong. George was an inspired comforter. Jim Tugg heard him, and grinned. Dominic heard him, and came to earth with a fine corrective bump that braced his nerves and stiffened his pride indignantly, and did him more good just then than all the sympathy in the world.

Having satisfied himself that his son was not a whit the worse, and still holding him tightly:

'You bat-brained little hellion!' said George feelingly. 'Just wait till I get you home!'

III

When they really did get him home, of course, they wanted to put him to bed and keep him quiet, and not let him do any talking until next day. Pussy and Io went straight into the kitchen with him, while the others shut themselves into the office, and presently telephones rang, and cars came and went. Dominic was preoccupied with more immediate things, little ordinary things the charm of which he had not noticed so clearly for a long time, like the coolness of Bunty's bare arms when she hugged him, and the rough place on her finger where she always pricked it when she sewed, and the skin on top of very creamy cocoa, and the worn place on his favourite velvet cushion. He had been so abstracted at tea that he had eaten scarcely anything, and now he was hungry. Bunty fed him, and didn't ask him any questions. She didn't know the half yet, but it was scarcely even late, and he was home, and safe, and apparently in some obscure fashion both a hero and a criminal. Since he was there within sight and touch of her, and eating his head off, Bunty forbore from either scolding or praising him, and waited without impatience for explanations. And when George and Chad came in, she got them at last in very fair order.

'He's away to Comerbourne,' said George, answering all the interrogatory eyes which turned upon him as soon as he entered the room. 'And the stick's gone with him. Plenty of work and fuss yet, but virtually, that's over.' He rubbed a hand over his forehead, and marvelled that he felt nothing of satisfaction, little of surprise, only a flatness and a weariness, such as come almost inevitably at the end of tensions. When the cord slackens, and there ought to be a joyous relief, there seems instead to be only a slightly sick indifference. But later things right themselves. You can get used to anything in time, even to the idea that Selwyn Blunden, J. P., the nearest thing to God around Comerford, is a murderer. He looked down at Dominic, half-immersed in cocoa, and said darkly: 'I ought to take the hide off you!'

But the tone was reassuring to Dominic's ears; he knew enough about parents to know that when they begin to talk about it as something they ought to do, the resolution necessary to the act has already left them. 'The stick!' he said, emerging from the mug with a creamy-brown moustache, 'I forgot about it! It was the one, wasn't it?' His face was beginning to melt from the slightly stunned immobility of shock to a rather painful excitement, with a patch of hectic rose on either cheek, and snapping yellow lights in his eyes. Bunty, having made room for everyone and given them all coffee, came and sat on the sofa beside him, and put a restraining hand on his arm. He liked the touch, and turned on her a brief, vague smile, but went back instantly to his question. 'It *was* the right one, wasn't it?'

'Not much doubt about it,' said George, eyeing him thoughtfully. 'The shield fits, even to the crumpled edge. The place has been stained over to match the rest, and very well done, too, but the holes are there to be seen, and the outline of the shape, too, in a good light. It's a ridged horn handle, well polished with use, but it has some very deep furrows. Even if it was washed in the outflow, there ought to be some traces to be found in those furrows.'

'And all this time,' said Io, staring fascinated, 'he just hid it by carrying it everywhere with him.'

'Can you think of a better way? And he didn't know actually that anyone was looking for it. The shield was never mentioned; it came too late for the inquest, and nothing was ever published about it even when it did turn up.'

'No, and in any case people had another new sensation then,' said Dominic, paling at the memory of Charles. 'But there are lots of things I still want to know – '

'Lots of things I want to know, too,' agreed George, 'but frankly, I think you've shot your bolt for tonight. It's time you and Pussy went to bed and slept it off. The urgent part's over, and well over. We can talk it out properly tomorrow.'

It was not their double grievous outcry that defeated him, but the resigned intercession of Bunty and Io, neither of whom saw any prospect of sleep for her charge if despatched to bed in this state. The crisis was too recently over. The echo of Pussy's enraged scream as she darted out of the bushes had scarcely ceased to vibrate in their ears, and Dominic was still shaking gently with excitement and erected nerves in Bunty's steadying arm. If he went to bed too soon he would probably wake up sweating with shock and leaping about in his bed to evade the fall of the terrible old man's loaded stick. If he talked himself into exhaustion and left nothing unsaid to breed, he would sleep without any dreams.

'Let him talk now,' said Bunty, smiling at George across the room. 'He'll be better.'

'I'm quite all right,' said Dominic indignantly. 'I was only scared at the time, and anyhow, who wouldn't be? But there's nothing the matter with me now. Only look, it isn't even my proper bedtime, quite – well, only just a little past it, anyhow.'

'All right,' said George, giving in, 'get it off your chest. I want to hear it quite as much as you want to tell it, but it wouldn't hurt for waiting a day. Still, go ahead! Tell me how you came to that performance tonight, and then I'll tell you what brought me to the same place. How soon did you start thinking in Blunden's direction, and what set you off on that tack?'

'Well, it was the dog,' said Dominic, frowning back into the past. 'I only started to get the hang of it today, really. I never thought of Mr. Blunden until this morning. I don't know why, but you know, he was sort of there like the rest of us, and yet not there. When we said everybody was in it, there were still people who weren't included in the everybody, and he was one of them. Until I saw the dog this morning, and I started to think, and I thought why shouldn't he be?'

He leaned back warmly into Bunty's shoulder; it was still rather nice, when he began remembering, to be sure that she was there. 'It was Charles dying when he did! It was almost the very minute he made up his mind to let the land be torn up, that's what made me think. One minute he'd won the appeal, you see, and he was going out shooting in the evening, all on good terms with himself and everybody; and the very next, almost, he was shot dead with his own gun in his own woods. And the only thing that happened in between was that he changed his mind about the land. He saw me, and told me, but that was just luck – nobody was supposed to know yet, he was just on his way home to tell his father. And then inside an hour he was dead. Well, I didn't think of it quite like that until today, because old Blunden still sort of wasn't there in the everybody who could have done it. But I did get to thinking awfully hard about the land, and it did seem, didn't it, that everything that happened round here was something to do with keeping that land from the coal people.'

'Everything? Previous events as well?' asked Chad, from the background.

'Yes, I think so. Only I know there were lots of other things about Helmut, he was just Helmut, almost anyone would have been glad to kill him. But even he fitted in, in a way, because, you see, it was Mr. Blunden who got him the job with the open-cast unit, and then all those things began to happen there, all the machines going wrong, and the excavator falling over the edge, and everything. And Helmut had lots of money that nobody knew anything about, odd-numbered notes that couldn't easily be traced. And though he wrote down everything, he hadn't kept any records to account for this extra money. Don't you remember, we all wondered what his racket could have been, because he wasn't known to have got into any of the usual ones? So there was he with lots of money, and the unit with lots of trouble, so much that they were thinking of dropping the claim on the Harrow land, and closing the site. And so when I just began to put everything together, today, all this fitted in, too, with the bit about the land. It looked to me as if Blunden had put Helmut into the job just to make it not worth their while to go on. I did tell you, I told Charles Blunden, Wilf Rogers on the site told me those accidents weren't accidents at all, but somebody pretty clever monkeying with the machines, only they couldn't get any real proof. You didn't listen much, I didn't much believe it myself, really, just because Wilf's an awful old liar. He *is* an awful old liar, only sometimes he tells the truth.'

Chad, staring down constrainedly at the notebook in his hand asked: 'You don't think – Charles was in on that deal, too?'

'No, I'm sure he couldn't have been. He might have backed up his old man in all the usual sorts of monkey business, you know, the legal ones. But I don't think his father would ever have let him in on anything like that, because he was – sort of honest. Even if he'd wanted to help, I don't believe he could have put it over.'

Chad's face warmed into a singularly sweet smile. He looked up at Dominic, and then beyond his shoulder to where Io sat on a hassock by the fire, with Pussy on the rug at her feet, coiled up and purring, the domestic pussy for once. 'Thanks Dom! No, I don't believe he could.'

'But according to this business of the stick,' said Jim Tugg abruptly, 'you're going to prove that Blunden skilled Schauffler. How does that fit in, if he'd put Schauffler in a position where he wanted him for his own purpose? He was doing the job all right, wasn't he? Then why kill him?'

'Yes, I know it does seem all wrong, until you think a bit further. You think what sort of a person Helmut was. And then, the pheasants, you see, they gave the show away. You know,' said

Dominic earnestly, turning his brilliant eyes on Jim, 'how it was with Helmut when he came to your place. First he was always as meek as milk, but as soon as he found his feet, and someone treated him well, he began to take advantage. Everybody who was decent to him he thought could easily be afraid of him, because he thought people were only decent because they were too feeble to be beastly.'

'That's hellish true!' said Jim. 'It was him to the life.'

'Well, of course, it was a bit different with old Blunden, because he knew from the start what Blunden wanted with him, and he wasn't being decent, particularly, he was just getting value for money. But if he hadn't got that hold over him, he thought he'd got a better. Just think how a man like Helmut would love it if he thought he'd got a local bigwig like Blunden just where he wanted him! It wasn't only the birds he could poach, or the money he could get out of him, but the pleasure of being able to swagger about Blunden's land as he liked, and if the old man tackled him about it, well, he'd only got to sneer in his face, and say, one word out of you, and I'll give the whole show away. Because Blunden had a lot more to lose than Helmut had, if it came out.'

'That's all good sense,' agreed George. 'But now you come to the real snag. Helmut wasn't trespassing on Blunden land when he was killed, and he hadn't got the pheasants on him, he'd been careful to dispose of them.'

'Yes, I know that's what we thought. But when I began to sort everything out today, and got to thinking all this I've told you about, of course that didn't make sense any more. Because if Helmut was just getting to the stage of being ready to spit in Blunden's eye, then of course he wouldn't bother to hide the birds. He wouldn't need to, and he wouldn't want to. He'd want to wave them up and down in front of his boss's nose, and say, want to make something of it? So then for a minute I thought, it's just coincidence, they can't have been Helmut's pheasants, but we know they were, they'd been in the lining of his tunic. So then I thought, of course, we've got it the wrong way round, the one who didn't want them connected with Helmut wasn't Helmut himself, it was the murderer. And why should the murderer care about giving Blunden a bit of a motive, unless he *was* Blunden? And I worked it all out that way. I think they met down beyond the well that evening, some time after Hollins had left the Harrow, and before Charles came home – between half-past nine and about half-past ten it would be, wouldn't it? I think Helmut *had* got the pheasants on him, and either Blunden knew he had, or Helmut boasted about it to him. Whoever started it, I think Helmut bragged how he could do as he liked, because he had the whip hand, and there was nothing the old man could do to stop him. Only, you see, they'd both picked the wrong man, but Helmut was even wronger about Blunden than Blunden had been about him. People couldn't threaten Blunden and get away with it. There *was* one thing he could do to stop it, and he saw he'd have to, sooner or later, and so he did it on the spot. When Helmut turned away from him he bashed him on the head with that walking-stick, just like he tried to bash me, and put him in the brook, and the stick in the outflow of the well, and the pheasants in the pit – so that no one should think his poaching had anything to do with his death.'

He paused, rather for breath than for words, and looked round the circle of attentive faces. 'And, of course, it hadn't, really. It wasn't for them he was killed, they were only a sign of the way things were going. You can't have two bosses in a partnership like that. They'd both mistaken their man, but Blunden was the first to see his mistake, and see he had to go all the way to get out of it. And you have to admit he could make up his mind fast, and act on it, too.'

'Oh, yes,' allowed George sombrely, 'he could do all that.'

'Well, and then things went on, and nobody connected him with the murder; and everything went his way, even the appeal, so he had everything beautifully arranged as he wanted it. Only Charles had to go and tip it all up again. He started to look at the whole question again as soon as he'd got his own way –

though it was really his father's way. And he went out with his dog and his gun, and thought it all out again by himself in the wood, and decided to hand the land over, after all. And going back towards the house he met his father, and told him so. The old man couldn't know, could he, that Charles had already told me? I mean, why should he? So he'd naturally think no one knew but himself, and it couldn't appear as a motive. He had to think very quickly that time, too, because Charles said he was going to tell them his decision first thing in the morning. He wasn't expecting any trouble with the old man, and when you come to think of it, the old man couldn't make any, because if he did it might all have to come out, the murder, too, and he couldn't trust Charles to feel the way he did about it. He could try to persuade him to change his mind again, but supposing he wouldn't? They were both pig-headed, and supposing he finally absolutely wouldn't? And after the next morning it would be done, too late to do anything about it at all. So he had to choose at once, and he did, and he took the gun from Charles on some excuse or other, to carry it, or to try a shot with it, or something, and he shot him dead.'

Everybody exclaimed at this, except George, who sat frowning into the bowl of his pipe, and Jim Tugg, who looked on darkly and said no word.

'But, his own son!' whispered Io. 'Oh, Dom, you must be mistaken there, surely. How *could* he?'

'Well, I don't know how he could, but I'm absolutely sure he did. Maybe it was done all in a minute, because he was in a rage – only he had to take the gun from him to do it, so I honestly don't think so. Anyhow, he *did* do it,' maintained Dominic definitely.

'But, just over a few acres of land and a little defeat?' Chad shook his head helplessly, though Chad had known people kill for less. 'It doesn't seem enough motive for wiping out his own family. It can't be true.' But he was shaken by the revelation of Charles's change of heart, and had to remind himself over and over that Charles and his father were two different human creatures. He remembered, too, Selwyn Blunden's fixed, competent, unmistakably sane face in the glow of Dominic's torch, in the instant when the stick was raised for a third murder. There wasn't much, after all, which could not be true.

'It wouldn't be enough motive for most people,' said Dominic hesitantly, 'but he was a bit special, wasn't he? I think – it wasn't the number of acres, or the littleness of the defeat. There wasn't any proportion about it, there wasn't any little or big. It was *his* land, and it had to be *his* victory. And when Charles changed his mind he – sort of changed sides, too. He *did*, you know. And so he was a sort of traitor from the old man's point of view.' He lifted his wide eyes doubtfully to George's face. 'I can't help it if it sounds thin. It happened, anyhow, didn't it?'

'Go on, Dom!'

'Well, when I was telling you about meeting Charles that night, I clean forgot about the dog. He had that spaniel of his with him, you know, the brown-and-white one that won all the prizes. But when Briggs rang you up to report about the death of Charles, and how he found him, and everything, he never said anything about the dog. And I wondered. You can't be *sure* what they'll do, but he was trained to a gun, he wouldn't be frightened by that; and I thought most likely he'd stay by the body until somebody came. There were plenty of people out shooting that evening, all round the village, one shot more or less made no difference. And then, it was done with Charles's own gun, and there didn't seem to have been any struggle for it, or anything like that, so if he didn't do it himself – and I was sure about that – then it must have been somebody who knew him well enough to walk with him, maybe to take the gun and carry it for him, or try it out as they went along. Anyhow, somebody who could get it from him without it seeming at all funny. That could still have been – ' his eyes avoided Chad ' – several people. But it *could* have been his father, easily. But it was the dog that really bothered me.'

281

'He bothered me, too,' said George.

'But I didn't tell you about him.'

'No, but if he was out with a gun it was long odds the dog would be there. And, as you say, Briggs found no dog. He was gone from the spot pretty quickly.'

'Yes, that was what got me. And then, when it really started with me, when I went up to the Harrow this morning, I saw the dog there chained up, and the old man told me he'd come home by himself after the shooting, and hidden himself in the stables and wouldn't come out – like they do sometimes for thunder, or shock, or fits. He said he'd been funny ever since, and they had to keep him chained up because he roamed off if he was loosed. Well, it all sounded on the level. But when he came near, the dog went into the kennel, and lay down right in the back and stared at him – you know, keeping its face to him wherever he went. It'd been all right with me – well, mopish, but fairly all right, it liked being petted. But he never touched it. And it was then I really started to think. I didn't believe him. I believe the dog came home after the shooting because he brought it home, for fear it should bring anyone there too soon, and give him away. But he only just had time, because by sheer luck Briggs found Charles very quickly. And if the old man dragged the dog home with him, and then told lies about it, of course it could only be because he'd killed Charles himself. There couldn't be any other reason for him keeping the dog out of circulation now, except because it acted so queer towards him that he was afraid to be seen with it. So then I was certain,' said Dominic simply. 'It came on me like a flash. And I thought, and thought, and couldn't see how we were ever to prove it, or get at him at all, unless he gave us an opening. Because what a dog would or wouldn't do isn't exactly evidence.'

'So you set to work to make an opening yourself. And a nice risk you took in the process,' said George severely.

'No, not really, because I knew you'd stand by me.' But he said nothing about the panicky moment when he had strained his ears after them with no such perfect trust. He flushed deeper; he was getting tired, but he wasn't talked out yet.

'I had to think in an awful hurry, it was a bit slapdash, perhaps. I told him I'd found a little notebook, down in the clay holes close by where Helmut was killed. I said I was scared to show it to Dad, because I'd got into a row already for interfering; so I wanted to find out first if it really was something to do with the case before I risked another row. I asked him if he could read German, and he cottoned on at once, though · he pretended he was just humouring me. He said he could. I don't know if it was true, but you see, don't you, that if I'd really found it where I said I had, and it really was in German, he couldn't afford *not* to jump at the chance of having first look at it – whether he could read it without a dictionary or whether he couldn't. If it had really been something of Helmut's, why, it might have had *anything* in it, all about their contract, and the money that passed, and the jobs that were done for it, and everything. You know what Helmut was like about all his other business, and Blunden knew it, too. So then I said I hadn't got the thing on me, but I'd bring it up to him if he really wouldn't mind looking at it for me. I was careful to tell him I hadn't shown it to anybody yet, so he figured if he could persuade me it was just rubbish, I'd take his word for it, and throw it away. Anyhow, he just *had* to find out. I bet he thought it probably would be rubbish, but there was always the little risk that it might not be. He'd got to be *certain*. But he was in a spot, because he had to go somewhere by train after the funeral, and he wasn't coming back until the nine o'clock train in the evening. That must have been something important, too, or he'd have given it a miss. But instead, he said would I meet him up at the forest gate when he came from the train, and go up to the house with him, and we'd have a look at it together. And he told me very specially not to mention it to anyone – the book, or where I was going, or anything – because he didn't want to make any fresh troubles for you harassed policemen, and also to keep myself out of trouble. So you see, he figured that if – well, it was always possible that he might have to – well, if I didn't come back, you wouldn't have a clue to where I'd gone.'

The same reflection had not escaped either George or Bunty.

'But if I produced some ordinary rubbish,' went on Dominic, stumbling a little in haste to get past a thought which he himself, on reflection, did not like very much, 'or even if it was really something, and I obviously didn't know it, and would take his word for it that it was rubbish – then he was O.K., he could just burn it and forget it, and I could forget it, too. Most likely that's really what he expected. Only he had to be *sure* I didn't know too much about it already, he couldn't take any chances on me. And I had to be sure, too. It wasn't any good half-doing it. So I went the whole hog. After school I got on to Pussy. I suppose she told you all that part – '

'I didn't know what you meant to do,' protested Pussy. 'I knew it was something desperate, by the way you looked, but I didn't know how bad. Or I'd have told your mother, right away, and put a stop to it.'

'You would not! And if you had, you'd have spoiled the whole thing. But you wouldn't! Well, then I went up to the well, and took my German vocabulary notebook from school – ' His eyes strayed rather dubiously towards Chad, who smiled, and laid the wreckage on the table. 'I'm afraid it's rather past it now. Do you suppose we can square it? I had to have something fairly convincing, and with a bit of faking the figures, and then doctoring it in the mud, and drying it again, it made a pretty good show. Anything that came through, you see, was at least German.'

'I dare say we can square it about the notebook,' said Chad gravely, 'all things considered.'

'Well, you know everything else, you were there. It wasn't as bad as it sounded, truly it wasn't. And I couldn't think of any other way. I had to make him think I knew too much to be let go, or he wouldn't have given himself away. I *was* scared, but it was the best I could do. Mummy, you're not awfully mad at me, are you?' The reaction was setting in. He was very tired, his eyelids drooping; but he wanted to get rid of all of it, and sleep emptied of even the last dregs of his seething excitement.

'Not tonight,' said Bunty comfortably. 'I'm saving that up for tomorrow.'

'But, Dad, if Pussy didn't bring you there, like I expected, how did you get there? I'm jolly glad you did, but *how* did you?'

'I followed Blunden,' said George simply. 'I'd gone part of the way you went, about Helmut's murder, about the way the land kept cropping up. But I won't say I seriously thought of Blunden, until the dog came into the picture, or rather didn't come into it when he should have done. I smelt the same rat. The spaniel more or less vanished. Nobody exercised him, he was never seen out with the old man. I got the same ideas you had. So I started a close watch on Blunden; and when he suddenly groomed the dog and took it down to the station after the funeral this afternoon, Weaver and I went after him. He went to get rid of it, of course, before anyone else could start noticing things.'

'He didn't kill the dog, too?' asked Pussy anxiously.

'No, he sold him – to a man who'd made several attempts to buy him from Charles before, for a very good price. Quite a known name in the spaniel world, lives in Warwickshire, right in the country miles from anywhere. We found out all about him quite easily. No, dogs were something it hardly occurred to Blunden to kill. He used them to help him kill other things. It didn't seem necessary to kill the dog, and it could have been dangerous. But it was quite natural to get rid of him, after what had happened – a gesture to get rid of a bereavement, and give the dog a fresh start, too. Besides, when he had a thing of value, he couldn't resist getting a price for it. Well, he sold the dog, and he came home, and we were on his heels – just in time to come in on your little scene, and a nice fright you gave us.'

'Do you mean you were close behind us all the time?' asked Dominic, opening his eyes wide.

'As close as was safe.'

'I wish I'd known! I'd have felt a lot better.' He yawned hugely. 'And do you mean, then, that you'd have got on to him just the same, without all that performance? I scared myself nearly to death for nothing?'

'I wouldn't say that,' said George, smiling. 'I was certain he'd killed Charles. I might have got hold of the stick sooner or later, and got him on that charge. But to date we hadn't a shred of real evidence. You provided that – at least enough to let us get our hands on him, and the rest followed.'

'I'm glad if I was useful,' said Dominic, 'anyway.' He yawned again. Io took the gentle hint which poised on Bunty's near eyelid, and rose from her hassock.

'It's time we went home. Dad might be wondering, and we'll have a lot of explaining to do for him. Come on, Pussy, you can see Dom again tomorrow, he's had about enough for tonight, and so have you, I should think.' And she turned with equal simplicity to Chad, and gave him the full candid look of her brown eyes, and her hand, too. 'Come back with us, Chad! Just for half an hour!'

Jim Tugg's dog was stretched out on the office rug. He rose at the first sound of his master's step on the threshold of the room, and fell into his place in the little procession, close at the shepherd's heel. Subdued good-nights drifted back to Bunty in the doorway, soft, relaxed murmurs of sound, tired, content. She watched them go, and her gratitude went after them down the moist October street, where the lamps were just winking out for half-past eleven. Chad with his hand protectively at Io's elbow, as if he had had the right for years, Io with her arm round Pussy's shoulders. A lot of knots had somehow come untied, and when the nine-days' wonder had passed over, Comerford could sleep easy in its bed. Bless them all, Jim and the collie, too, everyone who had stood by Dominic and brought him back alive.

She went back to the kitchen. Dominic had come down to the fire, and was kneeling on the rug to warm himself, shivering a little from the cold which follows nervous strain. But he was still talking, rather drunkenly but with great determination.

'There was something in it, you see, about the people who get to take killing for granted. Only Cooke had hold of the wrong ones, *I* think. It isn't the people like old Wedderburn who had to do it because there wasn't any other choice at all. You know, Dad, sometimes things get into such a jam that there isn't a right thing to do, but only a least wrong one. And that's how it was with the people like him, in the war. And then, even if you do the best you can, you feel dirty. And you hate it. You don't know how he's hated it! But it wasn't like that with Blunden at all. The only use he had for a lot of things was to kill them. He bred things to kill. He was brought up to it. The little things in the woods, that he could have left alone without missing much, the badgers, and foxes, and crows – anything that took a crumb of his without paying for it double, he killed. And the war didn't hit him, you see, because he was here, all he had to do was feel the excitement of it, a long way off, and talk about knocking hell out of the beggars. He didn't have to *do* it. He didn't have to feel dirty. Of *course* it came easy to him. Why shouldn't it? In a way it wasn't even real. Nothing was, that didn't happen to him.'

'And do you really think,' asked George, gravely and respectfully, 'that even Blunden – about whom I wouldn't like to say you're wrong – killed two people and was quite ready to kill a third, simply to preserve twenty acres of land?'

'I suppose so, yes. It was *his*, you see. Whether he even wanted it or not, it was his, and so it was sacred. It might as well have been his blood. It made no difference if it was only twenty acres, or if it was only one. That didn't have anything to do with it.' He rubbed a tired hand over his eyes. Bunty

287

came and put her hands on his shoulders, and he got up obediently to the touch, and gave her a dazed smile. 'Yes, Mummy, I'll go to bed. I *am* tired.'

George drew his son to him for a moment in his arm. 'Goodnight, Dom! Look – don't waste any regrets on Blunden. You did what you decided you had to do, what seemed to be the right thing, for everybody. Didn't you?'

'Yes. Well – I thought I did. I thought I was sure about it. Only they'll kill him, won't they?'

'He killed, didn't he? And hurt more people even than he killed. Couldn't we agree, at least,' he said very gently, 'that what you did was the least wrong thing? In the circumstances?'

'I suppose so,' said Dominic with a pale smile, and went away quietly to bed. But when Bunty went up to him, ten minutes later, he was lying with the light still on, and his eyes wide open, staring into the corner of the ceiling as if he would never sleep. She went to his bedside and leaned down to him without a word; and suddenly he put his arms out of bed and reached up for her, and clung to her desperately. She felt his heart pounding. He said in a fierce, vehement stammer: 'Mummy, I'm never going to be a policeman, never, never!' And then he began to cry. 'Mummy, don't tell him! Only I couldn't – I couldn't!'

She could have argued George's side of it, she could justly have told him that in an imperfect world *somebody* has to do the dirty work; but there was an answer to that, too, and she had a feeling that Dominic would put his finger on it. And in any case there would be a lot more days after tomorrow, time enough to get over this and be ready for the next inescapable tangle when it came. So she just hugged and soothed him, and said placidly: 'No, darling, no, you shan't! Of course you shan't!' and held him gently rocking in her arms until he stopped crying and went to sleep.

Chapter 10

Treasure Trove

I

He got over it, of course very quickly, almost as quickly as Comerford did. Only half the story was ever allowed to leak out, but it was enough to cause people to turn and look twice at Dominic in the street, and attract a comet's-tail of envious boys to trail after him on the way to and from school. Pussy shared his notoriety, but Pussy was a born iconoclast, and delighted in pushing even her own false image off its pedestal. But Dominic could enjoy being idolised, even while he saw through it; and the jealous scorn of Rabbit and his coterie was even sweeter to him than the adoration of the rest. Pretty soon it became necessary to take him down a peg. George had not saved his ammunition for nothing.

Not that there was anything peculiarly displeasing about Dominic on the gloat. He enjoyed it so, and laughed so wickedly at himself and his gallery at the same time, that it needed a serious-minded father to find the heart to burst the bubble. And then it was not an unqualified success.

'You are undoubtedly,' said George, laying down his office pen, 'no end of a clever devil, my lad. But let me tell you this, that *coup* of yours was the most barefaced fluke that ever came off to the shame of the really clever. And now I'll say what I've been storing up for you, young man, for a long time. If ever you put your private oar into my affairs again, and put me or anyone else to the trouble of lugging you out of a spot like that, look out for yourself afterwards, that's all! You'll be due for the nearest thing to a real hiding you ever had in your life, just as soon as I get you home undamaged. I ought to have done it this time, but next time I won't make any mistake.'

Dominic, when he could speak, gasped: 'Well, I like that! I save you no end of a long, dreary job, and maybe one that would be a failure, anyhow, and solve your beastly case for you, and that's all the gratitude I get!' But he was laughing even then, at George as well as himself, until hard paternal knuckles rapped at the back of his head, and jolted the grin from his face.

'Better take notice,' said George. 'I mean it.'

And he did. One sober look at him, and there was no more question about it. Dominic digested the steadying implications, and went away to think it over; but his spirits were too much for him, and he could not, in his present irrepressible state of gaiety, be put down in this way. Five minutes later he was back. He put his head in at the office door, and said sweetly: 'I told Mummy what you said. She says if you try it, you'll have to deal with her.'

'Tell her from me,' said George grimly, looking up from his work, 'that I'll be delighted to deal with her — after I've dealt with you! And if you come barging in here just once more today,' he added, warming, 'I'll start now.'

Dominic laughed, but he went, and he did not come back with any more impudence that day, which in itself was enough to suggest that he had decided to pay a little attention. And presently the exhilaration which had followed on the heels of his first revulsion went the same steady, sensible way into oblivion, so that before Christmas his days had settled again into a beautiful reassuring normality. People didn't forget. It was rather that events slipped away into perspective, and left the foreground for what was newly urgent, end-of-term examinations, cake-mixing, present-buying, and all the rest of the seasonal trappings. Not even the very young can iron out flat all the unevennesses of the past, but the mountains of today are the molehills of tomorrow.

So Comerford got over the shocks to its nervous system, and the place where Selwyn Blunden and his son had fitted began to heal over even before the winter had set in. He had already ceased to be the main topic of conversation in the village by the time he died in prison in November, before he could be brought to trial. Medically his death was curious. He was old, of course, and parts of his economy were wearing out with over-use; but there seemed no special reason why he should dwindle away and stop living as he did. Bunty said he had died of frustration and cumulative shock at finding that, after all, he was not above the law. He was a bad loser, because he had always used his position and privileges to avoid any exercise in the art of losing gracefully. It seemed seriously possible that spleen should kill him.

So there was never a verdict in either of the Comerford cases, except the verdict which had already been collectively pronounced by the village; but that was all that was required to set the village free to go back to its everyday occupations. The rift in the wall of society closed gently with the closing year. And there were other things to be discussed, other surprises to be assimilated, like Io Hart's quiet marriage to Chad Wedderburn, at Comerbourne registry office at the end of November. A quick decision, that was, said Comerford, considering the other one wasn't long dead; but this wasn't the first knot that had been cut by events when it couldn't be unravelled by humankind, and maybe it was all for the best.

Pussy confided to Dominic: 'You don't know how much trouble she had with him, even after that night. The time he spent trying to tell her he ought not to let her do it! It would have taken more than him to stop her, once she knew he was only trying to be noble. You men are a silly lot of dopes, if you ask me. But she nagged him so much, he had to marry her in the end to shut her up.'

The more usual interpretation of the affair was that Chad had managed to get Io at last, after infinite trouble, because Charles Blunden was no longer there to be his rival. But Pussy, though prone to sisterly derogations, was nearer the mark. The only thing for which her version did not quite account was the look of extreme and astonished joy on the bridegroom's face when the little registrar shut the book, smiled at them, and said: 'Well, that's all! You've done it now – you're married!'

Then the rumour started, and proved by Christmas to be no mere rumour, that Gerd Hollins was expecting a baby at last, after nine years of hoping and one of quietly giving up hope. They'd even thought of adopting one, when it began to seem certain that they would have none of their own; but now there was a fair chance of a son coming to the farm in his own right, and good luck to him, said Comerford, and to his mother, too; she'd had more than her share of the bad. A bit late, perhaps, to start a family, but she was a strong woman, and older and less sturdy wives had produced healthy first babies before now.

So what with births and marriages, Comerford could balance a death or two.

A distant cousin came to the Harrow after the old man's death. He seemed a nice enough young man, and he had a different name, which made things easier; and he came in time to have the last mild word upon the open-cast site. As far as he was concerned, they were welcome to go ahead, and so they did, as soon as the year turned and the mild, lengthening days began. Later surveys stated that the amount of coal to be harvested would be even larger than had at first been supposed, and the project would certainly pay for itself handsomely.

In the first days of the spring, therefore, the red-and-yellow monsters crept over the border of Harrow land, from which so many pains had been taken to exclude them, and began to rip

off the tangle of furze and heather and rank grass, to pile up
the gathered topsoil, to burrow deep into the entrails of pennystone and clay, and lay bare the old shallow shafts one by one,
the unfilled and the shoddily filled together, the ugly debris of
last century's not much comelier civilisation.

II

A worker from the coal site came to the police-station and asked
for George. 'You'd better come up, Sergeant,' he said. 'We've
found something we'd just as soon not have found. It's in your
line of business more than ours.'

George went up with Weaver, and stood beside the giant
excavator, on a broad shelf from which the topsoil had already
been stripped, in the heath beyond the Harrow farmhouse,
where were dotted the old shafts filled during the war years.
Debris of one of them, plucked out wholesale, had spattered
down the side of the new mountain where the pennystone and
clay was being shot. Old brickwork, half disintegrated, old rotten
timber, all the rubbish of a prosperous yesterday. The past had
come up the shaft and lay in the sun, slanting above the gouged
valleys where the water had drained off to a deep, cliff-circled
pool. The hole of the shaft, a ring of brickwork, gnawed by
time, filled with rubble, lay open to the noon light. They stood
at the rim, and stared into it, and were struck suddenly silent.

'Well, that's it,' said the manager, kicking at the crumbling
bricks and hunching a helpless shoulder. 'Your folks'd better
come and get it, I suppose. Unless you'd rather we just ploughed
it under and forgot it. I'd just as·soon forget it, myself.'

Weaver, very large of eye and solemn of face, looked into the
pit, looked at George. He said, breathing gustily: 'How long do
you suppose it – she – ' he looked again, and made up his mind
' – she's been down there?'

There was still perceptible cloth, shoes, a handbag; and

incomprehensibly there were two large suitcases, burst and gnawed and showing soiled colours of clothes. But the rest was bone. George said: 'A few years. Not above ten, I'd say.' For the skirt had a traceable length, the shoes a dateable fashion.

'But this is a skeleton,' said Weaver. He was chalky-white, too shocked to reason very closely. George didn't like to remind him that the workings were alive with rats. 'It must be longer than ten years. I don't know of anyone going missing as far back as I can remember. She must have fallen down?'

'Fallen down and taken her luggage with her?' said the manager.

'Then she must have committed suicide – wanted to vanish, I suppose. People do funny things.'

'They have funny things done to them, too,' said George. 'Do you see what I see round her neck? Quite a determined suicide, if she strangled herself with a twist of wire, and then carried her cases to a pit-shaft, and jumped down it.'

'My God!' said the sunshine miner blankly. 'That's right! You mean we been and found a new murder?'

'You dug up an old one,' said George. By now he even knew the date of it. Noon sun on covered places brings out a lot of facts in a very little time, and queer things happen when men begin making the rough places plain. There she lay, a short, tumbled skeleton, falling apart here and there in the dirty folds of cloth which had now only slight variations from the universal dirt-colour of buried things, among the soil and gravel and brick, jostled by the mouldering cases. A few fragments of skin still adhering to the skull, and masses of matted hair. Front teeth touched with distinctive goldwork standing forward in the jaw; and two things round her neck, a necklet of carved imitation stones and a twisted wire. Loose enough now, but once it must have been tight round a plump, soft throat.

'Plenty of identifiable stuff there to hang half a dozen men,' said the sunshine miner, in displeased but deeply interested contemplation.

'Yes,' said George, 'but it never will.'

For he'd got the hang of it at last. The cases had jolted him, but it was the necklet of stones that made everything click into place. He'd seen it before, not so long ago, round a soft, plump throat in a photograph. It was all very, very simple once one had the missing bit. A house without servants after six o'clock in the evening, a son away in North Africa, nobody home but a wife with a fair amount of money in jewels and securities, and a husband with his affairs in bad shape, and a position and reputation which rated well above other people's lives with him. A situation in which she could easily be persuaded to turn everything into cash, and a plethora of pit-shafts round the house, into which she could vanish some night when she had done it, with enough of her personal belongings to give colour to the story of her exit in quite another direction. A letter of farewell which didn't even have to exist, a lover who never had existed except in one proficient imagination. One man's word for everything, and an ingenious arrangement of circumstances which made it indelicate to probe too deeply. And then a broken, ageing, but re-established demi-god, who touched nothing he did not turn to profit.

Fill in the shafts, in a burst of local benevolence, and what have you left to fear? The war distracts attention from village events which might otherwise arouse too much interest; and Charles, the dumb, worthy Charles, comes home to swallow the story whole, and feel sorry for his father. What can you possibly have to fear?

Except, perhaps, red and yellow excavators ripping the bowels out of the secret places of the earth, laying bare the treasures of the mine, turning the soil traitor. For the land turned out to be neutral, after all. That was the one thing you hadn't bargained for. You were aware of ownership; but the land was not aware of being owned. And you had to fight some unexpected rear-guard actions; and there were casualties – a tool that turned in your hand, and a son who innocently went over to the enemy.

But you'd gone too far then to turn or to hesitate. And as for small, inquisitive boys, they should be kept out of the battle area; total war is not selective.

'I always had a feeling,' said George, 'that the motive as we knew it was a little thin to account for Charles. Well, now we know! I'm afraid we'll have to stop your operations here for a few hours. Go down and phone the inspector, Weaver, will you? Tell him we've found what's left of Selwyn Blunden's wife.'

Death and the
Joyful Woman

Chapter 1

The first time Dominic Felse saw Kitty Norris she was dancing barefoot along the broad rail of the terrace at the Boat Club, in a cloud of iris-coloured nylon, a silver sandal dangling from either hand. It was the night following the Comerbourne Regatta, the night of the mid-season Club dance, when such acrobatic performances were not particularly surprising, though the demonstrators were usually male. It was also the eve of Leslie Armiger's wedding day, though Dominic was not aware of that, and wouldn't have understood its significance even if he had been.

He was on his way home from his music lesson, an inescapable boredom which beset him weekly; and because the night was fine and warm he had let the bus go without him and set out to walk the mile and a bit to Comerford by the riverside road. At the edge of the town it brought him close beneath the club-house terrace, The strains of the band floated out to meet him, and a babel of voices was blown across the wooden balustrade with the music; and there along the railing, ten feet or so above his head, floated Kitty in her extravagant dress, hands spread wide dangling the absurd contraptions of cobweb straps and three-inch spike heels she called shoes. Several voices, all male, were calling on her entreatingly to come down and be sensible; two young men were threading a hasty way between the tables on the terrace to intercept her, and one of them in his extreme concentration had just failed to see a waiter with a loaded tray. Shrieks of consternation and a flurry of dispersing flounces marked the area which was now awash with short drinks. Kitty danced on, unheeding; the table lights illuminated from below a face set in childlike concentration, the tip of her tongue

299

protruding at the corner of parted lips. Dominic had never seen anyone so incandescent with gaiety.

His first thought had been a mildly contemptuous: 'If they're this high by a quarter to ten, what on earth will they be like by one o'clock in the morning?' But that was the automatic reaction of his youthful superiority, and tempered already by curiosity. He had experimented with tobacco so frequently during the last year and a half, unknown to his parents, that he had worn out its novelty without discovering its attractions; but now that he was beginning to contemplate alcohol hopefully from afar he did so with the same incorrigible conviction that it must be wonderful, since adults took such delight in it, and reserved it so jealously for their own use. These antics going on over his head were part of the rites; Dominic curled his lip at them, but stopped in the darkness beneath the terrace to take a longer look at the bacchanalia from which he was barred. And having seen Kitty he lost sight of everything else.

She was the centre of the din, but she herself was silent, and perhaps that contributed to the overwhelming impression of disembodied beauty. She was of no more than medium height, but so slender that she looked tall, and taller still because of being poised swaying above him against the dark-blue sky. She looked pale, too, white almost to transparency, though in fact she was sturdy and sun-tanned and as robust as a bull-terrier. Almost everything about her swam, like her body, in diaphanous clouds of illusion, but in the heart of the phantasm there was Kitty, a reality.

He stood gaping in his shadowy place below her, holding his breath for fear she would fall. One of the young men, a flash of magpie black and white lunging over the rail, made a grab for her, and she whirled round perilously and eluded him, her full skirts swirling about her. Dominic, staring upwards fascinated, caught a glimpse of long, slim legs, a smooth, pale golden thigh. He averted his eyes hastily, but made even more haste to raise them again. After all, who could see him? She wouldn't know. Nobody was looking at him, nobody knew he was there.

'Kitty, you'll fall! Don't be a fool!' implored the terrified young man above, catching at her hand as she drew back from him. She uttered a sudden high squeak of protest, and dropped one of her sandals plump into Dominic's startled hands; and there in microcosm was the solid reality that harboured within the iris-coloured cloud. A bit of silver nonsense it might be, but it was made for a healthy, modern, size six foot. Dominic stood holding it gingerly before him as though it might be charged with the incalculable properties of enchantment, so stupefied that it took him several seconds to realise what a quietness had fallen overhead. When at last he looked up it was to see three or four heads leaning over the wooden balustrade and staring down at him. Only one of them had any significance for him, he didn't waste any time looking at the others.

'I'm terribly sorry,' said Kitty. 'I hope it didn't hurt you? If I'd realised there was anyone there I wouldn't have been behaving so badly.'

A clear, round voice she had, direct and disconcerting, and so polite that it confused him even more than her former extravagances had done. She wasn't drunk, after all, she wasn't even elevated. As soon as she was aware of him she spoke to him as a punctilious child speaks to a stranger. And where was the gaiety now? She looked down at him from the shadow of her long, smooth, light-brown hair with large, plaintive violet eyes, and her expression didn't change when she had weighed up the person with whom she had to deal. Dominic was used to the look of indulgent condescension that visited so many faces when confronted with his want of years, but Kitty continued to gaze at him with the wondering, wary, courteous look of an equal and a contemporary.

He couldn't find his tongue, there wasn't anything for him to say that wouldn't sound idiotic, and he didn't know how to break out of the constricting moment. Disgusted with himself and crimson to the ears, he stood in a sweat of shame, wishing he'd gone straight home, wishing the night could be darker, wishing the morons up there with her would stop grinning, or better still, go away.

'You can throw it,' said Kitty simply. 'It's all right, really, I can catch.'

And she could and did. He measured the distance carefully, and tossed the sandal gently up into her out-stretched hands, and she lifted it out of the air as lightly as thistledown, held it up for him to see, in something between a wave and a salute, and stooped to put it on. And that was the end of the incident. One of the young men put his arm round her, and she let herself be led away towards the dance-hall. There was just one instant when she looked back, a last glance of reluctance and regret, as though she knew she had disastrously disturbed the peace of a fellow-creature who was in no case to defend himself. The oval face with its clear, generous features had a honeyed glow in the shadow of the burnished hair; the violet eyes were wide and dark and full of a rueful wonder. He had never seen anyone look so sad. Then she was gone.

She stayed with him, however, all the way home, and upset his life and all his relationships for months. His term results suffered a downward lurch from first place to fifth, his co-ordination on the Rugby field that winter went to pieces and he didn't get into his house fifteen. He couldn't talk about Kitty to anyone; his best friends, without malice, would have made his life a misery, and his parents were out of the question, for his mother was after all a woman, and he instinctively knew better than to confide in her about another woman whose image was elbowing her out of sole possession of his heart, while his father was a man, and good-looking enough and young enough to be in some degree a rival. Even if he had wanted to unburden himself to them, Dominic wouldn't have known what to say; he didn't understand himself what was happening to him.

At fourteen love can be an overwhelming experience, all the

more so for being totally incomprehensible. But Dominic was
as normal as his own predicament; his appetite didn't fail him,
if anything it increased, he slept well, he enjoyed most of what
happened to him, however disquieting, and he got over it. By
the time he saw the girl again, more than a year later, he was
back at the top of his class, mad about sports cars, and engaged
in a campaign to induce his father to let him have a motorbike
as soon as he was old enough. He had almost forgotten what
Kitty looked like. He had never discovered who she was, indeed
he had never tried, because any inquiries, in whatever quarter,
would have involved a certain degree of self-betrayal. She was
just Kitty, a recollection of absurd, melancholy beauty, already
growing shadowy.

The occasion of their second meeting was the autumn visit of
the mobile Blood Transfusion Unit to Comerbourne Grammar
School in the last week of September. Dominic had stayed late
for football practice, and after his shower had remembered
something he wanted to look up for his history essay, and
lingered an extra hour in the library. When he finally crossed
the forecourt on his way to the side gate it was already dusk,
and he saw the unit's van drawn up close to the gymnasium
block, and a nurse trotting across from the rear doors with an
armful of documents and equipment. The session was a quar-
terly occurrence, and he had never paid the least attention to it
before and would not have done so now but for the dark-red
Karmann-Ghia which was just turning in to park in the narrow
space behind the van. The car brought him up standing, with
a gasp of pleasure for its compact and subtle beauties, and when
its door opened he could scarcely drag his eyes from that chaste
thoroughbred shape even to satisfy his curiosity about its lucky
owner. But the next moment even the car was in eclipse. A girl
swung long, elegant legs out of it, and walked slowly across the
concrete to the door of the block, as if she was a little dubious
of her errand or her welcome when it came to the point. And
the girl was Kitty.

Dusk or daylight or unrelieved midnight, Dominic would
have known her. She had only to put in an appearance, even
after fifteen months, and everything that had to do with her
acquired a significance so intense as to blot out the rest of the
world. The parked van, the lighted windows behind which
the nurses moved busily, the whole apparatus of donating blood
suddenly became a vital reality to Dominic, because Kitty was
a donor. He knew he ought to go home and tackle his homework,
but he couldn't bring himself to move from the spot, and when
finally he did compel his legs into action he found that they
were carrying him towards the gymnasium block instead of
towards the gate.

In any case he'd probably missed the bus he'd intended to
take by now, and there was twenty-five minutes to wait for the
next. If he went away now he might never have such an opportunity again. She wasn't with a party this time, she wasn't on a
terrace ten feet above him; anybody could go in there and join
her at the mere cost of a pint of blood. After all, it was a good
cause, and even if they did have a list of regular donors they
surely wouldn't turn down another one. I really ought to think
about these services more, he said to himself virtuously,
especially with Dad being in the position he is, it's up to me to
do him credit, actually. It's now or never, warned some more
candid demon at the back of his mind, she's on her own as yet
because she drove herself here, but if you don't make up your
mind pretty smartly the official transport will be there, and you
won't have a dog's chance of getting near her. *And* you'll have
tapped off a pint of blood for nothing, it added spitefully,
demolishing the pretence that he was contemplating the sacrifice
out of any impulse of public-spiritedness. But he was beyond
noticing the intricacies of this argument within him, for he was
already pushing open the swing-door and shouldering his way
through into the hall.

She was sitting alone on one of the chairs ranged along the
wall, looking a little perplexed and a little forlorn, as if she

wondered what she was doing there at all. She wore a dark green jersey suit with a skirt fashionably short and tight, and the magnificent legs which had made his senses swim gleamed smoothly golden from knee to ankle, so perfectly tanned that he couldn't tell whether she was wearing nylons or not. She looked up quickly as he came in, pleased not to be alone any longer. The heavy coil of honey-coloured hair swayed on her smooth cheek, the disconcerting eyes smiled at him hopefully.

'Hallo!' she said almost shyly, almost ingratiatingly.

She didn't recognise him, he saw that at once, she was merely welcoming him as a fellow-victim. 'Hallo!' he said with a hesitant smile. He stacked his books on a window-sill, and sat down several places away from her, afraid to make too sudden a claim upon her attention merely because she found his company preferable to being alone.

'We're early,' said Kitty. 'They're not ready for us yet. I hate waiting for this sort of thing, don't you? Is it your first time?'

'Yes,' said Dominic rather stiffly, because he thought for a moment that she was making an oblique reference to his youth.

'Mine, too,' she said, cheered, and he saw that he'd been misjudging her. 'I felt I ought to do something about *something*. Every now and again it gets me like that. I'm not much use at anything much, but at least I've got blood. I hope! Was yours a case of conscience, too?'

She grinned at him. There was no other word for it, it was too wry and funny and conspiratorial to be called merely a smile. He felt his stiffness melting like ice in sunlight, and with it the marrow in his bones.

'Well, it was sort of on the spur of the moment,' he admitted, grinning back shyly, he who was seldom shy and frequently a good deal too cocky. 'I just happened to be late leaving and I saw the van here, and I thought maybe I ought – well, you see, my father's a policeman – '

'No, really?' said Kitty, impressed. The big eyes dilated; they weren't really the colour of violets, he saw, but of purple-brown pansies.

'Well, a detective actually,' said Dominic punctiliously, and then blushed because it sounded dramatic, and in reality he knew that it was normally nothing of the kind. The very name of the profession carries such artificial overtones, you'd never dream how humdrum is the daily life of a member of the County C.I.D.

'Gosh!' said Kitty, eyes now enormous with pleased respect. 'I see I must keep in with you. Who knows when I may need a friend? What with all these fifty limits around at week-ends, and no parking allowed anywhere less than a mile from the middle of town, I could be run in almost any minute.' She caught his fixed and fascinated eye, and laughed. 'I'm talking an awful lot, aren't I? You know why? I'm nervous of this thing we've got coming along. I know it's nothing, but somehow I don't like the idea of being tapped like a barrel.'

'I'm scared of it, too,' said Dominic.

It wasn't true, he hadn't given the actual operation a single thought; but it was generously meant, and it never occurred to him how difficult he was making it for her to hit upon a reply which would be equally graceful to his self-esteem. But she managed it, some natural genius guiding her. She gave him a pleased look, and then a doubtful one, and then a wonderful smile.

'I don't believe you,' she said confidently, 'but it's jolly nice of you to say it, anyhow. If I yell when they prick my ear for a sample, will you promise to yell, too, so I won't feel alone in my cowardice?'

'I shall probably be the first to yell,' he said gallantly, hot with delight and embarrassment.

A door opened with a flourish upon their solitude, and a plump young nurse put her head out into the hall. 'My, my!' she said, with that rallying brightness which is almost an occupational hazard in her profession. 'Two of us here before time! We *are* eager to help, aren't we?'

'Yes, aren't we?' said Kitty like a meek echo, dragging her eyes away from Dominic's before the giggles could overwhelm them both.

'If you'd like to get it over with, folks, you can come in now.'

They went in to the sacrifice together. A row of narrow camp-beds and two attendant nymphs waited for them expectantly, and an older nurse shuffled documents upon a small table, and peered up at them over rimless glasses.

'Good evening!' she said briskly. 'Names?' But she beamed at Kitty and didn't wait for an answer. 'Oh, yes, of course!' she said, ticking off one of the names in her list. 'This is a very nice gesture you're making, we do appreciate it, my dear. It does me good to see you young people setting an example.'

She was being very matey indeed, Dominic thought, evidently Kitty was really somebody; but then, a girl who drove a Karmann-Ghia was bound to be somebody. But if only the old battle-axe had let her give her name! He tried to read the list upside down, and was jerked out of his stride as the blue-grey eyes, bright and knowing, pin-pointed him and sharpened into close attention. 'Name, please?'

He gave it. She looked down her list, but very rapidly, because she was only verifying what she already knew. 'I haven't got your name here, apparently we weren't expecting you.' She looked him up and down, and the hard, experienced face broke into a broad and indulgent smile.

'No, I just came in – ' he was beginning, but she wagged an admonishing finger at him and rode over him in a loud, friendly, confident voice which stated positively: '*You're* never eighteen, ducky! Don't you know the regulations?'

'I'm sixteen,' he said, very much on his dignity, and hating her for being too perceptive, and still more for trumpeting her discoveries like a town-crier. She had made eighteen sound so juvenile that sixteen now sounded like admitting to drooling infancy, and his position was still further undermined by the unacknowledged fact that he had been sixteen for precisely one week. This formidable woman was perfectly capable of looking at him and deducing that detail to add to her score. 'I thought it was from sixteen to sixty,' he said uncomfortably.

'It's from eighteen to sixty-five, my dear, but bless you for a good try. We can't take children, they need all their strength for growing. You run along home and come back in a couple of years' time, and we'll be glad to see you. But we shall still need your parents' consent, mind.'

The younger nurse was giggling. Even Kitty must be smiling at him under cover of the gleaming curtain of her hair. Not unkindly, he had sense enough to know that, but that didn't make the gall of his humiliation any less bitter. And he really had thought the minimum age was sixteen. He could have sworn it was.

'Are you *sure*? It *used* to be sixteen, didn't it?'

She shook her head, smiling broadly. 'I'm sorry, love! Always eighteen since I've been in the service. Never mind, being too young is something time will cure, you know.'

There was absolutely nothing he could do about it, except go. Kitty craned round the nurse's shoulder from her camp-bed and saw him turn towards the door, crushed and silent. The old fool needn't have bellowed at him like that. The poor kid was so mortified he wasn't even going to say good-bye.

'Hey, don't go!' said Kitty plaintively after his departing back. 'Wait for me, and I'll give you a lift.' She made it as near a child's wail for company as she decently could, to restore him to a good conceit of himself, and threw in the bribe to take his mind off his injuries, and the sudden reviving gleam in his eyes as he looked round was full repayment. She put it down to the car, which was intelligent of her though inaccurate. 'You could at least come and talk to me,' she said. 'I was counting on you to take my mind off this beastly bottle.'

Nobody believed in her need to be amused and distracted,

but girls like Kitty are allowed to pretend to as many whims as they please.

'Well, if you really want me to – ' he said, recovering a little of his confidence.

'That's all right,' said the matron, beaming benevolently, 'by all means wait, my dear, nobody wants to drive a willing lad away.' He gave her a look she was too complacent to understand; she couldn't even pat a child on the head, he reflected bitterly, without breaking its neck, the kind of touch she had. But she was no longer so important, now Kitty had called him back.

'Here you are,' said the young nurse, planking a chair down beside Kitty's camp-bed. 'You sit down and talk to your friend, and I'll bring you both a nice cup of tea afterwards.'

Dominic sat down. Kitty was looking at him, and studiously avoiding looking at the bottle that was gradually filling up with her blood; but not, he observed, because she felt any real repugnance for it. She was shaking with giggles, and when his slender bulk was interposed between her and the official eyes she said in a rapid, conspiratorial whisper: 'These people *kill* me!'

That made everything wonderful by standing everything on its head. He made a fool of himself and she didn't seem to notice; they behaved according to their kind, only slightly caricaturing themselves, and they killed her.

'I really did think it was all right at sixteen,' he said, still fretting at the sore place, though he couldn't help grinning back at her.

'Sure,' said Kitty, 'I know you did. I never thought about there being a limit at all, but it's only sense. Am I done yet? You look, I don't like to.'

He didn't like to, either; the thought of her blood draining slowly out of the rounded golden arm gave him an almost physical experience of pain. 'Nearly,' he said, and averted his eyes. 'Look out, here comes our nice cup of tea.'

It wasn't a nice cup of tea, of course, when it came; it was very strong and very sweet, and of that curious reddish-brown colour which indicates the presence of tinned milk. When they were left to themselves again to drink it Kitty sat up, flexing her newly-bandaged arm, took an experimental sip, and gave the cup a look of incredulous distaste.

'I know,' said Dominic apologetically. 'I don't like it with sugar, either, but you're supposed to need it after this caper. It puts back the energy you've lost, or something.'

'I don't feel as if I've lost any,' admitted Kitty with some surprise, and looked thoughtfully at her bandage. 'I'm still not sure what they've got in that bottle,' she said darkly. 'Wouldn't you have thought it would be beer?' She caught his lost look, and made haste to explain, even more bafflingly: 'Well, after all, that's what I live on.'

He was staring at her helplessly, more at sea than ever. He hoped he was misunderstanding her, but how could he be sure? He knew nothing about her, except that she was the most charming and disturbing thing that had ever happened to him. And there *was* her performance that evening at the Boat Club dance.

'Oh, I don't mean it's actually my staple diet,' she said quickly. 'I just meant it's what I *live* on – it's what pays the bills, you know. I ought to have told you, I'm Kitty Norris. If that means anything? No good reason why it should,' she hurried on reassuringly. 'I'm just Norris's Beers, that's all I meant.' She said it in a resigned voice, as though she was explaining away some odd but not tragic native deformity to which she had long become accustomed, but which might disconcert a stranger.

'Oh, yes, of course,' said Dominic, at once relieved and mortified. What must she think of him for almost taking her literally? And he ought to have known. Katherine Norris the beer heiress was in and out of the local news headlines regularly, he must surely have seen her photograph occasionally. It couldn't have done her justice, though, or he wouldn't have failed to recognise her. Her name was prominent on about a third of the pub signs in the country, all those, in fact, which weren't the monopoly of Armiger's Ales. And hadn't she been going to marry old Armiger's son at one time? Dominic groped in his memory, but local society engagements and weddings did not figure among the events he was in the habit of filing, and he couldn't remember what was supposed to have happened to break off the merger. It was enough to be grateful for the fact, no need to account for it. 'I should have realised,' he said. 'My name's Dominic Felse.'

'Cheers, Dominic!' She drank to him in the acrid, sugary tea. 'Did you know this used to be a bottle of stout once? I mean they used to give the victims stout to restore them afterwards. Old man Shelley told me so. I'm being done, Dominic, that's what.'

'Norris's stout?' asked Dominic, venturing timidly on a joke. It had a generous success; she threw back her head and laughed.

'Too true! I'm being done two ways,' she said indignantly as she swung her feet to the floor and shook down her sleeve over the already slipping bandage.

It was nearly at an end, he thought as he followed her out. The transport had arrived and was disgorging its load of volunteers on the forecourt; the evening had closed in as it does in late September, with swiftly falling darkness and sudden clear cold. She would get into the Karmann-Ghia and wave her hand at him warmly but thoughtlessly, and drive away, and he would walk alone to the bus stop and go home. And who knew if he would ever see her again?

'Where can I take you?' she said cheerfully, sliding across from the driving-seat to open the other door.

He hesitated for a moment, worrying whether he ought to accept, whether he wasn't being a nuisance to her, and longing to accept even if he was. 'Thanks awfully,' he said with a gulp, 'but I'm only going to the bus station, it's just a step.'

'Straight?' said Kitty, poker-faced. 'That where you spend your nights?'

'I mean I've only got to catch a bus from there.'

'Come on, get in,' said Kitty, 'and tell me where you live, or I shall think you don't like my car. Ever driven in one of these?'

He was inside, sitting shoulder to shoulder with her, their sleeves brushing; the plastic hide upholstery might have been floating golden clouds under him, clouds of glory. The girl was bliss enough, the car was almost too much for him. Kitty started the engine and began to back towards the shrubberies to turn, for the transport had cramped her style a little. The bushes made a smoky dimness behind her, stirring against the gathering darkness. She switched on her reversing light to make sure how much room she had, and justified all Dominic's heady pride and delight in her by bringing the car round in one, slithering expertly past the tail of the transport at an impetuous speed, and shooting the gateway like a racing ace. They passed everything along Howard Road, and slowed at the traffic lights.

'You still haven't told me where I'm to take you,' said Kitty.

There was nothing left for him to do but capitulate and tell her where he lived, which he did in a daze of delight.

'Comerford, that's hardly far enough to get going properly. Let's go the long way round.' She signalled her intention of turning right, and positioned herself beautifully to let the following car pass her on the near side. The driver leaned out and shouted something as he passed, gesticulating towards the rear wheels of the Karmann–Ghia. Dominic, who hadn't understood, bristled on Kitty's behalf, but Kitty, who had, swore and grinned and waved a hand in hasty acknowledgement.

'Damn!' she said, switching off her reversing light. 'I'm *always* doing that. Next time I'm going to get a self-cancelling one. Don't you tell your father on me, will you? I do *try* to remember. It isn't even that I've got such a bad memory, really, it's just certain things about a car that trip me up every time. That damned reversing light, and then the petrol. I wouldn't like to tell you how many times I've run out of petrol inside a year.'

'You haven't got a petrol gauge, have you?' he asked, searching the dashboard for it in vain.

'No, it's a reserve tank. I thought it would be better, because when you have to switch over you know you've got exactly a gallon, and that's fair warning.'

'And is it better?' asked Dominic curiously.

'Yes and no. It works on long journeys, because then I don't know how far it will be between filling stations, so I make a point of stopping at the very first one after the switch-over, and filling up. But when I'm just driving round town, shopping or something, I kick her over and think, oh, I've still got a gallon, I needn't worry, plenty of time, pumps all round me. And then I clean forget about it, and run dry in the middle of the High Street, or half-way up the lane to the golf links. I never learn,' said Kitty ruefully. 'But when I had a petrol gauge on the old car I never remembered to look at it in time, so what's the use? It's just me. Dizzy, that's what.'

'You drive awfully well,' said Dominic, reaching for the nearest handful of comfort he could offer her. That self-derisive note in her voice, at once comic and sad, had already begun to fit itself into a hitherto undiscovered place in his heart like a key into a secret door.

'No, do you mean that? Honestly?'

'Yes, of course. You must know you drive well.'

'Ah!' said Kitty. 'I still like to hear it said. Like the car, too?'

It was one subject at least on which he could be eloquent, doubly so because it was Kitty's car. They talked knowledgeably about sports models all the way to Comerford, and when she pulled up at his own door in the village the return to his ordinary world and the shadow of his familiar routine startled him like a sudden blow. Those few minutes of utter freedom and ease with her were the end of it as well as the beginning. He had to be thankful for a small miracle that wouldn't drop in his lap a second time. He climbed out slowly, chilled by the fall back into time and place, and stood awkwardly by the door on her side of the car, struggling for something to say that shouldn't shame him by letting down the whole experience into the trivial and commonplace.

'Thanks awfully for the lift home.'

'Pleasure!' said Kitty, smiling at him. 'Thanks for the lift you gave me, too. I can't think of anyone I'd rather shed my blood with.'

'Are you sure you feel all right?' was all he found to say.

An end of muslin was protruding from Kitty's sleeve; she pulled it experimentally, and it came away in a twisted string, shedding a scrap of lint on the seat beside her. They both laughed immoderately.

'I feel fine,' said Kitty. 'Maybe I had blood pressure before, and now I'm cured.'

An instant's silence. The soft light from the net-curtained front window lay tenderly on the firm, full curves of her mouth, while her forehead and eyes were in shadow. How soft that mouth was, and yet how decided, with its closely folded lips and deep, resolute corners, how ribald and vulnerable and sad. The core of molten joy in Dominic's heart burned into exquisite anguish, just watching the slow deepening of her valedictory smile.

'Well thanks – and goodbye!'

'See you at the next blood-letting,' said Kitty cheerfully, and drove away with a flutter of her fingers to her brow, something between a wave and a salute, leaving him standing gazing after her and holding his breath until the blood pounded thunderously in his ears, and the pain in his middle was as sharp and radical as toothache.

But she saw him again earlier than she had foretold, and in very different circumstances; and the blood in question on that occasion, which was neither his blood nor hers, had already been let in considerable quantities.

Chapter 2

The latest of Alfred Armiger's long chain of super-pubs, The Jolly Barmaid, opened its doors for business at the end of that September. It stood on a 'B' road, half a mile from Comerford and perhaps a mile and a quarter from Comerbourne; not an advantageous position at first sight, but old Armiger knew what he was doing where making money was concerned, and few people seriously doubted that he would make the place pay. Those who knew the beer baron best were already wondering if he had any inside information about the long-discussed by-pass, and whether it wouldn't, when it eventually material-ised, turn out to be unrolling its profitable asphalt just outside the walls of the new hotel. It was seven months now since he'd bought the place and turned loose on it all the resources of his army of builders, designers and decorators, and everyone came along on the night of the gala opening to have a look at the results.

Detective-Sergeant George Felse of the County C.I.D. wandered in off-duty out of pure curiosity. He had often admired the decrepit stone-mullioned house and regretted its steady mouldering into a picturesque and uneconomic slum. Two old ladies had been living in it then, and like so many ancient sisters they had died within days of each other, leaving the place unoccupied for almost a year before their distant heir decided to sell and cut his losses. There was nothing else to be done with a place of such a size and in such a state; the only question had been whether he would ever find a buyer. But he had; he'd found Alfred Armiger, the smartest man on a bargain in three or four counties.

It still made no sense to George, even when he pushed open

the new and resplendent Tudor door and walked into a hall all
elaborate panelling and black oak beams, carved settles and
copper-coloured glass witchballs. He estimated that ten thousand at least must have been sunk in the restoration, and he
couldn't see how Armiger was ever going to get it back, short
of shifting the place bodily on to the main road, which was
liable to tax even his formidable powers. Even if he could
continue to fill it as he'd apparently filled it to-night, which was
very doubtful, it would still cost him more to run, with the
staff he'd need here, than he'd make out of it.

It was certainly lively enough to-night. In the crowded public
bar on the left, lantern-lit and period down to the fire-dogs in
the hearth, George recognised most of the Bohemian population
of Comerbourne, more especially the young ones. Ragged beards
and mohair sweaters gave the place the texture of goats and
something of their pungent smell. In the two small lounge-bars
on the right the eighteenth century had been allowed a toe-hold,
and there were some nice brocade chairs and some comfortable
couches, and a fair number of the more sober county posteriors
were occupying them. The dining-room seemed to be doing a
considerable trade, too, to judge by the numbers of white-coated
waiters who were running backwards and forwards for drinks
to the saloon bar. Most of them seemed to be strangers to the
district, probably newly recruited for this house. He saw only
one whom he knew, old Bennie from the White Horse in Comerbourne, no doubt transplanted here for his local knowledge. It
would pay to have someone about the place who knew all the
celebrities, and all the nuisances, too.

They were a mixed bag in the saloon bar, neither big shots
nor Bohemians. The big room had been virtually rebuilt, and
Tudorised with a monstrously heavy hand. The ceiling beams
were too low and too obtrusive, and hung with far too motley
an array of polished copper, much of it shamelessly new.
Armiger always knew exactly what he wanted, and if he couldn't
get it in period he'd have it manufactured specially, even if

it involved some surprising anachronisms. But at least the customers were genuine enough here, farmers, tradesmen, travellers, local cottagers and workmen, and scattered among them the occasional county elder who still preferred this kind of company.

George inched his way patiently to the bar and ordered a pint of mild, and a blonde with a topknot like the Prince of Wales's feathers and long pink finger-nails set the pot in front of him and informed him with a condescending smile that to-night everything was on the house, with Mr. Armiger's compliments. Hence the crowd, he thought, though the evening was yet youngish, and no doubt hundreds more would get wind of the party before closing-time. When drinks were free George stopped at one, indeed if he'd known he would probably have deferred satisfying his curiosity until another night, but he was here now. And the spectacle was undoubtedly interesting. More than half the members of the Borough Council were somewhere in the house, and a good sprinkling of the more widely scattered County Council, too. Armiger crooked his finger and people came running, but how many of them out of any love for him? You wouldn't need the fingers of both hands to count 'em, thought George, one would be enough.

He was carrying his pint pot to the most retired corner he could see when a heavy hand thumped him on the shoulder and a voice resonant and confident as brass, but tuned as truly as brass, too, bellowed in his ear: 'Well, well, my boy, is this an honour or a warning?'

Speak of the devil, and his bat-wings rustle behind you.

'Don't worry,' said George, turning to grin over his shoulder at the man who had bought him the beer. 'I'm off duty. Thirst brought me in on you. Thanks for this, I wasn't expecting it. Cheers!'

Armiger had a whisky in his other hand; he hoisted it to George and downed it in one quick swig. Not a tall man, hardly medium height, but built like a bull, shoulder-heavy, neckless, with a large head perpetually lowered for the charge. He ran head-down at business, at life, at his enthusiasms, at his rivalries, at everyone who got in his way and everything that acquired a temporary or permanent significance for his pocket or his self-esteem. He was dark, with thinning hair brushed across his sun-tanned scalp, and the short black moustache that bristled from his upper lip quivered with charged energy like antennae. His bluish chin and brick-red cheeks gave him a gaudy brilliance no matter how conservatively he dressed. Maybe he'd consumed a fair quantity of his own wares, or maybe he was merely high on his pride and delight in his new toy, and his ebullient hopes for it. Come to think of it, it was very improbable that he ever got tight on liquor, he'd been in command of it and manipulated his fellow-men by means of it too long to be susceptible to it himself at this late stage. He glittered with excitement and self-satisfaction; the bright, shrewd eyes were dancing.

'Well, how do you like my little place? Have I made a good job of it?'

'Terrific,' said George reverently. 'Do you think it's really going to pay for transferring the licence out of the town? Looks to me a costly house to run.'

'You know me, boy, I never throw money away without being sure it'll come back and bring its relations along. Don't you worry, I'll make it pay.'

He slapped George on the back again with a knowing grin, and was off through the crowd head-down, but shoulders swinging, distributing a word here and a hand-shake there, and radiating waves of energy that washed outward through the assembly and vibrated up the panelled walls to clang against the copper overhead. Self-made and made in a big way, Alfred Armiger; many a lesser mortal had been bowled over in that head-down charge to success. Some of the casualties were here to-night; more than one of the looks that followed his triumphal progress through his Tudor halls would have killed if it could.

'He's in high fettle,' said a voice in George's ear. 'Always is when he's been walking on other people's faces.' Barney Wilson of the architect's department slid into the settle beside him, and spread lean elbows on the table; a long, saturnine young man with a disillusioned eye. 'Don't take too much notice of me,' he said with a wry smile, catching George's curious glance, 'I'm prejudiced. I once had hopes of taking this place over myself, pulling down the rubbishy part of it and making the rest over into a house for my family. I still grudge it to him. What does he need with another hotel? He has more than he can keep count of already.'

'Biggish job for a private man, restoring this place, the state it was in,' suggested George, eyeing him thoughtfully.

'Biggish, yes, but I could have done the necessary minimum and moved Nell and the kids in, and taken my own time over the rest. And the way sales trends are running these days, a place this size and in that sort of state was the only kind of place I had a chance of getting. Everybody wants a modern, easy-to-run semi or bungalow, they fetch fantastic prices everywhere, but these bigger properties are going for next to nothing. You can't run 'em without servants, or so everyone supposes, and they cost the earth to maintain. But the maintenance would have just been my job to me, and Nell was raised on a Welsh farm, she knows all about managing a lot of house-room with a minimum of effort. Oh, we thought we were in. I'd even started drawing plans for my conversion, believe it or not, I was that confident. What a hope! The minute I clapped eyes on his man at the auction I knew we'd had it. If it hadn't been for him we could have got the place for the reserve, nobody else wanted it.' He gazed glumly into his beer and sighed. 'But no, he had to snatch it from under our noses and turn it into this monstrosity. You can expect anything of a man who'd turn The Joyful Woman into The Jolly Barmaid!'

'Is that what it used to be called?' asked George, surprised and impressed. 'I never heard that.'

'I'm well up in the history of this house, believe me. I read it up from the archives when I thought we were going to live in it. It was a pub, for centuries before it was used as a private house, and that was the sign – The Joyful Woman. Lovely, isn't it? Goes right back to about 1600. And before that it was a private house again, and before that, until the Dissolution, it was a grange of Charnock Priory. But now it's The Jolly Barmaid, and that's that.'

'Business is business, I suppose,' said George sententiously.

'Business be damned! He's willing to run this place at a loss rather than let his son have any part of it, that's the beginning and the end of it.'

'Was his son going to have some part of it?'

'He was coming in with me. We put together all we could raise between us to bid for it. We were going to convert the barn into a studio for him and Jean, and Nell and I and the kids were going to have the house. You know the barn? It's right across the yard there, beyond where he's laid out the car-park. It's stone, built to last for ever. It would have made an ideal studio flat. But somehow his loving father got to know about it, and he thought a few thousands well spent to spite his son.'

The Armiger family quarrel was no news to George, or indeed to any native of the Comerbourne district. It was natural enough that Armiger, self-made, ambitious and bursting with energy as he was, should intend his only son to follow him in the business, and marry another beer heiress who would nearly double his empire. Natural enough also, perhaps, that the boy should react strongly against his father's plans and his father's personality, and decline to be a beer baron. The story was that Leslie wanted to paint, and most probably the rift would have been inevitable, even if he hadn't clinched his fate by getting engaged to a humble clerk from the brewery offices instead of falling in with his father's arrangements for him. Variations on the theme were many and fantastic from this point on; what was certain was that Leslie had been pitched out of the house without a penny, and the girl had either left or been sacked, and they had married at a registry office as soon as they could. Once married they had dropped out of sight, their news-value exhausted. What was news was that Armiger should still be pursuing them so malevolently that he grudged them even a home.

'There must have been a limit to what he was prepared to throw away in a cause like that,' suggested George mildly. 'He likes his money, does Armiger.'

Wilson shook his head decidedly. 'We went to our limit, and he was still as fresh as a daisy. Maybe he does love his money, but he's got plenty of it, and he loves his own way even more.'

'Still, Leslie shouldn't have any difficulty in getting credit, with his expectations – '

'He hasn't any expectations. He hasn't got a father. This is final. And believe me, the news went round fast. They know their Armiger. Nobody's going to be willing to lend money to Leslie, don't think it. He has the thousand or so he got from his mother, and what he can earn, that's all. And can you think of anyone round these parts who's going to ally himself willingly with somebody on whom Armiger's declared total war?'

George couldn't. It wasn't just the money and power that would frighten them off, it was the sheer force of that ruthless personality. There are people only heroes would tackle, and heroes are few and far between. 'What's young Leslie doing?' asked George. Come to think of it, that made young Leslie a hero; and starting heavily handicapped, too.

'Working as packer and porter and general dog's-body at Malden's, for about eight pounds a week,' said Wilson bitterly. 'He's never been trained to earn his living, poor devil, and painting isn't going to pay the milkman. And a baby on the way, too, so Jean will have to give up her job soon.'

Armiger had erupted into the saloon bar again, sweeping newcomers towards the free drinks, dispensing hospitality in the grand manner. They followed the compulsive passage of the cannon-ball head through the crowd, their eyes guardedly thoughtful. He seemed to have a party with him now, he was busy seating them in a far corner of the big room.

'Parents usually come round in the end, however awkward they may be,' said George without too much conviction.

'Parents, yes. Monoliths, no. Leslie never had but one parent, and she died nearly three years ago, or she might have ventured to stick up for him when the crash came. Not that she ever had much influence, of course, poor soul.'

Wilson was craning to see past undulating shoulders to the group in the far corner, and the passage of a waiter with a loaded tray had just opened a clear corridor to the spot. Others were equally interested in the spectacle. A woman's voice said dispassionately: 'Vulgar little monster!' and a man's voice, less dispassionate, murmured: 'So that *was* Kitty's red bus I saw in the car-park. I thought there couldn't be two like it round here.'

There were three people with Armiger. The man was everything that Armiger was not, and valuable to him for that very reason; George was familiar with the contrast and all its implications. Into houses where Armiger's bouncing aggression would not have been welcomed Raymond Shelley's tall grey elegance and gentle manners entered without comment; where negotiations required a delicacy of touch which Armiger would have disdained to possess, he employed Shelley's graces to do his work for him. Nominally Shelley was his legal adviser, permanently retained by the firm; actually he was his other face, displayed or concealed according to circumstances. Middle-aged, quiet, kind, not particularly energetic or particularly effective in himself, but he supplied what Armiger needed, and in return Armiger supplied him with what he most needed, which was money. He was also Kitty Norris's trustee, having been for years a close friend of her father. And there was Kitty by his side now, in a full-skirted black dress that made her look even younger than her twenty-two years, with an iridescent scarf round her shoulders and a half of bitter in her hand. So that, thought George, admiring the clear profile pale against the subdued rosy lights, is the girl who gave our Dom a lift home the other night. And all Dom could talk about was the car! How simple life is when you're as young as that!

The third person was a handsome, resigned-looking, quiet, capable woman of forty-five, in a black suit, who was just fitting a cigarette into a short black holder. The movements of her long hands were graceful and strong, so was her body under the severely-tailored cloth. She let the men talk. Intelligent, illusionless eyes swept from face to face without noticeable emotion; only when she looked at Kitty she smiled briefly and meaningly, owning a contact with her which set the men at a slight distance. Women as efficient as Ruth Hamilton and as deeply in the business secrets of their employers frequently entertain a faint contempt for the temples they sustain on their shoulders and the gods they serve.

'His secretary,' said a man's voice in an audible whisper somewhere behind them. 'Has been for twenty years. They say she does more than type his letters.'

That was no new rumour, either, George had heard it bandied about for at least ten of the twenty years. The only surprising thing about it was to hear it mentioned at all; it had been taken for granted, whether believed or discounted, for so long that there was no point in trying to squeeze a drop of sensation out of it now. Nor was anyone ever likely to know for certain whether it was true or not. The legend had been more or less inevitable, in any case, for Miss Hamilton had virtually run Armiger's household as well as his office ever since his wife's long, dragging illness began, and that was a good many years ago.

Wilson emptied his pint and pushed the tankard away from him. 'Jean is quite a girl. But sometimes I wonder how Leslie ever managed to see her in the first place, with Miss Norris around. Not that I think he made any mistake, mind you. Still – look at her!'

George had been thinking much the same thing, though he did not know Jean Armiger. Young men frequently reject even

323

the most dazzling of girls, he reflected, when thrust at them too aggressively by their fathers, and if Armiger's mind was once made up he would certainly tackle this enterprise as he did every other, head-down and bellowing. Still – look at her!

She was the last person at whom he did turn and look when he left the saloon bar at about ten o'clock. She hadn't moved, she'd hardly spoken; she sat nursing the other half, but only playing with it, and though Armiger had vanished on one of his skirmishes and Miss Hamilton seemed to be gathering up her bag and gloves and preparing to leave, Kitty sat still; so still that the sparkles in the glittering scarf were motionless, crumbs of light arrested in mid-air. Then the swing-door closed gently on the grave oval of her face, and George settled the collar of his coat and strolled across the hall towards the chill of the September night.

Old Bennie Blocksidge, a lean, tough little gnome, was crossing the hall with an empty tray, all the copper witchballs repeating his bald pink dome as he passed beneath them. He stopped to exchange a word with George, jerking his head in the direction of the side door which led out to the courtyard.

'He's in high feather to-night, Mr. Felse. No holding him.'

'He' could be no one but Armiger. 'I noticed he's vanished,' said George. 'Why, what's he got up his sleeve now? I should think he'd had triumph enough for one night.'

'He's just gone off with a bottle of champagne under his arm, any road up, off to show off his new ballroom to some bloke or other. That's the old barn what was, off across the yard there. Wanted to open it this week, he did, but they've only just finished the decorations. Sets great store by it, and so he ought, it's cost him a packet.'

So that was what was to become of young Leslie's studio. George stepped aside to allow free passage to two people who had just followed him out of the saloon bar, and watched Miss Hamilton and Raymond Shelley cross the hall together and go out through the swing-doors and the nail-studded outer portals which stood open on the night; and in a few moments he heard a car start up in the car-park, and roll out gently on to the road, and caught a glimpse of Shelley's Austin as it swept round and headed for Comerbourne.

'Told us not to disturb him, neither,' said Bennie, sniffing. 'Says he'll be back when he's good and ready. Ordered his car for ten, and here it is turned ten, and he says, "tell him he can damn' well wait till I'm ready, if it's midnight." Clayton's sitting out there in the Bentley cursing like a trooper, but what's the good? There's never no doing anything with him. If you like your job you just go with him, nothing else you can do.'

'And you do like your job, Bennie?'

'Me?' said Bennie with a grin and a shrug. 'I'm used to it, I go with the stream. There's worse bosses than him, if you just go along with him and don't worry. These youngsters, they fret too much.'

'Well, let's hope he soon drinks his champagne and lets Clayton take him home.'

'It was a big 'un, a magnum. He thinks in magnums.'

'He does indeed!' said George. The Jolly Barmaid was a classic example of Armiger's inflated habits of mind. 'Good night, Bennie!'

'Good night, Mr. Felse.'

George walked home into Comerford, and gave his wife and son a brief account of his evening's entertainment.

'Your girl-friend was there, Dom,' he said, glancing mischievously at Dominic, who was in his homework corner still bent over a book, though it was a late start rather than an exaggerated sense of duty that had kept him at it until this hour. He slapped the Anglepoise lamp away from him and quickly switched it off, to hide the fierce blush that surged up into his cheeks, and assuming his protective colouring with the dexterity of a cornered animal, said eagerly: 'No, was she? Did you see the car? Isn't it a beauty?'

'I wasn't looking at the car.'

'Gosh, can you beat it! No soul!' said Dominic disgustedly, for once removing himself to bed without having to be driven. He had told his parents about coming home in the Karmann-Ghia because he was experienced enough to know that even if they had not witnessed his arrival themselves, someone among the neighbours was sure to have done so, and to retail the information over pegging out the washing or giving the lawn its last autumn mowing. Better and safer to give them an edited version himself, and the car made wonderful cover; but if his father was going to spring nasty little surprises like that sudden dig to-night, Dominic was going to have to stay in dark corners, or keep his back turned on his family.

Bunty Felse awoke just after midnight from her first light doze with a curious question on her mind, and stroked George into wakefulness with the gentle ruthlessness wives employ instead of open brutality.

'George,' she said as he grunted a sleepy protest into her red hair, 'do you remember that singer girl at Weston-super-Mare last summer? The one who dragged Dom into her act, the way they do?'

'Mmm!' said George, dazed by this seeming irrelevance. 'What about her, for goodness' sake?'

'He noticed *her* all right, didn't he?'

'Couldn't very well miss her,' admitted George, 'she was round his neck. How on earth did she get him up there? Some trick – I don't remember. I know I blushed for him.'

'Yes, *you* did,' said Bunty significantly. '*He* didn't. He bragged about it for days, the little ass. He said she was a dish.'

'That's all those paperbacks he reads.'

'No, I think it's pop records. The point is, apparently this Norris girl really is a dish. But he never said so. Why?'

'No accounting for tastes,' mumbled George. 'Maybe he doesn't think she is a dish.'

'Why shouldn't he? Everybody else does. *You* do,' said Bunty, and was drifting off to sleep again, still worrying over the discrepancy, when the telephone beside their bed rang.

'Damn and blast!' said George, sitting up in bed wide awake and reaching for the instrument. '*Now* what's up?'

The telephone bleated in a quavering voice which at first he hardly recognised for Bennie Blocksidge's. 'Mr. Felse?' it wailed. 'Oh, Mr. Felse, I dunno if I'm doing right, but I'd sooner it was you, and you're the nearest, and being as you were here to-night it's you I called. We got bad trouble here, Mr. Felse. It's the gov'nor, Mr. Armiger. He never come back. Past closing-time, and he never come, and eleven, and half past eleven, and the lights still on in there. And Mr. Calverley got worried, and one thing and another, even if he did say not to disturb him, they went to see was he all right –'

'Make it short,' said George, groping for his slippers. 'What's happened? I'm on my way, but what's happened? Make it three words, not three hundred.'

'He's dead,' said Bennie, making it two. 'There in the barn, all by himself, stone dead and blood all over.'

· Chapter 3

The moment of truth had overtaken Armiger in the middle of
an expanse of new flooring almost big enough for a bull-ring,
and of a colour not so far from that of fine sand. He lay in the
full glare of his brand-new lights, sprawled on his face with
arms and legs tossed loosely about him, his right cheek flattened
against the glossy parquet. If you stooped to look carefully the
thick profile in its bold, bright colouring still showed clear and
undamaged; but the exposed back of his head was crumpled
and indented, welling dark blood that oozed up out of the
splintered cavities and spilled sluggishly over into the puddle
gathering on the floor, where the crimson of blood and the thin
clarity of wine met and intermingled in long, feathery fronds
of pink.

All around his head and shoulders blood and champagne had
spattered to a distance of two or three feet, but not so lavishly
as old Bennie had made out, you could easily approach him
between the splashes, at least from the back, from which
position, George thought, squatting over the body, this ferocious
damage had been done. Any enemy of Alfred Armiger's might
well prefer not to face him when he hit out at him at last. The
neck of the magnum lay in the pink ferns of the pool, close to
the shattered head, and slivers of glass glittered on the bull
shoulders; two yards away the rest of the bottle lay on its side,
a thin dotted line of blood marking where it had rolled when it
broke at last.

Well at least, thought George grimly, we're spared the classic
hesitation between accident, suicide and murder; the one most
easily associated with Armiger was the one that overtook him,
and nobody's ever going to argue about it.

328

Death and the Joyful Woman

He had called his headquarters in Comerbourne before he left home, called them again after his first check-up on the scene, and turned everyone else out of the ballroom until the van should arrive. He had the place to himself for a quarter of an hour at the most. For Armiger he felt as yet nothing but a sense of shock and incredulity that so much demoniac energy could be so abruptly wiped out of existence. The blob of black in the acres of pallor looked like a squashed fly on a window-pane.

He stood back carefully, avoiding the splashes of blood, and looked round the room. No sense of reality informed this scene, it was a stage set, lavish and vulgar, the curtain rising on a run-of-the-mill thriller. The barn, pretty clearly, had once been the hall of the older house. Its proportions were noble, and its hammer-beam roof had been beautiful until Armiger got at it. His impact had been devastating; the hammer-beams and posts, the principals and curved braces and purlins had all been gilded, and the squares of common rafters between the gold had been painted a glaring glossy white, while from the centre beam depended four spidery modern electric chandeliers. The concentration of reflected light was merciless. All round the upper part of the walls he had built a gallery, with a dais for the band at one end, and a glass and chromium bar at the other, a double staircase curving up to it from the dancing floor with an incongruous Baroque swirl. Beneath the gallery the walls were lined with semi-circular alcoves fitted with seats, in every alcove an arched niche with a white plaster dancer; Empire, this part of it, if it could be said to have a style at all. Small tables nestled in the curves of the balustrade all the way round the gallery. The walls were white and gold and a glitter of mirrors. The palais crowd, thought George, dazed, will love it. Poor Leslie Armiger, he'd never see his beautiful bare, spacious studio home again. He'd never have been able to afford to heat it properly, in any case, it would have been Arctic in winter.

So much for the setting in general. Of notable disarrangements in this vacant and immaculate order there were only two, apart from the body itself. One of the plaster statuettes, from the alcove on the right of the door, lay smashed at the foot of the wall. There was no apparent reason for it, it was a good fifty feet from where Armiger lay, and apart from the broken shards there was no sign of any struggle, no trace even of a passing foot. The other detail struck a curiously ironical note. Someone, almost certainly Armiger himself, had fetched two champagne glasses from the bar and set them out on the small table nearest to the gilded dais at the top of the staircase. Evidently he had had no forewarning, he had still been in high feather, still bent on celebrating; but he had never got as far as opening the magnum.

George paced out thoughtfully the few yards between the sprawling feet in their hand-made shoes, and the foot of the staircase. No marks on the high gloss of the floor. He eyed the broken magnum; there was not much doubt it was the instrument which had killed Armiger. It was slimed with his blood right to the gold foil on the cork, and no artificial aids were necessary to see clearly the traces of his hair and skin round the rim of the base.

George cast one last look round the glaring white ballroom, and went out to the three men who waited nervously for him in the courtyard.

'Which of you actually found him?'

'Clayton and I went in together,' said Calverley.

There was a sort of generic resemblance in all the men Armiger chose as managers for his houses, and it struck George for the first time why; they were all like Armiger. He singled out people of his own physical and mental type, and what could be more logical? This Calverley was youngish, thick-set but athletic, like an ex-rugby-player run very slightly to flesh; moustached, self-confident, tough as fibre-glass. Not at his deb-onair best just now, understandably; the face made for beaming good-fellowship was strained and greyly pale, and the quick eyes alert for profit and trouble alike were trained on trouble now, and saw it as something more personal than he cared for. He'd even gone to meet trouble half-way, it seemed, by arming himself with a companion. People whose daily lives were spent in Armiger's vicinity soon learned to be careful.

'What time would that be?' They'd know, to the minute; they'd been watching the clock for him over an hour, waiting to get him off the premises and call it a day.

'About four or five minutes after midnight,' said Calverley, licking his lips. It was not yet one o'clock. 'We gave him until midnight, that's how I know. We'd been waiting for him ever since closing-time, but he'd said he didn't want to be disturbed, so – well, we waited. But from half past eleven we began to wonder if everything was all right, and we said we'd give him until twelve, and then go in. And we did. When it struck we left the snug at once, and came straight over here.'

'All the lights were on like that? You touched nothing? Was the door open or closed?'

'Closed.' Clayton fumbled a cigarette out of the pocket of his tight uniform jacket, and struck a match to light it. A lean, wiry, undatable man, probably about thirty-five, would look much the same at sixty; flat sandy hair brushed straight back from a narrow forehead, intelligent, hard eyes that fixed George unblinkingly and didn't mind the light. And his hands were as steady as stone. 'I was first in, I handled the door. Yes, the lights were on. We never touched a thing once we'd seen him. We only went near enough to see he was a goner. Then I run back to the house to tell Bennie to call the police, and Mr. Calverley waited by the door.'

'Had anyone seen Mr. Armiger since he came over here?' George looked at old Bennie, who was shivering in the background.

'Not that I know of, Mr. Felse. Nobody from the house has been across here. He never showed up after he took the champagne off the ice and walked off with it. I saw him go out of the side door. You know, Mr. Felse, you just come into the hall then yourself.'

'I know,' said George. 'Any idea who this fellow was, the one to whom he wanted to show the ballroom? You didn't see him?'

'No, he wasn't with him when I saw him go out.'

'He made quite a point of not wanting to be disturbed?'

'Well – ' Bennie hesitated. 'Mr. Armiger was in the habit of laying off very exact, if you know what I mean. It wa'n't nothing out of the way this time.'

'Can you remember his exact words? Try. I'm interested in this appointment he had.'

'Well, I says to him, "Mr. Clayton's 'ere with the car." And he says: "Then he can damn' well wait until I'm ready, if it's midnight. I'm just going over to show a young pal of mine my ballroom, he'll be right interested, he says, to see what you can do with a place like that, given the money and the enterprise – and I don't want anybody butting in on us," he says, "I'll be back when I'm good and ready, not before." And then he goes.'

'But he didn't sound upset or angry about it?' The words might have indicated otherwise in another man, but this was how Armiger habitually dealt with his troops.

'Oh, no, Mr. Felse, he was on top of the world. Well, like he was all the evening, sir, you saw him yourself.'

'Odd he didn't mention a name.'

'With that much money,' said Clayton in his flat, cool voice, 'he could afford to be odd.'

'He was laughing like a drain,' said Bennie. 'When he said that about showing off the ballroom he was fair hugging himself.'

'Somebody must have seen this other fellow,' said George. 'We shall want to talk to all the rest of the staff, but I take it all those who don't live on the premises have gone home long ago.' That would be the first job, once the body was handed over to the surgeon. 'Any of the waiters living in, besides Ben?'

'Two,' said Calverley, 'and two girls. They're all up, I thought they might be needed, though I don't suppose they know anything. My wife's waiting up, too.'

'Good, we'll let her get to bed as soon as we can.' He pricked his ears, catching the expected note of the cars turning in from the road. 'That's them. Go and switch the corner light on for them, Bennie, will you? And then I think you three might join the rest of the household inside.'

They withdrew thankfully; he felt the release of a quivering tension that made their first steps almost as nervous as leaps. Then the ambulance wagon came ponderously round into the yard, and Detective-Superintendent Duckett's car impatiently shepherding it, and the machinery of the County C.I.D. flowed into the case of Alfred Armiger and took possession of it. It was a mark of the compulsive power of the deceased that the head of the C.I.D. had climbed out of his bed and come down in person at one o'clock in the morning. Only the murder of his own Chief Constable could have caused him greater consternation. He stood over the body, hunched in his greatcoat against the chill of the small hours and the hint of frost in the air, and scowled down at the deformed head which would never plan mergers or mischief again.

'This is a hell of a business, George. I tell you, my boy, when you came on the line and told me, I thought you'd gone daft or I had.'

'I felt much the same,' said George. 'But there's not much mistake about it, is there?'

Death, like its victim, had never been more positive. Superintendent Duckett viewed the setting, the body and the instrument, and said nothing until the doctor was kneeling over his subject, delicately handling the misshapen skull. Then he asked briefly, growling out of his collar: 'How many blows?'

'Several. Can't be sure yet, but six or seven at least. The last few possibly after he was already dead. Somebody meant business.' The doctor was youngish, ex-army, tough as teak, and loved his job. He handled Alfred Armiger with fascinated affection; nobody had cherished him like that while he was still alive.

'And I always thought it would be apoplexy,' said Duckett, 'if it ever happened to him at all. How long's he been dead?'

'Say half past eleven at the latest, might be earlier. Tell you better later on, but you won't be far out if you consider, say, ten-fifteen to eleven thirty as the operative period. And most of these blows were struck while he was lying right here, and I'd say lying still.'

'The first one put him out, in fact, and then whoever it was battered away at him like a lunatic to make sure he never came round again.'

'Not like a lunatic, no. Too concentrated and accurate. He was on target every time. But you could call them frenzied blows – they went on long after there was any need.'

'So it seems. Didn't stop till the bottle broke. Marvel it didn't break sooner, but glass plays queer tricks. George, on the details of this we sit, but firmly,' said Duckett heavily. 'Dead, yes, of head injuries if we have to go that far, but keep the rest under wraps for the time being. I'll issue a statement myself, refer the boys to me. And warn off those fellows who found him. We don't want this released until I see my way ahead.'

'Very good,' said George. 'I don't think they'll be wanting to talk about it, they're too close to it for comfort. Can you make anything of that broken statuette?'

Duckett approached and stared at it, glumly frowning, then picked up its nearest neighbour, a couple locked in a tango death-grip. He grunted with surprise at its lightness, and turned it upside down to stare with disgust into its thin shell. 'Sham as the rest of the set-up.' He put it back in its place and thumped the wall beneath it experimentally, but light as it was it sat sturdily on its broad base, and never even rocked. 'Wouldn't fall even if you crashed into the wall beside it, you'd have to knock the thing off bodily. No trace of anything else in the wreckage, nothing was thrown. No scratched paint. And anyhow, if it fell it would fall slightly outwards from the foot of the wall, this is right in the angle of the wall. May be dead irrelevant, may not. Get a record of it, Loder, while you're about it. Not a hope of getting any prints off it, surface is too rough, but I suppose Johnson may as well try.' The photographer, circling Armiger's body, murmured absorbed acquiescence, and went on shooting.

'And the champagne glasses,' said George.

'I saw them. You know whose prints will be on those, don't you? Be a miracle if there are any others, unless it's the maid's who dried them and stacked them away here when they were unpacked. Still, we'll see. Door, of course, Johnson, all the possible surfaces, baluster of that staircase. And that disgusting mess.' He indicated the magnum with a flick of his foot. 'His own liquor turned traitor in the end.'

'Whoever was holding the neck of that,' said George, 'must have been pretty well smeared. Blood all over it, right to the cork. His shoes and trousers may be spattered, too, though maybe not so obviously as to attract attention. I figure he was standing this side. He took care not to step in it. Not a trace between these marginal splashes and the door.'

'Well,' said Duckett, stirring discontentedly, 'give me all you've got.'

George gave it, including his own accidental contact with Bennie during the evening.

'And those other two? What account have they given of their moves from ten o'clock on?'

'Clayton was sitting in the car out front when I left, which would be several minutes after ten. He says he moved the car into the yard about twenty past, as he saw no sign of Armiger coming back, and he was in the pub until closing-time, had one pint of mild, and that's all. From half past ten until nearly eleven he hung around by the car. Still no boss. Then Calverley asked him to come into his own sitting-room, and he was there with Calverley and Mrs. Calverley all the time from then on.

335

All three vouch for that. Bennie was clearing up in the bars with the other waiters, and keeping an eye open for Armiger returning, so that he could give Clayton the item. Around half past eleven Calverley and Clayton began to think they ought to investigate. They're all used to doing what Armiger says and making no fuss about it, but they'd also be blamed if anything came unstuck and they didn't deduce it by telepathy and come running, so whatever they did was pretty sure to be wrong, it was only a question of which was wronger, to butt in on him when he didn't want them or to be missing when he did. I won't say they were worried about him, but they were getting worried about their own positions with relation to him. Come midnight, they said to each other, better risk it. And they walked in solidly together and found him like this. The only period they don't cover for each other is approximately half past ten to eleven, but I fancy you'll find the indoor staff can account for Calverley for most of that time, too. Clayton could have moved around outside without being observed. I haven't had time to see the others yet, but they're waiting for me.'

'So many more mouths to shut,' said Duckett. 'Those three will have spread the load by now.'

'You know, I doubt it. Don't forget, this place only opened to-night, and all the staff except Bennie Blocksidge seem to have been brought into the district from all over. None of them knows the others yet. And when this drops on a bunch of strangers it's just as likely to shut their mouths as open them. After all, somebody killed him, it might be the bloke sitting next to you.'

'Get on to 'em, anyhow. When we finish here and take him away I'm leaving you holding it, George. Ring me early, and I'll send you a relief.'

'I'll stay with it all day,' said George firmly, 'if it's all the same to you.' He wanted to be sure of an undisturbed night rather than an uneasy and solitary sleep during the day. 'Want me to contact Armiger's solicitors, or will you do that?'

'*Cui bono?*' said Duckett absently. 'I'll get on to them myself. You make what you can of the bunch here, and I'll send Grocott to help you with the day staff when they come in, and the list of people who were in the pub last night.'

George left them still busy with cameras and flashes, and went to interview the frightened maids and waiters and the pretty, bleached blonde who was Mrs. Calverley. He got as little from them as he had expected, but deduced from the frozen silence in which he found them that they had justified his forecast by withdrawing into themselves rather than sharing their fears. Laboriously he put together an account of Armiger's movements during the last hour or two of his life. Shortly before ten, according to Mrs. Calverley, one of the waiters, a young man named Turner who lodged in Comerford, had come into the saloon bar and relayed some message to Mr. Armiger, who had excused himself to his friends and followed him out. A couple of minutes later he had returned, gone straight to his party and had a word with them, and then gone out again. It appeared that this must have been when the anonymous young pal arrived to see him, for what he did next was to bounce into the servery by the dining-room, help himself to a magnum of champagne, and make off in the direction of the side door, bumping into Bennie and giving him his orders with regard to Clayton and the car on the way. No one had again seen him alive.

By the time George had done with the last of them it was almost daylight, and the ambulance had long since taken the dead man away, though Johnson was still in possession of the ballroom, indefatigably combing every hospitable surface for prints. George took himself home for a bath and breakfast and a brief and troubled conference with Bunty, and then took himself off again before Dominic should come scurrying downstairs and begin to ask questions.

He called at the house where the waiter lodged, and found him sitting in his room poring over the day's runners, half-dressed and not yet shaven. Turner was a Londoner, pale with the city pallor on which summer has no influence, thin and sharp-eyed and dubious of Comerford already. He wouldn't last long, he'd be off back to town. Meantime he might well be detached about all the people involved in this case, since he knew none of them. He wasn't worried about being visited by the police, only puzzled and intrigued.

Yes, he said, some time before ten, maybe five minutes or so, he couldn't be exact, he'd been passing through the hall and a young man had walked in at the door and buttonholed him, and asked for Mr. Armiger. Didn't give a name, just said ask Mr. Armiger if he can spare a few minutes, say it's important and I won't keep him long. And he'd delivered the message, and thought no more about it, and Mr. Armiger had gone out to his visitor, who had waited in the hall for him. That was the last Turner had seen of either of them, because he'd been back in the dining-room after that. Did he know the young man? He knew nobody here, he'd only just come. Could he describe him? Well, there was nothing special about him. Young fellow about twenty-five or twenty-six. Dark overcoat and a grey suit. No hat. Tallish but not tall, clean-shaven, brown hair, nothing particular to notice about him. But he'd know him again if he saw him. Or a photograph? Well, probably, but you can't always tell with photographs. He could try. Why, anyhow? What did they want him for? What had happened?

George told him, in the shortest and most startling words he could find, watching the cigarette that dangled from a colourless lip. The ash didn't even fall, but at least Turner's eyes opened fully for the first time, staring at George with a curiosity and excitement in which he could see no trace of fear or even wariness. The unmistakable tint of pleasure was there. Nothing against the boss, you understand, but after all, he'd hardly clapped eyes on him a couple of times, and it isn't every day you get up this close to a murder.

'Go on!' he said, gleaming. 'Well, I'll be damned!' And so he might, but not, thought George, for anything to do with Armiger's death. 'You reckon it was this fellow I saw who done it?'

'It's merely one line of inquiry,' said George dryly. 'What I'm trying to do is to fill in all the details of the evening, that's all. What time did you leave the job last night?'

'About twenty to eleven.' The thought that he might have to account for himself had not shaken his confidence in the slightest. 'I got back here before eleven, the old girl'll tell you the same. What's more, one of the other blokes walked back with me, name of Stokes, you'll find him just up the street here, Mrs. Lewis's.' He pushed the paper aside, not even the runners could win back his attention now. 'Can you beat it!' he said, and whistled long and softly. 'And they think they've got all the life down home!'

George went down the dingy stairs turning over in his mind the irony of this last comment, and betting himself, though without relish because he was on a virtual certainty, that Turner would be in for work before his time that day, if never again.

The news hadn't got out yet, or at least it was not yet public property, for there was no crowd dawdling hopefully about The Jolly Barmaid when George returned to its bright new doors. He put in a call to Duckett, outlined his moves up to date, and the little information he had gleaned from them, and settled down to compile, with Bennie Blocksidge's help, a list of people who had been present at the gala opening on the previous evening. There would be no opening hours to-day, that was out of the question with the emperor dead; and once half past ten arrived and the first customer was brought up short against a closed door and a laconic notice, the secret wouldn't be a secret long.

By the time their list was as complete as their combined memories could make it, Grocott and Price were on the premises and waiting for orders. George unloaded the more promising of the routine calls on to them, and went to telephone Duckett again. By this time even solicitors should be working, and '*Cui bono?*' was still one of the leading questions. Had Armiger really cut off his son completely, or had he only threatened him and left him to stew a while in his own juice? Not in the hope of bringing him to heel, since marriage can't be sloughed off as easily as all that even to satisfy an Armiger; but perhaps merely out of spleen, to punish him for his rebellion with a taste of poverty, before taking him back chastened and amenable.

And plus an ex-clerk wife who would be a constant reminder of a defeat to her unloving father-in-law? No, it wasn't easy to imagine it, after all. George turned a thumb down as he dialled Duckett's number. About a hundred to one Leslie didn't figure in the will, unless in some peculiarly hurtful and humiliating way. And Armiger's wife was some years dead, and he had no other child. So somebody was due for a windfall. He wouldn't disseminate his empire, living or dead. Nor was it really conceivable that he would have neglected to make a revised will, or even postponed it for a period of reflection. He had never reflected, but always charged, and this time would be no exception.

'I talked to old Hartley,' said Duckett. 'The terms of the will won't be much help to us at first glance, but they're interesting, very interesting. Seems he had his old will destroyed and dictated the terms of a new one the very day he threw his son out. The boy isn't so much as mentioned. Might as well be dead, apparently, to his father.'

'I've been betting myself,' said George, 'that he wouldn't let his pile be divided up. Right?'

'Right. He was a born amasser, he didn't want things to disintegrate after he was gone, either. There's a long list of minor legacies to staff, not one of 'em interesting to us, you wouldn't consider killing a mouse for the amounts he considered a due reward for service. Mind you, he paid good wages living, I don't think it's meanness, it's just this empire-building tendency of his. But the residue of his property, after payment of these flea-bites, is left to – did I hear you make a guess?'

'You did not,' said George. 'My mind's a blank. He didn't, by any chance, think of the possibility of grandchildren, and leave it in trust for them?'

'Not a hope. The whole dynasty is cancelled, he's making a new and surprising start. The name is Katherine Norris, George. And what, if anything, do you make of that?'

Chapter 4

And what *did* George make of it? Just plain spite? A reaction towards Kitty Norris simply because Leslie had veered off from her and married someone else? A way of hitting Leslie as hard as possible by so pointedly deflecting his expectations into the lap of the girl he wouldn't marry? Not a gesture of consolation to Kitty, Armiger wasn't quite as clumsy as that, surely, even when he was angry. Or was there more to it than met the eye? Plainly this represented a move to amalgamate Armiger's Ales and Norris's Beers and vest the lot in Kitty after his death; but might it not be intended primarily as a move in a game which was to be played with Armiger very much alive and in shrewd command of his forces? Kitty would be welcome to the show after he was dead, provided he ran it while he was alive. His naming her as his heiress might well be an earnest of good faith designed to bring off a deal which had so far eluded him, and the deal could only be the acquisition of Norris's to add to his own barony here and now. After all, with Leslie out of the picture Armiger was making no sacrifice in declaring his intention of leaving everything he had to Kitty, since he had no other close relatives, and he couldn't take his fortune with him. He had to dispose of it somehow; how better than by buying a present gain with it, while he was here to enjoy it?

Supposing there existed a tentative proposition for a merger, thought George, and Miss Norris's manager was holding off – as he understandably might, for once the two firms were joined there wasn't much doubt who would turn out to be the boss – wouldn't such a disposition for the future strengthen Armiger's hand considerably? What had he to lose, in any case? If he failed to get what he wanted this will was as easily revoked as the previous one. It was at least worth a try. What Armiger wanted he usually got, hence the ferocity and finality of his reaction on the one occasion when he failed in his aims.

George got out his car and sat behind the wheel, and thought out his next move without haste. A rum set-up, when you came to think of it, old Norris making Armiger's right-hand man trustee for his daughter, but the three men had been fairly close friends, and nobody had ever questioned Shelley's integrity; it seemed to work well enough in practice. He didn't know whether the trust was wound up now that the girl was of age, or not. There were a lot of relevant things he didn't know, and on the face of it he had very little right so far to inquire into them. There was only one person he had a perfect right to see about Kitty Norris's movements and affairs, and that was Kitty Norris. She had been at The Jolly Barmaid last night, she had been with Armiger, he had spoken to her, among others, just before he went off happily to display his latest garish toy; and sooner or later George would have to see her. It might as well be sooner, he decided, and started the car.

Kitty had a flat in Comerbourne, not far from the main shopping centre, but tucked away in a quiet street in the lee of the parish church, and therefore clear of the business traffic which made the town bedlam all through the day. Even there, however, parking was a problem, and George had to take his Morris a good way past the house in order to find a vacant space into which he could insert it. He was lucky, the red Karmann-Ghia was there at the kerb, so Kitty was in. It was nearly noon when she opened the door to him, in a sweater and skirt and a pair of flat, childish sandals, and gazed at him for a moment with nothing in her eyes but patient bewilderment, waiting for him to state his business.

'My name is Felse,' said George. 'I'm a police officer, Miss Norris.' The bewilderment vanished so promptly, she stepped back from the doorway so instantly, that he knew she knew. 'You've heard already about Mr. Armiger?'

'Mr. Shelley telephoned me,' she said. 'Come in, Mr. Felse.'
She was looking at him, he noticed, with a certain grave
curiosity which he thought was not all for his office but partly
for himself, and he was human enough and male enough to be
flattered and disarmed by her attention. Some people cannot
look directly at you in conversation even when they have nothing
to hide; Kitty, he thought, would look straight at you even if
she had a guilty secret to hide, because it was the way she was
made, and she wouldn't be able to help it.

'I'm making investigations into Mr. Armiger's death, and
there are points on which I think you may be able to help me,
if you will. I promise not to keep you very long.'

'I wasn't doing anything,' she said, leading him into a big,
pastel-coloured room, lofty and unexpectedly sunlit, for she
lived on the fourth floor, and the buildings opposite were lower,
and showed her only their roofs. 'Please sit down, Mr. Felse.
May I get you a drink?' She turned and looked at him with a
small, wry smile. 'It sounds like a Raymond Chandler gambit,
doesn't it? But I was just going to have a sherry, actually. And
after all, you're not a private eye, are you?'

'More of a public one,' said George. It wasn't going as he'd
expected, but he was content to let it wander; it might arrive
somewhere very interesting if he let well alone.

'I hope you like it dry,' said Kitty deprecatingly. 'It's all I've
got.' The hand that proffered the glass was not quite steady, he
saw, but there was every excuse for that tremor.

'Thanks, I do. I'm afraid it must have been a great shock to
you, Miss Norris – Mr. Armiger's death.'

'Yes,' she said in a low voice, and sat down directly in front
of him and looked straight at him, just as he'd foreseen she
would have to do. 'Mr. Shelley and Miss Hamilton both rang
up to tell me,' she said. 'I didn't want to believe it. You know
what I mean. He was so alive. Whether you liked him or not,
whether you approved of him or not, there he was, and you
couldn't imagine the world without him. And there were things

about him that were admirable, you know. He was brave. He came up with nothing, and he took on the world to get where he got. And even when he had so much he wasn't afraid. People often learn to be afraid when they have a lot to lose, but he was never afraid of anything. And he could be generous, too, sometimes. And good fun. If you were a child he wasn't afraid or ashamed to play with you like a child – even though there was really nothing childish left in him. I suppose it was because children made good playthings for him, because we were satisfied with lots of action, and never made difficulties of principle for him like grown-ups do. It was very easy to get on with him then. And very hard afterwards.' She looked down into her glass, and for the first time George saw, as Dominic had seen, the essential sadness of her face, and like Dominic was dumbfounded and engaged by it, inextricably caught into the mystery of her loneliness and withdrawal.

She moved, he thought, as though her course was set, and her own volition had nothing to do with it, having aligned itself long ago with some other influence which was disposing of her. Not Arminger's influence, or she could not have talked of him like that. Perhaps not any man's, only a tide of events in which she felt herself to be caught, and which she had to trust because she had no alternative.

'We're all imperfect,' said George, trying to speak as simply as she had done, and hoping he didn't sound as sententious to her as he did to himself. 'I think he'd like what you've just said of him.'

'There was a great deal that I had against him,' she said, choosing her words with scrupulous care. 'That's why I want to be fair to him. If there's anything I can tell you, of course I will.'

'You were with him last night, at least for part of the evening. Towards ten o'clock, so I understand from one of the waiters, someone asked Mr. Armiger to spare him a few minutes, and Mr. Armiger went out to speak to him. He then came back and spoke to you and the other people at his table, before leaving again. Is that right?'

'I didn't look at the time,' she said, 'but I expect that's accurate enough. Yes, he came back to us and said would we excuse him for a quarter of an hour or so, he had to see someone, but he'd be right back, and he hoped we'd wait for him.'

'That's all he said? He didn't mention a name, or anything like that?'

'No, that's all he said. And he went, and then Ruth said she had to get back, because she was expecting a call from her sister in London about a quarter to eleven, she'd promised she'd be in at that time. That's Miss Hamilton, you know, Mr. Armiger's secretary. And as Mr. Shelley had brought her he had to leave, too, so I was on my own. I thought at first I would wait, and then I didn't, after all. I was tired, I thought I'd have an early night. I think it must have been just after a quarter past ten when I left, but maybe someone else might know. The car gets quite a lot of attention,' said Kitty without a trace of irony in her voice or her face, 'someone may have seen me drive off.'

Someone had; Clayton had, as he chafed and cursed in his boss's Bentley in front of The Jolly Barmaid, five minutes or so before he resigned himself to a long wait and moved the car into the courtyard. He had watched her drive out from the car-park and pull out to the right on her way to Comerbourne; and devoted car-enthusiast though he was, it was doubtful if he had been looking at the Karmann-Ghia.

'I see,' said George. 'So you'd be home by soon after half past ten, I suppose.'

'Oh, before, I expect. It only takes me ten minutes, even counting putting the car away. Oh God!' said Kitty, recollecting herself too late, as usual. 'I shouldn't be telling you that, should I?'

'I'm incapable of working it out without a pencil and paper,' George reassured her, smiling. But even when she made you laugh there was something about this girl that had you damn' near crying, and for no good reason. She wasn't heartbroken about Armiger, she'd stated her position with reference to him punctiliously; shocked she might well be, but that wasn't what had got into even her smile, even the sweet, rueful clowning that came naturally to her.

'May I ask you some personal questions about your affairs, Miss Norris? They'll seem to you quite irrelevant, but I think if you care to answer them you may be helping me.'

'Go ahead,' said Kitty. 'But if it's business it's odds on I won't even know the answers.'

'I understand that your father left his estate in trust for you, dying as he did when you were quite a child. Can you tell me if that trust terminated when you came of age?'

'I know the answer to that one,' she said, mildly astonished, 'and it did. I can do whatever damn-fool thing I like with my money now, they can only advise me. Actually it all goes on just the same as before, but that's the legal position.'

'So if a merger was proposed between Armiger's and Norris's it would be entirely up to you to decide whether you wanted to go through with it?'

'Yes,' she said, so quietly that he knew she had heard the further question he had not asked. 'He did want that,' she said, 'you're quite right. He's been working at it for some time. The people at our place weren't very keen, but he was like the goat in that silly song, and I dare say he'd have busted the dam in the end. But nothing had happened yet, and now it doesn't arise any more.'

'And what did you want to do?'

'I didn't want to do anything. I wanted not to know about it, I wanted to be somewhere else, and not to have to think about it at all. I'd have been glad to give it to him and get rid of it, myself, but after all, people work there, a lot of people, and it means more to them than it does to me. One ought not to own something that matters more to other people. If I knew how to set about it, or could persuade Ray Shelley to understand what I wanted, I'd like to give it to *them*.'

George had a sense of having been drawn into a tide which was carrying him helplessly off course, and yet must inevitably sweep him, in its own erratic channel, towards the sea of truth. He certainly wasn't navigating. Neither, perhaps, was she, but she swam as to the manner born with this whirling current, its overwhelming simplicity and directness her natural element. She meant every word she said now, there was no doubt of that, and she expected him to accept it as honestly; and confound the girl, that was exactly what he was doing.

Trying to get his feet on to solid earth again, he said: 'This idea of uniting the two firms wasn't a new one, was it? Forgive me if I'm entering on delicate ground, but the general impression is that Mr. Armiger had the same end in mind earlier, and meant to achieve it in a different way, by a direct link between the two families.'

'Yes, he wanted Leslie to marry me,' she said, so simply that he felt ashamed of his own verbosity. She looked up over her empty glass, and he saw deep into the wide-set eyes that were like the coppery purple velvet of butterfly wings. You looked down and down into them, and saw her clearly within the crystal tower of herself, but so far away from you that there was no hope of ever reaching her. 'But it was his idea, not ours. You can't make these things for other people. He ought to have known that. There never was any engagement between Leslie and me.'

A moment of silence, while she looked steadily at him and her cheeks paled a little. He had one more question to ask her, but he let it ride until he had risen to take his leave, and then, turning back as if something relatively unimportant had occurred to him, he asked mildly: 'Do you happen to know the terms of Mr. Armiger's will?'

'No,' she said quickly, and her head came up with a sudden wild movement, the velvet eyes enormous and eager upon his face. He saw hope flame up in her as though someone had lighted a lamp; a word, and something like joy would kindle in the crystal tower of her loneliness. What was it she wanted of him? Beyond the relatively modest needs of her car and her wardrobe and this almost cloistral flat of hers, money seemed to mean very little to her. He had to go through with it now, because he had to know if what he had to tell her was what she wanted to know.

'He's left everything to you,' said George.

The light in her was quenched on the instant, but that was the least of it. She stood staring at him open-mouthed, and the colour drained slowly from her face. Her knees gave under her, she reached a hand back to grope for the arm of a chair, and sat down dazedly, her fingers clenched together in her lap.

'Oh, *no!*' said Kitty in a gasping sigh that seemed to contain disappointment and consternation and rage inextricably mingled, and something else, too, a kind of desperation for which no effort of his imagination could account. 'Oh, *God*, no! I hoped he'd never really done what he threatened – or if he had done it I hoped he'd taken it back. I mean about *Leslie*! he always swore he hadn't and wouldn't, but then even if he had he wouldn't have been able to admit it, you see. And now – Oh, *damn* him!' she said helplessly. 'Why? There was no possible reason, the thing never arose. He knew I didn't need it, he knew I shouldn't want it. *Why?*'

'He had to leave it to someone,' said George reasonably, 'and he had a free choice what he did with his own, like everyone else. There's no need for you to feel responsible for someone else's deprivation, you know, it was none of your doing.'

'No,' she said dully, and let the monosyllable hang on the air as though she had meant to add something and then could find no suitable words for what she wanted to say. She got up again resignedly to see him out, punctilious in accompanying him to the door, but all the time with that lost look in her eyes. When the door had closed between them he made three purposeful paces away from it towards the stairs, and two long, silent ones back again. She hadn't moved from the other side of the door, she was leaning against the wall there, trying to think, trying to get hold of herself. He heard her say aloud, helplessly: 'Oh, God, oh, God, oh, *God*!' in childish reproach, as though she was appealing to an unreasonable deity to see her point of view.

What had he done to her? What *was* it he'd done? Granted she didn't want the money, granted she thought it ought to have gone to Leslie, she needn't have received the news as though it embodied some peculiarly insidious attack upon her. He couldn't say he hadn't provoked any interesting reactions, the trouble was he didn't know how to make sense of them now he'd got them.

He went down the carpeted stairs displeased with himself, almost ashamed, not even trying to make the odd pieces of jigsaw puzzle fit together, since they were so few and so random that no two of them touched as yet; and there, leaning negligently on the Morris, when he reached it, was Dominic.

He was a little out of breath, having run all the way to the car while George was coming down the last flight of stairs; but George was too preoccupied with other things to notice that. The bright inquisitive smile looked all right, the 'Hallo, Dad!' sounded all right, and George didn't look closely.

'Hallo!' he said. 'What are you doing here?'

It was the third time Dominic had skipped his school lunch and made do with a snack in the town, in order to have time to walk slowly up and down Church Lane in the hope of catching a glimpse of Kitty. The telephone directory had supplied her address, once she herself had told him her name. He hadn't yet quite recovered from the shock of strolling past the open door of the block and seeing the unmistakable shape of his father slowly descending the last turn of the stairs; and if it hadn't been for the sudden inspiration the sight of the car had given him, he would have been running still.

'I've been on an errand for Chuck,' he said, mastering his breathing with care. Chuck was the least offensive of the several names by which his house-master was known to the upper school.

'Here?' said George, divining an improbability even where he had no reason to feel suspicious.

'To the rector,' said Dominic firmly, jerking his head towards the corner of the churchyard wall. Blessedly the rector was a governor of the school and chaplain to its cadet corps. 'I saw the car and hung around on the offchance. As it's getting round to half past twelve I thought with a lot of luck you might buy me a lunch.'

On reflection George thought he might. Beer barons may die, but the rest of the world still has to eat. 'Get in,' he said resignedly, and took his offspring to a restaurant not far from the school, so that there should be no risk of his being late in the afternoon. 'What about Chuck? Can the answer wait?'

'No answer,' said Dominic. 'That's all right.' The odd thing was that he didn't feel as if he was lying at all; it was quite simply unthinkable to let the truth be seen or known, or even guessed at, though there was nothing guilty or shameful about it. Privacy as an absolute need was new to him. Ever since starting school at five years old he'd lied occasionally in order to keep something exclusively for himself, like most children, but without ever reasoning about what he was doing, and only very rarely, because his parents, and particularly his mother, had always made it easy for him to confide in them without feeling outraged. This was something different, something so urgent and vital that he would have died rather than have it uncovered. And yet he had to do things which would expose him to the risk of discovery; he had to, because what was his father doing there in the block of flats where Kitty lived? What was he doing there, the morning after old Armiger was killed, the morning after Kitty'd been with him at The Jolly Barmaid? 'Your girl-friend was there –' And now this visit. They'd have to see everyone who'd been there, of course, but why Kitty, so soon?

'You're on this murder case, aren't you?' he said, trying to strike the right note of excited curiosity. 'Mummy told me this morning old Armiger was dead. What a turn up! I never said anything to the fellows, naturally, but it leaked in around break, with the milk. It's all over the town now, they've had half a dozen people third-degreed by this time, and one or two arrested.'

'They would,' said George tranquilly. 'The number of people who can do this job better than I can, it's a wonder I ever hold it down at all. Who's the favourite?'

A sprat to catch a mackerel was fair enough. Dominic trailed his bait and hoped for a rise. 'That chap Clayton. I bet you didn't know he was under notice, did you?'

'The devil he is!' said George, wondering if Grocott had collected this bit of information yet, wondering, too, from which school theorist the item of news had come.

'Then you didn't know! Old Armiger's gardener's son is in our form. There was a blazing row three days ago over hours, Clayton pitched right in and said he wouldn't stand for being shoved around all hours of the day and night, and Armiger threw it up at him that he'd done time for larceny once and once for receiving a stolen car, and he was bloody lucky to have a job at all – '

'Language!' said George mechanically, drawing in to the kerb.

'Sorry; quoting. And then he fired him. Did you know he had a record?'

'Yes, we knew. A record ten years old. Not enough to hang him.'

'It isn't capital murder,' said Dominic.

'I hope you're not going to turn into a lawyer in the home,' said George. 'I was using a figure of speech.'

He locked the car, and ushered his son before him into the dining-room of The Flying Horse. They found a table in a corner, and settled purposefully over the menu. Bad timing, thought Dominic, vexed. I shall have to come right out and ask.

'Are you on to anything yet?' The ardent face, the earnest eyes, these would pass muster with George; it was Dominic himself who suffered, making this enforced use of travesty of something so real and so important to him. His father *was* wonderful, and he *did* feel a passionate partisan interest in any case his father was handling. But here he was putting on the appropriate face for his own ends, parodying his own adoration, and it caused him an almost physical pain when George grinned affectionately at him, and slapped him down only very gently.

'Just routine, Dom. We've hardly begun, there's a long way to go yet.'

'Who was it you had to see in Church Lane? There aren't any suspects there, are there?'

After a moment of consideration George said calmly: 'I'd been to see Miss Norris. Just as I told you, pure routine. I'm working my way through a whole list of people who were on the premises last night, that's all.'

'And no real leads yet? I don't suppose *she* was able to tell you much, was she?'

'Practically nothing I didn't know already. Get on with your lunch and stop trying to pump me.'

And that was all he was going to get, for all his careful manipulations. He tried once or twice more, but he knew it was no good. And maybe there was nothing more to extract, maybe this was literally all. But Dominic wasn't happy. How could he be, with murder passing so close to Kitty that its shadow came between her and the sun?

Chapter 5

'Yes,' said Jean Armiger, 'I've heard the news. It's in the noon papers, you know. I've been expecting you.'

She was a slender dark girl, with short black hair clustering closely round a bold, shapely head. Her face was short, broad and passionate and her spirit was high. She couldn't be more than twenty-three or twenty-four. She stood squarely in the middle of her ugly, inconvenient furnished bed-sitting-room on the second floor of Mrs. Harkness's seedy house in a back street on the edge of town, facing George and the full light from the window, and scared of neither. The slight thickening of her body beneath the loose blue smock had robbed her of her quick-silver lightness and precision of movement, but its unmistakable qualities were there in every motion she made with her hands and head. For some reason, perhaps because Kitty had a way of dimming everyone else around her, George hadn't expected anyone as attractive as this, or as vivid. Jean, as Wilson had said, was quite a girl. It wasn't so difficult, after all, to see how Leslie Armiger might contrive to notice her existence, even in Kitty's presence. He had grown up on brotherly terms with Kitty.

'You'll understand, I'm sure, that we have routine inquiries to make. Were you at home last night, Mrs. Armiger?'

She curled a lip at the phrase, and cast one flying glance round the room he had dignified by the name. True, there was a cramped make-shift kitchenette out on the landing to be added to the amenities, and a shed in the garden where Leslie was allowed to keep his easel and canvasses and colours. But – home?

'Yes,' she said, forbearing from elaborating on the glance, which had been eloquent enough. 'All the evening.'

354

'And your husband?'

'Yes, Leslie was here, too, except for a little while, he went out about half past nine to post some letters and get a breath of air. He was in the stores packing orders all day yesterday, he needed some fresh air. But it was only for about half an hour.'

'So he was home by ten?'

'I think it was a little before. Certainly by ten.'

'And he didn't go out again?'

'No. You can check that with him, of course,' she said disdainfully. At this very minute, if all had gone according to plan, Grocott would be asking Leslie Armiger the same questions, discreetly in the manager's office, at Malden's, so that the staff, no doubt already agog, shouldn't jump to the conclusion that he was due to be arrested any moment; but Jean didn't know that, of course. George wasn't even sure why he had taken the precaution of arranging these two interviews to take place simultaneously; he had no reason as yet to distrust this young couple rather than any other of the possible suspects, but he had learned to respect his hunches. And if they had no lies to tell he had done them no wrong.

'We shall do that, of course,' he said disingenuously. 'Tell me, Mrs. Armiger, have you had any contact with your father-in-law since your marriage? Ever seen him or spoken to him?'

'No, never,' she said firmly, with a snap which said plainly that that was the way she had wanted it.

'Nor your husband, either?'

'He hasn't seen him. He did write to him once, only once, about a couple of months ago.'

'Trying to effect a reconciliation?'

'Asking for help,' said Jean, and bit off the consonant viciously and clenched her teeth on silence.

'With your consent?'

'*No!*'

She wasn't going to much trouble to hide her feelings, but she hadn't intended to spit that negative at him so bitterly. She turned her head away for a moment, biting her lip, but she wouldn't take it back or try to soften it now it was out.

'With what result?'

'With no result. He sent a contemptuous answer and refused to do anything for us.' She had been grateful for that, it had salved the fierce pride Leslie had involuntarily injured by making the appeal.

'And there's been no further approach?'

'None as far as I know. But I'm sure none.'

After some inward debate George told her the terms of Armiger's will; it seemed a justifiable line of inquiry. 'Does that come as a surprise to you, Mrs. Armiger?'

'No,' she said steadily. 'Why should it? He had to leave his money to someone, and he had no relatives left that he hadn't quarrelled with.'

'You didn't know of this plan to make Miss Norris his heiress?'

'All we knew was that Leslie was written off for good, so it no longer concerned us. His father had made that very plain.'

She was turning the narrow wedding ring upon her finger, and George saw that it was loose. The cheek on which the dark hair curled so lustrously was thinner than it should have been, too, perhaps with too much fatigue and worry, carrying the child, running this oppressive, cramped apology for a home and working part-time to eke out the budget; or perhaps with some other strain that gnawed at her from within. Something terrifying and destroying had happened to her when Leslie caved in and wrote to his father, something he might never be able to undo. Thanks to that unrelenting old demon of a father of his, he had another chance to come up to her expectations, if he had it in him; but after that one slip he had to prove it, up to then probably she'd been serenely sure of him. And yet George could see Leslie's point of view, too. He must love his wife very much, or he wouldn't have burned his boats for her sake; and to see her fretting here, to think of his son spending the first months of his life here, was surely enough to bring him to heel, however reluctantly. You could even argue that his attitude was more responsible than hers. What was certain was that by that one well-meant gesture he'd come dangerously near to shaking his marriage to pieces.

'I won't trouble you any longer, Mrs. Armiger. Thank you for your help.'

He rose, and she went with him to the door, silent, disdaining to add anything or ask anything. Or hide anything? No, she would do that, if she had to. Maybe he'd soon know whether she was already hiding something.

The stairs were dark and narrow, the house smelled of oilcloth, stale air and furniture polish. Mrs. Harkness's frigid gentility would never stand many visits from the police, even in plain clothes. George had already observed that no telephone wires approached the house, and that there was a telephone box only fifty yards away at the corner of the road. He drove away in the opposite direction, but turning left at the next by-road came round the block and parked under the trees within sight of the bright red cage, and sat watching it for a quarter of an hour, twenty minutes, twenty-five; but Jean Armiger didn't come.

That pleased him; he had liked her, and he wanted her on the level, and though he had suffered some reverses in the past he had never yet learned to be sufficiently wary of the optimism with which he viewed the motives and actions of those people who made an instant good impression upon him. However, he went through the motions of scepticism; he wouldn't commit himself to believing absolutely in her until he'd called Grocott, who was back in the office by now waiting for the telephone to ring.

The call tended to confirm his view that Jean was honest, and her testimony reliable. Young Leslie, called discreetly into conference from his dusty warehouse behind the big shop in Duke Street, had told a story which tallied at all points with

357

his wife's. Instead of going straight back after posting his letters he'd gone for a walk round the park. He hadn't been away quite half an hour, because he was certain the church clock hadn't struck ten when he let himself into the house again. All very simple and entirely probable, and there had certainly been no contact between husband and wife. Yet the result, perversely, was to make George turn and take another look at his dispositions; and there was still room for doubt. As Jean had so unwisely revealed that she knew, Duckett's bald statement was in the noon papers. Armiger had been found dead last night on the premises of The Jolly Barmaid with severe head injuries; foul play was, by implication, taken for granted, though Duckett had avoided committing himself. That was enough to alert both the dispossessed son and his fiercely loyal wife; guilty or innocent, they would know they must shortly account for their movements on that evening, guilty or innocent they might find themselves without a surety except each other, and make haste to co-ordinate the details of their story before the questions were asked. There'd been time for a telephone call between the appearance of the early editions on the streets and George's two-thirty deadline. Depressed, George searched for the vindicating detail which should justify him in throwing this doubt overboard, but he couldn't find one. Given the intelligence Jean certainly did not lack, there could have been collusion.

'How did he look?'

'Not too bad. A bit shocked, naturally, but he didn't pretend they'd been on good terms, or that he was terribly cut up. Even if he was, actually, he wouldn't let you see it. A very reserved chap, and a bit on the defensive, too.'

'Scared?'

'I wouldn't say scared. But he's well aware that he's in a spot to attract, shall we say, the unwelcome attentions of the nosy public as well as ours. He's no fool, and he knows his affairs are common property. Knows his strongest card is that he had nothing to gain by killing his dad, too.'

'Did he take pains to call your attention to the fact?'

'You underestimate him,' said Grocott with a short laugh. 'He's giving us credit for seeing that much ourselves. He just seemed to me to be leaning back on it for reassurance every time the going looked a bit rough.'

'How does he get on with the drivers and warehousemen?' asked George curiously. Such little communities don't always take kindly to young men of superior education and manners accidentally dropped among them, especially if the alien tends to keep himself to himself.

'Surprisingly well. They seem to like him, call him Les, and let him mull in with them or keep quiet according to how he feels. Main thing is, I think, that there's nothing phoney about him. He doesn't try to be hail-fellow-well-met or drop his accent and pick up theirs. They'd soon freeze him out if he did, but he's a lot too sensible for that. Or too proud. Either way it's worked out to his advantage.'

The picture that emerged, thought George as he walked back to his car, was an attractive one, but he had to beware of being disarmed by that into writing off Leslie Armiger as innocent. Money is not the only motive for killing. There on one side was the heiress, already so wealthy that the money motive was no motive at all, and on the other side this young couple, very poor indeed but with nothing whatever to gain by Armiger's death. He was of some potential value to them still so long as he remained alive, since in time he might have relented and taken them into favour after all. Especially with a grandson or granddaughter on the way. On the other hand, those who knew him best had said that he was extremely unlikely to change his attitude – and anyone can let fly in a rage, even with nothing to gain by it but the satisfaction of an overwhelming impulse of hatred and a burning sense of injury.

And there were others who didn't love him, besides his own son. Clayton, that quiet tough in uniform, had turned out to be under notice, and Armiger had apparently tossed his prison record in his teeth when they fell out, and told him he was 'bloody lucky to have a job at all.' Had that been merely a shaft at random, or meant to suggest to him that Armiger could, if he chose, make it practically impossible for him to find alternative employment anywhere in the Midland counties? People have been killed for reasons a good deal less substantial than that. And there was Barney Wilson, who had been done out of the home on which he'd set his heart, merely to satisfy Armiger's spite against his son. That way the injury might smart even more fiercely than if the blow had been aimed directly at him. And others, too, people who had done business with Armiger to their cost, people who had worked for him.

Sitting there in the car contemplating the width of the field wasn't going to get him anywhere. George hoisted himself out of a momentary drowsiness and drove to the head office of Armiger's Ales, which was housed in a modern concrete and chromium building on a terrace above the cutting of the river. The main brewery was down behind the railway yards, in the smoke and grime of old Comerbourne, but the headquarters staff had broad lawns and flowering trees spread out before their windows, and tennis courts, and a fine new car-park for their, on the whole, fine new cars. Miss Hamilton's Riley was the only old one among them, but of such enormous dignity and lavish length that it added distinction to the whole collection.

She drove it well, too, George had often seen her at the wheel and admired her invariable calm and competence. As often as not there would be two or three callow teenage boys in the car with her when she was seen about at week-ends in summer, recruits from the downtown youth club she helped the probation officer to run. Maybe love of that beautifully-kept old Riley had been the saving of one or two potential delinquents within the past few years.

Raymond Shelley was just crossing the entrance hall when George appeared. He halted at once, obviously prepared to turn back.

'Do you want to see me? I was just on my way out, but if you want me, of course – ' He had his briefcase under his arm and his silver-grey hat in his hand; the long, clear-featured face looked tired and anxious, and there was a nervous twitch in his cheek, but his manners would never fall short of the immaculate, nor his expression fail of its usual aristocratic benevolence. 'One of your men was in this morning, so I rather assumed you'd done with us for to-day. I was going out to see Miss Norris. But I can easily telephone and put it off for an hour or two.'

'Please don't,' said George. 'I'll talk to Miss Hamilton, if she's free. You go ahead with whatever you were planning to do.'

'You're sure? Naturally if there's anything further I can do to help I'll be only too pleased. I'll bring you to Ruth's room, at least.' He reached a long, thin hand to the polished balustrade of the staircase and led the way. 'We have already accounted for ourselves, of course,' he said with a wry smile.

'I happened to see you leave the premises with Miss Hamilton last night,' said George, returning the smile. 'I was in the hall when you left.'

'Good, that puts us in a very strong position. I wish all the other problems were going to be as easily resolved,' said Shelley wretchedly. 'This is a beastly business, Mr. Felse.'

'Murder usually is, Mr. Shelley.'

The word pulled him up motionless for a moment. 'Is that absolutely certain, that it's murder? The official statement leaves the issue open, and your man this morning was very discreet. Well – ' He had resumed his climb, and turned right in the broad panelled corridor on the first floor. 'I won't pretend I'm surprised, everything pointed that way. At the moment I can't realise what's happened. I can think and understand, but nothing registers yet. It's going to take a long time to get used to his not being here.'

'I can appreciate that,' said George. 'You've worked with him a good many years. Known him, perhaps, better than anyone, you and Miss Hamilton. You're going to miss him.'

'Yes.' He let the monosyllable stand alone, making no claims for his affection; if anything, he himself sounded a little surprised at the nature of the gap Alfred Armiger had left in his life. He tapped on the secretary's door, and put his head into the room. 'A visitor for you, Ruth,' he said, and went away and left them together.

She rose from behind her desk, a tall, quiet woman in office black which had suddenly become mourning black, her smooth dark hair parted in the middle and coiled on the back of her neck. Twenty years she'd been in Armiger's service. There wasn't much she didn't know about him and his family, and maybe to understand all is to forgive a good deal, at any rate. Her calm was as admirable as ever, but her face bore the marks of shock and strain. He saw her fine black brows contract at sight of him, in a reflex of distress and reluctance, but she made him welcome none the less, and sat down opposite him in front of her desk, instead of withdrawing behind it, to mark her abdication from her official status.

'I've come to you as the person who can best help me to understand the family set-up here,' said George directly. 'Anything connected with Mr. Armiger's circle and affairs may be of vital importance now, I know you realise that. As one who is in a position to be fair to both of them, will you tell me the facts about Mr. Armiger's quarrel with his son?'

She set an open box of cigarettes and a heavy glass ash-tray on the edge of the desk midway between them, and allowed herself a moment for thought before she answered. He had time to take in the character of the room, which from long association had taken on her strong, austere colouring. The small black wall-clock with its clear, business-like face and good design was of her choosing, so were the elegant desk fittings. And there were two large framed photographs on the wall, and one smaller one in a stand-up frame on the desk, all of groups of boys from the probation officer's club. Two of the pictures she herself had probably taken at some summer camp; the third showed half a dozen boys grouped round her at a party on the club premises. She looked entirely at home among them, firm and commanding still, but flatteringly handsome and feminine, guaranteed to make any unstable sixteen-year-old feel six inches taller every time she allowed him to light her cigarette or embrace her in a foxtrot. Waste of an able woman, thought George, twenty years running nothing more personal than this office; she ought to have had a couple of promising boys of her own to worry about, instead of picking up the casualties after the kind of wastrel family that has a dozen and neglects the lot.

'There were faults on both sides,' she said at last, a little tritely after so much thought. She felt the inadequacy herself, and smiled. 'But in reality Mr. Armiger himself was responsible for all of them. I'm sure I needn't tell you that he was a most difficult man, whether as an employer or a parent. It wasn't wilful, he simply could not see another person's point of view. He was honestly convinced that everything and everybody ought to revolve about him and do what he expected of them. As a child Leslie was dreadfully spoiled. He could have anything he wanted provided it didn't cross his father's will, and while he was a child of course there wasn't any real clash. Every accomplishment such as his painting, everything he shone at, every superior possession, only flattered his father. And he was never punished for anything unless it annoyed his father, you see. After Mrs. Armiger began to be an invalid and kept to her room they asked me to move into the house. Mr. Armiger used to spend more of his time at home then, and manage a good deal of his business from there, before this place was completed. I won't say I didn't do my best to straighten up the accounts, the few years I was there, but it was a bit late to take Leslie in hand by then, the damage was done. Well, as soon as Leslie began to grow up and need a life of his own the clashes began, as you can imagine. They fought spasmodically for four or five

years before the break came, and all the earlier fights Mr.
Armiger naturally won. All the effective weapons were on his
side. But when the issues at stake became more and more
important it didn't work out that way any longer. Leslie paints
very well, he wanted to go in for it seriously, but his father
wouldn't let him, he made him come into the offices here.
Everybody had to fall in with *his* plans. Leslie was supposed to
marry Kitty Norris and go into beer in an even bigger way than
his father. And before they'd finished fighting out the battle
about his painting, he'd met Jean and there was an even bigger
row brewing up.'

'He got to know her right here, in the offices?'

'At first, yes, and then they began seeing each other casually,
not even secretly, and Mr. Armiger was furious. There was a
terrible scene, and he ordered Leslie not to see her again, and
laid down the law flat about what his future was to be, toe the
line or go. I don't think he meant it then, he was only trying
to bring Leslie to heel, but this was the real issue at last, and
it broke all the rules. Leslie should have given in and promised
to be a good boy. Instead, he went right out and took Jean
dancing and got himself engaged to her on the spot.'

'Not the best possible prospect for a marriage,' suggested
George, 'if he walked into it simply as a way of rebelling against
his father.'

'It wasn't that,' she said, shaking her head decidedly. 'All his
father had done was make him realise what was at stake, how
big it was and how very much he wanted it. And as soon as he
recognised it he grabbed it, like a sensible boy, and hung on to
it, though the repercussions were hair-raising. He walked right
in here to his father's office the next day, and stood in front of
his desk, and just blurted out like a gunshot that he was engaged.
Maybe that's the only way he could get it out at all. Mr. Armiger
really thought, you know, even then, that he could simply order
him to break it off. When he found he couldn't I expected a
heart attack from pure shock. Leslie dug his heels in and said

no, no, no, and went on saying no. He couldn't believe it was happening to him. When he really grasped the idea, he threw them out, and that time he did mean it. All right, he said, if you want her, if she's worth that to you, take her. Take her out of here now, this minute, and neither of you need ever come back. And Leslie said O.K., that suited him, and he went right downstairs and did just that, bundled Jean into her hat and coat and walked out with her. She stayed in her lodgings and he went to a hotel, and they spent the time while they waited to get married looking for somewhere to live. Leslie went to the house just once more, to collect his things, but as far as I know he never did see his father again. He couldn't find anything better for them than furnished rooms, and when it came to getting a job, of course, he'd no qualifications and no training. The only thing he'd taken seriously at Oxford was his painting. He had to go to work more or less as a labourer. I'm afraid he's collected all the arrears of discipline he missed in one dose,' she said ruefully. 'If he comes through it intact you can say he'll be able to cope with anything else life may throw at him.'

'Would he ever have relented?' asked George.

'Mr. Armiger? No, never. Crossing his will was an unforgivable blasphemy. I can imagine him as a senile old man in the nineties, perhaps, turning sentimental and wanting a reconciliation – but never while he had all his faculties.'

'Did anyone try to reason with him at the time?' She smiled at that, rightly interpreting it as meaning in effect: did you?

'Yes, Ray Shelley broke his head against it for weeks, and Kitty did her best, too. She was very upset, she felt almost responsible. As for me, I know a rock when I see one. I didn't say a word. First because I knew it would be no good, and secondly because if by any chance he did have a sneaking wish to undo what he'd done, arguing with him would only have made him more mulish than ever.'

'Did you by any chance see the letter Leslie wrote to his father two months ago?' asked George.

The level dark eyes searched his face. 'Did Leslie tell you about that?'

'No, his wife did. I haven't yet seen Leslie.'

Quietly she said: 'Yes, I saw it. It wasn't at all an abject letter, in case you don't know what was in it. Rather stiff-necked, if anything, though of course it was a kind of capitulation to write at all. They'd obviously only just settled for certain that Jean was going to have a baby, and the poor boy was feeling his responsibilities badly, and I suspect feeling very inadequate. He told his father the child was coming, and appealed to him to help them at least to a roof of their own, since he'd robbed them of the one they'd hoped to have. I don't know if you know about that?'

'I know,' said George. 'Go on.'

'Mr. Armiger made a very spiteful reply, acknowledging his son's appeal like a business letter, and repeating that their relationship was at an end, and Leslie's family responsiblities were now entirely his own affair. It was deliberately worded to leave no hope of a reconciliation, ever. He pretended he'd had no idea Leslie ever wanted the barn, but then he ended by saying that since he was interested in the place he was sending him a souvenir of its purchase, and it was the last present they need ever expect from him. As a would-be painter, he said, Leslie might find it an appropriate gift. It was the old sign, from the earlier days when the house used to be an inn.'

'The Joyful Woman,' said George.

'Was that its name? I didn't know, but that accounts for it. I saw it when Mr. Armiger brought it in for the people downstairs to pack. It was a rather crude painting of a woman laughing, a half-length. They found it in the attics when the builders moved in on the house. It was on a thick wooden panel, very dirty and damaged, the usual kind of daub. One of the firm's cars took it and dumped it at Leslie's landlady's house the day after the letter was written.'

Jean had said nothing about the gift, only about the curt and final letter. But there might be nothing particular in that omission, since the gift was merely meant to be insulting and to underline what the letter had to say. This is all you need expect from me, living or dead, and this is all you'll ever own of The Joyful Woman. Make the best of it!

'Leslie didn't write or telephone again?'

'Never again as far as I know. But I should know if he had.'

And all day, thought George, I've been writing off a certain possibility because I felt so sure that, firstly, if Leslie did go and ask for an interview Armiger wouldn't grant it, and secondly, if by any chance he did choose to see him it certainly wouldn't be to greet him with back-slapping heartiness, champagne and a preview of his appalling ballroom. But maybe, after all, that was exactly the way he might receive him, rubbing salt into the wounds, goading him with the shoddy miracles money could perform. On a night when triumph and success were in the air maybe this was much more his mark, not direct anger but this oblique and barbaric cruelty. 'He'll be interested to see what can be done with a place like that, given plenty of money and enterprise – ' 'He was fair hugging himself.'

'Miss Hamilton, have you got a reasonably recent photograph of Leslie?'

She gave him a long, thoughtful look, as though she was considering whether he could need such a thing for any good purpose, and whether, in any case, denial could serve to do anything but delay the inevitable. Then she got up without a word, and went behind the desk, and brought out from one of the drawers a half-plate portrait, which she held out to him with a slight, grim smile shadowing the corners of her mouth. It had at some time been framed, for George saw how the light had darkened the pale ground slightly, and left untouched a half-inch border round the edges. More recently it had been torn across into two ragged pieces, and then carefully mended again with gum and Sellotape. The torn edges had been matched as tenderly as possible, but the slash still made a savage scar across the young, alert, fastidious face.

George looked from the photograph to the woman behind the desk.

'Yes,' she said. 'I fished it out of his wastepaper basket and mended it and kept it. I don't quite know why. Leslie has never been particularly close to me, but I did see him grow up, and I didn't like to see the last traces of him just wiped out, like that. That may help you to understand what had happened between them.' She added: 'It's two years old, but it's the only one he happened to have here in the office. I'm pretty sure it wouldn't be any use looking for any of those he had at home.'

George could imagine it. A much-photographed boy, too, most likely. He saw bonfires of cherubic babies, big-eyed toddlers, serious schoolboys, earnest athletes, self-conscious young men-about-town, Armiger's furnace fed for hours, like a Moloch, on images of his son.

'Thank you, Miss Hamilton. I'll see that you have it back,' was all he said.

The face was still before his eyes as he went out to his car. Leslie Armiger was not visibly his father's son. Taller, with long, fine bones and not much flesh. Brown hair lighter than his father's curled pleasantly above a large forehead, and the eyes were straight and bright, with that slight wary wildness of young and high-mettled creatures. The same wonder and insecurity was in the long curves of his mouth, not so much irresolute as hypersensitive. No match for his father, you'd say on sight, if it came to a head-on clash either of wills or heads. But in spite of the ceremonial destruction of his image, young Leslie was still alive; the bull had pawed the ground and charged for the last time.

It was just four o'clock, and Dominic was walking up Hill Street on his way to the bus stop. Since he had to pass the main police station it was his habit to call in, on days when he hadn't biked to school, on the off-chance that George might be there with the car, and ready to go off duty; and sometimes he was lucky. To-day George picked him up at the corner and took him to the office with him while he filed his latest report; then they drove home together.

'One little call to make,' said George, 'and then we'll head for our tea. You won't mind waiting a minute for me? It won't take long.'

'And then you've finished for the day?' Dominic's anxious eyes were searching his face surreptitiously, and trying to read the mind behind it. He would have liked to ask right out if anything positive had turned up, if Kitty was safely and irrevo-cably out of the affair; but how could he? They had had a family code for years in connection with George's work, governed by rules none the less sacred for being unformulated; and once already to-day he'd been warned off from infringing them. One did not ask. One was allowed to listen if information was volunteered, and to suggest if participation was invited, but never to ask; and a silence as inviolable as the confessional sealed in all that was said within the framework of a case. He contained the ache within him, and waited faithfully, but it hurt.

'Don't know yet, Dom, it'll depend on what I get here.' He was turning into the empty parking-ground of The Jolly Bar-maid. 'If my man's here I shan't be five minutes, whatever the outcome may be.'

But it did not take even five minutes, for Turner was sitting in the curtained public bar, cigarette on lolling lip, devouring the racing results, and it needed only one good look at Leslie Armiger's photograph to satisfy him.

'That's him. That's the young bloke who come asking for Mr. Armiger. Stood on the doorstep to wait for him, but I saw him in a good light when he first come in. Different clothes, of course, but that's him all right, I'd know him anywhere.'

'You'd swear to him?'

'Any time you like, mate. About five to ten he walked in, and Mr. Armiger came out to him, and that's the last I saw of 'em.'

'Thank you,' said George, 'that's all I wanted to know.'

He pocketed the photograph and went back to the car thinking grimly: Home by ten, were you, my lad! So you've solved the problem I've always wanted to get straightened out, how to be in two places at once. Now I wonder if you'll be willing to tell me how it's done?

Chapter 6

Leslie Armiger was not a happy liar. There was almost as much relief as fright in his eyes as he looked from the photograph to George's face and back again. Jean came to his side, and he put his arm round her for a moment, with a curiously tentative gesture of protection, as though he had wanted to clasp her warmly, and either because of George's presence or his own predicament or her aloofness he could not.

'The best thing you can do now,' said George sternly, 'is tell me everything. You see what happens when you don't. You, too, Mrs. Armiger. Wouldn't it have looked infinitely better if you'd told the truth in the first place, rather than leave it to come out this way?'

'Now wait a minute!' Leslie's sensitive nostrils were quivering with nervous tension. 'Jean had nothing to do with this. She hasn't got a time sense, never did have. She merely made one of her vague but confident guesses, saying I was in by ten.'

'And picked on a time and a few details that matched your story word for word? That tale was compounded beforehand, Mr. Armiger, and you know it as well as I do.'

'No, that isn't true. Jean simply made a mistake – '

'So you backed up her statement rather than embarrass her? Now, now, you can do better than that. Have you forgotten that your statement and hers were made at the very same moment, something like a mile apart? My boy, you're positively inviting me to throw the book at you.'

'Oh, Christ!' said Leslie helplessly, dropping into a chair. 'I'm no good at this!'

'None at all, I'm glad you realise it. Now suppose we just sit round the table like sensible people, and you tell me the truth.'

371

Jean had drawn back from them, hesitating for a moment. She said quietly: 'I'll make some coffee,' and slipped out to the congested kitchenette on the landing; but George noticed that she left the door open. Whatever her private dissatisfactions with her husband, she would be back at his side instantly if the law showed signs of getting tough with him.

'Now then, let's have it straight this time. What time did you really come home?'

'It must have been about ten to eleven,' said Leslie sullenly. 'I did go to that pub of his, and I did ask to see him, but I give you my word Jean didn't know anything about it. All she did was get worried because of the times, because there was three-quarters of an hour or so unaccounted for. But I never told her where I'd been.'

George had no difficulty in believing that; it was implied in every glance they cast at each other, every hesitant movement they made towards each other, so wincingly gentle and constrained. It was clear that they knew how far apart they stood, and were frightened by the gap that had opened between them. That fiery girl now so silent and attentive outside the half-open door was suffering agonies of doubt of her bargain. Had he, after all, the guts to stand up to life? Was that disastrous appeal to his father only a momentary lapse, or was it a symptom of inherent weakness? George thought they had fought some bitter battles, and frightened and hurt each other badly; but now he was the enemy, and they stood together in a solid alliance against him. He might very well be doing them a favour just by being there.

'Then you'd better tell her now, hadn't you?' he said firmly. 'It'll come better from you than from anyone else. And she may be a good deal happier about knowing than about not knowing.'

'I suppose so.' But he didn't sound convinced yet, he was too puzzled and wretched to know which way to turn. He swallowed the humiliation of being lectured, and began to talk.

'All right, I went out to post my letters, and then I kept

going, and went straight to the pub and asked for my father. I didn't want to go in, I just stuck at the door until he came out to me. And I didn't happen to see anybody I knew – the waiter was a stranger – that's why, when this thing blew up this morning, I was fool enough to think I could just keep quiet about being there. But you mustn't blame Jean for trying to help me out.'

'We won't bring your wife into it. Why did you go and ask for this interview? To make another appeal to him?'

'No,' said Leslie grimly, 'not again. I was through with asking him for anything. No, I went to get back from him something of mine that he'd taken – or if I couldn't get it back, at least to tell him what I thought of him.' He was launched now, he would run. George sat back and listened without comment to the story of the first appeal, and the answer it had brought, the cruel and gloating gift of the old inn sign as a memento of Leslie's defeat and his father's victory. He gave no sign that he was hearing it for the second time that day.

'Well, then just two weeks ago something queer happened. He suddenly changed his mind. One evening after I got home old Ray Shelley turned up here positively shiny with good news. I knew he'd done his best for me at the time of the bust-up, he was always a kind soul, and he was as pleased as Punch with the message he had for me. He said my father'd thought better of what he'd done, come to the conclusion that though he'd still finished with me it had been a dirty low-down trick to needle me with that present of his. Said he now saw it was a mean-spirited joke, and he withdrew it. But being my father he couldn't come and admit it himself, he'd given Shelley the job. He was to take back the sign, and he'd brought me five hundred pounds in cash in its place, as conscience money – not forgetting to repeat that this was positively the last sub. we could look for. He said he couldn't leave me to starve or sink into debt for want of that much ready money, but from now on I'd have to fend for myself.'

Jean had brought in the coffee and dispensed it silently, and because her husband in his absorption let it stand untasted at his elbow she came behind him and touched him very lightly on the arm to call his attention to it. She could not have ventured contact with a complete stranger more gingerly. He started and quivered at the touch, and looked up at her with a flash of wary brown eyes, at once hopeful and wretched. The shocks that passed between them made the whole cluttered, badly lit room vibrate like a bow-string.

'Go on,' said George peremptorily. 'What did you say to his offer?'

'I refused it.' He was taking heart now from the very impetus of his own feelings, remembering his injuries and recovering his anger. The guarded voice warmed; there was even a note of Armiger's well-tuned brazen music in it when he was roused. 'I'd had it, I was done with the whole affair, it could stay as it was. It's a pity it was poor old Shelley who got the blast, after all he'd tried to do for me, but there it was. So the old boy went off very upset. He even tried to get me to accept a loan out of his own pocket, but even if I'd have taken it in any case, and I wouldn't, I couldn't from him. I know him, even with all he makes he lives right up to his income, sometimes over it. We tried to soothe him down as well as we could, because, damn it, it wasn't his fault. He said he hoped we wouldn't cut ourselves off from him completely, couldn't he come down and see us sometimes, he'd like to be sure we were all right and of course we said come any time, if he could bear the place we'd be glad to see him. And we gave him all the gen, because the old bag downstairs objects to having to answer the door for our visitors, though she never misses taking a good look at them, in case there's anything fat in it to shoot over the garden fence to the other harpy next door. She leaves the front door on the latch while she's in, so that anyone who comes to see us can walk right up. And we even told him where to find the key of our room, in case he ever called a bit too early and wanted to wait for us. I know,' said Leslie, catching George's faintly puzzled and inquiring eye. 'You're wondering if all this detail is really relevant. It's relevant, all right! The day before yesterday, while we were both out in the afternoon, somebody got into this room and pinched my father's letter.'

'The *letter*? The one accompanying the gift of the sign? But why should anybody want to steal that?'

'If you can think of more than one explanation you're a better man than I am. There *is* only one. Because my father really wanted that sign back. That was why he sent Shelley on his errand. He wanted it, and it was even worth five hundred pounds to him to get it. And when that attempt flopped his next move was to remove the only proof that he ever gave it to me. Without that, its ownership would be a matter of his word against mine, and where do you think I'd be then?'

'That's not quite true, you know,' said George reasonably. 'Miss Hamilton typed that letter, she knows exactly what was in it, and has already told me all the facts about that gift. There would also be the testimony of the people who packed and delivered it to you. So it wouldn't have been a matter of your unsupported word.'

Leslie laughed, with some bitterness but even more honest amusement. 'Really, you don't know the kind of set-up he had with his staff, do you? Hammie may have been beautifully open with you now he's dead, but if he'd been still alive she'd have done and said whatever he wanted, she always did, it's the cardinal point in her terms of reference. She wouldn't have remembered anything that could make things awkward for him, don't you think it, and neither would the lads in the office, or the bloke who drove the van. Oh, no, *that* wouldn't complicate things for him. The letter was the only evidence in black and white. My father wanted that thing back, he was prepared to give five hundred to get it, and when that failed he started to clear the ground so he could claim the thing anyhow, even though I hadn't seen fit to part with it.'

'Are you suggesting that Mr. Shelley was a party to this trick?'

'*No*! At least, not consciously. God, I don't know! I've never known how far he was aware of the uses Dad made of him. It went on all the time, whenever he needed a nice, benevolent front that would soften up the opposition. You must have seen them in action. *Can* you be totally unaware when you're being used as a cover man? For years and years? Maybe he shuts his eyes to it and hopes for the best, maybe he really doesn't see. Naturally he didn't simply go back and say: Easy, old boy, you just walk in, the door's on the latch, and they keep their key on top of the cupboard on the landing. Nothing like that. But he told him, all the same, consciously or unconsciously, because there's no other way he could have known. And he came, he or somebody else for him. *Somebody'd* been here, and the letter was gone.'

'You didn't ask Mrs. Harkness if she'd seen the caller? She must have been in, or the street door would have been fastened.'

'She was in, and I bet she knows who it was who called, but what's the good of asking her? She'd simply deny any interest in my visitors, and get on her high horse and turn nasty, because she knows damn' well I know she's always got her kitchen door ajar snooping and listening. I couldn't even begin to ask her.'

'Yes, I see it would be easier for us to do it. Though probably no more effective. And then another question arises. I notice you haven't mentioned the sign itself. If he was removing the evidence of the gift, why not remove the gift at the same time?'

'He couldn't, it wasn't here. I got sort of interested in the thing. It's been overpainted so many times you can't tell what may not be underneath, and there's something about the shapes and proportions of the painting itself that isn't nineteenth century by a long chalk. It isn't that I think it's worth anything, not in money, but I should like to know something about its history, and see if there's something more interesting underneath the top layers. So I talked to Barney Wilson about it. He said how about that dealer who has the gallery in Abbey Place, the other side of town, he thought he'd be willing to have a look at the thing for us. So I got him to take the sign over to him for an opinion, and it's still with him now.'

'When did you send it to him? Before the letter was abstracted, obviously. Was it also before Mr. Shelley came to see you?'

Leslie visibly counted days; colour had come back into his cheeks and something like excitement into his eyes. 'Yes, by God, it was! Shelley was here on Thursday evening. Barney took the sign away with him in the van on Monday morning, three days before.'

'Suggestive, you think?'

'Don't you? I'd had the thing six weeks, and Dad had shown no further interest in it. Then it's deposited with this dealer, and three days later Dad opens a campaign to recover it. Wouldn't you say there's a connection?'

'You think he got a direct tip from the dealer that it might be of value after all?'

'Well, I don't know that it need mean that, actually. It might be enough if it got to my father's ears that I'd asked for an opinion on it. If he thought he'd accidentally given me something valuable and turned the joke on himself it would just about kill him.' He shied at his own choice of words, the sharp realisation of his position coming back upon him with a painful jolt.

'All right, leave it at that,' said George equably. 'The letter vanished. What then?'

'Well, then, last night, as I said, I suddenly set off to tackle him about it, without saying a word to Jean. I didn't want to go home to see him, and last night I knew exactly where he'd be, and I suppose I was in the mood to pick a fight, too, smouldering mad. Not that mad, though,' he amended with a wry grin, meeting George's measuring eye. 'I never touched him. I suppose I got there a bit before ten, and asked this waiter of yours to ask him if he could spare a minute. I didn't give a name because I thought if I did he wouldn't come, but most likely he would have, anyhow, the way it turned out. He came out bouncing and laughing when he saw me, and banged me on the back as though I was the one thing wanted to make his evening complete. He said he'd just leave his friends a message and then he'd be with me, and then he shoved me out of the side door and said go on over and take a look at the barn now, see if you recognise the old dump. Walk in, he said, the door's unlocked, I was going over there in any case a bit later on.

'And I went on over, just as he said. I could guess what he wanted with me over there, but I wanted privacy for what I'd got to say to him, so it suited me, too. You've seen the place, I take it, you know what he's done to it. In a few minutes he came bounding in, bursting with high spirits, with a magnum of champagne under his arm. "Well, what d'you think of your ideal home now, boy," he says. 'Doesn't it shake you?" But I hadn't come to amuse him, and it was all rather water off a duck's back. I let fly with what I had to say, told him what I thought of his dirty tricks, and accused him of stealing the letter. He just laughed in my face and denied everything. "You're crazy," he said, "why should I want to steal my own letter?" I suppose I hadn't expected any sort of satisfaction except just in getting the load off my own chest, so I unloaded. I told him what sort of lying, cheating devil he was, and swore I'd fight him to the last ditch, over the sign, over my career, over everything.'

'And half an hour or so later he was dead,' said George deliberately.

'I know, but I didn't touch him.'

Jean moved her hand silently upon the table until it touched Leslie's hand; that was all, but the spark that passed between them quivered through every mass within the room.

'I didn't touch him,' said Leslie again, with a softer and easier intonation. 'He was running about the gallery there, getting out

378

champagne glasses from the bar, and I said was he celebrating the final break, because this was it. And he said, "this isn't for you, boy, I'm expecting better company." So I left. I walked out and left him there fit and well. It couldn't have been half past ten, because only one or two cars had moved out, and there was no sign of turning-out time. I walked home, and I walked fast because I was still burning. By about ten to eleven I was home.'

'Did you see anyone around when you left? Or on the way? Just to confirm your times?'

'Not that I noticed,' said Leslie, paling. 'I wasn't thinking about needing confirmation, or I'd have done something about it. I was inclined to fume off by myself, rather, the mood I was in.'

'I can confirm the time when he got in,' said Jean firmly, and the hand that had moved to touch her husband's now closed over it and gripped it tightly. 'There's a chiming clock at the church just along the road. I heard it strike the three-quarter hour just two or three minutes before Leslie came in.'

'Yes, well, there may be others who noticed him somewhere along the way, you know. We'll try to find them.' Even so, Armiger could just as well have been left behind in his ballroom dead as living. According to the surgeon he might have died as early as ten-fifteen. 'Mrs. Harkness didn't have to let you in, I suppose? You have your own key?'

'Yes. And she probably wouldn't hear me come in. She goes to bed early, and she sleeps at the back of the house.' He was going to the opposite extreme now, producing all the possible unfavourable circumstances himself before they could be un-earthed by others.

'Don't labour it,' said George with a slight smile, getting up from his chair. 'Others are having to account for themselves, too, you know. If you've done nothing wrong then you've nothing to hide and nothing to worry about. And if you'll let me advise you – hide nothing. And then stop worrying.' He buttoned his coat, stifling a yawn. The coffee had helped, but what he needed now was sleep. 'Meantime – you'll be here at our disposal, won't you?'

'I'll be here,' said Leslie, slightly huskily because his throat was dry with returning fright.

The last George saw of them, as he looked back from the top of the stairs, was the two pale, unwavering faces, side by side and almost on a level, with wide, wary eyes staring after him; and the two hands gripped together between their bodies, clinging to each other as though they defied the world to tear them apart.

Chapter 7

'I'm inclined to believe him,' said George, frowning over the litter of scribbled notes tucked under his coffee cup. 'When his father told him to go across to the barn, he says the old man said: "Walk in, the door's unlocked, I was going over there in any case a bit later on." And then about the champagne, which put me off in the first place: "This isn't for you, boy, I'm expecting better company." That strikes me as sounding true, and fitting in with the facts. If the champagne had been all part of heaving his triumph in Leslie's face he'd had time to open it. But it wasn't opened. And the alternative seems much more probable. He was expecting someone, he was preparing a cele-bration, but it wasn't for Leslie. Leslie was just a pleasant interlude of devilment thrown in by sheer luck, to pass the time until the other person arrived. The real business of Armiger's evening was still to come. And if I'm right, then it was because of this other person, not because of Leslie, that he didn't want to be disturbed. Why should he care who heard him tormenting his son? He'd have enjoyed it all the better with an audience.'

'Didn't you say Miss Norris told you he said he'd be only a quarter of an hour or so?' asked Bunty. 'That makes his time schedule rather tight, doesn't it?'

'It does seem so. And as a matter of fact only she used that phrase. According to Miss Hamilton and Shelley he merely said he'd be back, and he hoped they'd be able to wait. Maybe her recollection isn't quite accurate, maybe he was speaking rather loosely. And important meetings can take place in a quarter of an hour, of course.'

'Supposing Leslie did get back by ten to eleven, would he have had time to be the murderer? He has no car, there's no bus just then, it must be true that he walked, and even walking fast it would take him fully twenty minutes. So he must have left by half past ten at latest.'

When she was admitted into conference in this way she used a level, quiet voice, careful to break no thread of George's reasoning. Sometimes she put things into his head, sometimes she showed him things that were already there.

'Yes,' said George, 'there was time, though certainly none to spare. The surgeon's report confirms that death may have taken place any time between ten and eleven-thirty.'

'And it doesn't take long, of course,' admitted Bunty, 'to bash somebody over the head with a bottle and run for it.'

'Well, it's not quite so simple as that. It wasn't just one blow that killed him. Seems there were at least nine blows struck, all at the back and left side of the head. There are several fractures, and some splintering of the bone. Then there's also a large abrasion on his right temple and cheek, apparently from his fall when he was first struck. That wouldn't have killed him, in any case, he'd have been stunned but nothing worse. But at least four of the other blows could have been fatal. It may not take long to batter a man's head to pieces that way, but it takes longer than just hitting out once and running. It must have been quick work if Leslie did it.'

'Very messy work, too,' said Bunty.

'Yes, we're not forgetting that. And Johnson's report isn't much help, except in establishing that somebody must have had some badly soiled gloves to dispose of after the event. No prints on bottle or glass except Armiger's own, nothing to be got from that broken statuette, and all the prints lying at random about the room turn out to be Armiger's or else belonging to some of the decorators and electricians who were working on the place. Only one or two haven't yet been matched up. Clayton's prints are on the door handle, but nowhere else, and there are also some on the door we have to check up now with Leslie's.'

He shuffled the sheets of notes together, and reached for the toast. 'Well, if the chief agrees I'm going to follow up this odd business of the inn sign. May as well see if there's anything to it.'

Dominic was standing in the doorway of the room with his school-bag under his arm. He had been there for some time, waiting to be noticed, and unwilling to break into his father's concentration until he could catch his eye. The morning was bright, and the normality of everything wonderfully reassuring, and they had said not a word that could tend to cast a shadow on Kitty. Not that other people were expendable, of course, but he couldn't help being glad when Kitty slipped clean out of the discussion.

'Have I to bike to-day, Dad, or are you going in this morning?' he asked, seizing his opportunity.

'Yes, I'm going, I'll take you. Give me five minutes and I'm ready.'

Dominic had hoped that he would be communicative on the ride, but he wasn't, he remained preoccupied, and nothing was said between them until they parted at the corner by the police station. It was still an effort not to ask questions, but since the inquiries seemed to be veering well away from Kitty it did not hurt him quite so much to contain his curiosity.

'Can I ride back with you this afternoon? I shall be a bit late myself, because it's rugger practice. Say quarter to five?'

'I hope to be free by then,' agreed George. 'You can call in and see, anyhow. I shall be here.'

He watched his son shoulder his bag and stride away along the street. He was running to length these days, not so far off a man's height now, but still very slender. He was getting control of his inches, too, and learning to manage his hands and feet and all the other uncoordinated parts of him. Give him a year, and he'd be downright elegant in movement. Odd how they do their growing-up by sudden leaps, so that however constantly and affectionately you watch them they still manage to transmute themselves while your back's turned, and confront you every third month or so with another daunting stranger.

383

Freckled and chestnut-haired and no beauty, apart, perhaps, from those eyes of his; but like his mother, whom he so engagingly resembled, he didn't need beauty. George found them both formidable enough as they were.

He went in to his conference with Superintendent Duckett assembling in his mind the details of his evening interview with Jean and Leslie Armiger. Duckett found them no less interesting than George had done, and endorsed his proposition to follow up the curious affair of the inn sign. The dreary, dogged search for blood-stained clothing, the exhaustive interrogation of anyone and everyone who had been present at the opening night of The Jolly Barmaid, would go on all day and probably for a good many more days into the bargain; but if a promising side-track could shorten the journey, so much the better for them all.

George telephoned County Buildings before he set out, to check with Wilson.

'That's right,' said Wilson amiably, 'I offered to pick up the thing for Leslie and take it over to Cranmer's for him. Oh, yes, I think the chap's all right, knows his stuff, and all that. He's had one or two good things in since I've known the place. I don't know a thing about this panel of Leslie's, no. I've seen it, of course, but there's nothing exceptional about it on sight – except, perhaps, the quality and solidity of the panel it's painted on. I'd like to see the worm who could get his teeth in that. No, I can't say I know Cranmer, except just from looking round his place occasionally, and buying one or two small things. He's been there a few years now. Usual sort of antiquary, old and desiccated and hard as nails.'

The description fitted Mr. Cranmer very fairly, George thought, when he entered the small gallery in Abbey Place, and took stock of the person who hovered delicately in the background, refraining from intercepting him until he showed whether he wanted to gaze or do business. The neighbourhood was a part of the old town, mainly early Tudor, and the low black-beamed frontage of the shop was beautiful. English black-and-white, in contrast to some of its European kin, is so wonderfully disciplined, makes such a patterned harmony of a whole street, instead of a Gothic cadenza. The interior was also plain white beneath the enormous beams of the ceiling, and not cluttered. The man himself was of medium height, slightly stooped, grey of hair and complexion and clothing, and lean with an astringent leanness like that of roots and sinews and all that is most durable in nature. He wore thick-lensed glasses that made his eyes look enormous and incredibly blue. To approach him from the inoffensive side-view and be suddenly transfixed by that vast blue glare was electrifying.

The voice that went with the grey shape was old, prosaic and discreet; so discreet that until George identified himself as a police officer it produced no information whatever, and without even appearing to be wilfully stalling; as without any apparent volte-face it then became loquacious. Yes, he had the painting in question in his workshop, he understood that it had been the sign of an inn called The Joyful Woman. Yes, it might possibly turn out to be of some value, though questionably of very much.

'Several times clumsily overpainted, you know, and exposed to a great deal of weathering when in use as a sign, and therefore frequently touched up and varnished over, like most of its kind. But I have an idea – mind you, it is just an idea – that it may be based on an eighteenth-century portrait by a local artist named Cotsworth. You won't have heard of him, I dare say. Not important, but interesting, if it turns out to be his. Worth a few hundreds, perhaps, to a local collector.' He trotted away into his back room to bring forth a foot-square framed canvas, the head of some long-dead worthy. 'This is Cotsworth,' he said triumphantly. It seemed to George depressingly smug, clumsy and ugly, but he forebore from saying so.

'You've had the painting for about a fortnight, I understand. Are you making tests on it? Did young Mr. Armiger empower you to do that, or was he merely asking for an opinion first?'

'He asked for an opinion, but I should like, if he agrees, to try to uncover at least a corner of the old paint, and see if it confirms my guess. If it does, Mr. Felse, I may be prepared to offer Mr. Armiger as much as two hundred and fifty pounds for it myself.'

'Very handsome, Mr. Cranmer. Did you inform Mr. Armiger senior, or anyone in his employ, that you had the painting here, and that it might conceivably be valuable?'

The two hundred and fifty pounds had struck the first really phoney note; if he was ready to mention such a sum he was thinking in terms of a thousand and upwards. And once that false quantity had jarred on George's senses this whole room began to seem as much a façade as the magnified blueness of the eyes.

'Certainly not,' said the old man stiffly. 'It came to me as the property of Mr. Armiger junior, through Mr. Wilson, and I wouldn't dream of communicating with anyone else about it. Except, of course, the police when they require me to co-operate.' He made it a plaintive and dignified reproof, and George let him have it that way; but the fact remained that he had not been required to co-operate to the extent of naming a price, and there had been no need whatever for him to do so. Unless, of course, he wanted his offer to come back to the owner in this superlatively respectable fashion, relayed by the innocent police. It might not come off, but there was nothing lost in trying.

All very correct, thought George, halting for a moment outside to weigh up the three mediocre moderns in the low Henry VII windows; but then, he would be correct, and cautious too, now that Armiger's dead. The last thing he'd want would be to be involved. All the same, George suspected that Mr. Cranmer had indeed flashed the urgent warning to Armiger: look out, you're giving away something valuable. He probably didn't know that Armiger had gone as high as five hundred pounds in his attempt to recover it, or he wouldn't have stuck at two hundred and fifty himself, the discrepancy was too glaring to pass without comment. He hadn't, of course, actually made an offer, only hinted that he might be prepared to do so, but the implications were there. He would have collected a plump commission, no question of it, if he'd helped Armiger to get the better of Leslie, and acquired the great man's formidable patronage into the bargain. Now that that was knocked on the head, quite literally, he was going into the deal for himself. All that, thought George, strolling without haste back to his car, depends rather on whether Mr. Cranmer was acquainted with the painting's provenance; but since the thing came from young Armiger, and he evidently knows it to be the sign of The Joyful Woman, we may safely assume that he could guess Armiger had thrown it out as valueless, even if Wilson didn't tell him. And he probably did, he's a talkative soul, he confides easily.

The upshot, he decided, letting in the clutch, is that young Leslie ought to take back that picture very firmly, resisting all offers to buy it from him, and take it to some absolutely immaculate authority for an opinion. And so I'll tell him, if he's in a listening mood, and if no unforseen explosion blows him into gaol in the meantime.

He spent the rest of the morning in his office doing some of his arrears of paper work on the case, and the early afternoon with Duckett on a visit to the Chief Constable, who was anxious for quick results, partly because the case involved a family so well known in the Midlands, but chiefly because he wanted to get away from town for some shooting at the week-end. The visit comforted nobody, since the Chief Constable still thought of everybody and treated everybody as a classifiable item in a military hierarchy, and Duckett on an important case always became more and more laconic, until his gruffness amounted almost to dumb insolence.

'Waste of time!' snorted Duckett as he drove back towards Comerbourne at the solid, law-abiding pace which was also a symptom of his less amenable moods. 'Never let that boy of yours go into the police force, George.'

'He says he won't, anyhow,' said George. 'When it comes to the point he often seems to be on the side of the criminal.'

'All his generation are anti-social,' said Duckett disgustedly.

'No, it's just a natural sympathy with the hunted, I think, when the odds turn against them. Maybe a feeling that this society of ours makes its own criminals, too, and therefore deserves 'em.' He wondered if he was projecting his own occasional qualms on to Dominic's shoulders; better not look too closely in case he was. The depression that sometimes followed a successful conviction was bad enough, without being inhibited by doubts in the thick of the hunt. 'Never mind,' he said placatingly, 'who knows if something won't have broken while we've been away theorising?'

And when they turned the corner into Hill Street, and saw the concreted apron frontage of the station alive with staring, chattering people, it appeared that indeed something had. The station faced sidelong to the street on the outer side of a wide curve, with a small garden and two seats in front of its windows, and then the concreted forecourt lined out into parking space for four cars. One of the four spaces was now occupied by a flat two-wheeled cart bearing a tin trunk, a small pile of old iron bolts and oddments, a tumbled mound of odd clothing and rags, and a top-dressing of three small, silent, staring children. A somewhat larger child in his father's cut-down trousers and a steadily unravelling grey jersey held by the head a shaggy, fat brown pony. A uniformed constable, with the admirably detached, impervious solidity acquired only after innumerable public embarrassments, sauntered about between the door and the waiting family, gently shooing the shifting crowd along if it became too stagnant, and hypnotising it into pretending to an indifference as monumental as his own.

'God!' said Duckett, as he parked his car. The constable permitted himself a fleeting grin on the side of his face which was turned towards them and away from the public view. 'Has Grocott gone off his head and started bringing in all the tickney lot?'

'No, sir, this one brought himself. Claims he has important information.'

'So he got a load aboard before the pubs closed, and brought half the town along as well,' Duckett diagnosed disgustedly, and eyed the composed and dignified children, who looked back at him calmly, as though they had no doubts at all as to who was the alien and the savage. They were not full-blooded gipsies, they had not the soft, mysterious Indian features, the melting eyes, the delicate bones, but something in a coarser grain, olive and wild and sinewy, with a bloom of dirt. 'What are they?' said Duckett gruffly. 'Lays?'

'No, sir, Creaveys.'

'What's the difference? Nobody knows who's married to whom or which kids belong to which parents, anyhow. If you're a Creavey you are a Lay.'

He stalked into the station, and pounded up three flights of stairs to his own office, with George at his heels. Grocott was at the door before he had time to be called.

'All right,' said Duckett, 'let's have it. That's Joe Creavey's pony, isn't it?'

Joe was the Creavey (or Lay) who was almost no trouble; an occasional blind when business in wool rags and old iron was booming, and just once, with ample provocation, a determined assault with an ash-plant on his wife, but no major sins were recorded against him. He fed his kids, minded his own business without unduly annoying other people about it, and was unmistakably a happy and well-adjusted man.

'Yes, sir. Joe's below with Lockyer. He came in just over an hour ago, saying he'd got important evidence in the Armiger case.'

Joe was well known in the seedier outer districts of Comerbourne, where he made regular rounds with his pony-cart,

collecting rags and scrap, and a good many residents automatically saved their cast-off clothes for him. It was worth
making regular use of him, because he would take away for you
all kinds of awkward and unmarketable rubbish on which the
Cleansing Department tended to frown if it was put out for
their attentions; though what he afterwards did with some of
the items no one cared to inquire. On this particular morning
he had been round the shabby-genteel corner of town which
housed Mrs. Harkness, and in addition to collecting the contents
of her rag-bag he had thoughtfully lifted the lid of her dustbin
in case there should be anything salvageable there. People often
put old shoes in dustbins, sometimes in a state which Joe
regarded as merely part-worn. He didn't find shoes this time,
he found gloves, and the gloves were aged but expensive leather
gauntlets, with woven tapes stitched inside, lettered L.A. He
took them instinctively, and only afterwards did he examine
them closely, when he was pulled in at one of the suburban
pubs and had his first pint inside him. It was then he found
that the palm and the fingers of the right glove were stained
and stiffened with something dark and crusted, and the left
carried a few similar dark-brown stains here and there in its
frayed leather. Joe knew who lodged with Mrs. Harkness, she
was one of his regular clients; he knew what the initials L.A.
stood for; and he knew, or was convinced that he knew, what
had saturated and ruined those gloves, and why they were
stuffed into the dustbin. He knew his duty, too; the police must
be told. But his route to the station had taken him through four
more bars before it triumphantly delivered him, and if there
was anyone left in Comerbourne who didn't yet know that Leslie
Armiger had murdered his father and Joe Creavey had the proof
of it, he must have been going about for the last couple of hours
with his ears plugged.

'Blabbed it all over town, and pretty well brought a procession
with him. He isn't exactly drunk – not by his standards – but
well away. Do you want him?'

'No,' said Duckett, 'let him stew for a bit. I want the gloves, and I think I want young Armiger, too. If there's nothing in this, now's the time to talk to him, before we're sure there's nothing in it. But let's have a look at these first.'

The gloves were produced, they lay on the desk with palms upturned, displaying the reddish-black, encrusted smears that certainly looked uncommonly like blood.

'Well, what do you think it is, George?'

'Creosote, for one thing,' said George promptly, sniffing at the stiffened fingers, 'but that doesn't say it's all creosote.'

'No, traces of roofing paint, too. Johnson had better run them up to the lab, and we'll see.'

'You're not thinking of keeping Joe overnight, are you?' asked Grocott.

'Eh? Keep him overnight? What, and dump all that tribe of kids into the receiving home when there's no need? The Children's Officer would murder me! All right, George, you be off and fetch the boy along.'

George made the best of a job he never liked, approaching the manager's office discreetly without getting anyone to announce him, and making the summons sounds as much like a request as he could; all the same, Leslie, coming up in haste from the warehouse, paled and froze at the sight of him. Once he had grasped the idea it wasn't so bad colour came back into his face and a defiant hardness into his eyes, and he went out by George's side with a composed countenance and an easy stride, as though an old friend had called for him. They had to cross either the shop or the yard, and George hoped he was right in choosing the yard, where Leslie was better known and better understood.

Nobody was deceived, of course, they'd be muttering and wondering the rest of the day; but a van-driver caught Leslie's eye and cocked a thumb at him and grinned, and one of the packers walked deliberately across their path so that he could offer a crumpled cigarette packet in passing. The boy looked harassed rather than cheered, but he smiled all the same, and accepted the offering; and with the first deep drag the pinched lines round his mouth relaxed. He sat beside George in the car, drawing deep, steadying breaths, and trying too hard to prepare himself.

'Mr. Felse,' he said in a constrained voice, as George slowed at the traffic lights, 'could you do something for me? I should be very grateful if you'd go and see my wife for me.'

'You'll be seeing her yourself in an hour or so,' said George equably. 'Won't you?'

'Shall I?'

'That depends on what you've done, so only you know the answer.'

'I hope you're right,' said Leslie fervently. 'I suppose you can't tell me what this is all about?'

'You suppose correctly. You'll soon know, but I won't anticipate. Now let me ask you the one question I somehow never asked you before. Did you kill him?'

'No,' said Leslie without over-emphasis, almost gently.

'Then you'll be going home to your wife, and the worst that can happen is that you may be a little late. She'll forgive you for that, long before she forgives us for scaring you.'

Leslie was so unreasonably soothed and calmed by this tone that he forgot to take offence at the assumption that he was scared. He walked into the police station briskly, wild to get to his fence and either fall or clear it; and suddenly finding himself without George, had to turn back and look for him. He had stopped to speak to a boy in a grammar school blazer who was standing in the hallway.

'My son,' he explained as he hurried to overtake his charge. 'He's still hoping – and so am I – that I'm going to be able to drive him home. I should be off duty by this time.'

'Oh, now, look,' said Leslie with a faint recovering gleam in his eye, 'I should hate to keep you after hours, I can easily come some other time.'

'That's the stuff!' George patted him approvingly on the shoulder. 'You keep up that standard, and you'll be all right. Always provided you're telling us the truth, of course. Come on, three flights up, and I'm afraid the taxpayer doesn't provide us with a lift.'

Dominic watched them climb to the first turn of the staircase and pass out of sight like that, his father's hand on the young man's shoulder. Was it possible that it was all over already? Leslie Armiger didn't look like a murderer. But then, what murderer ever does? But he *didn't*!

Dominic was convulsed by the secret, uneasy part of him that couldn't help identifying itself with those in trouble, those trapped by circumstances and cornered, however deservedly, by the orderly ranks of the law-abiding. He felt the demon in his own nature, and trembled, knowing there was no end to his potentialities. He had to let part at least of his sympathy go out to the hunted, because the quarry could so easily be himself. Infinitely more terrible, it could be somebody who mattered to him so desperately as to make him forget himself. It could be Kitty! And yet he wanted not to be glad that it should be the young man in the worn, expensive suit, with the strained smile and the apprehensive eyes.

The surge of relief in his heart outraged him, and drove him out from under the desk-sergeant's friendly but inquisitive eye into the impersonal pre-twilight of the September evening, to wait on one of the seats in the strip of garden.

So it was that he saw the red Karmann-Ghia swoop beautifully inward from the road to park beside the ragman's cart, and Kitty swing her long, slender legs out from the driver's door. His heart performed the terrifying manoeuvre with which he was becoming familiar, turning over bodily in his breast and swelling until he thought it would burst his ribs.

She closed the door of the car with unaccustomed slowness and quietness, and walked uncertainly across the concrete towards the door; and as she came her steps slowed, until within a few yards of the step she halted altogether, her hands clasped tightly in front of her, in an agony of indecision. She looked to right and left as though searching for the courage to go forward; and she saw Dominic, motionless and silent in the corner of the wooden seat, clutching his school-bag convulsively against his side.

He couldn't believe, even when her eyes lit on him, that it would get him anything. He was just somebody she'd run into once, casually, and not expected to meet again. Probably she wouldn't even remember. But her eyes kindled marvellously, a pale smile blazed over her face for a moment, though it served only to illuminate the desperate anxiety that instantly drove it away again. She turned and came to him. He jumped to his feet, so shaken by the beating of his heart that he scarcely heard the first words she said to him.

'Dominic! I'm so glad to find you here!' He came out of a cloud of fulfilment and ecstasy to find himself sitting beside her, his hands clasped in hers, her great eyes a drowning violet darkness close before his face. She was saying for the second time, urgently, desperately: 'Is Leslie in there? They were saying in the shops the police fetched him from Malden's. Is it true? Do you know if he's in there?'

'Yes,' he said, stammering, 'he came with my father. Only a few minutes ago.' He was back on the earth, and the bump had hurt a little, but not much, because of her remembering his name, because of her turning to him so gladly. It wasn't as if he'd been expecting even that. And in any case he couldn't be bothered with such trivialities as his own disappointments, while she carried such terrible trouble in her face.

'Oh, God!' she said. 'Is he under arrest?'

'I don't know. I don't think so – not yet – '

'Your father's in there, too? I'd rather it be him than any of the others. I've got to talk to him, Dominic. Now I've got to.'

She released his hands with a vast sigh, and put back with a hopeless gesture the fall of smooth, pale hair that shadowed her forehead.

'I've got to tell him,' she said in a tired, tranquil voice, 'because if I don't they'll only put it on to poor Leslie, and hasn't enough happened to him already? I won't let them touch him.' She lifted her head and looked into Dominic's eyes with the practical simplicity of a child confiding its sins, relieved to exchange even for punishment a burden too great to bear a moment longer. 'I killed his father, you see.'

Chapter 8

Dominic tried to speak, and couldn't find his voice for a moment, and even when he did it tended to shift key unexpectedly, in the alarming and humiliating way he'd thought he was finished with; but Kitty didn't seem to notice.

'You mustn't say such things. Even if – if something happened that makes you feel to blame, that can't be true, and you shouldn't say it.'

'But I did it, Dominic. I never meant to, but I did. He came to me, and he said: "I'm just going to kick Leslie out of here once for all, and boy, shall I enjoy it. And then I've got something to tell you. Not here, you come out to the barn, we can be quiet there. Give me fifteen minutes," he said, "to get rid of his lordship, and then come on over." And I wasn't going to go, I'd made up my mind not to go. I got out the car and started to drive home, and then after all I didn't, I went round by the lane to the road behind the barn, and parked the car along under the trees by that little wood, and went into the courtyard by the back way. I thought if I begged him just once more he might give in and take Leslie back, and start acting decently to them. After all, he was his son. I couldn't get it into my head that it was really for keeps. People just don't act like that. Leslie wasn't there, only his father. He started telling me all his great plans for the future, all excited and pleased with himself, and he had a magnum of champagne and glasses set out on one of the tables. Oh, Dominic, if you knew how obscenely ridiculous it all was – '

His mouth ached with all the things he wanted to say to her and mustn't; his heart filled his chest so tightly that he could hardly breathe. 'Kitty, I wish there was some way I could help you,' he said huskily.

'You do help me, you are helping me, you're lovely to me. You keep right on looking at me as if I was a friend of yours, and you haven't moved away from me even an inch. But you will!'

'I won't!' he said in a gasp of protest. 'Never!'

'No, perhaps you wouldn't ever, you're not the kind. Let me go on telling you, it makes it easier, and my God, I need rehearsing, this is going to be lousy on the night whatever I do.'

He had her by the hands again, and this time the initiative had been his, and the warm, strong fingers clung to him gratefully, quivering a little.

'He'd had a brainwave,' said Kitty in a half-suffocated voice, laughing and raging. 'If Leslie wouldn't have me and join the businesses up, *he would*! He was going to marry me himself. That's what the champagne and the excitement was all about. He didn't even ask me, he *told* me. He didn't even pretend to feel anything for me. When he put his arms round me and wanted to kiss me it wasn't even sexually revolting, it was just like signing a merger. And I'd been trying to talk to him all the while about Leslie, and he hadn't even heard me. I was so mad, it was so mean and ludicrous and horrible, I was out of my mind, I couldn't think of anything except getting away. I just pushed him off like a demon. We were by the table at the top of the stairs, where he'd put the champagne and the glasses. I don't know how it happened – he went backwards, and stepped off the edge of the top stair, and went slipping and rolling and clawing all the way down and crashed on the floor. I ran down and past him to the door, I was terrified he'd get up and try to stop me. I wasn't afraid of him, it wasn't that, it was just that everything was so foul, I couldn't have borne it if he'd tried to speak to me again. But he just lay there on his face, and never moved. I didn't think anything about it, I didn't stop to see

397

how much he was hurt, I just ran back to the car and left him lying there. So you see, I killed him. And I've got to tell them. I never meant to, it never even occurred to me until I was in the car that he might be terribly hurt. But I did it. And I can't let them go on thinking poor Leslie had anything to do with it.'

When she had finished she lifted her eyes and looked at him closely, already half sorry and half ashamed that she should be so weak as to unload this cruel and humiliating confidence upon a mere child, too old not to be damaged by it, and not yet old enough to be able to evaluate it justly. But it wasn't a child who was looking steadily at her, it was a man, a very young man, maybe, but unquestionably her elder at that moment. He kept firm hold of her hands when she would have drawn them away, and his eyes held hers when she would have averted them.

'Oh, God!' she said weakly. 'I'm a heel to drag you into this.'

'No, you did right, Kitty, really you did. I'll show you. That was all that happened? You're sure that was all? You pushed him and he fell down the stairs and knocked himself out. That was all?'

'Wasn't it enough? He was dead when they found him.'

'Yes, he was dead. But you didn't kill him.' He knew what he was about to do, and it was so terrible that it almost outweighed the sense of joy and completion that he felt at knowing her innocent, and being able to hold out the image of her in his two hands and show her how spotless it was. Never in his life before, not even as a small, nosy boy, had he betrayed a piece of information he possessed purely by virtue of being George's son. If he did it he was destroying something which had been a mainspring of his life, and the future that opened before him without it was lonely and frightening, involved enormous readjustments in his most intimate relationships, and self-searchings from which he instinctively shrank. But already he was committed, and he would not have turned back even if he could.

'Listen to me, Kitty. All that was published about Mr.

Armiger's death was that he died from head injuries. But it wasn't just falling down the stairs that did it. It's only because of my father's work that I know this, and you mustn't tell anyone I told you. After he was lying unconscious somebody took the champagne bottle and battered his head in with it deliberately, hit him nine times, and only stopped hitting him when the bottle smashed. And *that* wasn't you! Was it?'

She whispered between parted lips, staring at him in a stupor of horror and incredulity and relief: '*No* – no, I didn't, I *couldn't* – '

'I know you couldn't, of course you couldn't. But somebody did. So you see, Kitty, you didn't kill him at all, you didn't do anything except push him away from you and accidentally stun him. Somebody else came in afterwards and battered him to death. So you see, there's no need for you to tell them anything. You won't, will you? There'll be nothing in this glove business, they won't touch Leslie, you'll see. At least wait until we know.'

She hadn't heard the half of that, she was still groping after the release and freedom he was offering back to her. The warm flush of colour into her face and hope into her eyes overwhelmed him with a kind of proud humility he had never experienced before.

'You mean it? You wouldn't just try to comfort me, would you? Not with fairy stories? But you wouldn't! Oh, Dominic, am I really not a murderess? You don't know what it's been like since yesterday morning, since they told me he was dead.'

'Of course you're not. It's true what I've told you. So you won't tell them anything, will you?'

'Oh, yes,' she said, 'I must. Oh, Dominic, what should I have done without you? Don't you see, I don't even mind now, as long as I'm not – what I thought I was. I don't mind anything now. But I must tell them, because of Leslie. I can show them that he'd gone, and his father was still alive. I can prove he didn't kill him.' She looked down at him, and was distressed by his consternation, but she knew what she had to do. 'I've got this far and I'm not turning back now. I've had enough of concealing information. At least I can see that Leslie's safely out of it.'

'But you can't,' protested Dominic, catching at her wrist and dragging her down again beside him. 'You can only prove he didn't kill him in the short time you were there. They might still think he came back. *Somebody* came. And don't you see, if you tell them what you've told me, they'll think you've left out the end, they'll think *you* stayed and finished him off.'

'I don't see why you should say that,' said Kitty, wide-eyed. '*You* don't think that, *you* believe me. Why shouldn't they?'

'Well, because their business is *not* to believe – and how can you prove it?'

'I can't,' she agreed, paling a little. 'But I can't turn back now, I couldn't bear to. You don't have to worry about me any more, the most wonderful thing anyone could have done for me is done already. *You* did it.'

If she hadn't said that, if she hadn't suddenly touched his hot cheek so lightly and fleetingly with her fingertips, he might have been able to protest yet once again, perhaps even to persuade her. But her touch snatched the breath from his throat and the articulation from his tongue, and he couldn't say a word, he had to stand and watch, suffocating, mute and paralysed, as she turned to leave him; and when she looked back just once to say quickly: 'Don't worry, I won't say a word about you,' he almost burst into tears of frustration and rage because he lacked the power to shout at her that it wasn't about himself he was worrying, that he didn't care about himself, that only she mattered, and she was making a terrible mistake, that he couldn't bear it, that he loved her.

She was gone. The darkening doorway swallowed her, and it was in any case too late. He sat down again, huddled in the far corner of the seat, and wrestled with himself painfully until his mind cleared again, and presented to him the most appalling implication of the whole incident, producing it with cruel aplomb, like a magician palming an ace out of the pack. He had robbed her even of the defence of ignorance! He, and no one else. If she'd gone rushing in there as she'd wanted to, and poured out her story as she had to him, they'd have seen the glaring hole in it at once, just as surely as he had. They'd have questioned her about the weapon, about the injuries, and she wouldn't have known what they were talking about, and her manner and her bewilderment would have rung true past any mistaking. But now he'd told her. She couldn't pretend ignorance worth a damn, she'd be certain to betray her knowledge. And worse, she'd never tell them about his treachery, and explain how she got her information, because that would get him into trouble. One slip to warn them that she knew how that death had come about, and they'd be absolutely sure she was responsible for it. The details had never been published, only a handful of people knew them – and one other, the murderer. He'd as good as convicted her.

His manhood, so recently and intoxicatingly achieved, was crumpling badly, slipping out of his hold. He ought to get up and march in there after her and tell them honestly about his lapse, but he hadn't the courage, the very thought of it made him feel sick. It wasn't just for himself he was such a coward, it was his father's job, his whole career. C.I.D. officers ought not to discuss their cases in front of their families. They'd been the exceptional family, proud of their solidarity, disdaining to doubt their absolute mutual loyalty, over-riding conventional restrictions because they were so sure of one another. All this had made perfect sense while that solidarity remained unbreached, but now he'd broken it, and how did it look now? His father was compromised. He would have to own up, it was the only way he could even try to repair the harm he'd done to Kitty; but he'd have to do it in private, to his father alone. Maybe there'd be some grain of evidence that would extricate Kitty, and make it unnecessary for confession to go any further. Supposing George felt he had to resign, supposing –

He longed for George to come and take him home, so that he could get the first awful plunge over. But when at last a step rang on the flags of the hallway and he jerked round in hope and dread to see who emerged, it was only Leslie Armiger, stepping lightly, buoyant with relief. He walked like a new man, for the old gloves he'd discarded after painting the garden shed where he kept his materials had yielded a great many interesting substances, creosote, bituminous dressing, several kinds of paint and lacquer, but not a trace of blood. As soon as he'd seen them he'd laughed with relief; he could have kicked himself for the imaginative agonies of anticipation he'd inflicted on himself, all on account of these ancient and blameless relics. His position now was actually neither better nor worse than it had been before this tea-cup storm blew up, but there was no doubt that the recoil had raised his credit all round. Especially with himself; this feeling of liberation was more than worth the scare.

Detective-Sergeant Felse had been called away from the inter-rogation to interview someone in his own room, but Leslie didn't know who it was, or whether the caller had anything to do with his father's death. He didn't know, and he didn't care. He was on his way home to Jean, still free and almost vindicated, and never again would he scare as easily as that.

It was ten minutes more before George came out to speak to his son, and then it was only to say tersely that after all he wouldn't be able to leave for some time yet, possibly several hours, and Dom had better get on home by bus. He wasn't going to have an opportunity to unburden himself here, that was obvious; his father was gone again almost before he could open his stiff lips to get out a word.

Miserably he took his dismissal and went home; there was nothing else to be done. He countered Bunty's queries with monosyllables, sat wretchedly over his tea without appetite, and refuged in his corner with textbooks he couldn't even see for the anxiety that hung over his eyes as palpable as fog. Bunty suspected a cold coming on, but he repelled her attempts to take his temperature so ill-humouredly that she revised her diagnosis. Something was on his mind, she reflected with certainty, and it isn't me he wants, so it must be his father. Now what, I wonder, have those two been doing to each other?

It was twenty to ten before George came home. He looked tired and frayed and in no mood to be approached, but there was no help for it. Bunty fed him and allowed him to be quiet, though she knew by old signs that there was something on his mind, too, that would have to come out before long. It was without prompting that he leaned back wearily at last, and said in a voice entirely devoid of any pleasure or satisfaction: 'Well, it's all over bar the shouting. We've just made an arrest in the Armiger case. We've charged Kitty Norris.'

Bunty's exclamation was drowned by the shriek of Dominic's chair. He was on his feet, trembling.

No!' he said faintly, and then, with the flat quietness of desperation: 'Please, Dad, I've got to talk to you. It's about that. It's important.' He looked imploringly at his mother, and his lips were quivering. 'Mummy, do you mind awfully – '

'That's all right, darling,' said Bunty, loading her tray methodically as though nothing out of the way was happening. 'I'm going to wash up. You go ahead.'

She made things sound so normal and calm, as she almost always did, that he longed to ask her to stay, but it couldn't be done that way, he had to have it out with George. She cleared the table, flicked Dominic's ear very lightly with the folded tablecloth as she went to put it away, and bore off the tray into the kitchen, closing the door firmly after her. They were left looking rather helplessly at each other, neither of them any longer able to doubt that this was a family crisis of the first magnitude. George flinched from it as much as Dominic did; he was tired and out of temper, and he knew it, and this luckless child was inviting trouble even their combined goodwill might not be able to avert.

What was the use of thinking how best to do it, when all that mattered was that it should be done?

'You know I was outside there this evening when Kitty Norris came to ask for you,' said Dominic in the drained tones of despair. 'I talked to her before you did. She told me all that tale about pushing Armiger down the stairs because he – he insulted her. But she told me she killed him. She didn't! You've got to believe me. All she did was go away and leave him there stunned. She said – '

'I don't know why it should be necessary for us to discuss it at all,' said George, laboriously patient with him but desperately unwilling to go on hammering at an affair of which he'd already had about all he could take, 'but if I'm supposed to humour you, I will. If she went away and left him there stunned, how did she know it was the champagne magnum that battered his head in? If she wasn't the one who killed him, if she was gone from the scene and somebody else came in and finished him off, how did she know how it was done? All that was ever made public was that he died of head injuries. So you tell me how she knew – how she *could* know and still be innocent?'

So they had tricked it out of her, questioned and cross-questioned and slipped in catch remarks until she gave herself away. Dominic hated them all, even his father, but not so much as he hated himself for making such an appalling miscalculation. He should have known she'd still insist on going through with her confession, because Leslie must be safeguarded whatever happened to her, Leslie who wouldn't marry her, thank God, the stupid fool, Leslie with whom she was still so crazily, desolately in love that she couldn't see anyone else for him. Dominic sat down slowly and carefully at the table, braced his sweating palms upon its glossy surface before him, and said loudly and hoarsely: 'She knew because I told her.'

He was glad he'd sat down, however it diminished his dignity, he felt safer that way; his knees would never have held him up, standing. George had lurched forward in his chair and come heavily to his feet. He spread his hands upon the table and leaned over his son, and in spite of himself Dominic wilted. He wanted to close his eyes, but he wouldn't, because whatever was coming to him, he'd asked for it, he couldn't complain.

'You *what*?' said George.

'I told her. I told her because I thought then she wouldn't have to tell you about being there at all. She was going to tell you she'd killed him, and yet she didn't know anything about him being battered to death, she just thought he'd cracked his skull when he fell down the stairs. So I knew she hadn't, and how could I let her go on thinking she had? I had to tell her. I couldn't not tell her.' Resolute in his desperation, he said with an altogether inaccurate suggestion of defiance: 'I'd do the same again.'

George said, after a blank and awful pause: 'I've a good mind to tan the hide off you.'

With all his sore heart Dominic almost wished he would, but with all his lively senses he knew he wouldn't. There was no getting out of things that way any more, the bolt-hole had been stopped at least two years now. Paying this debt was going to be a whole lot more complicated than that, a whole lot more long-drawn-out and painful. The compensations of being under juvenile discipline had never presented themselves to him before.

'I know,' he said drearily, 'but I had to do it. There wasn't anything else to do. And now I've made everything worse for her instead of better.'

'Whether you've done that or not, you've certainly made it impossible for us to judge how far she's telling the truth. And you know what else you've done, don't you?' said George, remorselessly.

Yes, he knew. He'd undermined the foundations of the house, and shaken the pillars that held up the roof. He wouldn't have believed himself that he could do such a thing; for a moment half of his heart was with George, astonished and reproachful,

405

half of it with Kitty, injured and imprisoned. Between the two of them he wished he could die.

'I shall have to report this to the chief, of course,' said George. 'I blame myself more than you. There's nothing to be done but tell him that I've been consistently indiscreet. I'd no right to allow you such easy access to information in the first place, it was thoroughly unconstitutional behaviour, and I should have known better. It was unreasonable to expect that you could refrain for ever from shooting off your mouth, I suppose.' But he had expected it; he'd been so sure of it, in fact, that it had never occurred to him to question his discretion at all. Only now that he'd lost that absolute trust did Dominic know how to value it.

'I didn't do it lightly,' he said, flinching. 'I never have before.'

'Once is all it takes. I shall have to see Superintendent Duckett in the morning and take the responsibility for this myself. That's putting it squarely where it belongs.'

'I'm sorry,' said Dominic abjectly. 'Do you have to?'

'Yes, I have to, in fairness to you as well as to Kitty. If he asks for my resignation he'll be within his rights.' That was cruel, because he was virtually sure that Duckett, things being as they were, the case as good as closed, and this particular item of evidence now so much less vital than Dominic supposed, would hardly even bother to listen to him, and quite certainly be unable to muster more than a token reprimand. 'In future, of course,' he said, 'I shall have to make sure I don't talk about a case when you're within earshot. I'll take good care this doesn't happen again. And you'll give me your word here and now not to meddle in this affair any more. You've done damage enough.'

'I can't! I *won't*! I tell you Kitty didn't know until I told her. You've got to believe me. Don't you see there isn't really any evidence against her apart from that? Dad, you've got to let her go now, don't you see that? You've no right to hold her now that I've told you about it. She's innocent, and if you won't prove it, I'll damn' well do it myself.'

George had had more than enough. He opened his mouth to say something for which he would quite certainly have been sorry next moment, and which would have cost Bunty days of patient, cunning negotiations to put right again between them; and then the violent young voice that was shouting at him cracked ominously, and stopped him in his tracks, and he was saved. He looked again, and more closely, at the pale, raging face and the anguished eyes that didn't avoid his searching stare, because the case was too desperate for considerations of dignity to have any further validity.

Understanding hit George like a steam hammer. Someone you're used to thinking of as a child, someone who sounds like a hysterical boy, suddenly looks at you with the profound, solemn, staggering grief of a man, and knocks the breath out of you. It won't last, of course, it isn't a constant yet, he'll be back and forth between maturity and childishness a hundred times before he loses the ability to commute. But it's the first plain prophecy of things to come, and it's hit him deadly hard. Oh, God, thought George, utterly dismayed, and I teased him about her! How dim can you get about your own kid?

Treading with wincing care, as though even a loud noise might start them both jangling again like shaken glasses, George went and sat down at the table opposite his son. In a soft, reasonable voice he said: 'All right, boy, you owed me that. I haven't been fair to you. This is the first time you ever let me down, and that's not a bad record, all things considered. I don't really think you did it lightly, I don't really under-value your reasons. I don't blame you for not being willing to contract out. Probably in your place I should do exactly the same as you've done. And since I'm the person who's to blame for breaking all the rules in the first place, and I've been doing it for years, I may just as well do it just once more, and tell you how the case really stands now. It won't make you any happier,' he said ruefully, 'but it may settle your mind. Since Kitty Norris told us her story to-night we've been working hard at the details.

We've questioned all the tenants of the block of flats where she lives, and we've found a couple on the ground floor who heard and saw her come in that night, not at half past ten, as she said at first, nor at ten past eleven, as she says now, but just after midnight. She declines to account for that missing time.'

'They could be mistaken – ' began Dominic strenuously.

'I didn't say she denied it, I said she wouldn't account for it.' The voice was gentler and gentler. 'And that's not all, Dom. We also brought in the clothes Kitty wore that night. I saw her, she had on a black silk dress with a full skirt, I didn't have any trouble picking it out. She had an Indian scarf, too, a shot red and blue gauze affair with gold embroidery. To tell you the one thing that fits in nowhere, since I'm telling you the things that do fit, only too well, the end of the scarf has a corner torn off, and we haven't been able to find a trace of it so far. The left side of the skirt of the dress has several smears along the hem, not easily visible because of the black colour, but enough to react to tests. They're blood. The same group as Armiger's. Her shoes I didn't notice, but we found them, by one spot of brown on the toe of the left one. That's blood, too, Dom. The same group. Armiger's group, but not Kitty's. We tested.'

Dominic shut his eyes, but he couldn't stop seeing the silver sandals glittering in her hands at the Boat Club. They wouldn't be the same shoes, but he couldn't stop seeing them.

'I'm sorry, old man,' said George. He rose and drew away gingerly; the front view of Dominic was beginning to be too precarious, he moved considerately to the rear. The slender shoulders were braced and motionless. 'It isn't the end of the world, or of the case, either,' said George, 'but it's no good pretending that the outlook's rosy, Dom. I had to tell you, in justice to you. Don't take it too much to heart.'

He laid his hand for an instant on Dominic's shoulder, and let his knuckles scrub gently at the rigid cheek.

Dominic got up abruptly and steered a blind course for the door, and blundering past Bunty fled for the stairs. Bunty looked after him, looked at George, and hesitated whether to follow. It was George who said warningly: 'No!' and shook his head at her. It couldn't be cured that way, either.

'Let him alone,' said George. 'He'll be all right, just let him alone.'

Chapter 9

By the time he came down to breakfast next morning he had thought things out for himself, and arrived at a position from which he did not intend to be moved; that was implicit in the set of his jaw and the pallid resolution of his whole face, which seemed to have moved a long stage nearer to its mature form overnight. By his puffy eyelids and the blue hollows under his eyes thinking was what he'd been doing all through the hours of darkness when he should have been sleeping. He arrived at the breakfast table composed and quiet, greeted his parents punctiliously, to show there were no dangerous loose ends dangling, and made himself more mannishly attentive to Bunty than she had ever known him. Gravely she played up to him; having two men in the house was going to be interesting. She had no real complaints against George, but having a rival around wasn't going to do him any harm, and she was going to enjoy herself. If only it hadn't had to happen to him this way! She and George had spent the early hours of the morning in subdued and anxious colloquy over him, and it was difficult not to betray that they were watching him with equal anxiety now, intensely aware of every consciously restrained movement he made, even of the hesitations and selections that preceded every word he spoke.

'About last night, Dad,' he said, embarking at last with a shivering plunge which he did his best to make look normal. 'I've been thinking what I ought to do. I've thought over everything you said, and – and thanks for telling me. But there's one thing I know absolutely, and it's evidence to me even if it isn't to you – I mean you can't possibly *know* it as I do. When she talked to me Kitty *didn't know* how Mr. Armiger was killed.

So she couldn't possibly be the person who killed him. I don't
expect you to be sure of that, because you didn't see her and
hear her, but I did, and I am sure. So all the other things you've
found out against her can't really mean that she's guilty, there
has to be some other explanation for them.'

'We shall still be working on it,' said George, 'trying to fill
up all the gaps. I told you, the case isn't closed yet.'

'No. But you'll be trying to fill up the gaps with one idea in
mind. The logical end of your gap-filling is a conviction, isn't
it?'

George, moved partly by genuine bitterness and partly by a
blind, brilliant instinct for the thing to say that would make
them equals, asked with asperity: 'Damn it, do you think I like
this solution any better than you do?' He didn't even care, for the
moment, whether Bunty caught the smarting note of personal
resentment in that, provided it bolstered Dominic's developing
ego.

The blue-ringed eyes shot one rapid, startled glance into his
face and were hastily lowered again. They would be stealing
measuring looks in his direction with increasing frequency from
now on.

'Well, no, I suppose not,' said Dominic cautiously. The tone
suggested that he would have liked to linger inwardly over the
implications, if there had not been something infinitely more
urgent to be considered. 'Only I start from what I know, and it
makes the whole thing different for me. And so – well, maybe
I might get somewhere different, and find out things that you
wouldn't. You can see that I've got to try, anyhow.'

'I can see you feel you have to,' agreed George.

'You don't object?'

'Provided you don't impede us in any way, how can I
object? But if you do happen on anything relevant, don't forget
you have a duty to pass it on to the police.'

'But I suppose that doesn't mean *you* have to tell *me* anything!'

The tone was so arrogant this time that George revised his

ideas of the nursing this developing ego needed; it seemed, on the whole, to be doing very well for itself, and there was no sense in letting it get out of hand. 'No,' he said firmly. 'And after what happened yesterday that can hardly surprise you.'

'O.K.,' said Dominic, abashed and retreating several years. 'Sorry!'

He rose from the table with a purposeful face, and marched out without saying a word about his intentions. It was Saturday, so at least he was saved from fretting barrenly over books he wouldn't even be able to see, and lectures that would be double-Dutch to him. Bunty followed him out into the garden, where he was grimly pumping up the tyres of his bicycle. She didn't ask any questions, she just said: 'Good luck, lamb!' and kissed him; she thought she might justifiably go as far as that, it was what she'd always done and said when she was sending him out to face some dragonish ordeal like the eleven-plus examination or his first day at the grammar school. He recognised the rite, and dutifully raised his head from his labours to offer his mouth, as engagingly and as inattentively as at five years old; but instead of scrubbing off the kiss briskly with the back of his hand and leaning hard on the pump again, he straightened up and looked at her with the troubled eyes that didn't know from minute to minute whether to be a boy's or a man's. The first three ages of man were batting him back and forth among them like a shuttlecock.

'Thanks, Mummy!' he said gruffly, preserving the ritual.

She tucked a ten-shilling note into his pocket. 'An advance against your expense account,' she said.

For a moment he wasn't sure that he was being taken seriously enough. 'I'm not kidding,' he said sternly, scowling at her.

'I'm not kidding, either,' said Bunty. 'I don't know the girl, but you do, and if you say she didn't do it that goes a long way with me. Anything on the level I can do to help, you ask me. Right?'

'Right! Gosh, *thanks*, Mummy!'

It wasn't just for the ten shillings, which at first he'd suspected of being a bribe to him to cheer up, it wasn't even for the offer of help and support, it was for everything she'd implied about his relationship with Kitty: that it was adult, that it was real, that it had importance and validity, and was to be treated with respect. He experienced one of those moments of delighted love for his mother, of startling new discoveries in his exploration of her, which are among the unexpected compensations of growing up. And Bunty, who knew when to vanish, sailed hastily back into the house feeling almost as young as her son.

Flashes of pleasure and warmth, however, did nothing to solve the problem of Kitty, and the shadow and weight closed on him again more oppressively than ever as he straddled his bicycle and rode out of Comerford by the farm road that would bring him out close to The Jolly Barmaid. In the grassy verge by the crossroads he put one foot to the ground and sat gazing at the house, thinking hard. People had almost given up standing about staring at the place by this time, the centre of attention had shifted now to wherever Kitty was likely to be. The news was out, in morning papers and news bulletins and by the ever-present grapevine that twined across the back fences of the villages and burrowed its roots into the foundations of the town. *Kitty Norris!* Can you *believe* it?

The vulgar new sign in its convolutions of wrought-iron gleamed at the edge of the road. The doors would not be opened for business until after the funeral, for which permission had been given at yesterday's adjourned inquest. How it would have annoyed Armiger to have to forgo a week-end's takings just because someone was dead. The funeral, they said, would be on Monday, and Raymond Shelley was seeing to the arrangements, not Leslie Armiger. The conventionally-minded, with magnificent hypocrisy, were already beginning to censure Leslie for want of filial feeling, and were quite certain in advance that he wouldn't go to the funeral. Why in the world, wondered Dominic, should he be expected to? He'd been expressly

413

dismissed from his position as a son, and forbidden to feel
filial; if he suffered any regrets for his ex – or late – father it
constituted a gesture of generosity on his part, it wasn't in any
way due from him. And what did he feel now for Kitty, who
had flown slap into the net to make sure he should not be
snared? He must know by now. Everybody knew. Even when
Dominic rode past the first farm cottages the air felt heavy and
tremulous with the reverberations of the news, and two women
with their heads together over the fence could only be retailing
the rich imaginary details of Kitty's fall.

Dominic began to follow the course Kitty had taken that
night. Here she had halted before sweeping out in a right-hand
turn and heading for Comerbourne; it had then been about a
quarter past ten. Somewhere on her way she'd changed her
mind and wished she'd stayed; somewhere before the next right-
hand turn into the lane that wound its way to Wood's End, and
there brought her into the rear farm road, the ridge-road from
the back of The Jolly Barmaid, that followed the old contour
track between the upland fields and the low, moist river
meadows. Probably she'd driven this stage slowly and cautiously;
she was a fast driver by inclination but not a reckless one, and
at night the frequent bends and high hedges of the lane contained and shrouded even the beams of headlights.

Natural enough, when she changed her mind, to go round
like this instead of turning and driving back along the high
road; natural enough, that is, if she only made up her mind
when the crossroads came in sight, and what could be more
likely? A crossroads is an invitation to pause, to think again and
confirm your direction. So she turned down here, saying to
herself: I will, I'll have one more go at making him see reason.

A third of a mile or so, and the lane brought her to the next
right-hand turn, under the signpost at Wood's End. Hardly a
village, just a few farm cottages, the long drive of the farm, one
tiny shop, and a telephone box. And from here to the right
again, into the old road, and maybe just over a quarter of a mile

414

to go to the tall boundary wall of The Jolly Barmaid. She had parked 'along there under the trees by that little wood.' When he reached the spot it was easy to see why, for the road broadened there into a wide stretch of trampled grass on the left, like an accidental lay-by under the hanging wood, and there she could get off the road. For by that time it must have been nearly, if not quite, half past ten, closing time at the pub, and though most of the customers would be using the main road, there was always the possibility that some of the countrymen would be leaving by this way.

Dominic dismounted, and pushed his bike slowly the last fifty yards or so from the place where she had parked to the rear exit from the courtyard. It was not a gate but a broad opening in the high wall, blocked with two iron posts so that no cars could drive out that way. The barn-ballroom was quite close, she had only to cross this remote corner of the yard to the doorway and walk in. And there Armiger had waited for her, full of his new plan, entertaining no doubts of her complacency.

How long had it taken, what happened in there? Not long, surely. She trying to get him to listen to her plea for Leslie, he riding over everything with his great schemes for the future, and convinced that she was with him; like two people trying to convey to each other two conflicting urgencies, without a word in common in any language. If she had reached this place about half past ten, or a little later, allowing for parking and locking the car and perhaps for some final hesitation, Dominic estimated that she must have taken flight well before eleven. Armiger would never let the exposition of his deal take him more than a quarter of an hour, he went straight at things. There was a pretty good indication of the times involved, too, in Kitty's declaration that she had reached her flat by about ten past eleven; granted that was discredited by the evidence of her neighbours, yet it must be the time she had felt she ought to give, the correct time to round off the version of her movements which she wanted to have believed. Between ten and five minutes to eleven she came running out of the ballroom and left Armiger lying at the foot of the staircase, thought Dominic with certainty.

And then what? She would want only one thing, as she herself had said, and that was to get away. Would she drive on to the next turning and go right round The Jolly Barmaid again to the main road? Or turn there under the trees and drive back by the way she had come? She'd turn, he decided, after only a moment's thought; this way was quieter and also shorter. There was plenty of room to turn under the trees. Almost certainly she headed back towards Wood's End. And in fourteen or fifteen minutes she should have been home. Why wasn't she?

He thought over and round it, and he was sure that was the only point on which she had lied. And why? There was an hour lost. Whatever she'd done with it, he was quite certain she hadn't come back and killed Alfred Armiger, so why wouldn't she tell them what had happened during that missing time? Because there was someone else involved? Someone equally innocent, whom she refused to harm?

Her whole desire had been to get away. If she hadn't done it it was because she couldn't.

He had begun to push his bike towards Wood's End, trailing his toes in the fallen leaves under the trees. He chose to walk because his mind was grinding over the meagre facts so slowly that his feet had to keep the same pace. Here she turned and drove back, and yet she didn't get home to Comerbourne until after midnight. She was going along here, probably fast, running away from her sense of outrage and frustration and shame; and somewhere along here fright fell on her, too, the dread that she ought to have waited to make sure how badly he was hurt; but by then it wouldn't stop or turn her, it would only drive her on all the faster. So why didn't she get home soon after eleven, as she should have done?

And then he knew why.

It was so simple and so silly that it had to be true. He heard the busy low note of the engine cough and fail, felt the power die away, and saw Kitty reach for the tap with one impatient toe, to kick it over on to the reserve, and then draw back furious and exasperated because it was on the reserve already, and yet once again she'd done her inimitable trick. Half the day she'd probably been saying to herself cheerfully: 'Plenty of time, I've got a gallon, I'll call at Lowe's before I leave Comerbourne, I'll look in at the filling station at Leah Green –' making easy promises every time the necessity recurred to her, until it didn't recur to her any more.

'I never learn. I run dry in the middle of the High Street, or halfway up the lane to the golf links.' He could hear her voice now, and remember every word she had said about her two blind spots. Nobody who didn't know Kitty as he did, nobody who wasn't in her confidence as he was, could ever have unearthed this simple explanation for her lost hour. She just ran out of petrol! She was always doing it; she'd told him so herself.

The next question was: Where did it happen? He thought that over and decided that it must have been somewhere close to The Jolly Barmaid and well away from Comerbourne. If she had been near the town when she ran dry she would simply have stopped a car on the main road and begged the driver either to let her have some juice or to call in at her garage and leave a message; to be immobilised on the main road near Comerbourne at around eleven o'clock would be innocent enough, just as good as being home by ten past eleven, and there wouldn't have been any missing hour, or any need for lies. But Kitty had lied, it was one of the main points against her. No, somewhere along here, somewhere unpleasantly close to the inn, she found herself stranded. And here she didn't want to stop a car and ask for help, she didn't want to have her garage man come out with petrol for her; she didn't want to call attention to her presence in any way, or let anyone know that she had been here.

Dominic was imagining her state of mind with so much passion that his own heartbeats quickened and his temples began

417

to throb with panic. Every minute that passed must have driven her a little nearer to hysteria. Supposing Armiger was desperately hurt, and she'd run away and left him? Supposing, even, that he should die? Maybe she'd thought of going back to him, but she simply couldn't face it. She hadn't meant to do anything so dreadful, but it had happened and she was to blame. In that state of mind she would have only one instinctive idea, and that would be to hide the fact that she had ever been near the place after she left by the main road at a quarter past ten.

Supposing it happened somewhere here, he thought, walking slowly along the left-hand side of the old road, she'd be in a spot about getting the car as far as possible off the fairway, because it's rather narrow and winding. If I keep my eyes open I may be able to spot the place, because she'd have to try and run it almost into the hedge, and I wonder if maybe her paint may not show some scratches, too?

He was almost within sight of the Wood's End cottages when he found one place at least where some vehicle had certainly been run as far as possible on to the bumpy grass verge, its near-side wheel-marks hugging the base of the hedge. There was no mistaking it; the crushing of the thick growth on the ground, the breaking of the overgrown shoots of the hedge, these were slight signs already partially erased by showers and winds and the passing of time, but the breakages were there to be seen if you looked for them, and the wheel-track was still evident. It might be Kitty, it might not, there was no way of knowing unless she chose to tell them.

However, supposing for the sake of the theory that this was where she ran dry, what would she do next? She would have to call on someone for help, and the obvious thing to do was to go to the telephone box at Wood's End, and from there ring up some private person, someone she could trust absolutely. And the someone came in response to her appeal, and brought her petrol enough to get her home. But what had determined Kitty's silence was surely the fact that this simple act had now laid her benefactor open to a charge as an accessory after the fact in a murder case. If they convicted her they could charge her helper. Kitty wouldn't allow that; no word of hers was ever going to involve the friend who had come to her rescue. That was the kind of girl she was.

This long communion with himself had brought Dominic to the telephone box. He stood and looked at it for a moment, and then, without any clear idea of what he hoped to find within, pulled open the door and looked round the dusty interior. Absolutely impersonal, a piece of the mundane machinery of modern living, with the usual graffiti. He was letting the door swing to when he caught an incongruous gleam of gold, and pulled it hastily open again. Clinging in the hinge of the door, shadowy as cobweb but for a few torn gilt threads, a scrap of gauze hung like a crushed butterfly.

He put out a hand to pull it loose, and then checked himself in the act, and did no more than smooth out the delicate scrap tenderly with his fingertips until he could distinguish the minute embroidered flowers of gold on the almost impalpable silk. A corner of an Indian scarf, shot dark blue and red, embroidered with gold thread; the scarf Kitty had worn on the night of Armiger's death. The one detail for which the police had no satisfactory explanation, the bit that didn't fit in; but for Dominic it fitted in miraculously.

He mustn't move it; he must let his father see it just as it was. He shut himself into the box and dialled with a hand trembling with excitement.

'This is Dominic Felse here. Can I speak to my father, please? I know, but this is important, it's something to do with the case.'

George was up to his neck in paper work, and impatient of interruptions, but too sore from his recent mistakes to take any new risks where Dominic was concerned. He listened without any real expectations, and heard, incredulously: 'I'm at the telephone box at Wood's End, Dad. I've found the corner you said was torn from Kitty's scarf.'

'You've *what*?'

Dominic repeated his statement patiently. 'It's caught on a rough place in the hinge of the door, she must have pulled it clear in a hurry and torn the corner clean off. I know, I *haven't* moved it. I'm keeping an eye on it until you come.'

'How on earth did you come to walk straight to it?' asked George, humanly aggrieved.

'I used me natural genius. Come along and I'll tell you.' He couldn't help the cocky note, but he wasn't really feeling elated; there was still too far to go, and too much at stake. He debated within himself, while he waited, how much he ought to tell his father, how much he was committed to telling. All that was really evidence was that scrap of silk, but it tended to consolidate his theories into something like facts, and perhaps he ought to confide everything. His accidental acquaintance with Kitty's idiosyncrasies in connection with cars, for instance, was evidence too, and so was the shaved place along the hedge. In the end he told George the whole process of thought which had brought him to the telephone box, and was listened to with flattering attention. He added his initials to George's on the envelope in which George enclosed the shred of gauze, though he had a faint suspicion that that was a sop to his self-love.

'It all makes remarkable sense, as far as it goes,' agreed George, inspecting the hedge. 'We can check the car and see if it shows any traces. This chap's wings were well into the strong growth.'

'I suppose,' said Dominic, very carefully and quietly, 'it wouldn't be possible for me to see Kitty, would it?'

'I'm afraid not, Dom. I'm pretty sure they wouldn't consider it. You'd need a solid reason like being her legal adviser or a member of her family to get in to her – yet, at any rate.'

'Yes, I see. I didn't think I could, really. But you could see her, couldn't you? You could ask her all my questions for me, if you would – like where she ran out of petrol, and whom she telephoned. I don't think she'll tell you, of course, but she won't be expecting you to know anything about it, and she may give something away without meaning to. She isn't very good at telling lies, really,' said Dominic, suppressing the slight constriction in his throat. 'She forgets and comes out with a bit of the truth, without thinking. Only if she's lying for somebody else she'll be twice as careful.' He scrubbed his toes along the deep grooves the wheels had left in the soft grass under the hedge, and scowled down at his feet. 'I suppose you couldn't give her a message from me, could you? Oh, nothing unconstitutional, I only meant just to give her my regards – and maybe tell her I'm doing what I can for her.'

'I'll give her that message with pleasure,' said George gravely.

He didn't tell him that Kitty's car had yielded two faint, minute smears of blood from the edge of the driving-seat, obviously brushed there from the skirt of her dress, or that the fine scratches on the near-side front wing had already been preoccupying their minds for several hours. It seemed ungenerous to keep these things back from him, when he was making so notable a contribution, but there was no choice about it. They'd agreed on their terms of truce; Dominic wasn't expecting concessions.

George went to see Kitty that afternoon. Raymond Shelley was just leaving her, his face worn and wretched, his bulging brief-case hugged to him defensively as he passed George in the corridor, as though he had Kitty's life locked in it. It wasn't easy for them even to talk to each other now, they had become representative of the two sides, and communication was an effort.

'You realise, of course,' said Shelley, 'that her defence will be an absolute denial of the charge. Any competent doctor will be able to show that no woman could have been responsible for the attack, on physical grounds alone.'

George said nothing to that. He had tentatively raised the

421

same point, and Duckett had given him a derisive glare, and said: 'Are you kidding? What, with a sitting target all laid out for her against a brand-new floor about as hard as ebony? A fairly lusty ten-year-old could have done it.'

'I can't realise it, even yet,' burst out Shelley, shaking his head helplessly. 'Kitty! I've known her all my life, she couldn't wilfully hurt even an insect. It just can't be true, Felse, it simply can't. I can't forgive myself for leaving her alone that night. If I'd realised he had any such thing in his mind I could have stopped it.'

Could he, wondered George, looking after him with sympathy as he flung nervously away. How much influence had he with Armiger, if it came to the point? What was it Leslie had called him? – a cover man. He was the one who was used; he was in his master's secrets only as far as Armiger chose to admit him for his own ends. No, Shelley would never have been effective in diverting the bull's rush, but if he'd tried he might have made one more casualty.

Kitty had survived the first anguish, the agonised tears of helplessness and loneliness and shame that had scarified his heart yesterday. Dominic, thank God, knew nothing about that half-hour of collapse, and never would know. Whatever his imagination inflicted upon him, it would not be the reality George had seen and suffered. The first thing to-day's Kitty did was to apologise for it, simply and directly, without embarrassment. It was past, it wouldn't happen again.

'I'm sorry I gave you such a bad time. I hadn't expected it myself, I was shocked. It just shows, you never know how you may react in a crisis. And I always thought I had an equable temperament.'

George said: 'My son sent you his regards, and said I was to tell you that he's doing what he can for you.'

She lifted her head and smiled at him, with a smile which he knew belonged by rights to Dominic. She looked pale and drained, but all her distress had done to her looks was to make her eyes look larger than ever, and the vulnerable curves of her mouth more plaintive and tender. She had on the same neutral-tinted sweater and skirt he had seen her in at her flat, and a book was turned down beside her; she looked like an over-earnest student surprised during the last week before a vital examination.

'Please thank him for me. He's almost the only one who believes me when I say I didn't do it. Out of the mouths of babes – ' She shut her hands suddenly on the air as if to snatch back the unforgivable indiscretion. 'No, don't tell him I said that. It isn't even true, and it would hurt him. Just thank him for me, and give him my love.' At that she had taken a careful second look before she ever let her lips shape the single signifi-cant syllable, but she didn't take it back. The soft bow of her mouth folded firmly, and let it stand.

'We found the place where you pulled the car into the hedge when you ran out of petrol,' said George in the same conver-sational tone. 'Why didn't you tell us about that? You might have known we were sure to find it.'

'*He* found it,' said Kitty, and smiled again to herself, and that smile, too, was for Dominic. 'What a boy!' she said. 'Fancy remembering that! But even he could be wrong, you know. Now I'm not talking about that any more, it isn't a subject I like, and you can't make me. Come to think of it, there's absolutely nothing you people can do to me now. Except, perhaps, stop visiting me. I'd much rather see you than nobody. Poor old Ray looks so desperately sad he breaks my heart. And who else is likely to come near me?'

'You have hordes of friends, and you know it,' said George, consenting to follow her disconcerting leaps.

'I *had*. The most popular deb. of her year, that was Kitty. Do you know how many eligible young men have wanted to marry me, since they knew Leslie was out of the market? Seven actually got as far as asking, and about five more were hovering pretty near the brink. And do you know how many have been to try and see me to-day, to show how much they loved me? One. And that was Leslie, the one who never pretended to.' She laughed and because Leslie had come it was a genuine, beautiful, even joyful laugh. Only then did George understand. Kitty had got something out of her disaster, after all.

'Did they let him in?'

'Oh, yes, he had a certain claim, you see, my victim's son, and brought up almost like a brother to me. He was sweet,' said Kitty, looking down into her cupped hands and smiling with a brooding tenderness for which any man would have performed prodigies of love and loyalty. 'And terribly upset.' She didn't care who observed her personal sorrow or her personal rapture here; life had become so precarious as to be simple, there was no time for dissembling or being ashamed. 'I believe he even feels responsible for me, simply because it was his father who got killed – as though he could help it. He feels almost as if it was he who got me into it. But I got myself into it – nobody else. You won't mistake that for a confession, will you? It isn't.'

'And kept somebody else out of it,' said George.

She turned her head and looked at him, not so abruptly that he could claim he had got a real reaction out of her, but at least so positively that he knew she was paying attention for once.

'The person you telephoned to come and help you out of your mess,' said George. 'We know you did, you left a bit of your scarf caught in the door of the telephone box at Wood's End. Did you think we shouldn't get wise to that call? You may as well tell us all about that interlude, you know, it's only a matter of time.'

'I'm in no hurry,' said Kitty, smiling, even teasing him, though the sadness that was in everything she did or said was in this perversity too.

'Who was it, Kitty? Better give us the name than have us give it to you.'

'I don't even know what you're talking about. Look, I've thought of something,' she said. 'If I'm convicted, I can't inherit from my victim, can I? So what happens to the money? I never thought to ask poor old Ray, I was so busy stroking his hand and saying: There, there! Do *you* know?'

'I'm not sure. But I should think it would automatically go to the next-of-kin, unless there's some express veto on that in the will itself.' He didn't know how much of this he could take, and still remember that he was a police officer, here on business. He wished he could think that she was doing it to him on purpose, to repay her own injuries, or out of bravado, to put them out of her mind, but he knew she wasn't. She was evading being questioned, but she asked her own questions because she wanted to know the answers.

'Good!' she said with a sigh of satisfaction. 'Then at any rate Leslie and Jean won't have to worry any more, they'll be loaded. I suppose I ought to make a will, too.'

George opened his mouth to answer her, and couldn't get out a word. She looked up, her isolation penetrated for a moment by the quality of his shocked silence, and searching for the reason in her own words, came up with the wrong answer.

'It's all right,' she said quickly and kindly. 'I didn't mean it like that. I know! Even if the worst comes to the worst, it isn't capital murder.'

Chapter 10

'There she is,' said Leslie, stepping back from the table. 'The Joyful Woman in person. I took your advice and fetched her back from Cranmer's yesterday. What do you think of her?'

If George had told the simple truth in answer to that it would have had to be: Not much! Propped against the wall to catch the light from the window, what there was of it on this dull Sunday morning, the wooden panel looked singularly unimpressive, its flesh-tints a sallow fawn–colour, its richer shades weathered and dirtied into mere variations on tobacco–brown. Not very big for an inn sign, about twenty by eighteen inches, and even within that measure the figure was not so bold as it could have been. Against a flat ground that might once have been deep green or blue but was now grained with resinous brown varnishes coat after coat, the woman was shown almost to the waist. At the base of the panel her hands were crossed under little maidenly breasts, swathed in a badly-painted muslin fichu. Her shoulders beneath the folds of muslin were braced back, her neck was long, and in its present incarnation shapeless, and inclined forward like a leaning flower-stem to balance the backward tilt of the head. In half-face, looking to the right, she raised her large bland forehead to the light and laughed; and in spite of the crudity of the flat masses of which she was built, and the want of moulding in the face, there was no doubt that this was the laughter of delight and not of amusement; she wasn't sharing it with an audience, it belonged to herself alone. Joyful was the just word for her.

'I know nothing about painting,' said George truthfully, and taking care not to sound complacent about it. 'Frankly, it's pretty ugly, isn't it? And a queer mixture. That frill round her neck, and those mounds of hair like touches of early Victorian realism. But her pose isn't Victorian – or realistic. More sort of hieratic – if I'm making any sense?'

'You're making quite remarkable sense. Which is it you find ugly, the mass or the detail?'

'The detail, I suppose. The mass balances – I mean the shape of her on the panel. The masses of paint are clumsy, but I suppose that's from years of over-painting by amateurs every time it got shabby.'

'You know,' said Leslie appreciatively, 'you'd better be careful, or you're going to turn into an art critic.' He had quite forgotten, in his excitement over this unimposing work of art, that his relationship with George had hitherto been one of mutual suspicion and potential antagonism. 'That's exactly what's happened to her, and been happening for probably a couple of centuries. Every time she needed brightening up, some ham-fisted member of the family took a brush and some primary colours and simply filled in the various bits of her solidly, line to line, like a mosaic. And every now and again one of the artists got carried away and started putting in twiddly bits like the corkscrew curls – which, as you so justly remarked, don't belong. I'm betting they don't go below a couple of coats at all. But the shape, the way she fills the panel and stands poised, and leaves these rather beautiful forms round her – that's there from the beginning, and that's *good*. And I want her out of that coffin. I want to see what she was like once, before she went into the licensed trade, because I'm pretty sure there was a before. She hasn't always been an inn sign.'

Jean, pausing for a moment on her way out to the landing kitchenette, stared intently at the laughing woman, and bit thoughtfully at the handle of the fork she was holding in her hand. 'You know, she kind of reminds me of something, only I can never think what. Do you think she always laughed?'

'Yes, I think so, it's in the tilt of the head. But with luck we shall see, some day. I'm taking her to the chap who runs the university gallery this afternoon,' explained Leslie contentedly. 'I telephoned him yesterday – Brandon Lucas, I find I used to know his son at Oxford, so that broke the ice nicely – and he said yes, she sounded very interesting, and he'd like to have a look at her.'

'Did you have any trouble getting it back from Cranmer?' asked George.

'No, no trouble. He wasn't very keen on parting, but I suppose he'd hardly be likely to commit himself to *too* urgent an interest, after your inquiries.'

'Did he make you an offer?'

'Yes,' said Leslie.

'How high did he go?'

Too late George felt the slight chill of constraint that had suddenly lowered the temperature in the room, and the tension that charged the air between husband and wife. He shouldn't have asked; money was something that had shadowed the whole of their short married life, the want of it, the injustice of its withdrawal, the indignity of stooping to ask for it.

'Six hundred pounds,' said Jean, distinctly and bitterly, and made for the door.

Leslie's fingers pinched out his cigarette, suddenly trembling. 'You didn't want to touch it when Dad offered five hundred,' he said indignantly. 'You said I did right to turn that down. What's so different about this offer?'

'It's a hundred more,' she said flatly and coldly, 'and it doesn't come from your father. It's straight money from a dealer, and it wouldn't burn me, and the things I could buy with it wouldn't be poisoned.'

So that was it. When the offer was pushed up to so tempting a figure she had wanted him to take it. Perfectly logical and understandable. She was a breeding tigress, she wanted to line a nest for her young; not at any price, but at any price that didn't maim her pride. If her confidence in Leslie had been still unshaken she would have accepted his estimate of their best course, and gone along with him loyally, but that one disastrous move of his had ended the honeymoon once for all. Now he had to prove himself, he would never be taken on trust again, and his every act was to be scrutinised and judged mercilessly, not because she was greedy for herself, but because she was insatiable for her child. Looking round the shabby, congested room that was their home, George couldn't blame her for preferring to clutch at certain benefits to-day rather than speculate on riches tomorrow.

'And if I'd taken it, and then the thing had turned out to be worth ten times as much, you'd never have let me forget that either,' said Leslie, smarting. He flushed at the petulant tone of his own voice, and to break off the unseemly argument went forward and plucked the panel from its place, his pleasure in it spoiled. He was ashamed of having displayed their differences before George, and probably so was she, for she said from the doorway, without turning her head: 'Well, it's no use worrying now, in any case, it's done. We may be lucky yet.'

'Believe me, Mrs. Armiger,' said George firmly, 'if Cranmer offered six hundred for it he was absolutely certain of clearing a good deal more than that. He isn't in business for fun. You hang on to it until you get a really disinterested opinion.'

He moved to Leslie's shoulder to take another look at it. There was a queer ornament pinned between the childish breasts, something that looked like an enormous oval brooch with some embossed pattern on it. It rested upright above the crossed hands, long, curved, inarticulate hands pallid under the crazed varnish. 'You've got some definite idea of your own about this, haven't you?' he asked curiously.

'Well, I have, but I don't dare believe it. It's too staggering, I'd rather not talk about it until somebody else has pronounced on it, somebody who knows a lot more about these things than I do.' He wrapped the panel in an old dust-sheet and stacked it carefully in a corner. 'I'm sorry, I've been so full of her I can't think of much else, but I'm sure you didn't come here to talk about *her*. Is it something about Kitty?' His face was grave enough at the thought of her, the vexation and the pleasure of his own affairs both overshadowed.

'It is about her, as a matter of fact,' said George. 'You paid her a visit yesterday morning, didn't you?'

'Yes, as soon as I could get away from the shop. I didn't even know she'd been arrested until I went to work. Why? It was all right, wasn't it?'

'Oh, quite. I was simply wondering if she'd been any more forthcoming with you that she was with us. There's an hour of her time, that night, from just after eleven until just after twelve, for which she refuses to account, and there's a possibility that her reasons for keeping quiet are concerned with some other person. My impression is that the best thing that could happen for her is that everything to do with her movements that night should come out.'

'Guilty or innocent?'

'Guilty or innocent.'

'From you,' said Leslie after some thought, 'I might accept that. But if you mean did she tell me anything yesterday morning that she wouldn't tell you in the afternoon, no, she didn't. Not a word about my father or that night. We didn't talk about it. We didn't talk a lot about anything. She just said she didn't do it, and I said I never thought she did. Which I suppose is a perfectly good reason for co-operating with you, now that I come to think of it.'

'It is, if that's what you honestly believe. You were with her – how long? Half an hour or so? If you weren't talking, what were you doing all that time?'

'Most of that time,' said Leslie, angry colour suddenly mantling over his shapely cheek-bones, 'Kitty was crying, and I was trying to comfort her.' He glared for a moment, but the flash of partisan indignation passed as quickly as it had flared up. 'Oh, nothing shattering, just she needed to, and with me she could. She didn't tell me anything about your missing hour.

430

And I suppose you know you're not the only one who's been asking me about it? Your boy came to see me yesterday.'

'I didn't know, but I'm not surprised.' Dominic had volunteered no information resulting from his inquiries in this direction, it seemed likely that he had acquired none. 'We have a working arrangement,' said George with a hollow smile. 'Did he ask you this one? If Kitty was in a desperate hole and needed someone quickly, someone who wouldn't hesitate to come out to her late at night and get her out of trouble, to whom would she turn?'

'No, he didn't ask that exactly, but maybe we covered much the same ground another way. There was a time when I'd have said she'd come to me. We've been good friends, she was like my little sister most of the time we were growing up, but that ghastly scheme of my father's broke it all down. What could you expect? Kitty's odd, sweet and funny and candid, but very much alone, too. I'm very fond of her, and I think she was of me until Dad spoiled everything. I did say to her yesterday, why on earth didn't she call on me if she was in a spot, but all she said was something daffy about my not being on the telephone any more, as though that was any reason for locking me out of her life. Did you say something?'

George shook his head. 'No, go on. If she wouldn't turn to you, then who would it be?'

'Well, of course she has fellows round her as thick as bees wherever she goes, and all that, but I can't imagine her going to any of them. I think it would be someone older, if she really needed someone. It would have been her aunt, the one who brought her up, of course, only she died a year or so ago. There's her manager – he's a nice old boy, and she's known him all her life – or Ray Shelley, he's her unofficial uncle, she always got on well with him, especially after he tried to stick up for me when the row burst. Someone like that. I'm not being much help?'

'You might be,' said George.

'Don't get me wrong. It's Kitty I want to help, not you. No offence, you're only doing your job, I know. But I'm not a policeman, I'm just a friend of Kitty's.'

'All right,' said George, resigned to his exclusion from humankind, 'that's understood. I suppose, by the way, that Dom made it quite clear where he stands?'

He saw by the fleeting gleam of a smile in Leslie's eyes that indeed Dominic had, and that he had been welcomed accordingly.

He got as far as the door, and then turned back to say: 'One more thing, you might like to know, we did find somebody who confirmed your timing that night. One of the colliers on late shift at the Warren happens to live at the bottom end of this road. He was coming off the miners' bus at the corner just as you turned in on your way home. That fixes the time pretty accurately at around a quarter to eleven, give or take a couple of minutes. So that's that. For what it's worth now.'

'I see,' said Leslie slowly. 'Well, thanks for telling me, anyhow. It would have been worth a lot a couple of days ago. As you say, it doesn't seem to matter much now.'

'It was only last night we got round to the idea of checking the miners' bus. If I'd known before I'd have told you. Well, good luck with your Joyful Woman this afternoon. How are you doing the trip? That's an awkward thing to tote around by bus. I could offer you transport, if you're in difficulties?'

'That's awfully kind of you, but we've got the use of Barney Wilson's van when he isn't using it himself. He lets me keep his spare key, so that I can fetch it if I want it. He stables it at the Department's depot just out on the main road, not having a garage at home, so it's nice and handy.'

'Trusting chap,' said George from the top of the stairs. 'Most people would rather loan you their wives.'

Well, he thought as he drove slowly and thoughtfully homewards, he hadn't come out of that encounter quite empty-handed, even if there were some annoying loose ends that didn't

432

tie in anywhere. Chief among them was The Joyful Woman, that unpromising work of art, of such commonplace provenance and ungainly appearance, for which nonetheless a shrewd dealer was willing to pay six hundred pounds. Had she anything to do with Armiger's death, or had she not? She didn't fit in with the theory which had been devouring him ever since his visit to Kitty yesterday, but if she was going to turn out to be extremely valuable the possibility became worth considering.

Yet if money was the motive for this murder there was surely a greater prize to be considered than the few thousands which might be involved even in an important art find. Not the money Armiger had been playing for at the end of his life, but all the money he already had, the quarter of a million or so that young Leslie had always lightheartedly assumed would come to him. Had he really resigned himself to doing without it? And even if he had been on the point of coming to terms with his new poverty, for want of the means to change it, what would be his reaction if fate had suddenly presented him with a wonderful, a unique opportunity of regaining his fortune?

No doubt about it, Leslie had left The Jolly Barmaid that night with no intention of doing anything more reprehensible than walking home. That was what he had meant to do, and that was what he had done; the collier's evidence proved that quite conclusively. There was no question of his having hung about outside and witnessed Kitty's panic flight, and then returned to finish the job she had accidentally begun. He had been in Comerbourne at that moment, a mile and a quarter away from the scene. If he had killed he had gone back to kill, and the intent had been conceived as instantaneously as a flash of lightning – or, say, a cry for help. A cry from Kitty.

George had arrived at this point when it dawned upon him at last that he was thinking in terms which indicated that he no longer entertained the slightest doubt of Kitty's innocence. Whether that was Kitty's own doing or Dominic's was something he couldn't determine. But it didn't surprise him; he was only belatedly recognising something which had been true for at least twenty-four hours.

Not Kitty. Someone else. Someone to whom she had telephoned from Wood's End? Supposing, for the sake of the argument, that someone had found out from an agitated Kitty that Armiger was lying unconscious in the barn, and supposing that someone had, or abruptly discovered at that moment, an overwhelming reason for wanting the job finished. There was Kitty all set up ready to take the blame, and herself alerting the murderer to his unique opportunity. A chance like that comes only once in a lifetime.

It was Kitty herself who had put the idea into George's head, without the slightest conception of the kind of seed she was sowing, merely clutching at a small satisfaction in her desolation of sadness: 'If I'm convicted I can't inherit from my victim, can I? So what becomes of the money?' And again, reassured and consoled: 'Good! Then Leslie and Jean won't have to worry any more, they'll be loaded.'

The setup, however accidental, was perfect. It didn't even involve the killer in conniving at Kitty's death, since, as she had said, this wasn't capital murder; but the division of murder into capital and simple murder did not affect the law that a murderer cannot inherit from his victim. Kitty convicted could forfeit her inheritance and still come out of prison at the end of her term a rich and comparatively young woman. With a quarter of a million at stake he might even have been able to persuade himself that he wasn't doing her such a terrible wrong. That much money can often drown out the voice of conscience only too effectively.

There had been, in fact, only two snags when George had set out to pay this unexpected Sunday morning visit. Leslie had no car he could have taken out that night to hurry back to the barn; and as he had so suggestively reported Kitty herself as reminding them, he wasn't on the telephone any more. He could be reached only during working hours, at the warehouse.

Insurmountable obstacles both; except that one of them had already been surmounted, for it seemed he had the use of Barney Wilson's van whenever its owner didn't need it. The spare key was in his charge and the van was close at hand in the yard of the depot. Now if the other obstacle should prove equally illusory?

The thing had been getting more complicated by the hour, and yet George had felt all along that in reality the truth must be one single thread that passed through the tangle as straight as a ruled line, and only by accident formed part of this proliferated web of motives and feelings. And here it was, the clear thread, the convincing motive, the irresistible temptation. A man who has a quarter of a million in his sights can afford to turn down a mere six hundred pounds.

But – Leslie wasn't on the telephone.

Chapter 11

Dominic sought out his father on Sunday evening with a face so determined that it was plain he was bent on a serious conference. Bunty had gone to church; George wouldn't have minded having her sit in on their counsels, but in all probability Dominic would, considering that mothers should be shielded from too close consideration of such shocking things as murder. In his present mood of newly appreciated responsibility he probably blamed George for subjecting her to his confidences all these years.

'Dad, I've been thinking about this glove business,' he began, squaring his elbows purposefully on the table opposite George's chair.

'Yes?' said George. It was not the precise opening he had expected, but it was apposite enough; there was no getting away from the gloves.

'You know what I mean. Those gloves of Leslie's were O.K., but somebody must have had some pretty fouled-up gloves to dispose of after that night, mustn't they? The bottle was plastered right to the cork. And I could tell, the way you all pounced on even the possibility of those old painting gloves being the ones, that that was what you were looking for and hoping for. I mean, anything else the murderer had on *might* be marked, but his gloves definitely *would* – and he definitely was wearing gloves. That's right, isn't it?'

'That's right. So?'

'Well, you never did say, but was Kitty wearing gloves that night?' He didn't ask it with any sense that the answer was going to prove anything, he wasn't as simple as that. But it was a necessary part of the development of his ideas.

436

'Not indoors,' said George at once. 'But she could very well have had some in the car. When she was dressed up for the evening she'd probably wear them for driving.'

'Yes – but you've never found any stained gloves among her things.' He didn't ask, he asserted, waiting with sharp eyes levelled for a reaction, and whatever he got satisfied him. 'Well, bearing this glove question in mind, I've been thinking exactly what happened that evening. If I've got it right, she dashed out of the barn to run home, and in a few hundred yards she ran out of petrol. There she is in a panic, she thinks she's done something dreadful, injured him badly, maybe even fatally, she's got to get away, she daren't call a garage or anything. She runs to the telephone box and calls up some friend she can trust, says where she is, says come and bring me some petrol, a can, or even a tube to siphon it, anything, just to get me home. Don't say a word to anyone, she says, and come quickly. I've done something terrible. And she blurts out all about it; she'd be in such a state she wouldn't be able to help it. Now suppose this person she calls has good reason to want Armiger dead. He might not ever have thought of doing anything about it until now, but now it suddenly strikes him, this is it, this is for me! There's Armiger knocked cold in the barn, a sitting target if only he stays out until I can get round there, and there's somebody else all lined up to take the blame. I don't say he's absolutely made up his mind to kill him, but it's just too good to miss having a closer look at the set-up. Obviously there are risks, he may only have been knocked out for a few minutes, he may be conscious by the time this fellow gets there, he may even have gone. But what is there lost if he is? If he's gone, that's it. If he's up off the floor and hugging his headache all you need do is fake concern, help him to his car, and go off and reassure Kitty. And if Armiger's still lying where Kitty left him, and still dead to the world – well, there you are, a chance in a million.

'So he goes all right, he goes like a shot off a shovel, not to

437

Kitty but to the barn. And sure enough, there's Armiger still out cold, and the chance in a million has come off.'

'Go on,' said George quietly, studying the intent face that stared back at him across the table. However hotly they both denied it, there must be something in this likeness Bunty was always finding between them, especially when they annoyed her. It was like having a mirror held up to his own mind. Often enough before, when the same interest had preoccupied them both, he had found Dominic hard on his heels at every check, like an echo; but now he was no longer sure who was the echo and who the initiator. 'Go on, let's see what you can do with the details.'

'I can fit them in,' said Dominic. 'All of them. This fellow's all keyed up for action, but he hasn't really believed in it until then. No weapon, you see, no real preparations. That would be like tempting providence. He's wearing gloves simply because he's been driving on a coldish night. Now he takes the chance that's really been offered to him at last. The minute he comes in at the door and sees Armiger still lying there, he grabs at the nearest weapon he sees – the plaster statuette from the alcove just on the right of the door. I heard you say what they were like, and how surprisingly light and hollow they turned out to be. He snatches it up to brain Armiger with that, but heaves it away again in disgust on the spot because it's such a silly, light thing it couldn't brain a mouse. It smashes against the wall, and he rushes up the stairs and grabs the bottle instead, and lets fly with that again and again until it smashes, too. And then he comes to his senses with Armiger pretty obviously dead, and he's got to get rid of the traces. Especially the gloves. And quickly, that's the point. Within a few hundred yards of where he is he's got to jettison those gloves. Because, you see, he's got to go on to Kitty and get her off the scene as he promised, otherwise whoever doesn't connect him with it when the murder comes out, *she will*. The whole beauty of the setup is that *nobody* shall know. He can afford to let the police find their own way to Kitty. He can't afford to leave her or her car where they are, and have her picked up in circumstances so tight that she'll have to come out with the whole story, and say: "I called so-and-so to come and help me, and he swore he would, but he never came." Because even if that didn't give her ideas, it would certainly give them to you people, wouldn't it?'

'We shouldn't be likely to miss the implications,' agreed George.

'He may not actually have planned on forcing Kitty to take the blame. If the chips fell that way, there she was. But probably he hadn't anything against her, and rather preferred that she should get away with it, too – as long as he was all right, of course. Anyhow, he had to go through with the rescue part of it as though he'd rushed straight to her. This part in the barn can't have taken many minutes, he wasn't long delayed. So he'd got to get rid of the gloves. He'd got to meet Kitty, talk to her, handle the petrol can. He couldn't afford to leave blood about in the wrong places, or let Kitty see it and take alarm. He daren't put the gloves in his pocket or anywhere in his own car, they'd be certain to leave marks. So you see, what it boils down to is that he'd got to jettison them or hide them somewhere *before he met Kitty.*'

'You have thought it out, haven't you?' said George. 'Go on, how does he get rid of them?'

'There's not too much scope and not too much time, is there? He hadn't time to go far from the road, he had to stay out of sight of Kitty. He lets himself out of the barn carefully, closing the door with his left hand, because that glove wouldn't be so saturated, it might only be splashed here and there. I don't think he'd leave the gloves anywhere inside, even if there was a hiding-place, because of the door handle. Better smears of blood on it than fingerprints. Then he peels off the gloves, letting them turn inside-out as he pulls them off, and probably rolling the right one inside the left, to get the cleanest outer surface he can. I've been over the ground, there's a drain grid close to

439

the back of the barn, that's tempting, but too obvious, because unless there was a strong flow of water going down, and there wasn't, gloves would lodge under the grid, and anyhow it's the first place the police would look – '

'The first place they did look. After the barn itself, of course. Go on.'

'Then there's just the road, the hedge-banks and ditches, and the hanging wood opposite. Seems obvious, but I should think it takes an awful lot of men an awful long time to search the whole of a wood that size, or even just the strip alongside the road – because he hadn't time to go very far inside. And all the ground there is so covered with generations of leaf-mould, they could hunt and hunt, and still might miss what they were looking for. Anyhow, that's what I should have done, rushed up into the wood and shoved them somewhere down among the mould. And then he goes on to Kitty's rescue, arriving all steamed up and concerned for her, dumps the petrol in her tank for her, and tells her to go home and not worry, she's making a fuss about nothing, the old fool's sure to be all right. And Kitty – you said she was wearing a dress with a wide skirt – she's so relieved to see him she keeps close to him all the time they're there together, and her skirt brushes against his trouser legs, where the blood's splashed – and a drop falls from his sleeve on her shoe. In the dark there neither of them would know. And that's it, all your evidence. Have I missed anything out?'

George had to own that he had not; he had accounted for everything.

'You're quite sure he must have killed Armiger before he sent Kitty home, and not after?'

'Well, of course! He wouldn't stay unconscious for ever. If this chap had gone first to Kitty I doubt if he'd ever had the impetus or the nerve left to go back and look if opportunity was still waiting for him.'

He had seemed utterly sure of himself until he came to the

end, but when George sat thoughtfully silent he couldn't stand the strain. He'd poured out all his hopes into that exposition, and he was trembling when it was done. His eyes, covertly hanging upon George's face, pleaded for a sign of encouragement, and the brief silence unnerved him. If he'd only known it, George was still staring into a mirror.

'Well, say something!' burst out Dominic, his voice quaking with tension. 'Damn you, you just *sit* there! You don't care if they send Kitty to prison for life, as long as you get a conviction. You don't care whether she did it or not, that doesn't matter. You're not doing *anything*!'

George, coming out of his abstraction with a start, took his son by the scruff of the neck and shook him, gently enough to permit them both to pretend that the gesture was a playful one, hard enough to indicate that it wasn't. The flow stopped with a gasp; in any case the onslaught had shocked Dominic a good deal more than it had George.

'That's enough of that. You hold your horses, my boy.'

'Well, I know, I'm sorry! But you *do* just sit there! Aren't you going to give me *anything* back for all that?'

'Yes, a thick ear,' said George, 'if you start needling me. If you'd been anywhere near that wood of yours since noon to-day you'd have found it about as full of policemen as it'll hold, all looking for your gloves – as they've been doing in various places, more or less intensively, ever since we were sure there must have been gloves involved. Maybe we're not as sure as you that they'll be in a logical place, but we're just as keen as you are to find them. We even have open minds, believe it or not, on such minor points as whether a few small smears of blood on the hem of a dress are really adequate – in the circumstances. You're not the only one who can connect, my lad. We'd even like to know *who* it was she called that night. You be working on that one, and let me know when you've got the answer.'

He was aware, by the sharpness and intelligence of the silence that followed, that if he had not said too much he had been

441

understood too well. Dominic resettled his collar with great dignity, studying his father intently from the ambush of a composed and inscrutable face.

So it's like that, said the bright, assuaged eyes. I *see*! *They* may be looking for the gloves to clinch their case, but *you*'re not, you're looking for them to break it. You don't believe she did it! What did I tell you? I knew you'd come round to my way of thinking in the end. He was understandably elated by the knowledge, comforted by not being alone any longer in his faith, but there was something else going on behind the carefully sustained calm of that freckled forehead, something less foreseeable and a good deal more disturbing. He was glad to have an ally, and yet he fixed upon him a look that was far from welcoming. He saw too much, recognised his own sickness with too sharp a sensitivity in someone else, and most penetratingly of all in his father. He'd longed for an ally, but he didn't want a rival.

'I am working on it,' said Dominic deliberately. 'What's more, I think I'm on to the answer.' But he did not say that he was going to share it, with his father or anyone. Saint George had sighted another banner on the horizon. It was going to be a race for the dragon.

Chapter 12

On Monday morning, about an hour before Alfred Armiger was escorted to the grave, against all predictions, by a grim-faced and sombre son, Kitty Norris made a formal appearance of about two minutes in court, and was remanded in custody for a week.

She sat quietly through the brief proceedings, without a smile or a live glance for anyone, even Raymond Shelley who appeared for her. Docilely she moved, stood, sat when she was told, like a child crushed by the burden of a strange place and unknown, powerful, capricious people. Her eyes, hollowed by the crying and the sleeplessness which were both past now, had swallowed half her face. They looked from enemy to enemy all round her, not hoping for a gap in the ranks, but not actively afraid. She had surrendered herself to the current that was carrying her, and whatever blows it dealt her she accepted mutely, because there was no help for it. It was heart-breaking to look at her. At least, thought George, who had brought her to the court, Dominic was spared this.

In the few minutes she spent in court the news had gone round, and there was a crowd waiting to see her come out, and one lone cameraman who erupted in her face before George could shelter her. He ought to have known that Kitty Norris, whose clothes and cars and dates had always made news, couldn't escape the headlines even on this first unheralded appearance in her new role. For the first time the lovely, hapless face came back to life. She shrank back into George's arm, frightened and abashed, mistaking raw curiosity for purposeful malignance. He half lifted her into the car, but even then the eyes and the murmurs followed her, gaping alongside the windows as she was driven away.

'Why should they be like that?' asked Kitty, shivering. 'What have I ever done to them?'

'They don't mean any harm, dear,' said the matron comfortably, 'they're just nosy. You get used to it.'

There ought to be something better to say to her than that, thought George, suffering acutely from the brushing of her sleeve against his, and the agonising memory of her warmth on his heart; and yet this queer comfort did seem to calm her. She expected nothing from him, and it was not upon his shoulder that she let her head rest as she was taken back to prison.

'You'll have to brace up, you know, Kitty,' he said as he helped her out of the car, himself unaware until he had said it that her name was there on his lips waiting to slip out so betrayingly.

'Why?' said Kitty simply, looking through him into a bleak distance.

'Because you owe it to yourself – and to your friends who believe in you.'

The cords of his throat tightened up, outraged that he could ask them to give passage to such unprofessional sentiments. And he told himself afterwards, nursing the smart of being misunderstood, that he deserved no better than he got. For Kitty smiled suddenly, affectionately, shortening her range so that for a moment she really seemed to see him. Then she said in a gentle voice: 'Oh, yes, I mustn't let Dominic down. You tell him I'm coming out fighting when the bell goes. With him in my corner, how can I lose?'

Well, thought George grimly as he drove back towards the centre of Comerbourne, that's properly accounted for me. The invisible man, that's all I am, an office, not a person, and an inimical office at that. And it hurt. He knew he was making a fool of himself, but that only made the smart worse. Jealousy is always humiliating; jealousy of your own young son is an indignity hardly to be borne.

The very soreness of his own nerves, and the small, nagging sense of guilt that frayed the edges of his consciousness, made him very affectionate and attentive to Bunty, and that in itself was dangerous, for Bunty had known him a long time, and was a highly intelligent woman in her artfully unpretentious way. But long familiarity had made George so unwary with her that even his occasional subtleties tended to be childishly innocent in their cunning. She loved him very much, and her security of tenure was unshakable.

After the long, fretting days with so little accomplished George would wake out of his first shallow, uneasy sleep to the ache of his own ineffectiveness, and reach for Bunty not as a consolation prize, but as the remedy for what ailed him; and she would open her arms and respond to him, half awake, even half awake knowing that she was called upon to be two women, and sure she could without extending herself be all the women George would ever want or need. It was mostly in the middle of the night that he confided with the greatest ease and benefit. It was in the early hours of Wednesday morning that he told her about his precariously based conviction that the person Kitty had called to her aid on the night of the crime was in all probability the murderer of Alfred Armiger.

'But wouldn't she have suspected as much herself, afterwards?' asked Bunty. 'She wouldn't keep silent about it, surely, if she thought it over and came to that conclusion herself? No earthly reason why she should protect a murderer, even if he did bring her some petrol.'

'Of course not, but naturally she must have called on some person she knew intimately and could trust absolutely. In real life nobody treats a murder investigation like an impersonal puzzle in a book, and suspects everyone who had an opportunity or a motive; to some extent you're bound to go by what you know of them. There are people it could be and people it couldn't be. Your family, your friends, they're immune. This man was immune. If you were in a hole, and you yelled to me for help and I came, and afterwards there was a body around to be accounted for, would it enter your head that I might be the killer?'

'Never in a million years,' said Bunty. 'But there's only one of you for me. I might look sideways at almost anyone else.'

'What, Dom, for instance? Or old Uncle Steve?'

She thought of her bumbling old sheep of a paternal uncle and giggled. 'Darling, don't be funny! That sweet old fool!'

'Or Chris Duckett, say?'

'No, I see what you mean. The only people you'd consider letting in on your scrape would be people you couldn't possibly suspect of anything bad. But if someone actually put it into your head afterwards, mightn't you just begin to wonder? Have you put it to Kitty that way?'

'I've put it every way I can think of.' The words that visited his lips when he thought of Kitty came spurting out of him in breathless bursts of indignation and anxiety, impossible to disguise however he muffled them by nuzzling in Bunty's hair. He could never deceive Bunty worth a damn, anyhow, he gave up trying. 'All along she's simply ignored questions about that telephone call. She knows we know she did ring somebody. But still she – no, she doesn't deny it, she just pretends not to understand, or else she doesn't even pretend, she just sits there and shuts her mouth and isn't with us any more. I've tried, and Duckett's tried. Nobody can get anything out of her. Of course I've told her whoever she called may very well be the murderer. I've urged her, I've threatened her, I've bullied her – it's only made it worse. She's more determined than ever not to give him away.'

'Because she doesn't believe he had anything to do with it,' said Bunty.

'No, she doesn't believe it. There's no talking to her.'

'So she thinks she'd only be shifting her own trouble on to someone else just as innocent.'

'And that we'd be just as dead set on getting a conviction against him as we must have seemed to be against her,' said George bitterly. Suddenly abjectly grateful for Bunty's presence and her oneness with him, that sturdily refused to be changed by any outer pressures or even by the helpless convulsions of his overburdened heart, he turned and wound his arms around her, burying his face in the warm hollow of her neck. She shifted her position gently to make him more comfortable, hugging him to her heart.

'And Chris Duckett still thinks she did it?'

He mumbled assent, too tired to free his mouth. The slight movement was like the beginning of a kiss; he turned it into one.

'So between the chief hellbent on getting a conviction against her, and you just as hellbent on getting one against someone she's certain is equally blameless, and who'd be equally helpless if she once dragged him into it, no wonder the poor girl's just giving up the fight and refusing to say a word.'

George came out of ambush to protest indignantly that he wasn't hellbent on any such thing, that nobody was trying to convict for the sake of a conviction, that there was a logical case for investigating X's movements very carefully. He outlined it, and in the quietness there in the small hours it sounded even more impressive than it had when Dominic had propounded it on Sunday evening, in terms that might have been conjured out of George's own mind as a direct challenge to him.

'If it's like that,' said Bunty at last, 'and she won't talk for you, why don't you turn somebody loose on her for whom she *will* talk? I don't know Kitty as you do – ' Her hand caressed George's cheek; he hoped she wasn't comforting him for the undignified pain of which she couldn't possibly know anything, but he was dreadfully afraid she was. ' – But I can't help feeling that if you got Leslie Armiger to question her she might break down and tell everything. I may be wrong,' said Bunty kindly, well aware that she was not wrong, 'but they almost grew up together, and I gather they're fond of each other.'

'But that's just what I can't do,' said George.

'Why not?'

'Because *he's the one*! Because in spite of one snag I can't get round I'm almost sure it was Leslie.' He felt her stiffen in disbelief, her fingers stilling in his hair. 'I know! He isn't on the telephone! He remembered to remind me of that. I know, but look what he has to gain, he and nobody else.' He poured out the whole of it, physically half asleep on her shoulder, but mentally, agonisingly wide awake, sensitive to every breath she drew, almost to every implication she was reading into his words.

'Still, I don't see how it could have been Leslie,' said Bunty firmly when he had done.

'I know, I told you, I don't, either. No telephone – there's no getting past it.'

'No, I didn't mean that. I meant I don't see how it could have been Leslie, because even if she could have called him, I'm pretty sure she wouldn't.' She told him why. When she ended he was asleep, his mouth against her cheek. She kissed him, and he didn't wake up. 'Poor old darling!' she said, and went to sleep embracing him.

But when he awoke before dawn he remembered everything she had told him, and sat up in bed abruptly. The whole thing had to be re-thought from the beginning, a new cast to be made. He lay down again very softly, to avoid disturbing Bunty, and began to go over the ground yet again in his mind, inch by painful inch.

He came home that night late and on edge after a day of furious but so far unproductive activity, and it was no pleasure, the mood he was in, to have Dominic spring out of the living-room at him before he could do so much as drop his brief-case and hang up his hat. The mirror had just presented him with the image of his forty-one-year-old face, fretted and drawn with tiredness, with straight brown hair greying at the temples, and he was afraid receding a little too, when there erupted into the glass, beside it the sixteen-year-old copy, fresh as new milk, just-formed, with lashes like ferns and a thatch as thick as gorse, a face as yet so young and unused that all the anxiety and trouble in the world couldn't take the springy freshness out of it. The contrast wasn't comforting; neither was the look Dominic fixed on him, waiting with held breath for the news he'd almost given up expecting.

'Sorry, boy,' said George, 'we haven't found them yet.'

Dominic didn't move. The anxious eyes followed every motion with a hopeless concentration as George hung up his coat and made for the stairs. In his own mind he had given them until this evening; if they hadn't found the gloves by now it was no use relying on it that they ever would, no use waiting any longer for the turn of luck it didn't seem as if they were going to get. Luck's hand would have to be forced. When logs coming down a river jam, somebody has to set off a charge to release them and start them flowing again. Dominic did not particularly fancy himself as a charge of dynamite, but extreme measures were called for. And this time it was in any case impossible to confide in George, because the kind of shock tactics Dominic had in mind would not, and could not, be countenanced by the police. One word to George, and the whole thing would be knocked on the head. No, he had to do this alone, or if he had to ask for help it mustn't be from his father. And before he ventured he had to make sure he hadn't left any loopholes for want of sufficient briefing. There were still things he didn't know; by the terms of their toleration agreement he couldn't go to his father for them, but what he wanted to know Leslie Armiger could tell them.

'I'm going out, Mummy,' said Dominic, following Bunty into the kitchen. It was already well past eight o'clock, and she was surprised, but she didn't ask him where or why, she merely said: 'All right, darling, don't be too late.' She was a nice mother, he was suddenly moved to engulf her in a bear's hug before he fled, but she was holding a hot iron, so he didn't do it. She hadn't even said: 'But you haven't finished your homework!' though he hadn't. Any other mother would have been all too liable to nag, the way he was skimping his work these days.

He got out his bike and rode into Comerbourne, and let himself into Mrs. Harkness's front garden by the low iron gate. There was an outside bell for the Armigers, but they didn't always hear it, you had to walk in at the front door and climb the stairs and tap on the door of their room.

Leslie was sitting over a pile of books at the table, in his shirt-sleeves and a cloud of cigarette smoke. Dominic might not be doing his homework, but Leslie was, with dedicated concentration. He'd come down from Oxford without a degree, having behaved there as his father had fully intended him to behave, tossing his liberal allowance about gaily, playing with zest, painting with passion, cutting an engaging figure socially and working only just enough to keep him out of trouble, and perhaps a little over to appease his tutor after every grieved lecture, purely out of liking for the old boy, and as a concession to his conservative ideas of what universities were for. That left him with a lot of leeway to make up now, when marriage and responsibility had put a sharp end to his prolonged adolescence.

'Oh, I'm sorry,' said Dominic, dismayed. 'I'd better not butt in on you if you're working.'

'No, come on, it's all right.' Leslie closed his book and pushed the whole pile aside, stretching his cramped shoulders. 'I'm glad to have an excuse to stop. There's nothing new, is there? About Kitty?'

Dominic shook his head. 'You haven't been to see her again, have you?'

'Not yet, it's no use asking too often, you know, they wouldn't let me. Is there something else I can help with?'

'Well, there is, as a matter of fact. You'll probably think it a funny thing to ask, but it's about this picture of yours. If you

450

wouldn't mind telling me all that stuff about how somebody tried to get it back, I think it might help me. Because I've got a sort of theory, but I don't know enough about the details to know yet if it makes sense.'

'You think The Joyful Woman may be mixed up in the business?' asked Leslie, studying him curiously through the haze of smoke. The queer thing about the kid was that there was nothing queer about him; tallish, pleasant-looking, reasonably extrovert, healthily certain of himself, taking himself a bit seriously at this stage, but then he'd be odd if he didn't. You could drop him among his kind in any public school, and he'd fall on his nice large feet and wriggle a place for himself on the spot. You could imagine him keeping well in the swim at whatever he touched, perhaps one notch ahead of average at games and two or three notches ahead at his books, with enough energy left over for a couple of reasonably intelligent hobbies, say climbing at one extreme and amateur theatricals at the other, and perhaps one amiable lunacy like an immoderate passion for fast motorbikes or a weakness for blonde bits on the side. Wonderfully ordinary, and yet here he was taking a proprietorial hold on a murder case, and bringing all his down-to-earth qualities to bear on a situation so unordinary that the result was pure fantasy. For a moment Leslie looked at him and couldn't believe he had his focus right, the components tended so strongly to fall apart into different dimensions. I suppose, he thought, in this setting we all look a bit out of drawing; it's only his being so young that makes it more marked in his case.

He sat down with him and told him the whole history of The Joyful Woman over again from the beginning, while Dominic followed with quick questions and hopeful eyes. Jean came in halfway through the story and brought him a mug of chocolate and some biscuits; she had grown up with three young brothers, and was used to feeding boys on principle at frequent intervals.

'So the idea is that this dealer, this Cranmer, had dropped

the hint to your father that the thing was valuable.' Warmth and eagerness had come back into Dominic's eyes, and a calculating gleam; it was working out as he'd thought it might. 'But it was Mr. Shelley who came to see you.'

'On my father's behalf, of course.'

'But why of course? You only know that because he told you so. Look, suppose it happened this way. Cranmer sees some definite possibility in the picture, he knows your father must have thrown it out as worthless, and he knows it may be worth a great deal. He decides it would pay him to keep in with your father, so he telephones the office to warn him. But just by chance he misses him. They put him on to Mr. Shelley, and he tells him what he thinks, that his boss should think again, he's giving away a small fortune. But instead of passing on the message Mr. Shelley does a bit of quick thinking. He's sure by then that you and your father are never likely to heal the breach, so you won't be comparing notes. And he sees a better use to make of this stroke of luck. You sit on it and keep quiet, he says to Cranmer, and you and I can do a deal and share the proceeds between us, never mind Armiger. And he comes to you with that story about your father having thought better of his mean joke, and sent him to offer you the five hundred pounds instead of the picture. You said he had the money in cash. Didn't that strike you as odd?'

'Not particularly. My father would think nothing of shuffling that much about in cash. But I agree it makes your version possible. I agree it might have seemed quite an easy way of getting hold of the sign too. But surely if the old boy had been in it for himself he wouldn't have dared to take it any farther after I turned him down? It was too risky.'

'But if the stake was big enough? You refuse him, so he comes back and steals your father's letter, which is the only actual proof of ownership. He's banking on it that you won't touch your father in any way, having seen how you feel – not to take anything from him, not to see him, not to talk to him, but also surely not to make a public accusation against him over this business. He's betting you'll just write it off in disgust, and not do anything about it at all, because of course you're not going to be told the picture has any value, Cranmer will see to that end of it. Just commonplace rubbish! So you were supposed to think, what's the point, the joke will be on him, let him have it and much good may it do him! The silly old fool jumped to conclusions just because it leaked out to him that we'd consulted a dealer, and now he's made himself just about as big an ass as he is a rogue, so let him hang the thing on the wall to remind him how he got too sharp and cut himself.'

Carried away by his own eloquence, Dominic had lapsed into language which he suddenly realised might by conventional standards be thought offensive in the circumstances. Even if you thought about the dead like that you weren't supposed to say it, and even if Leslie had no reason whatever to love his late father he was supposed to observe certain rules and maintain certain attitudes. And you never know how conventional unconventional people may be just beneath the skin. He paled to the lips, and then flushed bright red to the hair. 'I say, I'm sorry, I shouldn't be shooting off my mouth like this, it's terrible cheek. I really am sorry! I should have remembered he was your father, and all that – '

'That's all right,' said Leslie with a rueful grin. 'I might very well have taken it just like that. I probably should have, if I hadn't happened to reach my limit just about then. Don't mind calling my dad names, that's the last thing he'd have kicked about. One of the better things about him was that he didn't snivel about his virtue while he pulled off his sharp deals, he just slapped them down gleefully and said in effect: Go on, beat that! Carry on, you're doing all right.'

'You really don't mind? It was a hell of a cheek. But you see how important it could be if Shelley actually could have reasoned like that. There he is, sure you won't bother to claim the picture once Cranmer says your father's disputing its ownership,

but just let the whole thing go, and put all the dirty work down
to your father. So Shelley and Cranmer can quietly dispose of
the goods and share the proceeds. And then suddenly out of the
blue, when he's home after getting back from the pub that night,
Kitty rings him up.

'You said he was one person she might very well turn to in
her trouble. She blurts out everything to him, and asks him to
come and get her away. She doesn't realise she's telling him
anything very terrible when she says that you've been there in
the barn with your father – because you know he told her it
was you he was going out to see – but just think what it would
mean to Shelley! The very thing he was sure wouldn't happen
had happened. Instead of letting the whole thing drop you'd
gone rushing off to your father, to pitch into him about the
dirty trick he'd played you. Then of course he wouldn't know
what you were talking about, and he'd say so, and the whole
business would come out. And finish for Shelley! He'd been
with your father – how many years? Just think what it would
mean to him to be kicked out now and have to start afresh with
your father against him, maybe even to be disgraced publicly
and have a charge laid against him. But there's Kitty on the
phone, babbling that she's pushed your father down the stairs
and he's lying there in the barn unconscious. It's now or never
if Shelley wants to shut down on the scandal for good, and keep
hold of his share in the picture deal. So he tells Kitty yes, don't
worry, just stay there, he's on his way. And he gets out the car
and drives like hell back to the barn. And kills your father.'

They were both gazing at him with wide and wary eyes, in
wonder and doubt. Leslie said in a tight, quiet voice: 'It could
have happened, I suppose. It would certainly seem like the end
of the world to him if Dad turned against him. And I'm not
saying he wouldn't have gone the limit against him in the
circumstances. He didn't mind a little sharp practice, he
expected it and he could deal with it – but if there was a lot of
money involved – And then, his vanity would be desperately

454

hurt if he found out that for once he hadn't been the smartest operator around.'

'And when you pitched into him about pinching his own letter, he did deny all knowledge of it, didn't he?'

'He did,' agreed Leslie dubiously, 'but he could just as well have been lying like a trooper, I took it he was. Still, I suppose it could have happened like that.'

Jean had sat silent and intent throughout this exchange, her eyes turning from one face to the other as they talked, her chin on her fists. She made a sudden movement of protest. 'No, it couldn't,' she said, 'it didn't. I'm sorry, boys, there's just one thing wrong with it, but it makes it all wrong. Oh, I'm not saying it couldn't be Mr. Shelley who did it, but if so, it didn't happen like that.'

They had both turned to stare at her. 'Why not?' they asked together.

With the gentle reasonableness and absolute authority of a kindergarten teacher instructing her brighter charges, Jean told them.

Chapter 13

October came in cold and gusty, with squally days and ground frosts at night; the grass in front of the main offices of Armiger's Ales stopped growing and shrank into its winter sleep, and the leaves began suddenly to fall from the trees thicker than rain, until the pure, slender skeletons showed through the thinning, yellowing foliage against a blown and blustery sky. Inside, the full heating system was put into use for the first time that season. Ruth Hamilton, coming down the stairs at five o'clock on Thursday evening, listened to the moaning of the wind outside the long staircase window and hunched her shoulders. It was going to be a stormy night; the last fine spell had broken, and the last traces of summer had blown away in a day.

Old Charlcote, the pensioner who manned the janitor's desk in the hall, had come out of his cage and had his coat on already. Miss Hamilton was usually the last of the staff to leave, he often had occasion to curse her inflexible sense of duty, though never above his breath, she being the force she was in the affairs of the firm. He was just pulling on his home-knitted navy-blue mittens, the tail of one eye on the clock, the other on the stairs, and only a very small part of his attention indeed on the person who was doing his best to engage it. What on earth did a boy from the grammar school want here at this hour – or, for the matter of that, at any hour?

'What is it, Charlcote?' asked Miss Hamilton, sailing authoritatively across the polished floor from the foot of the stairs. 'Is anything the matter?'

Why couldn't she have been just one minute later? The kid would have been safely off the premises, and they all could have gone home. Now that conscience of hers would probably insist

456

on probing into the last recesses of whatever the little pest wanted, and he'd have to hang about for an hour or more before he'd be able to lock up and get out.

'Nothing we can do anything about, miss. This young fellow was asking for Mr. Shelley, but he's left about ten minutes ago. I don't suppose it's anything very urgent.'

The boy, gripping his school-bag very tightly under his arm, said vehemently: 'It *is* urgent. I did want awfully to talk to him to-night. But I suppose if he's gone – ' The constrained voice faded out rather miserably. The eyes, large and anxious and very bright, dwelt questioningly upon Miss Hamilton's face, and hoped for a sign of encouragement. She thought she saw his lips quiver. 'It's difficult,' he said. 'I don't know what I ought to do.'

'I'm sorry, Mr. Shelley left a little early to-night. He has a lot of work on his hands just now.' She didn't go into details; what could this child know about the case that was preoccupying Ray Shelley's time and thought? 'I'm afraid you won't be able to contact him to-night, I know he has an appointment, and they're liable to be at work most of the evening.' The appointment was with counsel, and would include an interview with Kitty. 'Won't tomorrow do? He'll be in tomorrow.'

'I shan't be able to skip school,' explained the boy with self-conscious dignity. 'I should have been earlier, to-night, only I had to stay for rugger practice. I did hurry, I hoped I might be in time.' He had certainly hurried his shower, there were still traces of playing-field mud beneath his left ear and just along the hairline beneath the thick chestnut thatch at his left temple. Miss Hamilton's shrewd eyes had not missed them; she knew quite a lot about boys. There was something decidedly wrong with this one, behind that composed, strained front of his; it showed no less clearly than the tidemarks.

'Haven't I seen you before somewhere? I'm sure I ought to know you.'

A pale smile relaxed the fixed lines of his face for a moment.

'We played your club a couple of times this summer, I expect you saw me at tea. I bowl a bit – spins, not awfully good. My name's Dominic Felse.'

'Felse? Not the same Felse – isn't that right, the detective-sergeant?'

'He's my father,' said the boy, and clutched his bag even more tightly, with a sudden contortion of nervous muscles, as though he had shuddered. 'It's something about the case that I wanted to talk to Mr. Shelley about.'

'But you father surely wouldn't – '

'He doesn't know,' said Dominic with a gulp. 'It's just an idea of my own that I thought I ought to put to Mr. Shelley.'

There was no doubt about it, some intense agitation was shaking him, and if he received the slightest encouragement he would let go the tight hold he had on himself and pour out whatever was on his mind. She was used to receiving and respecting the confidences of boys, some of them a great deal tougher propositions than this well-brought-up child. She cast a glance at the clock. Charlcote was looking significantly at it too. His time was his time, he had no intention of seeing anything pathetic in this nuisance of a boy, and he had been careful to block his ears against every word of this unnecessary conversation.

'Will I do?' she asked gently, and catching the eloquent roll of Charlcote's eyes heavenward in mute but profane appeal, suppressed a grim smile. 'If I can help you, you're welcome to come in and talk to me.'

The sharp jingle of the keys was like an expletive. 'It's all right, Charlcote,' she said, relenting. 'You can just leave the outside door and go. I'll lock up when we come out, you needn't wait.'

The old man had his coat buttoned and his cap in his hand before he could finish saying smugly: 'It's my duty to lock up in person, miss, but of course if you care to give orders to the contrary – '

She wanted to say: 'Get out, you silly old fool, before I call your bluff,' but she didn't; he had ways of manipulating the heating system when he was aggrieved, or mismanaging the tea round, it was never worth while taking him on in a long-term engagement. 'Consider it an order by all means,' she said briskly, 'and run off home to Mrs. Charlcote at once. I'll make sure we leave everything in order.' And she took Dominic firmly by the arm and marched him towards the stairs. 'Now, come along up to my room, we may as well be comfortable.'

'May I really? You don't mind?' He let himself be led away gratefully; she felt him trembling a little with relief and hope, though the trouble didn't leave his face. It was something that couldn't be so easily removed, but at least it could be investigated and possibly shared. She brought him to her own office and put him into the visitor's chair, and pulled up a straight chair to the same side of the desk with him, where she could watch his face and he wouldn't be able to evade her eyes. Not that he seemed to want to; he looked back at her earnestly and unhappily, and when she helped herself to a cigarette to give him time to assemble himself he leaped to take the matches from the stand and light it for her. Very mannish; except that his fingers were shaking so that she had to steady his hand with her own, and if the touch had been just a shade less impersonal she thought he would have burst into tears there and then.

'Sit down, child,' she said firmly, 'and tell me what's the matter. What is all this about? What is it you want with Mr. Shelley?'

'Well, you see, he's Miss Norris's solicitor, and I thought the best thing I could do was come to him. Something's happened,' said Dominic, the words beginning to tumble over one another on his tongue, 'something awful. I've just got to tell somebody, I don't know what to do. They've been looking everywhere – did you know? – for the gloves. The police, I mean. They've been looking for them ever since it happened. And now – '

'Gloves?' said Miss Hamilton blankly. 'What gloves?'

459

'The murderer's gloves. They say whoever killed Mr. Armiger was wearing gloves, and they must have been badly stained, and they think they must have been hidden or thrown away immediately after the murder. They've been looking all over for them, to clinch their case. And I've been looking for them, too, because,' he said, raising desperate eyes to her face, 'I was absolutely sure they wouldn't be Miss Norris's at all, if only I could find them. I was sure she was innocent, I wanted to prove it. And I have found them,' he ended, his voice trailing away into a dry whisper.

'Then that's all right, surely,' she said in carefully reasonable tones. 'That's what you wanted, isn't it? I suppose you've turned them over to your father, and now everything will be all right. So what are you worrying about?'

He had put down his school-bag beside him on the floor. His hands, deprived of this anchor, gripped each other tightly on his knees. He looked down at the locked and rigid fingers, and his face worked.

'No, I haven't turned them in. I haven't said a word to a soul. I don't want to, I can't bear to, and I don't know what to do. I was so sure they'd be a *man's* gloves. But they're not! They're a woman's – They're *Kitty's*!'

The knotted hands came apart with a frantic jerk, because he wanted them to hide his face, which was no longer under control. He lost his voice and his head, and began to cry, in shamed little gulps and hiccups he tried in vain to swallow. Miss Hamilton put down her cigarette carefully in the ashtray and took him by the shoulders, shaking him first gently and then peremptorily.

'Now, this is silly. Come along, tell me about it. *Where* did you find them? How did it happen that you found them, if the police couldn't?'

'I shouldn't tell you,' he got out between gulps, 'I oughtn't to tell anyone. It just *happened*. If I told you – you'd have to tell lies, too.'

'Oh, now, look, I'm trying to help you. If you don't tell me everything how can I judge the importance of these gloves? You may be quite mistaken about them, they may not be the ones at all. You may be fretting quite needlessly.'

'They are the ones, I know they are. And they'll say – they'll say she – ' He was trying to master the hiccups that were convulsing him, and to all her patient questions he could make no better answers than a few grotesque, incoherent sounds. It was quite useless to persist, he was half hysterical already. She released him and went into the small cloakroom which adjoined her office, and came back with a glass of water. She presented it to his lips with an authority there was no gainsaying, and he drank docilely, scarlet and tearful, still heaving with convulsions of subsiding frequency and violence. 'There's blood on them,' he gasped between spasms. 'What am I going to *do*?'

She stood back and looked at him thoughtfully, while he knuckled angrily at his eyes and muffled his hiccups in a crumpled handkerchief.

'Is that what you were going to ask Mr. Shelley?'

He nodded miserably. 'He's her solicitor, and – and I thought maybe I – I could just give them to him. I thought maybe he'd take the responsibility, because I – I – '

'You could destroy them,' said Miss Hamilton deliberately, 'if that's how you feel. Destroy them and forget all about it.'

'No, I *couldn't*! How could I? Don't you see how I'm placed? My father – I feel *awful*! He *trusts* me!' He struggled momentarily with an all too evident inclination to relapse into tears again. 'But it's *Kitty*!'

Sixteen-year-olds miserably in love are a pathetic sight, and his situation, she saw, was indeed pitiable. Whatever his resolutions the issue was certain; he'd never be able to bear the burden for long, sooner or later out it would all come tumbling to his father. Meantime, someone had to lift the immediate load from him.

'Listen to me, Dominic,' she said firmly. 'You're quite sure in your own mind, aren't you, that Kitty didn't kill Mr. Armiger?'

Where, she was wondering, did Kitty manage to pick up this improbable adorer, and how on earth did they get on to Christian name terms? But Kitty had always been incalculable in her attachments.

'Then have the courage of your convictions. Don't say a word to Mr. Shelley. He's a legal man, it would be cruel to pass the buck to him of all people. You can give the gloves to me. I'm not a lawyer. I'm not afraid to back my own judgment.'

Dominic's long lashes rolled back from large eyes gleaming with bewilderment and hope; he stared at her and was still.

'Law or no law,' she said with determination, 'I'm not prepared to help to send Kitty to prison for life, even if she did kill an unscrupulous old man in self-defence. And like you, I'm very far from convinced that she did. *I'll* take the responsibility. Let's consider that it was I who found them.'

'Oh, would you?' he said eagerly. 'If only you would, I should be so relieved.'

'You needn't even know what I do with them. Give them to me and forget them. Forget you ever found them.'

'Oh, I'd be so grateful! I haven't got them here, because I've just come straight from school, you see, and I couldn't risk carrying them about with me all day. The fellows can be awfully nosy, without meaning any harm, you know – and suppose somebody got hold of those? But I've got to come into Comerbourne again for my music lesson to-night, may I bring them to you then?'

'Yes, of course. I have to go to the club for part of the evening, though. Where does your music teacher live?'

He told her, brightening every moment now, his voice steady and mannish again. It was in Hedington Grove, a little cul-de-sac off Brook Street, near the edge of town. 'I leave there at nine. I usually catch the twenty past nine bus home to Comerford.'

Death and the Joyful Woman

'You needn't worry about the bus to-night,' she said good-humouredly. 'I shall be finished at the club by then, I'll pick you up at the corner of your teacher's road, on Brook Street, and drive you home. I'll be there at nine. Is that all right?'

'Fine, of course, if it isn't troubling you too much. You've been most awfully kind.' He scrubbed once more at his eyes, quickly and shamefacedly, and smoothed nervous fingers through his hair. 'I'm awfully sorry I was such an ass. But honestly I didn't know what to do.'

'Feel better now?'

'*Much* better. Thanks *awfully*!'

'Well, now suppose you trot in there and wash your face. And then run off home and try not to worry. But don't say a word to anyone else,' she warned, 'or we should both be in the soup.'

'I won't breathe a word to a soul,' he promised fervently.

She shepherded him down the stairs again into the silent hallway, and out into the darkness, and switching off the last lights after them, locked the door. The boy was beginning to feel his feet again now, and to want to assert his precarious masculinity all the more because she had seen it so sadly shaken. He hurried ahead to open doors for her, and accompanied her punctiliously across the forecourt to the parking ground where the big old Riley waited.

'Can I drop you somewhere now? I could take you to the bus stop, if you're going home?'

'Thanks a lot, it's awfully kind of you, but I've got my bike here. I put it in the stand near the gate.'

All the same, he came right to the car with her, opened the door with a flourish and closed it upon her carefully when she had settled herself in the driving-seat; and he didn't move away until she had fished her black kid gloves out of the dashboard compartment, pulled them on and started the car. Then he stepped back to give her room to turn, and lifted a hand to her with a self-conscious smile as she drove away.

463

When she was gone he awoke suddenly to the chill of the wind and ran like a greyhound for his bike. He rode back into the centre of the town as fast as he could go.

Some of the shops were already closing, and the dapple of reflected lights in the wet surface of the pavements blurred into a long, hazy ribbon of orange-yellow, the colour of autumn.

Chapter 14

It was on Thursday evening that Professor Brandon Lucas, on his way to a week-end art school which did not particularly interest him but at which he had rashly consented to put in an appearance, made a sudden detour in his most capricious manner and called on Jean and Leslie Armiger. The visit could have been regarded as planned, since he had with him the notes and sketches relating to the sign of The Joyful Woman, but he had not admitted his intention even to himself until the miles between him and his boredom were shortening alarmingly, and his reluctance to arrive had become too marked to be ignored. Why get there in time for dinner? His previous experiences at Ellanswood College had led him to write off the food as both dull and insufficient, whereas there was a very decent little hotel in Comerbourne; and if the slight ground mist didn't provide a plausible excuse for lateness his errand to the Armigers could be pleaded as important, and even turned into a topic of conversation which might save him the trouble of listening to fatuities about art from others.

Being too short-sighted without his glasses to read the lettering on Leslie's bell, and too self-confident in any case to bother about such details, he startled the silent evening street with a tattoo on Mrs. Harkness's knocker, and brought out the lady herself; but he was equal even to Mrs. Harkness, and made so profound an impression upon her that Leslie's status with her went up several notches on the strength of the call.

The professor climbed the stairs unannounced, to find Leslie in his shirt-sleeves washing up at the little landing sink, and the smell of coffee bubbling merrily from the hot plate, and demonstrated his finesse by exclaiming in delight that he'd come just in time, that the cooking at The Flying Horse was splendid, but their coffee hadn't come up to the rest. And having thus intimated that they need not attempt to feed him, he sat down comfortably and reassured them with equal dexterity that they were not expected to try to entertain him.

'I'm on my way to a week-end course, as a matter of fact. I mustn't stay long, but I thought I'd look in on you with a progress report. That's a very interesting job you've found me, my boy, very interesting indeed.'

Leslie came in rolling down his sleeves, and produced liqueur glasses and the carefully nursed end of the half-bottle of cognac Barney Wilson had brought back from his summer holiday in France. Jean had conjured up a glass dish he hadn't known they possessed, and filled it with extravagant chocolate biscuits which Leslie felt certain would be the wrong thing to offer this unexpectedly Corinthian old buck of a professor, until he saw how deftly and frequently they were being palmed. She had also shed her old blue smock and appeared in a honey-yellow blouse that made her hair look blue-black and her skin as clear and cool as dew. Half an hour ago they had been talking to each other with the cautious forbearance of strangers in order not to quarrel, but whenever events demanded from her a gesture in support of her husband Jean would be there, ready and invincible.

'Is it going to turn out to be anything? I was afraid to touch it myself, but I could hardly keep my hands off it, all the same.'

'You had definite ideas about it?'

'Well, rather indefinite, but very suggestive. Such as its possible date, and the genre it belongs to.'

'Have you shown it to anyone else?'

'A dealer in the town here. He put forward some theory that it was originally a portrait by some local eighteenth-century painter called Cotsworth.'

'Preposterous!' croaked Lucas with a bark of laughter, pointing his imperial at the ceiling like a dart.

466

'Well, not so much preposterous as crafty, actually, I think. Because he's offered as high as six hundred for it since.'

'Has he, now! And you turned him down. Good boy! So you must have had an idea you were on to something much more important than a dauber like Cotsworth. As indeed I'm pretty sure you are. Mind you, the actual market value may not be very great, I'm not sure how much commercial interest such a discovery might arouse just at this moment. Ultimately it's likely to be considerable, when the full implications are realised.'

Leslie was startled to discover that his hands were trembling with pure excitement. He didn't want to look at Jean, she would only think he was underlining the professor's vindication of his judgment; she would expect him not to miss an opportunity like that, not out of any meanness of spirit but out of his fundamental insecurity. And yet he was longing to exchange glances with her, and see if she was quivering as he was. There ought to be a spark still ready to pass between them, when they were on the verge of promised discoveries fabulous enough to excite this Olympian old man.

'Its possible date,' said Lucas, harking back. 'What did you conceive its possible date to be?'

If he wasn't actually teasing them he was doing something very like it, offering them marvels and then making them play guessing games for the prize. Well, thought Leslie, if he had to be tested, he'd better put a good face on it, and say what he had to say with authority.

'Before fourteen hundred.'

It sounded appallingly presumptuous when he'd said it, he would almost have liked to snatch it back, but now it was too late. He stuck out his chin and elaborated the audacity, refusing to hedge. 'It seemed to me that the pose couldn't be later, or the hands – that want of articulation, the long curved fingers without joints. And then the backward-braced shoulders and head, and even something about the way the blocks of colour are filled in to make the dress. If we get all those layers of repainting off successfully I shall expect to see a kind of folded drapery you don't get as late as the fifteenth century.'

'And the *genre*? You said you had ideas about that, too.'

Leslie drew breath hard and risked a glance at Jean. Her eyes, wide and wondering, were on him; he didn't know whether she was with him or only marvelling at his cheek and expecting to see him shot down the next moment.

'I think she's local work,' he said in a small voice, 'because I think she's been kicking about here for centuries, never moving very far from where she was first put in position. And that wasn't on any pub. The only thing out of tradition is the laugh – '

'Yes,' said Lucas, his eyes brightly thoughtful upon the young man's face, 'the laugh. Don't let that worry you. The laugh is one of those things that happen to any tradition from time to time, the stroke of highly individual genius nobody had foreshadowed and nobody ventures to copy afterwards. And extraordinary experiences they can be, those inspired aberrations. Go on. Out of what tradition? You haven't reached the point yet.'

Going softly for awe of his own imaginings, Leslie said: 'That oval inset that looks like a brooch, that's what first made me think of it. In its original form it was that odd convention, a sort of X-ray plate into the metaphysical world. Wasn't it?'

'You tell me.'

'It was then. It was an image of the child she's carrying. She's a Madonna of the Annunciation or the Visitation – something before the birth, anyhow – '

'Of the Magnificat, as it happens. You seem to have done very well without an adviser at all, my boy.'

'I haven't dared even to think seriously about it before,' owned Leslie with a shaky laugh. 'You as good as hinted that I could go ahead with my wildest guesses and they wouldn't be too fantastic. or I wouldn't have ventured even now. Do you really mean that a piece of work like that has been lying about in attics

468

and swinging in the wind in front of a pub ever since the fourteenth century?'

'More likely since about the latter half of the sixteenth. No doubt you know that the house from which the panel came was at one time a grange of Charnock Priory? And that the last prior retired there after the Dissolution?'

'Well, a friend of mine did dig out something of the kind from the archives, but until then I'm afraid I didn't know a thing about it.'

'You didn't? You cheer me. Neither did I, but it seems it was so. What struck me about this panel of yours was its likeness in proportion and kind to one of the fragments in Charnock parish church. I don't know if you know the rector? A scholarly old fellow, quite knowledgeable about medieval art. Glass is his main line, but he knows the local illuminators and panel painters well, too, and he's spent a good many years of his life hunting for bits of the works of art that were disseminated from Charnock at the Dissolution. What's now the parish church is the truncated remains of the old priory church, of course, and such relics as he's been able to trace he's restored to their old places. This head of an angel with a scroll is all he has of what seems to have been a larger altar-piece, probably from the Lady Chapel.'

'And you think we've found the lady?' asked Leslie, not meaning to be flippant, simply too excited to bear the tension of being entirely serious. An elevated eyebrow signalled momentary disapproval, but the knowing eye beneath it saw through him, and there was no reproof.

'I think it is a strong possibility. I went to see the rector. He has records which indicate that parts of the furnishings must have gone into retirement with the last prior, and some very interesting sketches and notes of his own, collected from many scattered sources. He holds that the angel with the scroll is the angel of the Magnificat, he has contemporary and later references to the painting which enable one to form a fairly detailed picture, and I'm bound to say there's every reason to feel hopeful that your panel is the Virgin from the same altar-piece. The master who painted it is not known by name, but various examples of his work have been identified, including some illuminations. One of them has an initial strongly resembling your Madonna.'

'Including the laugh?' asked Jean in a low voice.

'Including the laugh. Altogether the evidence is so strong that I don't anticipate much difficulty in establishing the authenticity of your fragment. The rector has seen it. If I am cautiously prepared to pronounce it genuine, he is absolutely convinced. He had made a careful reconstruction from the various references of what the lost Madonna should be. It bore an unmistakable resemblance to your panel. He has since made another sketch from the panel in its present form and from his previous sources to show what we should uncover.'

He slapped his briefcase open on the table, and drew out a wad of documents and papers, spreading them out before him with a satisfied smile.

'I've brought you his notes and drawings to examine over the week-end, if you'd like to. And here is his latest sketch. There she is. As she was, and as she will be.'

It was quite small, smaller than a quarto sheet of paper; they drew close together to look at it. The Joyful Woman had put off her muslin fichu and corkscrew curls and the Toby frills from round her wrists, and stood in all her early English simplicity and subtlety, draped in a blue mantle over a saffron robe, all her hair drawn back austerely under a white veil. She leaned back to balance the burden she carried, clasping her body with those hands feeble as lilies, and the symbolic image of the unborn son stood upright in her crossed palms. She looked up and laughed for joy. There was no one else in the picture with her, there was no one else in the world; she was complete and alone, herself a world.

Leslie felt Jean's stillness as acutely as if she had never before been still. He moistened his lips, and asked what would inevitably sound the wrong question at this moment; but he had to know the answer. He had to know what he was doing, or there was no virtue in it.

'Have you any idea how much she's likely to fetch if I sell her? Always supposing we're right about her?'

'It's a matter of chance. But the master's work is known and respected, and there are few examples, possibly none to be compared with this. And there's a local antiquarian interest to be reckoned with. I think, putting it at the lowest, even if you sell quickly, you should still realise probably between seven and eight thousand pounds.'

Desperately quiet now, their sleeves just touching, Jean and Leslie stood looking at the promise of fortune.

'And the rector – would he be in the market? He must want it terribly, if he's so sure – '

'He'd give his eyes for it, of course. You've stopped him sleeping or eating since he's seen this. But he's already appealing for twenty thousand to keep his poor old rotting church together, there's no possibility whatever of earmarking any funds for buying Madonnas.'

'Not even to bring them home,' said Leslie. He moved a little away from Jean because he wanted to see her face, but she kept it averted, looking at the little drawing. He wondered if she knew that she'd folded her own hands under her breasts upon the immemorial wonder, in the same ceremonially possessive gesture.

'Not even to bring them home. But there'll be other bidders. If you wait and collect enough publicity before you sell you may get double what I've suggested.' Professor Lucas closed his briefcase and pushed back his chair. The boy was obviously in need of money, small blame to him for relishing it in advance.

'I can't afford to pay for all the work that will have to be done on the panel,' said Leslie, his voice slightly shaky with the intensity of his resolution. 'Would your laboratory be prepared to stand that, if I give the thing back to Charnock?'

Lucas straightened up to look at him intently, and came to his feet slowly. 'My dear boy, you realise what you're saying?'

Yes, he realised, and he had to say it quickly and firmly and finally, so that there should be no possibility of withdrawing. Panic surged into his throat, trying to choke the words into incoherence. He was afraid to look at Jean now, he knew he'd done something she could never understand or forgive, but he'd had to do it, he couldn't have lived with himself if he'd let the moment go by.

'It isn't mine,' he said, 'only by the last of a long series of ugly accidents, and I don't like that. It ought to go back where it belongs. And it isn't because it's the church, either,' he said almost angrily, in case he should be misconstrued. 'I should feel the same if it was a secular thing and as fine as that. It was made for a certain place and purpose, and I'd rather it went back. Only it would be a bit rough if I gave it back to the rector and then he couldn't get the necessary work done on it for want of money.'

'If you mean what you've just said that point needn't worry you. I would be prepared to undertake the work in our workshop, certainly. Indeed I should be very unwilling to let it go to anyone else. But you spend the week-end thinking it over, my boy,' said the professor cheerfully, pounding him on the shoulder, 'before you make up your mind to part with it. I'll leave all this stuff with you, better see how good our case is before you decide.'

'I have decided, but I should like to read all this, of course. It isn't that I want to cut a figure,' he said carefully, 'though I shall probably enjoy that, too. But supposing I just took the highest offer and she went to America, or into some private collection here that does no good to anybody? I should never stop feeling mean about it. I want her to go back into her proper place, and if they can't pay for her they can't, and anyhow I have a sort of feeling they ought not to have to. Where she's going she'll belong to everybody who likes to look at her, and

472

they'll see her the way they were meant to see her – or as near as we can get to it. Then I might really feel she's mine. I don't feel it now.'

'I'm not trying to dissuade you, my boy, you don't have to out-argue me. I just don't want you to rush matters and then regret it. You make up your own mind and then do what you really want to do. Call me in a few days' time, will you, and we'll meet again, probably at the gallery if you can make it. I shall have to go now.' He tucked his flattened briefcase under his arm. 'Good night, Mrs. Armiger! Thank you for the coffee, it was excellent.'

Jean came out of her daze to add her thanks and farewells to those Leslie was already expressing. When Leslie came back from seeing his visitor out she was standing by the table, her face fixed in a grave, pale wonderment, staring at the rector's sketch.

He closed the door gently behind him, waiting for her to speak, or at least to look up at him, and when she did neither he didn't know how to resolve the silence without sounding abject or belligerent, either of which, in his experience, would be fatal. The tension which strained at his nerves she didn't seem to feel, she was so lost in her own thoughts.

'I couldn't do anything else,' he said helplessly, aware of the defensive note but unable to exorcise it.

She started, and raised to his face eyes in which he could read nothing, wide and dark and motionless, like those of a woman in shock.

'It was mine,' he said, despairingly abrupt, 'I could do what I saw fit with it.'

'I know,' she said mildly, and somewhere deep within her uncommunicative eyes the faint, distant glimmer of a smile began.

'I suppose I've disappointed you, and I'm sorry about that. But I couldn't have been happy about it if I'd – '

She moved towards him suddenly with a queer little gesture

473

of protest, and, 'Oh, do be quiet,' she said, 'idiot, idiot! I could shake you!' She came at him with a rush, taking him by the shoulders as though she intended to put the threat into effect, and then, slipping her arms under his and winding them tightly about him, hugged him to her and hid her face in his chest. 'I love you, I love you!' she said in muffled tones against his heart.

He didn't understand, he was hopelessly at sea. He never would be able to make sense of it, he'd be just as mystified about what he'd suddenly done right as about all the things he'd been doing wrong. Maybe he'd even come to the conclusion that she was simply female, illogical and responsive to a firm touch, and strain his innocent powers to keep the whip hand of her. It didn't matter, as long as he believed her. 'I love you,' she said. His arms had gone round her automatically, he held her carefully and gingerly, as though she might break and cut his fingers, but with the warmth of her solid and sweet against him he had begun to tremble, astonished into hope.

'I'm sorry about the money, Jean,' he stammered, floundering in the bewildering tides of tenderness and fright and returning joy that tugged at him. 'But we'll manage without it between us. I know you think it was irresponsible, but I couldn't help it, I couldn't feel it was mine. Oh, Jean, don't cry!'

She lifted her head, and she wasn't crying at all, she was laughing, not with amusement but with pure joy. She put up her face to him and laughed, and she looked like the woman in the drawing. 'Oh, do shut up, darling,' she said, 'you're raving!' And she kissed him, partly to silence whatever further idiocies he was about to utter, partly for sheer pleasure in kissing him. It was quite useless to try to put into words for him the revelation she had experienced, the sudden realisation of how rich they were in every way that mattered, he and she and the child that was coming. With so much, how could she have fretted about the minor difficulties? How could she have felt anything but an enormous pity for old Alfred Armiger, who had so much and couldn't afford to give any of it away? And how, above all, could she ever have feared dissatisfaction or disappointment with this husband of hers who had nothing and could yet afford to make so magnificent a gift?

'You mean you don't mind?' he asked in a daze, still breathless. But he didn't wait for an answer. What did it matter whether he understood how this sudden and absolute fusion had come about? It wouldn't pay him to question how he had got her back; the wonderful thing was that he had. All the constraint was gone. They hugged each other and were silent, glowing with thankfulness.

It was the unexpected tap on the door that broke them apart, the prim double rap that invariably meant Mrs. Harkness, and usually with a complaint. Leslie took his arms from round his wife reluctantly, put them back again for one more quick hug, and then went to open the door.

Mrs. Harkness was looking unusually relaxed and conciliatory, for Professor Lucas's influence still enveloped her as in a beneficent cloud.

'A boy brought this note for you a little while ago, Mr. Armiger. He said you were to have it at once, but as your visitor was still here I didn't care to disturb you.'

'A boy? What boy?' asked Leslie, thinking first of Dominic, though he knew of no particular reason why Dominic should be delivering notes to him at this hour of the evening, nor why, supposing he had any such errand, he should not come up and discharge it in person.

'Mrs. Moore's boy from just along the road. I thought it wouldn't hurt for waiting a quarter of an hour or so.'

'I don't suppose it would. Thank you, Mrs. Harkness.'

He closed the door, frowning at the envelope with an anxiety for which he knew no good reason. The Moore boy also attended the grammar school, and was much the same age as Dominic and probably in the same form; he might easily be a messenger for him at need. But what could be the need?

'What is it?' asked Jean, searching his face.

'I don't know, let's have a look.' He tore the envelope open, still lulled by her warmth close against his arm, and aware of her more intensely than of all the other urgencies in the world, until he began to read.

Dear Mrs. Armiger,

I've asked Mick Moore to bring you this on the dot of half past eight, because I need help with something at nine o'clock, and it's desperately important, but I daren't let it out more than half an hour before the time. If my father knew about it too soon he'd knock the whole thing on the head, but if he only knows just in time to be on the spot as a witness I hope he'll let me go through with it, I hope he won't be able to stop me. I don't want to telephone home myself because it might be Mummy, and I don't want to scare her. I don't want her to know anything about it until it's all over. So I thought the best thing was to leave this message for you.

This is what I want you to do. Please get on to my father and tell him to have the police watching the corner of Hedington Grove and Brook Street at nine o'clock. There'll be a car there waiting to pick me up and drive me back home to Comerford. Please *make them follow it*, be *sure* they do, it's urgent. I've done something to make things happen, but they *have to be there to see it*, otherwise it will be wasted, and no good to Kitty after all.

If anything comes unstuck for me, please try to help Kitty, I don't mind as long as she comes out all right.

Thanks.

DOMINIC FELSE.

'What the hell!' said Leslie blankly. 'Is he fooling, or what?'

'No, not about Kitty, he never would. He's dead serious. Leslie,' said Jean, her fingers clenching on his arm, 'he's *frightened*! What is it he's done?'

'God knows! Something crazy, stuck his neck out somehow

Death and the Joyful Woman

– Oh, *lord*!' said Leslie in a gasp of dismay as his eye fell on his watch. He sprang for the door and went clattering down the stairs. It was eleven minutes to nine, eleven minutes to zero hour. There was no time now to do anything but take the affair seriously.

He heard Jean's heels rapping down the stairs close behind him, and turned in the open doorway to shout to her to stay where she was, that he'd see to everything, that he'd be back. But she was still close at his elbow, tugging her way breathlessly into her coat, as he wrenched open the door of the telephone booth at the end of the street.

It seemed to take him an age to locate George Felse's number, and a fantastic time to get an answer when he dialled it, and even then it was Bunty who answered. Dominic's assumption that mothers were not to be frightened inhibited Leslie's tongue no less surely. No, never mind, it could wait, if Mr. Felse wasn't there. Never mind, he'd call him again. He slammed the receiver back and tried again.

'Police, Comerbourne? Listen, this is urgent. Please do what I ask *at once*, and *then* stand by for the explanation. It's the Armiger case, and this is Leslie Armiger, and I'm not kidding. If Mr. Felse is there, get him. Never mind, then, *you*, listen – '

Jean whispered in his ear: 'I'm going to fetch Barney's van. I'll be back.' She shoved open the door and ran, the staccato of her heels dwindling along the street.

'Corner of Brook Street and Hedington Grove, nine o'clock,' Leslie was repeating insistently. 'We'll be coming along from this end to meet 'em – you see you're there to follow 'em.'

It was two minutes to nine when he cradled the receiver for the second time.

Chapter 15

Dominic struck the hundredth wrong note of the evening, corrected it with a vicious lunge of both normally adroit hands, and said resignedly: 'Damn! Sorry! I'm making a hell of a mess of this. Wouldn't you rather I shut up?'

'I would,' said old Miss Cleghorn frankly, 'but your parents are paying for an hour, my lad, and an hour you're going to put in, even if you drive me up the wall in the process. I'm beginning to think I ought to revert to the old ebony ruler, though, and fetch you a crack over the knuckles every time you do that to my nerves.'

Dominic flicked a phrase of derisive laughter out of the piano and made a face at her. She was plump, sixty-odd and as lively as a terrier, and on the best of terms with her pupil, indeed from his point of view she was the one redeeming feature in these Thursday evening lessons. It was Bunny who had insisted that the ability to play at least one musical instrument was an invaluable part of any young man's equipment, and kept his unwilling nose to the keyboard; a feat which wouldn't have been nearly so easy if some part of his mind hadn't come to the generous conclusion that she was probably right about the ultimate usefulness of the accomplishment.

'Ebony ruler my foot!' scoffed Dominic. 'I don't believe you've even got one, much less that you ever hit anybody with it.'

'You be careful! It isn't too late to begin, and it doesn't have to be ebony. Come on now, you're not getting out of it by trying to side-track me. Try it again, and for goodness' sake keep your mind on what you're doing.'

He did his best, but the trouble was that his mind was very insistently and earnestly upon what he was doing, and it had

478

almost nothing to do with this harmless regular Thursday evening entertainment, which had merely provided the occasion for it. He set his teeth and laboured doggedly through the study again, but his thoughts were ahead of the clock, trying to speculate on all the possible developments which might confront him, and to compile some means of dealing with all of them. What worried him most was that he had had to base his actions so extensively upon speculation, that there was so much room for miscalculation at every stage. But it was too late to allow himself to be frightened by all the possible mistakes he had made, because there was no drawing back now.

'One certain fact,' said Miss Cleghorn, nodding her bobbed head emphatically when he had fumbled his way to the last chord, '*you* haven't touched a piano since last Thursday, have you? Own up!'

He hadn't, and said so. He quite saw that from her point of view it was reprehensible, and the tone in which he made his excuses was deprecating. He thought it would be nice if he could believe that some day such things would again have importance for him, too. The weight of the real world was heavy on his shoulders; the little cosy, everyday world in which mealtimes and music lessons mattered had begun to look astonishingly charming and desirable to him, but he couldn't get back to it. Like an unguided missile he was launched and he had to go forward.

'And how do you expect to learn to play well if you never practise? No, never mind soft-soaping me with fancy fingerwork, you take your hands off that keyboard and listen when I'm talking to you.'

He removed them obediently and sat meekly with them folded in his lap while she scolded him. It couldn't be said that he listened, though his eyes stared steadily at her round pink face with a rapt attention which amply covered the real absence of his mind. To look at her was comforting, she was so ordinary and wholesome and unsecret, knowing and knowable, no partner

479

to the night outside the closed curtains, which had begun to be terrifying to him. He dwelt earnestly upon her invariable hand-knitted twin set and short tweed skirt, the Celluloid slide in her straight, square-cut grey hair, the mole on her chin that bobbed busily as she abused him. He smiled affectionately, cheered by the human conviction that nothing sinister or frightening could exist in the same dimension with her; but as soon as he looked away or closed his eyes he knew that it could, and that he had invoked it and could not escape it.

'It's all very well,' she said severely, 'for you to sit there and smile at me and think that makes everything all right. That's your trouble, my boy, you think you can just turn on the charm and get away with murder.'

She could have made a happier choice of words, of course; but how could she know she was treading hard on the heels of truth?

'I know,' he said placatingly, 'but this week I've had things on my mind, and honestly there hasn't been time. Next week I'll do better.' I will if I'm here, he thought, and his heart shrank and chilled in him. He grinned at her. 'Cheer up, it's nearly nine o'clock, your suffering's almost over.'

'Yours will begin in a minute,' she said smartly, 'if you don't watch your step. You know what you're asking for, don't you?'

'Yes, please. With lots of sugar.' He knew there was cocoa in a jug on the stove in her kitchen, there always was on cold nights. She got up good-humouredly and went to fetch it. 'All right, pack up, we'll let you off for to-night.'

It was still a few minutes to nine, and he didn't want to be even one minute early for his appointment. If Leslie had done his part the police should be watching the corner of the street. To arrive ahead of time was to risk appearing there in full view, and having an irate father descend on him on the spot with a demand that he should explain himself, and wreck everything he had gone to such pains to build up. Even reasonable fathers were queer about allowing you freedom of action in matters

480

which infringed their authority and involved your own danger; and of the reality of the danger he had brought down upon himself Dominic was in no doubt whatever. That was the whole point. If he was not in any danger, then he was hopelessly off the track, and all his ingenuity would have proved nothing, and left Kitty as forsaken and encircled as ever. Moreover, this danger was something he must not ward off. He would have to watch it closing in, and sit still like a hypnotised rabbit to let it tighten on him. If he fought his own way out he might fail of proving what he had set out to prove. He mustn't struggle, he must leave it to others to extricate him and hope they would be in time. He was voluntary bait now, nothing more.

'You are in a state to-night,' said Miss Cleghorn, shaking him by a fistful of chestnut hair. 'You don't even hear when I offer you biscuits. Why I bother, when all you deserve is bed without supper, I can't imagine. What's the matter with you? Things being tough at school, or what?'

School! That was all they thought about. If you were sixteen, whatever worries you had must be about school.

'No, I'm all right, honestly. Just one of those days, can't concentrate on anything. I'll catch up by next time.'

'You'd better! Here you are, get this down you, it's freezing outside, you need something to keep you warm, waiting for that old bus. I always say that's the bleakest spot in town, that bus station.'

He made his cocoa last until the dot of nine. Better give her an extra minute or two, in case she got held up at the club.

'I'll tell Mummy you said I was making steady progress,' he said impudently as he pulled on his coat. 'That all right?'

'You can tell her I said you should be spanked, she might oblige. Now watch how you go, I can see the frost sparkling on the road already. Only just October and hard frost, I ask you!'

'Good night!' he said, already at the front gate.

'Good night, Dominic!' She closed the door on him slowly, almost reluctantly. Now what can be the matter with that child,

481

she wondered vexedly, he's certainly got something on his mind. Ought I to speak to his mother, I wonder? But he's at a funny age, probably it's something he doesn't want her to know about, and he'd never forgive me if I interfered. No, better let well alone. She switched on the television and put her feet up, and in a little while Dominic Felse passed out of her mind.

He walked to the end of the street with a slowing step, trying not to notice that it was slowing, not to let it slow. Normality, be with me! I've got a load *off* my mind, not on it. I've got to do it right, otherwise I'd have done better not to do it at all. Come on, you're in it now, give it everything you've got. Remember Kitty! He thought of her, and the tension within him was eased as by a sudden warmth relaxing every nerve. What, after all, does danger matter? You're making Kitty safe. What happens now can't hurt her, it can only deliver her. He took heart; he was going to be all right. Even when it came, he was going to accept it and not chicken out.

There was always, of course, the thought that she might not come to the rendezvous, that in all honesty she might have thought better of it. There was the possibility that she might come, but acting in all good faith, in which case she would simply take what he gave her, and reassure him and drive him safely home; and the thousand deaths he died on the way would be no more than he deserved, and the abject amends he owed her would be something he could never hope to pay. There were so many pitfalls, so many ways of being wrong; and yet all the time he knew in his heart that he was not wrong.

And she was there. When he drew near to the corner of the silent, frosty road, under the tinkling darkness and sparkle of the trees, he saw the long, sleek shape of the old Riley sitting back relaxed and elegant alongside the knife-edged glitter of the kerb. She opened the near-side door for him, smiling. Never before had he noticed how silent, how deserted this quarter of the town could be at night. There was not another person in sight, and only one lone car passed along the middle of the broad road as he approached. When it had gone everything was so still that his light footsteps sounded loudly in the quietness, reverberating between the frostlight and the starlight with a terrible, solitary singleness.

'Hallo, Dominic,' said Miss Hamilton, scooping up an armful of things from the front passenger seat and dumping them at random into the rear seat, scarf and handbag and a bunch of duplicated papers that looked like club notices, and a large electric torch that rolled to the far hollow of the hide upholstery.

'Hallo, Miss Hamilton! This is most awfully kind of you. You're sure I'm not being a nuisance? I could easily get the bus home.'

'Don't be silly,' she said placidly. 'Get in. It will only take me a quarter of an hour or so, I shall soon be home. And it's much too cold to hang about waiting for buses.' She leaned across him and snapped home the catch on the handle of the door. 'It's getting rather worn, I shall have to have a new handle fixed. I have to lock it or it might come open, especially on a bend. And as I'm apt to be carrying rather lively passengers sometimes it could be dangerous,' she concluded with a smile.

'None aboard to-night,' he said, glancing at the back seat.

'I've just dropped two of them. The club's still in session, but I don't have time to stay all the evening.' She settled back in the driving-seat, and looked at him with the indulgent smile that took into account both his youth and its extreme sensitivity, his helpless tears of the afternoon and his desire that she should forget them.

'Well, did you bring them?' she asked gently. 'Or have you thought better of it and turned them over to your father? Don't worry, I shan't blame you if you have, I shall quite understand. It was entirely up to you.'

'I've brought them,' he said.

'Then the best thing you can do is hand them over right now, and I'll take them and put them away, and you can forget the

483

whole thing. I'll never remind you of it again, and no one else can. You've not told anyone else?'

'No, not a word.'

'Good, then don't. From to-night on you're to stop worrying, you understand? Kitty'll come out of it all right if she didn't do it, and we two are agreed that she didn't. That's right, isn't it?'

'Yes, of course.' He withdrew from his music-case a small, soft bundle rolled rather untidily in tissue-paper, so loosely that a corner of Polythene protruded, and in the reflected light from the sodium street lights there was just a glimpse of crumpled black kid through the plastic, soiled and discoloured. He put it into Miss Hamilton's hand, his large eyes fixed trustingly upon her face, and heaved a great sigh as it passed, as though a load had been lifted from him.

Her eyes flickered just once from his face to the small package in her hand, and back again. She leaned across to open the dashboard compartment in front of him, and thrust the gloves into the deepest corner within. 'Don't be afraid,' she said, catching his anxious glance, 'I shan't forget about them. They're quite safe with me. Do as I said, put them clean out of your mind. You need never see or think of them again. Not a word more about them, now or at any other time. This closes the affair. You understand?'

He nodded, and after a moment managed to say in a very low voice: 'Thank you!'

She started the car. A motorbike whirred by them towards the town, its small, self-important noise soon lost. A solitary old gentleman on his way back from the pillar-box turned into a side road and vanished. They inhabited a depopulated world, a frosty night world full of waiting, ardent echoes that had no sound to reduplicate. He must not look round. His head kept wanting to turn, his eyes to search the street behind them, his ears were straining for another engine turning over reluctantly in the cold, but he must not look round or even seem to

484

wish to look round. He was an innocent, a fool without suspicions, a simpleton who had not said a word to anyone about this meeting. What should he be concentrating on, now that she had relieved him of his burden? Naturally, the car. It was worth a little enthusiasm, and at sixteen adults don't expect you to have any tenacity even in your anxieties, they take it for granted you can be easily seduced by things like cars.

'What year is it?' he asked, watching the competent movements of her hands as the car moved off, and capturing one genuine moment of pleasure in its smooth, quiet lunge forward. 'Is it actually vintage?'

It wasn't, but it missed it by only a few years. She smiled faintly as she answered his questions, the controlled, indulgent smile of a considerate adult allowing a child his preoccupations, even stooping to share them, but distantly envying him his ability to lose himself in them as a blessing long passed out of her own experience. Precisely the kind of smile to be expected from her in the circumstances, and it told him nothing. He could have done with a few pointers. There should have been something revealing in that one glance she had cast at his carefully assembled package, something to tell him if he was on target or if he had guessed wildly astray and utterly betrayed himself; but there had been nothing, no sudden gleam, no sharpening of the lines of her face. It was too late now to wonder.

'You do keep her beautifully,' he said without insincerity.

'Thank you,' she said gravely. 'I try.'

The road had narrowed a little, the pavement trees ceased abruptly, the garden walls and fences began to be interspersed with the hedges of fields. He wished he could lean far enough to the right to get a glimpse in the rear-view mirror, but he knew he mustn't. He wished he knew if they were following. It would be hell if he had to go through all this for nothing.

'We'll take the riverside road,' said Miss Hamilton, 'it's shorter. I suppose you haven't started learning to drive yet?'

'Well, it would be difficult, really. I can't go on the road yet, and we haven't got any drive to speak of, only a few yards to the garage. They did talk about starting lessons at school, there's plenty of room in the grounds there, but nothing's come of it yet.'

'It would be an excellent idea,' she said decidedly. 'In school conditions you'd learn very easily, from sheer force of habit. And it's certainly become an essential part of a complete education these days.'

'But I think they're scared for their flower-beds, or something, they swank frightfully about their roses, you know.'

It was possible to talk about these remote things, he found with astonishment, even when his throat was dry with nervousness and his heart thumping. He cast one quick glance at her profile against the last of the street lighting, the clear, austere features, the slight smile, the sheen of the black hair and the smooth shape of the great burnished coil it made on her neck. Then they had turned into the dark road under the trees, and the headlights were plucking trunk after slender trunk out of the obscurity ahead, sharp as harp-strings, taut curves of light that swooped by and were lost again in the darkness behind. Somewhere there on their right, beyond the belt of trees, the shimmer of the river, bitterly cold under the frosty stars. In summer there would have been a few cars parked along the grass verges down here, with couples locked in a death-grip and lost to the world inside, and more couples strolling among the trees or lying in the grass along the riverbank; but not now. The back rows of cinemas were warmer, the smoky booths of the coffee-bars had as much privacy. No one would come here to-night. And without the lovers this was a lonely and silent road.

It will be here, he thought, somewhere in this half-mile stretch, before we leave the trees. And he gripped the piped edges of the bucket seat convulsively, and felt his palms grow wet, because he wasn't sure if he could go through with it. It isn't just being afraid, he thought. How do you manage it when you see a blow coming, or a shot, and you mustn't duck, you mustn't drop for cover, you must just let it come, let it take you? How do you do it? He flexed his fingers, startled to find them aching with the intensity of his grip on the leather. He was strong, he could very well defend himself, but until the witnesses appeared he mustn't. They had to see for themselves what had been planned for him, his own word would never be enough. And if they weren't following, if they didn't arrive in time, then in the last resort what happened to him would have to be evidence enough to clear Kitty, Kitty who of all people in the world was safest from being blamed for whatever deaths might occur to-night.

Miss Hamilton put out her left hand and opened the glove compartment, rummaging busily among the tangle of things within until she brought out a packet of cigarettes. She had slowed down to a crawl while she drove one-handed, and she shook out a cigarette from the packet and put it between her lips with neat, economical movements which made it clear she had done the same thing a few thousand times before. She reached into the pocket again, groping for her lighter, and failed to find it.

'Oh, of course, it's in my handbag,' she said, letting the car slide to a stop. 'Can you reach it for me, Dominic?'

He looked over into the litter of things on the back seat; her bag had slid down into the hollow against the torch. The old car was spacious, with ample legroom between front and rear seats, and he had to turn and kneel on the seat to lean over far enough to reach the corner. He did so in an agony of foreknowledge, living through the sequel a hundred times before it became reality. Terrified, in revolt, forcing himself to the quiescence against which his flesh struggled like an animal in a trap, he leaned over with arm outstretched, presenting to her meekly the back of his brown hand. Oh, God, let her be quick! I can't keep it up, I shall have to turn round – I *can't! Oh, Kitty! And maybe you won't even know!*

487

The George Felse Omnibus

Something struck him with an impact that made the darkness explode in his face, and he was jerked violently forward over the back of the seat, the breath driven out of him with a second shock of pain and terror. Then the darkness, imploding again on a black recoil into the vacuum from which the burst of light had vanished, sucked him down with it into a shaft of emptiness and let him fall and fall until even the falling stopped, and there was no more pain or fright or anger or fighting for breath, no more anxiety or agonised, impotent love, nothing.

Chapter 16

'I wish we knew what we were looking for,' said Jean, crouched forward into the windscreen of Barney Wilson's Bedford van and peering with narrowed eyes to the limit of the headlight beams. 'A car – it might be any car, we don't know whose, it could be a taxi, or anything. We just don't know.'

'It won't be a taxi,' Leslie said with certainty. 'He's done "something to make things happen." It sounds like a man-to-man business.'

'And we don't even know that they'll be coming by this road, it could be the main road.'

'If it comes to that, we don't *know* they'll be on either. Anyhow, the police are covering both. What more can we do? I can only take this thing one way at a time, and this is the quietest and loneliest. Headlights ahead there, keep your eyes open.'

The approaching lights were still two or three coils of the winding road distant from them, and perforated by the scattered tress, but they were coming fast. One dancing turn carried them into the intervening double bend, and a second brought them out of it and into full view on one of the brief short stretches. Leslie left his headlights undipped, checking a little and crowding the middle of the road, setting out deliberately to dazzle and slow the other driver. The approaching lights, already sensibly dipped as they turned into the straight, flashed at him angrily, and failing to get a response, stayed up to glare him into realisation of his iniquity. He narrowed his eyes, trying to focus beyond the dazzle on the windscreen of the car. Only one face in view there, and not much hope of distinguishing whether man or woman. In a lighted road it might have been easier.

A horn blared at him indignantly. He said: 'Oh, *lord*!' as he pulled aside just far enough to let the long car by. Driven well and peremptorily, and going fast, going with purpose.

'No boy,' said Jean, and instantly gasped and clutched at the dashboard as he braked hard. 'Leslie! What are you doing?'

It was instantly clear what he was doing, and he didn't bother to answer her in words. He was in close under the trees at the side of the road, hauling on the wheel to bring the van about.

'What is it? What did you see? He wasn't there.'

'Not in sight,' said Leslie, and ran the van backwards with an aplomb he would never have achieved in ordinary circumstances. 'Didn't you recognise the car?' They came about in an accelerating arc that brushed the grass, and whirled away in pursuit of the vanishing rear lights. 'Hammie's! That *couldn't* be a coincidence. Thank God I know that car so well it can't even hoot at me in the dark without giving itself away. And she doesn't know this van. She's used to seeing me driving various missiles, but not this.'

Jean huddled against his arm, shivering, but not with cold. 'Leslie, if it *is* her – suppose he isn't with her any more? Suppose something's happened already?' She didn't say that it was unthinkable to suspect Miss Hamilton of crime and violence, because now nothing was unthinkable, every rule was already broken and every restraint unloosed. 'Could she have left him somewhere back there on the road?'

He hadn't thought of that, and it shook him badly. The Riley could be as lethal a weapon as any murderer would need. But he kept his eyes fixed on the receding rear-lights, and his foot down hard. 'The police car will be coming along behind.'

'Yes, but the road's so dark, that black surface – '

'She's turning off,' he said abruptly and eagerly, and stamped the accelerator into the floor; for why, if she was alone and upon innocent business, should she turn off this road to the right? There was nothing there but the remotest of lovers' lanes, a dead end going down to the riverbank. Not even a lane, really, just a cart-track through the belt of trees, once sealed by a five-barred gate, though it hadn't been closed for a year or so now, and hung sagging in the grass from its upper hinge. Leslie knew the place well enough from summer picnics long ago. There was a wide stretch of open grass by the river there, where cars could drive right down to the water and find ample room to turn. But what could a woman alone want down there on a frosty October night?

He swung the van round into the mouth of the track, and pulled up. 'You get out and wait here for the police car.'

'No,' she said in a gasp of protest, clutching at his arm, 'I'm coming with you.'

'Get out! How will they know, if you don't? They're nowhere in sight. Oh, God, Jean, don't waste time.'

She snatched her hand away and scrambled out. He saw her face staring after him all great wide-set eyes in an oval pallor, as he drove down into the darkness between the trees. She didn't like letting him go without her. They were loose among murders and pursuits and all the things that didn't normally happen, who could be sure there wouldn't be guns, too? But what sort of a team were they going to be in the future if they pulled two ways now? She watched the van rock away down the rutted track, and then stood shivering, watching the road faithfully. Leslie's ascendancy was established in that one decision, when he wasn't even thinking about their partnership or their rivalry, and it couldn't have been won in the face of a stiffer test. The hardest thing he could possibly have asked of her was to stand back and let him go into action alone, now, when she had newly discovered how much he meant to her.

The frozen ruts of the track gripped the wheels of the van and it slewed it in a series of ricochets down into the rustling tunnel of trees. He couldn't see the rear-lights of the Riley now, he couldn't hear its engine; he had all he could do to hold the van and drive it forward fast towards the faint glimmer of starlight that flooded the open riverbank. The trees thinned. He slowed, killed his headlights altogether in the hope of remaining undetected until he got his bearings, and cruised to the edge of the copse.

She had driven the car right out on to the low terrace of rimy grass above the water, sweeping round in a circle to be ready to drive out again. Both doors hung open like beetle-wings spread for flight, and midway between the car and the edge of the bank she was dragging something laboriously along the ground, something limp and slender that hung a dead weight upon her arms. Beyond the two figures moving sidelong like a crippled animal the flat breadth of the river flowed pallid with lambent light, at once swift and motionless, a quivering band of silver.

All down the rough ride under the trees Leslie's mind had been working coolly and lucidly, telling him exactly what to do. Don't leave the escape route open. Broadside the van across the track, there's no other way out. Make sure she shan't get the car out again. But in the end he didn't do any of the things his busy brain had been recommending to him, there was no time. She had such a little way to go to the water, and he knew the currents there and could guess at the cold. He didn't stop to think or consider at all, he just let out a yell of which he was not even conscious, slashed his headlights full on and drove straight at her, his foot down hard. Let her get away, let her run, anything, as long as she dropped the kid in time.

The front wheels left the track and laboured like a floundering sea-beast on to the bumpy shore of the open turf. Rocking and plunging, he roared across the grass, and his headlights caught and held her in a blaze of black and white. She was hit by noise and light together, he saw her shrink and cringe, letting the boy fall for a moment. She wrenched her head up to stare wildly, and he saw a face carved in light, as hard and smooth and white as marble, with panting mouth and gaunt eyes glaring. The eyes had still an unmistakable intelligence and authority, he couldn't get a finger-hold on the hope that she might be

492

mad. Then she stooped and seized the boy beneath the armpits, wrenching him up from the ground with furious determination, and began to drag herself and him in a stumbling run towards the water's edge. Heavy and inert, he slipped out of her hold and she clawed at him again, frantic to finish what she had begun.

Only at the last moment, as the van swerved and braked screaming to a stop a few yards short of her, did she give up. She flung the boy from her with a sudden angry cry, and ran like a greyhound for her car. Her hair had slipped out of its beautiful, austere coil, it streamed down over her shoulders as she ran, shrouding the whiteness of her face. Leslie, tumbling from the van before it was still, snatched vainly at her arm as she fled, and then, abandoning her for what was more urgent, plunged upon the boy who lay huddled where she had thrown him.

She had all but done what she had set out to do; a few seconds more and he would have been in the river. His head and one arm dangled over the downward slope of grass, the limp fingers swinging above the edge of the water. Leslie fell on his knees beside him and hauled him well ashore, turning him so that he lay face upwards in the grass. Under the tumbled chestnut thatch Dominic's face was pinched and grey, the eyes closed. He was breathing with a heavy, short, painful rhythm through parted lips, but at least he was breathing. Leslie felt him all over with hasty hands, and began to hoist the dead weight into his arms. He was just clambering gingerly to his feet under his burden when he heard the Riley start up and soar into speed.

He'd forgotten that she had a lethal weapon still in her hands. She hadn't finished with them yet. There was room between the water and the standing van for her to drive round and come upon them at speed, and what was there now to restrain her from killing two as readily as one? He was one man, apparently alone, there was room for him in the river with the boy.

The Riley's headlights whirled round the bulk of the Bedford, straightened out parallel with the river's edge, and lunged at him in a blinding glare. Caught off balance, staggering beneath the boy's weight, he broke into a lurching run. He couldn't hope to get into the trees, where she couldn't reach them, but he jumped for the van and tried to put a corner of its bulk between him and the hurtling car. She wouldn't crash the van, she wouldn't do anything to wreck her own means of escape; she was sane, appallingly sane, and at least you can have some idea of what the sane will do. The blaze of light blinded him, he couldn't see the van or the ground or the starlit shape of the night any more, he could only hurl himself straight across the car's path into the dark on the other side.

He caught his foot in the tussocky grass and fell sprawling over his burden beneath the back wheels of the Bedford. The car missed his scrabbling feet by inches, he felt the frosty clumps of the turf crunch close to his heels. Then the light and the rushing bulk were past, and his cringing flesh relaxed with a sob of relief. He eased his weight from the boy and put his face down into his sleeve for a moment, and lay panting, sick with retrospective terror.

The roar of the car receded, swaying up the rutted track towards where Jean waited. Leslie struggled out of his weakness and came to his feet and began to run, but what was the use? A couple of minutes and the Riley would be out on the road. He cupped his mouth in his hands and bellowed in a voice that shook the frost from the trees: 'Jean, look out! Stand clear!'

She surely wouldn't try anything crazy? Would she? How could you be sure with Jean, who couldn't bear to be beaten, and would die rather than give in?

Winding along the complex curves of the road from Comerbourne came the headlights of two cars, late but coming fast. Jean was standing in the middle of the road waving her arms peremptorily at the first of them when she heard the labouring sound of the Riley climbing back up the lane, and started and quivered to Leslie's shout. She ran back to stare frantically into the tunnel of the trees. Not the van, the car. What had happened down there? Where was Leslie? What was he doing? The Hamilton woman shouldn't get away now, she mustn't, she shouldn't, even if it made no difference in the end. Jean ran like a fury and wedged her shoulder under the top bar of the drunken old gate, and dragged it protesting out of its bleached bed of grass. She staggered across the track with it supported on her shoulder, and slammed it home against its solid gatepost on the other side. There was a great wooden latch that still dropped creakingly into place; she lodged it with a crash, and flung herself aside under the hedge as the Riley drove full at the barrier.

The impact burst the bars and sent the weaker gatepost sagging out of true. Wood and glass flew singing through the air, and splinters settled with a strange noise like metallic rain. The car had not the impetus to drive straight through the obstacle, it was brought up shuddering and plunging in the wreckage of the gate, the windscreen shivered, one lamp ripped away. The engine died. Jean crouched quivering in the midst of a sudden teeming activity that shuddered with movement and purpose, but made no more sound.

She opened her eyes and uncovered her ears and crawled shakily out of the hedge. Beyond the impaled Riley the van came rocking gently up the slope; she saw Leslie's disordered hair and anxious face staring over the wheel, and in the passenger seat beside him Dominic's unconscious head lolled above the fringe of Barney Wilson's old utility rug. Both the cars from Comerbourne were drawn up along the edge of the road, and five men in plain clothes had boiled out of them and taken charge of everything. Two of them were closing in one on either side of the wrecked car. Two more were dismembering the ruins of the gate and hoisting them aside to clear the way. And the fifth, who was George Felse, had made for the Bedford and climbed in beside his son, easing the dangling head into the hollow of his shoulder and feeling with gentle fingers through the tangled hair.

Dominic came round upon a rising wave of fear and pain, to feel himself held in someone's arms like a baby, and someone's fingers tenderly smoothing out the frenzied ache that hammered at his head. Making the inevitable connection, he settled more closely and thankfully into the comforting shoulder, and feeling the rush of tears stinging his eyelids, hastened to cover himself.

'Mummy, my head hurts!' he muttered querulously. But it was his father's voice that said gently in reply: 'Yes, old lad, I know. You lie quiet, we'll find you something to stop it.'

The discrepancy jolted him seriously, and he opened his eyes to make sure he wasn't dreaming, but closed them again very quickly because the effort was very painful. However, he'd had time to see the face that was bending over him, and there was no doubt about it, it was his father. Well, if that was how he felt about things it didn't look so bad, not so bad at all. Dominic had expected at the very best to find himself in the doghouse. Maybe if you're really going to kick over the traces in a big way it pays to get yourself half killed in the process. Even if it does hurt.

Drifting a little below the surface of full consciousness, he remembered the one thing he had to get settled, the only thing in the world that really mattered.

'It wasn't Kitty,' he said, not very distinctly but George understood. 'You do know now, don't you?'

'Yes, Dom, we know now. Everything's all right, everything's fine, you just rest.'

He was sinking unresisting into a stupor of weariness and relief, tears oozing between his closed eyelids onto George's shoulder, when a sudden appalling sound startled him into full consciousness again. Someone had laughed loudly and angrily, a discord harsh as a scream.

He opened his eyes wide, his wrung nerves vibrating, and beyond George's head and Duckett's solid shoulders, beyond

Jean and Leslie clinging hand in hand, he saw a wild creature in a torn black suit, her cheek cut by flying glass, long black hair dangling in great heavy locks round her face, a bloodstained Maenad wrenching ineffectively at her pinioned wrists, her mouth contorted as she spat defiance.

'All right, yes, I killed him. I don't care who knows it. Do you think you can frighten me with your charges and your cautions? All right, what if I did kill him? It isn't capital murder, don't think you're going to kill me, that's something you can't do. I know the law, I've had to know it. Twenty years,' she shouted hoarsely, 'twenty years of my life he had out of me! I could have married a dozen times over, but no, I had to fix my sights on him! Twenty years his bitch, being patient, waiting for that hag of a wife of his to die – '

Dominic began to shake in his father's arms, and then to sob convulsively. He couldn't help it, and when he'd begun he couldn't stop. All that black and white dignity, all that composure and discipline, she ripped them to shreds and threw them in his face. He couldn't bear it. He burrowed his throbbing head desperately into George's shoulder, whimpering, but he couldn't shut out the sound of her voice.

' – and then still waiting after she was dead, and still no reward. Bide my time, I've done nothing all my life but bide my time, and what did I ever get out of it but *him*? And then suddenly *her* on the telephone, that fool of a girl yelling for help to me – *me!* – and bleating that he was planning *to marry her!* And what was I to get, after I'd given him years of my life? Nothing, none of my rights, just the same old round, his letters to type in the daytime, and him in my bed when he felt like it – and her, *her* holding the reins! Yes, I killed him,' she panted, her breast heaving, 'but it wasn't enough. He ought to have been conscious. He ought to have felt it more – every blow! There ought to have been some way I could kill him ten times over for what he did to me!'

Chapter 17

He remembered nothing of the drive home in the van, with George nursing him anxiously in his arms, and Leslie driving as gingerly, so Jean said afterwards, as if he had an ambulance load of expectant mothers aboard instead of just one. He was conscious but totally astray. Very slight concussion, so the doctor said, and his recollections would sort themselves out coherently enough later on; but this part of the evening never came back. They put him to bed, and dosed him with something that gradually took the pain away but took the world away with it. 'He's all right,' said the doctor. 'We'll keep him under light sedation tomorrow, and by evening he'll be right as rain.'

He woke once in the night, struggling and crying out fiercely, loosing in his dreams the resistance he had restrained by force a few hours earlier. Bunty brought him a drink, and he gulped it down greedily, asked her wonderingly what was the matter, and fell asleep again on her arm. Towards dawn he began sobbing violently in his sleep, but the fit subsided when she bathed his hot forehead and soothed him back into deeper slumber; and in the morning he awoke hungry, alert and loquacious, though still somewhat pale and tense, and wanted to talk to his father.

'This evening,' said Bunty firmly. 'Right now he's busy arranging about getting Miss Norris released. That's what you were worrying about, isn't it? You take it easy and stop fretting, everything's under control.'

'Oh, Mummy!' he said reproachfully, almost offendedly, 'you're so darned *calm*.' He wouldn't, she thought, have chosen that word if he could have seen her face when they brought him home. He took a rapid retrospective glance at the memories that were beginning to assemble themselves into some sort of shape, and asked coaxingly: 'You're not very mad with me, are you?'

'Well, you know,' said Bunty amiably, putting away the thermometer which confirmed that his temperature was normal, 'maddish.'

'Only maddish? Well, look, Mummy, I overspent my expense account. Those gloves were twenty-three and eleven, I never knew they cost so much. Any good my putting in a claim?'

'We can't let the detective lose on the job,' she said comfortably. He wasn't feeling quite as tough and skittish as he pretended, but it was better not to notice that. 'I'm surprised you didn't just go to Haywards for them, and get them put down to my account.'

'Well, hell!' said Dominic, confounded. 'I never thought of that.'

By evening he was pronounced fit to talk as much as he liked. Later it might be necessary to take an official statement from him, but for the moment what mattered was that he should get the whole thing off his chest to his father as soon as George came home.

'Is it all right?' asked Dominic eagerly, before George could even move up a chair to the side of the bed. 'Kitty's free?' He couldn't altogether suppress the tremor in his voice when he uttered her name.

'Yes, it's all right, Kitty's free.' He didn't say any more, it was for her to do that. Dominic knew what he'd done for her, nothing George might say could add anything to his glory, and he certainly wasn't going to take anything away from it. 'You needn't worry any more, you did what you set out to do. How does your head feel now?'

'Sore, and I've got a stiff neck. But not so bad, really. What was it she hit me with?'

'You won't want to believe it. A rubber cosh loaded with lead shot, the kind the Teds favour.'

'No!' said Dominic, his mouth falling open with astonishment. 'Where would she get a thing like that?'

'Can't you guess? From one of her club boys. She confiscated it from him a few weeks ago, with a severe lecture on the iniquity of carrying offensive weapons.' Alfred Armiger hadn't survived to appreciate the irony, but by the grace of God Dominic had. 'What was it that put you on to her in the first place?'

'It was Jean's doing, really. I got to thinking how all the people involved had known Mr. Armiger for years, and wondering why one of them should suddenly pick on that night not to be able to stick him a moment longer. And I thought the real motive must be something that had happened that very evening, something that changed things altogether for that one person. So after we got to know about Kitty's phone call, and it seemed likely that the person she called might be the one, this sudden motive thing sort of got narrowed down into something that was said in that phone call. I made a smashing case on those lines against Mr. Shelley, and tried it on Leslie and Jean. And straight away Jean said no, it couldn't happen like that. She said Kitty wouldn't run to a man, but to a woman. She said,' said Dominic, steeling his hesitant voice to use the adult words Jean had used, firmly and authoritatively as became a man, 'that Kitty had just suffered a kind of sexual outrage, almost worse than the ordinary kind, with that beastly old man making a pass at her that wasn't even a pass, but just a cold-blooded business deal. And you see – what made it much worse – '

He turned his head on the pillow and stared steadily at the wall. He couldn't say it, even now. What made it much worse was that she was still in love with Leslie, and his father's complacent proposal must have seemed to her horribly shocking. 'Jean said in those circumstances she'd go to a woman if she had to have help,' he said, controlling the level of his voice with determination. He wasn't quite himself yet, he cried easily if he wasn't on his guard.

'I see,' said George, remembering how in the night Bunty

had reorientated him with much the same phrases and sent him off after the same quarry, though by slower and more orthodox methods. 'So you thought of one woman at least who was older, who was well known to her, and who'd been on the scene with her that evening.'

'Yes. And I thought what Kitty could have said to her that might make her suddenly want to kill Mr. Armiger, and you see, it was there as soon as I began looking for it.' Yes, it was there to be found, though he shouldn't have known enough to go looking for it. There isn't much boys miss; even the gossip they disdain their knowing senses record accurately. 'I wouldn't mind betting,' said Dominic, 'that Kitty's the one person who didn't even know what they said about him and Miss Hamilton. She's so *apart* from those things. Even if you told her something like that it would go in one ear and out the other. She doesn't hear what doesn't interest her.'

George wasn't prepared to follow him into the shadowy sweet hinterland of Kitty's mind; there was no permanent place for either of them there.

'So you decided as we couldn't find the gloves to try a gigantic bluff and pretend that you had. How did you set about it?'

Dominic told the whole story, glad to unburden himself; it was difficult to recapture the fear now, in this familiar and secure place, but there were times when he trembled.

'I went there after I knew old Shelley'd left, and pretended I wanted to talk to him, and that it was something about the case. As soon as she bit like that and suggested I should tell her instead I felt sure I was right about her. And when I told her I'd found the gloves, and they were a woman's – letting on I thought they must be Kitty's, and wanted to suppress the evidence – well, then it began to look even more promising, because right away she said I could give them to her and she'd deal with them. Meaning me to understand, she'd destroy them. Well, I mean people just *don't* stick their necks out like that, not to a chap they've hardly set eyes on before, and don't know at all.

Do they? Not without a pretty urgent reason of their own. She tried to make me tell where I'd found them, and what they were like and all that, so she could make sure whether she really had anything to fear or not, but I laid on a sort of hysterical act, and she couldn't get any sense out of me. And you know, she couldn't afford to take even the least risk of my tale being true. Even if the odds were a thousand to one against my having anything that mattered to her, she couldn't afford to let even that one chance slip by. So she said give them to her. And if I'd done it then and there I don't know what she'd have done, because long before that I could feel her thinking that I was just as dangerous to her as the gloves themselves, and she had to get rid of both of us. I was acting pretty emotional, I bet she was thinking to herself, this little ass will never be able to keep his mouth shut, some day he'll blab to his father. I think she'd have seen to it that something happened to me right there in the office, because everyone else had gone, and with the car she'd have been able to take me somewhere miles away to dump me. But I said I hadn't got them on me, on account of the chaps at school being naturally a bit casual with one another's things, and I'd bring them to her when I came in for my music lesson at night. You should have seen her jump at it! Nobody'd ever know we were going to meet, and if I vanished nobody'd ever think of her. She suggested she'd wait for me at the end of the road when she came from the club. And she impressed on me that I wasn't to say a word to a soul. So then I was absolutely sure. She *had* got rid of some bloodstained gloves somewhere close to the barn that night, and she *had* killed Mr. Armiger. Why else should she prepare a setup like that?'

'And why,' asked George gently, 'didn't you come to me then and tell me everything? Why did you have to go through with a thing like that all by yourself? Couldn't you have trusted me?'

The note of reproach, however restrained, had been a mistake. 'All right, I know, I know!' said George hastily. 'It wasn't proof, and you felt you had to provide the proof. But did it have to be by using yourself as live bait?'

'Well, having gone so far I sort of couldn't stop. And if I'd told you you'd have stopped me from going on with it. You'd have had to. *I* could *do* a thing like that, but *you* couldn't *let* me do it. You don't blame me, do you?'

'I don't blame you, I blame myself. I ought to have made it possible for you to rely on me more.' That wasn't the way either; self-reproach seemed to have a worse effect still on Dominic. 'Never mind,' said George gently. 'You did what you felt you ought to do, let's leave it at that for now. How did you know what sort of gloves to provide? That must have been a headache. If they were wrong, one glance and she'd know you were lying.'

'But then she'd also know I suspected her and was trying to trap her, wouldn't she? And that would have come to the same thing, she'd still think it essential to get rid of me while she had this chance. So it didn't matter. But I did try to do the best I could. I saw she hadn't got gloves on when we left the office, so I went along to see her to the car, and sure enough she had them there in the locker, and they were plain short black kid and quite new, hardly creased at the joints yet. So I thought the safest bet was that she bought a pair as like the ones she threw away as possible, and I rode back into town and got some like them. I ran the tap on them and crumpled and soiled them and tried to age them a bit, and even then I wrapped them up so she should only get a glimpse of them.

'And you know all the rest,' said Dominic, lying back in his pillows with a huge sigh. 'I couldn't know my note to Leslie Armiger would be held up like that, or I'd have said eight o'clock instead of half past.'

'I should think so,' said George warmly. 'Turned nine when they located me at the garage near her place, and no sign of you or the Riley by the time we got to Brook Street. If it hadn't been for young Leslie – ' He dropped that sentence quickly, for his own sake as much as for Dominic's.

'Suppose she goes back on her confession? Will you still be able to get a conviction without the real gloves?'

'Oh, there'll be no trouble there. Her car's full of traces of blood, all the seams of the driving-seat show it. The leather's been washed, but she made the usual mistake of using hot water, and in any case you can never get it out of the threads. And we've recovered the zip fastener of the black skirt she wore that night, and two ornamental buttons from the front pleat, all metal, out of the furnace ashes from the flats where she lives. The jacket she must have thought wasn't marked, she sent it to a church rummage sale, but we've traced it. The right sleeve is slightly splashed with blood, too. Oh, yes, we've got a case. She must have knelt on the floor beside him, I should think – anyhow she found it necessary to burn the skirt. No wonder the hem of Kitty's dress was stained where it brushed hers.'

Looking fixedly at the edge of the sheet which he was folding between his fingers, Dominic asked abruptly: 'Did you see her to-day?'

'Who, Ruth Hamilton?'

'No,' said Dominic stiffening. 'Kitty. When they – when she was released.'

'Yes, I saw her.'

'To speak to? How did she look? Did she say anything?'

'She looked a bit dazed as yet,' said George carefully, remembering the stunned purple eyes that had stared bewildered at freedom even when it was put into her hands. 'Give her a day or two, and she'll be her own girl again. At first the truth was just one more shock to her, but she was coming round nicely the last I saw of her. She said she was going out to get her hair done and buy a new dress.'

Dominic lay silent. His diligent fingers lagged on the hem of the sheet. He kept his eyes averted.

'And she said she'd like to come and see you to-night, if you were well enough to have visitors.'

Dominic rolled over and sat up in a flurry of bedclothes, eyes flaring golden. 'No! Did she, though? No kidding?' He had clutched at the bright promise with all his might, but caution made him give it a second look. 'I suppose you went and told her I had to be kept quiet,' he said suspiciously. They needn't think he hadn't heard them talking about him last night, even if he'd been in no mood to argue then.

'I told her there was nothing the matter with you but a swollen head. I don't suppose she'll manage to reduce that any,' said George, grinning, 'but anyhow she'll be here about eight o'clock. You've got a quarter of an hour to cover the worst ravages.'

Dominic was half out of bed, yelling for Bunty. George tucked him back again firmly, and brought him his new dark green silk dressing-gown, his last birthday present that was too good to be worn except on special occasions. 'You stay where you are, and don't squander your advantages. You look very interesting. Here you are, get busy on the details.' He dropped comb and mirror on Dominic's bed, and left him to his bliss.

He was already closing the door when Dominic suddenly cried: 'Hey!' And when he looked back: 'Somebody must have told her about me. I mean, about what I did. Otherwise how would she know – why would she want – '

'So they must!' said George. 'I wonder who that could be?'

He met Bunty on the stairs, coming up in haste to answer her fledgling's agitated cheeping. George spread his arms suddenly, on an impulse of gratitude and relief for which he didn't trouble to seek a reason, and swung her off her feet. He kissed her in mid-air, and put her down gently on the landing above him. She kissed him back warmly before she fled. She didn't know which of them she was sorrier for; but she knew they were both going to survive. George's heart, as a matter of fact, was lighter than she supposed; it had not occurred to him until this moment that he'd been so full of pride and excitement and joy for Dominic that he had somehow mislaid the sting of jealousy that belonged to himself.

Bunty was more respectful than George had been to her son's passionate and unaccustomed concern with his appearance. She didn't smile about it, she was as much in earnest as Dominic himself, though she did tend to go about it in a way that made him feel about seven years old. She brought him George's Paisley silk scarf and tied a beautiful cravat for him; and he was too agitated to resent her attentions provided they produced the desired result, and submitted to having his face sponged and his hair brushed like a convalescent child.

'Now you're not to make her too excited,' said Bunty artfully, busy with the comb, 'because you must remember she's been through a lot, and she may be easily upset. You be calm and gentle with her, and she'll be all right.' She was rewarded by feeling him put the trembling tension away from him very firmly, and draw a deep, steadying breath that filled him down to his toes.

Kitty came prompt to her hour. She was thinner and paler than when he had last seen her, and she wore that small, rueful smile of hers with a kind of wonder, as though she had rediscovered it after a long separation. She had done him proud. The new dress was a rough silk suit of a colour somewhere between honey and amber. The soft, floating motion of the sheaves of fair hair testified to the care someone had spend on the new hair-do, and the scent that shook out of it when she moved her head was enough to turn his. She sat by his bed and stretched out those splendid long legs in their almost invisible nylons, and looked at the toes of her absurd, fragile shoes, and then at Dominic.

A moment of shyness hung over them both like an iridescent bubble, while they held their breath for fear of breaking more than the silence. Then she suddenly wrinkled her nose at him and grinned, and he knew that it was all right, that it had all been worthwhile. The shadow hadn't lifted, the grin didn't ring quite true, not yet; but the time was coming when it would, and if not for him, then by his gift.

'What *am* I to say to you?' said Kitty. 'It just shows you a good deed really is its own reward. If I hadn't rashly taken a fit to give away a pint of my blood I might never have met you, and then where would I have been? Strictly up the creek!'

'They'd have found out without me,' said Dominic, humbled. 'Dad was on the right lines as it turned out, only I didn't know it. That's the way I am, big-headed. I thought nobody was working at it properly but me.' What would George have thought, or Bunty, if they could have heard him now? Adulation from Kitty made him want to go on his knees and confess all the things that least satisfied him in himself, and beg forgiveness for not being more adequate, and shout with joy at the same time because she saw him as so much more likeable and fine than he really was.

'I know the way you are,' said Kitty positively. 'You're sure you feel all right now? No pain? Nothing?'

'I'm absolutely fit, only they won't let me get up until to-morrow. And what about you?'

'Oh, I'm fine. I lost ten pounds in gaol,' said Kitty, and the grin was warmer and more sure of itself this time. 'That's what they call looking on the bright side. Don't I look all right?'

'You look marvellous,' said Dominic with unguarded fervour.

'Good! This is all for you.' She leaned forward, playing with the pleated edging of his eiderdown. 'I wanted to tell you about my plans, Dominic. You're the first person I am telling. About all that money. I don't want it. What I should like to do is just to refuse it, but before I do I have to make sure that *if* I do it will go to Leslie. Otherwise I shall have to accept it and find the best means of transferring it to Leslie and Jean afterwards. I'm determined they shall have it, it's just a question of which is the best way to arrange it. I'm going to see Ray Shelley about it to-morrow.'

'Leslie won't want to take it,' said Dominic, rather hesitantly because his knowledge of Leslie was so new that it seemed cheek to presume to instruct her in what he would or would not do.

'No, I know he won't. But I think he'll do it, because he won't want to make me unhappy.' She had almost said 'more unhappy than I am'; the boy was so grave and so sweet and so altogether a darling that it was hard work remembering that he was in a position to suffer, too. 'And I think Jean will let him, for the same reason. And as for me, I'm going away. If they want me for the trial I suppose I shall have to stay until that's over, but after that I'm going right away. I couldn't live here any more, Dominic, not now.'

She lifted her head, and the great purple-brown eyes looked into his, and he saw her there immured within the crystal of her loneliness, and felt the wonderful burden of responsibility for her settle upon his shoulders. Who else was ever going to get her out?

'Yes,' he said, swallowing the heart that seemed to have grown too big for his breast, 'I can understand that. I think you're right to go.'

'It isn't because of being in prison, or being afraid to face people, or anything,' she said. 'It isn't that. It's just that I have to get away from here.'

'I know,' said Dominic.

'Do you? *Do* you know what it's like, loving someone who doesn't even know you're there?'

He didn't say anything to that, he couldn't; the turbulent heart was back in his throat, quietly choking him. But suddenly she heard what she had said, and understood the answer he hadn't made. She slid from her chair and fell on her knees beside his bed with a soft, wretched cry of remorse and tenderness, and caught up his hands in hers and laid her cheek on them. The swirl of her hair spread like a wave over his knees.

His heart seemed to burst, and he could breathe and speak again. He took one hand from her gently, and began to stroke her hair, and then her one visible cheek, smoothing the long, silky line of her brow, laying trembling fingertips on her mouth.

'You'll find somebody else,' he said manfully. 'Just give it time. You'll go away from here, and it will all be different.' He listened to his own voice, astonished and awed. The words he had expected to find bitter were sweet as honey, and tasted not of renunciation but of achievement. 'Don't just settle somewhere else, Kitty, not straight away. You travel. Go right round the world, give him a chance to show up. You'll find him, you'll see.'

She lay still, letting him soothe her and listening to the deepening tones of the voice that was feeling its way by great forward lunges towards manhood. This was something she'd never meant to do. She had debated all day what she could bring him, what gift she could offer him for all he had done for her, and she had been able to think of nothing that would not diminish his triumph rather than complete it, so that in the end she had come empty-handed. And here without even meaning to she had made him the perfect return, her life for his life, the gift of her drifting, solitary self to be moulded and urged and cherished, and launched on a new course. He had recovered her, he had the right to dispose of her. And why not? Comerbourne wasn't the world. One man couldn't be the world, unless she shut all the rest out. I've got to live now, she thought, I'm a piece of his life, I owe it to him to live.

'You know what?' she said softly, moulding the words with her lips against his palm. 'You're absolutely right. That's just what I'm going to do.'

'Go to India, go to South America, all those places with the wonderful names. There are people everywhere. Nice people. You've only got to let them in.'

'Even a few as nice as you,' she said, and smiled up at him, cradling his hand against her cheek. She was in two minds about trying to prolong his pleasure, inviting him to plan with her where she would go and what she would do, but then she thought, no. One more thing she could do for him, and only one, and that was wind up this thing now and get out of his life clean, and leave him a perfect, immaculate, unassailable experience, safe for ever from any anti-climax. Wind it up on a high note, and finish! He'd be miserable for a while, but it would be wonderful misery. Not like mine, she thought, drawn out day after day, month after month in decline. My own fault, my own fault! I won't let that happen to him. I've been to blame. If I'd cared enough, if I'd felt enough, I could have saved all this. *He* could have been alive still, and poor, frustrated, calculating, vindictive Hammie needn't have been a murderess. But all I could see was *my* misery. Now I look at Dominic, and I no longer see myself so clearly, but I see him, he's real to me. With him I won't make any mistake.

'That's exactly what I'm going to do,' she said. 'And when I do find him, you'll be the first person to know.'

She rose on her knees, leaning towards him, and her face was where a woman's face should be, just below the level of his own. She put out a hesitant hand and passed it gently over the back of his head, where the thick hair was clipped short. The touch of her fingers on the dressing was almost too light to feel, and very close to his, all great warm eyes and sympathetic mouth, her face swam out of focus. He drew breath hard, and suddenly his arms went round her and caught her to his heart, and he kissed her three times, beginning at her throat and ending on her lips, inexpertly but not clumsily, with an abrupt, virginal passion.

His mouth was cool and fresh and smooth, and moved her to prodigies of hope and excitement and laughter and tenderness. She knew by every touch of him that there was nothing left in the world that he wanted or needed, not even from her. She let him begin the embrace and end it. She held him tenderly while he willed it so, and as soon as he recollected his role and gently and firmly disengaged himself under the impression that he was releasing her, she took her arms away and drew back, rising and stepping back from him in one lovely, fluid movement.

'Goodbye, Dominic! Bless you for everything! I'll never forget you.'

She was gone from the room, the door closing softly after her, before he managed to get out in a small, stunned voice: 'Goodbye, Kitty! Good luck!' He didn't say that he'd never forget her, either, but she knew it; never until the Greeks forget Marathon.

When Bunty looked in half an hour later Dominic was curled in his pillows fast asleep, smiling a little with fulfilment and content like a fed infant.

Kitty was as good as her word. Nine months later, one morning in the height of the summer, there was a picture postcard of Rio bay by Dominic's plate at breakfast. The text said:

I've found him, and you're the first to know. His name is Richard Baynham, he's an engineer, and we're getting married in September. Terribly happy. Bless you!

LOVE, KITTY.

Dominic read it through with a puzzled face, frowning over a hand which was totally unknown to him. He was not quite awake yet, and the message struck no immediate chord. Nine months is a long time. At the end he said blankly: 'Kitty?' And then, in a very different voice: 'Oh, *Kitty*!' That was all; but he didn't leave the postcard lying about, he put it carefully in his wallet and no one else ever saw it again; and he got up from the table and went about his business with a bright reminiscent gleam in his eye and looking several inches taller, a man with a future and a past.

A Nice Derangement of Epitaphs

Contents

MRS. MALAPROP: Sure, if I reprehend anything in this world it is the use of my oracular tongue, and a nice derangement of epitaphs!

SHERIDAN: *The Rivals*

Chapter 1

Wednesday

The boy in the sea was in difficulties, that was plain from the first moment Dominic clapped eyes on him. Only a seal could possibly navigate off the Dragon's Head in a tide like this one, racing out on the ebb with the impetus of an express train, checking and breaking back again like hammers on the toothed rocks, lashing out right and left in bone-white spray, and seething down through the wet sand in deep clawmarks, with a hissing like the old serpent of legend striking and missing his prey. For a mile off the point, far into deep water greener than emeralds, the sea boiled. Nobody in his senses swam there in an ebbing tide.

He cupped his hands and yelled, and the bobbing head, a small cork tossed in a cauldron of foam, heaved clear of the spray for an instant and turned towards him a pallor which must be its face. He yelled again, and peremptorily waved the swimmer inshore. The clamour of the ebb off the point might well have carried his voice away, but the gesture was seen and understood. And ignored. The head vanished in foam, and reappeared tossing off the spray, battling doggedly outward.

Dominic looked round wildly for someone else to take the decision from him, but there was nobody. This wasn't the populous Maymouth side of the Dragon, but the bleak bay of Pentarno on the northern side, and tea-time of a fine but blowy day, when nobody frequented those sandy wastes. Mile upon mile of drifted sand on his right hand, and inland, beyond the processional dunes, the first green of pasture and gold and brown of stubble; and on his left the craggy bastions of the Dragon's Head, running out to sea in a grapeshot of scattered rocks, the cliff paths a six-strand necklace above him, a tapering crescent of pebbles below. Not a local in sight to take the load from him. And if he didn't make up his mind quickly it might be too late. Better make a fool of yourself than watch some other fool kid drown himself before your eyes.

Oh, damn! Whether he was in trouble or not—!

Dominic launched himself from the path and went down the last slope of thinning grass and shale in a long, precarious slither, to arrive upright but staggering in the grey pebble shelf under the rocks, just clear of the hissing water. It was falling rapidly now, and this was no very good place to go in, but he had no choice. He shed his shirt and slacks, kicked off his sandals, and waded into water that ran back before him, snatching its last fringes away from his toes in a scurry of foam. He overtook it, felt his way as fast as he dared down the broken slippery descent, took one last rapid sighting, and struck out strongly towards the boy in the sea.

The first stages were easy, and he knew his own capabilities and could trust himself in this much of a sea, even if his own experience had been gained in the makeshift river-and-swimming-bath conditions of a land-locked county. But the currents off these rocks were something nobody would willingly venture in a fast ebb like this, and the thought of the jagged teeth ripping up the water into oil-green ribbons clung in his mind through every minute of that swim. Half a mile northward, and the mild, long rollers would be sliding innocently down the level sand, as harmless as the ripples in a baby's bath. Here he had a fight on his hands.

He dug his shoulders into it, head low, edging away from the rocks with every stroke. Once he hoisted himself out of the trough to take a fresh sighting, and found the boy by the glimpse of a slender arm flung clear of the water for an instant. Nearer than Dominic had expected. And perhaps still clear of the treacherous pull of the rocks. Maybe he'd known what he was doing, after all. Maybe he was one of the harbour kids, bred from some ancestry involving fish, and did this every afternoon for fun.

But no, that wouldn't do. The harbour kids simply didn't go in off the point, they had too much sense. The ones who can do nearly everything never push their luck to the last rim, because they don't have to prove anything, they know.

Well, if this kid was the strongest swimmer on the North Cornish Coast, he was coming ashore now, if his rescuer had to knock him out to bring him.

The sea flung them together almost unexpectedly in the end; two startled faces, open-mouthed, hair streaming water, glared at each other out of focus, six inches of ocean racing between them hard and green as bottle-glass. Dominic caught at a thin, slippery arm, and gripped it, pulling the boy round to lie against his body. The boy opened his mouth to yell, and choked on water, rolling helplessly for a moment; and then he was being towed strongly back towards the shore, and seemed to have lost all command of his own powers at the shock of such an indignity. He recovered almost as quickly, and suddenly he was a fury. He jerked himself free and tried to dive under his rescuer, but he had met with a resolution as grim as his own. The plunging head was retrieved painfully by its wet hair, and clipped smartly on the ear into the bargain. The sea effectively quenched the resulting yell of rage, and Dominic recovered his hold and kicked out powerfully for the distant sands.

For the first stage of that return journey, in the event more arduous and tedious than risky, he got no help from his passenger. But after a few minutes he was aware of a considerable skill seconding his own strokes; however sullenly, certainly to good effect. The kid had given up and resigned himself to being hauled ashore; and at least, having gone so far, he had sense enough to reason that he might as well make the journey as quickly and comfortably as possible. They came in like that, together, struggling steadily northward across the tug of the undertow into the sunny water off the beach, until they touched ground, and floundered wearily through the shallows, feet sliding deep into the soft, shaken sands.

Rising out of the water was an effort that sucked out their strength suddenly, and set them trembling and buckling at the joints with the realisation of their own tiredness. They fell together on their faces, toes still trailing in the receding foam, and lay gasping and coughing up seawater. And there was the late afternoon sun on their backs, grateful and warm as a stroking hand, and the soft, almost silent waves lapping innocently on the long, level beach that stretched for more than two miles beyond Pentarno.

Dominic hoisted himself laboriously on his hands, and looked at his capture with something between a proprietor's pride and a keeper's exasperation. A slim, sunburned body, maybe fourteen or fifteen years old, in black swimming trunks. Light brown hair – probably almost flaxen when it was dry – streamed sea-water into the sand. He lay on his folded arms, the fine fan of his ribs clapping frantically for air, like cramped wings. Dominic got to his knees, hoisted the limp, light body by the middle, and squeezed out of him the remainder of the brine he had swallowed.

Hands and knees scrabbled in the sand, and the boy writhed away from him like an eel. Under the lank fall of hair one half-obscured eye, blue and steely as a dagger, glared fury.

'What the *hell*,' spluttered the ungrateful child, from a mouth bitter with seawater, 'do you think you're – *doing*?' He choked and ran out of breath there. Dominic sat back on his heels and scowled back at him resentfully.

'Now look here, you daft little devil, you'd do better thinking what the hell *you* were doing, out there in a sea like that. Don't you know the bathing's dead dangerous anywhere off the point? Especially when the tide's going out, like this. This town marks all the safe places, why can't you have the sense to stick to 'em? And don't give me that drop-dead look, either. You can thank your stars I was around. You'd have been in a mess without me.'

'I would *not*! I wasn't in trouble – ' He wavered for the first time; fundamentally he was, it seemed, a truthful person, even when in a rage. 'I could have managed, anyhow. I know the tides round here a lot better than you do, I bet.' The still indignant eyes had sized up a summer visitor without any difficulty. 'Damn it, I *live* here.'

'Then your dad ought to tan you,' said Dominic grimly, 'for taking such fool chances.'

'I wasn't taking chances – not for nothing, I wasn't.' He heaved a great breath into him, and swept back the fall of hair from his forehead. 'I wouldn't – not without a good reason, my dad knows that. I went in because I saw a man in the sea – '

Dominic was on his feet in a flurry of sand. 'You saw a *man*? You mean, somebody in trouble? Where?'

'Off the point, where I was, where d'you think? There was *something* being pulled out in the race, anyhow, I'm *nearly* sure it was a man. I swam out to try and get to him,' said the boy, with bitter satisfaction in shifting the burden of his own frustration to more deserving shoulders, 'but you had to take it on yourself to fish me out. So if he's drowned by now, you know whose fault it is, don't you?'

Dominic turned without a word, and set off at a run towards the water, his knees a little rubbery under him from shock and exertion. He had gone no more than a few yards when a shout from the dunes behind him brought him round again. The coast road from Maymouth over the neck of the Dragon's Head to Pentarno dipped closer to the beach here, and a man had just left it to drop in a series of leaps towards the sands. He had come from Maymouth, by the angle at which he approached. A tall, agile, sudden man who could glissade down loose sand like a skier, and run, once he reached level ground, with the grace of a greyhound and the candour of a child. He came up to them full tilt, and checked in a couple of light steps, already reaching down to hoist the kneeling boy to his feet, examine him in one sweeping glance, and visibly sigh relief.

'Paddy, what's going on? Are you all right?' He turned an abrupt smile upon Dominic. 'What's he been up to? Did you have to haul him out, or something? But he can swim like a fish.'

'I haven't been up to anything, Uncle Simon, honestly!' The injured voice grew shrill, and snapped off into a light, self-conscious baritone. Dominic had thought and hoped this might be the father, but even an uncle was very welcome, especially one as decisive as this.

Gratefully he blurted out what most needed saying: 'He says he saw a man being dragged out to sea off the point. That's why he went so far out. But I was up on the path there, and I didn't see anyone except him. Maybe he'd have been all right – but I was afraid he might not. I thought I ought to fetch him in.'

'You were very right, and I'm most grateful. Even if he isn't,' said Uncle Simon with the briefest of grins. He stood Paddy before him firmly, and shook him by the shoulders. 'Now, what did you see? Somebody throwing his arms about? Shouting for help? What?'

'No, he wasn't doing *anything*. Not even swimming. It was like a head just showing now and then, and there was more of it sort of sloshing about under the water – like when you see a drift of wood or some old rags washing about.'

'It could have been just that, couldn't it?'

'Yes, I suppose so – only I don't think it was.'

'O.K., I suppose we'd better have a hunt round.' He stripped off his sportscoat and shirt, and dropped them beside the boy. 'Here, you stay here and mind these.'

'I'll come with you,' said Dominic.

'Stay well inshore, then. And get out when you've had enough. I know this coast, you don't, and you've tired yourself already.' He kicked his feet clear of his grey flannels. 'Paddy, you can make yourself useful, too. Get up on the top path, and give us a hail if you see anything.'

He was off down the beach and into the water, Dominic after him. Paddy's summer tan was only deep ivory compared with the tawny gold of Uncle Simon's long, muscular back, and the fine, lean arms and legs that sliced through the water without a ripple. His hair was not more than a couple of shades darker. Once in the deep water he swam like a dolphin. With unaccustomed humility Dominic accepted his own lesser part, and forebore from following too far. A man who could move with so much confidence and certainty, off such a thorny coast, had the right to deploy his forces as he thought best, and be obeyed.

He stayed in the water until he felt himself tiring again, and then he came out and made his way along the rocks towards the Dragon's mouth, as low towards the sea as he dared, watching Simon dive, and surface and dive again, achingly near to the cauldron of the rocks. The worst of the race was over now, the boiling had subsided a little. The swimmer worked methodically outward along the line of the receding tide, came back cautiously towards the rocks again where the worst spite was already spent, and clung to rest. He had torn his knuckles, Dominic saw a pink ooze of blood on the hand that grasped the rock.

'No dice, Paddy?' he called up to the boy above their heads.

'No, nothing.' The voice shouted down a little gruffly and anxiously: 'You'd better come in, hadn't you?' Even an Uncle Simon, presumably, may reach exhaustion finally, and with him Paddy was taking no chances. 'It's no good now, anyhow. Even if it *was* somebody.'

523

'All right – yes, I'll come.'

He dropped carefully into the water and swam back to the sand, preferring that to the slower climb along the rocks. The boys came down, scrambling after him, Dominic with his clothes bundled untidily under his arm.

The tall, tawny, sinewy man stood wringing water out of his hair and streaming drops into the sand. Deep brown eyes surveyed them as they came up, and he twitched a shoulder and shivered a little. It was early September, and the evenings were growing cool. They began to dress in damp discomfort and a sudden chill of depression.

'No sign of anyone.'

'Maybe there wasn't anyone,' said Paddy grudgingly. 'But honestly, I still think there was.'

'All right, Paddy, you couldn't have done more, anyhow. I'll notify the coastguard, just in case, if that'll make you feel better. That's all we can do. What we all need now is a cup of tea, and some towels. And maybe a drop of rum in the tea. Come on up with us to the farm – Sorry, but what should I be calling you?'

'My name's Dominic Felse. We're staying at the Dragon.'

'Well, Dominic, come on home with us, and get warm and dry. Can't let you run off now, without having thanked you properly.'

Dominic hesitated, half afraid that this might more properly be the time for him to disappear, but deeply unwilling to do so if he could gracefully remain. At eighteen years and one week he held the optimistic view that you can never know too many people or accumulate too many friends; and the success of a holiday depends on what you find for yourself on the spot, not what you bring with you.

'Well – if I shan't be in the way? I mean – I don't think Paddy particularly wants to come home with a lifeguard attached. Won't his people –?' It was a long time since he'd been Paddy's age, but with a heroic effort of the imagination he could still put himself in the other fellow's place.

524

'Now that's thoughtful of you, but take it from me, Dominic, this is one ego that needs no tenderness from you or anyone.' He took Paddy by the nape of the neck and propelled him briskly towards the rising path that led up through the dunes towards the stubble-fields. 'Come on, no argument!' He took Dominic, surprisingly but with absolute confidence, by the neck with the other hand, and hustled them into a trot. He was a man who could do things like that, and not only get away with it, but get himself liked for it, where someone less adept would have given electrifying offence.

'What about Paddy's clothes?'

'Oh, he came down from home in his trunks. Always does. First thing in the morning, and again in the afternoon. I told you, his parents gave birth to a herring. Come on, run for it!'

And they ran, glad to warm themselves with exercise; across the undulating coastal road, and through the hollow lane to the gate of Pentarno farm. A deep hollow of trees, startlingly lush and beautiful as always wherever there was shelter in this wild and sea-swept land, enfolded the solid grey stone house and the modern farm buildings.

'I don't live here,' explained Simon as he opened the gate. 'I'm just a long-standing nuisance from Tim's schooldays, that turns up from time to time and makes itself at home.'

The front door stood open on a long, low, farmhouse hall, populous with doors. At the sound of their footsteps on the stone floor one of the doors flew open, and Philippa Rossall leaned out, in denims and a frilly pinafore, her arms flour to the elbow.

'Well, about time! I thought I should have to start 'phoning the hospitals. When you two quit showing up for *meals* – '

She broke off there, grey eyes opening wide, because there were not two of them, but three. She was middle-sized, and middling-pretty, and medium about everything, except that all the lines of her face were shaped for laughter. She had a mane of dark hair, and lopsided eyebrows that gave her an amused look even in repose, and a smile that warmed the house.

'Oh, I didn't realise we had company. Hallo!' She took in suddenly their wet and tangled hair, and the way their clothes clung to them, and swung for an instant between astonishment and alarm, but beholding them all intact and apparently composed, rejected both in favour of amusement. 'Well!' she said. 'Never a dull moment with Simon Towne around. What have you all been doing? Diving off the pier for pennies? No, never mind, whatever you've been up to, go and get out of those clothes first, while I get my baking in and make another pot of tea. And be careful how you turn on the shower, the water's very hot. Simon, find him some of your clothes and take care of him, there's a lamb. Tim isn't in from the cows yet.'

Tim came in at that moment by the back door, a large, broad, tranquil person with a sceptical face and guileless eyes, attired in a sloppy, hand-knitted sweater and corduroys.

'Bodies, actually,' said Simon. 'Off the point.'

'Eh?' said Tim dubiously, brought up short against this cryptic pronouncement.

'Phil asked if we'd been diving for pennies off the pier. And I said, no, bodies. Off the point. But we didn't find any. This is Dominic Felse, by the way. Dominic's staying up at the Dragon. He was kind enough to fish Paddy out of the sea when he was in difficulties. Paddy says he wasn't in difficulties, but Dominic fished him out, anyhow. So we brought him back to tea.'

'Good!' said Philippa, with such large acceptance that there was no guessing whether she meant to express gratification at having her offspring rescued from the Atlantic, or receiving an unexpected guest to tea. The look she gave Dominic was considerably more communicative, if he had not been too dazed to notice it.

'He fetched me a clip on the ear, too,' volunteered Paddy, who would certainly not have mentioned this circumstance if he had not already forgiven it, and resolved to complete the removal of the smart by exorcism.

'Good!' said Tim. 'Somebody should, every now and again. We're much obliged to you, Dominic. Stick around, if you enjoyed it – there may be other occasions.'

The first, and brief, silence, which it must certainly have been Dominic's turn to fill, found him speechless, and drew all their eyes upon him in understanding sympathy. It appeared that the Rossall brand of verbal table-tennis had taken at a disadvantage this slender and serious young man who didn't yet know the rules.

'It's always this kind of a madhouse here,' Paddy told him kindly. 'You'll get used to it. Just muck in and take everything for granted, it's the only way.'

But it seemed that was not the trouble. Dominic had not even heard all the latter part of the conversation, and he did not hear this. He looked from Simon to Phil, and back to Simon again, and his eyes were shining.

'You did say *Simon Towne*? Really? You mean – *the* Simon Towne?'

'Heaven help us!' said Phil Rossall devoutly. 'There surely can't be *two*?'

Dominic rushed up the stairs of the Dragon Hotel just after half-past seven, made a ten-minute business of changing, and tapped at his parents' door. Bunty, who had been struggling with the back zipper of her best dress, relaxed with a sigh of relief, and called him in.

'Just in time, darling! Come and do me up.'

It was convenient to have him there at her shoulder, where she could watch him in the mirror without being herself watched, or observed to be watching. For the dark suit had surprised her. He was no fonder of dressing up, as a general rule, than his father. The look of restrained satisfaction which surveyed the sleek fit of the gold silk sheath over her shoulders, and the pleased pat he bestowed on her almost unconsciously as he closed the last inch of zipper, confirmed what the dark suit and the austere tie had suggested. Apparently she'd done the right thing. He was studying the total effect now with deep thoughtfulness. One more minute, and he'd have his fingers in her trinket-case, or be criticising her hairstyle. Something was on for to-night; something she didn't yet know about. But by the mute, half-suppressed excitement of his face she soon would. Provided, of course, that she didn't ask.

'I was wondering where you'd got to. You must have walked a long way.'

'Well, no, actually I never got very far. Something happened.'

'Something nice?'

'Yes and no. Not really, I suppose. But then, I don't think there ever was anyone there in the water, I think he just spotted some bit of flotsam. And then I had tea with some people I met.' That had been nice, at any rate; he shone secretly at the remembrance, and with difficulty contained his own radiance. A girl? Bunty didn't think so, somehow. When remembering and containing encounters with girls he wore another face, conscientiously sophisticated and a little smug. This, though it strove after a man-of-the-world detachment, was the rapt face of a second-former noticed by the skipper of the First Fifteen.

He perched suddenly on the end of the dressing-table stool beside her, and put his arm round her, half to sustain his position, half in the old gambit that made confidences easy. The two faces, cheek to cheek in the mirror, were almost absurdly alike, oval, fair-complexioned, with freckled noses and large, bright hazel eyes. The two thick thatches of chestnut hair – She turned, nostrils quivering to the faint, damp scent, and put up a hand to feel at his forelock.

'Hmm! I see there was at least one someone there in the water. I didn't know you even took your trunks with you.'

'I didn't, love! Look, I'll tell you!' But he'd do it his own way. He tightened his arm round her waist. The brightness was

beginning to burst through. 'Mummy, do you know who's staying in Maymouth?'

'Yes, darling, the distinguished Midshire C.I.D. man,
Detective-Inspector George Felse, with his beautiful wife, and
handsome and brilliant son.' And the said George was already
down in the bar, waiting for his family to join him for dinner;
and the only concession he had made to the evening was to add
a silk scarf to his open-necked shirt. Whereas it looked as if
Dominic had everything lined up for a very special impression.
She wondered if there'd be time to get George into a suit, and
whether she owed it to Dominic to demand such a sacrifice of
his father.

'Mummy, you said it! You look gorgeous. How about those
black crystals? They'd go beautifully with this dress.' He had
his fingers in among the few bits of finery she'd brought with
her, fishing for the necklace he approved. 'Keep still. No, but
really, Mummy, do you know who's here? Not in the hotel,
staying with some friends of his at the farm over at Pentarno.
Simon Towne!'

She opened her eyes wide at the gleaming, triumphant face
in the mirror. 'No! Is he, *really*?' Now who on earth, she
wondered for a moment, could Simon Towne be? This was a
difficult game to play unless you had at least an inkling. Or, of
course, there was always the deflationary play. The dead-pan
face, the sudden flat, honest voice: 'Who's Simon Towne?'

'Mummy, you shameless humbug! You were keener even than
I was on those articles he did on Harappa and Mohenjo-daro.
And that book on ancient and modern Peru – remember? Simon
Towne is just about the most celebrated roving freelance journal-
ist and broadcaster in the world, that's who Simon Towne is.
As you very well know! And he's staying with the Rossalls at
Pentarno until he sets off on another round-the-world
commission in October. And I met him this afternoon!'

And I'm going to meet him to-night, thought Bunty with
certainty; that's what all the fancy-work is for.

She took her exalted son by the arm and sat him firmly down beside her again. 'You tell me every word about it, quickly.'

He told her, and she paid him generously in reflected joy, and had no difficulty in appearing duly impressed; even *was* a little impressed. Yes, George would have to suffer; they couldn't let Dominic down. Meantime, she had to get downstairs ahead of him. It wasn't difficult; he'd given her enough clues.

'Sorry, Dom, I've mussed your hair a little. It's a bit fluffy from being wet so recently. Use George's cream. He left it in the bathroom, I think.'

He went like a lamb. She called after him: 'I'm going down, I'll be in the bar.' And fled. He'd be five minutes re-settling his crest to his satisfaction.

George was on a stool at the bar, leaning on his elbow; long and easy and thin, and physically rather elegant in his heedless fashion, but not dressed for a momentous meeting. Actually Bunty preferred him as he was, but a gesture was called for.

She dug a hard little finger into his ribs from behind, and said softly and rapidly into his ear: 'Collar and tie and suit, my boy, and hurry. Dom's captured a lion, and I think he's bringing the whole pride in to coffee, or something.'

George turned a face not yet shocked out of its comfortable languor. 'Don't be funny, girl, it's nearly eight o'clock. There isn't time. Even if I could be bribed to do it. I'm on holiday, remember?'

'So's Dom, and I tell you he's just aching to be proud of us. Just once won't hurt you. Look at me!'

George did, and smiled. 'You look good enough to eat.' He swivelled reluctantly on the stool. 'Oh, all right, I'll do it. But I won't perform.'

'You won't get the chance, Dom will be straight man to the lion, and the rest of us will be the audience. Go on, *quickly*! He's coming!'

George unfolded his long legs, looked at his watch, and shot away in time to meet Dominic in the doorway. 'Lord, I've left it late to change. Got talking to Sam, and never noticed the time. Go keep your mother company, I'll be down in ten minutes.'

Dominic, with a face of extreme maturity and dignity, wound his way between the tables to the bar, and perched himself without a word on the stool next to Bunty's. She gave him a sweet, wide look which never wavered before his severe stare. Behind the bar Sam Shubrough lifted an interrogatory eyebrow.

'Manzanilla, please,' said Dominic austerely, and slid an uneasy hazel glance sideways at his mother. She hadn't giggled; she hadn't made a sound or turned a hair, but the effect was the same. He had been eighteen for such a short time that he hadn't mastered his face yet on these occasions.

'It's all right, lamb,' she said in his ear wickedly, 'you're doing fine. You don't blush any more. But you haven't *quite* got over that tendency to a brazen stare yet.'

'Thanks for the tip, I'll practise in front of a mirror. All right, Mum-Machiavelli,' he said darkly. 'You needn't think I don't know what a clever minx you are, because I do. Which tie did you tell him to put on?'

'Anything you want to know about Maymouth and environs,' said Tim Rossall, over coffee in the lounge, 'just ask that well-known authority, Simon here. He's never been down here for more than three days at a time, not until this visit, but what he doesn't know about the place and its history by now isn't worth knowing. No, I mean it! He made a big hit with my Aunt Rachel, and she's given him the run of her library up there at the Place.'

'The Place? That's Treverra Place? That big pile with the towers, at the top end of Maymouth?'

'That's it. Phoney towers, actually, they built 'em on late in the nineteenth century. The old girl rattles round in that huge dump like a pea in a drum, but she's still got the money to keep it up, and nobody else has. When she goes the National Trust will have to take it, or else it'll simply have to fall down.'

531

'The National Trust wouldn't touch the place,' said Phil cheerfully. 'Tim's mother was Miss Rachel's younger sister. He's the last nephew, and he's horribly afraid she'll leave the house to him. There's a fine kitchen garden, though. She grows splendid apricots – a bit late ripening, but a lovely flavour. They'll be ready any day now, I must get her to send you some.'

Dominic sat back happily in his corner and surveyed his successful and voluble party. They were all there but Paddy, who had gone to a cinema with friends of his own age; but Paddy, thought Dominic in the arrogance of his eighteen years, would have been bored, anyhow, in this adult circle. And they were getting on like a house afire. They'd liked one another on sight. Phil Rossall looked a different but equally attractive person with her dark hair coiled on top of her head, and her boy's figure disguised in a black, full-skirted dress. And Simon – no one ever seemed to call him anything but Simon – was the centre of any group he joined, even when he was silent and listening. Everything was going beautifully.

'A wild lot, these Treverras,' Simon was saying, one wicked brown eye on Tim. 'I'm thinking of writing the family history. Unless you make it worth my while not to, of course.'

'Me? I'm relying on selling the film rights. Go right ahead. Two of 'em hanged for complicity in various faction plots, one time and another, several of 'em smuggled – '

'They all smuggled,' said Phil firmly.

'But the most celebrated of the lot was the poet-squire, Jan Treverra, in the eighteenth century. Go on, Simon, you're the expert, tell 'em about Jan.'

'On your own head be it! No one can stop me once I start. But let's adjourn to the bar, shall we? It's cosier down there.'

They adjourned to the bar. There was a panelled corner that just held them all, with one place to spare, and Phil spread her skirt across that, with the glint of a smile at Simon.

'That's for Tam, if she drops in later.'

'Tam?'

532

'Tamsin Holt, Aunt Rachel's secretary. It's only a quarter of an hour's walk from the Place, across the Dragon's neck. We're about on the same level, up here. And I should think the poor girl's had enough of Miss Rachel by evening. She is,' said Phil blandly, 'the real reason for Simon's passionate interest in the Treverra Library. She's re-cataloguing it and collating all the family papers. And when she takes off her glasses she isn't bad-looking. All right, Simon, go ahead, give us the story of Jan Treverra.'

Simon lay back in his corner and talked. Not expertly, not with calculation, it was better than that; halting sometimes, relapsing into his own thoughts, hunting a word and coming up with it thoughtfully and with pleasure, as if it had a taste. Some of his writing was like that, the lamest and the most memorable. Dominic had the impression that those particular pages had been born out of his less happy moments.

'Jan was an individualist who smuggled and wrote and hunted in these parts about the middle of the eighteenth century. You must have noticed St. Nectan's church, I suppose? You'll have read about it even before you came here, if you're the kind of person who does read a place up before he visits it?'

'We read about it,' admitted George. 'We're the kind.'

'Good, I like that kind. Then you know all about it, and anyhow you can see it from the top windows here. Over in the dunes, where they've been planting all the tamarisks to try and stop the sand marching inland. I don't know exactly what it is about this north coast, but there are several of these areas of encroaching sand, and nearly all of 'em have churches amidships to get buried. It's never houses, always churches.'

'They're surely digging out St. Nectan's, aren't they?' George looked across at Bunty. 'You remember, they'd uncovered all the graveyard when we were over there, and that's several days ago.'

'*We're* digging it out. With these two hands I've shovelled sand to get at what I want. The fact is, as Tim will tell you, they do get fits of conscience here every now and again, and dig the place out, but they always forget it again as soon as they've finished, and in a couple of months the sand's got it again. But the point is, that's where Jan Treverra's buried. He had a massive tomb dug out for himself there before he was fifty, right down into the rock, and he wrote his own epitaph, ready for when he died. He even wrote one for his wife, too. In verse. Not his best verse, but not bad, at that. And soon after he was fifty he did die, of a fever, so they say. Quite a character was Jan. His life was not exemplary, but at least it had gusto, and it was never mean. He was a faithful husband and a loyal friend. The whole district idolised him, and his wife pined away within six months of his death, and joined him in his famous vault. His poems were pretty good, actually. There's a tradition that some of them were buried with him, at his own orders, and now Miss Rachel's developed a desire to find out if it's true.'

'Not unprompted,' said Phil, 'by Simon. Any quest that gives him free access to the library will have our Simon's enthusiastic support. As long as Tamsin's in there, of course.'

'Not that it's getting me anywhere,' admitted Simon with a charmingly rueful smile. 'She's refused me eight times, so far. Funny, she doesn't seem to take me seriously. Where was I? Oh, yes. On the night following Mrs. Treverra's funeral there was a sudden violent storm. It drove all the fishing boats out to sea, and wrecked two of them. And young Squire Treverra, the new owner, was out walking by himself on the cliff path when the wind suddenly rose, and he was blown off into the sea and drowned. They never recovered his body. So there never was another burial in the old vault, because by the time the younger brother died it was past 1830, and they'd given up the struggle with the sand, and built St. Mary Magdalene's, right at the top end of Maymouth. They didn't intend to lose *that* one. So for all we know it may be true about the poems in the coffin. Anyhow, as Maymouth's in the throes of its periodical fit of conscience about letting St. Nectan's get silted up, we're in a fair way to find out.'

534

'You're thinking of opening the tomb?' asked George with interest.

'We've got a dispensation. In the interests of literature. If we miss this chance, who knows when we shall get another?' He thumped a fist suddenly and peremptorily on the oak table. 'And I propose – Hear ye! Hear ye! – I propose to do the job the day after tomorrow, as ever is.'

The whole public bar heard it, and several heads turned to grin in their direction; there was nobody among the Dragon's regulars who Simon did not know, or who did not know Simon. Sam Shubrough heard it, and beamed broadly over the glass he was polishing. And the girl just entering the bar by the outside door heard it, and turned towards them at a light, swinging walk, her hands in the pockets of her fisher-knit jacket.

'Hallo!' she said, over Dominic's startled shoulder. 'What's Simon advertising? Carpet sale, or something?'

'Tamsin!' The men shuffled to find foot-room to rise, and Phil drew her skirt close and made room for the newcomer in the circle.

'One thing about a man who announces his intentions through a megaphone,' she said as she sat down and stretched out her long and very graceful legs, 'you do at least know where he is, and how to avoid him.'

'You came straight here, a pin to a magnet,' said Simon promptly.

She looked round the table and counted. 'There are six of you here. Five would have been enough. Some,' she added, with a smile of candid interest that robbed her directness of all offence, 'I don't know yet. I'm Tamsin Holt.'

Tim did the honours. She smiled last and longest at Dominic, because he was looking at her with such startled and appreciative eyes. 'Hallo! Phil told me about you. You pulled her Patrick out of the water this afternoon.'

'Did she tell you he didn't want to come?' Dominic felt his colour rising; but the tide of pleasure in him rose with it. She

535

was so astonishing, after Phil's mendacious description. Glasses, indeed! The bridge of her straight nose had certainly never carried any such burden. And as for 'not bad-looking'!

'She told me maybe he didn't even *need* to come. But she said she'd like to think there'd always be you around whenever he even *might* need you. Take it from me, my boy, you're in. You've been issued with a membership ticket.' She looked up over her shoulder, where Sam Shubrough's granite bulk was looming like one of the Maymouth rocks, a monolith with a good-humoured beetroot for a face. Half of its royal redness was concealed behind a set of whiskers which looked early-nineteenth-century-coachman, but were actually ex-R.A.F., 'Hallo, Sam! Nice night for a walk.'

To judge by the small, demure glint that flashed from her eyes to the landlord's, this meant more than it said. But then, she had a way of making everything a fraction more significant. Ever since she had sat down beside him Dominic had been trying to assimilate the complete image of her, and she wouldn't give him the chance. She was always in motion, and all he could master was the lovely detail.

'That right, now,' asked Sam interestedly, peering down at Dominic from behind the hedge, 'that you fetched young Paddy out? That's the first time anybody's ever had to do *that*. Where'd he manage to get into trouble?'

'Off the rocks of the point, just in the ebb, the worst time.'

'Go on! What possessed a bright kid like him to go out there? He knows a lot better than that.'

'He thought he saw a body being pulled out to sea there,' Dominic explained. 'He went in to try and reach him. But we went in afterwards and hunted as long as we could – at least, Mr. Towne did. I didn't do much – and there wasn't a sign of anything.'

'A body, eh! Not that it would be the first time, by many a one. But I've heard no word of anyone being missing, or of anything being sighted. No boat's been in trouble for months, this is the best of the season. You reckon there's anything in it, Simon?'

'I doubt it,' said Simon tranquilly. 'He saw something, he's no fool. But I don't think for a moment it was a man. Bit of driftwood, or something, even a cluster of weed, that'll be all.'

'Well,' said Sam, comfortably, accumulating empty glasses with large, deft fingers, 'if it was a body, we'll probably know by tomorrow. Way the wind's setting now, the next incoming tide in the small hours will leave it high and dry on the Mortuary, same as it always does.'

'The Mortuary?' Simon looked up with raised brows.

'That stretch of sand this side the church at Pentarno, where all the weed builds up. Almost anything that goes out off the point comes in again next tide on that reach. Many a one we've brought in from there. They don't call it the Mortuary for nothing.' He stood brandishing his bouquet of dead men, and beamed at them cheerfully. 'What'll it be, Miss Holt? Gin and tonic? Any more orders, ladies and gents?'

George claimed the round, and Dominic backed carefully and gracefully out of it, because both his mother and his father had refrained from looking at him as if he ought to.

Something remarkable had happened suddenly to the circle. The two vehement people, the two who glittered and were always in motion, had fallen still and silent together. Simon was sitting with his hands folded before him on the table, all the lines of his long-boned face arrested in a Gothic mask, the brightness of his eyes turned inward. The stillness of the energetic often has a quite unjustified effect of remoteness and sadness. Their sleep sometimes has a look of withdrawal and death. And Tamsin – Dominic could see her whole for the first time, the pale oval of her face, the broad, determined brow under the smooth fringe of red-gold hair, the thoughtful, fierce and tender mouth, a little too large for perfection but just the right size for generosity and beauty; and the eyes, very dark blue under their startling black lashes, wide and watchful and withholding judgment, fixed upon Simon. If he looked at her she would lower the more steely blue of the portcullis, and her mouth would shape a dart quickly and hurl it. But now she studied, and thought, and wondered, and could not be sure.

'Gin and tonic,' said Sam, leaning between them with the tray. 'Bitter? Whisky on the rocks, that's Simon. Mild – that's Mr. Felse.'

Simon came out of his abstraction with a start, and reached for his whisky.

'Doing the job down at the church day after tomorrow, are you?' said Sam conversationally. 'That'll be a day for Maymouth. Nobody still kicking about it being irreverent, and all that?'

It was rather quiet in the bar. A frieze of benign local faces beamed at the corner table. A tenuous little cord of private fun drew them all close together for a moment.

'Only the cranks, Sam, only the cranks. Look at the top-weight we've got on our side. The church sanctions it, and Miss Rachel insists on it. Tim will represent the family's interests, and the Vicar'll be there to see fair play. How about you, Sam? Come and make a fourth witness? Ten o'clock in the morning, sharp!'

Just for a fraction of a second those two looked each other blandly in the eye, and the Maymouth regulars grinned like gargoyles along the wall.

'Wouldn't miss it, Simon,' said Sam Shubrough heartily. 'Any time you want a strong-arm man, you call on me. Ten o'clock sharp. I'll be there.'

From the hotel on the headland a broad path brought them to the slight dip of the Dragon's neck, where the road between Maymouth and Pentarno clambered over the humpbacked beast that slept in the moonlight. Their path crossed it and moved on through the highest roads, half backstreet, half country lane, of the quiet town of Maymouth, towards the towered monstrosity of Treverra Place.

'It's a lovely night,' said Dominic dreamily, halting at the edge of the road, unwilling to cross, and shorten the way he still had to walk beside her.

'Lovely,' said Tamsin.

'If you're not tired – '

'I'm not tired.'

'I thought we could walk along the cliff road towards Pentarno a little way, and then turn in by the other lane.'

'If you like, yes, of course.'

It was his day. She'd said yes to everything he'd suggested, the first dance, the offer to escort her home, and now this delicate prolonging of his pleasure. Perhaps to leave him room to expand and show his paces, because that was what he wanted, and she liked him well enough to give him his head, and certainly needed no help to manage him. Or perhaps to mark more clearly how firmly she had said no to everything Simon had asked of her. She had played Dominic's game neatly back to him, and she knew already what he didn't yet know: that he wasn't in love with her in the least degree, and never would be, though there would be times when he would feel that he was. Nobody was going to get hurt by the game, it wasn't going to get rough; but they would both enjoy it and learn something from it, and be a little bit the richer ever after. What she hadn't expected was that he would say anything in the least extraordinary or out of the pattern. And when he had, their relationship had opened out on quite another plane. The game would delight him while his holiday lasted, and make it memorable afterwards. But the second relationship might well last much longer, and be seriously valued by them both. And neither of them would break any hearts. So she went on saying yes; yes to everything.

They had reached the edge of the dunes, and halted there on the seaward side of the road. The moon laid rippling scallops of luminosity along the sea, and away on their right the squat spire of St. Nectan's tiny church protruded from its hollow of sand, half-obscured by the ruled hedges of tamarisks.

'Tamsin – may I call you Tamsin?'

'Yes, of course, Dominic.'

'Tamsin – how much do you really like Simon?'

She had never been more startled in her life. It hadn't taken her long to see that he was almost as dazzled by Simon as Paddy himself. She couldn't blame him; she knew all about that powerful magnetism, even if she herself was immune from responding to it. But he wasn't protesting or wondering, he was asking her, as one friend to another. Maybe he felt it flattering to be even a make-believe rival of the great man. Or maybe he just wanted to know. Or maybe, even more dangerously, he wanted to hear what she would say, because she wouldn't be answering him, and that would tell him a great deal.

'I like him well enough, but for certain attitudes. And those I don't like at all.'

'Then he really has asked you to marry him?'

At first she thought that his sophistication must have slipped very badly to permit him to ask such a thing; then the deliberation of his voice warned her that they were on the second plane, and this was in earnest.

'Yes, he has.'

'Eight times?'

'I haven't counted. Probably. Most times we meet.'

'Why don't you?'

'Why don't I what? Count?'

'Marry him.'

'Look,' she said, turning her back on the shining innocence of the sea, 'even if he meant it, the answer would still be no. But he doesn't. He's spoiled and flippant and mischievous, and in bad need of a fall. He's only had to smile at people all his life, and whatever he wanted has fallen into his lap. And he doesn't care what he breaks in the process. No, that's too steep.

He just doesn't realise that he breaks anything, all he sees is his own wants. He's just having fun with me.'

'*I* shouldn't think it much fun,' said Dominic, 'to ask you to marry me and get turned down.'

'You're not Simon, my dear. Do you think he'd be concerning himself with why I turned *you* down – supposing I ever did?'

'No,' agreed Dominic honestly, 'but then, he's in love with you, and – '

It was the first mistake he had made, fumbling between the two planes of his liking for her, and he was thrown out of his stride by the gaffe. To cover himself he took her rather agitatedly in his arms, gingerly in case she objected, but already almost persuaded she wouldn't. She was laughing; she shook gently with honest amusement against his chest.

'And you're not! Go on, say – '

He did not so much lose his head as throw it away, and without it he was much more adept. He felt gently downward with his lips to her mouth, and kissed her. It wasn't the first time, he knew what he was doing. But perhaps it was the first of its kind, warm and impulsive and affectionate, and quite untroubled.

When it was over he held her for some minutes still, not wanting to talk.

'That wasn't necessary,' she said in his ear.

'No, I know it wasn't.'

'Aren't you going to say you're sorry?'

'No. I'm glad. I enjoyed it very much, and so did you. But I won't do it again, because it would spoil it.'

'You,' she said helplessly, 'are an extraordinary boy.'

'I wouldn't be, if I were with an ordinary girl.'

His cheek against hers, the baffling unusualness of the day overwhelming him with the delicious conviction of complete happiness, suddenly he froze. His mind went away from her, somewhere there over her shoulder, down among the dunes. She pushed him away suddenly, and turned to look.

'Tamsin, do you see what I see? Look, there between the tamarisks.' One man, two, three, slipping along out of the landward hollow, keeping in the tenuous shade of the young hedges, moving towards the church in its deep nest.

Tamsin shivered and took his arm, turning him about and drawing him landward across the road. 'Ugh, it's getting cold. I'd better get home, Dominic. Come on, we've got ten minutes' walking yet.'

George was still on the hotel terrace, smoking his last pipe and watching the sea.

'Hallo!' he said, hearing the unmistakable step of his son and heir moving up on him quietly from the garden. 'How'd you make out?'

'Don't be nosy,' said Dominic austerely, and came and sat down on the arm of the chair.

'Dad – '

'Hmmm?'

'Do you suppose,' asked Dominic very casually, 'that there's much smuggling in these parts nowadays?'

After a long and cautious silence George said weightily: 'Now, look, I'm on holiday. I intend to remain that way. The local excisemen and police are quite capable of running their own show. And it's no business of mine where Sam gets his brandy.'

'That's what I thought,' said Dominic cheerfully. 'So, quite unofficially, of course, what d'you make of this?' And he told him exactly what he had seen in the region of St. Nectan's church, though not the precise circumstances in which he had come to see it.

'Going towards the church,' said George carefully. 'And Tamsin took good care to remove you from the vicinity as soon as she realised what was going on. Yes, quite interesting.'

'Especially,' said Dominic, 'since Simon made such a point of broadcasting in the bar exactly when he intended to open the Treverra vault. And then grinned at Sam, and invited him – '

542

'Or dared him?' suggested George.

' – to be present on the occasion. And the hint and the challenge were taken. On the spot.'

'Now I wonder just where the safe–deposit was?'

'I wonder, too. In the vault itself, do you think?'

'Now mind,' said George warningly, 'not a word to anyone else. We're only in this game by courtesy, if we're in it at all. It's the local man's manor.'

Dominic rose from the arm of the chair, and stretched and yawned magnificently.

'What do you take me for?' he said scornfully, and strolled away to bed.

Chapter 2

Thursday

'It's tomorrow, then,' observed Paddy, coming in damp and boisterous from his morning swim, and plumping himself down hungrily at the breakfast table.

Tim looked up from the paper. 'What's tomorrow?'

'The big day. The day we take the lid off the old gentleman. Mummy said Uncle Simon was alerting the squad last night. Wouldn't do if anybody got caught with his pants down, would it? Except the squire, I suppose it's all one to him by this time.'

Not at his most gay and extrovert in the morning, Tim squinted almost morosely at his son over his coffee cup, and wondered if anyone, even at fifteen, could really be as bright and callous as this before breakfast.

'I know!' said Paddy, fending off the look with a grin. 'That's no way to talk about the dead. Still, I bet he's the only one around Maymouth who isn't excited about this bit of research. *I* am! And if you're not, you ought to be. It's your family. And just think, we may be making history.' He reached for the cereal packet as if it had been the crock of gold, and helped himself liberally. 'Mummy, how's that fresh coffee coming?'

From the corridor Phil's voice retorted hollowly: 'Being carried by me, as usual.' She came in with the tray, and closed the door expertly with her elbow.

Paddy received his cup, laced it with brown sugar to his liking, and returned happily to his preoccupation.

'Think we really shall find anything, Dad? In the coffin?'

Phil stiffened, the coffee-pot suspended in her hand. She looked from her husband to her son, and inquired in suspiciously mild tones: 'And where did you get the 'we'?'

Paddy's eyes widened in momentary doubt and dismay, and smiled again in the immediate confidence that she must be pulling his leg. 'Come off it! You wouldn't go and spoil it, would you? Not when it's Uncle Simon's own personal project? I've got to be there, of course.' His smile sagged a little; her face hadn't melted. 'Oh, gosh, you *wouldn't* make me miss the only bit of real excitement there's ever going to be in Maymouth?' Inevitably he appealed to Tim across the table. 'Dad, you didn't say I couldn't. We were just talking about it, and you *didn't* say – '

'I didn't say you could,' said Tim, truthfully, but aware that he was hedging. He looked doubtfully at Phil's cloudy face, observed the set of her jaw, and could have kicked himself. He should have known that she wouldn't think grubbing about among tombs and bones a proper occupation for her ewe lamb. Mothers are like that. Especially mothers as achingly unsure of their hold on what they love as Phil.

'No, but I thought you understood that I was taking it for granted. You must have known I wanted to be there, you could have told me right away if you didn't mean to let me. I'm sorry if I should have asked, but I never thought. I'll ask now. Please, Mummy, is it all right with you if I go along with Uncle Simon and Dad to open Jan Treverra's tomb tomorrow?'

He recited this in a parody of his child's voice, wrinkling his nose at her provocatively; which, according to all the rules, should have been the right thing, and paid off handsomely. But it wasn't the right thing, and it wasn't going to pay off. He saw it at once, and was appalled to think he had so stupidly clinched the case against himself. Never reduce anything to a formula; if you do, you're stuck with it.

'No,' said Phil, gently but firmly. 'I'm sorry, but it isn't all right with me. You're not going, and that's that. Now forget it.'

Paddy pushed his chair back a little, brows drawn down over a level and injured stare. 'Why not? Why don't you want me to?'

'Because it's no place for you, and I'd rather you stayed away from it.'

'Think I'd be having nightmares?' he demanded, suddenly breaking into a broad but uncertain smile. 'Now, look, Mummy, I'm fifteen. I know what bones are like, and I know we're all going the same way in the end. It doesn't worry me a bit. You needn't be afraid I'll turn morbid.'

'*No!*' said Phil with unmistakable finality, refusing argument. She herself couldn't be certain of her motives, but she knew that the thought of letting him go down those sand-worn steps into the vault horrified her, and at all costs she wanted to prevent it.

Paddy recognised a closed and locked door, but would not acknowledge it as impassable. He made the mistake of casting a glance sidelong at Simon's place, where a carelessly folded newspaper left lying showed the state of the day. Apparently he'd breakfasted already, which was unusual and a pity. He could have diverted this disaster if it had threatened in his presence. Paddy pushed away his plate, and smoothed his forehead conscientiously, like a man-of-the-world tactfully recognising when to change the subject.

'Where's Uncle Simon?'

'No good,' said Tim, not without sympathy. 'You haven't an ally, my boy. He's gone up to the Place already.'

'Up early, wasn't he?' The implication that he was looking round for support he ignored, though he knew nobody was deceived.

'Now, look, Paddy,' said Tim with emphasis, 'let it alone. She's said no, and I say no, and that's all about it.'

Paddy's fist slammed the table. He jerked his chair back and was on his feet in a blaze of rage. That temper had cost them plenty in patience and forbearance in his early years, but they hadn't seen much of it lately, and this abrupt flare was as startling as lightning. It was almost a man's rage, quiet and quivering. The dilated nostrils looked almost blue with tension.

'What are you trying to do, keep me a kid? You can't! If I've got to grow up in spite of you, I'll do it that way, and be damned to it!'

He didn't even shout; his voice was lower than usual. And he turned and flung out of the room and out of the house before either of them could draw breath to stop him.

'The awful part of it is,' owned Phil, 'I don't know how honest I'm being about this. I don't want him to go, I don't think it's any place for an adolescent boy. But I know darned well I'm jealous of Simon. He only has to crook his finger, and Paddy comes running. You'd think no one else existed, this last week or so. It scares me.'

'Our own fault, I suppose.' Tim turned glumly from the window and looked her in the eyes long and sombrely. 'We ought to have known we should have to tell him, sooner or later. We should have done it long ago. I only wish we had.'

'But how could we know we should have to? I know it's supposed to be bad policy not to. But we were going to move here, everything was new. Nobody knew us, except Aunt Rachel. Nobody cared. I couldn't see any *reason*. And now – how in the world could we ever set about it, after all this time?'

'We couldn't. We daren't. There isn't a thing we can do, except just keep our fingers crossed, and let him alone. It won't be long now.'

'No,' she agreed, but only half-comforted. 'Tim – suppose Simon tells him?'

'No! He wouldn't do that. He's always kept his bargain so far, hasn't he?'

'He's never really wanted to break it before,' said Phil cynically, 'but this time he does. And much as I like him, I wouldn't trust him far when he's after something he wants.'

She got up with a sigh, and began loading the breakfast dishes on to the tray. There had been a time when she had been equally jealous of Simon's influence over Tim, until she found out by experience that Tim, after his quiet fashion, went his own way, and was very unlikely to be deflected from it by Simon or anyone else.

'Think I'd better go after him?'

'Tim, don't you dare give way to him, after I've gone and committed myself!'

'You've committed me, too,' said Tim with a wry grin. 'Don't worry – united we stand! Still, it was pretty much my fault he'd got the programme all set up like that. I think I'd better go and find him, and get him cooled down.'

But Paddy was not in the house, or the garden, or the yard, nor was he visible anywhere on the road to the sea. Tim came back empty-handed.

'His bike's gone from the shed. Never mind him, let him go. He'll be back for his lunch. Give him that, at any rate, he doesn't sulk for long.'

'What'll you bet,' said Phil sharply, 'he hasn't gone rushing up to the Place after Simon? I *bet* you! He thinks Simon will get round us. He thinks Simon can get round anybody.'

She plunged upon the telephone in the hall, and dialled the number of Treverra Place.

'Oh, hallo, Tam – '

But it wasn't Tamsin; the telephone was switched to Miss Rachel's room, and the old lady was wide awake and only too ready to talk. And perhaps that was better, for if it had been Tamsin and the library, more than likely Simon would have been there to hear one half of the conversation and deduce the other.

'Oh, it's you, Aunt Rachel. This is Phil. Listen, is Simon there in the library right now? No, I don't want him, I just want to know. Good, that's fine. Well, look, if our Paddy comes looking for him, don't tell him where he's gone, will you? And don't let Tamsin tell him. I know he'll find him in the end, but he won't think of the vicarage for a while, anyhow – long enough for him to think better of it, I hope.'

'Exactly why,' inquired Miss Rachel curiously, 'should he be on his way here, and why don't you want him to find Simon? Oh, I'll do what you say, naturally. But I do like to have reasons for what I'm doing.'

Phil sat down and drew the instrument into a comfortable position for a long session. Tim, recognising the signs, sighed and left them to it. What could you do with women? They were as dead set on not being outwitted or defeated as the kid himself, but it wouldn't be any use pointing out the illogic of their proceedings; they'd never be able to see the analogy.

By the time Paddy had pedalled furiously up the sunken lane and was breasting the climb into the outskirts of Maymouth, he had worked most of the spite out of him, and was coming to the conclusion that after all there was something to be said for his parents' point of view. Not much, of course, but something. Maybe, after all, he wouldn't go behind their backs and coax or trick Simon into promising him what they had denied. For pure pleasure he kept telling himself that he would, but the sight of the absurdly tall and ponderous gateposts of Treverra Place forced him to slow his pace and make up his mind. He took the long drive in a weaving course from rhododendrons to rhododendrons, like a contestant in a slow-bike race, fighting it out. He would, he wouldn't. He wouldn't! He was fifteen, not a spoiled kid in a tantrum. He'd go back at lunchtime and apologise.

Still, now that he was here he might as well drop in and say hallo to Miss Rachel and Tamsin. In fact, he'd have to, because one of them had spotted him already.

Miss Rachel was parading the stretch of gravel in front of the embattled Victorian front door, upright and stocky in a gaudy tweed skirt and hand-knitted purple jumper, the image of an elderly country gentlewoman from a distance. At close quarters she was more of a stage version of the same character, with a mobile, actress's face and bold, autocratic gaze, with a sort of instability about the whole impersonation, as if she was only waiting to complete her scene before whipping off the make-up and dressing for quite another role in quite another play. The one thing that didn't change was that she must always be the central personage. Sometimes she reminded Paddy of Queen Victoria, because of her imperious and impervious respectability and her general shape; at other times he thought of her as a local and latter-day Queen Elizabeth, because she had so successfully charmed younger men after her through most of her life, and could do so still when she really tried. Probably she had stayed single to keep her power, like her great prototype before her, though not for such grand and statesmanlike ends, but for her own personal pleasure.

He was very fond of her. She told him off and complained of him very often, but he didn't have to be a genius to know that she adored him, and that was nearly enough to ensure his affection in return. What clinched it was the unexpected amount of fun she could be at times, sometimes even his ally against the generation in between. She was all the grandmother he had, and grandmothers are a reassuring article of equipment in any boy's life.

So when he saw her stumping up and down examining her roses, it was natural enough to him to turn his bicycle from the main drive along the intricate paths between the flower-beds, and ride down upon her in a sudden flurry of fine gravel, circling her three or four times before he put a foot to the ground and halted to face her. He was at peace with himself by that time, and his face was sunny. They'd been stuffy, but he'd been a complete oaf. He wouldn't do a thing to widen the breach; he'd make his peace like a lamb as soon as he went home.

'Hallo!' he said, uncoiling himself at leisure from the bike and propping it against the huge scraper by the front steps. 'You'm looking very pert this morning, me dear.'

'Am I, indeed?' She tapped her stick peremptorily on the stones that bordered the rose-bed, and gave him a narrowed and glittering glance of her still handsome black eyes. 'Buttering me up will get you nowhere, my boy, let me tell you that for a start. I'm wise to you. You didn't come all the way up here to see me, did you? Oh, dear, no!'

'Well, for Pete's sake!' said Paddy blankly. 'What have I done to you this morning? Did you get out of bed the wrong side? I've only just set foot in the place, give me a chance.'

'Oh, I know! Innocence is your middle name. But it's no use, young man, you're wasting your time. You won't find Simon in the library. He isn't here. And Tamsin won't tell you where he is, either.'

'I wasn't going to – ' he began, stung and enlightened by this attack; and there, remembering in what a state of indecision he had arrived at the gate, he halted and flushed in guilty indignation.

'Oh, no, not *you*! You wouldn't dream of running to Simon behind your mother's back, would you? Don't think I don't know what was in your mind. You think he'll be able to twist your parents round his finger, and get you everything you want, don't you? Even when they've said no. Yes, you see, I know all about it.'

Yes, he saw, and he saw exactly how she had learned what she knew. It didn't take much imagination to reconstruct. His mother must have been on the line like a tigress. What galled him most deeply was not that she should be so determined to frustrate him, but that she should be able to see through him as through plate glass, and anticipate his moves so accurately. And he'd won his struggle and come to terms with her in his mind before it ever came to the point of action. But she'd never made a move towards reconciliation in *her* mind, never allowed for the possibility that he might relent and think better of it. Who was going behind whose back?

'Patrick, you're not listening to me!' The old lady was halfway through the expected lecture, and he hadn't heard a word.

'I am listening,' he said, with bewildering meekness, only half his mind present, the meek half. The rest, hurt, vengeful and obstinate, ranged bitterly after his mother's treason. If she wanted that sort of fight, if she could immediately accept battle on those terms, and never give him the benefit of the doubt, well, she could have it that way.

'If they've said no, that should be enough for you. You're not a little boy now, you know enough to realise they have your best interests at heart, and I thought you had sense enough to accept their judgment, even where you couldn't quite agree with it. Fancy losing your temper over a little thing like that! I'm ashamed of you!'

So his mother hadn't even kept *that* quiet. What could you do with women? They were all the same.

'I was ashamed of myself,' he said, with unexampled mildness; which pleased Miss Rachel so much that she never noticed the significance of the tense he had used. So he had been ashamed, for a few chastened and happy moments as he slow-biked up the drive. But not any more.

'That's better. I know you're not a bad boy at heart. Now you're to put it right out of your mind, you hear me? They've said no, and that's to be the end of it. You're not to pester Simon. You'll go right home and tell your mother you're sorry.'

Will I, hell! thought Paddy very succinctly. Aloud he said: 'O.K., I'm on my way, Aunt Rachel.' But he took good care not to say where.

She watched him mount his bike with exaggerated solemnity, salute her gravely, and pedal away down the drive again in a caricature of penitence and self-examination. He wasn't even ashamed of pulling her leg. Practically speaking, she wasn't in the act at all, she was just a miscalculation on his mother's part.

And now, since that was the way his mother wanted it, now he *would* find Simon, if it took him all day.

It didn't take him all day, but it did take him all morning. He'd tried the church in the sands, and the church in the town, and several other places, before he ran Simon to earth at noon in the lounge of the Dragon, snug in a corner between George and Dominic Felse, with three halves of bitter on their table. Paddy hesitated for a moment, somewhat daunted at having to prefer his plea before witnesses; but in the instant when he might have drawn back, Simon turned his head and saw him hovering.

'Hallo, there!' There was no doubting the welcome and pleasure in his face, but wasn't he, all the same, a shade sombre this morning, a Simon faintly clouded over? Tomorrow was, Paddy reminded himself with a start of surprise and a slight convulsion of an uneasy conscience, a very serious business. 'Looking for me? Anything the matter?' They made room for him, all three rearranging their chairs; he was in it now, he couldn't back out.

'No, nothing. I just wanted – But I'm afraid I'm interrupting you.'

'Not in the least. Oh, I forgot you two hadn't met before. This is Paddy Rossall, George. Say good-morning to Dominic's father, Paddy.'

He had got something out of his pursuit, at any rate. He fixed George with large and hungry eyes. Did he look like a detective-inspector? The trick, he supposed, was not to look like one, but at least George Felse would do pretty well. Tall and thin, with a lean, thoughtful face and hair greying at the temples; not bad-looking, in a pleasant, irregular way. Paddy paid his respects almost reverently, and accepted the offer of a ginger ale.

'What did you want to ask me?'

'Well – if it's all right with you, could I come along and help you tomorrow?' It was out, and in quite a creditable tone, though he had the hardest work in the world not to embroider it with all manner of persuasions and coaxings. His conscience suffered one more convulsive struggle before he suppressed it. If he hadn't confessed that his parents had already forbidden it, still he hadn't told any lies. It was a matter of his adult honour, by this time, not to admit defeat.

Simon sat looking at him for a few moments with an unreadable face, almost as though his mind had wandered away to ponder other and less pleasant subjects. 'It's like this, Paddy,' he said at last, almost abruptly. 'I can't very well say yes to you, in fairness, because I've just said no to Dominic here. There are good reasons, you know. Space is short inside there. And then, this isn't an entertainment, you see, it's a bit of serious research. It wouldn't be the thing to turn it into a spectacle. The witnesses are necessary for the record, not for their own satisfaction.'

In the few seconds of silence George and Dominic exchanged a brief, significant glance over Paddy's averted head. The boy studied his ginger ale as though the secret of the universe lay quivering somewhere in the globule of amber light suspended in it. His face was a little too still to be quite convincing, though the air of commonsense acceptance with which he finally looked up could be counted a success.

'Well, that all makes sense. O.K., then, that's it. You didn't mind my asking, though?'

'Paddy, in other circumstances I don't know a fellow anywhere I'd rather have to help me.'

'Thanks! I'll remember that. I suppose I'd better be getting back to lunch, then. You won't be coming?'

'No, I'm lunching here. I told your mother this morning.'

'Well, thanks for the drink.' He tilted the empty glass and slanted a quick smile up at George. 'Good thing it was only ginger ale.' He rose, his face still a little wry with swallowing his disappointment.

'Why, in particular?' asked Simon curiously.

The boy divided a bright, questioning glance between them. 'Didn't you really know? You've got a real, live detective-inspector sitting right beside you, watching your every move. Mr Felse would have pinched you in a flash if you'd stood me a shandy.' He waved a hand, not ungallantly. 'Goodbye!' He was gone.

'Well, I'm damned!' said Simon, blankly staring. 'Are you really?'

George admitted it. 'But I don't know how Paddy found out.'

'I told him,' said Dominic, a little pink with embarrassment at seeming still, at his mature age, to be boasting about his father's profession. 'When he walked back halfway here with me yesterday, after tea at the farm. We hadn't exactly got off on the right foot with each other, I was rather casting about for acceptable lures. There was Simon – ' He smiled rather self-consciously across the table at the great man. 'Anyone who knows your Harappa articles almost by heart is practically in with Paddy. And the next bid seemed to be you, Dad. He was duly impressed.'

'There's still a bit of Paddy left in me,' owned Simon. '*I'm* impressed. Would you, as a change from sordid modern cases, be interested in my little historical puzzler? Come up to the Place for coffee, this evening, all the family. Try your professional wits on Squire Treverra's epitaphs. There's no special reason why they should, but they always sound like cryptograms to me. Anyhow, the whole library is interesting. Not many such families were literate enough to amass a collection like theirs.'

'Thanks,' said George, 'we should like to, very much, if Miss Rachel has no objection to being invaded.'

'Miss Rachel loves it. Surround her with personable young

men, and she's in her element.' He smiled at Dominic, presenting him gratis with this bouquet. 'I'm sorry I made such shameless use of you just now. Thanks for taking it so neatly. It helped him to accept it, and frankly, I don't think it's going to be much of a show for kids, and I'd rather keep him out of it.'

'As a matter of fact,' confessed Dominic ruefully, 'I *had* wanted to ask, only I didn't quite like to. But of course it's settled now, anyhow. I don't mind, if it makes Paddy feel he's had a fair hearing.'

'I'm sorry to have had to do it, all the same. I suppose it wouldn't do to ask you to come along, after all? No, I'm afraid Paddy wouldn't forgive a dirty trick like that, and he'll be somewhere not far away.'

'Couldn't possibly risk it,' said Dominic firmly.

'But it really is a pity, because we *could* make room for *one* more sound man in the team.' And lightly Simon turned his deep-brown eyes, in their shapely pits of fine wrinkles etched paler in the bronzed skin, and looked innocently at George. 'So how about you, George? I'd be very glad to have you there. Will you come?'

Visitors to Treverra Place were treated to a personally conducted tour of the whole house and grounds, both of which, in their way, were well worth seeing. Miss Rachel, bright as a macaw in black silk and emeralds and a Chinese shawl, tapped her way valiantly ahead with the stick she used as an extension of her personality rather than an aid to navigation, and pointed out, even more meticulously than its beauties, the drawbacks and imperfections of her family seat. She loved visitors; they were allowed to miss nothing.

Treverra portraits filled the long galleries on the first floor, and stared from the lofty well of the staircase.

'Most of them very bad,' said Miss Rachel, dismissing them with a wave of her wand. 'All local work, we were not an artistic family, but we insisted on thinking we were.' The listeners got the impression that in her own mind she had been there from the beginning. 'There's just one very nice miniature here in the parlour – a young man.'

'It would be,' said Tamsin softly into Dominic's ear, bringing up the rear of the procession. But she said it with affectionate indulgence rather than cynically. In her own way she was very fond of her formidable old employer.

'The garden,' announced Miss Rachel, pounding across the terrace and threatening it with the silver hilt of her stick, 'is a disgrace. It is quite impossible to get proper gardeners these days. I am forced to make do with one idiot boy, and three days a week from the verger at St. Mary's. There's positively no relying on the younger generation. Trethuan promised he'd come in to-day and pick the apricots and Victoria plums. And has he put in an appearance? He has not. Never a sign of him, and never a word of excuse.'

'Maybe he wanted to finish scything the churchyard extension to-day,' suggested Simon vaguely, attendant at her heels. 'He left it half-done yesterday, so the Vicar says.'

'If he's going to be a jobbing gardener in addition to verger,' insisted the old lady scornfully, 'he should *be* one, and plan his time accordingly. He came in yesterday afternoon and picked just one tree of plums, and promised he'd be in to-day to finish the job. I was talking to him in the kitchen-garden not two minutes after you left here to go home to tea, Simon, and he said he'd only had an hour to spare, and he'd just looked in to let me know he'd give me the *whole* of to-day. And not a sign of him. You simply cannot rely on the young people nowadays.'

'Trethuan is not much above fifty,' explained Tamsin in Dominic's ear.

'And I particularly wanted to send some apricots down to Phil, while they're at their best. She has such a good hand with bottling.'

'I tell you what,' said Simon promptly, 'get Paddy to come and pick them for Phil tomorrow, and keep him out of our hair.

557

He's dying to get in on the act, it'll be a good idea to find him something to keep him out of mischief.'

Miss Rachel halted at the low balustrade of the front terrace, spreading her Chinese silks in an expansive wave over the mock marble. Her shrewd old face had become suddenly as milkily still as a pond.

'Paddy?' she said, in a sweet, absent voice. 'Absurd! Such a sensitive boy, I'm sure he wouldn't join you in your grave-hunt for any consideration. Certainly I'll get Phil to send him for some apricots, but whatever makes you think he has any interest in your undertaking at St. Nectan's?'

Simon laughed aloud. 'Just the fact that he came and asked if he could be there. Asked very nicely, too, but it didn't get him anywhere. It's no horror project, but still it isn't for growing boys.'

She had resumed her march, but slowly and thoughtfully. Without looking at him she asked innocently: 'When did he ask you?'

'This morning, around noon. Why?'

'Oh, nothing! I just found it hard to believe he'd do such a thing, that's all.' After I had expressly forbidden it, she thought, in a majestic rage, but she kept her own counsel and her old face bland and benign. Something drastic will have to be done about Master Paddy. This cannot be allowed to go on. The child is *shockingly* spoiled. If Phil and Tim can't take him in hand, *I* shall have to.

'And this,' declared Miss Rachel triumphantly, while the grandmotherly corner of her mind planned a salutary shock for Paddy Rossall, 'this is our library.'

She always brought her visitors to it by this way, through the great door from the terrace, springing on them magnificently the surprise of its great length and loftiness of pale oak panelling and pale oak bookshelves, the array of narrow full-length mirrors between the cases on the inner walls, and the fronting array of windows that poured light upon them. By any standards it was a splendid room, beautifully proportioned and beautifully unfurnished. There was Tamsin's desk at the far window of the range, and the big central table with its surrounding chairs, and two large and mutually contradictory globes, one at either end of the room. And all the rest was books.

On the nearer end of the long table a large, steaming coffee-tray had been deposited exactly ten seconds before they entered by the outer door; and the inner door was just closing smoothly after Miss Rachel's one elderly resident maid. When there were visitors to be impressed, the timetable in Treverra Place worked to the split second.

'There he is,' said Simon, 'the man himself.'

The painting was small and dark and clumsy, a full-face presentation in the country style; commissioned portraits among small country families of the eighteenth century were meant to be immediately recognisable, and paid for accordingly. There was a short, livid scar across the angle of a square rat-trap of a jaw, redeemed by the liveliest, most humorous and audacious mouth Dominic had ever seen. A plain, ordinary face at first sight, until you looked at every feature in this same individual way, and saw how singular it was. The jaw could have been a pirate's, the large, uneven brow might have belonged to a justice of the peace, and in fact had, for several years, until the squire had felt it more tactful to withdraw from the bench. The eyes were the roving, adventurous eyes of a lawless poet, and that joyous mouth would have looked well on the young, the gallant, the irresistible Falstaff.

Simon stood back from the wall, and looked the most cele-brated of the Treverras full in the eyes.

George thought: They really seem to be looking at each other, measuring each other, even communicating. And although they look so different, isn't there something intensely alike about them? Both privateers, a little off the regular track, not quite

559

manageable by ordinary rules, not quite containable by ordinary standards.

'He had one ship trading across the Atlantic, and three or four small craft fishing and coasting here. And smuggling, of course. They all did it. It wasn't any crime to them, it was business and sport – '

'Could it be,' whispered Dominic in Tamsin's ear, 'that Simon has his tenses wrong?'

She turned her head so rapidly that the fine red hair fanned out and tickled his nose. She gave him a lightning look, and again evaded his eyes.

'I hope they got everything away safely last night,' he said even more softly. He couldn't resist the innocent swagger, and it was hardly disobeying orders at all. This time she didn't look at him, but he saw her lip quiver and her cheek dimple, and she said to him out of the corner of a motionless mouth, like an old lag at exercise:

'You certainly are a sharp young man, Dominic Felse, be careful you don't cut yourself.'

'And here's his wife. Morwenna, her name was.'

'She was lovely,' said Bunty, surveying the unexpected charcoal drawing on grey, rough paper, heightened with white chalk and red. Fragile but striking, like the creature it encompassed. Fine, fiery dark eyes, a delicately poised head balancing a sheaf of piled black hair.

Miss Rachel beamed satisfaction from the background. 'I used to be thought very like her when I was younger.'

'Actually,' murmured Tamsin in Dominic's ear, 'she's the living image of Jan, if you cover up that jaw of his.'

'And these are the famous epitaphs?' George stepped close to the two framed photographs on the wall below Morwenna's portrait.

' "O Mortal Man, whom Fate – " '

560

A Nice Derangement of Epitaphs

'You'll find it easier from these transcriptions. Those photographs were made last time the church was cleared of sand, fifteen years or so ago. Whoever took them did a nice job on the angle of the light, and the lettering isn't much eroded, but it's eccentric. Here's the text.'

Simon read aloud, in the full, rapt voice of self-forgetfulness, as though the reflected image of Treverra stirred within him; and it was not often, Tamsin told herself, watching, that Simon forgot himself.

' "O Mortal Man, whom Fate may send
To brood upon Treverra's End,
Think not to find, beneath this Stone,
Mute Witness, bleached, ambiguous Bone.
Faith the intrepid Soul can raise
And pilot through the trackless Maze,
Pierce unappalled the Granite Gloom,
The Labryinth beyond the Tomb,
And bring him forth to Regions bright,
Bathed in the Warmth of Love and Light,
Where year-long Summer sheds her Ease
On golden Sands and sapphire Seas.
There follow, O my Soul, and find
Thy Lord as ever true and kind,
And savour, where all Travellers meet,
The last Love as the first Love sweet.'

'That was for himself. And this one is hers. Some say Jan wrote it before he died, knowing they wouldn't be parted long. Some say she wrote it herself in his style. Sometimes I think it's more remarkable than the other.

' "Carve this upon Morwenna's Grave:
NONE BUT THE BRAVE DESERVES THE BRAVE.
Shed here no Tears. No Saint could die

561

More Blessed and Comforted than I.
For I confide I shall but rest
A Moment in this stony Nest,
Then, raised by Love, go forth to find
A Country dearer to my Mind,
And touching safe the sun-bright Shore,
Embrace my risen Lord once more'."

There was a brief and curiously magical silence, and no one wanted to break it. It was not that the poetry was so lofty, but rather that it was so elusive, as though every phrase in it had at least two meanings, and therefore at any line you could lose your way, but if at every line you took the correct turning you would find yourself at the centre of a maze, always an achievement, and sometimes a revelation.

'Any reactions?' asked Simon, poking a deliberately brutal finger through the web of hallucination. 'Apart from the fact that here was a bloke who knew his folkverse and his Dryden equally well?'

Tamsin prodded Dominic in the ribs unexpectedly. 'Go ahead!' she hissed in his ear. 'Say something profound!'

Startled, he blurted out exactly what was in his mind. 'They make the after-life sound like a Christmas sunshine cruise to the Bahamas.'

Chapter 3

Friday Morning

'You,' said Miss Rachel, waiting for Paddy in the arched gateway of the kitchen-garden with silver-hilted stick at the slope, like a superannuated angel drafted to the gate of paradise in an emergency, 'you are a thoroughly bad boy.'

'Yes,' said Paddy in glum resignation, 'I thought I should be.' He hoisted the outsize basket from his carrier and dangled it sulkily. 'Well, you won. I'm here, and I'll pick apricots, even if I won't like it. What more do you want?'

'Come inside here, and put that basket down for a few minutes. I want to talk to you.'

He complied, but with an audible groan. He'd ridden up from the farm on his reluctant errand with nothing worse in his mind than scorn for all women and their conspiratorial tactics, a feeling which gave him a certain sense of detachment and superiority. A baby could have seen through this move to keep him away even from the sand-dunes on this of all mornings. His mother again, of course, enlisting Miss Rachel's aid. What else could it mean? Only women did things like that. Men came right out and said: 'If I see you within a quarter of a mile of St. Nectan's I'll skin you.' But women put their scheming heads together and concocted a job for you to do somewhere else.

'I suppose you and Mummy worked out how long it would take me to fill this thing,' he said, dropping the basket on the grass, 'and took jolly good care to make it an all-morning job. All right, I'll fill it. And she'll have to get down to it and bottle the lot to-day, and serve her right.'

'Your mother has nothing whatever to do with this. If you want to blame anyone for it,' she said grimly, 'you can blame yourself and me – no one else. You went straight out from here, yesterday, and hunted out Simon. After I'd expressly told you not to! Didn't you?'

'All right,' he said, roused and scowling, 'I did. How did you know about it? But I'd have told you, anyhow, if you'd asked me.'

'Simon let it out, last night. Oh, quite innocently, don't worry, *he* didn't know you'd gone flatly against my orders and your parents' wishes. Paddy Rossall, how *could* you!'

'They asked for it,' said Paddy, goaded. 'If you want to know, I *wasn't* going to go after Simon, by the time I got here I'd got over it, and it seemed mean and silly. But it didn't seem mean and silly to *her*, did it, to get together with you just to balk me? That's different, isn't it? It doesn't count if you gang up on your son, but it's a crime if you do the same to your mother.'

'Now, you stop this nonsense this minute,' commanded the old lady, quivering with indignation. 'Your parents have a perfect right to check you – and to expect at least obedience from you, if nothing else. They're responsible for you, of course they're entitled to take whatever steps they think necessary for your good. You don't realise how much you owe to them, or how badly you're behaving to them. You take all their love and care for granted. Well, let me tell you, young man, if you had any gratitude in you, you'd never be able to think of enough ways to repay them for all they've done for you.'

He couldn't bear it. To have the most secret, penitent and loving promptings of his heart ripped out and brandished in front of him, made cheap and public and sanctimonious like the disgusting parables in some old-fashioned moral book for children – it was too much. He reacted violently against it, with

flooding colour and reckless rage, crying out things he didn't
mean and didn't believe, in an effort to restore at least a balance
of decency.

'So only one side's got any rights! What about *my* rights?
Did I ask them to have me? *They* could have helped it, couldn't
they? But *I* couldn't, I didn't have any choice. I'm their *son*,
remember?'

Whether Miss Rachel can be said at this point to have taken
any actual decision to resort to extreme measures, or whether
she was quite simply pushed over the edge of action before she
realised it, the result was the same. She drew herself to her full
modest height, looking more like Queen Victoria than Paddy
had ever seen her, and in a half-smothered voice of shocked and
royal rage, with judgment in every syllable, she said what could
never again be unsaid.

'*No*,' said Miss Rachel, full into his angry, miserable face,
'you are *not*!'

His first instinct was quite simply not to hear her, to pick up
his basket and back out of this argument now, before events
overwhelmed him. Such a thing could not have been said, and
therefore it had not been said. He cast one desperate glance
round him, looking for a way of escape.

'Which tree am I supposed to – to start – '

It was no use, the words were still there in his ears, stinging
like an echo, and he could not get rid of them by pretending
they were mere meaningless sound. His second impulse was to
laugh. If this was her way of punishing him, it was a splendidly
silly one. But she stood there squarely before him, watching his
face intently and maintaining her unrelenting gravity, and there
wasn't the ghost of a chance that she was just being spiteful. The
laugh collapsed in ruins. He stared at her, his eyes enormous and
stricken, pushing the inconceivable thing away from him with
one last convulsive effort at regaining the normal ground of
everyday.

'It isn't true,' he said passionately.

'However angry I may be with you,' said Miss Rachel harshly, 'I wouldn't lie to you.'

'No,' he owned forlornly, 'that's right, you wouldn't.' He began to shake. 'But I *must* be, I *have* to be, I *am*. I *can't* start being somebody else – '

'Now, don't be silly. You're old enough to understand these things, and there's no need to get upset about it. Here, come and sit down, and listen to me.'

She took him by the arm, unresisting, and led him to the stone seat under the sunny wall, and there plumped him down before her, diminished strangely in years, a lost small boy. Big, stunned eyes stared at, and round, and through her, and saw nothing at all. She tapped his cheek lightly, and nothing whatever happened. It took quite a sharp slap to startle those eyes back into focusing, and jolt a spark of warmth and feeling back into the fixed face.

'Oh, come along, now, you know people often adopt children, there's nothing so strange about it. Tim and Phil adopted you, you're *not* their own child. They took you legally, as a very young baby, from a friend of theirs whose wife had died. And don't run away with the idea that you were chosen for the part, either. They took you against their inclinations at the time, out of pity, because your father didn't want you.'

That brought the live and angry colour back to his cheeks, and a flare to his eyes that still looked like mutiny, even in the face of the firing-squad.

'Yes, you heard me correctly. Didn't want you! He could perfectly well have afforded to pay for proper care for you, but a baby was a nuisance to him. He took advantage of the fact that Phil had lost a child of her own, and couldn't have another, and he worked on her feelings until she took you off his hands. That's how much your father cared about you. Tim and Phil took you out of pity, and they've loved and cared for you ever since. And this is how you behave to them in return! You'll see,' said Miss Rachel with stern emphasis, 'if you go on like this, *no one* will be able to love you.'

Somewhere deep inside him that started an echo that hurt and frightened him. He shut himself fiercely about it to contain the fear and pain, unwilling to give her the satisfaction of having moved him.

'I don't believe it,' he said obstinately. But he did, that was the worst part of it, that he couldn't even hope for it to be a lie. 'You're making it up, just to scare me.'

'You know quite well I'm doing nothing of the kind. And there's no occasion at all for being scared. You're theirs now, and you know they love you, even if you don't always deserve it. And you know that everything will go on just the same as always. This doesn't alter anything. Except, I hope, the way *you*'ll look at things from now on.'

Doesn't alter anything! Only the whole of his world, and worse still, the heart of his body and the mind in his head, and the memory of a lordly childhood he had always supposed to be simple, unassailable, and his by right.

In the flat, practical voice of shock, which she had no way of recognising, he said: 'Why did they never tell me? I wouldn't have minded so much if I'd known all along, I could have got used to it.'

'That was their mistake. I know it, I always told them so. They thought you need never know, because it happened just about the time they were thinking of moving here to Pentarno. By the time they realised how foolish they'd been, they'd left it so late they didn't know how to go about it. So they kept quiet and hoped for the best. But *I* think it's high time you knew what you really owe to them. Maybe now you'll show a little more gratitude and consideration.'

'I didn't know I wasn't. I mean – I didn't know I had to be more grateful than other boys – '

'Now, there's no need to feel like that about it. You just think it over quietly, while you pick the apricots for your mother, and see if you can't make up your mind to behave a bit better to her in future.'

He looked at his hands, which were gripping the edge of the stone seat so hard that the knuckles were white. He wasn't sure whether he could detach them without having them start shaking again, but he tried it with one, cautiously, and it was quite steady. He picked up the basket. Everything seemed to work much the same as before, and yet he felt a long, long way from his own body, as though he were looking on at a play.

'All right. Which tree shall I start on?'

She told him, piloted him to it, not without certain careful sidelong glances at the chilled quietness of his face, and left him to his labours, firmly determined not to fuss over him now and undo the good she had done. He'd needed a sharp lesson. All boys get above themselves at times, even the nicest. It would be disastrous to hang over him anxiously at this stage, and betray the fact that he had only to manufacture a look of distress to twist her round his finger again. So she tapped away stubbornly out of the kitchen-garden, without once looking back. It was going to take her the whole of the next hour to convince herself that she had done the right, the necessary, the only possible thing, and there was not now, and never would be in the future, any cause to regret it. But she would manage it eventually, and then forget that she had ever been in doubt. What she did must be right, as it always had been.

Paddy set the basket on the edge of the gravel path, and began methodically to strip the apricot tree. Somewhere infinitely distant and dark, his mind groped feverishly after the full awful implications of what he had heard. Fifteen is a vulnerable age. Once the possibility was presented to him, he found it only too easy to believe that nobody could love him, and to imagine that nobody ever had. When he came to consider himself in this new light, stripped of privilege, he didn't find himself a particularly lovable specimen. The people you rely on, the people you're sure of, even though you don't deserve them –

what happens when you suddenly lose them? Like having the world jerked out from under your feet as neatly as a mat.

Now he wasn't sure of them or of anything. Oh, he knew, just as positively as ever, that they were wonderful, that he adored them, that they would never let him down. They'd always been marvellous to him, and always would be; that wasn't what dismayed him. But now he found himself horribly afraid that it was only out of pity for his forlorn estate, unwanted by his father, a rejected nuisance, badly in need of someone to take pity on him. The shock of feeling himself uprooted, of not even knowing who or what he was, was bad enough. But the shock of turning to look again at the parents he had hitherto taken for granted as his undisputed, cherished and misused property, of seeing them suddenly strange, forbearing and kind, and not his at all, only suffering him out of the goodness of their hearts, of feeling his inside liquefy with fearful doubts as to whether they could ever truly have loved him or felt him to be theirs – this was too much for him to grasp or face. He shrank from it into protective numbness, clinging desolately to the job he had been given to do, and dreading the time when the shell of habit would crack and fall away, and leave him naked to the chill of what he knew. Furiously he plucked apricots he was not aware of seeing and loaded them into the basket he hardly knew he was filling.

'You might,' said Miss Rachel, making an unexpected appearance in the library at about half past eleven, 'take out some ginger-beer and cake for Paddy. I daresay he'd like something by now.'

'I daresay he would,' agreed Tamsin, 'if he hasn't eaten himself sick on apricots. I know which I'd rather have.'

'Paddy isn't afraid of spoiling his figure,' said Miss Rachel nastily.

Tamsin rose from her work with a sigh, and took the peace-offering the old lady had prepared with her own hands. And very nice, too, she thought. Chocolate layer cake, and the almond biscuits he likes best. What did he do to be in such high favour to-day? Or what's she trying to smooth over? Come to think of it, why doesn't she take it out to him herself?

She was back very quickly, and still carrying the tray.

'He's not there.'

'Nonsense, he must be there.' Miss Rachel's resolutely confident face grew indignant at the suggestion that things could slip out of the comfortable course she had laid down for them. 'You haven't looked properly.'

'Under every leaf. He isn't there, and his bike isn't there, and his basket isn't there. And the apricots from that first tree aren't there, either. He must have worked like a demon. Probably to get away and down to the dunes before the matinée's over.'

'Ah!' said Miss Rachel, seizing gratefully on a solution which permitted her to keep her self-righteousness, her indignation against him, and her cheering conviction that children were as tough as badgers. 'That's probably what it is. The little wretch! I just hope Tim will send him home with a flea in his ear.'

They rode down to the church promptly at ten, in Tim's Land-Rover and Simon's grey Porsche, dropping from the coastal road through the dunes by a pebble-laid track among the tamarisk hedges, silted over here and there by fine drifts of sand. The tang of salt and the straw-tinted pallor of salt-bleached grasses surrounded them, the fine lace of the tamarisks patterned the cloudless but windy aquamarine sky on either side. The small car led, with Simon driving it and George beside him. The Land-Rover, used to being taken anywhere and everywhere by Tim, ambled after like a good-natured St. Bernard making believe to chase a greyhound pup. Tim and Sam Shubrough up in front, the Vicar behind for ballast, with the additional tackle they had brought along in case of need.

A formidable team, thought George, considering them. Simon and George himself would have passed for presentable enough physical specimens by most standards, but here they were the light-weights. Tim stood an inch or two less than either of them, but was half as broad again, and in hard training from the outdoor life he had led in all weathers. Sam Shubrough was a piece of one of the harder red sandstones of the district, animated. But the greatest surprise was the Reverend Daniel Polwhele.

The Vicar of St. Mary's, Maymouth, stood six feet three in his socks, and looked like the product of several generations of selective breeding from the families of Cornish wrestlers. He wore the clothes of his calling with a splendid simplicity, and was neither set apart by them nor in any way apologetic for them. Shouldering a couple of crowbars, he looked as much at home as with a prayer-book, because he approached everything in the world with a large, curious and intelligent innocence, willing to investigate and be investigated.

He was probably forty-five, but dating him was the last thing you'd think of trying to do. He had a broad, bony Cornish face, without guile but inscrutable, and a lot of untidy, grizzled dark hair that he forgot to have cut, and eyes as thoughtful, direct and disconcerting as a small boy's, but more tolerant.

The great waste of sand opened before them, and the great waste of sea beyond, a vast still plane and a vast vibrating plane. Through the tamarisk fronds they saw to the left the fanged head of the Dragon jutting out to sea, and nearer, at the southern end of the length of Pentarno sands, the low pebbly ridge of the Mortuary, dark with the rim of weed that built up there with every incoming tide. To their right was the clean, bright sand where young Paddy ran down to bathe every morning and every afternoon during the holidays. And here, tucked away on their left at the blown limit of the dunes, was St. Nectan's church. They saw it first by the small, squat tower and the little peaked roof over the empty lantern where once there had been a bell. Then, as they entered the small, cleared bowl, the whole building stood before them; very small, plain as a barn, with tiny, high lancet windows pierced here and there without plan or pattern, a narrow, crooked, porchless door with a scratched dog-tooth border almost eroded away, and a rounded tympanum with a crude little carving that could barely be distinguished now.

'Saxon, all the base of the walls,' said the Vicar, bounding out of the back of the Land-Rover and approaching George as he stood contemplating the relic. 'Windows and door and lantern very early Norman. The roof was re-slated not long before they gave it up as a bad job and built St. Mary's. The foundations go right down to the rock. We keep losing this, but St. Mary's will fall down first.'

The permanence and elemental quality of the sea pervaded the little church, the laboriously cleared graveyard with its stunted stones and erased names, the feathery curtains of tamarisks. Only the large grey bulk of the Treverra tomb, a stone cube rising about three feet above the surrounding ground, still obstinately asserted its own identity.

Before the tomb there was a railed-in pit, stone-lined and narrow, like a Victorian area. The iron gate swung freely on its newly-oiled hinges, and the fresh drift of sand was already filming over the steps of the staircase that descended to the low, broad door.

'I thought we should be sure to have an audience,' said Simon, coming from the Porsche with a large iron key in his hand.

Tim laughed. 'We have. Don't you know 'em yet? Half Pentarno and a fair sprinkling of Maymouth is deployed wherever there's cover along the coast road, moving in on us quietly right now. By the time we're down the steps and inside they'll be massing all round the rim. Only just within sight, they won't cramp you, but they won't miss a thing.'

'One of my choirboys,' said the Vicar brightly, 'borrowed my binoculars this morning. I didn't ask him why. I fancy most of the trebles are up on the Dragon's Head, passing them round. It's more fun that way. Shall we go down?'

They already had their gear piled outside the sunken door. Simon trod gently down the steps, disturbing the furls of blown sand, and fitted Miss Rachel's key into the huge lock. It turned with ready smoothness, a fact on which, George noted, nobody commented. Sam Shubrough's benign red face was serene in ambush behind his noble whiskers, his eyes as placid as the sea. They entered the vault, letting in daylight with them to a segment of rock flooring, thinly and idly patterned with coils of sand that must have drifted under the door. It fitted closely, or there would surely have been much more. A well-sealed place, dry and clean, the walls faced with stone slabs, shutting out even the saltness of the sea air. Treverra had made himself snug.

Tim switched on the electric lamp he was carrying, and set it on the stone ledge that ran all round the walls at shoulder-height. Sam added a second one at the other side. And there they were, the two massive stone coffins, each set upon a plinth carved clear and left standing when the vault was cut deep into the rock. They occupied the whole centre of the chamber between them, a narrow passage separating them, a narrow space clear all round them. There was nothing else in the vault.

Plain altar tombs, their corners moulded into a cluster of pillars, the lips of their lids decorated with a scroll-work of leaves and vines, and a tablet on each lid brought to a high finish to carry the engraved epitaph. By these they were identifiable, even if the one coffin had not been larger than the other, and perhaps two or three inches higher.

'O Mortal Man – '

This was Treverra. And the other one, close to his side as in life, was the lady, that frail beauty with the brilliant and daring face. She must have been every inch his match, thought George tracing the deliberate misquotation from Dryden spelled out in challenging capitals over her breast:

'NONE BUT THE BRAVE DESERVES THE BRAVE.'

Did a man ever think of that? Surely not! It was a woman making that claim for herself. Not wanting to be understood; wanting, in fact, not to be understood, but delighting in the risk. Why should she give that impression even in dying? She pined away. Only somehow it hadn't looked like a pining face.

The Vicar hefted the crowbars into the tomb. He stood holding them upright by his side, like the faithful sentinel, and looked again, long and thoughtfully, at the two coffins.

'I'd like to say a prayer first.'

He prayed with his head unstooped and his eyes open, and in his own unorthodox way.

'Help us if we're doing well,' he said, 'and forgive us if we're not. Lord, let there be peace on all here, living and dead.' He looked at the bold words on Morwenna's coffin, with respect and liking in his face. 'And reunion for all true lovers,' he said.

Simon said: 'Amen!'

'And now, how do you want to handle it?'

Simon disposed his team as practically as the Vicar prayed, and with the same sense of purpose.

'I thought we could easily lever the lid from Jan's coffin over to rest on hers. It's more than broad enough to span the space between without overbalancing, and the drop's not more than two and a half inches. We'll cover her over with these thick felts – I brought them down on purpose – we don't want to damage either stone. Let's have two of you over on Morwenna's side. Right. We three will hoist the stone up on the clear side first, and you can get some thin wedges in. Then we'll see if there's a deep rim to deal with, and ease your side out gradually if there is.'

George was at the head of the tomb, the Vicar in the middle,

574

Simon at the foot. They got their crows started into the well-fitted chink of the stone, and eased it enough to get the first wedges in. After that it was merely a matter of patience. There was a rim to lift free on all sides, but a shallow one, and they got it clear without difficulty.

'It isn't so massive,' said Tim, surprised. 'Two of us could hoist it off in no time if we didn't have to be so careful about damaging it.'

'True enough, but we do.' Simon felt along the under edge where the crow had prised, and grimaced. 'Matter of fact, it has chipped a bit. Hmm, here, too. Not much, but it seems to fret easily.'

The Vicar measured the thickness of the stone slab with an unimpressed eye, and found it thinner than he had supposed. He stooped and set his shoulder under its deep overhang, and hoisted experimentally, and the thing perceptibly shifted.

'We could lift it, Simon. Between the five of us, and taking it steadily together, now she's out of the socket we could manhandle her over. Try it!'

Simon eyed the stone doubtfully, and added another thickness of felt to the protective covering over Morwenna. 'All right, we can but try. One at each corner, and I'll take the middle here. Everybody set? Here we come, then. Gently – heave!'

The stone moved, slid along in response to their hoist a couple of inches, and disclosed a hair-line of darkness along the near edge of the coffin as the overhanging lip drew clear.

'It's coming! Right, together – heave!' The hair-line of blackness became a pencil, an ebony ruler. Out of it came a breath of cold and the odour of the sea and of dust. Strange, the two together, as though the inimical elements had settled down together in the grave. 'Again, heave!'

'Child's play!' said Sam cheerfully, and shifted his large feet to brace himself for the next hoist.

'Once more – heave!' The stone slid with their persuasion, and again settled, and this time as they relaxed their efforts it swung in delicate counter-balance, ready at a touch to tilt gently and ponderously, and come to rest against the felt padding on the lady's tomb. Nine inches of uncovered dark gaped below George's face, and the odour, faint but persistent, made his nostrils dilate and quiver. A more precisely defined odour now, not just the vague salt tang of the sea. Something more homely, and extraordinarily elusive – he thought, in a sequence of kaleidoscopic images, of sheep in salt pastures, of wire-haired terriers in the rain, of washing Dominic's woollies sometimes, long years ago, when Bunty had been ill. *Damp cloth! Woollen cloth!*

'Once more, and let her down gently. Ready – heave!'

Over slid the stone, and nested snugly on top of Morwenna's coffin, only its edge still propped upon the side of Treverra's own uncovered grave. The light of the two lamps fell obliquely into the stony space, and they all loosed their hold of the stone and leaned forward eagerly, craning to see what they had unveiled.

Only George, though with equal alacrity and a gasp as sharp as any, lunged back instead of forward. For that last strenuous lift and thrust had brought him up lying across the open coffin, almost face to face with the man who occupied it, as the stone slid from between them. The long, gaunt bony pallor of a lantern face gaped at him open-eyed from the dark, heavy jaw sagging towards a broad, barrel-staved chest in a dark grey pullover. Large, raw-boned hands jutted from the slightly short sleeves of an old black jacket, and lay half-curled against long black-clad thighs. And the smell of damp cloth and damp wool and damp human hair gushed up into their faces and sent them all into recoil after George.

Amazed and aghast, they stared and swallowed.

'If that's Treverra,' said George with conviction, 'I'm a Dutchman!'

The Vicar said: 'Lord, have mercy on us all when the day comes! It isn't Treverra, but it is Trethuan.'

'You know him?' George looked round at them all and saw by their appalled faces that he was, indeed, the only person present who did not know the incumbent of the coffin.

'I should. He's – he was – my verger at St. Mary's.'

George stared down at the long, lank body that lay so strangely shallowly in the stone pit, and his mind went back some hours, after an evasive memory, and recaptured it, and was confounded. It seemed Miss Rachel had complained unjustly of the unreliability of the young. Her truant gardener, even if he had not been able to communicate it, had had the best of all reasons for not turning up yesterday. He had picked his last apricot, and scythed his last churchyard. He lay, minus one shoe and sock, and reeking of the clammy, harsh damp of sea-water from feet to hair, stone dead in Jan Treverra's coffin.

'Lift him out,' said Sam urgently, starting out of his daze. 'He may not be dead.'

'He's dead. Whoever he is, however he got here, he's dead enough. Don't touch him.' George looked at Simon, looked at the Vicar across the coffin. Four intent, strained faces stared back at him with stunned eyes. 'I'm sorry, but it looks as if this has got out of hand. Out of our hands, anyhow. We've got a body here that was apparently alive a couple of days ago, and is very dead now. I've got no official standing here. Do you mind if I take charge for the moment? I suspect – I'm pretty sure – it isn't going to be for long.'

'Whatever you say,' agreed Simon in a shaken voice. 'This wasn't in my brief.'

'Then leave him where he is. Don't move anything. Tim, bring that lamp over, and let's have a careful look in here.'

Shocked into silence, Tim brought it, and tipped its light full in upon the dead man. George felt carefully at the well-worn, respectable black suit, the lank, dun-coloured hair, the hand-knitted pullover, the laces and sole of the one remaining shoe. All of them left on his fingers the clinging, sticky feel of salt.

He felt down past the bony shoulder, and touched a flat surface beneath the body, not cold and final like the stone, but with the live, grained feel of wood about it.

'I thought he was lying very high. There's a wooden coffin below him.' He tapped on it, and the small resulting sound was light and hollow. 'Not very substantial, just a shell to go inside the stone. That should be Treverra. But this one – '

'There appears to be some injury to his head,' said the Vicar, low-voiced. 'Do you think – ?'

'I *think* he drowned in the sea, but the doctors will settle that. Shine the light here, Tim.'

Tim illuminated the bony, dark-skinned face. A darker, mottled stain covered the outer part of the socket of the left eye, the lower temple and the cheekbone, the mark of a large, broken bruise.

'Could he have got that in the sea?' Sam's big voice was muted.

'I don't think so. I think it was done before death. And I think,' he said, looking round them all and stepping back from the coffin, 'we're going to have to turn this over at once to the Maymouth police. They'd better have a look at the whole set-up. Because it looks very much as if they've got a murder on their hands.'

There was a moment of absolute silence and stillness; then Simon heaved a cautious breath and dusted the powdering of stone from his hands.

'One of us had better take the car and go and telephone,' he said in the most practical of voices. 'Will you go, George, or shall I?'

But the most incomprehensible thing of all about the St. Nectan project came later still, past noon, when the photographers and the experts and the police surgeon had all had their way with the Treverra tomb, and the long, lank body of Zebedee Trethuan, verger and jobbing gardener, had been taken out on a covered stretcher and driven away in an ambulance, watched silently and avidly by a gallery of fishermen, children, respectable housewives and solid townspeople from all the dunes around, and no doubt just as eagerly by all the trebles of St. Mary's choir, fighting over the Vicar's binoculars on top of the Dragon's Head.

They were left with the plain, light wooden coffin on which he had lain; and at the first touch the lid of it gave to their hands, and came away, uncovering – surely, this time? – the last resting-place of Jan Treverra. And there they were, the expected bones.

This body had certainly been there longer than its bedfellow. It was almost a skeleton, shreds of perished clothing drifted about the long bones and the dried and mummified flesh that remained to it. But had it, on closer inspection, really been there for two centuries and more? It had a hasty and tumbled appearance, with no composed, hieratic dignity. The fragments of cloth still had enough nature left in them to show a texture and a colour; a colour which had been very dark navy blue, a texture that looked suspiciously like thick, solid modern woollen, meant to withstand all weathers. And here, about the chest, clung bits of disintegrating knitted stuff.

Among Treverra's eccentricities it had never been recorded that he wished to be buried in a fisherman's Meltons and a seaman's jersey.

By the middle of that Friday afternoon it was all over Maymouth that Jan Treverra's tomb had yielded not one body, but two; and that, positively though quite incomprehensibly, neither of them was Jan Treverra.

Chapter 4

Friday Afternoon

Detective-Sergeant Hewitt was pure Maymouth from his boots to his sober utilitarian haircut, a stocky, square man of middle age with a vaguely sad countenance, who used few words, but in some curious fashion turned other people voluble. In taking his last look round the Treverra vault before they locked it and left it to its ravished quietness, he said nothing at all. Only his solemn eyes lingered thoughtfully along the propped edge of the stone lid, with its specks of pallor where the iron had bitten into the stone; and Tim, following their reproachful survey, said apologetically: 'I know, it's a pity we had to use crowbars and foul up the possible traces. But we couldn't possibly have *known* – ' The grieved gaze moved lower, to the trampled patterns in the dust of the floor, and five pairs of feet did their best to appear smaller. 'I'm afraid we have rather driven the herds over everything,' said Simon ruefully. 'It was dead smooth when we came in, though – just a blown layer of sand, as usual.'

'Yes, well – if you gentlemen will go along with Snaith to the police station, right away, we'd like to have statements from all of you. Your individual observations may help us.' He didn't sound hopeful, but he probably never did. 'Mr. Felse, if you wouldn't mind, I'd like to have you along with me for a call on the way. We'll join the others in half an hour or so.'

'Glad to, if I can be any help,' said George.

580

'And I'll take the key, Mr. Towne.' Simon surrendered it, and watched it turned in the great lock, with a soundless efficiency which did not fail to register with the Detective-Sergeant. 'I see you've been preparing for to-day. This is the key from the Place?'

'Yes, the only one, as far as I know. I've had it three days now. Miss Rachel gave it to me when I wanted to bring down some of the gear.'

'Yes, I gathered from what you said just now that you'd been in the vault before to-day. How often?'

'Twice. On Wednesday morning – the Vicar was with me that time – we came down to clear the steps and clean and oil the lock, and tried the key to be sure how it worked. But we didn't go farther than than just inside the doorway.' And that, thought George, was probably when Simon spotted the illicit stores there, hence his discreet withdrawal, and the public declaration of his programme that evening. Nor had he actually said that they had in fact cleaned and oiled the lock, merely that they had come here with that intention. This job at least had proved unnecessary. 'Then I came in again yesterday afternoon, and dumped those sheets of felt.' To make sure that the hint had been taken?

'Notice anything at all different then? Or when you came in to-day?'

Simon considered. 'Not that I recollect.'

'You didn't sweep the floor clean of sand?'

'No. Never occurred to me, even if I'd had a broom. I was surprised how dry and clean it was in here, only a blown layer of sand. Just like now – except for our hoof-marks, of course,' said Simon ruefully.

'Ah, well, you'll have time to think it over. Mr. Felse and I will be with you shortly.'

They climbed the narrow steps on which the sand whisked softly like blown spray, and closed the latchless gate upon the solitude so bewilderingly void of Treverra, and so

over-populated with others who had no business there. The
Land-Rover and the Porsche set off for the police station in
Maymouth, Detective-Constable Snaith, son of a long line of
fishermen, ensconced in George's place beside Simon. Only
when the little convoy was well away did Hewitt climb ponderously into his Morris.

'We shan't be going far out of our way. Just along the quay
to where his girl lives. I thought a detached witness might come
in handy, if you don't mind being used. I've known Rose since
she was first at school. Being this close to a place has its
drawbacks, as well as its advantages.'

'I know,' said George, thinking of his own home village of
Comerford, where every face was known to him. 'Trethuan's
daughter?'

'Yes, only relative, as far as I know. She's been married a year
to a decent young fellow, Jim Pollard. Fisherman, of course,
they all are. Lives about three minutes' walk from where
Trethuan lived.'

'Alone, I take it? Now that the girl's married?'

'Yes, alone. Did for himself most of the time, and Rose did
the real cleaning for him. Thought I'd better see her and tell
her myself.'

It should have been a daunting prospect, but though he
maintained his aspect of professional and permanent discourage-
ment, Hewitt did not, in fact, appear at all daunted. And wasn't
there, perhaps, something in that gaunt, powerful, unprepossess-
ing corpse in Treverra's tomb that ruled out any harrowing
possibilities of family lamentation? There are people it's almost
impossible to love, however the blood may struggle to do its
duty.

They drove over the neck of the Dragon, the coastal road
rising to its highest point near the hotel. A fair portion of the
juvenile population of Maymouth was still deployed along
the cliff paths looking towards Pentarno; no doubt armed with
fruit and sandwiches, and with an organised errand-service for

ice-cream. Then the road dipped again, and the slate-grey cottages of the upper town closed in upon it, backgrounds for their small, crowded flower-gardens, that blazed with every possible colour. From the steep High Street they could see the harbour below them, locked between the huge bulk of the Dragon's Head and the crook of the mole, all the invisible streets doddering down towards it, seen only as thread-like channels between the slate roofs. Uniformly grey from this aerial view, the houses flowered into apple-blossom pinks and forget-me-not blues as the car descended, every shade of peach and primrose and pale green, foaming with window-boxes full of geraniums.

In the square, four-sided about an ugly Victorian fountain and embattled with solid shop-fronts, they saw the Porsche and the Land-Rover parked. But Hewitt drove on imperturbably, down towards the harbour, and the clusters of colour-washed houses that clung like barnacles to the rocks along the sea-front.

A row of leaning cottages, six in all, propped their backs against the outlying rocks of the Dragon, and stared out to sea over beached boats and a flurry of gulls. Each was painted its own individual shade, two different pinks, a daffodil yellow, one blue, one green, and one dazzlingly white. Hewitt parked the car on the cobbled shoulder of the quay, and led the way to the second pink house. A little horse-shoe knocker rapped on the jet-black door. The whole row looked like toys in a child's box.

Rose Pollard opened the door. At first glance Rose looked like a round, soft, primrose-haired doll to go with the toy house, but this illusion lasted only for the fraction of a second it took her large, inquiring eyes to recognise Hewitt. The round face, as delicately-coloured as a nursery-rhyme dairymaid's, nevertheless had some form and character when it sharpened into awareness; and there was nothing doll-like about the small, bright flares of fear that sprang up in her eyes. Hewitt was known to everyone, as surely as he knew everyone. But why should she be frightened at the very sight of him? Or, wondered George ruefully, was it occupational naivety on his part even to ask such a question?

She mastered her face, and rather nervously invited them in. The front door gave directly into the tiny living-room, which was as neat and frilly as the exterior of the house suggested it would be. The mind behind that pretty, plaintive face was probably itself furnished in the same innocent fashion; not much style, and no sophistication, but shining with cleanness and prettied up with pouffes, scatter cushions and net curtains. Not a very clever girl, but meant to be gay and bright; and certainly not meant to habit with things or people or thoughts that could frighten her.

'Sorry to butt in on you at dinner, Jim,' said Hewitt placidly, looking over her shoulder at the young man who rose from the table as they entered. 'Just a few things I ought to ask you and Rose, if you've got a minute or two to give me.'

'That's all right,' said Jim Pollard, uncoiling his tall young person awkwardly. 'We're finished, Mr. Hewitt. I was late coming in, or we'd have been all cleared away. Is there something the matter?'

He was a brown, freckled boy in a loose sweater and faded dungarees, with a face that must normally have been pleasant, good-natured and candid, but at this moment was clouded with the slight blankness and uncertainty consequent upon being visited by the police. It happens to the most law-abiding, it need mean nothing; but the barrier is instantly there, and the trouble is that there's never any telling what's behind it.

'Well, there's just this matter of Mr. Trethuan's movements,' said Hewitt with nicely calculated vagueness. 'Have you seen him to-day?'

Rose said: 'No!' She moved nearer to her husband, and the small, wary lights in her eyes burned paler and taller. The boy said: 'No,' too, but in a mystified, patient tone, ready to wait for enlightenment. His steady frown never changed.

'Or yesterday? Well, when did you last see him, Mrs. Pollard?'

'Wednesday morning,' she said, 'when I went in to clean. I usually go in Wednesdays and Saturdays and give the house a going-over. He was finishing his breakfast when I went. I only saw him for a few minutes, then he went off to work.'

'And you haven't seen him since? You don't know whether he came home that night?'

'Why should she?' said Jim Pollard evenly. 'He's capable, he can look after himself. Often we don't see him for days on end.'

'Even though he only lives just round the corner in Fore Street?'

'Maybe he does, but it is round the corner, we don't run into one another going in and out of the back doors. Thank God!' said Jim with deliberation, eyeing Hewitt darkly from under his corrugated brow.

'Now, Jim!' said Rose in a faint murmur of protest.

'Never mind: Now, Jim! Mr. Hewitt knows as well as you do there's no love lost between your old man and me. Less I see of him, the better. I might as well say so.'

'So you might, lad,' agreed Hewitt placatingly. 'Then I take it you don't know anything about him since your missus saw him Wednesday morning?'

'No, I don't, Mr. Hewitt. I haven't set eyes on him since last Sunday in church. What's he done to interest you?'

Rose shrank under her husband's hand, and turned her head to shoot him a look of panic entreaty, but all his attention was on Hewitt, and whatever his own disquiet, he seemed to feel nothing of the urgency of hers.

'It isn't what he's *done*,' said Hewitt heavily. 'I'm afraid this is going to be a bit of a shock to you, Rose, my girl. Your father was found this morning by Mr. Towne and the others, when they went to open the Treverra vault – '

Her soft, round face lost its colour in one gasp, blanched to a dull, livid pallor. Her eyes stared, enormous and sick. Her lips moved soundlessly, saying: 'In the vault – ?' Then her mouth shook, and she crammed half her right fist into it, like a child, and swallowed a muted cry.

'Yes, in the vault. He's dead, Rose. I'm sorry!'

Her knees gave way under her, and Jim caught her in his arms and held her, turning her to him gently. 'Now, love, don't! Come on, now, Rose, hold up!'

She clung to him and wept, but they were not tears of any particularly poignant grief, only of excitement, and nervous tension, and — was it possible? — relief. She cried easily, freely, with no convulsive physical struggle. Even fear was submerged, or so it seemed, until Hewitt added rather woodenly: 'It looks like foul play. We shall have a lot of work to do on the case before we have full information. We'll be in close touch with you. And if you can think of anything that may help to fill in his movements in the last days, we shall be glad to have it.'

'Are you trying to tell us,' demanded Jim Pollard, scowling over his wife's blonde head, 'that old Zeb's been *murdered*?'

'Yes,' said Hewitt mildly, 'that's exactly what I'm trying to tell you.'

Then they were both absolutely still; and perceptibly, even while they stood motionless, they withdrew into themselves, and very carefully and gently closed the doors to shut the world and Hewitt out. Jim tightened his hold on his wife, and that was the only reaction there was to be seen in him. Rose — and how much more significant that was! — Rose drew a long, slow, infinitely cautious breath, and stopped crying on the instant. She needed her powers now for more urgent purposes.

'Well,' said Hewitt, turning the car uphill again at the corner of Fore Street, 'what do you make of them?'

'Rose is frightened,' said George. 'Very frightened. Her husband, as far as I can see, is merely normally cagey. When the police come around asking about one of the family, nobody's at his most expansive. But what's more interesting is that she was frightened before you even asked a question. And most frightened of all when you mentioned the Treverra vault, before — I think — she realised you meant he was dead.'

'Ah!' said Hewitt cryptically, but with every appearance of

satisfaction with his own thoughts. 'You do notice things, don't you? I just wanted to know. Then you can't very well have missed the broom-marks.'

'Broom-marks?' said George carefully.

'On the steps of the vault. And the floor, too. Mr. Towne didn't have a broom down there, but somebody did. Very delicately done, but still it showed. Take another look at the corners, where none of you stepped to-day. Somebody had moved around that room, and then carefully swept it, and dusted a layer of sand over it again to wipe out the prints. Almost impossible to do it as smoothly as time and the wind do it.'

He slanted a knowing look along his shoulder at George's wooden face.

'Ah, come off it! I'm not in the excise. It's a murderer I'm after. I'm not interested in what a whole bunch of people were doing in there just ahead of the researchers. Murder is a solitary crime, Mr. Felse. No easy-going muddle of local brandy-runners put Trethuan in Jan Treverra's coffin, that I'll bet my life on. But what I am interested in – '

'Yes?' said George with respect.

'Is the key they let themselves in with. And who else may have had access to it.'

'Oh, no,' said the Vicar, emerging from deep thought, 'I don't think he had any actual *enemies.* Only people who're positive enough to have friends have enemies. When you're as glum and morose as he was, people just give up and go away.' He glanced round the circle of attentive faces in Hewitt's office, and ruffled his untidy hair. 'I don't think he wanted or needed liking, you know. Not everyone does.'

Hewitt gave him a brief, baffled look, and returned with a sigh to his summing-up.

'Well, we've got him to Wednesday morning. He worked on the churchyard extension, hedge-clipping and then scything, all the morning, or at least he was at work on it when Mr.

Polwhele and Mr. Towne came home to lunch after their trip down to the vault. He had his meal in the vicarage kitchen, and went back to work, and he was there when Mr. Towne left to go on to Treverra Place. Both Mr. Towne and Mr. Polwhele agree that would be about a quarter to three. Mr. Towne exchanged words with Trethuan in the churchyard as he walked through. Mr. Polwhele saw him put away his tools shortly afterwards and leave. That was nothing unusual? He arranged his own work as he pleased?'

'Yes, I never interfered unless I wanted something special. He got through everything if you left him to it. He could be awkward if you tried to give him orders.'

'So it was nothing surprising if he was missing from round the church for a couple of days or so in mid-week. He fitted in his gardening jobs for Miss Rachel as he thought best. And it looks as if he did go down to Treverra Place that same day, after he left the churchyard. Anyhow, the next we hear of him is there. About four o'clock he brought into the house a basket of plums he'd picked, told Miss Rachel he couldn't stay longer on the job then, but he'd come in next day and get in all the plums and apricots for bottling. Then he left. She saw him start down the drive. And so far that's the last we do know of him, until he turned up this morning in Treverra's coffin. According to the doctor's preliminary estimate, he was dead probably before nine o'clock, Wednesday night. Well, gentlemen, that's how it stands. Has anyone got anything to add? No second thoughts?'

'Yes,' said Sam Shubrough, and: 'Yes,' said Simon at the same moment. They looked briefly at each other, and Simon waved a hand: 'After you!'

'I've got a key,' said Sam modestly. 'One that belongs to that vault. I never bothered to mention it, because it wasn't needed. Miss Rachel was providing the one for official use. But it's plain now that you need to know about all the ways there are of getting in there, since somebody did get in and dump a body.

So that's it. It's the only other key I *know* of, and I've got it. I'll turn it in if you want to have it in your own hands.'

Hewitt closed his notebook with a movement of terrible forbearance. 'Oh, you have a key. Well, that's helpful, at any rate. Would you mind telling us how you got it in the first place?'

'Not a bit. When I was a kid, St. Nectan's was our favourite playground. I found the key, once when we dug our way into the church for some game or other. It was down in the sand, under a nail on the wall, where I take it it used to hang. The wire on the bow was frayed through. I brought it home and cleaned it up, and it didn't take me long to find out it fitted the Treverra vault. We were a bit scared of going in,' said Sam, smiling broadly under cover of his whiskers, 'but sometimes we did. I've had a key ever since. It's in a bunch on a nail in my shed right now.'

'Where, I take it, anyone could get at it? Do you keep the shed locked, even?'

'No, there's nothing special in it, and anyhow, we don't lock things, you know that. So I suppose anyone could get at it. But he'd have to know it was there, or else have an extraordinary stroke of luck, happening on it and finding out where it fitted. Do you want me to turn it in? I'll go and get it right now, if you've finished with me for the moment.'

'If you'll be so good.' And there were not now, and there never would be hereafter, any awkward questions about how, and how often, that key had been used. Hewitt was after a murderer, he was not going to be sidetracked. Sam rose and left the conference with only one bright, backward glance in Simon's direction.

'Now, Mr. Towne, you were going to add something, too?'

'Yes, I was. I didn't think much of it at the time – I don't now, for that matter – but you know all the talk there was when I first let it get round that I meant to open the Treverra tomb? A lot of people went off at half-cock, as usual, about the attempt

589

being irreverent and blasphemous, about how a curse would fall on us, and so on. You must have heard it. Then when we made it known that it was a serious project, and the bishop had given permission, and Miss Rachel was positively egging us on, then all the fuss died down. All but this chap Trethuan. Well, of course, he was the verger, and I made allowances for certain prejudices, but he did begin to be a bit of a nuisance. He took every occasion he could to buttonhole me and try to persuade me to drop it. At first he just denounced it as ungodly, and said there'd be a judgment if we went ahead. Then he began to get threatening. I listened politely at first and made soothing noises, but I got tired of it finally and gave him the brush-off. But he didn't give up. He got more urgent.'

'And was that what he spoke to you about on Wednesday,' asked Hewitt, 'when you came away from the vicarage?'

'It was all he ever spoke to me about. He saw me coming through the churchyard, and he came and stood right in the path, blocking the way, with the scythe in his hand. Something between Father Time and Holbein's "Death",' said Simon wryly, 'that long, bony man with his lantern face, clutching a scythe and pronouncing doom.'

'Did he actually threaten you?'

'Physical threats? Not exactly. Just hints that I should regret it if I went ahead. But he did seem desperately disturbed about the whole thing, as if it was a matter of life and death to him.'

'And what did you say to him?'

'Told him to do his worst, of course. Bring on your lightnings, I said, and pushed past him and left him standing there.'

'By the Vicar's account,' said Hewitt sharply, 'he didn't stand there long. He didn't, by any chance, *follow* you to Treverra Place? He turned up there shortly afterwards.'

'If he did, I never looked back to see. I didn't see him at the Place, either, I didn't know he was there. I spent the next hour or so with Miss Rachel, sitting talking in the garden. So it must have been after I left that he took his plums into the house and talked to her. I left around four o'clock, I suppose.'

'You didn't say anything about Trethuan's queer behaviour to the old lady?'

'No, why should I? Oh, because it was her pet project – no, I didn't. I'd forgotten all about him by then, and anyhow, why bother Miss Rachel with it? We weren't even talking about Treverra that day, only about personal things.'

'And after you left?'

'I hadn't brought the car out that day. I walked down into Maymouth for some cigarettes, and then took my time walking back over the Dragon's neck on my way home to Pentarno to tea. And that's when I came upon George's boy and our Paddy, down on the Pentarno beach. I saw them from the road and ran down to them. Dominic had just hauled Paddy out of the sea. And that reminds me,' he said, stricken, 'of why he said he went out so far. He said he'd seen a man in the sea.'

'A man in the sea?' Hewitt's head jerked up smartly at that. 'This is the first I've heard of any man in the sea.'

'We didn't believe there ever was one. But, my God, now I'm beginning to wonder. It's like this, you see. There were these two boys, and it seemed Dominic had seen Paddy swimming dangerously far out off the point, and felt he ought to go and bring him in. But when he did, Paddy up and swore he thought he'd seen a body going out with the tide, and was trying to reach him. Dom and I went in again to see if we could see anything of him, but never a sign. Neither of us thought there was anything in it. But now – if Trethuan really drowned in the sea, as it seems he probably did – '

'About what time would that be?'

'Past five, maybe as late as half past, or even a little later. *Could* it have been? As early as that?'

'And only young Paddy actually claims he saw anything?'

'Even he wasn't positive. But he was worried. I promised I'd notify the coastguard, just to satisfy him, and I clean forgot.

Not believing in it, you see, and then there was no report of anyone missing. I wish now I'd taken it more seriously.'

Hewitt looked at Tim. 'We'd better get hold of your boy, Mr. Rossall, and let him tell his own story. There may be nothing in it, but we can't afford to miss anything.'

'I'll call him and tell him to bike over here. He'll come like a bird.'

'Do. And maybe we'd better get your boy, too, Mr. Felse. He was on the scene before Mr. Towne arrived, there just may be something he can tell us.' He handed the telephone across his desk, and Tim dialled his own number.

And thus began the great hunt for Paddy Rossall.

'No, he isn't,' said Phil. 'He didn't come home to lunch. I took it for granted he's sneaked round to the dunes to watch your operations from a distance, since you wouldn't let him in on the ground floor. Maybe he cadged a lunch with Aunt Rachel. Try there. I'm waiting for those apricots, the monkey!' She added at the last moment, with the first faint and distant hint of anxiety in her voice: 'Call me back if you find him, Tim, won't you?'

'No, he isn't,' said Miss Rachel, with some asperity because of her own irrepressible conscience. 'Tamsin took a snack out to him about half past eleven, and he'd already filled his basket and gone. Naturally I took it he'd taken them home to Phil. Oh – and he hasn't been near the church, either? He'd want to keep out of sight, of course. Well, don't fuss over him, Tim, that's fatal. He'll come home when he's hungry'

She replaced the receiver with unnecessary violence, and found Tamsin studying her very narrowly across the desk.

'I gather Paddy didn't go home.'

'No, he didn't. You said yourself where he'd most likely be,' snapped Miss Rachel.

'I know I did, but it seems he isn't. And I didn't know, when

592

I published my estimate, what you'd been saying to him – did I?'

'You still don't,' pointed out Miss Rachel, all the more maliciously for the alarm she couldn't quite allay, and wouldn't acknowledge. 'He'll come home when he's got everyone nicely worried, that's what he's after. I'm not going to fall for that, if you're stupid enough to buy it. Children are born blackmailers.'

He was perfectly all right, of course. He was simply hiding somewhere and sulking, and gloating over the uneasiness he was causing everyone. Well, it wasn't going to work. He'd run away once, as a very small boy – like many another before him, in dudgeon over some fancied injustice. But he'd come home fast enough when it began to rain. Children are realists; they know which side their bread's buttered.

'No, he isn't,' said Dominic, surprised. 'Have you got Dad there? No, not to worry, only we heard the rumours that are running round, and we couldn't help wondering. But we haven't seen anything of Paddy. Yes, of course I'll come, like a shot. Well, I've been out there on the Head part of the morning, it *is* like a grandstand, but I haven't seen hide or hair of Paddy. Look, suppose I scout round now, before I come down, and see if I can find out anything? No, there's hardly anybody hanging about round the church now, only a handful of people who were late coming, but I'll have a look there, too. Sure, I'll be down as soon as I can make it.'

'He isn't anywhere,' said Tim, banging down the receiver for the tenth time. Dominic was already with them by then, with a negative report and a curiosity that positively hurt him, though he was containing it manfully. 'That's all his closest friends crossed off. And he hasn't had anything to eat! I don't like it.'

Hewitt didn't like it, either. His solid face, conditioned to the suppression of all feeling except the deceptive pessimism he used for business purposes, was letting anxiety through like a slow leak.

'He wouldn't go off anywhere out of town without telling anyone. He isn't irresponsible. It isn't that he'd do anything harebrained. But anyone can have an accident.'

'I'm wondering,' said Hewitt heavily, 'if he saw something else, when he saw – or thought he saw – that body in the water. Maybe without at all realising the significance of what he was seeing. I'm wondering if he saw *someone* else, say up on the Head above the rocks, just at the crucial moment. Or whether somebody who was up there may *think* Paddy saw him, even if he didn't.'

'You don't think he could be in danger?' asked Tim, shaken and pale.

'I'd have said no, up to this noon. But now it's all over this town that Trethuan's body has turned up, and the hunt's on. Whoever killed him will be pretty desperate now to remove anyone who may – even may – have noticed and recognised him, and may blurt out to the police what he knows.'

'Then we've got to find Paddy, quickly. My God, if anything happened to him – '

'Nothing will happen to him,' protested Simon strongly. 'He'll turn up soon, safe and sound, and with a perfectly simple explanation, you see if he doesn't.'

But Hewitt was already on his feet, and reaching for the telephone. 'I'd rather not wait, Mr. Towne. What was he wearing this morning? Oh, Blakey, I want every man we can spare, we've got a full-scale hunt on our hands. We've lost a boy – young Paddy Rossall, most of our fellows will know him on sight. Missing with a bike, since this morning. Yes, we need everybody.'

'Well, if it's like that, you've got a handful of volunteers right here,' said Simon, solid and calm at Tim's shoulder. 'You're the boss, where do we start?'

Tamsin turned from her uneasy pacing along the range of the

library windows, and marched through the doorway into Miss Rachel's sitting-room. The old lady looked up with a face resolutely complacent, and told herself for the twentieth time that day that young people nowadays had no stamina. No wonder all modern children were spoiled.

'They still haven't found him,' said Tamsin. 'I'm sick of this, I'm going down to help look for him.'

'You're going to do nothing of the sort. Don't be foolish. His parents are bad enough, there's no need for you to start. The boy is where he went of his own will, you may be absolutely sure, and he'll turn up when it suits him. When he's demoralised everybody so much that he needn't fear reprisals. Not before!'

'You,' said Tamsin forcefully, 'are a heartless old woman, that's what you are. I wish you'd tell me what you did to him this morning. I know there's something.'

'What I did to him, indeed! Don't be impertinent! I'm the old woman who pays your salary, at any rate,' said Miss Rachel tartly, because no matter how firmly she held the door, the demons were getting through it. 'You'd better remember that, miss. I hate dining alone, and you know it. And I haven't had my game of chess. So stop being melodramatic, and get the board.'

'You'll have to make do with patience,' said Tamsin. 'I shan't be here.'

Miss Rachel called after her towards the door, in high indignation. 'If you go, you needn't bother to come back.'

'Goodbye, then,' said Tamsin pleasantly, and closed the door after her without even a slam.

Miss Rachel, left alone, was astonished and annoyed to find herself crying.

Chapter 5

Friday Evening

The tide was two hours past the full, and it was getting dark. The cauldron off the point was just going off the boil, slivers of slate-grey pebbly beach showed between the fangs of the Dragon, rimmed with scummy foam. The Dragon's Hole, which pierced clean through the headland near its narrowest point, and acted as a spectacular blow-hole as the tide streamed in to its highest, was merely breathing spume now in a desultory manner, as though the Dragon was falling asleep. Soon the dripping crown of the arched entrance would heave clear of the water, and the level would sink magically fast, to leave the whole rocky gateway clear. At low tide you could clamber and walk right through it, and emerge in the snaky little haven on the Pentarno side. Certain regions of the complex of caverns inside were always above water, but for three hours before and after high tide both entrances were submerged.

They were all in the hunt by then. Phil had driven in from the farm in the Mini, pale and strained and violently silent, matched herself with the first partner who happened to come in with his periodical, and negative report, and gone off with him to scour the most distant of the Maymouth beaches. Fate dealt her George, for which she was grateful, because that compelled her to behave sensibly and contain her terrors; she

596

couldn't have borne to be with Tim just then, to double his anguish and her own.

Bunty had come down from the hotel, determined not to be left out, workmanlike in slacks and a windjacket, and was quartering the country fringes of Maymouth with the Vicar, in case Paddy had had a fall or a crash somewhere on his intended way home. There were precipitous lanes he might have chosen to use, to vary the monotony of his journey, and a cyclist can come to grief on even the quietest of roads, given a little carelessness or a too-optimistic local driver who assumes no one uses these byways but himself. Everyone who was at all intimate with the boy had been telephoned and asked to keep in touch. What more could they do but just look everywhere, and go on looking?

Tamsin and Dominic had worked their way the length of the harbour, down on the mud, following up the receding tide, and come empty-handed to the remotest rocks under the wall, where ashlar gave way to granite and shale, and the jagged scales of the Dragon leaned over them. The sea still lipped the cliffs here, they could go no farther as yet. They turned inland, hugging the cliff wall, winding in and out of its many razor-edged alcoves, and the crying of the subsiding waves followed them mournfully. They were drenched with spray and very muddy. Dominic had the torch, and sometimes turned to empty its light carefully before her feet in the rough places, and give her a hand. She knew every inch of this shore, but she took the hand, just the same. They were both glad of the touch. This had been going on for such a long time now, and where can you lose a sensible, responsible boy of fifteen, where, at least, that hadn't already been searched? Except in the sea! They wouldn't think that, they couldn't, it was unthinkable. Paddy was strong, shrewd and capable, and knew his native coast. He was alive, he must be alive.

They climbed slowly out of the pebbly fringes of the sea, towards where the first steep path plunged down from the Dragon's Head. A surging rush of air was all the warning they had. They sprang apart before the hurtling onslaught of something that came bounding down the slope, flashed between them, and was dragged to a noisy stop by a toe horribly scoring the turf. Small, invisible things hopped and rolled under their feet. A voice, anxious, urgent and low, panted: 'Tam, is that you?'

Stumbling and slipping on the rolling missiles, Tamsin groped for a tweed sleeve. Dominic turned the torch, and Simon's face started out of the dark, abrupt in black and white, strained to steel-sharpness, for once utterly bereft of its light, world-weary smile.

'Simon, for God's sake! What are you trying to do, kill yourself? Fancy riding a bicycle down – '

Tamsin stopped, swallowed, drew breath hard and was silent. The light of the torch passed briefly over the frame of the bicycle, the carrier on the front, the basket spilling small oval fruit. They had no colour by this light, but Tamsin knew them for apricots. She whispered, 'Where did you find it?'

'In the gorse, up by the cliff path there. Put down quite carefully, the basket lifted out. Near the edge,' said Simon, low-voiced and ashen-faced. 'Not exactly hidden. Laid down out of the way.'

'He did it himself?'

'I think so. I hope so. I'm going to turn it in at once, in case it can tell us anything.'

'*Where* along the path?' she demanded intently. Her voice had lost its reserve in Simon's presence, and its sting, too, as his face had lost its assured sophistication. It was as if they had never bumped into each other without masks before, and now that they had, they couldn't even see each other.

'Farther out. Over the blow-hole, about. Have you been down there?'

'We couldn't yet, not so far. It's going out fast now, though, we'll follow on down.'

'Do, Tam, please. I'll be with you as soon as I can.'

'Do you think he could have fallen?' she asked, desperately quietly.

'I don't know. I won't think so. I – Oh, Tam!' said Simon suddenly, his voice almost inaudible, and caught at her hand for a moment; and instantly pulled away from her, climbed unsteadily on to the bicycle that was too small for him, and wobbled away recklessly across the bumpy waste of turf to the road and the town. Soiled and dishevelled and faintly ridiculous, and for once wholly, passionately intent upon someone other than himself, without a thought for the preservation of his image or his legend.

Dominic switched off the torch; and after a moment he put an arm delicately but quite confidently about Tamsin, and turned her towards the sea.

They followed the receding tide down the beach yard by yard, ranging along the edge of the water and coasting round into every new complexity of the cliff wall, which ran down here in striated, shaly strata into the litter of flat, blue pebbles and eroded shell. A certain amount of lambent light showed along the breaking foam, and gleamed from the streaming rocks, and their torch, a thin pencil in the dark, probed the corners where even the starlight could not reach.

'That *was* Simon?' said Tamsin suddenly, all the old obduracy back in her voice.

'Well, that's what you called him,' said Dominic cautiously.

'Thanks. Just making sure. It's the first time I ever saw him when he didn't have an imaginary mirror in front of him. He must be really fond of Paddy.'

'He is,' said Dominic.

'Do I detect a note of reproof in your voice, Mr. Felse?'

He said nothing. What was the good? Only a tiny corner of her mind fretted at the memory of Simon off his guard, and that was to make their one overwhelming anxiety bearable, like pinching yourself to take your mind off a hideous toothache.

Any serious thinking she was going to do about it would be done later, in repose, when, please God, they'd have Paddy Rossall safe in bed, and Simon restored to his old image. And then he'd start rubbing her up the wrong way all over again.

'You'll notice,' she said perversely, her shoes slipping in the weedy crevices of the rock, 'he never asks me to marry him when there might be the slightest fear of me saying yes.' She slithered into the edge of an invisible pool, and Dominic caught her by the arm and drew her back on to safe ground.

'All right?'

'Fine! Just a shoe-full of sea. It can't make me any wetter.' She held on to him for a moment, steadying herself. Her hands were very cold. He saw her face close to him, feathers of wet hair plastered to her cheek, her eyes sombre and wretched. 'Dom – we shall find him, shan't we?'

'Yes,' he said, very firmly. 'He's a sensible kid, I don't believe he'd let anyone creep up on him, and I don't believe he'd do anything daft himself.' Which from eighteen to fifteen, when Tamsin came to think of it, was pretty generous, but he sounded as if he really meant it. 'He'll be found intact,' said Dominic strenuously, 'and with any luck, we shall be the ones to find him. So hang on, and let's have a look round the next corner.'

They had looked round a good many by then, with their hearts in their mouths at every turning, but so far there'd been no slight, tumbled body under the cliffs, and nothing washing about in the edge of the retreating waves but casual weed.

'Yes,' she said docilely. And after a moment, very quietly at his shoulder: 'You're a nice boy, Dominic Felse, I like you.'

'Good! I like you, too, I like you a lot. There, you see, nothing!' He couldn't help reflecting, as soon as it was out, that nothing was a pretty poor return for all their hunting, and a pretty lame reassurance for Paddy's mother. But it was all they had, and it was better than the wrong thing, at any rate.

The sea sighed away from them, down the more steeply tilted shingle. They stood close under the overhang of the cliff, on a washed and empty shore, and right above their heads must be the necklace of the lofty path that circled the Dragon's Head, and the scattered hollows of gorse where Simon had found the bicycle. The waters had left the arched entrance of the cave now, it stood tamed and dark above a faint glimmer of salt puddles penned among the boulders.

They halted for only a second, contemplating it together.

'He wouldn't,' said Tamsin, 'would he?'

'Not without a reason, but he may have had a reason, how do we know?'

'But he knows the tides, he wouldn't let himself get caught.'

'Something may have happened that didn't leave him any choice. Anyhow, we're not leaving anything out.'

'Careful, then,' she cautioned, drawing him to the right, to the landward side of the thin channel of water that lay prisoned among the pebbles in the cavern's mouth. 'This side's the smoothest going. And look out, there are holes.'

Dominic fell into one at that moment, cold salt water gripped him to the knees, and the chilling shock surprised a muted yell out of him. Deep in the blackness beyond the beam of the torch, echo took the shout and volleyed it back to him redoubled.

'Dom!' Tamsin caught at his arm. 'Did you hear that?'

Floundering out of the crevices on slippery oblique rock, he supposed that she was as startled by the force and complexity of the echo as he had been, and merely went on scrambling noisily up to safer ground. 'Hear it? I started it. It wasn't that good an imitation – '

'No – listen!' She shook him impatiently, and he froze into obedient silence, straining his ears.

Nothing at first, not a sound; then they were aware of the ceaseless, soft, universal sound of the dripping of seawater from every jutting point of the stone ceiling above them and the contorted walls around, and the soft, busy flowing of a dozen rivulets draining down between the pebbles into the central

601

channel behind them. The place was full of the sounds of water, but empty of the sounds of men.

'But it wasn't all echo. I'm sure!'

Almost fearfully, Dominic called upward into the invisible spaces of the cave: 'Paddy?'

The call came eddying back to him from a dozen projections he could not see, repeated in a dozen hopeful, fearful inflections, ricocheting away into silence. Then a last faint and distant sound, out of turn, out of key, started a weak reverberation away on their right.

'There! Here that? There *is* someone!'

But Dominic was already scrambling wildly up the rattling scree of sand and gravel and shell, the pencil of wavering light wincing away from rocks and water-drips before him, clawing his way up towards the drier reaches of the cave. He stretched out a hand to her and dragged her after him. Stumbling, slipping, panting, they climbed inland; and somewhere ahead of them, distant and faint but drawing nearer, unmistakable sounds of someone else's stumbling, slipping, panting progress came down to meet them.

Into the beam of the torch blundered Paddy Rossall, wiping his dirty face hastily with an even dirtier hand; pallid, wet, and shivering with cold, but alive, intact and alone.

'You don't mind,' said Phil, turning in at the drive of Treverra Place, 'if we call in here? I don't know that it will do any good, but I just thought, while we're so near – She might remember *something* he said, anything that will give us the faintest clue. I know we've asked the same questions already, but it's worth one more try. Oh, George, my poor little boy! I wish I hadn't said no to him. I wish I'd let him go with Tim and Simon – at least he'd have been safe with them.'

It was the most she had said in all the hours they had hunted together. As long as there'd been more places to search, more possible people to contact, Phil had been a silent, ferocious force of nature sweeping all before her. Only now, when they had almost exhausted the possibilities, was the edge of desperation audible in her voice, and the shadow of breakdown a perceptible cloud over her face.

Miss Rachel was sitting over the fire in her sitting-room, huddled like a broody bird, with her solitary dinner untouched on a little table beside her. She stiffened her old spine and snapped the imperious lights on again in her eyes when Phil stalked in with George at her elbow, but she knew her back was against the wall.

'Aunt Rachel, didn't he say *anything* about where he was going? There must have been something. You did see him yourself, didn't you? Well, what *did* he say? I *know* we're snatching at crumbs. Damn it, crumbs is all we've got.'

'Yes, I talked to him, certainly.' Miss Rachel looked smaller than usual, but fiercer. Attack is the best defence. 'What passed between Paddy and me can't possibly have anything to do with any danger to him. But it may – I say *may* – account for his naughtiness in staying away like this. If you ask me, that's all it is, and you are just playing into his hands. I was justified in being cross with him. He was exceedingly impertinent and very disobedient, and it was high time someone took steps to bring him to more chastened frame of mind.'

Quivering and aghast, Phil demanded: 'But what – for God's sake, Aunt Rachel, what *did* you do to him?'

She couldn't stall any longer, it would only make it worse when it did come out. And besides, she was lonely and frightened and she wanted Paddy back, impertinent or not, disobedient or not, she just wanted him. So somebody had to find him for her.

'It's too much to hope that you'll approve, of course, but I was concerned only for you and Tim, and for the child's own wellbeing. I told him what he should have been told as soon as he was old enough to understand – that he has to thank you and Tim for taking him in and giving him a good home and the love of good parents, when his own father wanted to get rid of him. I told him he was adopted, and that he should consider how much he owed to you, and try to behave better to you in future, not take everything for granted as he does. That's what I told him, and you'll have reason to thank me for it yet.'

Stricken, Phil stood clinging to the back of a chair as to the rocking remnants of her world. 'Aunt Rachel! You couldn't! You *couldn't* be so cruel!'

'Cruel, nonsense! It was high time he was told, you'd have had to do it in the end. I don't believe it's done him one jot of harm, either, so – '

'No *harm*!' Groping through the blankness of her misery, Phil arrived at a positive and tonic fury. Her cheeks flushed scarlet, and paled again to a pinched and frightening whiteness. 'No *harm*! You drive that poor boy away with the bottom knocked out of his world, not knowing who or what he is, and you say you've done him no *harm*!'

'It means we're probably all wrong about his being in danger from our murderer,' pointed out George quickly, with a gentling hand on her arm. 'He's shocked and hurt and wretched, he wants to hide, that's all understandable. But it means he's probably staying away of his own will, and when he's come to terms with it he'll come home. It isn't as bad as what we were afraid of.'

'It is, George, it's almost worse. He'll be in such a state he might do *anything*.' She turned frantically upon Miss Rachel, who was backed into her great chair with hackles erect, ready for a fight. 'How would *you* feel, you wicked old woman, if you suddenly found you weren't who you thought you were, and your parents weren't your parents, and everything you had was borrowed? Even your identity?' She gripped the edge of the table, and demanded urgently: 'Did you tell him *who* he was? But you couldn't – we never told you, thank God, so you didn't know.'

'Oh, yes, my dear Phil, I did know. His father told me himself

– right here in the garden, no longer ago than Wednesday afternoon. He told me quite a lot. But I didn't tell Paddy. I don't have to tell everything I know.' She drew breath before Phil could ride over her again, and pursued belligerently: 'But *you'd* better. Oh, I know, Simon thinks he can twist me round his finger. Maybe I like it that way. But don't think I've got any illusions about him. I like him very much, but sooner or later he'll make a bid for what he wants. And if you haven't noticed that he's beginning to want Paddy, very much indeed, you'd better wake up, quickly.'

George, whose experience in breaking up fights between women was still somewhat inadequate to such a situation as this, felt profound gratitude to the telephone for ringing just then. It gave him something to do, more constructive than listening to family secrets it would be his duty promptly to forget again, and it distracted the attention of both the embattled females. He picked up the receiver thankfully.

'Treverra Place. This is George Felse. Oh, yes – yes, she's here. Phil, it's Tamsin Holt for you.'

Phil clutched the receiver convulsively, afraid to hope. 'Tamsin, what is it? Have you – *You have*! Thank God! He's all right?'

Her knees gave under her, she was suddenly limp as silk, and George slid a chair under her and eased her into it.

'*He's all right!* They've found him. In the Dragon's Hole. The tide caught him inside there. Aunt Rachel, it's all right! They've found him – Tamsin and Dominic. I don't care now, nothing else matters. I don't care what you told him, he's all right. Tam – we're on our way down, we'll meet you. Take care of him! Don't you let him out of your sight again. The little *demon*! Honestly, I'll murder him! You're *sure* he isn't hurt? God bless you, Tam! We're on our way.'

She let the receiver slip nervelessly down into its cradle. She was in tears, and trembling. 'George, can you drive a Mini? I – don't think I'm capable – Oh, George, *I want Tim*!'

George got her to her feet and out to the car. No one had even a glance to spare for Miss Rachel, braced and defensive in her high-backed chair.

As soon as they were out of the doorway she hopped suddenly out of her sanctuary behind the cold dinner-tray, and danced the length of the room and the library, like an agile girl, until her piled grey hair came down round her shoulders, and she was out of breath. Then, having carefully reassembled her magnificent coiffure and her even more magnificent personal assurance, she rang the bell for Alice, and demanded food.

On their way down through the town they picked up Tim. Phil clung to him in the back seat, pouring out the best and the worst of the news, and swinging breathlessly between rage and joy. Tim held her in his arms and shook with the vehemence of her trembling, and implored her first, and then ordered her, just as ineffectively, to be calm and matter-of-fact, and take the whole thing easily. Hadn't they agreed from the beginning that with a child not your own you must take nothing for granted, that you had to exercise twice as much care and self-control as natural parents, and earn every morsel of your gift-son's affection? Restraint, no too greedy love, no too lavish indulgences and no too exacting demands, that was the way. If she let herself go now, she'd push the boy right over the edge, and break something.

'Here they are,' said George at the wheel, and drew the Mini in to the kerb just below the square, the dilapidated trio before them caught and dazzled in its lights. A slim, taut, brittle figure toiled up the hill between two muddy supporters just recognisable as Tamsin and Dominic. He had been drooping badly a moment before, but now he was braced to meet them. The moment was on top of him; he wasn't ready, but he never would be ready, it might as well happen and get it over. A pale, grime-streaked face stared, all enormous, shocked eyes. Phil

lunged for the door-handle and was half out of the car before
it came to a halt.

'Phil, you must be *calm* – '

'To hell with being calm!' shouted Phil, in a splendid flare of
wrathful joy, and hurled herself upon her stray in a flurry
of abuse, endearments and reproaches.

Paddy's parent problem was swept away in the warm, sweet
hurricane. After all, he didn't have to make any decisions about
how to behave, he didn't have to do anything at all. The meeting
he had been dreading was taken clean out of his hands. He was
plucked from between his henchmen, hugged, shaken, even he
seemed to remember afterwards with respect and astonishment,
slapped, a thing he couldn't remember ever having happened to
him before in his life. Tim snatched him from Phil to feel him
all over, swear at him heartily, strip him of his wet and filthy
sweater, and bundle him into a warm, dry sportscoat much too
big for him. He could hardly get a word in edgeways, all he
managed was: 'I'm sorry!' and: 'I didn't mean to!' and: 'I
couldn't help it!' at intervals. And he had been shrinking from
the thought of moderated voices and careful handling, into
which he would inevitably have read all sorts of reservations!
There weren't any moderated voices round here, he couldn't
hear himself think; and the way he was being handled, he was
going to start coming to pieces shortly. This sort of thing there
was no mistaking. He was loved, all right. She was frantic about
him, and Dad wasn't much better. This, he thought, hustled
and scolded and abused and caressed into dazed silence, this is
exactly how parents behave.

'Into that car,' ordered Tim, growing grimmer by the minute
now that he had satisfied himself that he had his son back with
hardly a scratch on him. 'You're going to apologise to Mr.
Hewitt for all the trouble you've caused everybody, and you'd
better make it good.' And when he had him penned into the
back seat, with Phil to cushion him comfortably, he had to

rummage out the old car rug and tuck him into it like a cocoon, and all to go the two hundred yards to the police station.

The rest of the evening always remained to him a crazy confusion, from which fleeting remarks emerged at times to tickle his memory. The one overwhelming thing about it was that all of it, every bit, was good, better than anything had ever been before, or perhaps ever would be again. To have happiness and know that you have it, and know how wonderful it is to know it, that's almost too much for any one day.

He was bundled into the warmth and light of the police station, blinking and exhausted, and made his apologies with quite unexpected grace, out of the fullness of his own plenty. He said thank you to everyone who had gathered there from the great boy-hunt, and requested that his thanks be conveyed to all those who were not there to hear for themselves. Hewitt received the offering with considerable complacency, out of pure relief, but maintained a solemn face.

'Don't you think you've heard the last of it, young feller-me-lad. Your next six months' pocket-money's going to be needed to pay for police shoe-leather. I'll be sending you in a bill.' He grinned at Tim over the tow-coloured head that was beginning to be unconscionably heavy. 'Take him home, clean him up and put him to bed, Mr. Rossall. I'll talk to him in the morning, he's out on his feet now.'

He remembered looking round a whole ring of faces when he said goodnight. Mr. Felse was there with his wife, Tamsin was there, and Dominic, and the Vicar, and Uncle Simon. Uncle Simon was looking at him in an odd sort of way, smiling, but without the sparkle, and twice as hard as usual. And he didn't come with them. Why didn't he? Oh, yes, of course, he probably had his own car here, so he had to drive it home. But it didn't look as if that was in his mind, somehow, when he shook his head at Dad, with that odd, rueful smile on his face, and said: 'No, I'll follow you down later, old boy. This is a family special.'

That reminded Paddy of how this extraordinary day had

started. There were things he still had to know about himself, but somehow all the urgency was already gone. In the back seat of the car, rolled up again snugly in the rug, with Phil's arm round him, and Phil's shoulder comfortable and comforting under his cheek, he drowsed gloriously, too tired to know anything clearly except the one wonderful, all-pervading fact that it was all right. That everything was all right, because his belonging to them was everything.

And whoever he might have belonged to in the beginning, he was certainly theirs now. Heaven help anyone who tried to take him away from them, or them from him!

'I'm glad you know I know,' he said out of his pillows, bathed, fed, warmed and cosseted, and drowning in a delicious, sleepy happiness. 'It did come as a bit of a shock at first, that's why I sheered off from Aunt Rachel's without telling anybody. I wasn't trying to frighten anyone, or run away from home, or anything daft, like that. Honestly! I'm not such a clot.'

'I should hope not,' said Tim.

'No, but I was afraid you might think – I just felt shaken up, and not wanting to see anybody, or be talked to. You know! I started for home, and then I couldn't face it, not until I'd had time to think. I went up on the Head, instead, but it was *swarming*. People everywhere. I just ditched the bike, and nipped down the cliff path and into the cave, where I knew I could be quiet. Just till I got a bit more used to it, that's all. But then some kids came in, playing, and I backed up as far as I could, to get out of their way.'

Having, thought Phil, who had not failed to distinguish the tear-marks from the general stains of seawater and cave-grime, an entirely visible and possibly temporarily uncontrollable distress to hide by then.

'Never mind now, darling, you go to sleep. There's time for all that tomorrow. You're home, and that's all that matters.'

'Yes, but I just wanted you to know I wasn't sulking, or

anything childish like that. It was just by accident I happened
to find this passage in the top end of the cave. Only a low sort
of hole, you have to crawl through it on hands and knees. I was
backed up into this corner, and I shoved my shoulder through
it in the dark. It goes a long way. That's how I lost time, having
to be careful because of not having a light. In the end I did call
it a day and decide to come back some other time with a torch,
but what with not being able to see my watch, and forgetting
because I was interested, by the time I crawled back through
the hole I'd had it. The water was almost up to the top of the
cave mouth, and I didn't dare dive for it, it was too rough. I
had to lie up and wait, there wasn't anything else to do.' He
looked up with the remembered terror suddenly brilliant in his
eyes, squarely into Tim's face. 'I was scared green,' he said.

'So would I have been. Even knowing that the top part of
the Hole's above high water, I'd still have been scared.'

'And even there you get a bit battered. And deafened! I
couldn't wait to get out, it seemed for ever. I couldn't tell what
time it was, you see, I just had to follow the water down, and
you have to be super-cautious feeling your way in the dark. But
I was on my way out as fast as I dared when they came and
found me.'

Phil turned the shaded light away from her own face, for fear
he should see his ordeal reflected there all too plainly, stroked
the fuzz of fair hair back from his forehead, and said: 'Yes, well,
it's all over now. You just forget it and go to sleep.'

'Yes – all right, I will. I just wanted you to know how it was.
I'm sorry I caused everybody so much trouble.' Half asleep and
off his guard, he said with shattering simplicity: 'I was just so
miserable I didn't know what to do.'

Tim hooked a large right fist to the angle of his son's jaw,
and rolled the fair head gently on the pillow till a shamefaced
grin came through.

'Did you say you weren't a clot? You could have fooled me!
Sure you know now where you live?' The drowsy head nodded;

the grin had a curious but happy shyness. 'And what time the tide comes in? All right, then, you sleep it off. If you want anything we'll be around.' He rose, rolled Paddy over in the bed, and smacked the slight hummock of his rump under the clothes. 'Good-night, son!'

'Good-night, Dad!'

All the years they'd been saying exactly the same words, and they'd never meant so much before!

Phil kissed the spot where the blonde hair grew to a slight point on the smooth forehead, and was following Tim from the room when a small, self-conscious voice behind her said: 'Mummy!'

The tone of it tugged her back to him in a hurry. He hadn't said it without thought, it had a ceremonial solemnity. She stooped over him, and he pushed away the bedclothes suddenly and reached up his arms for her, burrowing his face thankfully into the hollow of her neck.

'Just making sure,' he said in a muffled whisper. 'You *are*, aren't you?'

'Yes, I am, Patrick Rossall, and don't you dare forget it.'

She gathered up his clothes when she left the room. The flannels would have to go straight to the cleaners. She sat down on the rug beside Tim, and extracted from the pockets, smiling over them with a ridiculous tenderness because they were small projections of Paddy's personality, one exceedingly grubby handkerchief, sticky with seawater, a ball pen down to its last inch, the end chewed, two or three foreign stamps, a used bus ticket, one dilapidated toffee, and a few coins, which she stacked carefully on the arm of Tim's chair.

'He's all right, isn't he?' said Tim, ears pricked for any sound from upstairs.

'Yes, he's all right.' Her smile was heavy, maternal and assured. 'Don't worry about Paddy. Tim, I'm glad! I'm glad she told him. It's a once-only. He knows now.'

'He's a nice kid,' said Tim. He took up the little pile of coins to play with, because they were Paddy's. 'Look, a brand-new halfpenny.' He looked again, and froze. 'It isn't, though! What is it? Phil, look! It isn't copper. It looks like gold!'

She dropped the crumpled, dirty flannels, and held out her hand curiously for the coin. It lay demurely in her palm, showing a thick-necked female profile, with a curled lock of hair draped over one plump shoulder.

'Tim, it must be a guinea! Or a half-guinea – but it's too big, isn't it? ANNA DEI GRATIA. And VIGO underneath her portrait. What does that mean? There's a date on the other side, 1703. REG. MAG. BR. FR. et HIB.' She looked up at Tim over her spread palm, open-mouthed. 'Tim, where on earth did our Paddy get a Queen Anne guinea?'

Chapter 6

Saturday Morning

Phil looked in at Paddy's door as soon as she was up on Saturday morning. The early sunlight came in softened and dimmed through the drawn curtains, and the boy lay curled comfortably, with cheek and nose burrowed into his pillow, fast asleep. She looked at him with her love like a warm, golden weight in her, and was drawing back silently when a faint movement in the shadows of one corner arrested her.

Simon was sitting in a chintz-covered chair, drawn back where the light could not reach him. He was looking at her by the time she saw him; but she knew very well that until that moment he had been watching Paddy's sleep. He looked as if he had been there half the night. Maybe he had. He had his own key, and she hadn't heard him come in.

Only a few days ago she would have stiffened in jealousy and suspicion, willing him away, and stared her orders unmistakably. Now she stood looking at him thoughtfully and calmly, and in her heart she was sorry for him. It was the first time she had ever achieved that. This morning she was sorry for everybody who wasn't herself or Tim, and hadn't got a son like Paddy; and sorriest of all for Simon Towne, who had had one and lacked the sense to hang on to him while he had him. She smiled, meeting his tired and illusionless eyes. He got up very quietly, as though she had warned him off, and followed her out of the room and down the stairs.

'I'll grind the coffee,' he offered, following her into the kitchen. He was handier about the house than Tim, and quieter. She supposed widowers of long experience – nearly fifteen years now – easily might be. She began preparing breakfast. Even the solid blue and white crockery looked new, as if to-day everything began afresh. But not for Simon.

Not because she had the better of him, and knew it, but because he was a figure so much more appealing now that he was shaken and vulnerable and fit for sympathy, she had never liked him so much before. But you couldn't alter Simon, or teach him anything, just by liking him better. He would have to learn the hard way.

'Have you been to bed?' she asked, slicing bread.

'No. I brought the Land-Rover down with Paddy's bike aboard, and then fetched the car and went for a long ride. Then I came home and lay down for a bit, and had a bath. I hope I didn't disturb you when I came in?'

'No, I didn't hear you. How long have you been guarding Paddy's sleep?' She didn't sound either suspicious or resentful; he found that surprising, and for some reason it pricked a spring of resentment in him.

'I don't know. A couple of hours or so. I enjoy looking at him. Do you mind?'

'No, I'm glad. I enjoy looking at him, too.' She came from the pantry with a bowl of eggs balanced on one hand, a jug of milk in the other. Simon left his grinding to take the eggs from her, and being so near, leaned impulsively and kissed her cheek, without apology or explanation. Phil smiled at him. 'It's all right, Simon. I know what happened to you, when you were afraid Paddy was gone for good. But do you know what happened to him? A fifteen-year-old bubble burst, my dear, and we're none of us ever going to be the same again. Miss Rachel got annoyed because Paddy was cheeky to her, and because she thought he didn't appreciate his good home as he ought. So she told him he only enjoyed it on sufferance. He knows now that he – ' She couldn't say: 'He isn't ours,' because it wouldn't be true; it would be more monstrously untrue now than it had ever been before. 'He knows we adopted him. That's what happened to Paddy.'

Simon put the eggs down very carefully on the kitchen table, and straightened up to turn upon her the gravest face, and the least concerned for the effect it might be producing upon the outside world, that she had ever seen him wear. After a long moment of quietness he asked in a voice that was avoiding strain with some care: 'Did she tell him he was really mine?'

Phil smiled. He hadn't chosen the words as a challenge or a claim, in a sense he hadn't consciously chosen them at all, but they still indicated his implicit belief in their truth. 'No, she didn't. But she told me she could have. After all this time, why *did* you tell her?'

'I don't know,' he said honestly. 'I suppose I simply wanted *somebody* to know, just so that I could talk about him and be understood. Preferably somebody who'd feel sorry for me, to tell the whole truth. But I never meant this to happen, Phil. I suppose it's because of what I told her that she had this thing in her mind, a stick all ready to beat him with when he offended her. I'm sorry! I never thought of anything like that.'

'I know, I'm not blaming you.'

'But since he knows so much – I don't know that I'd feel there was anything now to stop me from telling him the rest.' He turned on the gas ring and put on the kettle with steady and leisurely movements. A fine spark of intent had kindled deep in his eyes, and that meant mischief. The faintest hint of the usual bold quirk twitched at the corner of his mouth, and again his face had a wayward acquisitiveness about it. Tamsin's hackles had risen at sight of that debonair and much-admired face with which he pursued his dearest objectives, but it hadn't taught him anything.

'You won't have to bother,' said Phil. 'I'll tell him myself.'

'You?' He was surprised into a genuine laugh.

'I haven't much alternative now, have I? You must know very well that the first thing he's going to ask me, when he gets round to thinking about it seriously, is: Who am I? Of course I shall tell him.'

She turned and looked at him sharply, and saw exactly what she had expected to see, the sleek glow of triumph and speculation and hope warming his face into golden confidence. She closed the oven door with a crisp slam.

'Look, Simon, wake up, while there's time. It isn't going to do you any good, you know.'

'Isn't it? Phil, you're positively inviting me to see what I can do. Aren't you afraid I'll sneak him away from under your nose even now? Don't you think I could?'

'I know you couldn't,' she said steadily. 'I don't think you'd even try, if I begged you not to. But I'm not begging you – am I? I don't have to, Simon, that's why. You couldn't get him away from us now whatever you did, fair or foul. You've had a long innings, charming the birds from the trees, and getting golden apples to fall into your lap whenever you smiled. You can't realise, can you, that it isn't going to last for ever? The high days are over, Simon, middle age is only just round another corner or two. You'd better start settling for what you can get, because the long holiday's running out fast. And whatever you do, you won't get Paddy.'

For a moment it seemed to her that his brightness had grown sharp and brittle, and his eyes were staring at something he would rather not have seen. Then they took heart and danced again.

'What will you bet me?' he said with soft deliberation.

Remembering the long years of friendship through which Tim had followed him around patiently, picking up the things Simon dropped and putting together the things Simon broke, she wondered for a moment if her motives were as pure as she would have liked. But if it was vengeful pleasure that was prompting her to invite him to his downfall, why was this moment so sad, so strangely the shadowy reverse of the serenity and joy that made this morning a portent and a prodigy? And why should she feel so much closer and kinder to him than she had ever felt before?

'I should be betting you Paddy, shouldn't I?' she said, gently and quietly. 'What more do you want?'

Paddy opened his eyes and stretched delightedly, and then remembered why everything felt and looked different to-day. Not necessarily better or worse, not yet; just different. And as if in answer to a call which had certainly never been uttered except, perhaps, in his mind, Phil was suddenly there in the room, bringing him a clean pair of slacks and a shirt from the airing cupboard.

'Good morning, mudlark! How do you feel this morning?'

He felt strange; larger than usual, more responsible, and more subdued. Big with all the things he had to think about. But beyond all question, he felt good. Good, in a state of wellbeing; and good, virtuous.

'I feel fine. Is it really that time? And I've got to go to the police station, haven't I?' He sat up, solemn-faced, remembering.

'Mummy!' The sudden charged softness of his voice warned her what was coming, but he was longer about framing it than she had expected, and the end-product, when it emerged, was a revelation.

'Mummy, *who was I*?'

Her heart gave a leap of joy and triumph. She thought: Poor Simon! She laid Paddy's clean clothes on a chair, and came and sat down on the edge of his bed. Flushed and bemused from long sleep, he faced her earnestly and trustingly, and waited for an answer. It mattered, just to the private thinking he had to do about himself; but it couldn't affect what they had between them now.

'You know,' he said, 'what I mean.'

'Yes, I know. Your mother was a very nice girl, a good friend of ours, Paddy. She was only twenty-one when she died, from some illness that came on after you were born. And her husband – your father – You know him, Paddy. You know him very well, and he's very fond of you. You know him as Uncle Simon.'

He didn't exclaim, his face didn't show surprise, or consternation, or relief, or pleasure, or anything else but the same charged gravity. He accepted it, and sat digesting it.

'His wife died,' said Phil, 'and left you on his hands. He was just beginning to be well-known then, and he had a contract for his first big tour. He couldn't take a baby with him. And I'd lost one only a few months before, and the doctors said I couldn't have another. So you mustn't blame him too much. He loved his wife very much, and he was wretched about losing her, and wanted to get away. It wasn't just fear of losing his big opportunity.'

Since she had invited this single combat, she felt obliged to conduct it scrupulously; and besides, one should never allow a child to contemplate the possibility that he may have failed to make himself loved. But was this a child facing her? The fluffy crest and slender neck and unformed forehead said yes; the grave eyes and something in the set of the face suggested that this juvenile image was already a little out of date.

'It doesn't mean he didn't love you,' said Phil firmly. But he didn't, she thought honestly; he wasn't a person to whom babies were quite human beings at all, and he isn't alone in that, it's something he couldn't help. 'Well, you've got to know him pretty well, this visit. He hasn't shown any want of affection, has he?'

Paddy received the revelation in silence, and continued to ponder with an almost forbidding concentration.

'O.K., Mummy, I see. Thanks for telling me. Now we're all straight.' He slid his legs out of bed. 'I'd better get a move on, or Mr. Hewitt will be sending an escort for me. But I don't know that I'm going to be much use to him, am I? I mean, my little trek isn't going to tell him who knocked old Trethuan on the head and tossed him in the sea, is it?'

'That reminds me,' said Phil, glad of the distraction. 'Do you know what I found in your pocket last night?' She brought the little gold coin, and displayed it triumphantly in her palm.

'Oh, that!' he said, rather disappointingly. And then, as his eyes took in the design and the colour of it, which seemed to be totally unfamiliar: 'Gosh, is *that* what it turned out to be? But it looks really something.' He took it and turned it about curiously, examining it with astonished delight. 'What is it? Do you know?'

'You're a fine one!' said Phil, amused. 'First you say: "Oh, that!" Then you start goggling at it as if you'd never seen it before.'

'But, silly,' he said, laughing, 'I never have seen it before. It was pitch dark in there, I told you, that's why I had to give up and turn back in the end. I've *felt* it before, though.'

'You found it in this passage in the cave?'

'Yes, way along it as far as I went. I fell over a bit of rock and went down on my hands, and this thing was sticking in my palm. Well, I could tell it was a coin, but all I thought was, somebody else exploring must have had a hole in his pocket, and I was a shilling up. It looks like *gold*,' said Paddy, disbelievingly. 'Could it be?'

'I think it could, you know. Guineas and half-guineas were minted in gold, and this seems to be a Queen Anne guinea. You could show it to somebody at the museum, to make sure.'

'You mean it's really worth a guinea?' His eyes were wide with visions of wealth, and had lost for a moment their look of solemn preoccupation.

'More, I should imagine, if it's genuine, and I can't think of a reason why it shouldn't be. But it might be treasure trove, technically, we should have to find out about that.'

'I thought there'd be a catch in it.' He grinned at her

cheerfully enough, still having at least the thrill of discovery. 'But there might be more of them, did you think of that? Smugglers might have hidden them somewhere there.' She could feel him suddenly planning, and checking, and contemplating a barrier he might have to get round before he could proceed. Moments of crisis boil up so abruptly out of nowhere. 'Mummy!'

The careful, gentle, tentative voice nerved itself, moving in on her. Here it comes, Phil, she thought, and whatever you do there mustn't be any hesitation.

'Mummy, you don't mind if I go back there and take another look? With a torch, of course, this time.'

It was a stiff fence for both of them. Knowing he'd frightened her half to death once, and she'd hardly had time yet to get over it, terrified of being babied, but aware that it might be hard for her to give him his head to frighten her in the same way again, he couldn't quite manage the right easy tone. But that was something she mustn't let him realise she had noticed.

'No, of course I don't mind, darling. Take Daddy's big torch, there's a new battery in it. Don't want to risk getting left in the dark again. Do I get a commission, if the hoard turns out to be legally yours?'

After a brief, blank instant of astonished relief and admiration, shaken to the heart at finding himself trusted without even a caution, he said gruffly: 'You bet you do! We'll go halves.'

'Low tide's about a quarter to twelve. You'll be able to get in any time after ten. So hurry and get up to Mr. Hewitt, and then you'll have time enough before lunch.' Blessed reassurance, he wouldn't risk missing his lunch, not on a day when he was happy, not for all the guineas Queen Anne ever minted.

'I'll be careful,' he volunteered even more gruffly, and dug his toes hastily into his slippers and headed for the door.

There he checked, ears suddenly pricked, catching the unmistakable sound of Simon's Porsche starting up in the yard. Phil saw him stiffen, and the resolute shade of thought came down again upon his face. There was a relationship still to be adjusted somehow, and it wasn't going to be easy.

She wished she could guess what was going on in his mind, but the set of his face told her nothing. All that charm and glamour and excitement suddenly his for the claiming, and more than ready to fall into his lap – if only he would say something to give her a clue! But when he did make his one pregnant comment, it wasn't much help to her.

'I suppose I'm more fun now,' said Paddy bafflingly, and whisked away to the bathroom.

'I'm sorry,' he was saying, three-quarters of an hour later, in Hewitt's office overlooking the square, 'I don't seem to have been much help. But I really didn't look up at the Dragon's Head at all, and I didn't see a soul until Dominic came yelling at me. It isn't as if I'd seen anyone fall from up there, you see. I don't even know anything accurate about times, because I ran down in my trunks, like I always do, and I didn't have my watch. I'm sorry!'

'Well, there it is,' agreed Hewitt, no more nor less lugubrious than usual, but distinctly more loquacious, solid and fresh behind his shabby desk, with George Felse and Simon Towne in silent attendance, one on either side. 'Can't be helped, laddie. Don't you worry about it any more.'

'And you don't think my passage in the cave, and that guinea – if it really is a guinea? – you don't think they're anything to do with Treverra?' –

'I didn't say that, Paddy, my boy. I think it's unlikely, but I didn't say I wasn't interested. But I've no time to investigate that to-day.'

'Well, is it all right if I go and explore there again myself? I haven't got much time left, you see, I go back to school Monday.' School was the boarding-house of the best local grammar school, twelve miles inland. Its shadow cast a light cloud over the last week of his holidays, but promised escape, at least, from his present difficulties. He hadn't once seemed to look at Simon since he balked in the office doorway on finding him there, but he hadn't missed a single shade of expression that crossed the somewhat drawn and sombre face. He saw it tighten now, saw the quick flash of uneasy brown eyes in George's direction.

'My mother's given me permission,' said Paddy, with immense dignity.

'I've no objection, laddie,' said Hewitt heartily. 'You go ahead, and good luck. Let me know if you find out where the treasure's buried.' He saw Paddy's eloquent eyes rest calculatingly upon the small gold coin that lay before him on the desk, and palmed and tossed it to him so smoothly that the act seemed spontaneous. 'Here, better keep your sample by you. You'll let me see it again if necessary, I'm sure.'

Paddy's smile blazed like the sun. The little glitter of metal vanished into his ready palm and into his pocket. 'Yes, of *course*!'

'Why don't you show the place to Dominic?' suggested Simon, lightly and quickly. 'You just about owe him that.'

And Mr. Felse, equally easily: 'He'd certainly be glad to come with you. I look like being busy for a while, and he won't want to go souvenir-shopping with his mother, that's sure. Give him a ring, Paddy.'

'I will,' said Paddy politely. 'Thank you.'

He was pretty quick on the draw, was Mr. Felse, but of course a detective-inspector would have to be. He got Uncle Simon's message as fast as I did, thought Paddy, withdrawing aloofly from the room. He didn't want me to go back in the cave alone. Mummy still trusts me, but he doesn't. He's afraid something may happen to me.

And in the instant he saw it in reverse, and was dazzled. Uncle Simon, who can do everything better than anyone else, who goes everywhere, and ventures everything, and doesn't know what it is to be afraid for himself, he's afraid for *me*. He *does* care about me. Uncle Simon that was. Now I don't know what to call him. I don't know what he is.

I know what I am, though. I know *who* I am. And Mummy cares about me, too, and maybe she was just as afraid – more, because she's a woman. But all the same, she trusted me, and didn't even say: Take Dominic with you.

Meantime, it was hardly Dominic's fault, and you could see their point of view, and all that. So he'd do just what he'd said he'd do, and call him and invite him to come along. He was a little bit prefect-type, to be honest, but it was difficult not to be at that age; and he'd been jolly decent last night, and had the tact to vanish into the background as soon as the fussing began. He deserved to be rescued from souvenir-shopping.

'Well, that didn't get us much forrarder,' observed Hewitt, when the door had closed and Paddy's feet were clattering down the stairs. 'No surprise, really, I didn't think it would. So here we still are with two bodies that shouldn't have been there, and – don't forget this little detail – minus one that should.

'With the older body we still haven't got much to go on. The first job is to identify him. According to the reports so far he was about thirty years old, about six feet tall, and a pretty husky specimen. His ears were pierced, and there's a thin gold ring still in one of 'em. The body shows no injuries except to the skull, and those were clearly the cause of death. It looks as if he was bashed on the head from behind, maybe two or three blows, with a solid and probably jagged object, such as a lump of rock. The fragments of cloth suggest he was a seaman, most likely a fisherman.'

'Which means probably a local man,' said Simon intently.

'It doesn't necessarily follow, but everything rather indicates it as a probability. He's been dead between two and three years – certainly not two centuries. The one really good lead for identifying him is in his jaws. He's got a lot of very good dental work, most likely all done in one series of treatments after a long period of neglect. Whoever did that job on him will have it on record, and he'll know his own work again. It means we've got to get on to every dentist here and maybe up and down the coast, but it's only a matter of time, and we'll find him. And then, with any luck, we'll know who we've got down there.

'Now the other one, he's a very different matter. Here we have a fellow everyone knows, who was seen alive as late as four o'clock last Wednesday, and according to the medical evidence and the set of the tides must have been dead before ten o'clock the same night. The blow or blows that left that mark on his face didn't do more than knock him out, which seems to have been the object. He's otherwise more or less undamaged. He drowned in salt water, and was then put in the Treverra vault. And though Miss Rachel's key was in your possession during the material time, Mr. Towne, we now know that another key exists, and was kept in a place where anyone who had a little inside knowledge or a bit of luck could get at it. That leaves us a pretty wide field. It may have occurred to you, as a limiting factor, that surely only somebody who didn't know the vault was about to be opened could think of it as a good hiding-place for a murdered man. But even if we accept that – and I wouldn't put too much reliance on its importance – the field's still wide open.

'Now here we've got an unfriendly man who kept himself very much to himself, and usually managed to grate on other people so much that they were glad to let him. Obviously we're obliged to make a pretty thorough check on the movements of his son-in-law, because it's no secret that young Jim had a good many breezes with Trethuan before he got Rose away from him, and relations have been strained, to say the least of it, ever since. I'm not saying I think Jim Pollard makes a very likely murderer, but he's got a temper, and these things happen without much warning sometimes. There are holes in Jim's alibi that won't be easy to fill. He was down to the yard at the south end of Maymouth, Wednesday afternoon, for some timber for a little repair job at home, and then he did one or two more errands for paint and stuff round the town, and ended up working late on an old boat he's got beached in Pentarno haven, so he says. Which makes him mobile and at large but for the times of his various calls, and leaves plenty of time between for an unexpected brush with Rose's dad, supposing he met him in a nasty mood.

'However, he's just one possibility among many. If I should ask you, now, what's the oddest thing about Trethuan's own behaviour in the last days of his life, what would you say?'

He had looked at Simon, but Simon held his tongue. When the guileless stare turned upon George he responded promptly: 'Why was he so insistent that the vault must not be opened?'

'Exactly! Why? Religious objections? Superstition? That would account for anyone in his position criticising and prophesying evil, yes. But by all accounts this was more than that. He was desperate about it. Is that too strong, Mr. Towne?'

'No,' said Simon shortly, 'that's how he struck me.'

'So what was it that made it so urgent? Now I hear most of what goes on around here, and I don't mind telling you openly, I know all about your sporting warning issued in the Dragon bar on Wednesday night, Mr. Towne. And I saw – and so did Mr. Felse, if you didn't – the signs that the vault had been artistically swept and garnished and sanded over again before I got to it, and presumably before you did, on Friday. It's an old and time-honoured profession, is smuggling. You know it still goes on, I know it still goes on. I doubt if there's a licensee along this coast who doesn't get a drop of the real stuff that way. We know the vault was used as a liquor store, we know there was a nice, handy key, the one Sam Shubrough came by as an innocent child. And we know they won't use the same place again, if it's any reassurance to you – not since they cleared out their contraband, whenever they did. There wasn't any sense of desperation there. *They* didn't care a toot when you tipped 'em the wink, they just took the tip, and shifted their store to a safer place. And slipped you one on the house as an acknowledgement, I shouldn't wonder. Only one person was really concerned, and that was Trethuan. A lone wolf who wouldn't be wanted in any such confraternity, and who wouldn't want to be in it, anyhow.

'So I'm telling you, I don't believe smuggling or contraband had anything whatever to do with Trethuan's death, and I don't think you need worry about any of the otherwise law-abiding chaps around here who don't feel it any sin to slip a few kegs of brandy past the preventives. They're not my job. Murder is. And we're left with Trethuan and the something that made it absolutely vital to him that Treverra should rest in peace. Always supposing he'd been resting there at all, which as it turned out he wasn't. Did Zeb have something private and dangerous of his own that came over with the brandy? I doubt it. No, more likely his preoccupation was about something quite separate from theirs. It was somewhere in the vault. Why else should he be so desperate to stop you from opening it?'

'And why couldn't he move it,' said George, 'since apparently he could put it there in the first place?'

'*And where is it?*' added Simon. 'The place is as bare as the palm of your hand but for those two stone coffins. One of those we've exhausted already. There's nowhere left but Mrs. Treverra's coffin.'

'And that's exactly it, Mr. Towne. You represent Miss Rachel's interest in this matter. I'm going to suggest to you that we ought to open the second coffin, too. The Vicar thinks he can justifiably sanction it, on the strength of the permission already given for her husband. If you're prepared to join me and come along down to St. Nectan's right now, we can at least see if there's anything there to account for Zeb Trethuan's acting like a desperate man.'

'For the record,' said Simon, his eyes kindling golden-brown with curiosity, 'maybe we should. If it turns out to be full of Swiss watches that have never paid duty, then we shall be getting somewhere.'

'According to precedent to date,' said George dryly and

ruefully, as they went down the stairs, 'the one thing that certainly won't be in it is Mrs. Treverra!'

But that was where George was wrong. For when they had carefully lowered Jan Treverra's coffin-lid with slings to the floor of the vault, and prised the smaller stone lid beneath it, with its fine, defiant flourish of cryptic verse, out of its seating, when they had levered it clear and lowered it to rest beside its fellow, when they stood staring into the coffin, it was plain to be seen that the lady was all too surely there.

The shadow slid from over her almost reluctantly. A gush of fine dust ascended into the beam of their lanterns, and a dry, dead, nostalgic scent, as though pressed flowers, long since paper-fine and drained of nature, had disintegrated into powder at a touch. The outer air spilled in upon her, flowing over the broken and displaced lid of the wooden coffin that had once held her, and the frozen turbulence of silks and woollen cloth that overflowed from the box, stirred by the displacement of air, billowed for one instant buoyant and stable in their sight, and then collapsed together with a faint, whispering sigh, crumbling away at hems and folds into fragmentary rags.

A subsiding drift of dust and tindery cloth settled and fluttered down into the grave, disclosing the small, convulsed bones of hands and arms and drawn-up knees that thrust vainly and frenziedly upward, a shapely skull arched back in anguished effort among a nest of crumbling silks and laces, and the withered black of once-luxuriant hair, powdered over with the drab of perished silk and the fine, incorruptible dust of death.

Morwenna did not rest in peace. Contorted, struggling, fighting to force her way out, she seemed for a moment to be about to rise and reach her fragile, skeleton hands to them. Then even her bones began to rustle and crumble stealthily, settling lower and lower before their eyes into the stone tomb in which she had quite certainly been buried alive.

Chapter 7

Saturday Noon

'Oh, it's you at last, miss, is it?' said Miss Rachel into the telephone, in her most belligerent tones, for fear she should be suspected of even the least shade of penitence. 'And about time, too! What do you think you are doing, absenting yourself in this undisciplined way, and where, may I ask, are you doing it?'

'I'm at the Dragon. You told me not to bother to come back, remember? But as a matter of fact, I did 'phone Alice, pretty late, after we found Paddy. I beg his pardon, after he came back, I should have said. He wasn't lost, he knew only too well where he was. And all your fault, in case nobody else has raised enough courage to tell you. Me? What have I got to lose? You as good as fired me.'

'I did nothing of the sort! But if you're not back here pretty quickly, miss, I will! You can't leave without giving me a month's notice, and even if you did, I wouldn't take it, so don't be so uppish. Is Paddy there? I thought I heard his voice a minute ago.'

'Yes, he's here.' He was giggling like a girl in the background, but a little conscience-stricken, too. 'He came up to ask Dominic to go out somewhere with him, and if you want to know, I'm going, too. I like handsome young escorts, and now I've got two of 'em. Don't expect me back before lunch, and I'll be late for that. What? No, don't be silly. We were just rather late, and I was very dirty and hungry, so I accepted Mrs. Felse's offer to come here with them for dinner and borrow some clothes from her. Then I called Alice, and she said you knew Paddy was O.K., and you were just about exhausted with worry and then relief, and had gone to bed. So I thought I might as well stay here overnight, as Bunty was kind enough to lend me everything I needed. O.K., so you weren't worried. Then why were you carrying on like a broody hen? Well, tell Alice you weren't, she told me. Halfway up the wall, she said – Yes, sure you were right, cleared the air like a thunderstorm. All right, I'll be home this afternoon. Yes, he's all right. Do you want a word with him?'

Paddy smoothed her in one breathless sentence: 'Hallo, Aunt Rachel, I'm terribly sorry about the rest of the apricots, it was all a mix-up, I meant to come back. Would some of them be all right tomorrow? Mummy's making jam with those. No, I don't mind, really I don't. I'm glad. Yes, I do mean it. Can we keep Tamsin for to-day? She was the one who found me last night – one of the two, that is, Dominic was the other. 'Ess, me dear, I'll be up-along soon as I can. Tomorrow for sure, because I'm going back to school Monday, you know. O.K., I'll tell her. 'Bye, Aunt Rachel!'

He hung up, grinning. 'She says to tell you Alice has instructions not to keep lunch hot for you.'

'Good!' said Tamsin, linking her other arm in Dominic's. 'That means I've got the whole day off. Come on, let's go and pan gold in Paddy's cave.'

They went down the steep path from the Dragon, where Simon had risked his neck on Paddy's cycle, three abreast, linked and light-hearted. At the edge of the harbour they halted to buy three immense cones of candyfloss, and went down the harbour steps in single file, flourishing them like torch-bearers in a procession, and nibbling the fringes like fire-eaters. They paid no attention to anyone or anything but their own mid-September holiday happiness, reprieved from yesterday's

629

shadow. But a girl who was just hurrying out of the narrow, rocky alley behind the six colour-washed cottages of Cliffside Row checked and drew back at sight of them, and stood in the shadow of the rocks, watching them recede, linked and hilarious, down the slate-coloured sands.

The tide was nearing its lowest ebb, and beyond the pebbly stretches the finer sand gleamed moist and bright in a watery sun. The three young people, the taller boy, the visitor, on the right, young Paddy Rossall on the left, Tamsin Holt in the middle with her arm about Paddy's shoulders and the other boy's arm about hers, bore steadily sidelong into the cliff face, and halted to finish their hectic pink torches before they vanished into the black mouth of the Dragon's Hole.

Paddy looked back up the beach towards the coloured cardboard stage set, the impossibly charming and gay toy theatre of the harbour and the town. He saw another flare of candyfloss, primrose-gold, burning at the corner of the dark alley behind the cottages, and recognised Rose Pollard, a round, soft, appealing doll in neutral Shetland sweater and tartan trews, standing there braced and alert. She seemed – he couldn't be sure, but that was how it struck him – she seemed to be watching them, and wondering, and hesitating. And when she moved at last, it was to draw back softly into the shadow; but his eyes, following movement rather than colours, assured him that she had not gone away, and his intuition, already sharpened beyond ordinary this morning, warned him that she had not stopped watching.

'I can't believe it,' said Tamsin disgustedly. 'We've walked how far? – more than half a mile underground, and suddenly the whole thing folds up in a blank wall. And you said yourself the stone's been worked with tools in places, so somebody was interested in improving the passage for use. Why would it just stop, without arriving anywhere?'

Dominic's eyes followed the beam of Paddy's torch from stone ceiling to stone floor. To call it a blank wall that faced them was simplifying things; it was a rough confusion of broken planes, sealing off the small chamber into which the passage had opened. But quite certainly there was no cleft nor hole in it through which they could pass. This was the end of the journey.

'Maybe the passage was an end in itself,' he said. 'There's room among some of these side-pockets we've passed to store any amount of contraband. The whole complex could be a pretty good hiding-place. And they may have taken steps to hide the entrance even better, when it was in use.'

'But, look,' said Paddy acutely, 'if the passage was to be the cache, they didn't need half a mile of it, a hundred yards would have done. They could have got a ship-load of stuff in that first bulge. You don't chip your way along half a mile underground unless you're aiming to *get* somewhere.'

'I have to admit,' agreed Tamsin thoughtfully, after pondering this for a minute, 'that he's got something there.'

'Do you suppose we've missed a turning somewhere? It may go on in another direction.'

'We could have a more thorough look on the way back. We've got time, it's not much after twelve. And there's nothing for us here.'

They turned back rather reluctantly, all the same; nobody likes going back by the same route. It is, as Paddy had rightly observed, a fundamental predilection of human nature to want to get somewhere, even if most arrivals turn out to be disappointing.

The floor on which they walked had been smoothed in places by stones deliberately laid. Sometimes it was naked rock, sometimes this levelled causeway, and sometimes, especially where the narrow cleft opened out into a broader passage, there was deep, fine grey sand. With a light, the whole half-mile of it was easy, no more than a stony walk; and all these later reaches were dry, for over the entire length the level climbed very gently, and bore away inland from the Dragon's Hole at a brisk right incline.

'Where do you suppose we are?' asked Paddy as they turned back, playing his light ahead of them on both rough walls. 'Half a mile is farther then the neck, we must be right under the high part of the town.'

'I don't think we've borne as far to the right as that,' objected Dominic. 'I'd say somewhere just the other side the Head, under the dunes.'

'It's so straightforward here,' said Tamsin, stepping out merrily in the lead, 'you hardly need a light.' And promptly on the word she tripped over a stone that tilted treacherously out of the sandy floor, and went down with a squeak of protest on hands and knees.

Dominic and Paddy both reached solicitous hands to help her up, but for a moment she sat scowling, dusting her hands and examining her nylons. 'Damn! Somebody owes me a new pair of stockings.' A ladder was trickling playfully downward from her right knee.

'I'll buy you some new ones with my guinea,' offered Paddy generously. 'That was pretty much how I found it, actually, only I had more excuse, because I didn't have a light that time. You sure you're not sitting on a pirate's hoard?'

'Not unless he hoarded granite sand. But there was something sharp, look, it broke the skin.' She sifted fine sand through her fingers, probed the indentation her knee had made, and raised from beneath the surface a thin ring of yellow wire, with edges that barely met. 'That's the secret weapon. Not a pirate's hoard, but maybe a smuggler's earring.' She rubbed it on her sleeve, and it gleamed encouragingly. 'I believe that's what it is. It looks like gold wire.'

They ran the torch carefully over every corner of the sanded floor, but found nothing more. Tamsin pocketed her find, and they resumed their methodical walk back. There were broken bays in the rocks here and there to be explored, but all of them

632

proved to be dead ends; and as they drew nearer to the Dragon's Hole tiny trickles of water filtered down from the walls and channelled the sand of the floor.

They reached the seaward end of the tunnel, where the low, screened entrance hole shrank to thigh-height, and doubled upon itself midway in an optical illusion of solid rock. They crawled through on hands and knees, and stood upright again in the upper reaches of the Dragon's Hole.

When they had dropped down the slopes of shale and shell to where the light of the September day penetrated, there were still a few children playing on the sand, but even these were being called away to lunch by parents and elder sisters. The midday quiet was descending on Maymouth's beaches. Far down the glistening shore the tide had turned, and was beginning to lip its way back towards the town, but it would be two hours yet before it covered the cavern again.

'You could come and have lunch with us,' said Dominic, 'if you'd like to. Tamsin's staying. We could ring up your mother and tell her.' But he made the offer rather hesitantly, and was not surprised when it was politely refused. Paddy hadn't seen his mother for all of three hours, and there are times when three hours is a long time. Moreover, he had to demonstrate, rather than claim, that he was a responsible person who paid attention to the times of high and low tide, and could be trusted not to take any more chances.

'Thanks awfully, but I think I ought to go home.'

'Well, come and have an ice with us, anyhow.'

Paddy jumped at this offer. They climbed the steep path from the harbour to the Dragon's Head, and turned in by the first pale cliff-track towards the Dragon Hotel.

'Better put this with your guinea,' said Tamsin, extracting the thin gold ring from her pocket. 'I don't suppose it's anything much, but hang on to it, and time will show.'

'Do you think we should tell Mr. Hewitt about it? I told him

I was coming to have another look at the passage, but he wasn't much interested.'

'Question of priorities,' said Dominic with courteous gravity. 'Tell him about it, but leave it till he's got time for it. He's probably got a dozen lines to follow up, and some of 'em more urgent than this. He'll work his way round to it.'

They were walking close to the grassy edge of the cliff, where it overhung the beach and the harbour. Paddy looked down, from the painted operetta-set of Cliffside Row to the mouth of the blow-hole. The children were all gone now, the whole sickle of moist shore was empty. Only one lance of movement caught his eye.

From the narrow alley behind the cottages darted the figure of a girl, hugging the shadow of the cliff. She had tied a dark chiffon scarf over her candyfloss torch of pale hair, but Paddy knew her all the same, by her fawn-coloured sweater and Black-Watch-tartan legs. She ran head-down, hugging something small and shapeless under her arm. Because of the overhang he lost sight of her for a full minute, then she reappeared close to the deep shadow of the Dragon's Hole, and darted into it, and vanished.

He opened his mouth to call the attention of his companions to her, and then after all he held his tongue, and walked on with them in silence. But he couldn't get Rose Pollard out of his mind. And the more he thought of her, the clearer did it seem to him that she had been in the act of launching herself on this same errand earlier this morning, and then had drawn back when she saw them go down the beach ahead of her, and enter the cave. She had watched them every step of the way, he recalled now the stillness and tension of that small figure standing at the edge of the sunlight. The tide had dropped just clear of the entrance then, the beach had been otherwise almost deserted, only they had prevented whatever it was Rose wanted to do. Almost certainly she had watched them emerge again into sunlight and walk back to the harbour steps and the cliff path.

Then, with the last of the playing children called home to lunch, she had found the coast clear at last.

For what? He had known her since he was a small boy, she had acted as babysitter several times for his mother, and he had liked her because she was kind and pretty and soft, and he could twist her round his finger, stay up as long as he liked, make all the mess he wanted in his bath, and ignore the finer points of washing. She wouldn't have the resolution to do anything dangerous or underhanded, and she wouldn't have the wits to cover it up for long even if she tried it. Unless, perhaps, for Jim she could rise to things she wouldn't dare attempt for herself? It was her father who was dead, and she hadn't liked her father any better than anyone else had, and Jim had detested him, because of her. But they couldn't have done anything bad, he wouldn't believe it. They were both too open, not for darkness and secrecy. Not for caves! Rose was frightened of the dark. What *was* she doing there?

Mute and abstracted, he ate his way through a cassata, and made his farewells. But once he was out of sight of the hotel terrace and back on the cliff path, it was towards Maymouth that he turned. He slid recklessly down the whitening, late-summer grass to the harbour, clattered down the steps, and homed like a racing pigeon into the gaping mouth of the Dragon's Hole.

She wasn't in the open part of the cave, he knew that intuitively as soon as he crept into the dark interior. There were no echoes, only the very faint and ubiquitous murmur of water, that was inaudible when there were voices and movements to drown it. She might have gone right through into the haven at Pentarno, which would still be dry at this hour; but he scrambled purposefully straight through until the daylight met him again, and the great waste of the beach and the dunes lay within sight, and there was no Rose to be seen crossing the sands.

In his heart he'd known all along where she must be. He

abandoned the stony channel, and climbed inland, as quietly as he could, until he stood hesitating unhappily over the entrance to the tunnel.

He couldn't follow her in there without meeting her face to face, and somehow he couldn't bring himself to precipitate a situation like that, at least not until he knew what he was doing. He looked round him for the best cover, compressed his slight .person into a screened corner as close as he dared to the passage, and sat there silently, his arms wound round his knees, his heart thumping. She couldn't possibly stay long, whatever she had to do there, because she had to return by the same way, and to make good her retreat from the cave before the tide engulfed it. But if she didn't come, what must he do? Get out in time himself, and tell Jim? But Jim must surely know already. Husbands and wives were in each other's confidence, weren't they? Tell Hewitt, then? Or ought he to stay there and take care of Rose? But he *couldn't* do that to his mother, not again! He was getting hopelessly confused as to where his duty lay.

Rose spared him a decision. Before he heard her footsteps he saw a thin, pale pencil of light filter out of the rock wall, and waver across the shaly floor. She was hurrying, perhaps afraid of the tide, though she had still plenty of time by his reckoning. He heard the pebbles rasping, and uneven, running steps suddenly ending in a soft thud, as she threw herself down to creep through the low opening. The light of her torch leaped and fluttered with every thrust of the hand that held it. She clawed her way through, careless of the noise she made, as though a demon had been hard at her heels. When she scrambled to her feet, he saw the flickering light cast from below upon her pale hair, from which the scarf had been dragged back on to her shoulders. He saw her face twisted hopelessly into a child's mask of anguish, smeared with tears, the soft mouth contorted, the round chin jerking.

She blundered away from him down the slope, slipping and recovering in her frantic haste, and he heard the convulsed sobbing of her breath, and a faint, horrified whimpering that made the short hairs rise in the nape of his neck. The rattle of pebbles from under her feet receded and was still.

He sat for some minutes hugging his knees and shaking, reluctant to creep out after her where he must be seen. It didn't seem decent to let her guess that he'd been spying upon her in that condition. It didn't seem decent now that he had ever thought of doing it, but he had, and he hadn't meant any harm to her, rather the opposite. Better not to say anything to anybody, because whatever she was so frightened and so unhappy about, Rose couldn't have done any wrong, she had no wrong in her, she was too soft and mild. Better to go through the Hole to the Pentarno side; he might have to roll up his slacks and wade out at the entrance that side, because it lay a couple of feet or so lower than the Maymouth end. But it wouldn't be any worse than that, and he could still be home before his mother began to get worried.

He scurried down the slope to the thread of water that was gathering in the channel, and clambered hastily through the Hole again, to splash through the first encroaching foam and take to his heels up the Pentarno beach. The remembered vision of Rose Pollard hung before his eyes every step of the way, both arms spread for balance, the glow of the torch flailing in her right hand.

One thing at least was certain. When she came back from her mysterious errand, she had no longer been carrying anything under her arm.

Chapter 8

Saturday Evening

Phil was washing up after tea when Hewitt called. She put her head in at the door of the living-room to report: 'For you, Simon. Mr. Hewitt says the pathologist's come to have a look at Mrs. Treverra's body, and if you and Tim would care to be present, he'd be grateful. I suppose he wants to have the family represented, so that there can't be any complaints or anything later. Shall I tell him you'll be along?'

All three of them had looked up sharply at the message, Paddy sensitive to the quiver of feeling on the air, and stirred out of his unnaturally subdued quietness. All afternoon Tim and Phil had been exchanging anxious glances over his head, and wondering how long to let him alone, how soon to shake him out of his abstraction. A very dutiful, mute, well-behaved boy who sat and thought was not at all what they were used to.

'How about it, Tim? I don't say it's the pleasantest thing in the world to see, but if we can learn anything from it, I think we should.'

'I'll come, I want to. It's a hell of a thing,' said Tim soberly.

'Then he says in a quarter of an hour, at St. Nectan's. They don't propose to disturb her, not unless there's absolute need. I'll tell him you'll be there.'

Tim looked at Paddy. There was no guessing what was in his head, but it could only be the shocks and readjustments of

638

yesterday that were still preoccupying him. Unless directly addressed, he hadn't once said a word to Simon, and they had refrained from discussing the inexplicable tragedy of Morwenna in front of him. But sooner or later he had to learn to move and breathe in the same air with Simon again, and find some sort of terms on which he could live with him, and he might just as well begin at once.

'How about you, Paddy?' invited Tim after a moment's hesitation. 'Come along with us for the ride?'

The serious face brightened, wavered and smiled. 'I bet that means I don't get to come in,' he said, but he got up from his chair with every appearance of pleasure.

'I think I'd rather you didn't. But I'll tell you about it as we go.'

'O.K., Dad, I'll come, anyhow.' He hadn't been with Tim very much during the day, and he found that he wanted to. To sit by him in the front seat of the Mini, and touch shoulders with him now and again, was comfort, pleasure and reassurance. Subdued and amenable, he wasn't going to ask any favours; if he was required to sit in the car while they went down into the vault, he'd do it, and not even creep to the top of the steps to peer down in the hope of a glimpse of forbidden sights. It was his pleasure to please Tim. You can be demonstrative with mothers, but showing fathers how you feel about them is not quite so simple, you use what offers, and hope they'll get the idea.

They threaded the sunken lane, halted at the coast road, and crossed it to the track among the dunes. The smell of the evening was the smell of the autumnal sea and the fading grasses.

'I didn't know they were thinking of opening Mrs. Treverra's coffin, too. Why did they? Was that this morning?'

Any other time he would have been asking Simon, hanging over the back of the seat and feeding on his looks and words like a puppy begging for cake. Now he sat close and asked Tim, in his quiet, young baritone, touchingly grave and tentative.

'Yes, this morning. After you left, I suppose it must have been. I wasn't there. Mr. Hewitt thought it necessary to search every possible place in the vault, because it seems there must have been something there to account for Trethuan's not wanting it opened. And the only place that hadn't been searched already was Morwenna's coffin. So they opened that, too.' Tim eased the Mini down into the rutted, drifting sand, and was silent for a moment. 'She's there, Paddy. It isn't like the other one, she is there. Well, this chap's going to tell us whether the body that's there is from the right time, and so on, but I don't think there's much doubt. But what's terribly wrong is that she – well, she isn't at peace. She's fully dressed – she *was* – and she was trying to get out. She – must have been alive when they left her there. It could happen. Sometimes it has happened.'

He had felt the young, solid shoulder stiffen in unbelieving horror, and he wanted to soften the picture, to set it two centuries away, like a dream or a sad song.

'They hadn't modern methods or modern knowledge. There could be conditions like death. They weren't to blame. And thank God, they couldn't have known. Only we know, when it's all over, two hundred years and more. Like "The Mistletoe Bough." It wouldn't be quite like you think. The air would give out on her, you see. She'd only have what was inside the stone coffin, and then, gradually, sleep. It wouldn't be long.'

Simon might not have been there. There was no one else in the car. Paddy leaned closer by an inch, delicately and gratefully.

'It could look like a struggle, but be only very brief. Very soon she grew drowsy. Only she stayed like that, you see, fighting to lift the lid and get out. She slept like that. And when she was dead – Well, you've read her epitaph. This makes me think she wrote it herself. I don't even know why, but it does.'

Paddy said, in a small but still adult voice, perhaps even a note or two nearer the bass register than usual: 'I always thought she was so beautiful.'

'So did I. She'll find him again, you can bet on that. She wasn't the sort to let death stop her.'

The Mini turned in to the left among the dunes. The little open lantern of St. Nectan's stood clear against the sky.

'It wasn't ugly,' said Simon unexpectedly from the back seat. 'A scent, and a puff of air, and a little dust. She was very little, like in her picture, and all muffled up in a travelling cloak with a hood – at least, I think so. She had masses of black hair, and such tiny bones.'

Paddy said nothing more. He sat almost oblivious when they got out of the car and left him there between the shadowy dunes. He woke out of his daze when he heard the strange voices, and turned his head to see them met and greeted by Hewitt, with George Felse in attendance, and a stranger who must be the police pathologist. He watched them unlock the padlock on the gate, and go in single file down the steep staircase. He heard the heavy door below swing wide, but he didn't move. If the window of the car had not been open, he would not have heard the raised tones of their voices, like gasps of amazement and consternation rising hollowly out of the grave.

Something was wrong, down there. Something was not as they had expected it to be. Paddy put out a hand to open the door of the car, and then drew it back, shivering, afraid to want to know.

But you can't turn your back on knowledge, just because it may be uncomfortable. Supposing someone else should need what you know? Someone who belongs to you, and doesn't know how much you know already?

He slipped out of the car, and crept close to the rail of the vault. The open doorway showed him nothing but a corner of Treverra's empty tomb, and half of George Felse and all of Tim, hiding from him even the foot of the second coffin. But the

641

voices sailed up to him clearly, roused and brittle, and in signal agreement.

'None of it was there this morning,' said Hewitt. 'There was *nothing* with her in the coffin. All of us but Mr. Rossall were here, we know what we uncovered.'

'We couldn't possibly have missed seeing this,' said Simon. 'Even if we didn't disturb or touch her, we looked pretty carefully. It's enough to make you look carefully, isn't it? Well, she'd none of all this with her then. Nothing!'

'But if you've had both keys in your own hands all the time, and you locked up again carefully this morning,' said the one strange voice with dry mildness, 'it would seem to be impossible.'

'It is, damned impossible, but it's happened.' It was the first time Paddy had ever heard Hewitt sound exasperated. 'Take a look at this, this is real enough, isn't it? That wasn't here, none of this was here spilled round her feet, at eleven o'clock this morning. But it's here now at six in the evening. And I'm telling you – I'm telling myself, for that matter – this place has been locked all that time, and I've had both keys on me. And tell me, just tell me, why should anyone, guilty or innocent or crazy or what, bring *this* here and leave it for us to find?'

He plunged a hand suddenly into something that rattled and rang like the loose change in a careless woman's handbag, and brandished across the coffin, for one moment full into Paddy's line of vision, a handful of coins and small trinkets that gleamed, in spite of all the discolorations of time, with the authentic yellow lustre of antique gold.

He shut himself into the front passenger seat of the car, and held his head, because it felt as if it might burst if he worked the brain within it too hard. One little guinea in the sand of the tunnel, and a fistful of them in Morwenna's coffin. And the door locked, and both keys in police custody, and the whole thing impossible, unless – it was the last thing he had overheard as he retreated – unless there was yet another key.

Or another door! Nobody had said that, but he couldn't stop thinking it. Not an ordinary door, a very retiring door, one that wasn't easy to find.

Under the ground he'd had almost no sense of direction, but Dominic had said – somewhere under the dunes. Paddy took an imaginary bearing from the church towards the blow-hole under the Dragon's Head, and tried frantically to estimate distances. It was possible. It had to be possible, because there was no other possible way of accounting for everything.

They were down there a long time, nearly an hour. He stayed in the car all the time, because it had dawned on him that if he spied on them, or even asked them questions when they returned, he would have to tell them things in exchange; and he couldn't do that, not yet, not without other people's consent. No, there was only one thing to do, and that was go straight to the Pollards, and tell them what he knew, and try to make them see that the next move was up to them.

But there was no reason why he shouldn't use his eyes to the best advantage when the five men emerged from the deep enclosure of the Treverra tomb. Hewitt climbed the steps only to cross to his car, take a small rug from the boot, and make a second trip down into the vault with it. When he came up again he was carrying the rug rolled into a thick, short bundle under his arm. What was inside it, allowing for the bulk of the rug itself, might be about the size of a three-pound bag of flour, but seemed to be a good deal heavier. Say, a small gunnysack full of coins – or maybe a little leather drawstring bag, such as they used for purse and wallet in the eighteenth century. About the right size, at any rate, to match that small, shapeless bundle Rose had carried under her arm at noon.

Tim got into the car prepared for questions, and there were none. 'Don't you want to know if it is really Morwenna?' he offered, concerned at such uncharacteristic continence.

643

'Well, yes, of course!' The boy brightened readily. 'I thought you'd tell me what I'm allowed to know. I didn't want to poke my nose past where the line's drawn.'

'Such virtue!' said Tim disapprovingly. 'You're not sickening for something, are you?'

He started the engine, and the Mini came about gently in the trodden space before the church, and followed the police car back to the road.

'Is Uncle Simon riding with them, this time?'

'Yes, he wanted to talk to the pathologist. We're pretty sure it's Morwenna. Right age, right period, right build, no reason to suppose it would be anyone else. There'll be some work to do on fabric, and all that, but it looks authentic.'

'Where are we going now?'

'Back to the police station. We've got a bit of conferring to do, if you wouldn't mind amusing yourself for a hour or so. Or would you rather I took you home first?'

'No,' said Paddy, almost too quickly and alertly. 'I'll come down into town with you, that'll suit me fine. While you're in your official huddle, there's somebody I want to see.'

He knocked at the front door of the second pink cottage in Cliffside Row just as the church clock was chiming half past seven; and on the instant he recoiled a step or two nervously, almost wishing he had let well alone, for the consequences of the knock manifested themselves before the door was opened. Something – it sounded like a glass – shattered on a quarried floor. A girl's voice uttered a small, frightened cry, and a young man's, suddenly sharp with fury and helplessness, shouted: 'For God's sake, girl, what's up with you to–day? Anybody'd think a gun had gone off. It's only the door. If there's something wrong with you, I wish you'd have the sense to tell me. Oh, come out! I'll go.'

The door, suddenly flung wide, vanished with startling effect, as if Jim Pollard's large young fist had plucked it off. Levelled

brown eyes under a thick frowning ridge of brow stared dauntingly at Paddy.

'Well, what's up?' The eyes, once they focused upon him,
knew him well enough. 'Oh, it's you, young Rossall. What do
you want?' Less unfriendly, but as anxious as ever to get rid of
him and get back to whatever scene they had been playing
between them there in the doll's-house living-room. The knock
on the door had been only a punctuation mark. Paddy felt small,
unsupported, and less certain of the sacred harmony of marriage
than he had been two minutes ago. But he'd started it, and now
there was no backing out.

'I'd like to talk to you and Rose, please. It's very important.'

'Mrs. Pollard to you, my lad,' said Jim smartly. 'All right,
come in.'

'I'm sorry! She used to let me call her Rose, but I won't do
it if you don't like it. It was only habit.'

He stepped over the brightly-Cardinalled doorstep into the
pretty toy room, and Jim closed the door behind him. Rose,
clattering dustpan and brush agitatedly in the minute kitchen
beyond, was sweeping up the fragments of the glass she had
dropped. The door between was open, and Paddy saw her slide
a furtive glance at him, and take heart. All the same, her eyes
were evasive and her hands unsteady when she came in.

'Hallo, Paddy, what's the matter?'

'Nothing with me,' he said, making straight for the essential
issue, head-down and ready for anything. 'It's *you!* I came to
tell you I know where you went this morning, and what you
did. I saw you take something with you into the Dragon's Hole,
and I know where you left it. Don't you see how silly it is to
act as if you've done something bad, when you haven't? Mr.
Pollard, you must get her to tell the police everything, it's the
best thing, really it is. I know about the money and the jewellery,
you see, I know she put them – '

His impetuous rush had carried him thus far through a
silence of stupefaction on one side and desperation on the other,

but now, in a subdued way which didn't carry beyond the walls, hell broke loose. Rose burst into tears and flung herself face-down into a chair. Jim gaped open-mouthed from one to the other of them, and with a muted bellow of rage clouted Paddy on the ear with an open right hand as hard as a spade. The blow slammed him back against the wall, from which one of Rose's pretty little calendar pictures, a golden-haired tot with a bunch of forget-me-nots, promptly fell and smashed.

'You nasty little brat!' growled Jim through his teeth. 'You come here slandering my wife, and see what you'll get! Who d'you think you're threatening with the police, you – '

Nobody had ever hit Paddy like that before. Instead of taming him it infuriated him. Clasping his smarting cheek, he shouted back into the menacing face that leaned over him: 'I wasn't threatening her, I wasn't slandering her. I said – '

'I heard what you said. Accusing her of taking money and jewellery – '

'Don't be so bloody stupid!' yelled Paddy, blazing with rage. 'I never said she took them, I said she *put them back!* Why the hell don't you listen?'

It was not language of which either his parents or his teachers would have approved, but it stopped Jim, in the act of loosing a damaging left at him, as though the breath had been kicked out of him. His hands dropped. Shades of doubt and conster-nation and suspicion pursued one another over his candid face. Rose, through her desperate sobs, implored indistinctly: 'Don't hurt him, Jim! He doesn't mean any harm.'

Her husband turned and looked at her, quaking in the frilly chair. 'Now, look! There's one bloke around here who doesn't seem to be in any of the secrets, and that's me. And I'm going to know, and pretty sharpish, so you can both make up your minds to that. Maybe what this kid's saying has got something in it, after all. The way you've been acting the last couple o' days, there could well be something queer going on, and you mixed up in it. If there is, I want to know. Now!'

646

His voice had worked its way down from the peak of anger to an intimidating quietness. He plucked Paddy away from the wall by the shoulders, and plumped him down hard in a chair.

'If I went off at half-cock, and you're being straight with me, I'm sorry, kid. But first I've got to know. Come on, let's have it. The lot. I've been trying to get some sense out of her for days, and she's been putting me off and swearing there was nothing, and going round like a dying duck in a thunderstorm. I'm about sick of it. If you know anything, let's have it, and know where we are.'

Paddy took a deep breath, and told him everything he knew and everything he guessed. Rose, subsiding into exhausted silence, still hid her face.

'I came to tell you,' said Paddy, with dignified indignation, 'that I know very well you can't have done anything wrong, and it's dead silly to carry on as if you have. I don't know what's behind all this, but I do know you'll only get yourself into trouble if you go on hiding things. What you ought to do is go straight to the police, and tell them all you know. That's the only way to help yourself.'

Jim took his hands from the boy, and looked down at Rose's heaving shoulders. There was hardly any need to ask, but he asked, all the same, his voice baffled and exasperated, and painfully gentle.

'Is that right, Rose, what he says? *Did* you – '

A fresh spurt of tears, but she scrubbed them away with the stoical determination of despair. 'I had to get them out of the house. I didn't want you to know. It wasn't my fault, but it was even less yours, and I wanted you kept out of it.'

'Go and wash your face and pretty yourself up,' said Jim. 'We're going to the police. Now.' He turned to fix a stern but no longer unfriendly eye on Paddy. 'All three of us,' he said with emphasis.

'Yes,' said Rose, bolt upright and pale of face on one of Hewitt's hard chairs, 'it's true, there is a way in. I'll show you. If somebody'd leaned against the right edge of the right stone, there in the vault, he'd have found it, only it's placed so nobody's likely to, not by accident. It's one of the facing slabs in the corner. It swivels on an iron bar that runs through it from top to bottom. I reckon they put it all in when the vault was made. It'll only swivel one way, and you'd have a job to find it from the tunnel side unless you know.

'And it's true, I did go there, like Paddy told you. I went and put the things back in the poor lady's grave – but I never took them in the first place. I wanted to give them back, and I didn't know how else to do it. I was going to put them loose in the vault, because I couldn't have shifted the stone. But she – she – you'd uncovered her. I saw her – ' She put her hands up to her cheeks and drew breath in a single hysterical sob, her eyes fixed and horrified. Jim put his hand on her shoulder, and his index finger stroked her neck surreptitiously above the collar of the smart cotton shift-dress, with a quite unexpected tenderness. It calmed and eased her, reminding her of life. Death was a long way off, and she could make a good fight of it if events threatened her tenure or Jim's. She stooped her cheek to his hand fleetingly. They all saw it, and could not help being moved.

A nerve of awareness quivered in Paddy, and troubled his innocence, but the sensation was pleasurable and private, and he kept it to remember and ponder afterwards.

'How did you know about the tunnel and the entrance to the vault?' asked Hewitt, in the neutral tone he found so productive.

'My dad showed me.'

'And how did he discover it?'

'I don't know. Accident, I suppose. He was a questing kind of man, he liked nosing things out. It was going to happen to somebody, sometime, and it just happened to be my dad. He never told me how it happened. But he found it. About three years ago, it would be. He began to bring home little things he hid, and in a small house it isn't easy to hide that you're hiding things. And I'm curious, too. I hunted for them. I found some gold buttons. I didn't know they were gold, not till he told me.'

'You asked him about them then?'

'Yes, I did, but at first he wouldn't tell me anything. Then he got a bit above himself, and started showing me more things, a ring it was, once, and another time three gold coins. And then one day he made me go with him, and he took me and showed me the tunnel in the rock, and showed me how to get into the vault at the end of it. That was the first time I ever saw the coffins. He told me he'd got the stuff he was bringing out of the smaller one – the lady's coffin. I didn't want anything to do with it, I begged him to put them all back and leave them alone, but he never took any notice of anything I said. I was scared, but I didn't like to tell anyone, not on my own father. Even if there'd been anyone to tell, then,' said Rose, simply, and fondled Jim's hand on her shoulder. 'And there wasn't. Not close to me.'

'Was he, do you know, disposing of any of these pieces he lifted out of the grave?'

'Yes, he began to. I think he didn't know how to go about it himself, but after a bit he took up with a fisherman who used to come after me, a queer fellow he was, name of Ruiz. Spanish he was, only way back. I mean, he'd always lived in Cornwall himself, and his folks, too. My dad started encouraging him, and wanted me to be nice to him, but I didn't like him much. He got to be quite a crony of Dad's, and that was queer, because he didn't have many. They used to knock about together quite a bit. I got to thinking maybe this Ruiz chap was shipping some of the things out abroad for him, because he knew a lot of people over there, in France and Spain, and he spoke the languages, too. They went on like that for about six months, and then they fell out. I think this here Ruiz wanted a bigger share, and was threatening to give the show away if he didn't get it.'

'Did they talk about it in front of you?'

'No, only that one time, when they fell out, and then it wasn't

649

much. Ruiz flung off out of the house, and my dad went after him, and they made it up. Anyway, they came back together, and they had their heads together all the rest of the evening, as thick as ever. But then a bit later this Ruiz was drowned at sea. I don't know if you remember, his boat never came back from fishing, one blowy night. His body was washed up on the Mortuary a few weeks later. Then I did hope my dad would give up, not having anyone to sell the things for him, and I think he did for nearly a year. But then he began to bring things again, and started going off sometimes for a couple of days at a time, and wouldn't tell me where he was going.'

'And where did you think he was going? You must have had some ideas on the subject.'

'Not about where, not exactly. But I did think he'd started selling the things himself where he could, round antique shops, and like that. I tried to get him to stop, but he only told me not to be a fool. And by that time Jim had started coming after me.' She flushed warmly even at the mention of his name. 'We had a bit of a fight for it, because Dad didn't want to lose his housekeeper. But we did it in the end. And was I glad to get away to a home of my own!'

Hewitt turned his pen placidly on the desk, regarding her with his most benevolent and unrevealing face. 'But that didn't end it, did it?'

'It did, until about a week ago.' She thought back, biting her lip. 'Last Monday it was – five days ago. Dad came when Jim was out, and brought this whole bag of coins, and some rings and things, all there was left. He said so. He said to hide them and keep them for him. I know I ought to have refused, but I was scared of him. You can't just stop being scared of somebody,' said Rose, with unexpected directness and dignity, 'when you have been all your life. He said he'd take it out of Jim if I didn't do what he wanted. It seemed the easiest thing then to put them away out of sight till I could see my way. But then,' she said, apprehensive eyes on Hewitt's face, 'you came yesterday and told us he was dead. And I knew you were sending men to ask questions all over about Jim and me. I didn't know what to do, I was terrified you might search the house, and find those things there. I had to get rid of them, and the only thing that seemed even halfway right was to put them back where he took them from. And that's what I did. Only she – I never can forget it – seeing her – '

'You should have told me,' said Jim reproachfully, 'and not tried to do things by yourself, that way.'

'Jim never knew anything about it until now. He never knew the things were in the house. And I never wanted them. I never wanted anything to do with it.'

'All right, Rose! Now you've done what you should have done in the first place, and if ever you find yourself in a spot like that again, don't you run the risk of putting yourself under suspicion, you just come to me, and bring the whole thing into the open. Now there's one thing you can do to help us, as well as showing us the entrance into the vault. Can you remember any of the pieces your father brought home in all that time?'

'Yes, some I can,' she said hopefully. 'They were all that old, you know, they were different from the sort you see now.'

'Well, when you go home, you try to make out a list of the ones you remember, and describe them as well as you can, so that we can try to find them again. Will you do that?'

'Yes, Mr. Hewitt, I'll try.'

'And don't keep secrets from your husband from now on, if you want a peaceful life. All right! I may want to ask you some more questions tomorrow, for now we'll let you rest and think it over. Jim, I'd like you to go with her, Snaith will drive you down to the old church, and I'll follow in a few minutes and join you there. After that you can take her home and keep a strict eye on her, see she doesn't get into any more mischief.'

'She won't,' said Jim grimly, and twisted a finger furtively in her fair hair, and tweaked it tight.

On the way out, still holding his wife very possessively by

651

the arm, he halted squarely in front of Paddy, and stood looking down dubiously but not particularly penitently at the print of his fingers on the boy's swollen cheek and ear. The kid looked tired, dazed, battered but content. Large eyes stared back just as appraisingly, withholding judgement but assessing quality. They liked each other. They liked each other very well. True, Paddy did burn for one moment in the dread that Jim would blurt out an apology for the clout, and call everyone's attention to it; but he should have known better.

'Thanks, mate!' said Jim calmly. 'I'll give you as fair a chance, some day, and we'll get even.'

'That's all right, mate,' said Paddy, wooden-faced, and eyeing the precise spot at the angle of Jim's jaw where ideally he should connect. 'And I'll take it.'

'Come three or four years,' observed Jim, looking him over critically, 'I reckon you'll be about ready, too.' There wasn't much muscle on the light body yet, but he had a nice long reach, and speed, and spirit enough for an army.

'I reckon so,' said Paddy; and with mutual respect they parted.

A concerted sigh of relaxation and wonder and speculation went round the room as soon as the door had closed, and the sound of feet descending the stairs had ebbed to a distant, lingering echo. They stirred and rose, drawing together round the desk.

'You believe her story?' asked Simon.

'Yes, I believe it. All of it, maybe, most of it, certainly. Maybe Jim's clever enough to put over an act of knowing nothing about it, but I don't think so.'

'He didn't know,' said Paddy, standing up in the middle of events with authority, for hadn't he precipitated this single-handed? 'They were rowing when I got there, before I ever got in the house. She was all nerves and cried if he looked at her, and he was just about frantic trying to get sense out of her. Why should he act when there was nobody else there?'

'I'm prepared to accept that,' agreed Hewitt benevolently.

'Rose has cleared up quite a number of things for us, but she hasn't shed any light on who killed her father. There's nothing to put Jim out of the running for that, so far.'

'He didn't know about the tunnel into the vault,' said Paddy doggedly, 'so he couldn't have put him there.'

'Oh, yes, he could, laddie. Finding a back way in doesn't block the front door. There was a key almost anyone could get at. There could be others who knew about the back door, too, of course. Don't worry, I wouldn't say Jim makes a good suspect, but he isn't out of it. We've got plenty to do yet – looking into Trethuan's finances, for one thing.'

He reached for his hat, smothering a yawn. 'Well, I'll be off down and take a look at Rose's swivelling stone. Care to come along?'

'Not me,' said Tim firmly, after a quick glance at his son. 'Paddy and I are off home.'

Paddy wasn't really sorry. He'd had enough excitement for one day, and a mere hole in the wall isn't so wonderful, once located. Secret tunnels sound fine, but they're two-a-penny wherever there was organised smuggling a couple of hundred years ago, whether on a sporting or a commercial scale. It would keep. He went down the stairs after the others, Tim's arm about his shoulders.

'Well, at any rate,' said Simon, as they emerged into the faint, starry, salty coldness of after-summer and not-yet-autumn, 'we do know now what Trethuan was acting so cagey about, why he didn't want the tomb opened.'

'Do we?' asked George Felse.

'Don't we? With all that stuff there to be found – '

'Ah, but it wasn't there. There was nothing there this morning but the body – remember? He must have made a special journey, last Sunday, and taken away all that was left of Morwenna's treasure. At any rate, on Monday he gave it to Rose to hide for him. Once that was done, what was there to betray him? No one would know he'd been stealing it, no one would ever know it had been there at all. Oh, no,' said George pensively, 'we haven't found out yet why Trethuan was so mad to keep you out. It certainly wasn't because of Mrs. Treverra's money and jewels, removing them was no problem. They were a good deal more portable than the – purely hypothetical, of course – brandy. No, the most puzzling thing about that little hoard is something quite different.'

They had halted beside the cars. 'Such as what?' asked Simon.

'Such as: What was it doing there in the first place?'

'That's it! That's it exactly! The way it looks,' sighed Hewitt, sliding into the driving seat, 'no one ever told Mrs. Treverra that you can't take it with you.'

Chapter 9

Sunday Afternoon

Dominic came down to lunch in his best suit, and with a demure gait to match, threaded his way between the tables in the bar, and slid on to the stool next to his mother's, in the approved casual manner.

'Dry Martini, please, Sam.'

'Darling, you *have* come on!' said Bunty admiringly. 'You even sound as if you expect to get it.'

'Careful, now!' cautioned Sam, with a face so straight that apart from the moustache it was practically featureless. 'That vermouth's powerful stuff.' He spared a moment, in spite of the noon rush of business after church, to admire his young guest's grave Sabbath appearance. 'I hear you've got old Hewitt coming to lunch.'

Dominic centred the knot of his tie more severely. 'This won't stay on past two o'clock, if it lasts that long. But it's the least I could do. After all, Dad did put on a collar and tie for me, the night we got to know Simon and the Rossalls. Not unprompted,' he added, looking down his nose into his glass.

'Look who's talking!' said Bunty. 'Twelve minutes ago he looked like something a water spaniel had dragged in off the beach. If anyone gets the credit for his present appearance, it should be me.'

'Well, congratulations, Mrs. Felse,' said Sam reverently, 'it's very, very beautiful.'

Dominic began to get down from his stool with great dignity, but not so purposefully as to suggest that he had any real intention of leaving. 'Look, I'll go away if I'm cramping your style at all.'

'Leave the glass,' said Bunty accommodatingly, 'I'll take care of it.'

'You touch it!' He took care of it jealously himself, spreading both elbows more comfortably. Through the windows that over-looked the terrace, half-empty to-day because the wind was in the wrong quarter and the sunny air deceptively cool, they saw George and Hewitt approaching in earnest conversation.

'They're here. Good, I'm hungry. And, Sam, talking of powerful stuff, don't you think you could find us a drop of the real McCoy to go with the coffee? The special, for Mr. Hewitt. I think you really should offer it with the compliments of the house.'

'I might, at that,' said Sam, grinning.

'And serve it yourself. Just to show your conscience is clear.'

'My conscience is always clear. I've got it properly trained.'

'I bet you you daren't,' said Dominic, glittering with mischief.

'You bet me what I daren't?'

'The price of the brandy.'

'Plus duty?'

'Oh, have a heart!' protested Dominic, injured.

Bunty slid from her stool and shook out the peacock-blue skirt that made her chestnut hair take fire in opposition. 'I hate to admit an impediment to this marriage of true minds, but I'm not really sure that this is the right time to tease Detective-Sergeant Hewitt. Are you both sure of your alibis? He might have a warrant in his pocket right now.'

George and Hewitt were already entering the doorway. Sam watched them approach, his face benign and childlike. Apart, of course, from the whiskers. Those whiskers, Dominic reflected, must be worth a fortune to him.

'Don't you worry,' he said, momentarily serious, 'the old boy knows all about my alibi long ago. He may look stolid, it's his stock-in-trade, but there isn't much he misses. I'm checked up on and passed harmless, that's for sure, or we should have seen more of him around.'

'Well, hang it,' said Dominic, 'I was one of the blokes trying to pull the victim *out* of the sea. Everybody knows where *I* was.'

'That could be very good cover for anyone who'd just thrown him in,' pointed out Bunty darkly, and took her son firmly by the elbow. 'Come on, we have a guest. Put your company face on.'

'It is on,' he said indignantly.

'It's crooked, then. Straighten it.'

Sam appeared at Bunty's shoulder with the coffee, beaming and benign, and distributed the delicate, tall-stemmed balloons he kept for special occasions.

'With the compliments of the house, Mr. Felse,' he said ceremoniously, catching George's inquiring eye, and began to pour the brandy with reverence.

'That's very handsome of you, Sam,' George acknowledged civilly. He looked at Bunty, and her face was limpid and innocent. He looked at Dominic, and his was pleased and bland.

'Not at all,' deprecated Sam, rubbing thumb and forefinger together gleefully at Dominic from behind Hewitt's back. Dominic remained seraphic, flattered and serene, just artful enough to retain a pinch of the schoolboy in his impersonation of the man-of-the-world. It didn't fool George. But good brandy is good brandy.

'What is it, Sam, a drop of special?'

'My own favourite,' said Sam fondly and truthfully, and judiciously withdrew the bottle, leaving only a very modest dose in Dominic's glass. That should have shaken the practised calm, if anything could, but Dominic merely flicked one glance at Sam, unreadable to the others, and contained his displeasure to loose it at a more opportune time. His small, delighted smile never wavered for an instant. 'Give me your opinion, Mr. Hewitt, I know you're a good judge.'

Hewitt caressed and warmed the glass in his large palms, and let his nose enjoy itself. 'Lovely bouquet, Sam! Not a trace of that overtone of brass you sometimes get.'

'That's just what I like about it,' said Sam, feelingly. 'I'm glad to have my judgment confirmed by an expert. You don't mind if I quote you, Mr. Hewitt? Try the flavour, you won't be disappointed.'

Hewitt tried it, and was not disappointed. One heavy eyelid lifted from the happy contemplation of his glass, one round, bright eye examined Sam minutely, shifted from him to Dominic, and lingered thoughtfully. Dominic retired coyly into his glass, but slanted one glance across it, so quickly that it should have slid harmlessly by. Hewitt winked. Dominic looked down his nose and appeared to have noticed nothing unorthodox. Honours were approximately even.

'That's lovely stuff, Sam. You go on buying it as long as it's on offer, that's all the advice I can give you.'

'I will, Mr. Hewitt, glad to know it has your approval.'

It was a pity that Mrs. Shubrough should have to loom up at that moment from the direction of the bar, and strike the one discordant note: 'Telephone for you, Mr. Hewitt. It's Mr. Rackham calling from the police station. He says it's very important.'

The little bubble of comedy burst damply round them. They watched the stocky figure shoulder its way out through the glass doors, and they were back with an unsolved double murder.

'I feel cheap,' announced Dominic, after a moment of self-examination.

'Don't be self-important,' said George witheringly. 'You don't think fate's got time to cast a disapproving eye on your little capers, do you? Besides you don't feel cheap at all, you only feel you ought to. Now if you want to make yourself useful, take your mother out for the afternoon, because I suspect I shall be out of circulation. And kick your heels all you want – there won't be any nemesis listening to you. Nemesis has got more important things to do.'

'I've had two men out since Friday,' said Hewitt, slowing at the beginning of the steep drop into the town, 'looking for the dentist who put in all that work on our unidentified corpse's teeth. Rackham's found him. At least, it seems likely it's the right fellow, but he's a cautious one, won't say for sure from the charts. Wants to see the molars before he commits himself, but is sure he'll know his own work again if it is the bloke he thinks.'

'If he's as cagey as that,' said George, 'I take it he's naming no names yet. Where did your man find him? Evidently he isn't a Maymouth man.'

'Plymouth. Just got back with him.'

'What sort of a fellow is he? I hope he knows what he's going to see.'

'Small, dapper and highly-strung,' said Hewitt, 'according to Rackham. He'll be all right. It's the big, husky ones that keel over.' He turned into the square, almost deserted at this hour on a fine Sunday, the old-fashioned shop-fronts gated, shuttered and still. 'Well, if we can't do much on the Trethuan case until tomorrow, maybe we can get somewhere on this other one. Didn't have more in his deposit account or in the house – Trethuan, I mean – that you could account for as a careful man's savings, but I fancy he's got a lot put away somewhere in cash from this antique traffic of his. Maybe in a safe-deposit box somewhere, maybe under the floorboards at home. We haven't been over the house properly yet. It'll be somewhere. And we'll find it. As far as we can tell, all of the stuff that he hadn't already disposed of piecemeal, we've got in custody. Rose has identified what we've got, and furnished us with a nice little list of things he brought home earlier. We should be able to trace some of them through the trade. Here we are! Don't come down to the mortuary with us unless you want to, George. You've had all that once.'

'I can stand it. I might learn something. I like to hear an expert on his own subject.'

Rackham was a deceptively simple-looking young local man, fresh-faced and bright. Beside his cheerful, extrovert bulk the dentist from Plymouth looked meagre and unreal, and as highly-strung as his companion had indicated, but a second and narrower look corrected the impression. He was wiry, durable and sharply competent, and he had come armed with all his relevant records and charts, ready to go into extreme detail. So firmly astride his hobby-horse, he was not to be thrown by any corpse, however fragmentary, provided its jaw was still intact. In the chill basement mortuary he probed, matched and demonstrated in complete absorption; and at the end of his examination he snapped the rubber band back into place round his records, and declared himself satisfied, and prepared to swear to the dead man's identity in court as soon as it might be required of him.

'I was practically certain from the charts your man brought with him, but it was essential that I should see the work for myself. Yes, it's mine. I can give you dates for the whole sequence of treatments. They went on for about eight weeks in the spring of 1961, and occasionally we had to adjust the appointments because of his sea trips. He should have come back to me for a check-up six months later, but he never came. That does happen, of course, it needn't mean anything. But it could mean that by then he couldn't come. He was a fisherman, and he gave me a Maymouth address – I've got it here in the records. His name,' said the little man blithely, unaware that he was springing a land-mine, 'was Walter Ruiz.'

A Nice Derangement of Epitaphs

'On the face of it,' fretted Hewitt, prowling the length of his small office like a restive tiger, 'it's damned impossible. Walter Ruiz is buried in St. Mary's churchyard, up the town, with a stone over him to prove it. There was an inquest, and he was identified.'

'He's just been identified again,' said George dryly. 'Very impressively, for my money. It seems that one or the other of two equally positive identifications must be mistaken. The question is, which?'

'You heard him. That amount of dental work in one course of treatment, fully documented as such things have never been before, coupled with the individual formation of the bones, and all the rest of it, makes this man's jaw about as unique as a set of fingerprints. That evidence would stand up at any inquest.'

'But so did something else, presumably something that looked equally sound, at the previous inquest. According to what Rose told us last night, Ruiz and his boat failed to come home after fishing in rough weather, and his body was washed up on the Mortuary a few weeks later. A few weeks in the sea don't make a body any easier to identify, even a landsman knows that. But somebody did identify this one. Who was it? His parents? A brother? His wife? But no, he didn't have a wife, he came courting Rose, and her father wanted her to be nice to him. Her father found him useful, until he got a bit too demanding, and knew a bit too much.'

Hewitt came back to his desk, and stood gazing at George across its empty surface for a long, dubious minute of silence.

'If you're trying to put ideas in my head, George, you're too late. They're there already.' He reached out a large hand, and picked up the telephone, and with deliberation began to dial.

'I'm trying to sort out the ones I've got in mine,' said George. 'It looks as if we're both being driven on the same shore. Did he have any family? It seems to me that a solitary like himself would be most likely to appeal to Trethuan as an ally, if he found it expedient to look round for one at all.'

661

'You're so right, Ruiz didn't have any family. You're neck and neck with me, George.' His head came up alertly as the burr of the telephone was answered. 'Hallo, Henry! This is Tom Hewitt. Sorry to interrupt your Sunday nap, but I need a quick reference to something about two and a half years back, and you're the quickest and most infallible referee in town. Nip down to your files and look it up for me, will you? You probably know the answer, but look it up anyhow, I want to have it officially. An inquest on a seaman drowned and cast up on the Mortuary, I think it will be in March or April, 1962. Name of Walter Ruiz. A routine job, it seemed at the time. But now I want to know *who identified him*. Just that. Call me back as soon as you can. And thanks very much!'

He hung up, laying the receiver so softly in its cradle that there was no sound to break the slight tension in the room. He sat down gently and folded his hands, and looked at George.

'No family. No brothers, no sisters. There was his widowed mother, up to about seven years ago, I remember. They had a cottage down the south end of the sea front. After she died he lived alone, kept himself to himself, and bothered nobody. The excise people did have their suspicions about him, though not, I think, over the occasional drop of brandy. He was never actually caught out over anything. Just another lone wolf. If he needed hands he took on casuals, and dropped them again afterwards. Nobody ever worked with him regularly. Nobody was ever in his confidence.'

'That was your local paper?' Local papers are formidable institutions. They may ignore national events, but they must get every name right, and every date, and every detail, within their own field. 'Proprietor? Editor? Or both?'

'Both. Henry still lives above his offices, he won't be long looking it up, his files are kept in applepie order. I could,' admitted Hewitt, 'have got the same information at least three other ways, but not so quickly.'

It was barely a quarter of an hour before the telephone rang.

A Nice Derangement of Epitaphs

Hewitt lifted it out of its cradle before it could cough out a second call. He listened for a moment with an unreadable face. 'Thank you, Henry! That's exactly what I wanted to know. I'm very grateful. Goodbye!' He replaced the instrument, and sat looking at George.

'The body that came up on the Mortuary and was buried as Walter Ruiz was identified by the man who was considered to be his closest, maybe his only, friend. Zebedee Trethuan.'

It accounted for everything. They sat and looked at it, and details of Rose's story fell into place like bits of a jigsaw puzzle, filling in what had seemed, until this morning, the most mysterious third of the whole picture.

'Well, I know now which identification I'd trust,' said Hewitt with curious mildness, pacing the room again, but with a longer, easier stride. 'A handy and unrecognisable corpse turns up on the Mortuary, and you have need of just that to lay a ghost. The ghost of someone known to have been associated with you, and now missing, supposedly drowned at sea. How nice and easy to say this is it, and get it put away under a stone with your man's name on it, so that no one will ever start asking awkward questions. Walter Ruiz is dead and buried respectably, and everybody knows it. Everything beautifully tidy and safe. And then this interfering Simon Towne comes along, and puts it into the old lady's mind, of all crazy things, to *open the Treverra tomb!*'

A cool voice from the doorway said deprecatingly: 'I'm afraid he's interfering again. I'm sorry, I did knock.'

They both swung round in surprise. So intent had they been on their revelation and its implications that they had failed to hear Simon's light feet climbing the stairs. He stood in the doorway, eyebrows cocked obliquely, smiling a little. 'The desk sergeant told me I could come up. Don't blame him, I told him I had something that might be relevant to tell you. I really did knock, but you didn't hear me. And I was just in time to hear no good of myself. Would you rather I waited downstairs?'

'No, that's all right, Mr. Towne, come in. You might as well hear the context as well,' said Hewitt good-humouredly. 'I wasn't calling you interfering on my own account, it was what you might call an imaginative projection. Come in, and close the door.'

'I seem to have missed a lot.' Simon hitched a knee over the corner of the desk, and looked from one to the other of them, frowning. 'Did I hear you talking about Ruiz? That's the fellow Rose Pollard talked about last night, the one who was shipping pieces of jewellery abroad for her father? What's he got to do with the Treverra tomb? I thought he was buried in St. Mary's churchyard.'

'So did everybody else, Mr. Towne, except one person, the one who knew he was somewhere very different. In Jan Treverra's coffin, where we found him.'

'*We found him?*' Simon drew breath sharply, and flashed a doubtful glance at George. 'This is serious? Then you're telling me that the unidentified one – the one underneath – *that* is *Ruiz*? But they wouldn't bury a man under that name without good authority. Someone must have vouched for him.'

'Someone did. He came up practically naked and featureless, after six weeks in the sea. What could be better? The man who'd put the real Walter Ruiz in Treverra's coffin, where he hoped he'd lie uninvestigated till doomsday, jumped at his chance when it offered, and got another body buried as Ruiz, publicly and decently. And that would have been the end of it, if you hadn't conceived this notion of finding out whether Treverra really did have his poems buried with him. Imagine how this fellow would feel when he heard it! Wasn't it enough to make him frantic? Wasn't it enough to account for his threatening you, pestering you, trying to frighten you off? Anything to get you to go away and leave well alone.'

A Nice Derangement of Epitaphs

Open-mouthed, eyes huge and blank with astonishment, Simon whispered: 'Trethuan?'

'Who else? Doesn't it make sense of everything? He got Ruiz to help him dispose of the valuables he'd been steadily lifting from Mrs. Treverra's coffin, they were partners for about six months, so Rose says. Then they quarrelled, and she thinks Ruiz was demanding a bigger share of the proceeds, maybe threatening to make trouble if he didn't get it. And shortly after that Ruiz's boat vanished one night, and never came back and Ruiz was presumed drowned. And the next possible and unidentifiable body that came up on the Mortuary – Trethuan identified it as Ruiz. Isn't it plain what his reason must have been?'

'It looks,' said George, 'as if Trethuan killed him either actually in the vault, or very close to it, maybe in the rock tunnel. Why else hide him there? He was a big man. Admittedly Trethuan was a pretty powerful person, too, but he wouldn't want to move the body any farther than necessary. Ruiz had a skull fractured by repeated blows. No passing that off as the work of the sea. A drowned man, like Trethuan himself later, is another matter.'

'I see two possibilities,' said Hewitt. 'Either Ruiz pretended to be reconciled, and then spied on Trethuan on his next trip, confronted him in the act, and was killed – for you can bet your last bob a man like Trethuan would want to keep the source entirely to himself and Rose, he'd never willingly let his partner into the secret. Or else – and perhaps this is the more likely – Trethuan pretended to agree to whatever Ruiz wanted, offered to prove his good faith by showing him where their profits were coming from, and took him there with the fixed intention of killing him and hiding him there. If he'd looked in the lady's coffin, he'd looked in Treverra's, too, he wouldn't miss anything. He knew the coffin was empty. He supplied it with a body.'

'Could it be done by one man alone?' asked George, and turned his head and looked at Simon.

'Yes, it could. One man couldn't possibly get either of the

665

stones off and replace it again unbroken. But he could prise it sidelong, all right. Enough to probe inside. Enough to dump a man inside, and cover him again – ' He drew breath in a deep gasp, realising the full implications of what he was saying. He sat voiceless and motionless, his eyes blank and colourless as glass, staring inward at his own imaginings.

'It could be done, all right,' said Hewitt. 'Trethuan did it repeatedly, didn't he? Morwenna's stone is lighter than the other, that one he must have shifted whenever he went back for another raid, enough to get his arm down into the poor thing's belongings. The other, presumably, he moved only twice, once when he made his assay and found the coffin empty, once when he filled it.'

'There was still the boat to dispose of,' said George.

'That wouldn't be any problem. Trethuan was an amphibian like all the rest of Maymouth. His folks were fishermen. He had a dinghy of his own. To scuttle Ruiz's boat by night and get back to land safely wouldn't cause him much trouble. You don't have to go far off this coast to find deep water. And he had time. Ruiz lived alone, nobody was going to raise a hue and cry immediately he didn't come home to supper. We'll go through all the circumstances again. We'll find out who first called attention to the fact that he hadn't come in from fishing. And when. It may even have been a couple of days later, time enough to wait for a pretty blowy night.'

'And wouldn't there be a certain risk in rushing to claim a corpse, like that?' suggested George. 'Suppose he said it was Ruiz, and then somebody else really did recognise it – by a ring, or something?'

'Ah, but he didn't rush! He was canny. He waited for one nobody else was claiming. Henry tells me – it wasn't my department – the police had been appealing for help in identifying that body for several days before he stepped in. And even then, if it had been obviously the wrong height or age, or shape, he only had to let well alone and say no, I don't know him. No, he had everything sewed up. And he lay low with his thefts for a year or so, and left the stuff where he thought it was safest, before he started hawking pieces round the buyers in this country. And then you came along, Mr. Towne, and heaved a brick through all his plans and precautions. Nobody'd ever shown any interest in the tomb before. He made haste to shift the rest of the valuables, but he was terrified to move the body. No wonder he tried all he dared to scare you off. He knew it wouldn't pass for Treverra, once the scholars and antiquaries got their noses into it.'

Simon lifted a dazed face from between his hands, and stared before him. George had not noticed until this minute the blue rings under his eyes, the copper shadows hollowing his lean cheeks. He might not have noticed even now, if he had not possessed knowledge acquired by the accident of being with Phil Rossall on the evening of Paddy's disappearance. Not everybody had reason to see beyond the bright, handsome public image of Simon Towne to the marginal failures and deprivations that crippled his private progress.

'Look, do you really mean to say that whoever killed Trethuan took him in there, and dumped him into the coffin with – *the man he himself had killed*?' He said this very slowly and deliberately, as if his lips were stiff, and had to be driven to form the syllables.

'That's exactly what I mean to say.' Hewitt was triumphant. 'I haven't the slightest doubt that that's what happened. And a supreme bit of irony it is!'

'A supreme bit of cheek!' said Simon furiously. 'If I wrote that and published it, I'd be hooted out of journalism. Nobody, not even a novelist, could get away with a bare-faced coincidence, like that.'

'Not a coincidence at all,' Hewitt objected brusquely. 'There were completely logical reasons why Ruiz should be disposed of precisely there, and in that way. As we've demonstrated. And there'll be equally logical causes leading to the precise effect we're left with, the presence of Trethuan's body in the same hiding-place. Don't forget there's a waste of sand all round it. Don't forget that a stone coffin is good cover. But I grant you we've still got to find out what the precise causes were in Trethuan's case. He drowned at sea, that's definite. He was taken dead into the vault. Why, and how, we don't know yet. It may have been through the door, with one of the two keys. Or it may have been through the tunnel. If young Paddy really saw him in the water about half past five, then the body might well be brought ashore on the Mortuary after the next high tide. He might be cast up fairly close to St. Nectan's. And anyone who didn't know the vault was going to be opened might still think it a pretty safe hiding-place.'

'There couldn't have been many who didn't know,' said Simon. 'I advertised my intentions loudly enough, for obvious reasons.'

'Well, that's just one of the things we shall have to look into. That case remains. But this one is as good as closed. A few details to fill in, some back history to verify, but I'm in no doubt of the result myself. It's kind of tantalising,' he said thoughtfully, 'to know the middle of a story, and not the beginning or the end.'

'That'll come, all in good time,' said Simon, rising. He felt through his pockets for a crumpled packet of cigarettes, and offered them, and again began to search for matches. 'Lord, I'm forgetting what I came for!' It was some small object at the bottom of his trouser pocket that had reminded him. He fished it out, a tiny, folded square of tissue paper.

'Paddy forgot to mention this last night, what with all the excitement, and to-day he's on duty, Tim being his own cowman on Sundays. I said I'd bring it in to you. They found it yesterday in the tunnel, not far from the entrance into the vault.'

He leaned across to the lighter George was offering, and drew in smoke deeply and gratefully before he completed the unwrapping of the minute thing, and held it out on his open palm. A thin, broken gold ring, bent a little out of its true circle, the two ends pulled apart about a quarter of an inch. Hewitt took it up between his finger and thumb, and stood staring at it warily, as though it might close on him and bite.

'I don't suppose it means a thing,' said Simon apologetically, 'but I said I'd deliver it, and I have. Can I run you back to the Dragon, George? It's on my way.'

'Mr. Towne!' Hewitt had threaded the ring on the tip of his large brown forefinger, and was still gazing at it, a small, smug flare of pleasure in his eyes. 'Where did you say this was found?'

'In the tunnel from the Dragon's Hole to the vault. Only about twenty yards from the vault end, Paddy says, but I daresay he can show you the exact spot. Tamsin actually found it. Does it matter?'

'The spot where this was found may very well be the actual spot where Ruiz was killed,' said Hewitt happily, 'that's all. It happens to be the identical twin to the one ring he's still wearing in his left ear.'

Chapter 10

Sunday Night

On their way up through the quiet Sunday reaches of the town they passed the narrow opening of Church Street, and Simon suddenly braked hard as they overshot it, and began to reverse along the empty road.

'You don't mind a few more minutes' delay, George? I suddenly thought I'd like to have a look at the other fellow's grave, the one who isn't Walter Ruiz.' He slowed the car beside the small lunette of gravel at the churchyard gate. The young lime trees, leaves just ripening into the yellower green of autumn, leaned over him.

'A sad sort of end he had,' said Simon, threading the maze of little paths between the graves, 'dying solitary in the sea, and then cast up here among humankind again, only to be used as a pawn in a dirty game, and have another man's name wished on him for all time. That's the sort of ghost I'd expect to haunt us. Somebody we've deprived even of his identity. After all, he was a man, too, somebody may have loved him, he may have had children. Suddenly he seems to me the most injured of all. I'd like just to see what they gave him to last him till doomsday. You did say there was a stone?'

'Hewitt said so. I wondered who paid for it.'

'I wonder, too. Where do you suppose he'd be? It's a burial

only two and a half years old. I should think that would be the new part.'

They passed by the vestry door, and the Vicar came out in his cassock, and joined them as naturally as one stream joins another. He had the hymn-board for the evening service in one hand, and a fistful of numbers in the other, and went on placidly slotting them into their places as he walked.

'Dan, you're just the man we need,' said Simon. 'We're looking for a grave. The man you buried as Walter Ruiz, a couple of years or so ago.'

'You're heading the wrong way, then,' said the Vicar tranquilly, neither missing nor acknowledging the doubt thus cast on the recorded identity, as though it did not matter one way or the other. 'He was a seaman, we made room for him among the older graves, where all the mid-nineteenth-century sailors are. I thought he'd be more at home. This way!'

He led them, skirts fluttering round his Great-Dane strides, along a thread-like path swept darker in the high grass, to a remote corner in the angle of the stone wall, shaded with thorn trees.

'Two hundred and thirty-five,' read Simon aloud, deciphering the numbers on the hymn-board upside down. 'Abelard's hymn. Maybe I should come to church to-night.'

'Maybe you should, but don't expect me to tell you so.'

'You won't believe this, but I used to sing in the choir. Alto. I could sing alto before my voice broke, and after. I still can, it's a technique I was somehow born with. There's a splendid alto to *"O Quanta Qualia"*.' He began to sing it, softly, mellifluously, afloat above the pitch of his own true baritone speaking voice, and in Latin.

' "Vere Jerusalem est illa civitas,
Cuius pax iugis et summa iucunditas,
Ubi non praevenit rem desiderium,
Nec desiderio minus est premium." '

Wish and fulfilment can severed be ne'er, nor the thing prayed
for come short of prayer! That always seemed to me the most
perfect of all definitions of heaven. But then, look who wrote
it, poor devil! He knew all about wish and non-fulfilment, and
things falling short.'

'Simon,' said the Vicar, 'I don't know whether I really ought
to admire you for it, but you must be the only fellow I ever met
with the effrontery to think of Abelard as a poor devil. Here
you are, here's – ' He had been about to say 'Walter Ruiz';
instead he said, courteously but serenely; ' – the man you're
looking for.'

A low, cropped grave, turfed over within a granite kerb, under
the bough of a hawthorn tree. Grey old stones, seamed with
fine viridian moss, leaning all round. A plain pillow stone at the
head of the small enclosure, and inscribed on it:

WALTER RUIZ
Born May 8th, 1929,
Drowned, March, 1962.
'I will bring my people again
from the depths
of the sea.'

'He wasn't Ruiz, you know,' said Simon, standing gazing down
at it with a shadowed face. 'Nobody'll ever know now who he
really was. I don't know why, but I feel bad about that. Even if
we could think of him by a name, and a face, and say: Poor old
Smith, three years next month since he was washed up! – even
that would be something, give him a place to exist in, a dimension in which he'd be real. But now he's nobody.'

'He's as surely somebody,' said the Vicar placidly, 'as you are.
And nothing could be much surer than that.'

'But who? Doesn't that matter?'

'It matters who. It doesn't matter that we should know who.
He's been identified,' said the Vicar, tucking his hymn-board

under his arm, 'a long time ago, in the only way that matters in the least now. And by a witness who doesn't make mistakes.'

'Yes – I see your point. "I will bring my people again from the depths of the sea." Yes, he might have done worse. Who provided the stone? You?'

'It's always been the tradition that the dead from the sea, who had no families here to bury them, should be a charge on the church. Look round you, if you think a foreign name makes a man a stranger here.'

They looked. Half the seafaring nations of the west lay there quietly enough together, with the scent of the salt shore for ever in the wind that stirred the pale grasses over them. Edvard Kekonnen, seaman. Hugh O'Neill, master-mariner. Alfonso Nuñez, master-mariner. Vassilis Kondrakis, seaman. Two Spanish shipmates, unknown by name. Sean MacPeake, master-mariner. Jean Plouestion, fisherman. Walter Ruiz, or X, fisherman, seaman, or master-mariner. 'I will bring my people again from the depths of the sea.' It didn't much matter if no one else knew what to call them, the voice they were listening for would have all their names right.

'Yes,' said Simon, a small, wry smile curling the corners of his mouth, 'this is the point of departure for a good many heavens, seemingly, Valhalla, Tir-nan-Og, the lot. It's the sea-going men who made the western islands heaven, I suppose.' He slipped into song again, very softly:

' *"Far the cloudless sky stretches blue*
Across the isle, green in the sunlight."

It sounds like Jan Treverra himself designing that paradise, doesn't it?

"There shall thou and I wander free
On sheen-white sands, dreaming in starlight".'

'I was thinking much the same thing,' agreed George, smiling. 'What was it Dom said about your two epitaphs, that first evening we were up at the Place with you? Something about making the after-life world sound like a sunshine cruise to the Bahamas.'

Simon had begun to turn back towards the gravelled walk, his hands deep in his pockets, the air of the Hebridean song still soft and sweet in his mouth. He halted suddenly, stiffening; for a moment he hung perfectly still, then he turned a face sharp and pale beneath its gold contained excitement.

'Dom said *what?* Would you mind saying that again?'

'He said the Treverra epitaphs made the after-life sound like a sunshine cruise to the Bahamas. Why? What nerve did that prick?'

'The nerve it should have pricked then, if I'd been even half awake. And I was there?' he protested furiously. 'I heard this? And I didn't connect?'

'You laughed. Like the rest of us,' said George, patient but mystified.

'I would! The fate of many another pregnant utterance in its time. Why do I never listen properly to anyone but myself? My God, but I see now how it all began, all the first part of the story. You only have to put one bit in place, and all the other pieces begin to slide in and settle alongside. George, come to the Place to-night, will you? We're dining with the old lady, because Paddy has to go back to school tomorrow. Bring Bunty and Dominic, and come to coffee afterwards. You, too, Dan, please. I'd like you to be there.'

'With pleasure,' said the Vicar equably, 'if you want me.'

'I do. I want you all, everyone who was involved in this investigation from the beginning. Because I can see my way now,' said Simon, suddenly shivering in the chilling air of early evening and the tension of his own incandescent excitement. 'I believe I can clear up the strange, sad case of Jan and Morwenna, the mystery that set off all these other mysteries. And I will, to-night.'

They gathered round the long table in Miss Rachel's library, ten of them. The curtains were drawn, and the tide, already well past its height, lashed and cried with subsiding force off the point, in the soft, luminous dark. Miss Rachel sat at the head of the table, dispensing coffee royally and happily, with Paddy at her left because she would not let him out of her reach now that he was regained in good condition and angelic humour, and had forgiven her freely under the pretence of being freely forgiven. On her right, Simon, curiously quiet and strained and bright. Tamsin moved about the foot of the table handing coffee-cups, helped by Dominic. George and Bunty on one side of the table, Tim and Phil and the Vicar on the other. It was a long time since the old lady had assembled such a satisfactory court, she didn't even seem to mind that it was turning out to be Simon's court rather than hers. The more he disclaimed it, the more honestly he abdicated, the more surely this evening belonged to him.

'I wasn't the one who put my finger on the spot,' he was saying with passionate gravity. 'That was Dominic. I had to have my nose rubbed in the truth before I could even realise it was there.'

'Me?' said Dominic, staggered. 'I didn't do anything, how on earth did I get in on the credits?'

'You took one look at the Treverra epitaphs, and put your finger on the one significant thing about them. "They make heaven sound like a sunshine cruise to the Bahamas," you said.'

'Did I? It must have been a joke, then. *I* didn't see anything significant.'

'You did, though you may not have realised it or taken it seriously. All that pretty verse about year-long summer, and golden sands, and sapphire seas – you saw intuitively what it really meant, and that it was very much this side the grave.

Whether you ever examined what you knew or not, you offered it to me, and I didn't have the wit to look at it properly, and learn from it.'

They saw now, dimly, where he was leading them. They sat still, all eyes upon Simon. His thin, long hands were linked on the table before him. The cigarette he had lighted and forgotten smoked slowly away to a cylinder of ash in the ashtray beside him. The tension that held them all silent and motionless proceeded from him, but only he seemed unaware of it.

'If ever there was a crazy bit of research, this was it. There we were, with Treverra's own tomb – well, not empty, but empty of the man who should have been in it, and his wife's coffin unhappily not empty, but most tragically occupied, by the poor lady who had died there, and, as we found out afterwards, by a pretty large sum in old money and jewels. This crazy, sad puzzle, and those two epitaphs for clues, and nothing else.

'You remember Treverra was the adored leader of the smugglers round these parts. We know he also had at least one ship trading legitimately with the West Indies and America. We can guess, now we know about the tunnel from his vault to the Dragon's Hole, that he must have had the tunnel improved and the tomb dug out at the end of it to provide a safe runway to the harbour and Pentarno haven, for a very practical purpose. What could be more respected than a family tomb? And what could make better cover for the secret road to the sea and the ships? He completed it about six years before he died. Maybe he always had in mind that it might eventually provide a way of retreat, if Cornwall ever got too hot to hold him.

'Well, now, suppose that the authorities and the preventives were closing in on this local hero, and finally had something on him that he wasn't going to be able to duck? I think there are signs that they would have welcomed an opportunity to bring him down. Most of the gentry dabbled in smuggling, but in a mild, personal way. Treverra went beyond that. Not for profit, probably, so much as for fun. He liked pulling their legs, and leading them by the nose. They wouldn't forgive him that. He resigned from the bench, where by all accounts he was a pretty generous and fair-minded Justice. I think he knew his scope here was narrowing. And then, you see, any of the local people who heard of any threat to him would warn him. He was the idol of the coast. Yes, I think he knew time was getting short, and made his plans accordingly. Among other things, he wrote his epitaph. And hers, I'm almost sure, was written at the same time, by her, by him, or by both together, I can't be sure. But I like to think of them sitting here, in this very room, with their heads together, capping each other's lines, and laughing over the supreme joke of their shared and audacious career. Look at Morwenna's face! That lovely, fragile creature was a lot more than a sleeping partner.

'So there's Treverra, only fifty-two years old, in the very prime of his life and vigour and powers, and the authorities closing in for the kill. And what happens?

'Treverra "dies", and is buried. In the tomb he had made for himself, with the swivel-stone in the corner giving access to the cave and the harbour.

'And at night he arises, this "dead" man, after all the decorous funeral business is over and the mourners have gone away. Maybe he was provided with a good crowbar inside the coffin for the occasion, even more probably he was also visited and helped out by his older son after dark. He had two sons. The elder was just twenty at this time, the younger was a schoolboy of fourteen. I think the elder was certainly in all the plans, you'll see why when we come to the case of Morwenna. Treverra, then, emerges from his tomb exceedingly alive and lusty, and retires gaily by his back way, from which, at low tide, he can reach either Maymouth harbour or Pentarno haven. What does it matter which he used? At either one or the other a boat is put in for him, to take him aboard ship – his own ship or another – and ship him away to the reserve fortune he's been

677

salting away in readiness in the year-long summer of the West Indies.

'A sunshine cruise to an island paradise, just as Dominic said, if I'd only listened to him. But not Tir-nan-Og! Not even the Bahamas, perhaps, but near enough. According to the records most of his trading had been done with Trinidad, Tobago and Barbados. Somewhere there, I judge, we might still pick up his traces.

'How many were in the know? It's guesswork, now, but I'd say just the three of them, Jan, Morwenna and their elder son, and maybe the skipper of his ship. There may have been a family doctor in it, too, to cover the deaths, but if so, he kept his mouth tightly shut afterwards to protect himself, and who can blame him? They may have managed without him? It hardly matters now. I'm sure that's what happened. It accounts for the empty coffin, that was later to be filled and over-filled. And it accounts for what followed.

'For, you see, Morwenna would never have agreed to such a plan if there hadn't been provision in it for her to join him. Act two was to be the translation of Morwenna. She was to pine away – her own touch, that, I'd swear – and to be reunited with her lord in an earthly, not a heavenly, paradise. After six months the same programme is put in motion for her. She "dies" of a broken heart, and is buried in the tomb prepared for her.'

He broke off there, startled, for someone had uttered an almost inaudible sound that yet had the sharpness of a cry. A quiver passed round the circle, and a rustle of breath, as if they had all been shaken out of a trance. Paddy, flushing hotly, drew back a little into shadow, 'I'm sorry! I was only thinking – She was so *little*!'

'They took every possible care of her, Paddy. Or they thought they had. Yes, she was very slight and frail, she couldn't deal with tombstones herself, they knew that. She had to lie patiently in her coffin until dark, when her son would come to release her, and see her safely down the passage and abroad. The light

678

wooden coffin in which she was carried to the vault was pierced in a pattern of fine holes just above her face – did you notice that, George? The air in the stone coffin would easily be enough to keep her going until night. And she was well provided with funds for the journey, in money and jewellery. The wooden lid would be only very lightly fastened down, so that she could move it herself. And all she needed besides was the heart of a lioness, and that she knew she had. *She* was the one who misquoted Dryden, that I'd swear to. "None but the brave deserves the brave." To lie and wait several hours alone in the dark didn't seem terrible to her, not by comparison with what it bought.

'But that night of her funeral, you remember, is recorded as the night of the great storm, when the fishing-boats were driven out to sea. And young Treverra, the new squire, was blown from the cliff path in the darkness, and drowned. A young man in mourning, wandering the cliffs alone – no one would ask what he was doing there.

'I'm afraid, I'm terribly afraid, he was on his way down the cliff path to the church and the vault, to see his mother resurrected and put safely aboard ship for Barbados.

'And no one else, you see, knew anything about her.

'No one else. She was dead, they'd just buried her. *If* the doctor knew, he'd assume everything was going according to plan, or at least that her son was taking care of her, until he heard of the boy being missing. And that may not have happened until well into the next morning. By then a doctor would know she'd be dead. He'd be afraid to speak. It couldn't help her, and it could, you see, harm not only himself but Treverra, too. He'd be a wanted man again as soon as it was known he was alive. And nothing and nobody could give Morwenna back to him now.'

'But the ship,' ventured Dominic huskily. 'There was a ship lying off for her. Wouldn't they try to find out what had happened?'

'That's what makes me think that this time it wasn't their own ship. It would be risky to chance having it stopped in these waters, obviously. No, this time I think it was a matter of a simple commercial arrangement with some other skipper, in which case they wouldn't know anything except that they were to put in a boat at such and such a spot and pick up a lady. If they ever did manage to put in a boat in such a sea, it's certain she didn't come to keep the appointment. They couldn't know what that implied, to them it just meant their passenger hadn't turned up. Maybe they waited as long as they could, maybe they were driven out. What could they do but sail without her?

'And all that money, and the valuables she was to have taken with her, just lay uselessly in her coffin with her for two centuries, until Zeb Trethuan found it and started methodically turning it into money again. Thus setting the stage for the next death.

'Nobody knew about it, you see. Young Treverra's body was never found, so the vault wasn't opened for him. His young brother came home from school and took over the estate, but he'd never been in the secret. To him his mother and father had died and been buried, no mysteries, no tragedy but the ordinary, gentle tragedy of bereavement, that happens sooner or later to everyone. By the time *he* died and was buried, St. Nectan's was already fighting a losing battle with the sand, and they'd built St. Mary's, high up in the town, and abandoned the old graveyard by the shore. And Morwenna lay there alone, separated from her Jan, and he – God knows which was the unluckier of the two.'

Tamsin had got up from her place very quietly, and gone to her desk. She came back with the folder of the Treverra papers in her hand, and slid out upon the table the two epitaphs.

'Not that I don't know them by heart,' she said in a low voice. 'But suddenly they seem so new and so transparent, as though we ought to have been able to read the whole story in them from the beginning.'

A Nice Derangement of Epitaphs

'You think I've made out a case, then?' Simon's eyes met hers down the length of the table, and there was nothing left of challenge or antagonism on her side, and nothing of pursuit or self-indulgence on his. They looked at each other with wonder and grief, and a certain frustrated helplessness, but with no doubt at all.

'I think it's so unanswerable a case that I don't know how we missed following the clues Jan left us. It's all *here*! Don't you hear him? He couldn't play any game without making it danger-ous to himself, there wouldn't have been any sport. He told them just what he was about. He made his exit snapping his fingers under the nose of the law, and daring them to follow his trail if they had the wit. But they hadn't, and neither had we.

> *"Think not to find, beneath this Stone,*
> *Mute Witness, bleached, ambiguous Bone –* "

You see, he told them, don't look for me here, you won't find me. And then, his "trackless maze," "the labyrinth beyond the tomb" – what was that but the real tunnel that opened beyond *his* tomb? He told them how he made his getaway, kicked up his heels at them and invited them to go after him if they were smart enough. And then, the last four lines, those are for *her*.

> *"There follow, O my Soul, and find*
> *Thy Lord as ever true and kind,*
> *And savour, where all Travellers meet,*
> *The last Love as the first Love sweet".'*

Simon sat looking at her with a face very still and very pale beneath its tan, and eyes that had no lustre; his voice was gentle and impersonal enough as he took up the recital from her.

'Now listen to Morwenna, and I don't think you'll doubt that this really was Morwenna herself speaking:

> *"Carve this upon Morwenna's Grave*:
> NONE BUT THE BRAVE DESERVES THE BRAVE.
> *Shed here no Tears. No Saint could die*
> *More blessed and comforted than I.*
> *For I confide I shall but rest*
> *A Moment in this stony Nest,*
> *Then, raised by Love, go forth to find*
> *A Country dearer to my Mind,*
> *And touching safe the sun-bright Shore,*
> *Embrace my risen Lord once more."*

Well, do you hear the authentic voice?'

They heard it indeed, suddenly fierce, impious, arrogant and gay, the reverse of its own conventionally presented image. Miss Rachel stirred uneasily, unwilling to acknowledge but unable to deny what she now saw in that delicate and beautiful creature in the drawing on the wall. Not the first and not the last in history to spit unwise defiance at the lightning.

'Why, she was the wilder of the two! That's surely more than a little blasphemous! And then such a terrible fate, poor girl. Mr. Polwhele, do you think that what happened to them was a kind of *Judgment*?'

'No!' said the Vicar, with large and unclerical disdain, and looked a little surprised at his own vehemence. 'I should be ashamed to attribute to God a malice of which I don't find even myself capable. And I don't think the spectacle of two daring and exuberant children egging each other on to say outrageous things about me, in my hearing, would even drive me to knock their heads together, much less drop a mountain on them and crush them. I think I might even laugh, when they weren't looking. It would depend on the degree of style they showed. And Morwenna certainly had style. No, I don't think there was any rejoicing in heaven when there was nobody left to lift the stone away. Rather a terrible sense of loss. She was brave, loyal and loving, enough virtues to offset what the Authorised Version would call a forward tongue. No, I suppose one must say that they played with fire so persistently that it was inevitable they'd get burned in the end. But to them playing with fire made life doubly worth living. You can't have it both ways.'

'If she was blasphemous,' said Phil, shivering, 'she certainly paid for it. She had the more terrible fate.'

'Did she?' Simon looked up, looked round the table with a brief and contorted smile. 'I wonder how long Treverra watched and waited for her, or for news of her? He couldn't come home, you see, he couldn't even send letters, there was no one left here who knew he was alive. He had to stay dead in his old identity, he was still a wanted man. Maybe he thought she'd changed her mind, and found it quite convenient to be a widow. Maybe he thought she'd married again. Maybe he even began to fear she'd been planning her own future and laughing at him even while she helped him to arrange his elaborate joke. She was only forty-one, and a great beauty. And he couldn't come back and fight for her. His joke had turned against him. Oh, believe me, if there was anything he had to pay for, he paid. There was only one agony he was spared – at least he didn't know how his darling died.'

The moon was up when they went out to the cars, not too late, because Paddy had to leave by the traditional mid-morning train, and there were still the last little things to pack. The tide was halfway out, the moonshine turned the wet beach to silver, and the scattered clouds were moist with reflected light.

'I trust,' said Simon, finding George Felse close beside him as they went down the steps to the drive, 'you were duly impressed with my performance?'

The voice was deliberately cool and light, but tired. He had walked rather stiffly past Tamsin, when she hesitated and waited

683

for him in the doorway. For several days now he had been walking past Tamsin, with aching care and reluctant resolution. It had taken her a day or so to realise it, and longer to believe in it. She had the idea now, she had betaken herself promptly where she was welcomed, between Paddy and Dominic. They stood chattering beside the Mini, all a little subdued. The soft voices had a sound of autumn in them, too, as gentle as the salt wind.

'Yes, you're quite a detective,' conceded George. Simon's eyes were on Paddy, and the slight, brooding smile was unwary; he had no reason to suppose that George possessed the knowledge necessary to make it significant. 'Now what about tackling the only mystery that's left? I'm sure you could put a finger just as accurately on Trethuan's killer, if you really tried.'

The smile stiffened slightly for an instant, and then perceptibly deepened. 'Maybe I will, yet,' said Simon. 'But there's just one more question I have to ask before I shall know what I've got to tell you about that case. Give me till tomorrow.'

'I'll do that.'

'Can I run you back to the hotel? It isn't too comfortable for four, but it's bearable for that distance.'

'Thanks, but we'll walk. It's not far, and rather nice at this time of night. And I think we'll make our farewells to Paddy now. Tomorrow,' said George quite gently, 'had better be left to the family. Don't you think so?'

The question that was to determine the ending of the Trethuan case was asked later that same night. And the person who had to answer it was Paddy Rossall.

They were all together round the fire before bed, Paddy's packing done, the last pot of tea circulating, when Simon said in a careful and unemphatic voice, so that the shock came only gradually, like the late breaking of a wave:

'I hadn't intended to do this, and if the truth hadn't come out without any act of mine, I never would. But now we all know where we are. Paddy, you're fifteen, for all present purposes you're a man. You know I'm your father, as well as I know it. Now I want to talk to you, here, now, with Tim and Phil present, the only honest way.'

The silence that fell was extreme. There might never have been sound or movement in the world.

'Simon,' began Tim quietly, when he had his voice again, 'do you think this is fair?'

'Yes, I think it's fair. I think it's absolutely necessary. We've been stalling it since yesterday morning, since we all knew where we stood. It's necessary for us all, if only to clear the air. I am who I am, and Paddy knows it now, why not say it? Paddy, you *do* know. Say it!'

'Simon, you've no right – '

Phil laid her hand restrainingly on her husband's arm. He had expected her to blaze into indignation, and she was silent; it confused and calmed him at the same time, effectively silencing him.

'Yes, I know,' said Paddy in a small, tight voice. He had a cup of tea in his hand; he laid it down carefully on the tiled hearth, and wiped his palms slowly on his thighs. His face was taut and expressionless.

'Then listen to me. This once listen to me, and be sure I respect you and trust you to be honest. We all want you to be happy, to have a full life and a satisfying life. I'm going to speak up for myself now. It's the first time I've been able to do that, and I don't see why I shouldn't take advantage of it. I know I'm very late in making my bid, Paddy, but I've got a lot to offer. I've got an assignment that's going to take me practically round the world for a series of articles and broadcasts. If you choose, you can come with me. It's entirely up to you. Everything I can give you, I'll give. Everything I can do for you, I'll do. I want you, Paddy, I want you very much. I'll do everything possible to try and deserve you, if you'll come with me.'

'Now look!' growled Tim.

'No, Tim, let him talk.' Phil drew him down again to his chair and held him there, charmed into quiescence by her bewildering serenity. It was too late, in any case, to deflect the encounter. The matter had been taken out of their hands, but for all that it was not yet in Simon's. Paddy was a person, too. They must place as much reliance in him as Simon did, they had better reason. Nobody must argue back. Their arguments were already on record, fifteen years of them, without any world-tours, without any glamour, inexpert, imperfect, intimate arguments. But Phil knew their weight, and had already bet her life and Tim's on their validity.

So Simon was the only one who talked; and Simon was an unmatched talker when his heart was in it. He was ruthless, too, now that he was in pursuit of something he really wanted. Miss Rachel had been a shrewd prophet.

'That's all, Paddy. You know what you've got here, and now you know what I'm promising you. It's up to you. If you decided to come with me, I don't believe Tim and Phil will stand in your way.' It was a fighting case he'd made, he felt drained with all that had gone out of him. And Paddy sat there with his hands clenched on his thighs, and his face white with tension, staring into the fire.

'Paddy, look at me!'

Paddy raised his head obediently, and met Simon's eyes full. His mouth and chin were set like stone, as if he felt the threat of tears not far away.

'Will you come?'

Paddy's lips parted slowly and painfully. He moistened them, and tried for a voice that creaked and failed him; tried again, and achieved a remarkably steady, loud and controlled utterance.

'I'm sorry, but this is where I belong. With my parents. I like you very much, and of course you're my father's best friend. But I'm not going anywhere, except back to school tomorrow. But thank you,' he ended with punctilious politeness, 'for asking me.'

686

He uncurled his closed fingers with a wrench, and got to his feet abruptly, all his movements slightly stiff and careful.

'If you'll excuse me, I'll to go bed now. Goodnight, Mummy!' The quick, current touch of his lips on her cheek forbade her to manifest either surprise or concern. 'Goodnight, Dad!' His hand patted Tim's shoulder lightly in passing. He was halfway to the door, magnificent and precarious, passing close to where Simon stood stricken mute and rigid with shock. And then he spoiled the whole gallant show.

It was not a deliberate blow; he had hesitated and cast about him frantically for a second to find some formula he could use, but there was none, and the instant of silence grew enormous in his own ears, and had to be broken. You can't just excise a human being from your life, and pretend he doesn't exist, you can't call him 'Uncle Simon' when he's just reminded you that he isn't anything of the kind, you can't say 'Father' when you have a father already, and have just been at pains to point out that you have no intention whatever of swopping him for anybody else on earth. There wasn't anything left but that inalienable possession, a name, and only the respectful form was even halfway appropriate.

He said: 'Goodnight, Mr. Towne!', fighting off the silence in sheer panic, and instantly and horribly aware that even the silence had been preferable.

Simon jerked back his head and drew in breath painfully, as if he had been struck in the face. He reached out a hand in incredulous protest, and caught the boy by the arm.

'My dear *child* – !'

Paddy turned upon him a pale face suddenly and briefly convulsed by a bright blaze of anger and desperation, and struck as hard as he could, frantic to end this and escape.

'That's just the point! I'm not a child any longer, I'm not all that dear to you, and above all, I'm *not yours*. You gave me away, remember?'

For one electrifying instant Phil saw the two fierce, strained faces braced close to each other, staring in mutual anguish, more alike than they had ever been before. Then Paddy tugged his arm free and stalked out of the room; but in a moment they heard him climbing the stairs at a wild run, head-down for the privacy of his own room.

Simon hung still for a long, incredulous moment, his hand still extended, unable to grasp what had happened to him. Its finality there was no mistaking, but it took him what seemed an age to comprehend and accept it. He turned from them in a blind man's walk, and went and groped out a cigarette from the box on the table, to find his shaking hands something challenging and normal to do.

Phil had risen instinctively and taken a couple of hasty steps towards the door to follow Paddy, but then she checked after all, and sat down again slowly. She felt for Tim's hand, and closed her fingers on it gratefully. Simon's fair crest, pale against the dark curtains, Simon's rigid shoulders and patient, obstinate hands at work with matches, seemed to her suddenly close kin to Paddy's beloved person, and infinitely more in need of pity.

'I ought to take you apart,' said Tim roused and scowling.

'Think you could do a better job than Paddy just did?' asked the taut voice.

'You asked for it.'

'I know I did. And I got it. Between the eyes.' He was ready to turn and face them now, the faintest of smiles wry at the corners of his mouth. 'Don't worry! I know when I'm licked. Even if I never had much practice, I can still be a sporting loser when there's no help for it. I apologise, Tim, it was a dirty trick. It won't happen again. Ever.'

'I tried to warn you,' said Phil in a very low voice.

'I know you did. I ought to have remembered that most women never bet anything that really matters to them, except on certainties. I won't forget again.'

'Simon,' she said impulsively, gripping Tim's hand tightly, because of course Tim didn't understand, and probably never would, 'settle for what you can get. There *is* something that belongs to you. I know it isn't what you wanted, but it's too good to throw away.'

Simon came across the room to her, took her chin in his hand, and kissed her. 'God bless you, Phil! I'll take any crumb that's offered. But I don't deserve a damn' thing, and I won't ask for anything again. After tomorrow, I promise, you won't be bothered with me any more.'

Chapter 11

Monday Morning

Paddy came down next morning pale and quiet, but resolutely calm, and very much in command of himself and circumstances. There were the blessed, beastly, ordinary details of returning to school to be taken care of, and no drama at all, and no opportunity for introspection. He had worked out his own course overnight, even before his mother had looked in almost guiltily to kiss him goodnight all over again, and found him composed and ready for sleep. He had been glad to be visited, all the same; it's fine not to need comfort, but it's nice to know that it's ready and waiting if you should want it.

'I hope I wasn't rude, Mummy. I didn't mean to be. I was a bit pushed, not having any warning.'

'I know. Don't worry, you weren't rude.'

She tucked him in, a piece of pure self-indulgence, for Paddy had never looked so adult and self-sufficient as he did now. He smiled up at her with understanding and affection, but very gravely.

'Mummy – will *he* be all right?'

'He'll be all right. We'll see that he is.'

She was quick to know what he wanted. It was she who made a point of inviting Simon to drive in with them to the station, and so gave Paddy himself the opportunity of seconding the invitation.

'Yes, do come. Of course there's plenty of room. My trunk's gone on ahead, there's only a small case to take.'

So there were four in the Mini on the way to the station, Simon in the front seat beside Tim, the pair of them taciturn as yet; Paddy and his mother in the back, cosy and a little disconsolate together. There's something at once damping and heartening about the beginning of a new term.

'It was a lovely holiday, darling, I'm sorry it's over. Don't forget to write every week-end. There'll be ructions if you don't.'

'I'll be chivvied into it, don't worry. But I wouldn't forget, anyhow. Cheer up, it won't be long till Christmas.' It seemed an age away, but he knew from experience how soon it would be sitting on the doorstep. He nuzzled Phil's shoulder briefly and happily; and presently a corner of his mind defected flightily to consider the Middle School's football prospects for the new season, even before he had taken care of all his responsibilities here at home.

They disembarked beside the blonde wooden fence of the station approach, and unloaded the suitcase with due ceremony, already worrying vainly about whether anything had been forgotten.

'I'll say goodbye here,' said Simon, with the right lightness of tone, if not of heart. 'I've got a call I want to make in the town. So long, Paddy, have a good journey. And a good term!'

'Thanks very much!' He had saved it until then, to give it its maximum effect. He gripped Simon's hand with warmth, but still with some reserve. 'Goodbye, – ' His face flamed, but the blue eyes never wavered. ' – *Uncle Simon*!'

Simon turned away briskly, and walked the length of the light-brown barrier with an even pace and a jaunty bearing, balancing with care the great, hollow ache of Paddy's charity within him; and alongside the extreme end of the platform a lean quiet man was propped against the fence with arms folded, watching the lower school starlings gather and shrill greetings, and the self-conscious young cock-pheasants of the sixth stroll from their parents' sides to knot themselves into world-weary conversations with their own kind. They had about as much control over their sophistication as over their feet, and their graces were as endearing as one's first-born's fledgling efforts on the amateur stage. The in-between's, like Paddy, had the best of both worlds, rollercoasting without pretence from lofty dignity to uninhibited horseplay, and back again. They could even stand and wait, as Paddy did, warmly linked with their parents, and openly happy to have them close for a few more minutes; for they had out-grown homesickness, and quite forgotten the ancient dread of tears, but had not yet grown into that extreme state of senior self-consciousness which scorns to have had a human origin at all, and prefers not to have its parents around for fear they shall somehow fall short of the ideal image.

'On the whole,' said George Felse, turning from the spectacle with the small, private smile still on his lips, 'I must say they inspire me with a degree of self-satisfaction. Wouldn't it be simpler, though, to put boy and trunk and paraphernalia into the Land-Rover, and just drive them the twelve miles there, and tip 'em out?'

'They wouldn't consider it for a moment. This always has been the school train, and it always will be. It's better for the little ones,' said Simon. 'By the time they get there the ice is well and truly broken, and they've been doused a couple of times, and got over the cold and the shock, even begun to enjoy it. Twelve miles is just long enough.'

'I see,' said George, falling into step beside him, 'you've got the basic knowledge necessary to a father.'

'But not the other basic requirements. Cigarette?' They halted for a moment over the lighted match, faces close, and again fell into step together. Simon drew in smoke hungrily, and let it go in a long soundless sigh. 'Yes – I promised you a solution, didn't I?'

692

'You promised, at least, to let me know whether you could provide one or not. When you'd asked your final question.'

'I've asked it. And it's been answered.' He walked for a minute in silence, his eyes on the ground. 'Not that I really have anything to tell you. You already know – don't you?'

'I've known all along,' said George, 'who put him there. I didn't know who'd killed him until Miss Rachel mentioned that you were sitting on the lawn talking to her about Paddy, the afternoon *he* was there in the garden, picking plums. Only a few hours before he died. And even now,' he said with intent, 'I couldn't prove it.'

'I shouldn't worry,' said Simon. 'You don't have to prove it. Paddy turned me down.'

Silence for a moment. They walked together equably, down the cobbled paving of a narrow street leading towards the town. Behind them, in the healthy fringes of the uplands, a train whistle sounded.

'If Paddy had opted for me – but I see I was mad ever to think he might – I'd have kept my mouth tight shut and ridden it out, and let you prove it if you could. I'd have taken him and got out. But he turned me down. Flatter than I've ever been turned down in my life, and harder. And now, do you know, on the whole I find myself preferring it this way. My instincts are incurably on the side of justice, after all.' He dug his hands deep into his pockets, hunching his shoulders against the sudden cold wind from the sea. 'I gathered last night that you knew already Paddy was – or rather used to be – mine.'

'I happened to be with Phil, the night we were hunting for him, when Miss Rachel finally admitted what she'd done. Phil said in any case she couldn't have told him *who* his father was, because she didn't know it. And the old lady said oh, yes, she did, she'd learned it from you yourself, no longer ago than Wednesday afternoon, sitting in the garden. Don't worry, I haven't told anyone else. I never shall.'

'And how did you know the rest of it? What was it that told you?'

'A number of small things. First, that you asked me to be there at all. I'd been with you most of one evening and part of the next morning, and you hadn't found it necessary to draft me in. But five minutes after Paddy had let it out that I was C.I.D. by profession, you asked me to make one in your team. I knew there had to be a reason. You hardly knew me as a person, you'd invited me as what you did now know me to be, a policeman, but a policeman on holiday, out of his own manor, without any local connections or loyalties. I couldn't imagine why you wanted such a person, and why you wanted him suddenly on the last day. Not until we were confronted with a body. Then I knew. You wanted an accurate and unbiased observer. You wanted no one involved because of haphazard evidence. You wanted to be fair to all those who might otherwise come under suspicion. So you'd known he was going to be found there. So you'd put him there. It was as simple as that. Everything else had to fit in. And the whole organisation of that affair, the whole setup in the vault, did fit in. The discovery had been staged. And there was only one possible stage-manager. And other, personal things, fitted in, too. You began to avoid Tamsin. Forgive me if I'm trampling rather crudely through things you'd prefer to keep well apart from this. But you asked me how I knew. You've kept carefully away from her for the last five days. But not – forgive me again! – not because you stopped wanting her. And then, when Paddy went missing, you were the one who said he'd turn up safe and sound. Knowing, of course, that he had nothing at all to fear from our supposed murderer-at-large. It was only later, when time wore on and he still didn't show up, that you got really frightened about him. Do you want me to go on?'

Simon broke step to tread out his cigarette at the edge of the pavement. The incredible hydrangeas of Cornwall foamed over a garden wall and filled his eyes with blue and rose and violet.

'Yes, go on. I'm interested.'

'Every soul in this district knew the tomb was going to be opened, and nobody knew it better than you. So when you put the dead man there, or at least when you elected to leave him there, it was because you *wanted him found*. Well, that didn't surprise me very much. Supposing you were responsible for his death in some way, you might well prefer it like that, if you could arrange it in circumstances that wouldn't point straight at you. You'd want, other things being equal, to be fair to his family, not to leave them on thorns, not knowing whether he was alive or dead. But if you wanted him found, and if, as seemed likely, he'd drowned in the sea and been washed up on the Mortuary, then why not just leave him to be found there? And there was an answer to that, too. All the time we've been staying here, the first bather on that beach every morning has been young Paddy.

'And you wouldn't want Paddy to be the one to find him. Not even just because of the ugliness. This man had died, in a way, because of Paddy, and you couldn't bear that there should be any closer link than existed already in your mind. It was shock enough when you heard he'd glimpsed him in the sea, the evening before, wasn't it? And then, you'd promised Paddy to tell the coastguard, and I know you didn't, even after Dominic mentioned it in the bar at night, and reminded you. You didn't forget. You don't forget promises to Paddy.

'But there wasn't a ghost of a motive. Not even when it came out that Trethuan had been trying to threaten or persuade you into leaving the vault alone. What did you care for his threats? He had no hold on you. No, what I was inclined to think, up to then, was that you knew who *had* killed him, and were covering up for the guilty party because you didn't think of him as a murderer, but at the same time trying to protect the innocent from suspicion. And then Miss Rachel let it out that he'd been there in the kitchen garden of Treverra Place, just at the time when you were there with her on the lawn, telling her that

Paddy is your son. Trethuan had followed you down from the churchyard, after you brushed him off for the last time. He was desperate to stop you, by any means. Whether he would have tried to put *you* out of the way, too, if everything else had failed, one can't be sure. But it's worth considering, isn't it?'

He flashed a glance along his shoulder, and saw Simon's clear profile beside him, fixed as bronze, the lines of jaw and cheekbone pale with tension. 'I suppose he might have tried it. I hadn't thought. He didn't, though.'

'No, what happened wasn't in self-defence, I realise that. All the same, he was dogging your steps, in search of anything, any mortal thing, that could be used to bring you to heel or shut you up for good. And he was in the kitchen garden. Picking plums, maybe, but only because where the plums were he could listen to your conversation, and be ready to continue his pursuit of you.

'I don't suppose he heard everything. What he did hear meant just one thing to him, didn't it? Just one obvious, crude but possibly useful thing.

'And then you left the Place, and went out along the Dragon's Head, alone, at an hour when it was deserted. Having a lot of not very happy thinking to do, and plenty of time before you were expected home to tea. And Trethuan made his excuse to Miss Rachel in a great hurry, promised to finish the job next day, and made off after you. He thought he could make you dance to his tune. He came to you, I judge, somewhere near the point, up on the cliff path. He'd want a solitary place. I can guess what he said.

'Yes – he had a simple sort of mind. Not nice, but simple. It wasn't Paddy *he* threatened to tell – was it?'

They had come down to the southern corner of the harbour, and halted there to lean on the railings shoulder to shoulder, looking out over the smooth brown mud and the stranded boats close to them, and the gleaming quiet water beyond, lipping so softly now at the masonry of the mole. Watery sun gilded the small, scalloped waves. The tide was well out, but not yet at its lowest. Simon clenched his hands on the rail, and stared blindly before him, and the screaming flight of gulls wheeling round them was only a pattern of sound to him for a moment. He shut his eyes hard, and shook his head, and the dizziness passed.

'I'm sorry!' he said. 'I haven't been sleeping so well.' He passed a hand over his eyes, and in a moment he said: 'No, it wasn't Paddy!' and again was silent.

'You'd better tell it,' George said reasonably. 'You know best.'

'You know already. It was just as you said. It was the blind, bloody meanness and stupidity of it that got me,' he said, suddenly shivering with detestation. 'I blow up, sometimes. One thing Paddy's got from me, worse luck! – wouldn't you know it would be something like that I'd give him? – is that temper of his. If you've ever seen it in action? No, I suppose not. Tim's the patient one, Tim's done wonders with him. But it can still happen, to Paddy and to me. And there was this creature capering and crowing that he'd heard me admit Paddy was my son! You're so right, to him that meant just one thing, and he thought it was all he needed. If I wouldn't call the whole thing off, *he'd tell Tim*!

'It was ludicrous, it didn't mean a thing, it was no threat to anyone, how could it be? I burst out laughing in his face. And then he called Phil – the sort of name – *Phil*! The truest soul alive, and the one I've injured most already!

'And *I hit him*.

'I don't know if it makes sense to you. It was somehow the one thing I couldn't stand. After all I'd done to them, making use of them for my own ends when it suited me, and then wanting to steal Paddy back – because I did want to, very badly. And then on top of everything, this futile, meaningless, humiliating bit of dirt. You can't imagine how horribly it offended.'

'I think,' said George mildly, 'I can. You're sure he didn't lose his head and hit out at you first? Or shape towards it? when you laughed at him, for instance?'

'Don't tempt me, George. I'm a dodger but not a liar. He never raised a hand.'

'Did you ever, even for an instant, mean to kill him?'

'Good lord, no! Well, – I don't think so. I don't know that I *meant* anything. I just blew up. I hit him with everything I'd got, but I give you my word I only hit him once. I even woke up in time to make one wild grab at him as he dropped, but he slipped through my fingers. I'd turned, you see, when he came up to me, there was the rise of the Dragon's Head on my right, and the drop of the deep water outside the haven on my left. If I lash out, it's always with the right. I hadn't thought how it would swing him round. I hadn't thought at all, it was too quick for thought. It wasn't quite a sheer fall, we weren't that near the edge. He went lurching two or three strides downward, and then lost his footing and rolled. Before I could slither after him he was over the edge. He dropped into the deep water. I think he must have been stunned, because he never came up.'

The lines of strain had eased a little, blood was coming back to his face. He drew breath deeply, and let go of the rail.

'We'd better be moving along, hadn't we?'

'When you're ready.'

'You're not in any hurry to turn me in, are you?' said Simon, with the first reviving smile.

'I'm not turning you in. And there never was any hurry. We hadn't got a murderer at large to worry about. Go on, if you care to. You went in after him, didn't you?'

'How did you know that?' He was capable of feeling surprise again.

'Because you went in again with Dominic afterwards, so long afterwards that it couldn't have been with any hope of finding him alive. It must have been full tide when he fell, if there was deep water off the haven. It was at least half an hour past when you showed up on the beach with the boys. So either it was just for the look of the thing generally – which isn't entirely convincing where you're concerned – or because you wanted to account satisfactorily for wet hair and wet underclothes. The boys wouldn't be noticing that you were wet already, before you went in, they were much too preoccupied then.'

'That's pretty good, but I can tell you one more reason. I'd skinned my knuckles on the right hand, when I hit him. Diving and swimming round those rocks, I made the other hand match. I hadn't thought about that the first time. You can get cut about quite extensively if you're not careful. Paddy was quite concerned, when we were cleaning up afterwards, and he saw them.' He looked down with a dark, remembering smile at the backs of his hands, the points of the knuckles still marked with small, healed lesions. 'Yes, I went in after him. I scrambled down the rock path, and shed my top clothes, and dived and dived for him until I was worn out, and by then it would have been no good, anyhow. It was pretty rough going, but I'm a strong swimmer. And after that, I suppose, it came over me what I'd done, and I knew I had to get away from there, fast. I couldn't get through the Dragon's Hole, or I'd have beat it through there and let myself be seen along the harbour. But it was deep under water at that time. All I could do was put on my clothes and bolt back up the cliff path, and work round by the Maymouth side on to the road. And when I came up over the neck on my way home I saw your boy hauling Paddy out of the rough water. I ran down to them, and you know the rest. I went in and worked hard for the complete answer to why my hair was wet and my knuckles skinned. Praying we wouldn't find him. Praying he'd never be found.

'And that's all. Except that Sam said, that night, he'd probably come in on the Mortuary with the next high tide. That gave me a shock. I'm not a native, that was something I didn't know.'

'And the first thing you thought of was Paddy running down to the beach about seven o'clock in the morning and finding him.'

'Wouldn't it be the first thing that would have occurred to you? If the body was going to be cast up here, I wanted to be the one to find it, not Paddy. I was awake all night, brooding about it, and before it was light I got up and dressed, and snaked out while everybody else was asleep. High tide was about a quarter past four that morning. I bet I was down on the shore before five.

'And he was there! I hadn't really believed in it till then, but he was there. Miles of sand every way, and he was a big fellow, and dead weight. And the sea was no good, the sea wouldn't have him. There was only the church anywhere near for a hiding-place. And the key of the vault was in my pocket. So I put him in there. We had crowbars and wedges down there, already, waiting for the big job. I suppose I thought I could move him again the next night. Maybe I didn't think at all, just huddled him out of sight. It was getting light, and all the time I had Paddy on my mind. It was quite a job, single-handed, but it can be done if you're pushed.'

'So you very honestly explained to me,' said George, 'when I asked you, yesterday.'

'Well, by instinct I am honest. I've never had any reason to be anything else, before. It gets everything snarled up, though, when you do get into a jam. Well, I got him into the coffin. I thought I was putting him in with Treverra. And all the time I was shutting him in with the man he'd killed two years before. Who says providence hasn't got a sense of humour?

'And yet it doesn't make me feel a bit better about it, that he turned out to be a murderer. It doesn't alter anything.

'And then afterwards, when I began thinking where I'd move him to, I thought, well, why? Why move him at all? For all I knew then, he had a loving family. I don't think I'd ever wanted to deprive them of him, and I didn't really like the thought of them waiting and worrying, and looking for him, not even knowing whether he was alive or dead. *Never* knowing. I'd killed him, and that was bad enough. But I found my conscience was going to give me double hell if I tried to sneak out and leave them to fret, and justice to fumble around without any hold on me. But most of all, I suspect, I simply hated and dreaded the thought of touching him again, and going on with this awful game of hide-and-seek. Oh, I wanted to get off scot-free, if I could. Half of me did, anyhow. But not quite on those terms. So I thought, all right, let it just happen. We're going to open the tomb, right, we'll open it. Murder will out, let it at least out in a decent, orderly fashion, with no kids and no women to happen on it unawares, and nobody to give emotional and mis-leading evidence that can land some innocent person in trouble. That's why I asked you to make one.'

They had walked the length of one little shopping street from the end of the harbour, and emerged into the square. Without consultation, but quite naturally, they crossed the cobbled space of parked cars towards the door of the police station.

'I'm glad I did,' said Simon, producing suddenly, even out of his profound depression, the smile that drew people after him.

'You didn't need me,' said George. 'This has been your show throughout.'

They reached the apron of paving before the steps, and halted there by consent to take breath before entering. Neither of them noticed the light flurry of steps on the cobbles, heading for them at a confident run from the newsagent's shop at the corner of the square.

'Well, that was exactly how it happened. Pointless and need-less. Nobody even wanted it. But it happened, and I was the one who made it happen.' Simon filled his lungs deeply, as though there was going to be less to breathe inside. Very soberly he asked: 'What do you think I shall get?'

The running feet broke rhythm, suddenly and very close to them. A breath caught on a half-sound, as if someone had been about to speak quite loudly and gaily, and then swallowed the word unspoken. George swung round, and found himself staring into the wide, wary, golden-hazel eyes of his son.

'Dad, I – I was only – ' His voice wavered away into uncertainty and silence. He looked from one face to the other with that bright, uneasy, intelligent glance, and drew back a step. 'I'm sorry, I didn't mean to butt in. I'll see you later. It wasn't anything.'

'That's all right, Dom,' said George calmly. 'But not now, we're occupied. Run off and take care of your mother, I'll be with you at lunch.'

'Yes, of course. I didn't realise you were busy. Sorry!'

He drew back at once, gladly, quickly, but the stunned look in his eyes had begun to change before he turned his back on them and walked away rapidly out of the square, and the imagination behind the eyes was at work frantically with what he must certainly have heard. 'It happened, and I was the one who made it happen. What do you think I shall get?' His innocent approach couldn't have been better timed to tell him everything in two sentences. And he was exceedingly quick in the uptake.

'I'm sorry about that,' said Simon with compunction, looking after the slender figure as it walked too steadily, too thoughtfully, away from them. 'But he'd have had to know pretty soon, I suppose. What *do* you think I shall get?'

'With luck,' said George, 'a discharge. At the worst, up to three years for manslaughter. If you tell it as you've told it to me.'

'Ah, but I shan't be doing that. And neither will you, George, not quite. If they reduce the charge to manslaughter, or unlawful killing, or anything less than murder, I'm going to plead guilty. Then they won't have to call evidence at all – will they? So everyone will be spared.'

'You'll do nothing of the sort,' said George with equal firmness. 'You'll employ a good lawyer, and be guided by him how to plead. You just tell the truth and leave the law to him. With any luck he'll get you off.'

Simon's tawny face had recovered something of its spirit and audacity, and all of its obstinacy. 'I'll tell the truth, and nothing but the truth, but not quite the whole truth. I'll say he came following and threatening me, I'll say he was abusive. And with what's going to come out about Ruiz, that won't be at all hard for them to believe and understand. But I won't bring Paddy and Tim and Phil into it. They're back safely on the rails, and running like a train, and I'm not going to do anything to shake them again, and neither are you. I'd rather plead guilty ten times over. I'm not what I'd call a good man, George, but that's one thing I won't do, and won't let you do, either. And unless you promise me here and now to keep them out of it, it's your word against mine for all this. I won't co-operate. I'll turn back here and deny everything, and make you sweat your case up as best you can. I don't believe you could ever make it stick.'

'You wouldn't be happy,' said George, smiling.

'No, I wouldn't. I'd much rather go in there and get it off my chest. But not at that price.'

'I told you,' said George, '*I*'m not turning you in. You brought yourself here. It's your show.'

'Good, then they're out of it. For keeps. I look upon that as a promise, George. But – would you mind coming in with me? And will you be kind enough to let Tim know, afterwards? Don't let them worry. They'll know best how to tell Paddy. It isn't that I wanted to keep him from knowing,' he said, as they climbed the steps side by side. 'I just wanted him safely off the scene until I'd got the worst over.'

The shadow of the doorway fell on him, softening the tight, bright lines of his face, braced again now for the ordeal.

'Oh, well,' he said, with a small hollow laugh, 'I've never been in gaol before. It should be a rest-cure.'

From the corner of an alley at the far end of the square, Dominic watched them disappear into the dark doorway. When they were gone he came out of hiding, and began furiously to climb the

703

steep streets inland, towards the upper town and Treverra Place. Inside him a weakening sceptic was still clamouring that it was impossible, that he was making a fool of himself, that there were dozens of possible interpretations of what he had heard, besides the obvious and yet obviously inaccurate one. But he went on walking, at his longest climbing stride, and with lungs pumping.

'Nobody even wanted it. But it happened, and I was the one who made it happen.' And then, in that quiet voice: 'What do you think I shall get?'

It had to mean what he thought it meant, there was nothing else it could mean. But in that case it could tell him more, if he looked closely enough and carefully enough. 'Nobody even wanted it.' It wasn't intended, it wasn't done deliberately. Not murder, then. 'But it happened, and I was the one – ' Still not murder, something that happened by Simon's act, possibly by Simon's fault, but not deliberately. Manslaughter, culpable homicide, but *not* murder. And he wasn't expecting extremes in the penalty, either. 'What do you think I shall get?' Dominic wished he'd been clever enough to blunder in just two or three seconds later, in time to hear the reply. To make it easier to tell, to answer some of the frantic anxieties that would result, before they could even be voiced. Because there was still just one thing a knowledgeable friend could do for Simon, in this extremity. And Dominic was the one person who knew exactly how to do it.

He arrived blown and panting at the absurd, top-heavy gates of Treverra Place, and took the drive a little more soberly, to recover his breath.

Tamsin was in the library, copy-typing catalogue notes, her underlip caught between her teeth, the reddish-gold fringe on her forehead bouncing gently to the slight vibration of her head. He marched straight to her desk, leaned a hand on either side the typewriter, and looked down into the startled face that warmed immediately into a smile for him. He wondered why he felt like the bearer of good news, when he was only the messenger of disaster. Still, you may as well pick up the better pieces even of a catastrophe, and see what they'll make when you put them together.

'Tamsin, I've got something very urgent to tell you. I just ran slam into Dad and Simon outside the police station, and from what I heard, Simon has just given himself up for killing Trethuan.' That's the way news should be delivered, if you want to know what people really feel about it.

'*Simon?*' cried Tamsin, eyes and tone flaring into partisan anger and derision. She was on her feet. 'Simon *murder* some-one? You're out of your mind.'

'I didn't say murder, I said killing. They were perfectly calm but deadly serious. And they've gone into the police station. I'd say what's in the wind is manslaughter, at most. But it *was* Simon, I heard him say it himself. He said: "Nobody even wanted it. But it happened, and I was the one who made it happen." And then he asked Dad: "What do you think I shall get?" Now you know everything I know. And what,' demanded Dominic, jutting his jaw at her, 'are you going to do about it?'

She was a remarkable girl, he'd always known it. She had exclaimed once, and there was no more of that. She caught him by the shoulders and held him before her, so hard that she left the marks of her fingers on his arms, while she searched his face with wild blue eyes that had been like cornflowers a moment ago, and were now like spears.

'So *that's* why!' she said in a rushing whisper. 'Five days, and he hasn't touched or looked at me. You'd have thought I had plague. Ever since it – And I thought he'd just been having fun with me! What does he think I *am*?'

'He wouldn't let you be dragged into this. And you said he was spoiled and in bad need of a fall, anyhow.'

'Dragged in? Let him try and keep me out! The big, brilliant, incapable *idiot, how* did he get himself into this mess?'

'It's nothing to you, anyhow,' pointed out Dominic, tasting a kind of slightly bitter but still unmistakable joy. 'You wouldn't have him. You don't even like him.'

'I know I don't. I could wring his neck! And anyhow, what do you know about it, Dominic Felse? The last time he asked me I didn't tell him yes or no, I just walked away.' She had been all this time ricocheting about the room like an uncoiled spring, slamming the cover on her typewriter, grabbing her coat from a closet, sweeping the papers from the table into a drawer anyhow, just as they fell. 'And now I'm walking back,' she said, turning the blue blaze of her indignation on Dominic, as if he had dared to challenge her. 'Whether he likes it or not. I bet he hasn't even got a lawyer. Can you get bail in a case like this?'

'I don't know, I'm just the errand boy.' She had caught him by the hand and was towing him with her through the doorway; and there, caught close together, they turned to spare one hurried glance for each other, and she stretched across the remaining few inches, and kissed him on the mouth.

'With me, you're royalty plus! But right now, if you can drive, you're the chauffeur. I've just started lessons. Can you?'

'Yes, I've got a licence. But we can't possibly take –'

'We can, we're going to. We've got to get down there quickly. She's out with Benson in the Morris right this minute, but the Rolls is in the garage.'

'*Rolls*? Not likely!' gasped Dominic, appalled. 'I'd be terrified to *touch* it. Suppose I went and scraped the paintwork?'

'You won't!' she said, commanding, not reassuring.

And he didn't. And perhaps that was all that was needed to crown this mad holiday with the right extravagant finale, the impossible fantasy of himself driving that glossy, purring, imperial monster doggedly and gloriously out of its garage and down through the steep, narrow streets of Maymouth to the square, with Tamsin bright and fierce as a fighting Amazon beside him, and parking it with the superb accuracy of sheer lunatic chance in a painted oblong only just big enough to contain it.

Tamsin patted his shoulder, and said something wild and fervent and complimentary, that he never even heard in his daze of retrospective terror, and was gone like an arrow across the square.

Dominic sat quivering with reaction, still clutching the wheel. He wasn't even sure he could stand up now, he thought his knees would give under him if he climbed out and attempted to walk away. They didn't; he got out, closed the door with reverent gentleness, tried a few steps, and had hard work not to take to his heels. One thing was certain, as soon as he turned to look again at the majesty on which he had just laid impious apprentice hands: the chauffeur would have to fetch it back. Nothing in the world would have induced Dominic to tempt providence a second time.

George, humanely withdrawn to the window of Hewitt's office, and thus having half the square in his sight, saw the resplendent car insert itself with the delicacy of desperation into the tight parking space, saw the brave red head sail flaming out of the opened door like a torch, and blaze across towards the doorway below him. And in a minute more he saw the driver's door open, and his son emerge. George's brows rose; he permitted himself a small, appreciative smile. Taking away cars without the owner's permission, now. No need to ask if Miss Rachel had been consulted. Dominic's charge-sheet was becoming interesting. But George was not an exclaiming man. The speaker and the listeners behind his back knew nothing of the storm-wind that was blowing rapidly their way.

Simon, having reached simultaneously the end of his cigarettes and the end of his story, felt lighter, but with the lightness of emptiness. If you can see your whole life clearly as you drown, so you can when events go over you like a tidal wave, and effectively drown the person you have been up to now. Simon saw his life as a dust-sheeted room, the occupant of which had gone gallivanting so often and so far that he had never actually had time to live in it at all. Such a lot of time wasted, looking elsewhere for the impermanent. He'd left it too late to realise the potentialities of a son, and far too late to fall in love with a girl twelve years his junior.

I'm a thirty-seven-year-old widower, he thought, looking into the last coils of cigarette smoke as into a mirror, and a pretty harsh mirror, too. I'm going to be doused head-first in the kind of publicity I'd rather do without, and I shall learn to live with it. I'm going to be hurt, and survive it. I'm going to be stripped of my privileges, and fight my way back into a competitive world as best I can. But at any rate, the distress to other people is only going to be marginal.

He offered himself this, despondently, as a worthy and comforting thought, but instead it made him feel even more depressed. It's too late for me to change, he thought, I've revolved round myself too long. Much the best thing I can do is keep my own company. No wonder I could never find the right note with Tamsin, no wonder I always managed to sound as though I was insulting her. I suppose in a way I was trying to protect her, wanting and not wanting, begging for her and warning her off. And Paddy – what was he to be? A consolation prize? Thank God they both have sound instincts. They know a heel when they see one.

The quietness of the room was suddenly shaken by raised voices below, one of them, and the one that seemed to be laying the law down most emphatically, unmistakably a woman's. They all pricked up their ears, Simon most sharply of all. But it couldn't be! She couldn't even know anything about it yet, and even when she knew, why should she interfere?

George crossed from the window; Hewitt rose from his desk in mingled irritation and curiosity, and stalked across to open the door and call down the stairs: 'Who is that? What's going on down there?'

The tones which had disrupted the desk-sergeant's calm echoed imperiously up the well like a trumpet-call: 'Oh, Mr. Hewitt! Good! I'm coming up.' High heels pattered rapidly up

708

the uncarpeted stairs like a scud of hail. 'Is Simon here with you?'

Simon was on his feet, shaky and disrupted with hope and dismay, and an absurd, shamed apprehension; half hoping against his own heart that Hewitt would manage to send her away, half smiling in spite of his own conscience, because he knew that that was more than the entire Maymouth constabulary and the county regiment could have managed between them.

'You can't come up now, Miss Holt, I'm occupied,' Hewitt blocked the doorway with a broad body and an extended arm.

'I *am* up. He is there, isn't he? What's he told you? What have you charged him with?'

'He hasn't been charged with anything yet,' said Hewitt dryly. 'He's made a statement, which is now being typed. And you've got no business here, my girl, let me tell you that.' He had known her since she was a pig-tailed imp doing acrobatics on the swings in the park; if he couldn't control her, he could still make satisfactorily stern noises.

'Oh, yes, I have. I bet he hasn't even done anything about a lawyer yet. I want to talk to him. Let me in!' Not a request, a command.

She appeared beyond Hewitt's solid shoulder, pale and bright and formidably angry, her red-gold hair in ruffled feathers on cheek and temple, her forehead smudged with carbon. Her eyes, levelled lances, flashed across the room and pierced Simon to the heart. Faint flags of colour had come to life in his tanned cheeks, warming the grey of sleeplessness out of them. An incorrigible spark of mischief reappeared in his eyes, a shadow of itself and veiled in desperation, but alive. The two roused faces locked glances like the beginning of a battle or an embrace. Difficult to be sure which, thought George, edging unnoticed towards the door. Maybe both.

The first words of love sounded like the clash of arms, if that meant anything.

'You're a fine one!' said Tamsin hotly. 'What the devil have you been up to, to get yourself in this mess?'

'If it's a mess, at least it's my mess,' said Simon, all the more loudly and angrily because of the longing he had, and knew he must suppress, to welcome her in and grasp at this unbelievable happiness while it offered. 'What do you think you're doing here? For God's sake, girl, go home and behave yourself.'

' "Go home and behave yourself," he says,' Tamsin rolled bitter blue eyes to heaven in mute appeal. 'Listen who's talking! And he isn't fit to be let out alone!'

'I doubt if he's going to be let out at all for the next year or two,' snapped Simon, man-alive again, and surrounded by a live, thorny and rewarding world. 'So you can make your mind easy, *you* won't be needed for a keeper. Now get out and leave me alone!'

Maybe it was the note of entreaty he hadn't been able to suppress, or maybe she possessed an intuition that didn't even need such aids. However it was, Tamsin knew her moment. The blue of her eyes softened to its calmest gentian darkness.

'It's the forty years or so afterwards I'm worrying about,' she said sternly. She looked at Hewitt, looked him levelly in the eyes, and smiled.

'You'd better let me in. Give me ten minutes with him. I have got a certain right here, you know. That's my fiancé you've got in there.'

She had unfurled her colours, and nobody would ever be able to trick, bully or persuade her into striking them again. Seemingly they all knew it. She breasted Hewitt's large arm, and it gave before her and let her in. She looked as if she could have marched through walls just as irresistibly. She marched straight at Simon, all pennants flying.

'Ten minutes!' said Hewitt, and shoved George before him out of the office, and closed the door upon them.

BLACK IS THE COLOUR OF MY TRUE LOVE'S HEART

Ellis Peters

Various singers and musicians are gathered for a folk music course that will occupy a weekend in the fantastic country mansion called Follymead. Most come only to sing or to listen, but one or two have non-musical scores to settle. When brilliant talented Liri Palmer sings:

'Black, black, black is the colour of my true-love's *heart*!
His tongue is liked a poisoned dart,
The coldest eyes and the lewdest hands...'

she clearly has a message for one of the audience. Passions run high;. there is murder brewing at Follymead.

Among the music students are Tossa Barber and her boyfriend Dominic Felse. When disaster strikes, Dominic can privately enlist the aid of his father, Detective Inspector George Felse, to unravel the tangle of events.

THE KNOCKER ON HEAVEN'S DOOR

Ellis Peters

The knocker hung on a very special door – oak, heavy,
with a late-Gothic arch, and apparently a late-Gothic
curse. Then the door was moved from an old house, once
an abbey, to the village church. Legend held that sinners
who seized the knocker had their hands burned by the
cold iron. But Gerry Bracewell didn't die of burns, neither
did a second victim. Had they knocked on death's door,
or was a more down-to-earth killer at large?

Detective Chief Inspector George Felse, returning from a
weekend in Wales, had passed through the village of
Mottisham and watched the ceremony enacted to
re-dedicate the door. Little did he know that soon he
would be called back to investigate murder . . .

RAINBOW'S END

Ellis Peters

The sleepy village of Middlehope is suddenly jerked into life by *nouveau riche* antiques magnate Arthur Rainbow. In a whirlwind of activity he extravagantly refurbishes the Manor House, joins the Golf Club, Angling Society and Arts Council – and, in a ruthless coup dislodges the old church organist to take over the position himself.

But for all his reforming zeal, the Middlehope community rejects him. 'He won't do, you know', is the villagers' judgement, an opinion spearheaded by Miss de la Pole, the local artistocrat. And when Rainbow's crushed body is found in the graveyard of St Eata's church, there is very little surprise or sorrow – but much speculation as to who the murderer could be.

After all, there are so many candidates – from his young, beautiful, flirtatious wife to the usurped organist and his mutinous choir. It falls upon Superintendent George Felse, newly promoted head of the Midshire CID, to solve this most perplexing murder.